Reclamation Series
Volume 1
For the Want of a Pill

Vic Broquard

Published by Broquard eBooks, East Peoria, IL 61611

i

Reclamation Series Volume 1
For the Want of a Pill
First Edition
Copyrighted © 2010, 2013, 2014, 2015
by Vic Broquard
ISBN: 978-1-941415-75-7

This is a work of fiction. All characters, organizations, and events portrayed in this novel are products of the author's imagination and are used fictiously.

Published by:
http://www.Broquard-ebooks.com
Broquard eBooks
103 Timberlane
East Peoria, IL 61611
author@Broquard-eBooks.com

Artwork by Crooked Willow Studios.

For Morgan and L. Ron Hubbard

Table of Contents

Part I Establishment

Part II Organization

Part I Establishment

Chapter 1—Terrorist Strike

Excerpt from <u>The History of the Twenty-first Century</u>, by Professor Herbert Finglebottom, PhD. 2201 Edition, Random House Publishing.

"With the world's economic and financial collapse during the early years of the twenty-first century, an escalating over-population problem, global warming wreaking havoc on what had been prime agricultural areas of the world, and massive unemployment, world leaders took advantage of breakthroughs in modern medicine, pharmaceuticals, and psychiatry. They launched the Total Care Program, based crudely on the failed Affordable Care Act, which had earlier bankrupted the United States. Total Care answered everyone's prayers, living up to their motto, 'From the Cradle to the Grave.'

"Total Care promised everyone full-time employment, inexpensive housing and food, and free medical care, watching over a person from birth until death. I believe they delivered on their promises and then some. I'm told the complete handling of both global warming and overpopulation was unexpected byproducts of the Total Care Program. I would point out that Total Care's success is based primarily on their use of the anti-psychotic drug, Pytalon, and the psychiatrists' invention of the Implant machine. Pytalon is the wonder drug, which not only prevents insanity but also the common cold and flu. It also had a surprising side benefit, the removal all criminal tendencies in people, making police forces obsolete before the beginning of the twenty-second century. Further, the electronic implanting of people has guaranteed everyone performs their assigned work perfectly."

Federal Elimination Division and Security Bulletin of 8 June 2270

Most Wanted:
1. A hacker known as the Weasel
2. A hacker known as the Wart

Missing and wanted for questioning:
EE Woman Jessica Alexandra
EE Woman Amanda Pottingham

It was 09:00 on June 8, 2270. Two conspirators, Ben Hadwell and Fred Singer, waited patiently just inside the hanger housing the Pytalon Corporation's giant Air Liner at New O'Hare, Chicago, Illinois. They were dressed in the ill-fitting baggy, brown coveralls of the two baggage handlers they had knocked out, stripped, and who now lay hidden inside the hanger out of sight. Ben and Fred were members of a loose knit underground, fighting against the drugged and implanted society of the world, specifically here in Chicago.

The world-famous hacker known only as the Weasel had relayed the key information. Today at nine o'clock, two vice-presidents of the Chicago Pytalon Corporation were scheduled to hand-deliver the newest reformulation of the anti-psychotic drug Pytalon to the San Francisco office, where it would be further tested and put into mass production worldwide. This drug turned people into mindless, totally controlled zombies, as Ben called the normal person on the street. While others in the underground suggested other means to stop them, Ben was a young man of action and had decided enough was enough. Today, he would put an end to this new, improved drug and send an unequivocal message to the Pytalon drug CEOs. Nothing could go wrong, not with the world filled with these mindless zombies. The pair waited.

***

A week before, Jason Hamilton, one of the executives at Pytalon Inc, Chicago branch, announced, "Ladies, Bill and I have some exciting news for you." He and Bill Wells were vice-presidents of the huge pharmaceutical company. He was thirty-five and Bill was thirty. Both wore only the finest light grey business suits with silk shirts and ties, as befitting their top positions. Their eyes were bright and full of youthful enthusiasm, wholly unlike the hundreds of others who worked in their skyscraper, including the two fabulously looking young Exotic Escort women sitting at their sides. The two EE women had long ago had their EE implants, but they were not on heavy doses of Pytalon, unlike the general population who were.

Jessica Alexandra was Jason's permanent escort; she went everywhere with him, just as her roommate Amanda Pottingham did with Bill. She batted her overly long eyelashes, thick with extended mascara, at Jason, a flirting move that he could not resist. He grinned, "Devilish of you, Jessica. Okay, I'll tell you the big surprise. We are all going to take an extended trip to San Francisco! Bill and I need to make some changes at our plant there. We'll be gone a month, ladies, so pack everything."

The week had passed quite uneventfully for the men, but it had been quite a different story for the two EE women, who had somehow come off Pytalon, recovered their memories, and had decided to flee and start a new life in San Francisco. At nine o'clock, both women hastily checked their makeup, and then slipped their compacts back into their purses. Why? Jason and Bill had just called to tell them that they were on their way to pick them up and take them to the airport. Amanda helped Jessica stand and they moved to their door, arriving in time to answer Jason's knock.

"Wow! You look great, Jessica," Jason exclaimed. "New outfit? Did you miss me?" Both women were wearing their new gowns, sky blue satin with accompanying, matching outer corset, which accentuated their perky G cup bosoms. Their heels matched their dresses as well as their eyes. Both women looked stunning, as expected of EE women.

Jessica slipped her arms around Jason. "You like them? We picked them out especially for you guys. Miss you? My god, we've been so utterly horny all week! You are going to have to make this week up to us big time, tall, handsome fellow! You aren't going to get any sleep tonight; I guarantee it!" She planted a loving kiss on his lips but had to wipe traces of her red lipstick off his lips, though doing it in a very sensuous manner with her fingers. As she did so, Jessica realized just how easily she could play this new game, keeping her real self from being discovered. Neither Jason nor Bill had any idea their EE women were now off the heavy effects of Pytalon. So far, so good, Jessi thought.

"Okay, we're wasting time. We have a plane to catch. Porters," Jason summoned three men who entered and stacked the women's suitcases onto a large rack, all the while muttering something about sanity and doing a good job, wholly ignored by the four. Jason put his arm around Jessica and gently supported her, while nudging her forward. "We are going up,"

4

he added, as she made a motion towards the elevators. "We are taking an EMAC to New O'Hare, dear." EMACs or Electro-Magnetic Air Cars long ago replaced all cars and helicopters, just as the Air Liners had to airplanes.

"Oh, this is going to be so much fun, dear," Jessica replied, watching him press the topmost button. Shortly, they exited onto the roof where the EMAC port was located. A large EMAC was waiting for them. The glassy-eyed porters followed the foursome and stowed the many bags into the cargo bay, while the men helped the women up the three steps and into the luxurious company EMAC with the Pytalon logo boldly emblazoned on each side of it.

Jason was careful to make sure Jessica got safely to her seat and strapped in. The uneven flooring made her steps rather challenging, and he felt her wobbling several times in her sky blue ballet boots. Amanda had little such trouble since her heels were merely six inches tall, a contrast in their heels. Jason didn't mind at all, for he had his wish: an EE woman who was only an inch shorter than he was. Likewise, Amanda stood an inch shorter than her sponsor, Bill, did. Such adaptions in height were often a consideration in the footwear of EE women. Both men knew they had chosen wisely.

Soon, the impressive skyline of Chicago passed by their windows, though none of the four noticed it. Both women continued flirting with the two men, who enjoyed every minute of it. Jessica sensed Jason had really missed her this past week and wondered what that might mean. Still, she did not intend to abandon their plans to escape once they got to San Francisco. A half hour and a dozen passionate kisses later, they landed at the nearly deserted airport.

These days, few people ever flew across country. The old jet airliners had long ago been replaced with luxurious Air Liners, based upon the EMAC technology. These airplanes used electro-magnetic propulsion systems and were completely "green." Further, either the air towers or the liners own built-in geo-navigation systems automatically controlled their entire flight. However, pilots were still required in case some unexpected event occurred. No such thing had happened for years, and these days, the pilots were doped up on Pytalon. Today, Jessica surmised that if an emergency arose, these so-called pilots wouldn't be able to handle it.

Their EMAC hovered near the great Air Liner and then set down some twenty feet from it. Two brown clothed baggage handlers walked up and began removing their suitcases, loading them onto the liner, again saying something about sanity and doing a good job. Meanwhile, the two men assisted the two EE women out of the EMAC. While Jessica could easily walk up a ramp, going down a ramp in her boots was more than a challenge. Even Amanda had a most difficult time going downhill. Noticing Jessica's bent knees, Jason slipped a steadying arm around her, "I've got you, dear. I won't let you fall." She flashed him a flirting thank you.

His arm around Amanda and playing to her EE implant, Bill whispered, "I've got you. I can see going down the ramp is hard on your knees, but you do look gorgeous and sexy." She flashed him a flirting smile as required by her EE implant.

Once down, they led them over to the Air Liner, which also prominently displayed the company logo. After getting the women safely inside and seated, Bill explained, "We'll be back in a moment. Couriers are bringing our special top-security briefcases. We're taking them to the San Francisco Pytalon Headquarters." Promptly, the two men exited and stood on the tarmac, awaiting the arrival of the couriers. The two women smiled at each other, silently communicating they were pulling their escape off without a hitch!

Shortly two glassy-eyed couriers wearing business suits arrived, unlocked the briefcases handcuffed to their wrists, and then fastened the cuffs onto the two men. Amanda whispered to Jessi, "What's in those cases that's so very important?"

Jessica replied, "I can't imagine. Gosh, I hope the men don't have to be chained to the briefcases all the way there. It's going to be hard to flirt with them tied up like that."

As they watched the two couriers turn around to leave, the two baggage handlers pivoted, facing the group of men. They had something in their hands, but the women couldn't see what. Several loud popping sounds startled the women. "What's happening?" Jessica called out, but then wished she'd kept quiet. Something was going horribly wrong. The two women saw Jason, Bill, and the two couriers collapse unconscious onto the concrete tarmac. Were the men dead? Was this a robbery or a murder? An insanity outbreak?

Shocked, Amanda and Jessica watched the two baggage handlers undress Bill and Jason, and then drag the couriers out of sight. Shortly, the baggage handlers returned to drag the two nearly naked executives away as well. "What's happening?" whispered Amanda. "Why are they bringing Bill and Jason's suits onto the plane? Where are Bill and Jason? Are they dead? Are they going to kill us next?"

Amanda didn't get a chance to reply. One of the men climbed into the Air Liner, and both women expected to be killed.

Moments before while Ben and Fred were dragging the unconscious bodies of Jason and Bill inside the hanger and handcuffing them, Fred whispered, "Damn it, Ben. We didn't count on those EE women being here. Now what do we do?" His hands shook slightly.

In a steely voice, Ben replied, "Should have expected them to be bringing their sex dolls along with them, the creeps. Doesn't change a thing. Follow my lead." Carrying the executive's clothes with them, they boarded the Air Liner. Ben answered Jessica's questions. "Don't worry EE women; they aren't dead, though they will soon wish they were. Time for you to get off this Air Liner, unless you want to die."

Surprised she wasn't shot, Amanda replied, "We want to live. Come on, Jessica. I'll help you. Please, sir, can you get our bags off the Liner too, please?" Amanda bravely asked, knowing their bags contained most of their cash, but she observed the man's eyes carefully, as she helped Jessi to her feet. His eyes were not glassy, and she rightly concluded he was also not under the influence of Pytalon, scaring her further. Ben faked a grumble and signaled Fred to carry their many bags off the Air Liner.

Amanda helped Jessica move slowly to the exit. By the time the two faced going down the steps to the tarmac, Ben and Fred already had their bags unloaded. Since neither of the men offered to assist them, the two EE women held onto each other as they carefully stepped down. As they descended, Jessica wondered why the men hadn't killed them, and why they had returned their luggage. *Are they going to kidnap us?*

"Come on; hurry it up ladies," Ben grumbled.

Once on the tarmac, Amanda spoke up. She'd already determined these men must be murderers and thieves and were not drugged zombies. On the other hand, so far they didn't seem to be actually interested in the EE women. She was confused. Other than the executives, she knew of no one else who wasn't drugged, but here were two who weren't. "What's going on? You're not drugged on Pytalon. Neither are we. We're trying to escape Chicago somehow." She guessed these men were probably terrorists or worse, but they might respond to the fact the EE women were also off Pytalon. At least she hoped this would work in their favor. Her math-oriented mind calculated the odds as being fifty-fifty, which is why she spoke so boldly.

Ben looked at her eyes; his were cold and drilling. "Damn, she's right! Hell, we didn't plan for this."

Nervous Fred spoke up, "But we can't just abandon them here. All hell will soon break loose."

Ben sighed and explained, "Look ladies, nothing against you, but we're stealing this EMAC and the Air Liner. In a little while, everyone will believe you two are dead. If you are sincere in wanting to disappear, this is your chance." Ben's voice sounded quite harsh and gruff.

Amanda thought better than to ask why everyone would believe they were dead. She also wisely decided not to attempt to use her EE charms on these men. She found them disgusting, if not downright revolting. They had just committed a serious crime; perhaps their two men were dead or badly injured. Instead, she picked up on his last words. "Yes, we want to disappear, but we don't know how or where to go."

Fred suggested, "Boss, we don't have time for this. We only have minutes left. Let them find the professor. Dump them on his plate."

Evidently, this made sense, for Ben replied, "Okay. Take your bags and go to this address. Ask for the professor. Give us your cell phones so they can't track you. Now get going before you get captured." He handed her a scrap of paper, while they dug their cells out of their purses and handed them to the man. "Give me your spare pair," Ben ordered Fred, who handed over a pair of new phones. Hastily, Ben downloaded each woman's phone information into one of the new phones and handed the two new cells back to the women. "These are untraceable disposable phones. Nav chips are disabled so they can't track you. They are safe to use. All your old phone info on is now in these. You can thank me later. Now get going."

While this was happening, Jessica spotted Fred loading their bags onto a single baggage pull cart. With their phones safely in their purses, the two women walked over to the cart. "I'll pull," Amanda suggested, "and you do your best to push it." She knew that Jessica in her boots could push better than she could pull. Slowly, the two women got the cart rolling along, passing on through the main terminal, which was mostly deserted. Few traveled these days. Several nervous minutes later, they came out onto the MTE. Mass Transit Escalators: every city now had a complete MTE system in operation. More than two centuries ago, the MTE invention was first used at larger airports to speed passengers down the long corridors, but in today's world, they had nearly replaced all other forms of transportation in towns of any appreciable size.

Hastily, Amanda grabbed a map, and then the two pushed their cart onto the escalator, which moved them along at a brisk pace.

Finally alone and safe, Jessica asked, "Where are we going? Who were those men? What are they going to do? I think it can't be good. What did they mean by we'll be presumed dead? Amanda, I'm really scared. Should we report this to the AP-cops?" She meant the anti-psychotic police officers, who were also implanted and on Pytalon. It was their job to arrest those who went "insane" in public.

"No, we should find this professor fellow and see what that brings. Somehow, we have had a very narrow escape, I think. We have to disappear like he suggested. Why don't you sit down while I try to figure out how to get to this address? I think it's way out in the suburbs. It's going to be a long ride on the MTE for us," Amanda sighed and sat down on their bags too.

They watched the outskirts of the suburbs fly by them along with numerous women going shopping and an endless array of billboards all displaying the usual messages concerning Total Care's ongoing war against Insanity. Neither woman now believed there even was such a war. Rather, both were extremely frightened. Something unexpected and potentially deadly had totally disrupted their planned escape to San Francisco. "We're on the run, aren't we?" Jessica whispered fearfully.

Amanda bit her lip, nodded, and then added, "At least those two men were not on Pytalon too, though they must be criminals. Maybe there are more of us who are off the drug. He said to go to this professor fellow. I think professors aren't the criminal type, at least I hope so. I don't know what else we can do. We don't dare go back to New O'Hare and book a flight to San Francisco ourselves."

"No, we can't do that," Jessica replied. "EE women never do such things. We don't really have much choice but to check out this professor. We certainly can't stay in Chicago any longer."

***

Ben and Fred watched the two unexpected women entering the terminal and then moved swiftly. They loaded several hundred pounds of explosives into the Air Liner. That done, Ben quickly re-programmed the autopilot, while Fred returned to the stolen EMAC, readying it for their hasty departure. Shortly, Ben joined him. "Is it done?" Fred asked nervously.

"Yep. We've done it, Fred, just as I said we would. Stupidly easy. Now we're going to send these drug kingpins a message they'll never forget. Look. It's taking off. Time we split too. Get us out of here, Fred," Ben ordered.

Fred lifted the EMAC off. "So where do we go now? Won't they come after us?" That was Fred's biggest fear.

"Look, you hold up at the factory. I'll take the EMAC and drop it off where they'll never find it, down by St. Louis. We've done it, Fred! No more Pytalon for Chicago," Ben declared.

"I don't know, Ben. Surely, they'll just bring in more from other cities," Fred countered.

"Doesn't matter. We've stopped them from making an even more powerful version of Pytalon. That's what really matters. Now shut up and fly this thing," Ben ordered. Neither man knew their lives would soon be over.

***

Millions watched the noon news on the Communications Network. The WGN reporter talked in her usual Pytalon emotionless monotone, "This morning, insane terrorists flew one of Pytalon Corporation's Air Liners into their Lakeside skyscraper, killing hundreds. Firefighters have the fire confined to four floors where they manufacture our desperately needed Pytalon pills. Company officials have said the vital pills, which everyone needs, will be flown in from other manufacturing plants until they can rebuild here. The Insanity Police captain has said earlier this morning the Air Liner was hijacked. Two company executives were incapacitated at New O'Hare and the liner hijacked. The two executives were taken to the hospital and are expected to recover fully. However, the execs report two EE women were also aboard the Air Liner. No trace of the missing women have yet been found around New O'Hare, and officials now presume they were onboard the Air Liner when it flew into the building and are presumed dead at this time along with the two hijackers."

***

Curiously, one of those who died in the attack, Josh Hamilton, Jason Hamilton's uncle, actually was very pleased and relieved to die! Why? A week ago, the soft feminine voice spoke in a monotone through the white, commonplace box known as the Communications Network, "Time to wake up, Josh Hamilton, Technician Fourth Class. Remember, sanity is always rising on time. It is seven o'clock on the first of June, 2270." Josh's eyes were still closed. Though forty-eight years old, he'd not yet gotten to sleep. Why? All night long, he'd stared at the swirling grey mass that was always visible when he closed his eyes. How long had it been since he'd had a good night's sleep? Josh simply could not say. His mind barely functioned. As if somehow sensing the man had not yet risen, the voice added, "Sanity is always rising on time!" This time, the voice was louder and placed more emphasis on the words.

"Dear, it's time to get up. I have breakfast ready for you," the gentle, but monotonous, voice of his wife broke the silence. "Sanity is having a good breakfast ready for your husband. Sanity is looking your best for your husband when he rises so that he can have proper start for the working day," she whispered her implanted mantra softly to herself again, devoid of any real emotion. Following the same daily routine she'd followed for the last twenty-eight years, she mechanically checked their table, finding it precisely laid out: orange juice in the small glasses, toast nicely brown with a light coating of butter, two eggs sunny side up, two strips of bacon artfully arranged around them. Perfect, she thought and then glanced at her appearance in the mirror. "Sanity is looking your best for your husband," she recited in a whisper. After pouring two cups of freshly brewed coffee, she sat down to wait for Josh.

Five minutes later, a bleary-eyed Josh stumbled out of their bedroom, struggling to get his jacket on properly. "Sanity is having a good breakfast ready for your husband," she greeted him, and then waited expectantly for his reply.

Absentmindedly, Josh mumbled, "Sanity is having a good breakfast." He sat down and stared at the food. Am I hungry? I can't tell, he thought, staring at the small cup that held their morning pills. Mechanically, he found himself reciting, "Sanity is taking your meds on time. Protect yourself from insanity." Across the table from Josh, his wife repeated the same words and downed her pills with her orange juice. Josh sighed and did the same. Josh watched disinterestedly as his body ate the food before him, just as his wife did too, emotionless as well.

He rose. She said, "Sanity is having a good day, Josh." He repeated her words and mechanically leaned over, placing a brief kiss on her red lips. Later as he stepped outside their apartment complex, he heard her reciting, "Sanity is washing the dirty dishes."

Outside, the late spring morning air was crisp, and Josh began his short walk to the MTE, the Mass Transit Escalators. He knew it was 2270 only because the billboards displayed the date. As he watched his body being moved along, great billboards flashed their incessant messages. Vaguely, they registered in his fuzzy mind. Total Care: From the Cradle to the Grave. Public Enemy Number One: Insanity. Fight Insanity; take your daily pills. We will win this war on Insanity! Sanity is doing a good job. Sanity is being on time to work. Sanity is being polite to others. Finally, Josh's mind stopped registering their messages. He'd seen them every day for longer than he could remember.

At this hour, the MTE was densely packed with others going to work as well—all standing motionlessly erect, most in work clothes, but a few in suits or plain, drab dresses. No faces displayed a smile, and no one spoke to each other. Glassy-eyed stares met Josh's. Many younger men and women were whispering their implanted mantras softly to themselves. Josh didn't. He was worn out from saying them for the last twenty-eight years. As his body was moved down Lake Shore Drive, his eyes saw the blue lake to his right, but his mind didn't register it any longer.

He spotted a group of children using the MTE to get to their school. For a moment, he remembered the fact he hadn't yet been given permission to have a child. Josh had a faint notion he still wanted to have one, if his wife was still able to bear one. If so, they would be officially informed, and he would be given a pill that would allow him to function sexually. Otherwise, a side effect of the anti-psychotic drug, Pytalon, left him unable to perform in that manner. He had the notion this was to prevent over-population of their world. Somewhere in the back of his mind, he recalled having seen billboards stating that, but the memory was too fuzzy to bring into focus. Little was in focus in Josh's mind this morning. Perhaps he was in need of another psych implant, he mused.

Now he approached the giant Pytalon Manufacturing plant, a converted tall skyscraper, where he worked on one of the many assembly lines. His eyes spotted Joe, the window washer, five years older than himself, slightly overweight, and wearing brown bib overalls. Every day for the last twenty years, he saw old Joe cleaning the windows on the ground floor. Rain or shine, sleet or snow, Joe was there polishing the windows, every day, wearing the same bib overalls.

For a moment, Josh wondered how the windows could get so dirty that Joe would have to spend all day cleaning the hundred plus feet of windows, repeatedly. Then, he spotted Ted, the brass polisher. Like Joe, Ted was a fixture here at the huge entrance doors. He carried a bag of cleaning supplies stuffed with bottles, rags, wipers, and poles, and spent his working day cleaning the inside windows and polishing and re-polishing the brass of the doors. Once more, Josh wondered how the brass door handles could get so dirty that they needed continuous polishing all day long.

Entering the massive skyscraper, Josh saw other familiar faces. A few were well-dressed women wearing tall, black spiked heels, black or grey skirts, and white blouses—the many secretaries, his mind registered. Most, however, wore drab work clothes like himself. A communications network speaker blared loudly, "Total Care: From the Cradle to the Grave. Fight insanity, our common enemy. Remember, sanity is doing a good job. Work your very best today; deliver a solid blow to insanity." Josh's mind didn't register the words, however. He walked mechanically to the elevators and waited his turn, along with dozens of other equally glazed employees.

A few minutes later, Josh arrived at his workstation on the tenth floor. A loud speaker barked, "Sanity is doing a good job. Help us fight insanity. Do your part." Just then, the assembly line began moving, and Josh's body reacted. As each giant batch of proto-pills appeared before him, his fingers pressed a red button, which injected the proper dose of Pytalon into the proto-pills. Then, the batch moved on down the line where they were counted and packaged into distribution bottles. From there, Josh lost sight of them. Long ago, he had a vague notion the whole process could be done by computer-controlled machinery, but then he wouldn't have a job. Neither would so many others, if that were true.

Josh pushed and pushed the red button. However, as the endless day passed, the grey fog in his mind took over. He doped off, believing he was swimming in this sea of grey. "Sanity is doing a good job. Fight our common enemy, insanity." Somewhere that voice continued to speak to him. He woke from the fog only to see that he'd missed pressing the red button.

"I wonder what happens now?" he thought, though he didn't feel any real emotion and certainly not fear. Reprisals? Perhaps his supervisor would pay him a visit now. Should he tell his boss about his grey fogginess? Josh felt a faint pang of concern, the most emotion he'd felt in a long time. "No! You don't want to endure another of those psych implants!" a dim voice spoke from somewhere inside his head. Josh, like nearly everyone, heard voices in his head—disembodied voices that often told him what he ought to do. He knew he had to obey that voice or endure another severe headache. "Okay, I won't tell my boss," he muttered, sensing the disappearance of the budding headache. He felt better now.

Still he didn't press the red button as the next large batch appeared before him. Instead, mindlessly he watched them move on down into the packaging machine. Nothing happened. Another batch appeared. Again, Josh merely watched them, hundreds of little red pills in their containers awaiting the needle injections from the machine just above them. After a minute, the automated assembly line activated, transporting the pills on down to the packaging assembly. Nothing else happened.

Josh became slightly amused. The next batch appeared, and this time, he pressed the red button and watched as a hundred needles injected Pytalon into the proto-pills before they moved on down the line. The next batch appeared. This time, Josh did nothing. Soon, it became a grand game. "Press or not to press—that is the question," he said softly to himself, vaguely amused.

Farther down the assembly line, Supervisor Third Class, Emil watched a red light flash. Mechanically, Emil whispered, "Red light. Means something is wrong. I must act. Sanity is doing a good job." His hand moved slowly to the button labeled "Stop." If he pressed it, the whole assembly line would come to a halt. Then, he would have to work out what had gone wrong and fix the problem. That meant he would have to think. His hand paused above the button. "My head hurts so! God, I don't want to think! Not today! My mind hurts!" He paused again. "Ah, the red light is off now. All fixed. It seems I've done a good job," he whispered to himself and relaxed.

Again, the light came on, but just as swiftly, it turned off. On, off, on, off. This seemingly random pattern continued, hypnotizing Emil, who merely stood and watched, fascinated by the pretty patterns the light made in his mind. Bong! The lunch break buzzer sounded, and the assembly line halted. Mechanically, Emil rose and joined the other technicians, including Josh, as they made their slow, mindless way to the company cafeteria, oblivious to the salient fact that one hundred thousand defective Pytalon, anti-psychotic pills, were already packaged and being loaded onto distribution vehicles. Pytalon had also been the total answer to many other societal problems, not just over-population. There were no sex crimes now. Actually, crime was nearly non-existent, since the worldwide distribution of Pytalon.

Josh's fingers continued to push the red button off and on that afternoon. When the gong sounded ending the workday, he inserted his ID card into a slot beside his machine. Automatically, it logged his hours. The company computer system then sent his pay credits into his bank account. Josh headed down the elevators, joining the crowd exiting the tall skyscraper. He walked the short distance to the MTE and stepped onto the moving escalators for his long ride back to his apartment complex.

Suddenly, he heard screaming—wild yelling off to his right. Although still moving briskly along the MTE, he turned to see the commotion. Two women were shrieking and yelling, wildly waving their arms around. "Demons! Demons have invaded my mind!" one woman shrieked, pulling at her hair. Already Chicago's finest were on the scene, Josh noted. AP-cops or anti-psychotic police officers—the four men in blue hastily subdued the two ranting and obviously insane women. Josh thought, "Insanity is still among us. Damn, we haven't won the war yet." He had no other reaction though.

That evening in bed, Josh found himself staring at the grey fog surrounding him when he closed his eyes. He longed for total blackness. *How can I sleep if it is so light around me?* His mind registered such thoughts a few minutes before the soft feminine-sounding voice spoke in a monotone through the white Communications Network, "Time to wake up, Josh Hamilton, Technician Forth Class. Remember, sanity is always rising on time. It is seven o'clock on the second of June, 2270." Josh groaned, vaguely wondering when the miserable life of his would end, wishing it were sooner than later. In fact, it did end in just seven more days.

Chapter 2—Two EE Women

The fleeing EE women had a long way to go on the MTE system. The address on the paper indicated the distant suburb of Joliet. With little to do but sit, Jessica reflected back on the past seven eventful days that led up to today's perilous flight. It had begun at lunch on June 1 when Jason Hamilton announced, "Ladies, Bill and I have some exciting news for you." He announced they were going to take an extended trip to San Francisco. He had said, "We'll be gone a month, ladies, so pack everything." Jessica could now remember what had happened after that, and the memories replayed in her mind.

After Jason made his surprise announcement, she'd replied, "Oh, terrific." Jessica attempted to muster up some enthusiasm, so terribly hard to do these days. The mental grey fog only allowed her and her companion to express a few very specific emotions and feelings, though those were drastically more than those in other occupations could feel, and those were carefully channeled to what was expected of their profession as escorts. "Can we see the Golden Gate Bridge?" she asked, trying hard to recall anything about that large city in northern California. Vaguely, she thought there was this impressive bridge or perhaps it was another city or something else entirely.

"Absolutely, dear. We'll even spend some time on the beaches there, if the waters are warm enough. I promise you both we'll take an extended sightseeing trip. Nothing is too good for our lovely escorts," he wisely punched in that last bit, knowing it re-enforced their EE implant programming.

"Oh, terrific," Jessica replied, wholly unable to think of any other response that was more appropriate. Thinking was so hard to do, so very hard, unless the thoughts were aligned to her implant programming as an exotic escort.

"I thought you both would love the trip," Jason continued. "We'll leave a week from today. However, the bad news is you both will be on your own until then. Bill and I are going to be tied up in critical meetings until we leave. Business comes first, of course. I'm sure you two can entertain yourselves for a week."

"Oh Jason! I don't know how I can possibly be away from you for a whole week!" Jessica responded with great emotion as dictated by her mental implant, slipping her slender arm around him. She ran her long, red nails gently down his cheek, resting them seductively on his lips. "A whole week without you," she protested sensually.

He bought her tease, adding, "I'm sure you and Amanda can find a way to get by without us for seven days." He teased her back, and Jessica gave him a flirting pout with her wet, red lips. He laughed, "My dear, Sanity is doing a good job. Bill and I must attend these closed meetings. There's no way we can sneak you into those meetings and you know it. Amanda, I hereby charge you to make sure my Jessica here is fully satisfied each day." Amanda grinned, revealing her bright white, perfect teeth outlined by the lush red of her lipstick. Both men knew well how to play to the implanted training patterns of their EE women.

"But Jason, dear, who will satisfy you each evening?" Jessica pleaded, again batting her long lashes accompanied with a perfectly formed flirting grin on her moist lips.

He made an exaggerated sigh. "Somehow, my darling Jessica, we will have to manage. Come on; it's time to be seen once more. Back to work." He gently helped Jessica rise to her feet. She appreciated his steadying arm. Rising on her ballet boots was always challenging. He stood six-six and standing on her toes in the boots allowed her to be barely an inch shorter than he was. Somewhere in the back of her mind, she assumed she had been programmed to wear only these ballet boots with their towering eight-inch heels so she would match Jason's height well.

Jason's eyes took in her shapely form, his eyes rising up her long legs covered in black seamed, fully fashioned nylons, to her black satin, short gown which only came down to her upper calves, to her massive bosom, and finally to her particularly beautiful face with its perfectly done makeup. "I will miss you, Jessica," he whispered in her ear, "but in a week we will have more fun, I promise you." She grinned in an automatic sexual response.

Behind them, Ben took Amanda's arm. She wore red patent oxfords with a steel, six-inch heel, and contrasting black sole. Her gown was also satin, red, matching her heels. She tossed her wavy, shoulder-length, brown hair and took his arm securely, giving him a playful, sexual nudge that brought a pleased grin to his lips. In her heels, she was also an inch shorter than Ben was, a perfect match, her mind noted, as it always seemed to do whether or not she desired that thought.

Once they had been escorted to the top floor where many other eyes followed their every move, the two men released them. Jason explained, "The meetings start now, so you two have the afternoon off. Go start packing. Use your cards to purchase any new outfits you think you'll need for this lengthy trip."

"Oh perfect!" Jessica replied seductively. "I'll surprise you with a sexy new outfit. Bye dear." She made a kissing motion, as he left her standing at the meeting room doorway. After Ben stepped inside, Jessica reached out to Amanda to help steady herself. The two EE women were inseparable, having lived together for over seven years. In her ballet boots, Jessica definitely appreciated the support Amanda always gave her while standing or walking.

"We best go shopping first," Amanda said more mechanically than anything else. With their men gone, they slipped into their usual blank states—their minds, a grey fog. Carefully, arm in arm, the two made their slow way back to the main elevators. Before long, they passed Ted, who was polishing the inside brass doors, though they surely didn't need it, and then passed Joe, who was cleaning the already spotless windows for the tenth time this day. Soon, they reached the MTE and relaxed. All they had to do was hold on and let the escalators take them to their favorite shopping center, Lacy's EE Apparel. They purchased all their outfits from this store, which catered solely to EE women. Each bought matching sky blue satin gowns and heels, along with five pairs of black, seamed nylons for the trip. Jessica's idea was to have their dresses match their eyes this time.

Several hours later, the pair stepped off the MTE just outside their apartment complex located in the wealthier section of Chicago opposite the lake. Again, Amanda put her arm around Jessica steadying her as she walked on her toes into their building, passing by two workers who were shining the door trim and washing the windows, just as they did every day. They took the elevator to the tenth floor and moved down the long hall to their apartment door. The plush red carpeting made walking more difficult for Jessica, and Amanda held her securely just as she had done every day for years.

Once inside, they noticed their new supply of meds had arrived, and Amanda divided the package between them. Neither had any idea these many bottles didn't contain the light dosage of Pytalon they were supposed to contain. In effect, they were placebos, nothing more, perhaps thanks to the blunder of Josh. As she stored them in their medicine cabinet, Jessica called out, "Dear, how about ordering pizza tonight? Since we are on our own, I feel like pizza, though for the life of me, I can't say why I feel this way. I've been feeling kind of funny all day."

Amanda walked back into their living room. "How strange. Me too, funny-like all day. Pizza sounds fine with me, dear." She sat down beside Jessica on their plush couch and felt her passions rising as usual. Jessica flushed; she felt a sudden strong need for passionate pleasure with Amanda. Without exchanging a word, the two fell into a strong, sensual rapport with each other until each broke into a sudden burst of intense pleasure and satisfaction. Amanda whispered, "If only a man could give us this kind of pleasure." Jessica smiled, agreeing wholly.

These two EE women had been together for more than seven years and shared a very similar history. In high school, they had both been strikingly attractive. When they turned eighteen, the time of their Total Care Choosing, they received notification they were to become EE women. Neither had considered EE as a career, but like everyone else, they had no choice in the Total Care Choosing. When a youngster reached eighteen, Total Care told him or her what their lifetime employment would be, based on the country's needs and not on the person's skill, ability, or educational level. Certainly none of these mattered in the choice of the young women to become EE women where only physical beauty mattered. At this time, neither Jessica nor Amanda could recall what they had been interested in studying before they had been chosen to become EE women.

Vaguely, they recalled how they had been taken from high school during their senior year and admitted into some clinic, where they received beauty augmentations. Both women's breasts had been greatly enhanced to a perky G cup, a full sixteen inches difference between their over-the-bust size and their band size. No EE woman had sagging breasts. Additionally, some minor blemishes were removed. Once healed, they were then taken into the dreaded white building, the IS, Implant Station. Neither could remember what had happened there, only a grey mental fog had appeared, along with massive behavioral modifications, and of course the migraines, which appeared whenever they went against their programming.

In fact, what did happen to them was simple. The psychs placed a metal headband over their heads and injected them with a special drug. While unconscious and in great pain from the electrical discharge into their brains, the psych spoke clearly and precisely into their ears, reading from a pre-arranged, time-proven script. (Note: before the end of this year, both women would know precisely what had been said to them during this procedure.) "My body is hypersensitive to sensual touches. My body needs sexual sensations and stimulations several times each day. I exist to provide elegant and sensual experiences to men and women of power. I am an exotic escort. I must look my very best at all times. I must be ready to flirt at any time. I must be ready to engage and satisfy the sexual fantasies and satisfactions of both men and women at any time. I am a super-sexual, hypersensitive woman. I must wear only the finest and exotic gowns and heels. I must look perfect at all times. I will repeat to myself these words several times each day. I must not forget these words."

After receiving the pain-drug-hypnosis (PDH) implant, both women forgot who and what they had been and began reciting the implanted words, just as everyone who received an implant did. However, shortly after that, both became frantic, trying to find the proper apparel to wear. Right on cue, their handler took them shopping to purchase their first outfits.

Both were already assigned to their sponsors, Jason and Bill. This dictated their heels, since perfection in personal escorts demanded the woman be one inch shorter than her sponsor, male or female. Jessica was given knee-high ballet boots to always wear, while Amanda was given the six-inch stilettos. Further, they were given this very apartment to share, along with female "toys" with which they could carry out their implanted orders on each other, since their sponsors weren't always around. It took Jessica some time to learn to walk in her boots, but that too had been carefully planned. As always, they were given a Pytalon pill every day, which only added to their zombie-like state and their shared mental grey masses, though their dosage was substantially less than the usual amount. Why? Given the standard dosage, they would be almost unable to follow their EE implant commands.

Now nearly eight years later, both women's feet had adjusted to the constant wearing of their exotic footwear. Amanda's high arch no longer permitted her to wear any heel of a lesser height. Her foot simply couldn't rest flat on the floor. Without her heels, she was forced to tiptoe around. Jessica fared worse. Her feet had more or less fused into the en pointe position, and she couldn't even walk without wearing ballet shoes or boots.

On the other hand, neither knew that all week they had been taking the non-Pytalon pills that Josh, presumably, had failed to inject with the drug. All their new supplies were also lacking the anti-psychotic drug, yet the bottles were clearly labeled as "Pytalon—For Sanity, take one each morning." The effect of the drug was now beginning to wear off, which was why both women were feeling "funny" this evening.

Having satisfied each other's hunger, Jessica volunteered, "You know, I feel sort of detached from everything. We're so utterly useless—just sexual toys, if the truth be told."

"Me too, I've felt funny all day, like everything is going by while I sort of watch, but then I had the usual craving which you more than satisfied," Amanda grinned at Jessica, who involuntarily flirted with her eyes.

"See—my body just reacted, but I didn't cause it—did I? I feel so weird, Amanda. God, I hope we don't have to get the implants redone. I can't remember the experience, but it must have been horrid. I sure don't want to become insane!"

"Me either, Jessica. We can't be insane, not really. We're just feeling strange somehow, but I know what you mean about feeling utterly useless. Bill and Jason—they are doing really important things and what do we do? Nothing but walk around and look sexy."

Jessica laughed nervously, "I'm afraid we do a whole lot more than that with the men. Still, it's pointless—not like a real job. Yet, look at us, Amanda. We live in this luxury apartment, only wear the finest clothes, dine in the most elegant restaurants, and have money credits in the bank. But what do we do to earn all this? Fulfill our boss' sexual fantasies? Are we glorified whores?" She shuttered as she said that last.

"No, we are Exotic Escorts, Jessica. You know that. Our bodies are hypersensitive to sensual touches, and we know our bodies need sexual sensations and stimulations several times each day. We exist to provide elegant and sensual experiences to men and women of power." She looked rather shocked that she'd just said all this aloud. "What's happening to us? I have this voice in my head that keeps telling me to say this all the time."

"Me too, Amanda, me too. It's a little voice saying I must look my very best at all times. I must be ready to flirt at any time. I must be ready to engage and satisfy the sexual fantasies and satisfactions of both men and women at any time. I am a super-sexual, hypersensitive woman. I must wear only the finest and exotic gowns and heels. I must look perfect at all times. It—it keeps telling me this. But am I? Are we really this? I seem so detached from it all right now," Jessica admitted.

"Me too. I didn't have these strange feelings last week, not that I can recall. Remembering anything is so terribly hard to do, you know. I just keep seeing a grey fog in my mind," Amanda confided in her best friend.

"I don't think we should tell anyone about how we're feeling though. I'm scared they'll turn us in as having gone insane," Jessica suggested. "Everything is just so utterly hopeless."

"Right, but we can easily keep on being EE women. That's super easy, and God, Jessica, I'm getting horny again! Let's get to bed and do it once more," Amanda admitted, rubbing her head, which had begun to throb once more.

The next morning, both women rose, pleasured each other, took their pill, and ate a quick breakfast of leftovers. "At least we have seven free days now. We don't have to go out or go anywhere at all," Jessica said calmly. However, she felt anything but calm this morning. In fact, she felt hysterical, but couldn't find any real reason for it.

Amanda said nervously, "Jessica, I'm feeling really, really weird. Like I'm supposed to do something, but I can't think what it must be. I feel sort of freaked right now, like I could suddenly start crying like a baby or something."

"Oh god! Me too, Amanda, me too. Look at my hand! It's shaking so. I can't hold it still. I'm sure something is wrong with us. There has to be. We've never felt like this before, have we?"

"Jessica! You are shaking! No, I can't remember ever feeling like this. Are we poisoned? Are we drugged? Was there something awful in that pizza last night? Maybe it was bad, spoiled or something. Maybe we're just sick, but I don't feel like vomiting. Do you?"

"No, not really. We could have been drugged—slipped something into our pizza. But why? Almost no men can even get aroused, not unless they are given the pill for it. I think we should lock our doors in case they try to break in and rape us or something!" Amanda gushed hysterically. She moved as quickly as she could in her heels to check the door. It was locked already.

Jessica was just as hysterical as Amanda was. Rising on her toes, she moved over to inspect the door herself. "Come on; that puny lock won't stop them from breaking in. Let's move the couch in front of the door." Amanda agreed and the two moved over to the couch. Jessica tried her best to push on the couch, but in her ballet boots, she had virtually no traction at all. Amanda fared little better. Soon both women gave that up, and Amanda carried a chair to the door, wedging its top against the doorknob. "Thanks, Amanda, that ought to stop them," Jessica gushed and sat back down on their couch.

Amanda joined her, admitting, "God, Jessica, I feel like I am bouncing off the walls! What's wrong with us? Are we going insane? Has insanity struck us? Was it in the pizza? Can you get insanity from pizza? We shouldn't have ordered it. I'm sure that must be it."

"I'll never eat pizza again! It must have been doctored pizza!" Jessica exclaimed, finally finding an outlet for her hysteria. "Hold me, Amanda. Hold me." The two EE women held each other tightly for a long time.

Suddenly a new thought struck Jessica. "My god, Amanda! What if the perpetrator is already inside our apartment! I thought I saw someone moving towards our bedroom!"

"Oh God! You're right! Something's in here, Jessica, but I think it is a python snake. I swear I saw it slithering into our bedroom just now. Didn't you see it?" Amanda shrieked. "I hate snakes."

"A snake? No, I thought it looked more like a man bent over. Crap, our cells are in our bedroom! We can't call for help!" Jessica whispered, afraid of attracting the man's attention or the snake's, whichever it was. In fact, their cell phones were lying where they had left them last night, on the kitchen table. Cell phones had evolved into highly powerful computer systems, but the average person, implanted and on Pytalon, was barely able to make use of .01% of the phone's capabilities, that is, make an emergency call to 911. The EE women were better off than most, for they could actually call their sponsors, their men, but little else, which is why they had them, though they often misplaced their phones.

"Maybe we can sneak into our bedroom, grab our cells, and run out here," Amanda suggested.

"I can't run, not in these boots. I can barely walk if I'm careful. Can you do it?" Jessica admitted.

Nervously, Amanda agreed. Stealthily, she got to her feet and moved silently over their plush carpet into their bedroom, leaving Jessica sitting like a statue on their couch, completely out of sight. Shortly, both women began screaming, but for different reasons.

"Amanda! Amanda! Help me! Help me! Rats are everywhere! They are crawling up my legs!" Jessica shrieked.

"Jessica, the python is killing me! It's strangling me! Help me, help me," Amanda wailed, struggling to get out of their bedroom and back to Jessica who might be able to save her before she suffocated to death.

Waving her arms wildly in an attempt to knock the rats off her, Jessica got to her toes and began making her slow way towards the bedroom. Both women met halfway. "Where are the rats?" Amanda said, startled to see Jessica before her and flailing her arms around as if knocking rats off her.

Jessica looked up. "What's my dress doing around your neck, Amanda?" she asked startled.

Amanda looked sheepishly at Jessica's dress and hastily removed it, tossing it on a nearby chair. As they returned to their couch, both women saw several pillows now lying on the floor. Because it was so hard for Jessica to pick things up, Amanda hastily retrieved the pillows, and Jessica put them back into their proper positions, looking very sheepish all the while. Both then sat down.

"I think we're hallucinating now," Amanda whispered.

"We are. I could have sworn a flock of rats was crawling up my legs. Damn, I've ruined my hose with my long nails," Jessica admitted, feeling rather silly.

"Sorry about freaking out over your dress. We're hallucinating, but why? Was that part of the drug that was in the pizza last night?" Amanda asked.

"I surely don't know, dear. Still, you'd think we would have been hallucinating last night. It's nearly suppertime a day later. Somehow, I don't think it was the pizza. Do you?" she asked, adding, "I'm surely not thinking straight today."

"Thinking. Jessica, that's it. We are sort of thinking, and we don't normally think, do we?" Amanda pointed out. Both sat stunned for some time, pondering the meaning of this.

After a time, Jessica said determinedly, "Amanda, I don't think we were hallucinating. Rather, I think we were just being delusional. Right now, nothing seems real to me at all."

"Delusional? Maybe you're right. Nothing seems real to me, excepting you. God, maybe we ought to go pleasure each other. Maybe that's what's wrong with us. We've not done it enough today," Amanda suggested. The two women headed to their bedroom.

The next day, both women merely sat around their apartment. Neither said much to the other at all. Somehow, Jessica found herself pondering that grey mass in her mind, going over how useless she was, how pathetic her life had become. She had no idea then that Amanda was introverting in a similar manner. Amanda repeatedly had the thought, "I am nothing more than a victim of the government." She couldn't get that notion out of her mind. Unknown to her, Jessica had similar thoughts. By afternoon, Jessica now thought, "It's all my fault. I've brought this on myself, somehow." Amanda had similar thoughts, and both believed they were wholly unworthy to be EE women, though both were too ashamed of their intense feelings to say anything about it to the other.

The third day found both women utterly numb all morning, sitting motionless and silent on their couch for hours. Finally, their implants kicked into high gear; each began craving sexual sensations. In a burst of energy, they frantically pleasured each other in a wild frenzy of activity. A half hour later, they lay sweating on their bed, gently stroking each other's shapely body with their long talons. Jessica broke the silence, "Thanks Amanda. I was suffering something awful. My body felt as if it would somehow burn up if you hadn't pleasured me."

"Same here, Jessi. I ached something awful too. Suffering, God do we ever suffer if we don't pleasure each other at least three times each day! We've rather forgotten to do that, Jessi. Maybe that's all that's wrong with us—not getting enough sexual stimuli. We're hypersensitive to it all, aren't we?" Amanda asked.

"You're right. That must be it. The men have left us completely alone for what? Three days now. That must be it. We're hyper-sexed for sure. We should write ourselves a note to have sex three times each day, just in case we forget it tomorrow," Jessica suggested. They did just that, pasting stick-it notes all around their apartment. No matter what room they found themselves in, there was a note plainly visible. Satisfied, they retired for the night.

The fourth day was filled with utter despair. Nothing was working right. Toast burned up; coffee spilled and was bitterly strong; their scrambled eggs were inedible. The only relief either felt was for the few minutes when they were highly aroused. Neither said too much all day, merely languishing in their own personal despair while sitting on their couch, side by side. Grief overwhelmed both young women. They cried much of the day, oblivious to the other beside them. Finally, around suppertime, Amanda realized she was very hungry. "Chinese?" she asked. Jessi agreed, and they ordered Chinese. An hour later, the two women sat around their kitchen table eating chicken with snow pods and chicken with broccoli.

"You know, Amanda, all this is ruining our lives," Jessica began philosophizing. That seemed to be the right thing to do, she thought. "Here we've a week to ourselves without any real work to do, and we're being basket cases. It wasn't like this before when we were in high school. I remember those days now. Funny, I can remember some things just now. I don't know how, but I can."

"My God, Jessica! You're right! Something is ruining our lives! Jessi, I'm able to remember things too! I used to love math when I was in high school! I wanted to be a math teacher back then! I can recall my childhood now. Jessi! I've not been able to remember anything for the last eight years or so, not since I had my Total Care Choosing. This is really freaky, Jessi!"

"Amanda! You're right! I haven't been able to remember anything either, not for the last eight years too, not since my Choosing. The last thing I remember is someone saying they would be upping my Pytalon dosage, since I was an adult. After that point, it all became a grey fog. I remember now. In high school, I loved to program computers and study history. I wanted to either be a history teacher or work with computers and the Internet," Jessica admitted.

Just then, both of their cell phones began ringing. It took the women six rings to get to them; both moved slowly, and their cells were still where they'd left them in the kitchen. "Hello Jason. What's up? I thought we wouldn't hear from you for a week. Missing me badly? I miss you," Jessica said. Amanda said similar words to Bill.

"I miss you, sexy. Still in the big meeting, but something's come up. An emergency. Somehow, a bad batch of

Pytalon pills was made. Well, actually they didn't get made. The pills don't contain any Pytalon, but there is no way to tell that they don't, not without a lab test. I called to see if you were all right. Lord knows who has gotten the bad batch."

"Wow. How could that have happened, dear?" Jessica asked demurely. "I thought you said everything was foolproof."

"We don't know yet. I just wanted to warn you. If you start having bad reactions, send for a new batch of Meds. Promise me you will," he insisted.

"Sure dear. I feel fine now. I'll tell Amanda. We will be on the lookout for them. Thanks sexy man." She found herself flirting in spite of her intentions.

"Okay, see you in a few more days. San Francisco here we come," he replied and hung up. Shortly both women looked at each other; their mouths opened.

"That's what's been ruining our lives!" Jessica finally found words.

"Right, but Jessi, it's the wrong way! I feel better now than I've felt for eight years. I'm finally able to remember things. My god, Jessi, the Pytalon has been what is ruining our lives, not helping us!"

Jessica exclaimed, "Amanda! You're right! Pytalon has been keeping us more like zombies for the last eight years. Oh wow!" After a startled pause, Jessica added, "Amanda, everyone is on Pytalon to keep insanity at bay. All of us—we must all be in that grey fog. No one can remember things or think for themselves. Everyone's lives are being ruined by this Pytalon!" Both women sat silently on their couch for quite some time, stunned by this revelation.

At last, Amanda broke the silence, "It's ruining our lives—this Pytalon stuff. Worse, we're the total effect of it all, Jessi. Look, we escort two of the Pytalon manufacturing vice-presidents. We can't escape this nightmare. Besides, everyone is on Pytalon now. It's supposed to be the cure for the terrible insanity disease, which is our number one enemy—the world's number one enemy for that matter. We can't escape it. Everywhere we look, everyone is on Pytalon. If Jason or Bill finds out we're coming off it, they'll surely dope us back up. We're doomed, Jessi. We really are the total effect of the government, the psychs, the doctors, the company, the world, and even our own sponsors. Statistically speaking," Amanda added, her math education finally returning in some small measure to her, "the odds against us are many billions to us

28

two. I can't imagine a more total effect than this."

"Amanda, if we don't take Pytalon, we'll get insanity, eventually. That's what the Total Care billboards all say. I'm really, really scared. I'm shaking. Pleasure me, please. I can't take this anymore," Jessica pleaded with her friend and constant companion. The two made their slow way into their bedroom. Once more, they found a temporary release of all tensions, fears, and emotions by following the dictates of their EE implant.

The sixth day, the two oscillated between fear and a lighter anxiety over their discovery and physical condition. Their nerves were frayed, and they pleasured each other six times that day. After one of those rounds, the two satisfied and now relaxed women lay beside each other's naked body, gently touching each other with their fingers. Amanda volunteered, "Jessi, you know it's only going to get worse for us. Lord knows how Jason and Bill will react when they find out about us. I think I would rather die than go back onto that horrid Pytalon."

"I know. I couldn't even think right or remember anything. My memory is returning pretty well now. I don't want to lose that again and be a zombie like I was, living from moment to moment in a sort of blissful stupor. I can't. I won't," Jessica said trying to muster some modicum of force behind her pronunciation.

"Right, dear, we somehow need a change from all this. We need a change," Amanda declared, her voice filled with anxiety once more.

"Right," Jessica agreed, adding, "but how? Where can we go if the whole world is hooked on Pytalon? Besides, we're also the awful effect of this EE implant thing. We can't escape being exotic escort women. The Pytalon isn't affecting that. If we don't do our EE thing, we get these blinding, debilitating headaches. We're so screwed, Amanda, so screwed!"

Suddenly, Amanda burst out laughing. "Screwed! That's funny, Jessi. Screwed. That's our job, our employment—to flirt and be screwed. You are right. The EE thing isn't even slightly impacted by Pytalon. It's still there full force. What are we going to do?"

Laughing as well, Jessica added, "Yes, but screwed by only the finest of clientele." Suddenly, her face tensed. She grew quite serious. "Amanda, look, we can't even get most men to be aroused. They can't. The Pytalon keeps them from getting aroused or being able to even flirt with us, let alone do it. The only men who can are definitely *not* on Pytalon, the corporate bigwigs. We're like company dolls, I think. We're being used by Jason and Bill. No, they made us into what they wanted as doll escorts. Look at what Jason wanted me always to wear—these awful ballet boots just so I'm an inch shorter than he is. No, we're the victims of those who we're supposed to be escorting, showing a good time, and satisfying. Damn, damn, damn. We need a change, Amanda; we certainly do need a change."

"I agree completely, dear," Amanda declared.

"I know," Jessi suddenly had an idea. "We can still play EE to Jason and Bill. As long as we act normally, they'll never know the difference. We flirt, excite them, and satisfy them just as before, and they'll never suspect we're off Pytalon," she suggested hopefully.

Amanda smiled coyly. "Oh, how devious! I love it. Let's! They'll never know the difference, not really. When have either ever asked for our opinion of something? Never. They treat us as if we were things, dolls, okay, sex dolls. As long as we continue to perform that way, they'll never know. Besides, we're supposed to pack up everything and go to San Francisco with them tomorrow. We might not be back here for a long time. We can do this, Jessi. I know we can. Somehow, we can change."

"True, we might even be able to run away from them while we're in San Francisco. Surely, they'll eventually have to come back to Chicago, leaving us behind. We can start a new life there," Jessica added hopefully. "They'll never know about us."

"Right. Wait, if we flee them, we'll need money credits," Amanda countered.

Recalling her computer training from high school days, Jessica explained, "Right, if we use our ID cards to withdraw money credits in San Francisco, they can trace our banking transactions. So we just take all our money out now before we go. After all, Jason did tell us to bring *everything* with us," Jessica added covertly. "That silliness would be just what someone on Pytalon might do when told to bring everything." Both women laughed; she was right about that point.

"Come on; let's get presentable and go to the bank. Then, we best pack," Amanda agreed. A half hour later, their makeup perfectly done, arm in arm, the two left their fancy apartment, making their slow, careful way to their bank. At first, both women felt as though everyone was staring at them, recognizing they were different, that they were no longer so heavily under the influence of Pytalon. Soon that feeling left them completely. Out there among the drugged population of Chicago, no one paid them the slightest real attention. Their elegant gowns, giant busts, and extreme heels told even the casual passerby they were simply EE women. Rare was the person who even glanced at their exotic appearance. Their confidence in pulling this off began to rise.

At the bank, they noticed the glassy-eyed look of the tellers and other customers. Again, no one even remotely questioned them. A half hour later, they left, each carrying a small bag containing over ten thousand dollar credits. Their accounts were nearly empty, but they had met Jason's order to bring everything with them. As they rode along the MTE, crowded with women doing their family's shopping, Jessica whispered, "One good thing, dear. No crime. We don't have to worry about someone stealing our bags. That would require thought, and they can't think, not anymore. Pathetic. What has happened to our whole world? How did we get this way? I want to find out, you know. I used to love history. My curiosity is roused." She flashed Amanda a flirting grin, in keeping with their implant programming, which was still in operation.

An hour later, they began packing up their many dresses and heels. By the time they finished packing their collection of apparel, each had three large suitcases filled, barely closing. Additionally, each had a carrying bag with their various cosmetics they had to have so they could always look their best as the EE implant dictated they must. While they could fight against the lingering aftereffects of the Pytalon, they were powerless against the psych's EE implant. Yet that implant was their ticket out of their ruin. Cleverly, the two had put part of their money credits into each of the three suitcases and their cosmetic bag, keeping a little spending money credits in their purses. Now they sat on their couch to wait word from their men. Somehow, someway, Jessica Alexandra and Amanda Pottingham were determined to start a new life, free from the horrid effects of Pytalon.

***

Time passed slowly for the two women, who sat on their bags on the stolen cart from New O'Hare, while the MTE moved them along through the many suburbs of Chicago. Both were lost in their reflections of the past week. Hours later and after several goofs, the two finally walked off the MTE close to the indicated address.

They found themselves on a tree-lined side street with quaint old homes, some of which must be over a hundred years old, Jessica surmised from their appearances. Many were rather rundown, but still serviceable. Now they had no choice but to push their baggage rack along the street as they hunted for the right home in Joliet. Jessica did her best to push, but her ballet heels were not conducive to such things. Amanda continued to do most of the work, pulling the cart along the street. By the time they found the address on the paper, their feet were aching. They pushed their cart up the driveway, and arm in arm for much needed support, they made their way to the front door. Amanda knocked, not seeing any doorbell button. She knocked again. "What're we going to do if he's not home?" she whispered. She knocked once more.

The door opened slowly, revealing a bearded man, perhaps fifty-five with slight streaks of grey in his beard and brown hair. He was a short man, barely five-six with beady eyes. "Yes, whatever you are selling, I'm bloody well not buying." He had an English accent and started to close the door on them.

"Wait sir. We are looking for the professor. A man gave us this address," Amanda spoke up hastily. He opened the door a bit more and stared at the two women.

"A pair of EE women? Who sent you?" he demanded, but looked up and down the street. Seeing no one, his eyes met hers.

"We don't know his name. He told us to come here and find the professor. Sir, can you help us?" Amanda repeated her plea, but decided against using her flirting skills on him just yet.

"Now what on earth could a pair of sex dolls want with a professor? You know a professor is a learned man who teaches others, don't you?" His tone was definitely hostile and condescending, treating them as he might some uneducated bumpkin.

"Sir, are you the professor? We are off Pytalon and can remember. I wanted to be a math teacher, and Jessica wanted to teach history or work on computers," Amanda decided to reveal a bit more to this strange man. She rightly guessed if she didn't, he'd shut the door on them.

"Hum, how very strange. Two sex dolls off their meds. So why do you want to see this professor fellow anyway?" he replied.

"Sir, can we please come inside. We've walked a very long way, and our feet are killing us. Besides, it's not something we ought to talk about out here in public," Amanda encouraged him. She felt Jessica's arm tightening on her shoulders and knew that her toes must be aching horribly. She'd never done this much walking at one time before.

"What about your bags out there?" he asked.

"Please sir, if you wouldn't mind bringing them inside for us. We're about done in from walking all the way here from New O'Hare," Amanda pleaded, flirting ever so slightly with her eyes.

He opened the door fully. "All right. I'll bite. Go on inside and have a seat on my couch. I'll bring your bags inside for you. All the way from New O'Hare, bloody interesting." They entered and found themselves in the small living room. Both hastily made for the couch, just as Jessica's knees gave out. The man made several trips bringing in their six suitcases and two cosmetic bags. Meanwhile, Amanda hastily began massaging Jessi's feet through her boots. While Jessi desperately wanted to take them off for a spell, such would be wholly unseemly in a total stranger's home. Besides, he could soon kick them out if he wasn't the professor or didn't believe them.

He finally closed the door and took a seat opposite them. After studying them for a moment, he said, "Suppose for a moment I am this professor fellow you're looking for. Why don't you tell me what is going on and how you got this address? Start at the beginning, elegant sex dolls or rather Exotic Escorts, I believe you're called over here in the colonies."

"We got off Pytalon last week, bad pills, or something, and made plans to sort of disappear when we got to San Francisco. You see, we are or were the personal escorts of two company vice-presidents, Jason and Bill, who had to make an extended trip to San Francisco today. We all got to New O'Hare and onto the Air Liner when these men showed up and shot Jason and Bill, along with two courier men who brought them two briefcases, which they kept handcuffed to their wrists. We think the four might be dead, but we're not sure. Anyway, the men took us off the Air Liner after they told us that we would die if we stayed onboard. We want to live, and we did as asked. One of the men gave me this note with this address. He told us to find the professor and that he could help us disappear," Amanda explained, giving Jessica time to deal with her cramped feet.

"I see. Off Pytalon. You went through hallucinations or delusions I presume?" he asked.

"Yes, they were really bad. I thought a python was strangling me, and Jessi thought rats were crawling all over her. Silly us. It was just a dress and some pillows, but for a time, it was so real, sir," Amanda added truthfully.

"All right. So you claim to have wanted to be a math teacher. Tell me, if X squared minus sixteen equals zero, what are the three roots of the equation?" he asked pointedly.

"Two roots only, sir, since it's only X squared. If it was X cubed, then there could be three roots. In this case, the roots are plus four and minus four," Amanda replied with a wry grin. She realized the man was testing her, and that seemed to her to be a most hopeful sign. *Thank god, I can remember things now!*

He grinned. "Right you are. Mind you, in these times, you cannot ever be too careful. People are often not what they seem to be. Your tale rings true, especially in light of the news. Have you seen the news today?"

"No, we've been walking here ever since the attack," Amanda replied. He rose and turned on the Communications Network. Startling images of the skyscraper in flames filled the scene. It was the very building in which they and Bill and Jason worked.

The reporter was talking in her usual monotone, "This morning, insane terrorists flew one of Pytalon Corporation's Air Liners into their Lakeside skyscraper, killing hundreds. Firefighters have the fire confined to four floors where they manufacture our desperately needed Pytalon pills. Company officials have said the vital pills will be flown in from other manufacturing plants until they can rebuild here. The Insanity Police captain has said that, earlier this morning, the Air Liner was hijacked. Two company executives were incapacitated at New O'Hare and the liner hijacked. The two men were taken to the hospital and are expected to recover fully. However, they reported two EE women were also aboard the Air Liner. No trace of the missing women have yet been found around New O'Hare, and officials now presume they were onboard the Air Liner when it flew into the building and are presumed dead at this time along with the two hijackers."

"I feel sick," Jessica whispered. "They killed all those people!"

The professor turned the news off. "So you must be the two missing EE women who are now presumed dead. How convenient, unless you were seen walking here to my home. That would raise far too many questions, I'm afraid. The dopey IP will certainly think we three were somehow involved in the hijacking. Damn Ben anyway! I told him this was a terrible idea, but he and his group just wouldn't listen. They wanted to stop Pytalon production, if you hadn't already worked that out. We three could be in deep trouble, if anyone reports seeing you two coming here. Damn, damn, damn."

"Sir, how are we to disappear? Where will we go? How will we live? No way do we ever want to get back onto that awful Pytalon stuff," Amanda asked what was bothering her. If more trouble came here, she had no idea where she and Jessi could possibly go. The whole world was doped up.

He ran his hands through his hair and beard. He sighed, "Well, living is always a problem, you see, what with all the Insanity Police around looking for violators who are off their meds. The best advice I can give you is when you are out in public act as if you are still doped up. Act as you used to when you were under its influence. I take it you both were also implanted?"

"Yes, sir. We were made into EE women when we were eighteen. No matter what we do, we can't seem to break out of that, but we're managing to get by anyway. As long as we don't have to go back onto Pytalon, we can probably fake it well enough," Amanda admitted and suggested hopefully. "Can you tell us, sir, how are we to disappear? Where will we go? How will we live?" She repeated what she and Jessi desperately wanted to know. Was there even any real hope? If not, she toyed with the idea of begging this older man to become their sponsor.

"I don't have all those answers just yet. Let me make some calls first, ladies. Have you had lunch?" he countered. They hadn't. "Go to the kitchen and fix yourselves something to eat." As they rose to do that, he got out his cell phone and began making some discrete calls out of earshot of the two women.

Sometime later, the two women rejoined him in his living room. "You certainly have a lot of books," Jessica volunteered, having passed through his study to get to the kitchen. One wall was lined with books.

He smiled. "That I do. I prefer the real thing, not the electronic books so popular today. Well, they used to be popular. I'm afraid those on Pytalon don't read anything anymore. Sad really. Our world is dying. Say, weren't you interested in history?"

She smiled, "Yes, I am. Why?"

"Considering the circumstances, I have just the book for you: A History of the Twenty-first Century. You will find it fascinating, I'm sure. I'll loan it to you. Bring it back sometime when you are finished with it." He went into his study and retrieved the two-inch thick volume. Then, he was back to the business at hand.

"Look, we're very likely in hot water, bloody hot water. I'm going to have to disappear myself for a while. I've located a place where you two can stay for a time until you get things more sorted out. You can drive an EMAC, can't you?" he asked.

"Er, sorry sir. We don't drive. Is that bad? Can we learn?" Amanda replied growing more and more worried about everything. Somehow, nothing seemed to be going their way this day.

"Okay. I rather figured you sex dolls couldn't drive one. No offense intended." He looked rather worried and fidgeted some. Amanda guessed he hadn't liked what he'd heard on his phone. "Okay, I'll program it to take you partway there. When it stops, a man will get inside and drive you the rest of the way. If all goes well, he'll return my EMAC here. If not, it's been nice meeting you. When you get to the destination, probably late tonight, you'll get to meet Weasel. He'll take care of you for a while, until you get things sorted out. You'll be safe with him, that much I can promise, if you can actually get to him. Me, I'm going to a different place. No sense in all of us being apprehended over Ben's foolish act of terrorism. Come on. My EMAC is out back. Let's get you inside, and I'll bring your bags."

A half hour later, the two women were sitting in the comfortable seats, their many suitcases piled on the other seats. The professor spent some minutes fiddling with the controls, setting up the automated portion of their drive. "There we go. Okay, it's all programmed. Remember, when it stops, a man will get in and take over. Don't expect him to say anything at all to you. Silence is golden in this case. Best of luck. Perhaps we'll meet again at a later date."

"Thank you, sir, for helping us. We really do appreciate it. I don't know what we would've done without your help. Thank you," Amanda replied. She was very sincere, and he knew it.

He shut the door, and the machine activated on its own. The two women sat back and relaxed a little. "God, I'm in dire need of pleasuring," Jessica admitted. Amanda smiled; she was long overdue and felt a slight headache coming on if she didn't obey the implant and obtain some pleasure soon. For once, the two were glad to be alone for a time.

Finally satisfied and their headaches gone, the two began to look out the windows and to try to figure out where they were at and going. They saw rolling countryside. "We're not in Chicago anymore," Jessica whispered, somewhat concerned. "Where are we going? Ideas?"

"From the sun's position, which must be in the west about now, since it's late afternoon, we have to be going south. Chicago must be far behind us now, because there are only farmer's fields around. Where are we going?" Amanda replied.

"Well, we were in the suburb of Joliet. So now, we must be far south of there. What's way down there?" Jessica asked. "Geography was not my specialty. Maybe St. Louis?"

"Don't know. I'll try to watch for signs so we can get some idea," Amanda suggested. "Gosh, it's so great to be able to think again! Two weeks ago, we'd be just sitting here in a sort of stupor, wholly dependent on Jason and Bill. Nevertheless, I'm glad they're going to be okay though."

Around sunset, the vehicle pulled up a farmer's lane and stopped before a large white barn. Both women looked very confused, but had little choice but to trust what the professor had said. Shortly, a hooded man stepped out of the barn and looked in all directions for a minute. Seeing nothing, he then walked swiftly to the EMAC and climbed inside. He didn't speak, as the professor had warned them, even though the women did say hello and thanked him for helping them. He merely climbed into the driver's seat and got the vehicle moving once more. The two sat back and waited.

Time passed. Although it was now full dark, the two saw the lights of a city appearing and realized they were entering it, though they knew not which city; maybe it was St. Louis. Their driver took a circuitous route and finally came to a stop outside what appeared to be a darkened warehouse. No one was around. Both began to worry once more. Their silent benefactor opened the door, handed Amanda a flashlight and a piece of paper. He pointed to the paper, and she read it.

"We are to follow these instructions?" she asked politely. The man nodded and began carrying their bags out of the vehicle and inside the warehouse. Amanda helped Jessica down and then held on to her. Both needed the support of the other. The gravel just outside the warehouse was tricky to handle in their heels. Once inside, they spotted the elevator the directions mentioned. Already, their silent benefactor had placed four of their suitcases inside. By the time that they got themselves over to the elevator and inside the warehouse, he returned with the remainder of their baggage and the rolling cart they had taken from New O'Hare earlier this morning.

"Thank you sir," Amanda whispered. The hooded man merely nodded and left them alone in the vacant warehouse. "Okay, you hold the light, and I'll follow the directions." Jessica did as she asked. "Press the D button." She did so, and the elevator began descending below ground. "I think this must be the basement level. There are no lower buttons."

"I wonder what's down here," Jessi whispered. "What are we getting ourselves into this time?"

"Safety, I hope," Amanda tried to keep her morale up. This was anything but encouraging. In fact, nothing had gone as they had planned for this day. By now, they ought to have been in a penthouse suite somewhere in San Francisco and planning their escape from their two men. Now, they were likely presumed dead until their bodies were not found in the Air Liner wreckage, at which point they were likely to be wanted fugitives, in a strange and unknown city, in an abandoned warehouse, heading underground, and had no idea what lay ahead of them. When the elevator stopped, the two began loading their things back onto the rolling cart.

They were in some kind of hallway, but it was pitch black. Their tiny flashlight only barely illuminated their cart and the directions. "We have to go a long way down this hall according to the directions. Can you still push some? I don't think I can pull it far all by myself. My feet are rebelling," Amanda whispered.

"Mine too, but we have too. I'll push as best I can. It'll help if I lean on the cart some. I hope it's not too far. I'm getting rather scared. I suppose there are rats down here," Jessica whispered back, her voice wavering a little. Slowly they made their way along the hallway. All manner of discarded junk lay around them. Twice they had to stop and move obstacles out of their way so their cart could pass by. Finally, they arrived at a sliding metal door, and they stopped to read what to do next.

"It says to knock three times, then once, then twice. Okay, here goes," Amanda whispered. "Keep your fingers crossed." She knocked in the proper sequence. They heard something metal sliding, and then the hallway around them was suddenly brilliantly illuminated. Both blinked furiously at the sudden, unexpected light. They noticed the hallway was both filthy and quite cluttered, but somehow they'd negotiated it. Then the lights dimmed way down, for which they were grateful. The heavy metal door, which they later learned was a blast door, slid open, revealing a clean, but cluttered room. A young man about their own age stood before them.

Chapter 3—Weasel and Wart

"Holy shit! You two are knockouts! Incredibly impressive," the strange man eyed the women, undressing them from head to toe. "Here you are in Weasel's Den. Nobody's going to believe this one. Oh! Where are my manners? Hello, I'm Weasel. Wart is off on a mission right now. Come on in. Ignore the mess. Been working. Damn, the professor sure knows how to pick them," the overly excited young man rambled, gushing without thinking. Jessica thought he had probably never seen an exotic escort woman close up.

He was wearing a T-shirt that read: If it ain't broke, don't fix it. She thought this was rather strange, but soon the whole place seemed strange to the two women as they entered his den. Weasel's jeans were a bit dirty, and she concluded he'd been on his knees doing something. His sneakers were quite worn. His hair was rather long and brown, but in need of a good brushing or combing, and he definitely needed to shave. His blue eyes were bright, and his smile and enthusiasm seemed genuine. He said, "You're safe here. None of us is on Pytalon, and we've never been implanted. So you really are going to be very safe here."

Jessica tried to relax for the first time on this long day. "Thank you for taking us in, Weasel. I'm Jessica Alexandra and she's my constant companion Amanda Pottingham."

"Come on. I'll show you around the den. Leave your stuff for now; I'll bring it to your room later. Because I'm a computer whiz, there are lots of electronics around here. Please don't touch any of the equipment." They walked through a large room filled with computers and sound equipment. They heard exotic music splatted with peppy and pounding rhythms, but sounding foreign to the two women.

"What is that music? It's strange, but cool," Jessica asked, forgetting how badly her feet were aching just now.

"I am into ancient music. It's from the Crusades times, medieval times. It dates back to the 14th century, Celle qui m'a demande—my French is pitiful. It's really cool with a change from binary to ternary meter between the verse and the refrain. I have my play list on auto-repeat. Keeps me energized when I'm working. We're on a crusade, you see, to rid the world of the psychs, Pytalon, and the damnable PDH implants that they do."

"Incredible! What a worthwhile goal," Jessica replied. "Now that we're off Pytalon, I can see just how incredibly vital this crusade of yours is. Are there others helping you?" she asked.

"Yes, quite a few. You've met one, calls himself the Professor. Alas, we're still kind of a small group. It's hard finding anyone who isn't drugged or implanted these days," Weasel replied.

As they walked past his big control center, they spotted three poster-sized images of other EE women wearing exotic outfits. He flushed, "Don't pay them any attention."

"You have good taste in posters," Jessica teased him a little, adding to his embarrassment.

"Well, you two are incredibly sexy, no doubt about that. I can't imagine how you can even walk in those boots, Jessica," he replied, changing the subject a little.

"Right now my feet are killing me. I've walked more today than ever before. Is our room close?" she asked, trying not to whine.

"Just past mine and Wart's. Come on. I have it all fixed up for you two. The Professor called me before he sent you off in his EMAC. The bathroom is next to your room, and the kitchen and play areas are further down the hall. I'll go get your bags now," he offered.

Both women smiled and thanked him. Their room was small with one regular sized bed, a circular table, two chairs, one small chest of drawers with an old mirror on it. A small rug lay before the bedside hiding the concrete floor.

Jessica sat down on the bed and began massaging her feet. "I'm starving, but I've got to rest my feet a while, Amanda."

"Don't worry, mine ache too. I'll get our things arranged. When you are up to it, we'll see what's in the kitchen. I'm famished, but I want to get out of this tight corset as soon as possible," Amanda answered.

Weasel made several trips with their suitcases. They filled up the empty floor space. "Once you get things stored, we can put the empty cases outside along your wall. I suppose I should fix you something for supper. I'm not much of a cook, but I'll fix you something while you're getting settled."

"Thanks Weasel. We really appreciate it. Our feet are cramped and killing us," Amanda replied with a sigh, as she took off her heels to massage her feet. "Is there a shower in the bathroom?"

"Sure and a tub. Probably don't have all the right soaps and things you're used to having. Guess you're going to have to rough it until we can get what you need." He smiled and left, heading off to the kitchen with his fingers snapping time to the music.

A half hour later, the two women walked to the kitchen. They had removed their tight corsets and freshened up, but the smells of dinner made their stomachs growl. Once they found the kitchen, they saw Weasel bent over a pot on the stove. "Hi Weasel, what's for dinner?" Jessica asked with a flirting grin, as her eyes took in the room. The kitchen was a concrete block room some twenty feet square, with a microwave, a refrigerator that had seen better days, a small electric stove that was in need of a cleaning, and a sink piled high with dirty dishes. The table was a plywood board resting on four barrels, with four cushioned folding chairs around it.

"Hi, I've got dinner reheated. Hope you like tea. Wart's the coffee drinker, and I'm not allowed to mess with his machine when he's not here. Have a seat. I know it's not what you are used to, but it's the best we've got here." He carried two pots over to the table. "Chicken, mashed potatoes, gravy, and peas. Help yourselves." He sat down and poured himself a cup of tea from the yellow flowered porcelain teapot. The teacups were also fancy porcelain. "I take my tea seriously," he grinned. The two helped themselves.

"Thanks, we're hungry," Jessica said and began to eat, noticing that the food seemed to taste much better than it had when she was drugged.

"So, the professor said you two somehow got yourselves off Pytalon. That's really something. You know most people end up committing suicide or go insane and don't survive the awful withdrawal symptoms. You had hallucinations and all that?" he asked curiously.

Jessica gave a little chuckle. "I can laugh about it now, but it was really awful. I really thought my pillows were rats, crawling all over me. I hate rats. I can see why people might succumb to harming themselves. It was scary, but Amanda and I helped each other through it all."

"Impressive, indeed, most impressive," he validated them, though he appeared deep in thought.

"What a relief it is to be able to remember things again. I can't believe I went almost eight years, unable to remember anything about my life, just living from moment to moment," Jessica added.

"No kidding. The worst part of it was always seeing a sort of grey fog when I closed my eyes," Amanda added. "That's mostly gone now, thank God. I can't believe people live like that."

"I know. We call them zombies. They can hardly think for themselves. Rather pathetic if you ask me," Weasel admitted. "So the awful withdrawal symptoms are totally gone?"

"As far as we know," Jessica suggested, "unless there are other things that'll happen to us. We have our memories back, and we've been rather stable these last couple of days. Say, will we be getting flashbacks or other things happening to us later? Are there symptoms we should be watching for?"

Her voice sounded a little worried. Weasel reassured, "Have to ask Wart that. I know very little about getting off Pytalon. I've never been on it, thank God! If you're stable, the worst is over," he suggested, hoping to put the women at ease. He saw he'd caused them to worry and knew he should've waited for Wart before discussing such things. "Wart knows about Pytalon. I know more about psych PDH implants, since they deal heavily with electronics—that's my area, computers and all things electronic."

"Our implants are still in us," Jessica felt she should at least let him know that they were not "normal" yet.

"Of course. Those have nothing to do with the Pytalon drug, separate and far worse for you, though many might disagree with me on this point. Certainly, Wart and the professor do. We argue about which is worse frequently. I know what the psychs say to EE women when they are being implanted, and I know all about their behavioral patterns they must follow," he broached the topic that really interested him. "I hope you don't mind my talking about the implants. You see, I've never had the chance to study anyone who was implanted but not on Pytalon. So you two are exceptional cases."

"It's okay," Jessica replied, taking a sip of tea. "Good tea. Earl Grey?"

He smiled. "Yes. Do you get headaches if you don't follow the implanted behaviors?"

Jessica laughed. "How did you know that? Yes, excruciating, totally debilitating headaches. We both get them if we don't follow what the voices in our heads tell us."

"Naturally, that is part of the implant—getting the pain if you don't obey. Can I ask you something about it? If it's too personal, you don't have to answer." Jessica nodded, and he continued. "From what I think I understand about the EE implants is you have to be pleasured at least three times a day and that you have enough free will or reasoning powers to be able to flirt with the men you escort. Is that right? What do you do if the man can't do it that often?"

Jessica laughed. "Wouldn't you like to know?" she teased him, and he flushed. "Seriously, Weasel, you're right. We need pleasuring three times a day. If we don't, the headaches start and slowly increase until we do. That's why EE women are often paired up with another EE woman. We often have to pleasure each other to get by and avoid the crushing headaches. Now that we're off Pytalon, we find this very embarrassing too, and we still get the implant headaches."

Amanda added, "You are right about the reasoning powers. We call it the ability to think, at least a little. From what we've seen, EE women have a lot more ability to think than anyone else, but our thinking powers were limited to our 'trade,' if you follow me. What a difference being off Pytalon is making! Now we only have to deal with the implant behavior and headaches."

"Got it. Makes sense. I bet that extra reasoning power helped you get off Pytalon, but Wart can answer that better. Say, it's late and you two must have had quite a day. I best let you get some sleep. In the morning, we can chat more and try to figure out what to do next. If you need anything, just holler. I'll keep my music down."

A while later, the two women had changed into their nightgowns and dealt with the mounting low grade headaches they were feeling. Then, Jessica whispered, "I'm going to stay up a while longer and read some of the professor's history book." An hour later, Jessica finally put the book down and slipped under the covers, her mind reflecting over what she'd been reading. Because it explained so much, this was the most important book she'd ever begun to read—she was certain of that, and very timely, considering what had happened to the two of them.

The smell of eggs and bacon roused the women. As usual, when they finally walked into the kitchen, they were fully dressed with their makeup nicely done. The command that an EE woman must always look her best at all times was still fully functional with the two women. "Morning, Weasel," Jessica announced, as she entered the room, Amanda following her.

"Morning. Things are a brewing—I mean the recent events of yesterday. Help yourselves. While you're eating, there are some things we should discuss," he stated formally.

"Like what?" Jessica asked, scooping some of the scrambled eggs onto her plate.

"Like your new identities. You can't use your ID cards anymore. That'll be the first thing the IP-cops will be monitoring. Use the card and they'll be on you in no time. I can make you a new ID card that will pass all screening. You can keep your first names, but we're going to have to change your last names. You'll still be logged as EE women. There's no point in changing your occupation. The implants will prevent that, you see." He went on, "The worst thing is you can't access your bank accounts any longer. Again, they'll be watching that like a hawk, but then you've already handled that one."

"We did. We took out most of our money before we went to San Francisco. How did you know that?" Jessica asked, suddenly becoming very curious about Weasel.

"I checked your accounts late last night. Hey, I'm Weasel. There's hardly nothing I can't get access to when I want it. Very smart move on your part. Actually, I was very much impressed you had the insight to do that." The two women smiled, pleased at his observation.

He went on, "Of course, the IP-cops have already discovered you withdrew the funds. Unfortunately, that has led them to believe you both were somehow involved in the terrorist attack on the skyscraper yesterday morning and that you are now dead or fleeing."

Both women's faces twisted. "Oh damn! We're fugitives for real now!" Jessica exclaimed. The reality of their plight took on a new dimension.

"No problem. We're all fugitives, in one way or another. The professor was right. Only an hour after you fled from his place, the IP-cops swarmed in, but found only his note saying he was out of town for two weeks teaching a course at a high school. Of course, he didn't tell them what high school," he grinned mischievously. Seeing the concern on their faces, he added quickly, "He's fine, just in hiding at another of his homes. That man has nine lives, like a cat. Strange Englishman. Anyway, Jessica, you're now going to be Jessica Wales, and you'll be Amanda Walsh. Hope you like the new names." Both grinned.

Once they finished eating, he took them to his main control center where his ancient music was playing softly. He brought up their new ID cards on his big flat screen for their approval. "One thing you have going for you is that on your old cards, your pictures are old, taken when you were eighteen. You look different now, better, cooler, sexier," he grinned. "I'll put your current images on these new cards. They'll pass everything except for a close facial recognition program that ages your eighteen-year-old senior pictures. I doubt the IP-cops will have enough reasoning power to think of doing that. Now the Feds—they might. The Feds are involved now, since Ben's dumb move made it a terrorist action. Still, let's not give the Feds any reason to reprogram your photo ID. Let's get your pics taken and get these cards finished up, shall we?"

"Let us check our makeup, please. We must always look our best, but you know that," Jessica began to explain. He knew precisely why she said that. She flushed. Ten minutes later, they pocketed their new ID cards.

"Okay, I've got to do some other work now. I have to leave some false breadcrumbs for the Feds to find. We'll talk more later," Weasel said.

"Fine, we'll wash the dishes for you," Amanda offered.

"Thanks. I only do them when I run out of dishes." The women laughed.

"Turn up the music if you like," Jessica suggested. He did so and began typing away. As much as she wanted to stand beside him and watch, she felt obligated to help Amanda. Then there was that history book calling her back too. After cleaning the kitchen, Jessica went to read, while Amanda lay down on the bed to relax.

Around noon, she finished the book. "This was fascinating and so revealing! Amanda, you should read it now."

"Can't you just summarize it for me?" Amanda pleaded. "I'm into math, not reading history books."

"Okay. Back near the start of 2000, many kids were into playing video games, so the psychs added a new mental disorder, similar to their fictitious attention deficit disorder. They called it GAD, games attention disorder, and they put such kids onto the predecessor to our Pytalon drug. By 2020, nearly all children in the developed countries were hooked on the drug, which rendered them much like us, unthinking zombies. Also, in 2012, something called Affordable Care was passed, providing healthcare for everyone."

"So what happened after that?" a strange voice broke in on them. Both looked up to see a stranger standing in their doorway. "I'm Wart, by the way. Please, do go on with your explanation. You must be Jessica and you, Amanda." He stood six feet tall and wore jeans and a yellow cotton pullover shirt. His hair was longer than Weasel's was, and Amanda thought he looked rather handsome.

"Right. Hello. Pleased to meet you, Wart. Okay, by 2020, these doped up children began to take over all manner of jobs as the older generation retired. By then, everyone was dependent utterly on the national healthcare and unemployment was staggering. Worse, that Affordable Health Care system bankrupted the US government. With nearly everyone demanding a government handout, they passed the Total Care bill, you know, from the cradle to the grave. Total Care took over everyone's lives, promising everyone total security for their entire lives."

"By 2030, these drugged adults were running nearly everything. That's when the psychs convinced them that Insanity was the number one enemy of the country and the world. You see, their drugs actually often induced insanity in these people. So it began—the war on insanity. Then along came Pytalon, the new improved anti-psychotic drug. How am I doing?" Jessica asked, flashing Wart a flirting grin.

"Fine so far," he replied with an equal grin. "Do go on."

"Ah, then, Doctor Bo Bin Lin, a psychiatrist, worked out the fundamentals of how to do a much better PDH implant. By drugging the person, hitting them with intense pain delivered via electronics, and then laying down words in the middle of it all, he was able to modify greatly a person's long-term behavior. Of course, it's been refined a whole lot since then, but he invented it back in 2022. By 2030, its use became widespread. They claimed enormous benefits from it. Crime dropped to nearly zero. Of course it did. Drugged and implanted people can't think, let alone do anything they aren't told to do. Now the war against Insanity took a huge leap forward. Based on the supposed benefits, the implants and Pytalon spread worldwide. Here in the US, by 2030, even the normal police were given the treatments, since there wasn't any crime for them to handle. Total Care was then finally implemented everywhere. I wish there was more on the last hundred or so years though, but the book ends there."

"Excellent summary, Jessica," Wart complimented her. "So, Amanda, you're supposed to be a math person. What can you extrapolate from what she's said to our world? Statistically speaking, of course," he added, nudging her in the right direction.

"Oh, statistically. Well, that's another angle, certainly. Those under the dual influence can't think. We should know. People would just continue to do what they had always been doing, so one would expect that nothing new would be invented. This explains why we have our current totally stagnant world," she suggested in a rush of thought.

"Precisely, Amanda. Nothing new is ever invented. It's as if the evolutionary time line has simply stopped. Everyone does only what they have always done. Culture, society, music, the arts, even the entertainment industry is non-existent. No one plays games; no one listens to music; no one reads any more than they have to read. No one creates anything new; they just keep on doing their job over and over like Weasel and his ancient music that keeps repeating itself."

"Hey, I heard that Wart!" Weasel shouted in mock anger from his console. Both men laughed, and the women grinned.

"Well, to be honest, we owe the MTE system, EMAC vehicles, and Air Liners to a bunch of women engineers, who took over when the men in those industries were drugged on Pytalon. Of course, some years after that, they too were turned into zombies," Wart explained. He went on, "So here we are a century or more later, and the world is wholly stagnant—an awful status quo, so to speak."

Weasel stuck his head in the doorway and added, "Yes, and don't forget to tell them about what's been happening to those who underwent PDH implants. That's my research project, you see."

"Right, this impacts you both. Weasel has discovered that in time, the awful command values implanted in people tend to break down. While they don't totally go away, they tend to have less and less of an effect on them. Coupled with the Pytalon in their systems, they tend to do very goofy, bazar things. At this point in time, the psychs are re-implanting those who are messing up too badly to continue with their work."

He went on, "That, in part, was what your former sponsors were planning to do in San Francisco. They were on their way there with a new modified version of Pytalon—that is, an experimental version—plus new guidelines on when to pull someone in to get re-implanted. Thanks to Ben and his Air Liner mess, that's been delayed for some time. However, many of us think Ben's actions were just plain wrong. We've been monitoring Pytalon manufacturing in your skyscraper, where your former sponsors worked, and have noted that already some of the assembly line workers' implants were breaking down. The result was Pytalon pills containing no Pytalon. You two must have somehow gotten a hold of some of those failed batches and thus inadvertently got off the drug. My calculations indicated in time, more and more of these failures would have occurred, and hundreds, perhaps thousands, would have come off the drug. In my opinion, that would have been a far, far better outcome than what Ben, on his own, has dealt us. All those whose implants were breaking down are now dead. Damn him anyway."

"How do you know what our sponsors were going to do?" asked Amanda, whose curiosity was definitely pricked. She'd learned more about her world and situation in the last twenty-four hours than she had in her whole life. She had dozens of questions bouncing around her head, but settled on this one. *How can these two men know what our sponsors were planning to do?*

"Simple, we've been hacking into your company's computer systems for years, monitoring their plans. Moreover, Ben sent me the contents of the two briefcases your vice-presidents were given before they were attacked, because he thought I might know what to do with them. I've forwarded them on to others in our group, after reading the documents, of course," Wart replied. "Mind you, Ben acted on his own. None in our group wanted him to kill all those people."

"So what happens to us now?" Amanda asked, while a multitude of questions swarmed in her mind.

"That depends a lot on what you want to do. Now that you know the truth of our world, it's your call. You can stick around with us and lend us a hand in trying to undo all this mess or you can go to whatever city you desire and live your lives as you had planned, more or less," Wart answered truthfully. "We could use the help, though. Hint, hint." He grinned.

Amanda grinned back. After a nod from Jessica, she replied, "Okay, we'll help as we can. What do you want us to do? I hope it isn't cooking. Neither of us is particularly good at that."

He chuckled. "Thanks, Amanda. We'll manage on the cooking somehow. I heard you used to be good at math. I need some help with some calculations right now. Jessica can help Weasel with his computer backups."

"Okay, I'm probably very rusty, but I'll do my best," Amanda replied.

Wart took Amanda into his small study area and gave her some complicated equations. "I want you simply to do the calculations using these values for the variables," he explained. "I'll tell you what it means after you get your answer. That way, you won't be biased in any way." She set to work on his calculations, while Jessica sat down beside Weasel.

"We're backing up all the files, Jessica," he explained and got her going on the project. With her long nails clicking on the keyboard, Weasel smiled. "I've got to check on the professor's EMAC."

"Why? Isn't it just outside or with that farmer?" she asked, entering the next command on the keyboard.

"No, it was here only for the brief time it took for you to get out of it. The Feds can track it down, so—ah ha. Yes, it's halfway to Boston right now. Hopefully, if they're tracking it, it'll lead them far astray," Weasel explained.

"So where are we? St. Louis?" Jessica asked softly, unsure if she should even ask about this location. If she didn't know, she couldn't be forced to tell someone.

"In the basement of an abandoned warehouse in East Peoria, about halfway to St. Louis from Chicago," he replied. "Oh, don't worry; it's not a secret, now that you're with us."

"Cool. Say, what is your real name and why are you called Weasel? Why is he Wart? You don't have to answer if you think I'm out of line in asking, Weasel."

He chuckled, as if remembering former times. "Ben Snells. He's Tim Hickory. I got my nickname ages ago, because I can weasel into any computer system in the world, and I've never been caught nor detected. Hence, Weasel. He's Wart because of his insidious plans. He keeps on getting the authorities to do what he wants them to do, and they don't even know he's pulling their strings. He's like an ugly wart they can't get rid of by any means. Everyone knows us by our nicks, not by our real names. Heck, we haven't used our real names, not for at least the last ten years or so. How are the backups coming?" He looked over her shoulders. "Good, you do know something about computers. I've never met any woman who knew much about them, but then there aren't many women that aren't zombies these days."

"Thanks, I used to love programming computers and making web sites when I was in high school," she replied, "that and history."

Wart let out a curse. "Okay, Amanda. This is quite important. Please redo all the calculations once more. Let's double-check the result, because it's bad for us." Amanda didn't quite know what to make of his outburst. She'd just showed him the final resulting number, seventy-five.

"Did I do something wrong?" she asked, worried she'd made a huge error.

"No, I don't see anything wrong. It's just the resulting number. Please, it's very important. Do the calculations one more time, and I'll watch you as a triple-check." Amanda felt very nervous with him staring at her figures, but she took a deep breath and began redoing the rather extensive calculations. Minutes later, she arrived at the same answer and looked up at his grimacing face.

"What's it mean?" she asked nervously.

Wart called out, "Weasel, time to put Plan X into high gear. Seventy-five percent chance the Feds will come knocking on our door in the next twenty-four hours."

"Shit! Damn Ben anyway! Well, Jessica and I are about done with the backups. Why don't you and Amanda start packing," Weasel suggested.

"What's going on? Why are the Feds coming here? How do they know about this place?" Jessica asked, suddenly growing very worried again. She'd only just become comfortable here, and her world was being turned upside down again.

"The professor took a gamble sending his EMAC here with you two aboard. While it was stopped here for ten minutes at most, according to Weasel who sent it on its way to Boston after returning the farmer, my probability formulas are suggesting the Feds will in all likelihood come here to check this place out, particularly so, once they find the EMAC and see it's empty. They'll be looking for you two women, because they think you might have been somehow involved in the terrorist act. Of course, you weren't, but they would certainly force you back onto Pytalon, if not insist you get your implants redone. Amanda, that's what you were calculating, the probability the Feds would check on this place," Wart explained. "Seventy-five percent chance they'll come here."

"I'm so sorry! We didn't mean to cause you all this trouble. We just wanted to get away somehow," Jessica fought hard to keep her eyes from watering, which would mess up her eye makeup. Part of her continued to insist she look her best no matter the circumstances.

"Hey, no problem. We knew the Feds would find this place eventually. No problem. We planned for it, so let's get packing," Wart said in a calming tone.

Jessica asked, "Who or what are these Feds? I take it they are really bad men."

Wart replied seriously, "Federal Elimination Division and Security or Feds. Officially, there are about three hundred men who are not either implanted or on Pytalon in the United States, at least that we know about. Some are the leaders of key companies, such as us, theoretically. These men are extremely well armed and trained, like an army's Special Forces. We suspect they take orders from the heads of the drug companies. Their job is to handle terminally dangerous situations, such as Ben's ill-conceived attack on your skyscraper, and provide top quality security for their bosses. Obviously, the local AP-cops, who are on Pytalon, can't think or reason, but they can pick up those who display outward signs of Inanity. If Ben and everyone else only had to worry about the AP-cops, why, we would all still be back in our headquarters, and you two would still be in the professor's house in Joliet. These Feds are utterly ruthless and go to any extremes to get their jobs done. Nasty bunch of fellows. So we'd best get packing."

"Pack my stuff for me, will you, Amanda? I'm still helping Weasel here," Jessica pleaded.

"Sure thing. As soon as I have our things ready, you have to tell me what to do here, Wart," Amanda volunteered. He nodded, and they headed off in different directions.

An hour later, they had everything they were taking stowed in some kind of huge bus that neither woman had ever seen before. All the gear they were leaving behind had been cleverly concealed behind secret panels. The finishing touch was handled by the men, who scattered more junk around the place, making it appear abandoned, but that perhaps a tramp had lived here at one time or another. The two men helped the women into the large cab. Both men had changed their clothes and were now wearing business suits.

With a broad grin, Wart explained, "Ah, Miss Amanda, you're now formally the EE for Mr. Hickory. Miss Jessica, you're the EE for Mr. Snells. We two are the co-presidents of Acme Manufacturing who are taking a traveling business trip in search of a new company expansion location. Plan X is that we go mobile for some time. If we ever get stopped, that is our cover story, one which will check out, thanks to Weasel, who has installed us and you two into the National Corporate Database. This is our modified EMAC bus, fully equipped with all the amenities one could ask for, save food. To maintain our cover, we'll need to stop and dine at some fancy restaurants along the way. Shall we get rolling?"

"Let her rip," Weasel replied with a chuckle. "I've always wanted to go touring. Actually, Jessica, Amanda, with you two EE women along, our cover story is far, far more believable. When we thought of this plan years ago, we figured we'd have to go hire a couple of EE women or kidnap them. So ladies, your timing is impeccable."

"Still, Weasel, I'm sorry we have brought you both so much trouble," Jessica said sincerely.

"Ah, don't worry about it. Just having two gorgeous, young women with us makes it all worth it," he teased, but she sensed his tease was hiding the truth about their situation. Jessica believed neither of these men had been with a woman for a very long time, if ever. The bus was on a huge elevator and slowly rose up to the ground level. After Wart drove it off the elevator floor, Weasel hopped out and moved more junk over the surface of the elevator, further disguising it.

"That should do it. Looks like the rest of the place, abandoned junk. We're good to go," Weasel relayed to Wart.

"We're off to see the world," Wart called out. "Weasel, get on the monitoring station, please. We don't want any surprises for a while." Silently, the large bus moved out of the alley and onto the main streets of the city. It was late afternoon when they pulled out of Peoria, heading south. "Find us a nice restaurant in St. Louis, Weasel, where we will fit in nicely. Amanda, supper will be elegant tonight, more like what you were used to having." He grinned at Amanda, who was sitting beside him. She returned in kind, as the bus silently picked up speed.

Chapter 4—Countermoves

Fifty year old Tom Fredricks, the CEO of Pytalon LLC Chicago inherited his position from his father, who had helped form the Great Civilization also known as Total Care, ending wars, crime, and for the most part insanity. Three years ago, he'd slipped Pytalon into his parents' drink and taken over the Chicago operation. After all, he justified, dad might have had the onset of dementia, and besides, he was tired of waiting to take over for his father. Now he was peaceful and calm. Tom, one of the actual rulers of the world, kept himself fit. He was handsome, but had never married. He couldn't stomach marrying a "normal," as they called those on Pytalon, nor did he desire children, who always seemed to get in his way.

No, he preferred the constant company of his current beautiful doll, the EE woman Elana. Her constant flirting kept him aroused, and she knew how to satisfy him, which was the whole point of her PDH implant after all. Besides, the EE women could at least think independently, if only along one channel of thought, how to please him sexually. No, life was grand. Of course, in a few more years, he could "acquire" a new, younger EE woman.

His technicians had just developed a possible Pytalon variation, which promised to have longer lasting effects. The San Francisco office had volunteered to mass test the new drug variation. Why? They had the highest abnormal reactions rate of all the major US cities. What better place to test it? Jason and Bill were entrusted to take the supplies and formula to San Francisco. They should be taking off from O'Hare about now, Tom thought, glancing at the wall clock.

"Baby, why do you look at that silly clock and not me?" Elana asked demurely. "Am I not prettier than a clock?" She pursed her red lips slightly, as though annoyed. She had long raven hair, augmented breasts, a small nose, and thick, black eyebrows and lashes. Centuries ago, she could have been a top model. Such things did not exist these days, however.

"Raven honey, it reminds me that it's time for you to come sit on my lap," he replied. She smiled, rose, tottered slightly on her extremely high heels, and slunk sexily over to him, wiggling her hips and waist seductively. As she sat, his arms encircled her thin waist. Together, they peered out of the massive windows here in his office on the top floor of the skyscraper. To the north, Lake Michigan stretched, a line of blue contrasting with the billowing clouds of the sky. He brushed her long hair aside and gently kissed her exposed neck.

They spotted the company Air Liner coming their way. "That's strange. Jason and Bill ought to be heading for San Francisco," he mused, as he watched the large craft growing steadily larger. "My god! It's heading straight for us!" he exclaimed, nearly dumping Elana onto the floor as he rose. She grabbed onto him to keep her balance and stared uncomprehendingly at the great form coming at them.

She screamed, and he swore when the Air Liner smashed into their building a number of floors below theirs. Both their knees buckled from the jarring collision, magnified by the metal and concrete structure. They landed hard on the floor. Mechanically, he helped Elana to her feet, but ignored her screams. He tried the intercom, but all power to the building was temporarily gone. He was isolated on the top floor, as mass chaos erupted and flames from the chemical processing floors rushed up the side of the skyscraper.

Just then, his chief Feds, Peter Delius, a muscular and fit man of thirty, came dashing into his office. "Evacuate now, Tom. To the EMAC on the roof! We're under a terrorist attack!" Though he tried to get them to head to the roof, Tom hesitated.

"Wait. I don't see any other liners out there. The attack is over. We must see to the damage and what happened to Jason and Bill. Their mission is vitally important, and that is their Air Liner. Elana and I saw our logo. Send men to New O'Hare; see if their mission has been compromised, Peter," Tom ordered, dusting himself off. "I'll take charge here."

An hour later, Tom brought Jason and Bill down from his EMAC on the rooftop. Both were wearing blankets over their underwear; both looked haggard. "Well, what the devil happened, Jason?"

"Boss, we got the EE women onto the Air Liner when the two couriers arrived. We just made the briefcase switch when the baggage handlers shot us. Must have been stun guns because we're still alive. My God, our women—they were still onboard the liner!" Jason fumbled for words, his body still shaking some.

Tom griped, "Hell, you can always get new EE women. What of the secure cases?"

"No sign of the women or the briefcases, but we found the two couriers and two baggage handlers not far away. Stunned too," Peter added, flexing his muscles. His anger was quite visible. "Wait until we catch them, Tom! I'll show them what terror really is!"

"You don't need my permission to do that, Peter. First, you have to find them and find the briefcases! They knew precisely where to cause us the most damage. All our production lines are destroyed, as well as the experimental lab. Without those notes and samples in the briefcases, we won't be able to recreate the new drug for at least a year," Tom grimaced. The adrenaline had long ago gone from his system, and he felt terribly tired and weak.

"No Pytalon production, boss?" Jason tried to focus on what he thought was important. His mind was still fuzzy; the shock had very nearly killed him. "Chicago is going to need more supplies before a year, aren't we? How?"

"Jason, Bill, you go get cleaned up, rest. I'll handle it. Elana, get us some coffee. I have to make a series of video-calls now. Damn the terrorists to Hell!" Peter saluted and left, while Elana, still in shock herself, walked off to see about making some coffee.

Normally, Elana would just order it from the cafeteria, but that was destroyed, at least she thought she'd heard that. *I'm so confused. Terrorists. So many people killed. Surely, this is insanity striking us. I thought we were winning the Insanity War. I'm so confused. How do I make coffee anyway? I don't know how to cook. I need pleasuring right now; I can't take any more of this confusion, I really can't. I must look my best at all times.* She paused before a mirror to check on her makeup and appearance, making a few minor adjustments. Eventually, she found the coffee maker, but soon realized she had no idea how to work the machine. "Oh dear, is it the red button that I push or the green one?" she called out to Tom.

"Oh forget it; bring me a bottled water, Elana," he replied. At least backup power was on, and now he could get the video-meeting going. There would be hell to pay this time. All the other major plants and CEOs had to know of this brazen attack and take preventative measures. An hour later, he ended the online conference, having gotten promises from the other plants to make up his shortfall of Pytalon pills until his manufacturing capabilities were restored. To that end, he issued orders for the massive cleanup and rebuilding process to begin, even though rescue workers were still removing the dead bodies from the rubble.

"Tom, you have to see this," Peter broke in on his conference calls. Peter played back some video clips from surveillance cameras in and around New O'Hare. "The two EE women were not onboard. Apparently, the terrorists removed them and their baggage," Peter pointed out the obvious. Only key locations still had operational cameras. Crime was almost non-existent for the last century, and no one bothered to repair all the cameras throughout the city. Such was more or less pointless these days, and besides, who would monitor the feeds? Other doped-up people?

"Yes, I can see them, but why didn't they return here? Where the devil are those two women going?" Tom asked, growing more and more curious about their strange behavior. He glanced at Elana, who was still trying to figure out how to make coffee and pleasure herself at the same time. "Their actions are inexplicable. Just look at how Elana is handling this," Tom pointed out. "Those two women should be running around in circles, but they seem to possess some kind of motivation."

"That's what I'm thinking, Tom," Peter said with a snarling grin. "It's almost as if they may have played a role in the terrorist strike. It's more as if they're running away or trying to at least. My men are following them. I've put out a Wanted Bulletin already. We should have them apprehended in an hour or two. Then, I will question them personally." He pounded his fist onto the table rather hard, shaking Tom's half-empty water bottle.

"Best not tell Jason or Bill their EE women were not on the liner just yet. They aren't above suspicion as far as I'm concerned. They are thinking men and should never have allowed this disaster to happen in the first place. I know. I should have listened to you and sent along a couple of your Feds. Hindsight is perfect, you know. Keep me posted, Peter." Peter saluted and left the CEO, rejoining his men in their time-consuming efforts to trace where the two EE women had gone.

An hour later and after making a fast trip to Joliet, Peter barked, "I don't care if the note says the owner is out of town. Break the damn door down. The women must be inside hiding or something." Two of his men did just that, splintering the front door of the home. With their bulletproof vests on and protective headgear, his two Feds charged into the professor's home, guns drawn. Shouts of "Clear!" echoed for a couple of minutes, and then Peter walked inside. The place was empty.

"Okay, search for signs the women were here, men," he barked. "They have to have been here." After some searching, they found two lipstick smears on two cups, which Peter took as conclusive evidence that the two EE women had indeed been here, probably not very long ago. He sat down in the professor's lounge chair for a moment to think. Was this professor somehow tied to the terrorist attack? Why had the two women fled here of all places in Joliet? Why had they not taken the first EMAC back to their apartment? He had more questions than answers. He picked up his cell and made another call, one that sent another of his trusted Feds to the EE women's apartment. A few minutes later, the return call sparked his interest even more. The women had apparently taken all their possessions with them. Again, he mused; Jason and Bill had told them to bring all their things with them for the extended stay in San Francisco. Thus, an empty apartment was not unexpected.

Still not satisfied one way or the other, he made another call. "Now this is interesting," he said with a snarl as he hung up. "They took out all their money from the bank. The professor's EMAC is missing. Someone check on the professor and see if he has his EMAC with him." One of his men saluted and made a call of his own. Minutes later, he reported the professor had used public transportation on his trip. However, he had not yet arrived at his destination. Well, when the professor did arrive, one of his men would be there to question him.

"Okay, then, let's assume the two EE women took the professor's EMAC, with or without his permission. We must track where that EMAC is located now. Get on it men!" Peter barked. He began to believe these two EE women had played a role in the terrorist attack. Too many things now pointed to that conclusion. With nothing more to be learned here, he returned to his office in the top floor of the damaged skyscraper, reporting his findings and suspicions to Tom.

"But how could the EE women be involved, Peter? They're nothing more than intelligent sex dolls," Tom asked, growing confused. "They've been implanted properly. That I *do* know. I double-check all the EE women around here. They should be acting more as Elana has been. Something isn't right here, Peter. Keep digging," he ordered. Peter didn't need his order to do that. He fully intended to get to the bottom of these women's strange behavior patterns.

Late the next afternoon, other Feds stopped the professor's EMAC while en route to Boston! They found the vehicle empty and on automatic pilot! Immediately, Peter ordered a full trace on the route the vehicle had traveled since leaving the professor's home in Joliet. It was not until late the following afternoon that they had recovered the complete route taken.

Five Feds then proceeded to raid the single stopping point where the vehicle had halted long enough for the EE women to get out and retrieve their many suitcases. It was an abandoned warehouse on the west side of East Peoria, filled with rats, rusted machinery, and other abandoned junk. There were no surveillance cameras within a half mile of this place. Their cursory examination of the warehouse turned up little of interest. One called in and asked, "Boss, you want us to go over this warehouse with all of our fancy detection gear?"

Peter fumed, "How the devil could two idiot EE women simply vanish without a trace? They were implanted EE women, for God's sake!" Calming down, he replied, "Hold on that. Let's see if we can find them using easier ways. Head on back now. We can always go over that warehouse later." Fuming, he took his anger out on some of his men. A bit later, Tom took his anger out on him, though.

"So the despicable terrorists have vanished without a trace and so have two implanted EE women, who can only think of sex. My God, Peter, you'd think you Feds are all on Pytalon too! Find those damn terrorists. Forget the EE women for now, Peter. That's a direct order. Do it!" He fumed.

"Calm down, honey. You know anger makes you irritable. I know just what you need, Tommy. Come on. Let's use the couch for a while. Let Elana show you a good time," she flirted and suggested. It was hard to resist her mischievous grin and those red lips of hers. He succumbed to her charms once more.

***

Two weeks later, the cleanup operations were in full swing. More importantly, the Feds forensics team had finally produced results. From DNA samples recovered around New O'Hare and some fingerprints, they had identified one of the two terrorists, a Ben Hadwell. A nationwide dragnet was ordered. His capture was top priority among all active Feds everywhere. Of course, the databases contained virtually nothing on this man; Weasel had seen to that. Peter finally relaxed; it was just a matter of time now before this Ben Hadwell would be located and apprehended. He began to make plans on the best way to get the key information out of him and put an end to this terrorist organization permanently.

He set his mind to work on how to locate the two missing EE women, whom Jason and Bill still claimed simply couldn't have had anything to do with this mess. They were merely good sex dolls. Nevertheless, both men couldn't understand why the women had fled, but they theorized the terrorists had told them to flee for their lives. Unconvinced, Peter installed a Watcher program. If they ever used their ID cards for anything at all, and folks used them many times each day, his program would instantly alert him to their location. This was preferable to wasting time at that abandoned warehouse in East Peoria, and cheaper.

After a few days, Peter became very frustrated. The Watcher program reported nothing at all. How could anyone go for days without using their ID card? It was needed for damned near everything these days. He ran his hands through his hair. What was going on with these two EE women? Had they been kidnaped? Perhaps that would explain some of their strange behavior. That made some sense in his mind. After all, Tom, as well as Jason and Bill, assured him repeatedly that they were fully EE implanted, on Pytalon, and had no reasoning powers beyond flirting and being attractive sex dolls. Still, the trails had all gone cold, and Peter was most unhappy with this, vowing somehow to find more clues.

"Hey, Pete, we have a hot lead on the location of our bomber!" his second in command, Lech, brought him out of his deep thought and malaise. Within minutes, Peter geared up—flak-proof vest, bulletproof helmet, and five guns, one huge. Lech grinned. It was good finally to get some real action! Peter, Lech, and ten other Feds climbed into their EMAC and headed off to the south side of Chicago, now called Old Town. They stopped by a rundown factory that made bedsprings. It was some twenty miles from New O'Hare. A few people were on the street, but as the dozen Feds jumped out of the vehicle, they wisely moved away quickly. Obviously, here was more of the dreaded insanity, and they wanted no part of it. Their implants and Pytalon told them so via little voices in their heads.

Without any warning, the Feds burst into the factory. Ten men and women were going about their tasks working the machinery. None took more than a cursory notice of the dozen well-armed Feds. Many recited, "Sanity is doing a good job," in hushed tones. Quickly, the dozen men fanned out and began looking for the two rebels. Figuring this was merely a cover for the two rebels, Peter found the stairs and headed down into the basement. Over his helmet intercom, he barked, "Basement. Found something. Secure bunker!" A steel blast door blocked his way, and he was wise enough to wait for the others before trying to gain entrance. His adrenaline was flowing, action! He felt very much alive, for once.

Peter watched, as Lech and two others set the charges. Boom. The explosion forced the blast door open, and the dozen Feds charged in, taking Ben's accomplice by surprise. Fred raised his hands and called out, "Sanity is doing a good job." He was obviously pretending to be just another factory worker. His ruse failed at once. Peter recognized his face from the surveillance camera that had caught them entering New O'Hare. "You are under arrest for blowing up the Pytalon Headquarters. Where's the other man, Ben?" Peter barked out loudly, while the others rapidly searched the bunker.

"Clear!" several other Feds soon called out.

"Don't know what you are talking about, sir. Sanity says to help our Feds. I would help, but I don't know," Fred tried to talk his way out of this mess. Too late. He realized he should've fled when Ben had.

"Lech, take six others and search this place from top to bottom," Peter ordered. Roughly, he manhandled Fred out to the EMAC. Within minutes, Fred was securely chained to a chair in the basement interrogation room of the Feds building in downtown Chicago, the last place he wanted to be! He was sweating now. Would they torture him? If so, he wouldn't reveal where Ben was. He didn't know!

Relishing the moment, Peter walked into the room. "Fred, we can do this the easy way or the hard way. Your call, but I'd prefer to do it the hard way." He slapped Fred hard across his face. "Where are your accomplices?"

"I don't know, really I don't know," Fred answered. "We split up," he added hastily, hoping Peter would halt his fist, which was headed towards his face again. It didn't. Pain shot through his face.

A half hour later, Peter's hands throbbed from the severe beating he'd delivered to Fred. To Fred's credit, he didn't reveal any new information that Peter didn't already know.

Next, Peter injected Fred with the usual truth drug. After waiting the proper time, he again pounded the terrorist with his battery of questions. "Damn," Peter cursed. Fred had told him the same answers as before. In his drugged state, Fred thought, *The Feds aren't asking the right questions, and I sure as hell am not volunteering them.*

Hours later after the drug's effects wore off, Peter was convinced he wasn't going to get anything more out of Fred. "Okay, Fred. For your act of sabotage and the willful murder of nearly five hundred men and women—an act of raw insanity," Peter began to pronounce judgment. The Feds now tried, convicted, and sentenced all criminals. There were no more courts of law. No need for them.

Fred interrupted him, bleeding from his nose and cheeks from the beating he'd received, "Oh shut up! Go ahead and kill me. It won't stop a damned thing. Be quick about it, you fat pig!"

Peter slapped him again, splattering his blood on the adjacent wall. "Hell, I'm not going to kill you, though you damn well deserve it. A century ago, you would be executed on the spot. No, we're civilized now. You're going to the psychs and be implanted. You'll spend the rest of your miserable life polishing a doorknob!"

Fred shrieked, "God! No, anything but that. Kill me! Kill me, you fat pig!" For the first time, terror filled Fred's mind and body! He reeled from the thought that he would be spending the next fifty years or so mindlessly polishing some damnable doorknob and all the while believing he was doing a wonderful, useful job! He was about to become what he hated most, what he'd spent his young life fighting against, a mindless zombie! His shrieks died down, as he was dragged up and out of the basement. Peter merely grinned. A new notion entered his mind, one that he promised to look into as soon as this nasty business was wrapped up.

Peter then headed back to the rusting factory to check firsthand on the search. "Hi boss, we found something," Lech called out, seeing Peter enter the bunker. "This note suggests there is a safe-house down in St. Louis, a warehouse of some kind. We should check it out and see if Ben has fled there."

"Excellent, Lech! I'll arrange a raiding party at once. As soon as word of our raid here gets out, Ben may flee again. Say, who owns that warehouse down there anyway?" Peter asked, becoming slightly curious about it.

"Hum, Acme Refrigerator Manufacturing. I did a quick Web search and found they make refrigerators, as the name says. Owned by Mr. Snells and Mr. Hickory. They seem clean, boss. No records," Lech reported.

"Good work. We should investigate them as well. They could be part of a larger conspiracy. You keep looking here. I'll go back to HQ and see what more I can dig up on those two. They probably live in St. Louis, but we'll see," Peter barked, glad to have something he could really sink his teeth into. This was working out well, he thought.

Back in his office an hour later, Peter paused to reflect on what he'd uncovered. According to the Acme company website, the two company executives weren't on Pytalon nor were they implanted. They'd been exempted from both by the St. Louis Pytalon CEO so they could ensure a steady supply of refrigerators. Well, everyone needs refrigerators, he mused. According to the company site, the two bosses were traveling now, looking for possible factory expansion sites in other states. Peter couldn't imagine making refrigerators would be an expansion industry, but accepted it at face value. He set his mind on working out how to locate these traveling men.

Around suppertime, he got a phone call from the head of the St. Louis Feds. "Peter, good news and bad news." The voice sounded upset, Peter thought.

"Good news first. Please tell me you got our insane terrorist," Peter replied.

"Yes, we found him at that location, an old abandoned warehouse in East St. Louis, actually. The bad news is that he wore a suicide bomb vest. Ben detonated it when it could do the most damage to us. He killed twenty of my Feds! You should have told us he was a mad bomber!"

"Damn! Sorry, we didn't know that detail. Here in Chicago, he stole an Air Liner and drove it into a skyscraper. No bombs. We didn't have any clue he was also a bomber. Twenty? Damn. My apologies," Peter replied sympathetically, very glad it wasn't his twenty Feds!

"Well, you can close this case, Peter. We got your man. Next time, tell us, for God's sake. You owe me big time!" Peter agreed with him, and they chatted a little longer before hanging up.

Just then, Lech returned with a grim face. "Sorry boss, nothing more. The place was mostly empty. We did find the two stolen briefcases, but their contents weren't there. Lord knows what Ben and Fred did with them, probably destroyed the papers and samples. That would be my guess. Any word from St. Louis?" Lech asked. He sensed something was up from the slightly tense Peter.

After Peter explained what had happened down south, Lech said softly, "Damn! Sure glad it wasn't us who charged in there. Well, we can close this case now anyway. That's something at least."

"Yes, officially closed, but I'm still curious about any connections they had with the owners of that abandoned warehouse—this Mr. Snells and Mr. Hickory. It'll give me something to investigate for a while." Lech smiled; that it would. He turned and left. Peter turned on the nightly newscast.

"Crap, more troubles," he sneered. Ordinary citizens were reporting an alarming number of newly insane individuals, who were already on Pytalon, though some were also implanted as well. Clearly, the Pytalon drug was not working well. Peter called up Tom Fredricks to report in.

"Well, we've captured your two rebels. One is being implanted and the other is dead. What's going on with all the insane people here in Chicago? It's all over the news," Peter reported and then accused.

"Well, this isn't for public release—keep it between us," a nervous Tom replied. "You see, someone in our manufacturing floors somehow failed to inject Pytalon into the proto-pills. A large number have been distributed, and they are simple placebos. They don't do anything, and the ones who are acting up are displaying withdrawal symptoms. I have a new shipment coming in from the Twin Cities and from Detroit tomorrow. We will have it under control soon. Trust me," he said nervously. What he didn't report was the simple fact that other major manufacturing sites were now beginning to experience similar troubles. Quality control in the plants had failed utterly. "It's just one bad batch," he added hastily. "Be over soon."

Peter smiled, thinking the hell it would be over soon. If it happened here in Chicago, what would prevent it from happening in other cities? No, these drug lords were no longer fit to rule the world!

After hanging up, Peter reflected on recent history. Originally, two branches of the Total Care system, the psychs and the drug companies, formed an alliance to distribute

Pytalon to the masses. The psychs declared war on insanity. Their word alone forced people onto Pytalon, as well as getting implants. The drug makers made vast fortunes, as did the psychs. Then, some thirty years ago, the drug makers secretly dosed the psychs with Pytalon. Now all the psychs were hooked, mindlessly going about their implanting work as needed. The drug lords or the CEO's of the giant Pytalon Corporation Worldwide now controlled the entire world or so it seemed to most everyone who wasn't drugged. "Well, they're making a damned mess of it all!" Peter cursed softly, fearing to be overheard. "Why should we continue following those stupid men? Hell, we are the only real force left in the whole world who can honestly think, and intelligently too." A plan began to form in his mind and a huge grin formed.

Peter thought for a moment. He was one of the most powerful and influential Feds in the world. Chicago had always been in the lead in the Pytalon race and in the psychs' PDH implanting. He likened them to the ancient Al Capone mob. Well, the mob was history, dying along with all crime when Pytalon took over. Still, he chuckled at his own analogy. Al Capone. He, Peter, could be the ruler of not only Chicago, but also the world. He picked up his secure phone and formed a conference call with the three other most powerful and influential Feds in the world: Jim Edgeworth of Miami, Arnold Bucks of Los Angeles, and Yen Chinto of Tokyo.

After exchanging news, he explained the reason for his secure conference call. He watched the three men's faces on his video screen, as they watch his. After he finished, Yen replied, "Yes, I agree with you, Peter. Something must be done. It's getting out of hand. We should be running the show. But can we pull it off?"

Jim suggested, "Yes, with the greatest of ease. We meet with our CEO daily. It would be trivial to dose his drink. Once he's good and under, we take him to get a good implant. Easy as pie. We can then order the other Feds leaders to do the same. When shall we begin?" he grinned, loving the whole idea.

"Peter, you're a genius. Why didn't we think of doing this years ago?" Arnold added enthusiastically. "I say let's have at it tomorrow." The four men discussed details for a few more minutes before breaking the secure connection. Peter failed to hear the electronic click of a fifth party, who had been listening in on his secure connection. Although he didn't know it, his secure connection wasn't very secure.

After supper, he finalized his own plans for the next day. Then, he sat back and did more research on the refrigerator makers. A search of their officially registered EMAC vehicles turned up a large bus affair, suitable for extended travel in relative luxury. He logged into the Universal Surveillance Satellite or USS and entered the vehicle's ID code. "Ah, it is approaching St. Louis now. Hum, how interesting. I wonder if I can somehow get a video on these two men." Of course, he could tie into any number of surveillance camera networks, but he had to know where the men were currently located. Since they were approaching St. Louis, he'd have to wait a while until they stopped somewhere. He took another route of investigation and pulled up any recent records involving these two men.

"Now this is curious!" He sat up straight and stared at his computer monitor. A few mouse clicks brought him more information. "Well, I'll be damned! They have recently acquired two EE women, but look who they acquired! If it isn't our two missing EE women, Amanda and Jessica! They've changed their last names, but they look just like the digital images Jason gave me from his cell phone. So they've changed employers. This is getting more and more interesting every minute. Who would have ever given EE women enough credit to pull this one off? None, I'll wager. Looks like I need to make a little trip down south soon. Inconvenient timing, though. Still, they are a minor matter; the CEO is the more important person. I'll handle him first, tomorrow." He chuckled at his good fortune, his good sleuthing. "This is why I'm the most powerful and important of all the Feds!" he said to his monitor.

Chapter 5—No More . . .

As Tim drove their large bus towards St. Louis, he, Ben, Jessica, and Amanda worked on their *story*, in case anything unexpected happen. Then, Ben began to teach Jessica how to operate his various electronic devices. "Jessica, it's great you can help me with this monitoring I have to do. I wish we'd run into each other years ago."

She gave him a flirting smile, not the fake EE one, but a real one. Her passions, long dead, had begun to awaken. Jessica really liked this young man, though she didn't know the reason. The implant still interfered with her thinking, though nowhere near as bad as it had been when she was nearly a zombie. She felt as if her life had undergone a massive change for the better, even though they were on the run from the Feds.

Tim said, "St. Louis is just ahead. For appearances, we need to stop at a fancy restaurant. Suggestions?"

"Let me surf the web and see what I can find," Jessica called out.

Amanda smiled and added, "Pick a fancy one, dear. The fellows are treating us well." Tim and Amanda chuckled.

"Oh I will, love," Jessica teased her dearest friend. *Friend! God, it feels so good to be able to think of that word again. How long has it been? Eight years.* Ever since she turned eighteen and gotten implanted, she'd been a living zombie. Now she felt more like a real human again just as she did when she was a small girl. She remembered taking ballet lessons and suddenly made the connection with her implanted command to wear ballet boots. She'd been able to handle the ballet boots because of all her en pointe work as a young girl. They must have known that, whoever *they* were, she mused, as she scanned her monitor looking for a plush restaurant. "Hey, how about Edwards Inn? Looks expensive."

She called out the coordinates, and up front, Amanda punched them into their onboard navigation system. An hour later, they pulled up to the restaurant on the northern edge of sprawling St. Louis. As they stopped, the two EE women's implants kicked in. "Oh, we must look our best," Jessica whispered involuntarily to herself. Up front, Amanda did the same. Both men looked at them, and said nothing. Obviously, they too needed to straighten their suits and ties. The women's implants were just re-enforcing that behavior.

As they prepared to get out of the bus, Ben reminded them, "Okay, ladies. Remember, you're supposed to be our EE women, so act accordingly. We don't want to raise any suspicions."

Amanda grinned. That would be easy enough to do, for she'd been doing nothing else for the last eight years but flirting with Bill. Today, she realized she detested Bill and didn't want to flirt with Bill, but had to. Instead, she had already grown fond of Tim and wanted him. *What is happening to me?* "You'll need to help us down."

Tim had already parked their bus, but the parking attendant came up to him anyway, just as he stepped down. "Sanity is doing a good job. Do you need me to park your vehicle, sir?" he said in a monotone.

"No, we're good here, if this is an acceptable place for us to park it," Tim answered. It was, and he put his attention on helping Amanda step down. He couldn't help notice her long, black hose-covered legs.

She smiled coyly. "I do hope you like them and my overly large, perky breasts." Amanda added that last as her bosom approached his head.

"God, I can't take this, Amanda! I like all of you," he teased her back, grinning broadly.

"Well, you should. We EE women are, after all, only the prettiest of women." She tossed her long hair into position and took his arm, moving slowly out of Ben's way, who next descended the three big steps. He turned to help Jessica manage them, which she did gracefully and very carefully.

"I hate steps," she whispered to Ben. "There, thank you, dear." She battered her eyes and smiled at him. She whispered, "Smallish steps. There, perfect. Do I look elegant enough for you, dear?"

Ben chuckled, "Anymore elegant and we'd not be stopping to eat." Both laughed at his taunt, following Tim and Amanda up to the fancy doors, which had a pair of bears carved in them.

As they approached, a doorman opened them for the group. His eyes were glazed over, and they heard him mutter, "Sanity is doing a good job of opening the door for the customers." In a louder voice he added, "Welcome to Edwards Inn." All four nodded to the man as they passed by him, but his glazed eyes didn't register their appreciation. Just inside, they stepped onto a plush red carpet.

Jessica held on tighter to Ben, whispering, "It's harder for me to keep my balance on such soft carpeting, same with Amanda." In a louder voice, she added, "Oh dearest, this is such a nice place."

Just then, another EE woman stepped out from behind the counter. She wore an elegant gown, probably silk Amanda thought, and heels similar to hers, quite high with a thin, metal spike. "Welcome to Edwards Inn. I'm your hostess, Emily Edwards. Table for four?" she asked, batting her eyelids in a flirting manner.

"We're company Presidents, here with our EE escorts, ma'am. We want your finest and private booth," Tim replied pleasantly, with a hint of authority in his voice. He was dubious if an EE woman could respond to his pronouncement. He needn't have worried.

"Ah, yes, I can see that. Our best is the Penthouse Room. Will that be satisfactory, sirs?" she replied with a flirting grin that would have disarmed any man.

"Yes, perfect," Tim countered, rather pleased she had duplicated him. He rationalized, *she is an EE woman and not the usual Pytalon zombie.*

"Excellent, gentlemen. My daughter, Lisa, will escort you to the Penthouse Room, and she will serve as your liaison this evening. Anything you desire, you only have to ask her, and she will see that it's done," Emily replied, uncommonly straightforwardly, Tim thought. Then, he realized EE women did have more reasoning power than the normal person. *Her position was fitting.* She nodded and her young daughter stepped forward.

Lisa was almost eighteen, tall and slender. Her blonde hair fell to her waist, covering her shoulders. It was obvious she had her mother's spectacular looks. Lisa was a very attractive, young woman, alive and intelligent, because she was not yet an adult. Hence, her dosage of Pytalon was very low. Inwardly, Tim grimaced a little as he realized soon the sparkle in her eyes would be dimmed out when she would be given the adult dosage, turning her into just another mindless zombie. *Such a horrid waste.* Unlike her mother who wore hose and spiked stilettos very similar to Amanda's, Lisa's legs were bear, but smooth. She wore flats.

"If you four will follow me, I'll take you to the Penthouse Room. We don't often get such fine guests as yourselves. You must be important men. Oh, don't mind me; it's a birth defect, but I get by just fine with my feet. This way," she hastily explained, as the four suddenly realized what she was missing, her arms. She led the way, going at a perfect pace for the two EE women. Ben thought she probably had a lot of experience because of her mother being one herself.

"I do hope this room will meet your expectations," she said charmingly, after opening the door with her foot for them.

"Ah, perfect, Lisa, perfect," Tim answered, leading Amanda into the spacious, candle-lit room. Several ancient paintings graced the walls. A stuffed bear rose high in one corner. A fireplace crackled at the opposite end of the room. The faint odor of pine filled the room. The table and chairs were walnut and highly polished. In short, this was a truly elegant dining room and quite costly, but the four cared little for its cost. Four menus sat on top of the plates. Graciously, the two men helped the two women get seated before sitting themselves. Tim noticed there was a fifth chair off to one side. Lisa walked over to it and sat down.

She noticed him noticing her and added, "I'll sit here while you're dining, so I can assist you with anything you might need or desire."

He smiled and then decided. "Say, why don't you come up here by the table so we can all talk more easily?"

Lisa didn't need to be asked twice. She got up, pushed her chair up to the table, and sat down before Tim could rise and do it for her. "My you're fast. I was about to help you with your chair."

She grinned. "Well, thank you sir. I don't really need help. Besides, I'm here to assist you, not the other way around. When you have looked over the menu and are ready to order, I'll take your orders. Will you desire cocktails?"

"No, we don't drink alcohol," Ben replied.

"In that case, may I recommend the punch? It makes a superb appetizer," Lisa replied unfazed. "Not many executives drink alcohol anymore. I don't see why dad still insists I ask about it."

Ben grinned. "Say, what is the house specialty? We're hungry, so why waste time looking the menu over? We want the best meal you serve here, don't we ladies."

"Why, certainly dearest," Jessica agreed with him, giving him a smile that melted his heart.

If she only weren't play acting! My God, what a woman, that Jessica. Ben smiled.

"Oh, in that case, you should have the strip steaks. Dad, or Phil rather, is famous for his juicy, tender steaks. I'd recommend a tossed salad for your women, though most men hardly ever finish theirs." Lisa chatted on, and Tim took all of her suggestions, which pleased the young woman. She left to deliver their order to the chef, returning with another server who poured their punch.

"Say, this is delicious. Slightly tart—it does seem to make me even hungrier," Ben complimented Lisa on her recommendation.

She giggled. "Of course. Glad you like it. I think it sets up the rest of the meal splendidly."

"So have you always helped out here at your dad's inn?" Ben made polite conversation.

"Well, yes, since I was in high school. It was hard though, with ballet lessons during grade school. My parents thought the lessons would give me better grace and poise. I suppose they have, but in high school, I was allowed to pursue karate lessons. I've graduated already, so those have ended. Those were more fun than ballet lessons, but a lot more difficult. I want to be a physical therapist someday. I've studied a lot about history and ways of helping people. I can see you both aren't on that awful Pytalon drug. I sure wish dad wasn't, because he could do such a better job of running his inn if he wasn't, but mom is, a little, but she's an EE woman like yours are, so she's not a glassy-eyed zombie like dad is."

"How can you tell we aren't on Pytalon?" Ben asked, curious if her reasoning was sound.

"Lots of ways. First, your eyes don't have that vacant look. Second, you talk coherently. Third, you aren't whispering Sanity things to yourselves, so you haven't been implanted, though your EE women have been. Need I go on?" she grinned at Ben, who laughed.

"No, your observations are spot on. Well done. I take it you're against folks taking Pytalon?" he tried to probe a little. Her answer had to wait a spell, as another server entered with their main course and placed the dishes perfectly on the table, allowing the men to serve their women, while whispering something about sanity and doing a good job.

When they began to eat, she then replied in a heated manner and rapidly, "No, I think it's just awful. It turns people into mindless zombies, like my dad and everyone else around here, but then, I suppose there are good reasons for doing it. You see, after Pytalon was widely introduced, there have been no more murders. No more rapes, no more break ins and thefts. No more robberies. No more marijuana, coke, and other drug use. No more drug addicts and no more drug lords and dealers. No more wars. No more violence to speak of. No more nasty political elections. No more income taxes. No more corrupt politicians. No more criminals. No more jails. No more law courts. No more lawyers. No more law suits."

She took a deep breath and continued, "No more policemen; the AP-cops don't count. No more private detectives. No more federal marshals. No more traffic cops. No more speed traps, whatever they were. No more pedophiles, thank God. No more sex offenders. No more con men. No more stock market with its wild fluctuations. No more wild swings in the value of our money. No more inflation. No more deflation. No more recessions. No more depressions. No more wildly changing laws. No more personal arguments. No more fist fights or beatings. No more spousal abuse. No more speeders on the roadways. No more drunken drivers. No more criminality. No more wars. No more conflicts. No more profiteering. No more hunger. No more homeless; everyone has a home of some kind. No more joblessness. Everyone has some kind of job these days." She finally stopped to take another deep breath.

"All those are good things, thanks to Total Care, but then, there are others. No more music being made or listened to, well mostly though a little is kept alive in the ballet lessons. No more TV entertainment—only the news and rules for everyone to follow. No more actors and actresses. No more video games. No more movies. No more of the arts, if the truth be told. No more reading books, except for us kids in school. No more prohibitively expensive colleges. No more colleges at all. No more writers. No more artistic painters. No more new inventions. No more changes in our everyday world. No new appliances, that sort of thing, I mean. It's always the same ones, only newly made. No new dress designs. No fashion shows." Again, she paused to take another deep breath before continuing.

"Of course, there are other things missing too. No more love. No more friends. All that ends when the adults get on Pytalon. Maybe that's a good thing. There's no more population explosion. No more overpopulation of one country. No more intercourse to speak of, excepting with you EE women, of course. Mom and dad did get one waver to have one child, me, but that was eighteen years ago, almost anyway. No more thinking, that is, by adults on Pytalon. No more complaining and angry outbursts. No more emotions at all as far as I can tell. No more will power. No more Insanity, though I'm not so sure about this one. I do hope I'm not boring you with all this."

Ben laughed, "Not at all, Lisa. It is refreshing to hear someone speak openly about such things. I bet you don't do that around your parents."

She giggled. "Of course not. I wrote my senior paper on this topic. I'm not on Pytalon. Can you keep a secret?" she leaned over expectantly. All four agreed. "I've this hole in my upper gum line. Another birth defect. So when they give me my Pytalon pill, I simply use my tongue and push it into the hole. Later on, I spit it out in the toilet. I've seen what Pytalon does to everyone, and I want no part of it, if I can help it. I bet you both don't either."

"No, we certainly don't, Lisa," Ben admitted. "Your secret is safe with us." She smiled appreciatively.

Embolden by their listening to what she had to say, Lisa ventured, "You know something else? I've worked out a way to get people off Pytalon and get the aftereffects of the drug out of their bodies. However, I don't know if anyone will ever want to try my treatment. Once you are on it, no one has enough will power to want to get off it. Pytalon is terribly addictive. If you take one adult dose, you're hooked on it!"

Her words hit home to Jessica. For eight years, such a thought never entered her mind. Only when she began taking the pills that lacked the active Pytalon did she come off the drug and with nearly fatal withdrawal symptoms and delusions. However, she was wondering if Lisa's treatment would help her body get rid of the lingering after-effects. She dared not ask, though, for that would blow their cover. Instead, she continued running her long nails long the side of Ben's face, occasionally passing them seductively over his lips, sensing his arousal every time she did so.

They chatted more until they'd finished desert and it was time to leave. As they prepared to rise, Ben said, "Thank you for a lovely evening, Lisa. I wish you only the very best in succeeding with your career in physical therapy. I do hope your method for getting someone off Pytalon works well. If you need something later on, contact me. Here is my card. You can leave a message for me at this number." He handed her his business card. His face reddened slightly, but she slipped off her shoe and took it between her toes, deftly depositing it into a pocket in her dress.

"Thanks. If you'll follow me, I'll take you to the cashier station. It's been a really fun night for me," she explained, and then led them out.

Once safely inside their spacious bus, Ben whispered to Jessica, "You did well. You have me so aroused that I was nearly going out of my mind all night long!"

"Of course, that's what we EE women are supposed to be doing," Jessica replied sweetly. Then, she became quite serious, "Ben, I meant it, all of it. I wasn't just being an EE woman flirting with you. I meant it. I like you more than I can say, more than I've ever felt about a man before." Up front, Amanda admitted pretty much the same thing to Tim. The four spent a very enjoyable evening, while their bus continued on its way on autopilot, heading towards Denver.

The next day, they saw the Rocky Mountains and took an extended sightseeing trip along the eastern edge of the great mountains, near Rocky Mountain National Park. Then, they headed south and west to take in the Grand Canyon. Tim hadn't said that their objective was Phoenix. He'd left the impression they were sightseeing for a time, while things cooled down.

The third day out from St. Louis, Ben's phone rang. "Hello Professor. Okay, I'll put you on speaker phone." Jessica actually pushed the button for Ben, bringing a smile to his face as well as hers.

"Hello you four. How are things going? Well, I hope?" The women recognized the professor's British accent. After exchanging pleasantries, the professor's voice became serious.

"Say, I called you because I need your help rescuing someone. I would have sent Ben Hadwell, but the Feds caught up with him, and he blew himself up, taking twenty Feds with him." They hadn't heard about this and spent a few minutes being briefed by the professor.

He continued, "There's a young woman in St. Louis whom we desperately need to rescue so she can help us. As you know, I keep myself well apprised of the progress of all high school teens around the country. This one has shown exceptional intelligence and has tremendous potential for us, though I admit, she also comes with a good deal of liabilities. This will be a dangerous mission, fellows, no discounting that, but it's to our great advantage to snatch her away from her parents and home. Take her to Phoenix with you. I know you're already on the run, but I'm a little desperate now. She's turned eighteen, and you know what that means."

"Right professor. If they get to her, she'll be lost to us, just another mindless zombie. You can count on us," Ben replied before Tim got the chance.

"Ben's right, professor," Tim butted in. "Give us the specifics, and we'll snatch her one way or the other."

"Thanks, boys. I do hope we're in time. Her name is Lisa Edwards. Her father," he began to relay the necessary information.

Ben interrupted him, "We met her. She was working at her father's inn. She was our hostess for our evening meal. She is brilliant. Say no more; we're turning around now. We'll get her, and I'm sure she'll want to come with us. Count on us, professor. Wish we knew about this three days ago; we could have snatched her then."

"Small world, I know, but with all this upheaval caused by Ben Hadwell's stupid ramming of the Air Liner into the Pytalon skyscraper, my schedule has been shredded. I have others rescuing six other promising young teens as we speak. Good luck. I'll stay in touch with you." They chatted a bit more, and then the professor hung up.

"He was really worried we'd not get to her in time, wasn't he?" Jessica suggested. "At least that's how it seemed to me. I admit I'm only now beginning to sense other people's emotions again."

"No, you're spot on, my love. I've never heard him be this worried before. He must think Lisa will be an extremely valuable ally or asset. Maybe she does know how to get people safely off Pytalon. Come on, Tim; burn rubber as the ancients used to say," Ben called out.

"On it, but there's no rubber in this vehicle. Amanda is plotting a new course straight for St. Louis. Be there in two days at most, highballing it all the way. No stops," Tim countered, nodding to Amanda who fed him the readout from the navigation computer.

"I'll go fix up a bed for her," Amanda suggested, adding, "it's too hard for Jessica to maneuver in the moving EMAC." Tim nodded.

Jessica continued to monitor the communications, while Ben worked on other actions, including hacking into the psychs database. He had a hunch if they were not in time, surely, Lisa would be implanted. With her bright mind, Pytalon probably would be insufficient, especially since she always used her secret method to avoid taking the pills.

Just then, Jessica interrupted him. "Honey, listen to this. We've picked up some kind of secret conversation here— among the Feds, I think." Ben pushed his rolling chair over to her position and listened in as she replayed the conversation.

"Hey, listen up everyone. Jessica has just picked up a vital conversation. It seems the Feds are secretly planning to get all the Pytalon corporation heads, the CEOs, onto Pytalon and implanted too. Worldwide. The Feds are taking over control of the whole world and will be the only ones running things now. Incredible. The professor needs to know about this development. My God, he predicted this would happen two years ago! That man is unbelievably smart!" He did just that and then returned to his snooping. Around one in the afternoon, gloom struck Ben. He was successful, but the result was not.

"Damn, damn, damn, we're too late for Lisa!" he called out loudly. "She's already been taken and PDH implanted. She's been turned into an EE woman!" Silence. Only the very low drone of their EM engine could barely be heard.

Jessica was the first to speak up, "Perhaps it's not too bad for her. You see, EE women have a whole lot more reasoning and thinking powers. We have to be able to flirt with men and all that. So even in the worst case, she isn't a mindless zombie. Rather, she's more like Amanda and me. We're doing pretty well, I think."

"You are doing splendidly, Jessica," Ben praised her. "Okay, maybe it's not the end of the world. We're still going to rescue her. Let me do some more digging."

"Honey, an EE woman needs an escort. Perhaps you can apply to get her," Jessica suggested, trying to help him somehow.

"Say, that is a good plan, Jessica. I'm on it." Ben began typing away on his computer. A while later, he called out, "We are in luck. Because of the swiftness of the action with her, they

76

have assigned her to her mother's care for now. She hasn't yet been assigned a sponsor. I've put in my request for her with the EE Women's Association of Greater St. Louis. So far, I'm the only one. Keep your finger's crossed."

The next day, Ben received both good news and bad. "Hey, great! I've been granted sponsorship of Lisa. She's being assigned to me as my second EE woman." The others cheered him. A bit later, the professor called again and Jessica put him on the speakerphone, turning up the volume.

"You've been made! The Feds are on to you, Ben, Tim. They've tied the safe house in St. Louis to you, Tim. They are tracking your bus right now and want to take you both in for questioning. Also, the Chicago Feds head, Peter Delius, is on to Jessica and Amanda. He knows who you are and wants to talk to you about your role in the sabotaging of the Pytalon skyscraper. Whatever you do, get the hell out of there. Forget Lisa. Save yourselves. Get to Phoenix pronto!"

After he hung up, Tim said, "I've never heard him be so worried before. Damn, they're on to all four of us. We'd best triple check our stories. Are we going to turn around?"

"Look, Lisa has to be in very bad trouble, dealing with implants and drugs. Feds or no Feds, I say let's sneak into St. Louis and rescue her as planned. Then get the hell out of there as fast as we can," Ben answered.

"I'm with Ben, if we matter," Jessica added. Amanda echoed her.

"Of course you matter. You're one of us now," Tim countered. "Your opinion counts as much as mine or Ben's does. Besides, I'm in love with you, Amanda." His face reddened as he finally admitted what he'd been feeling.

She leaned over and gave him a loving kiss. "And I'm in love with you too, Tim. It feels so fantastic to have such feelings again." In the back of the bus, Jessica and Ben were also sharing their deeply felt love.

"Okay, as someone once said in ancient times, damn the torpedoes, full speed ahead. Whatever torpedoes are," Tim called out. Amanda explained what they were. She'd read about them in history class.

A few hours later, they pulled into St. Louis and had to slow down. Amanda said, "Whatever happens to us, I want you all to know that I love you all. We're doing the right thing. They can't ever take that away from us." The others echoed her sentiments. Before long, they pulled into the Edwards Inn, once more parking in the reserved spot.

"Gang, you all stay inside and keep the motor running, as the saying goes. This is my responsibility. I'm to be her sponsor. I'll bring her out as quickly as I can," Ben suggested, but they sensed it was more of an order. If he was apprehended, perhaps they could still flee.

Ben stepped down and walked up to the entrance, more or less ignoring the mindless greetings of the valet and doorman. He walked up to Emily, who recognized him. "Oh, it is you! Ben Snells, isn't it?"

"Yes, Mrs. Edwards. I am to sponsor Lisa; she will be my official EE woman," he replied.

Ben detected the faint trace of concern in her voice, but her EE appearance gave no such hints. "I have been notified of your selection and have been given the proper forms for you to sign." Flirting with him, Emily handed them to him, and he signed them as rapidly as he could. "Er, don't you want to see how pretty she looks first?" At last, she began to display some slight emotion.

"I'm a business executive and on a tight schedule, ma'am. We met a few days ago, and she can only be prettier than before. I'm certain she will be perfect, just as you are a perfect EE woman," Ben replied, hoping to appease her.

"Yes, but she needs so much help now—with her makeup and dressing," Emily added, her voice shaking a little. Underneath her implanted behavior pattern, her true motherly emotions were surfacing, as much as her mental state would allow, Ben guessed.

"Emily, please don't worry about Lisa. I will give her the best care. I already have asked our other EE women to help her with her many needs, and they, like all good EE women, assure me they'll help her always. I'll treat her well and with the highest respect," Ben added, hoping somehow to reach through the woman's implants and give her some faintest peace of mind. It was the least he could do, the only sane thing, as a matter of fact. For a second, he believed his message had actually arrived.

"Okay then. She needs help walking. I have her few things packed. She will need to purchase more gowns and heels soon. She is only a day out of surgery and the implant, so please be extra gentle with her for some time," Emily explained. "This way. She is sitting and waiting for you, but you'll have to support her while she walks. In time, she will walk well on her own; we all do, it just takes time. Usually, we are given time to adjust and learn," Emily explained as she made her slow way into the next room. Ben saw Lisa sitting on a plush chair, a small duffle bag beside her, and a purse on a long strap slung over her shoulder, looking very different than she had before.

Somehow, her blonde hair seemed longer, her lips thick and full, much as Jessica's were. As with all EE women, her breasts had been greatly enlarged. Ben had no idea why. Hers protruded as much as her mother's did and those of Jessica and Amanda, for that matter. She wore a red satin gown with the typical black, seamed nylons. What stopped him were her boots. She too wore ballet boots, just as Jessica wore. They were tied tightly around her calves and reached to just below her knees. They matched her bright red dress and lips. Her eyes were overly made up with striking blue eye shadow and extensive mascara, giving her lashes a more than full look.

As they entered the room, she was whispering to herself, "My body is hypersensitive to sensual touches. My body needs sexual sensations and stimulations several times each day. I exist to provide elegant and sensual experiences to men and women of power. I am an exotic escort. I must look my very best at all times. I must be ready to flirt at any time. I must be ready to engage and satisfy the sexual fantasies and satisfactions of both men and women at any time. I am a super-sexual, hypersensitive woman. I must wear only the finest and exotic gowns. I must always wear nylons and ballet boots. I must look perfect at all times. I will repeat to myself these words several times each day. I must not forget these words."

Lisa looked up. "Oh, it is you. Help me," she pleaded, but immediately lapsed back into her implant. "My body is hypersensitive to sensual touches. I must look my very best at all times. Mom, do I look my very best for Ben?" she asked, coming slightly out of her recitation.

Quickly, Ben spoke up, "Lisa, you look absolutely stunning, perfect in all ways. Come. Shall we go now?" He moved to her side and put his arms around her, beneath her now massive bosom.

"Yes, I must make you sexually satisfied," she replied from beneath her mental fog. As she tried to rise, her panic broke through. "Ben, help me! I'm so utterly helpless now! I can't walk without help!" She spoke in a whisper, but very much full of emotion.

"I'm here, Lisa. One step at a time. There you go, my gorgeous EE woman." At the mention of EE woman, a brief, flirting smile appeared on her face. Slowly, they made their way out of the room. Her father noticed her leaving but said nothing. His glassy-eyed stare told Ben that he probably didn't even know he had a daughter, much less that she was going off with him. Emily led the way, but kept looking back to make sure Lisa was able to continue walking. Without Ben's help, she wouldn't have gotten much beyond the ten feet to the room's doorway. After what seemed an eternity to those waiting in the bus, Ben, Lisa, and her single bag finally made it outside.

"I must look beautiful for you. Oh! I'm coming again," she interrupted herself. He felt her body tremble and wondered what was happening to her now. She stood still for a minute before he finally got her moving once more. Again, it happened. Just as they finally reached the steps of the bus, her body shook, and she had to stop all motion, this time for even longer, while biting her lower lip.

"Come on; just a little further, Lisa. Can you go up the three steps?" Ben asked.

She tried, but simply couldn't on her own, so Ben lifted her up and carried her inside. The other three stared at the huge changes in the appearance of what had been a precocious young woman. As soon as Ben got her to a seat, her legs gave out, and she sat down rather ungracefully. Tim started the bus up and headed out of St. Louis, so far so good, the four thought.

Lisa was exhausted from her walk, and once more, she began reciting her litany. Jessica motioned for the others to listen carefully to what Lisa said. Ben and Tim realized this would give them clues to Lisa's future behavior and the problems that she'd be having. She finished and then broke down. Crying, she gushed, "I can't! I can't! Like this, I'm completely helpless. Ben, help me, please," Lisa begged. "I've been implanted. Look what they've done to my body. I can hardly see my feet anymore. My breasts ache, my lips feel funny, and my feet are cramping. Help me, please." As soon as she'd said this, her eyes glazed over, and she began reciting the implant words once again.

Jessica whispered, "Her implant is pretty much the same as ours. She has just some minor variations, wearing nylons and the awful boots. We know how to massage her breasts to ease their pain. Ben, you take off her boots and massage her feet." The three quickly began attending to Lisa's immediate needs.

"Oh! Yes, like that. The aching is going away," she whispered to Jessica. As Ben began massaging her feet and toes, she perked up a little and then lapsed back almost at once. "But I always have to wear the boots. I must look perfect at all times."

"You can't look perfect if you are in pain, Lisa. Don't your feet feel better now?"

"Well, yes, yes they do. Oh, but I haven't practiced my ballet for four years. That's why they hurt so much. Put them back on please; I'll toughen up soon." Her expression suddenly changed again, "But I'm helpless with them on. Please leave them off, Ben." Then her mood changed once more, "Wait, I must always wear them! I simply must. Put them back on me, please," she begged. Ben complied, knowing at least that he had massaged the cramps out of her feet temporarily. As soon as she had to walk or stand, they would begin to cramp once more. As soon as he had them tied securely, Lisa seemed to relax. The awful mental pressure abated, and the breast massage really helped as well.

"Heads up, everyone! Here come the Feds. Stick to our stories!" Tim yelled frantically from the driver's seat. He had no choice but to halt. Six other EMACs descended, surrounding their large bus. While he could ram them and probably wreck one of the Feds' EMAC, which were much smaller, such would be out of character for a couple of company presidents. Hence, he halted and watched as several Feds climbed out of their vehicles and walked up to his door. He recognized one as Peter Delius, the head of the Chicago Feds, a long way from home.

Chapter 6—Explanations and Implants

Peter smiled, satisfied with the simple capture of his *Wanted for Questioning* suspects. With textbook style apprehension, he asked, "You're Mr. Tim Hickory?"

"Yes sir. Co-president of Acme Manufacturing. My partner, Mr. Ben Snells. Our official EE women. What's the problem?"

Peter ordered, "Follow these EMACs back into St. Louis to their Feds headquarters. I want to question all of you, including your EE women," he replied frankly.

"Certainly, sir," Tim replied. Surrounded by the six other Feds vehicles, Tim drove them back into the heart of the city, stopping outside the tall, Feds building in downtown St. Louis.

Once parked, Peter came aboard again and ordered, "You two men, go inside with Lech there. I'll question the EE women here first." Ben and Tim had no choice but to do as asked, hoping to bluff their way out of this mess. Mentally, Ben cursed the two men who had flown the Air Liner into the skyscraper. There seemed no end to the damage that ill-conceived action was wreaking.

"Well, Miss Jessica Alexandra or Walsh as you're now calling yourself. Miss Amanda Pottingham or shall I say Wales. We finally meet. You've given us quite a challenge in finding you women," Peter began.

Jessica batted her long eyelashes at him, "I'm sorry sir, but I didn't know you were looking for us. If I had known that you wanted to see me. . ."

He interrupted her, "Yes, yes. Now let's talk about that day when you were going to fly out to San Francisco with Jason."

She feigned a shudder. "Oh, no! Horrible day. Worst day of my life. I must look my best at all times. Do I still look good, sir? I hope so." She pretended to be having an inner conflict between something awful and her implanted behavior patterns. It worked.

"Yes, please tell me what happened to you women that day," he brought her back to the topic.

"Well, we were all packed to spend a month or so in San Francisco with Jason and Bill. They said to bring everything with us. So we took out all our money, and we bought new dresses, light blue, with matching outer corsets, and heels," Jessica began to relate it.

"Yes, yes, I don't want to know about your dresses. I'm sure they're very elegant. What happened at New O'Hare?" he again fought to get her back on track, becoming convinced these two were nothing more than confused EE women.

She related what had happened at the airport that their sponsors were shot, presumed murdered, but that the terrorists told them to take their bags, run away, and never come back. Eventually, when they couldn't walk any longer, they stopped at some house and borrowed and EMAC there. Jessica added, "We had to do as they asked and go far, far away, you see. I hope whomever that EMAC belongs to has gotten it back. We just began pushing buttons until one made it go. We don't know how to drive, but it just went, you see, and we were very pleased because we were going far, far away from the insane men. We want to live."

She described how it nearly ran into this bus, and thus, they met Mr. Snells and Mr. Hickory. "We told them of our plight, and they decided to become our sponsors so we can still be proper EE women. Mr. Snells told us to change our last names when we registered with EE Women International and signed our contracts with them, so that the bad men wouldn't be able to find us. Please, don't let those bad men find us. We don't want to die," Jessica flashed him her very best flirting, pleading look.

"I see. And what about this third woman here?" Peter asked.

"We met her last week at their fabulous inn. You simply must try their steaks. Ben really liked Lisa. We were in Denver when he learned Lisa had become an EE woman, just like us, so he came back here to become her sponsor too. Isn't Mr. Snells just the greatest?" she again batted her long eyelashes at Peter.

He couldn't help but grin. "Okay, Miss Jessica. Your story makes sense. You three stay here in your bus, while we question the two men."

"Thank you sir. Please, don't let those bad men kill us," Amanda added.

"Don't worry miss. Both bad men are dead. You are safe now." It was a partial lie; while Ben was dead, Fred was still alive, though he was now a doorknob polisher.

"Oh thank you, thank you, thank you," Jessica gushed. Peter turned and left them.

As Peter walked inside the Feds building where the two men had been taken, he thought, *Silly EE women! It's just as I suspected; they were forced to flee. Idiot women anyway—still they are sexy. I think I'll have to get me a pair once I'm in total control of Chicago.*

After the Feds left, Jessica whispered, "Amanda, do you think he bought it?"

"Absolutely, Jessi. You were superb! Whatever happens, we did our part perfectly. Now, let's see what we can do for Lisa."

***

At the Feds headquarters, no one asked the two men anything, but kept them locked in a room. Eventually, Peter arrived and the grilling began. Tim did most of the talking, much to Ben's relief. Peter asked, "So what are you two doing traveling around the country?"

"We are looking for a good site on which to build a new, more modern refrigerator manufacturing plant. You see, our existing plants are aging rapidly. Our studies suggest if we don't build a new plant soon, eventually we simply will not be able to produce enough of them. In ten years, a working refrigerator may be worth its weight in gold. We thought about St. Louis and spent some time there looking for a compatible and affordable new site. That's where we ran into the two EE women, who were fleeing for their very lives. Something about a double murder in Chicago. Well, actually, they ran into our bus here. Silly EE women—they can't drive an EMAC."

"I see. And did you find your site here?"

"Er no. So we headed further west. We were checking out the Denver area when we learned that Lisa had become an EE woman. Ben here liked her and wanted to sponsor her, so we returned to close that deal. He has the proper papers and all, if you'd like to see them."

"I see. And do you know what else happened in Chicago?"

"Er, no sir, just that our two women witnessed a double murder of their sponsors and were told to flee for their lives. Why? What's happening in Chicago? Do you need more refrigerators there soon? If so, we can arrange for some new ones to be shipped there yet today," Tim added naively. Ben

84

noticed Peter seemed to be buying the story completely.

"No, thanks anyway. Wait here while I check on your story further," Peter ordered. He rose and left.

Outside the room, Peter thought, *Everything makes perfect sense. The two women are too stupid to have been involved, and these fellows are just dumb CEOs. Quite why they weren't implanted and put on Pytalon long ago eludes me. Then again, who knows why the Pytalon lords did what they did. Well, they won't any longer. All the Pytalon CEOs are now properly implanted and on the drug. We Feds run the whole world, well most of it. Yet, we still have other cities to handle. What to do about these two fools?*

As if reading his mind, Lech asked, "So boss, what do we do with these two men? Their story checks out. They're just a couple of minor company presidents."

"One thing is for sure, Lech, and that is we're going to get all those that the drug lords excluded from being implanted or put on Pytalon taken care of. Their exemptions are now void. The only ones not implanted or drugged will be us, the Feds. After that, there will never be another saboteur attack, not ever. We know how to run a tight ship. All these exemptions are canceled," Peter declared.

"Right boss. Once we have rounded up those few who were exempt and have taken care of them, there'll be no more rebels anywhere in the world. Might be somewhat boring after that, but I can live with a little boredom. Might take myself one of those EE women," he grinned mischievously.

Peter returned his grin. "Okay, I'm going to see the psychs and see what I can have done to these two. Don't tell them a thing. Put some knockout drops in some sodas and see that they drink it. Once they are unconscious, have them transported over to the psych facility." Lech saluted and left to make the arrangements, while Peter had one of the local St. Louis Feds take him to their psych facility.

A bit later, Peter stepped out of the EMAC and stood before the imposing, white concrete structure that looked like an enormous pillbox. Standing some fifty feet tall and windowless on all sides, the building was a perfect square. However, massive power lines were attached to one side of the building, supplying the enormous power needs of an implant. He walked briskly inside and soon sat in the psych's office. The man was barely coherent, heavily dosed on Pytalon.

"I have two corporate presidents who need to be implanted," Peter explained. Ben and Tim were going to be the first of many previously exempt company presidents who were now going to be implanted and put on Pytalon.

"Let me see. I don't recall having such an implant for company presidents," he replied mindlessly. He brought out an extensive listing of just what implants were available, giving it to Peter, while smiling. "I'm sure you can find what you need among these. Door polishers, window washers, doctors, nurses, EE women. . ." His monotone voice trailed off.

Peter scanned down the listing and saw nothing that was remotely suited to company presidents. Again, he saw that these people were being treated special. Well, now that was going to change, no more implant-Pytalon exemptions. Peter's disgust rose. He was about to explode on the pathetic psych man when something the man had just said rang a bell in his mind, EE women. Slowly, a sadistic grin formed on Peter's face. *So these two men have a healthy lust for EE women and their exaggerated breasts, eh? Why not give them the same treatment? Serve them right.*

He looked up at the glassy-eyed psych man. "Can I have the two men turned into EE women, and yet have them keep their manhood?" He had no idea what ramifications his sadistic impulse would ultimately have. At this moment, he merely though this was funny, treating the presidents like the women they admired.

For a second, he saw a flicker of recognition beneath that vacant stare. "Well, that is highly unusual, but certainly doable. They'll need the breast expansion surgery and lip enlargement. Hair will pose a problem. Men wear their hair shorter than women do. I take it you wish them to appear to be women on the outside?"

"Yes, look like women, act like women, but still be a man. Perfect torture for dirty old men, wouldn't you say?" Peter insinuated and asked, pleased with his sadistic choice.

For the briefest instant, Peter saw a flicker of recognition in the psych man's eyes, replaced almost at once by the glassy stare. "Yes, it can be done. No problem. Sanity is always doing a perfect PHD implant. How soon? Where are they? Any other special requests? We had one just a few days ago." He consulted his notepad. "Ah yes, an EE woman requested her daughter always wear ballet boots and nylons. We can add in special requests," he explained mechanically.

Peter laughed. "Yes, one of these men needs just that—to always wear ballet boots, just like the women he most admires and wants around him. Oh, this is just too delicious for words. You've made my day." *Refrigerators? Hah.* The psych man merely nodded vacantly; the subtlety was lost on him completely.

Right on time, Lech arrived with the two unconscious men. The Feds carried them inside, and Peter told the psych man which one was to have the special request. He left them in the man's capable hands, capable meaning the implants always worked well. Peter had seen enough of that. While Pytalon was sometimes unpredictable, the implants were not. It was a shame no new implants could be developed, since the psychs themselves were now mindless zombies, capable of merely following their own routines, not inventing new ones. Like all others, they could no longer think.

As Peter and Lech left, Peter thought about this singular absence, no effective president or CEO implant. He knew he had many other exempt company leaders to implant and had taken a copy of the psych's list of available implants to study. *Well, I'll just have to do the best with what's available.*

"Lech, we should visit the EE women in their bus briefly before we head home. We should at least tell them their men will be returned to them in a few days."

Lech grinned wickedly. "Boss, their implants will be diabolical to say the very least."

Peter replied, "I call it justice. Lord knows how long those men lusted after their EE women. This will teach them a valuable lesson, even if they never realize it. Best order new refrigerators for our building soon. I doubt they will be effectively running their company any longer."

Lech roared. "Hell, they'll probably never be able to get out of the bed with their EE women."

Later, both men laughed heartily as they boarded their Air Liner, headed for Chicago. Peter felt as if he were ruling the entire world! A few more isolated Pytalon plants, round up the remaining exempt company presidents, and the world was all his.

***

Ben and Tim underwent surgery, though they didn't know it. The last thing they remembered was drinking a welcome soda. Once the minor operations were done, their heads were shaved, and they were placed in the implant chair.

Electrodes on a metal band were fastened snugly around their heads. Then, a powerful drug was injected into their bodies. Their minds took on the color of a grey mass. Powerful electrical bolts shot intense pain into their bodies, building on the grey mass. Yet, the pain was not deadly; rather, it just hurt. Finally, the monotone voice of the psych spoke into earphones attached to their head harness.

Ben heard: "My body is hypersensitive to sensual touches. My body needs sexual sensations and stimulations several times each day. I exist to provide elegant and sensual experiences to men and women of power. I am an exotic escort. I must look my very best at all times. I must be ready to flirt at any time. I must be ready to engage and satisfy the sexual fantasies and satisfactions of both men and women at any time. I am a super-sexual, hypersensitive woman. I must wear only the finest and exotic gowns. I must always wear nylons and ballet boots. I must look perfect at all times. I will repeat to myself these words several times each day. I must not forget these words. If I fail, I will get an intense migraine headache." Tim heard the exact same words, less the ballet boots sentence.

A half hour later, the implant ended, though both were still unconscious. Now, two local EE women arrived and dressed the two men, following the psych man's orders. Seeing their male organs, both questioned him about it. First, they applied glue to their baldheads and then firmly attached a long human hair wig to each, making sure that they were firmly stuck in place. The glue would hold their wigs tightly for three months, at which time they would have to redo the process themselves. They attached long acrylic nails to their fingernails and painted them appropriately. Finally, they finished dressing them and applied their makeup. They left the typical beginning EE woman's basic supplies with them in a bag, along with detailed instructions about the care and handling of their wigs, and a supply of the glue. As always, the two EE women then closely inspected their handiwork. The two men were sitting in plush chairs as the women went down their final checklist. The checklist was mandatory, since as implanted EE women themselves, they could forget some detail. All must be perfect on each new EE woman—that was the inviolate rule. Satisfied, they handed the checklist to the psych man and left.

The psych now added the men's names to the official list of EE women, even though they were technically not women. Nothing in his training allowed him to do otherwise. Finally, he summoned an EMAC to transport the soon to be reviving men back to their EMAC bus, following Peter's written orders. That done, he headed home, terribly tired this evening and with a dull headache. He was certain he'd forgotten something with these two EE women, but what? In fact, he'd forgotten to give them their first Pytalon dose.

Upon seeing their men, Amanda gasped, "Oh my God! What happened to them?" Two men just carried Ben and Tim up and into their bus, depositing them on a pair of seats.

"Sorry ladies, we're delivery men. Sanity is making a good delivery. Here are their new things," one of the glazed-eyed men said, handing her their two bags. They turned and left the bus, quickly departing in their EMAC, leaving Amanda and Jessica still aghast.

"Well, the Feds man did say that from now on, no one is going to be exempt from Pytalon use and implanting, but Jessica, this is something else. Are they women now? I recognize Tim's face, sort of," Amanda finally began to recover from her shock.

"It sort of looks that way. I guess they only have one size fits all for us EE women. Their breasts are the same size as Lisa's and ours. No, wait, Ben's still a man. Oh, this is really weird!" Jessica gasped, looking very confused. Amanda quickly felt Tim's crotch and looked relieved.

"I don't understand this, Jessica. They still have their male organs, but in all other ways, they look like us, EE women. Even so, they should have been given a three-day recovery period and then a month to get used to everything, like we were given. They're still unconscious."

"In that case, I bet they don't even know what's happened to their bodies," Jessica began theorizing. "Look, can you drive this bus? Get us the hell out of here. I don't know—head back towards Denver. I'll look after them some and try to make some sense of this."

"Okay. I agree, we have to flee again." Amanda got into Tim's seat and began activating the EMAC controls, setting a course for Denver, mostly retracing their previous route, thankful Tim had shown her how to operate the machine. Finally, she set it on automatic pilot and made her way back to Jessica, Lisa, and the two men.

She found Jessica was writing what appeared to be notes. "What's happening with them?" Amanda asked growing more concerned. The men were still unconscious for the most part, though they were occasionally mumbling and moaning.

"I think they're still heavily under the PDH implant process. I'm writing down the words they are mumbling. Those are probably the words the psych man was implanting in them. Ben is in real trouble, Amanda. He's being forced to always wear ballet boots, and he's never had any ballet training. He won't even be able to walk, not for a long time. Amanda, they rescued us when we were in dire need. Now it's our turn to rescue them," Jessica pronounced.

"I want to help too, but I can't do much," Lisa whispered from the seat beside Tim. She was watching over him for Jessica.

Realizing Ben would have a horrid time trying to walk in the boots, she thought about adding some new commands, since Ben was still unconscious, but decided against that. Jessica sighed, "God, how are they going to survive now? Their voices haven't been altered, so they will still sound like men too. So confusing. I wish there was some way to undo these awful implants, Amanda," Jessica countered. "You know, there should be a way to undo them. After all, if the psychs can put this stuff into our minds, there should be a way to take them out, don't you think?"

Amanda pointed out that after much time passed, they'd gotten over the worst of their own implants. She suggested, "Perhaps, if we could just take them somewhere safe, where it's very quiet, and devoid of other people, they might come out of it quicker. Look, right now, all three of them need a safe, quiet, distraction-free safe house where they can relax, come to grips with what's happened to them, and learn how to cope and get by," Jessica pointed out, thinking quickly.

Hastily, the two women decided it would take days to reach Denver and the men would be waking sooner. Further, Ben, Tim, and Lisa had only the dress they were wearing and needed much more apparel. Hence, they decided they didn't have time to travel across country.

Amanda came to the rescue. *Oh, we need to get an apartment.* In every large city, there was an AEEW, an Association of Exotic Escort Women. The association looked after their own, particularly those EE women who were in need, such as having just lost their sponsors or newly created women. Well, there were three newly created ones here, she reasoned. She reversed course, heading back to St. Louis. After checking with the St. Louis AEEW hotline, Amanda arranged for a safe house.

A half hour later, the bus came to a halt in a quiet residential area on the northern edge of the sprawling city. As the AEEW promised, Amanda spotted an EE woman stepping out of the shadows. The woman made her way up to the bus door, as Amanda opened it and stepped carefully down, lamenting that the men were no longer able to assist her.

"Welcome, sister. I'm Joy. This is one of our safe houses. It's empty right now, so we feel it is perfect for your needs. I've brought my sponsor and his brother to help get your women safely inside. Things don't always go as others plan, do they? Sanity is always making things work out right. We'll make it right, won't we? We do have to always look our best, even if the situation is a bleak one." Joy was perhaps forty, but Amanda sensed she was still somewhat under the influence of her implant and Pytalon. Still, Joy was far more coherent than many of the other younger, newer EE women Amanda had met during the last eight years. She spotted two young men moving towards the bus. Joy's sponsor was probably twenty years younger than she was, which brought a grin to Amanda's face.

Soon, the two men joined Joy, carrying Ben, Tim, and Lisa inside the safe house. They sat the two unconscious men on the couch in the living room, and Lisa now sat beside the pair. Amanda was truly grateful that Tim and Ben were still out, for there were far fewer questions being raised.

Joy said, "It's late. I'll give you a call tomorrow and see what else is needed. You're going to have your hands full, Amanda. Ta ta for now. I've two men to pleasure," Joy teased Amanda, who grinned appropriately.

Once they left and the door was shut, Jessica exclaimed, "Amanda! You're a genius. This is perfect. We have a whole house to ourselves. We'd best see what is where. Lisa is going to need the bathroom soon, I expect."

Chapter 7—Unexpected Developments

"My God! What's happened to me? Oh no! No! No! No. Oh? Still male? No, this can't be!" Ben screamed. He'd just regained enough consciousness to be aware of his body and surroundings. Gaping and in shock, he involuntarily began talking in a normal tone of voice, "My body is hypersensitive to sensual touches." He continued until finally reaching the end, "I will repeat to myself these words several times each day. I must not forget these words. If I fail, I will get an intense migraine headache."

His screams brought Tim around, who added his similar shouts and exclamations to Ben's. Lisa was sitting quietly on Ben's other side. Hearing their recitations of their implanted behavior patterns, she too began reciting hers, just as she was ordered to do by the implanted words. Sitting in a sofa across from them, Jessica's heart went out to the three. From her implanted point of view, the men were being horribly misused. Either they should've been given a complete body alteration so they could really be the EE women they were now implanted to be or they shouldn't have been given this type of implant. Half-way, they were being forced to live in a limbo state. While they outwardly appeared to be EE women, they still had their male anatomy and voices , which would betray them the instant they spoke. There would be no place for them in the world.

As Jessica listened to the three reciting their programmed mantras, she knew better than to try to say anything to them. They wouldn't even hear her words. They were wholly wrapped up in the grey mental masses from the pain and drugs they'd been given. She reflected, however, on her own mental state. It had been eight years since she endured what these three were facing. Time had done one thing for her; it had allowed Jessica's own grey mass from her implant to move off her head some distance, thereby lessening the EE implant's affect upon her. For a minute, her attention focused on this phenomenon.

Jessica thought. *At first when I awoke, my head was entirely inside that mass. Eight years ago, I was a puppet, just as they are now, but now that ball-shaped mass has moved off my head, sitting about six inches up and in front of my head, outside my body, but I can see it clearly. Jessica, what does this have to do with anything?* She chided herself. "Well, it's not affecting me so much now," she explained to herself, "and that is very important." As if answering the question put to her by the men, she added, "But they can't wait eight years to regain control over their implants and behavior patterns."

She also knew Ben wouldn't be able to walk much at all, and Lisa, who used her feet as hands, desperately needed her feet back. "If only there was a way to modify their implants or to desensitize them before eight years passes," Jessica muttered to herself, biting her overly large lips. As she gazed on the three, the thought struck her again. She said to herself, "You know, there seems to be only one physical pattern that all EE women are given. We all have the same sized monster boobs and thick lips—sort of one size for all. I bet it is mostly the same with the wording of our implants too; all are done the same way. Does this help me?" she asked herself.

Amanda entered the room, having heated up some soup, and she overheard Jessica's question. "Does what help you?" Amanda asked. Her memories of doing a little cooking were slowly coming back to her, having been obliterated by her implanting and life over the last eight years. "I've got some soup heated up for everyone. They have to eat something. I bet they're starving."

"Pee, I have to go," Ben wailed and tried to get up. He failed and fell back down onto the couch. The two women struggled to get him up, and together, they managed to get him to the bathroom. Jessica had to help him deal with the unfamiliar apparel. As soon as he was done, the two led him into the dining room, where he suddenly declared he was starving. While they left him there greedily devouring the chunky soup, they helped Tim to the bathroom. He was only a bit dizzy, but could walk on his own. After he joined Ben at the table, the two supported Lisa, as she made her unsteady way to the bathroom. When they finally got her seated at the table, Ben was already done eating.

"What did they do to us? We can't live like this! I feel really bad. My breasts are throbbing and my head is killing me. My feet are so cramped I can hardly move. Oh God! I have to . . ." He never finished his thought, but immediately began reciting the implanted script once more. Not long after that, Tim followed suit.

"Come on; let's get them into bed. Sleep is what they need now," Amanda suggested. A half hour later, the two men were sound asleep, and the two women helped Lisa walk back to the living room couch.

"What a mess, Jessica. Now what are we going to do?" Amanda said disgustedly. She slumped into the sofa, while Jessica sat beside Lisa.

"Time will desensitize them, Amanda, as it has for us, but we can't wait eight years," Jessica began to relay the ideas that had been filling her head earlier. She saw Amanda was about to protest, and Jessica quickly added, "So we're going to have to do something to speed this along. If we don't, Lisa will be totally helpless, and both her and Ben's feet will become all messed up like mine are, Amanda, and they'll be stuck having to wear these awful boots all their lives."

"I know. I've thought about that too. While you do look sassy and sexy in them, you're mostly hobbled up. But what can we do? Their implants demand they wear them," Amanda countered.

"Desensitize. I have an idea. I'm going to try something on Lisa, since she's recovered the most from her implanting," Jessica offered.

"Please, I'll do anything," Lisa whimpered, but then once more began reciting her implanted speech, almost as if it had somehow realized she was trying to remove her ballet boots.

"Okay, Lisa. I want you to say quite forcefully, 'I must always wear nylons and ballet boots.' Say it like you mean it," Jessica asked.

"But I have to wear them," Lisa protested. "Okay, I must always wear nylons and ballet boots."

"Good. Say it again and again and again," Jessica asked.

"I must always wear nylons and ballet boots. I must always wear nylons and ballet boots. I must always wear nylons and ballet boots. Oh, I don't feel so good," Lisa whimpered. "My head is hurting again. I feel groggy."

"That's okay, Lisa. Say it again and again. You can do it," Jessica encouraged her, while Amanda watched without knowing what Jessica was doing, though grimacing, realizing firsthand what poor Lisa must be enduring.

For the next half hour, Jessica continued to make Lisa say that single sentence repeatedly. At first, Lisa's headache only worsened, as did her grogginess. Then to everyone's amazement, the pain and disorientation began to subside. This encouraged Jessica and Lisa continued her chant. She whispered to Amanda, "See, we're desensitizing that one sentence, like time has done for us. Lisa, you're doing great. Continue to say it like you really mean it."

An hour after they had started this process, Lisa finally felt better. "You know, maybe I don't have to wear these. Can you please take them off me, Jessica?" Jessica was more than willing to remove the boots, nylons, and garter belt.

"Oh this feels so much better! Now, I'm not helpless any longer. See, I can finally scratch my nose," Lisa exclaimed. "Oh, but I'm an EE woman. I have to look my best," she began to protest a little and looked very confused.

"Of course, you are, dear. Around the house, we don't have to look elegant. We'll get you some flats. Amanda will get you some nice heels like hers to wear when you go out. Not all EE women wear nylons, because not all men like them. Some men prefer to see bare legs," Jessica affirmed.

"Oh, I didn't know. I don't know how to flirt or provide pleasure to men. I've never seen mom do it to dad. They always had their bedroom door shut. What do I do? I'm so embarrassed; I don't know how to be an EE woman. I'm doomed!" Lisa began to sob. Her implant was forcing a behavior pattern on her, and she analytically realized she didn't know how to fulfill it.

"There, there, darling, don't fuss. Amanda and I will teach you everything you have to know." Turning to Amanda, she fumed in a whisper, "They didn't even educate Lisa. My God, they have really bungled this one! She's probably never even had sex before."

Amanda groaned. She thought this might be the case with Lisa. "That's criminal on their part, pure insanity if I ever saw any. Don't cry, Lisa, that's why we're here in this safe house, so you and the men can learn what you need to learn." Lisa stopped fussing and thanked them profusely.

"At least, I can help around the house. I'm not helpless now," she admitted, "but I feel so funny. I have to get more pleasure soon." Lisa was fighting against the drive of the implanted orders still.

"Okay, you've done well for today, Lisa. I'm very proud of you. Come on. Let's go to bed, and Amanda and I will show you how to do some things," Jessica suggested.

The next morning, Lisa began to help with the many domestic chores. This emboldened Jessica, who began to believe her approach to desensitizing the implant behavior patterns might just be working. Of course, Ben and Tim were more than a handful this morning. Both were vacillating between outrage and anger over what had been done to them, combined with frantic attempts to fulfill their implanted sexual behavior patterns. However, their tremendous upset was quickly buried by their nearly overwhelming desires to obey the orders. Migraine headaches left them little choice. Thus, the two women had to help the men get fully dressed, once they finished breakfast.

With finally a brief breather and the men sitting on the couch, Jessica encouraged, "We have no choice but to keep trying to desensitize them. It worked on Lisa, so come on, Amanda. You work with Tim, and I'll work with Ben. I need at least to get Ben not to have to wear these boots. Lisa, you take care of everything else around here, please."

The teen grinned, "Yes, I can help now, but I'll need to get pleasured first." Both women ignored her, as she pleasured herself. Instead, the two pulled chairs across from their respective men and began by asking the men to repeat the one sentence that was causing the currently most debilitating actions.

It took all morning, coaxing and pleading with the men to continue the chants in spite of their headaches, but Jessica and Amanda persisted. By lunchtime, Ben agreed to remove his boots and Tim, his heels. Lisa had warmed up some soup for them, and the four walked into the dining room to eat.

"We need vitamins and more nourishing food," Lisa commented. "Good nutrition really helps people."

"Okay, after lunch, I'll do some shopping for us all, Lisa. Let's make a list of what we need, including outfits for you and the fellows," Amanda replied.

"What good is it going to do for us?" wailed Ben. "We can't go out in public like this! We aren't women; our voices aren't right. We can't live like this." Unfortunately, as soon as he uttered his protest, his implant kicked in, and he began to recite his pattern, which the women ignored.

While Amanda was gone, Jessica sat before all three and worked on desensitizing the same phrase in all three of her patients. She chose the sentence for them to repeat: I must look perfect at all times. Her reasoning for this sentence was simply if this were no longer a dominating factor, they could take a breather from dressing up formally, eliminating a whole lot of work on their part.

After many head pains, protests, and much grogginess, all three were agreeing voluntarily they no longer had to look perfect all the time. They could tolerate lounging around inside their home. Jessica was greatly relieved by this little progress, for her burdens were lessening. When Amanda returned, she was very much impressed with what Jessica had achieved and felt true hope for the first time.

Amanda and Jessica were both in agreement in wanting to stop their three patients from continually having to need sexual sensations and stimulations several times each day." Amanda gushed. "I know it's pleasurable, but their behavior is starting to annoy me. Plus, I still have that same urge!" Amanda flushed, admitting why their behavior was bothering her so much. Jessica giggled, adding that she too felt that urge.

Later, the five sat in the living room, and the two women forced the three to constantly repeat the line about needing sexual sensations and stimulations several times each day, many times. Naturally, their symptoms and headaches returned full-force, but Jessica and Amanda continued to persist, soothing and comforting the three, while insisting they continue to repeat the mantra. Interestingly enough, Jessica and Amanda also began to feel headaches coming on, because it was affecting them. Still, the two didn't give up. By bedtime, all five had finally gotten some relief from that command. For the first time, none of the three insisted on pleasurable acts before going to sleep. Lisa also insisted they take many vitamins before bed to help their bodies fight off this implant mantra.

Embolden by the progress she'd made, Jessica kept at it during the following days. The three quickly adapted and began to look forward to each day's session. Day by day, more and more of the command words and sentences were desensitized in Lisa, Ben, and Tim, and to a much lesser extent in Jessica and Amanda. Good nutrition and vitamins were also helping their physical condition. Still, Amanda alone handled all trips outside of the home. Lisa wouldn't be too much help on shopping trips, and the men dared not face the world as they were now.

A week after they rescued Lisa, the professor called on Jessica's cell phone. Hastily, she explained what happened and that Amanda had taken quick action to get them to safety. She also told him about her success in getting the three people desensitized from the implants.

"Bloody hell, Jessica! Do you realize you're the first person I know of who has been able to defeat the damnable implants! You are truly a genius! Please keep at it with Ben and Tim. I'll see what I can figure out. Give my thanks to Amanda too, will you dear? I'll be in touch," the professor said.

After he hung up, Jessica said, "Amanda, that was the professor. He said thank you for saving all of us. He sounded amazed we were desensitizing these implants and affecting their behavior patterns.

Around August 1, she and Amanda finally finished getting the last phrase knocked out of all three. No longer were Ben, Tim, or Lisa reciting their pattern or getting headaches if they didn't obey them fully. While not actually gone or erased, their implants had destimulated, giving them vastly more control over their lives, actions, and activities.

That first morning over breakfast when Jessica explained she'd finished with all the phrases, Ben declared, "Jessica, Amanda, we owe you our lives. I feel alive once more, totally screwed up, but alive. Of course, the real question is what do we do now? I suppose if Tim and I keep our mouths shut and play dumb, we could get by outside of this house. We can't put on our usual clothes. These boobs of ours are mammoths."

Jessica laughed. "But Ben, mine are the same size. You know, one size fits all is the EE motto, at least, it seems that way, and you seem to love mine." Ben flushed, while Tim roared.

Tim commented, "Well, you do have a point."

Lisa asked quietly, "Why do men like such large boobs anyway? I can't see my feet because of them."

No one provided an answer. Ben continued his line of thought. "Look, with these nails, boobs, and hair wigs, we don't have much choice, but to wear EE women's outfits. We could cut our nails back and peel the wigs off. However, there's not a damn thing we can do about the breast implants, unless we want to try cutting them off."

"That'd be one bloody mess—no way," Tim protested, looking rather shocked that Ben would suggest such a thing. He added, "No, somehow, we have to make do. With our knockers, we've no choice but to dress as EE women for now. God help us if we have to speak out there in the world at large. I swear if it's the last thing I do, I'm going to see the Feds Peter Delius pays dearly for what he's done to us!"

Amanda spoke up, "In that case, Tim, you, Ben, and Lisa had better learn to dress yourselves properly, and most importantly, learn to walk gracefully in the heels we're supposed to wear out in the public arena."

"Jessica, thank heavens you were able to get me out of those heels!" Ben gushed.

She smiled. "I know. You didn't have ballet lessons, so there was no chance you'd be able to walk in them, not without building up your muscles. Besides, as you know, after wearing them as long as I have, my feet and legs have totally been altered. The good news is since we've been lounging around here for a month, my toes are starting to bend again. I think maybe if I work at it, I may eventually be able to wear regular heels. So don't get any ideas of leaving here soon, please."

"Wow, dear! That's the best news yet," Ben replied sincerely. "I mean you're terribly sexy in them, but they hobble you up too badly."

"Say, I know something about physical therapy," Lisa butted in. "Let me work on your feet and legs some. Maybe I can help you, Jessica."

Amanda added an additional caution. "Fellows, remember if you wear the heels for too long a period, your legs are going to alter like mine have. Once that happens, you can't wear anything but them. Remember to take it easy. Don't wear them all the time. Like Jessica, my legs are starting to stretch out a bit, but I couldn't wear Lisa's flats."

"Hey wait a second, Tim. We forgot all about the stupid makeup. Are we going to have to learn to put all that on our faces too?" Ben looked pale.

"Fellows, there's two schools of thought. One is that less is more. Not all EE women wear garish makeup. The sponsors and their desires in their escorts mostly dictated it. I suggest we go minimalist with you fellows and with Lisa. Come on; we best get you three practicing."

The next day, the professor called Jessica again. "Great news. I've found a doctor who can remove the men's breast implants! I reasoned if they could be inserted, they could also be removed. The trick was finding someone reliable who would do it without asking questions, if you get me. I found one who is in New York City. I'm texting you the coordinates and his name. By the way, have you been watching the news at all?"

"Thanks. No, we've been too busy with all this to watch TV. Why?"

"Put Ben on please. I'll tell him, and he can relay it." She handed the phone to Ben, indicating the professor wanted to talk to him.

After greetings, the professor explained, "Well, it's been happening just like I predicted. The various manufacturing lines for Pytalon are allowing placebo pills accidentally to leave their factories. Of course, those who take them are no longer getting their Pytalon and are undergoing the horrific withdrawal symptoms, Ben. It's happening in all the major cities—outbreaks of so called Insanity, giving the AP-cops a real workout."

Ben asked, "Is this happening because those workers on the manufacturing lines are doping off?"

"I believe so, but there is no way I can know for sure, son. In all honesty, it is time we move up to Phase Three of our long-range plan. I know your predicament is nasty, but son, this might be our big chance."

"Great. Okay, I'll talk it over with Tim. Say, Lisa here thinks she might know a way to help them come off Pytalon without the awful consequences," Ben replied.

"If so, that would be a real blessing, one that we didn't anticipate years ago. I guess if Jessica could find a way to nullify the implants partially, then there should be a way to help them come off the drug. If you want to pursue it with her, then you should go to our Phoenix site. If her ideas work, then I can devise a whole program around it. That would be bloody great, you know. We could add to our numbers at a vastly escalated rate than we planned for."

"Okay, this is really important. I'll talk to Tim. Maybe we can endure our misfortune a little longer for the greater good, but mark my words, professor, one day soon, I'm going after that Feds man, Peter Delius! Tim and I have a score to settle with him."

The professor laughed. "Son, that you bloody do have. Let me know if Phoenix is on. Bye for now."

"So what was that all about?" Tim asked, growing curious with the mention of Peter. "Remember, that Feds man is mine!"

Hastily, Ben relayed the news. "That's great he's found a doctor who can remove your boobs," Jessica commented sincerely. She felt much relief after hearing that such a procedure was possible.

Amanda asked, "But what's this Phase Three thing he mentioned? We should let Lisa have a go at getting people off Pytalon. It's a hideous drug. Jessica and I still have recurring symptoms from it, and we've been off it for months now."

Tim commented, "Ben, they've a right to know about Phase Three. After all, they've saved our lives." Ben nodded and Tim explained. "You see, some of us have been studying the world situation for years trying to figure out just how we can undo this century and a half of insanity, I mean the whole PDH implanting thing and the damnable Pytalon drug. Our best models predicted that eventually the zombies would really start to goof up, especially those on the manufacturing lines. Apparently, that's been happening big time while we've been stuck here. Hundreds have accidentally come off Pytalon, because the pills they're taking don't contain Pytalon. In Phase Three, we who are free and not on Pytalon or implanted are supposed to reach out to those who are coming off it and get them whisked away to some safe house, where they can recover in time. The idea is to have them join our ranks and help the others. Of course, it may take years and years to get everyone off and our world restored in some fashion. That's the idea behind Phase Three."

"If my idea works, it will help them come off Pytalon," Lisa commented. "That's what I wanted to do when I graduated, through things like physical therapy. I'd still like to try, if I can."

Ben looked at Tim. Then, he said, "Okay, Tim. I think we owe it to Lisa to give her a chance to see if she can also work a miracle. We can always go to New York City later on. The doctor will still be there."

"Glad you see it that way too, Ben. There is more at stake here than ourselves. Amanda, we'd best get to practicing so we at least appear to be proper EE women, even if we're men," Tim suggested. Lisa smiled. Finally, she would get a chance to see if her ideas had any real merit to them.

They spent another week getting comfortable with their EE apparel. Eventually, the five ventured out to do some shopping at the local EE apparel store, adding several new outfits to those that Amanda had purchased some time ago. They also stocked up on groceries for the bus. Finally, Amanda called the association to check out of the safe house. She left a sizeable monetary contribution to the association. On August

10, the five EE women walked slowly out of the home and boarded the bus, each assisting the other with the steps. Amanda drove the bus, pulling away from the curb, while Tim carefully punched in the coordinates for Phoenix. He found this more difficult to do with his longer nails.

Chapter 8—On the Road

During the long drive to Phoenix, Lisa busied herself working on Jessica's feet. She was convinced massage therapy would eventually undo Jessica's eight years of wearing the exotic boots. Already Lisa had worked a minor miracle in that Jessica was now able to wear the usual regular EE stilettos, but only for a short time. From Jessica's point of view, this was a most welcomed change, and she eagerly let Lisa work on her feet, despite the pain she felt as the teen continued to bend her toes back to a more normal position. "No pain, no gain," Lisa chatted whenever Jessica grimaced or groaned.

To keep Jessica's mind off her feet, Ben continued her education in the operation of his many electronic devices and insisted she continue to monitor the mostly silent communication channels. Much of their spying had died down because the CEOs of the Pytalon companies were now zombies, like those they'd created everywhere else. Monitoring the local AP-cops channels was now more interesting. Outbreaks of Insanity were spreading around nearly every section of the major cities, overwhelming the AP-cops. The Feds were called in to help, but thanks to the power play by their top leaders, these men were also zombies.

On the Feds' channel, Jessica learned an interesting fact. Only the top Feds' leader in each of the key cities was still normal. That person was not implanted or on Pytalon. They'd followed the example set by Peter Delius of the Chicago Feds. One communication now reported there were only twenty Feds left who were not cured of future Insanity, meaning they weren't yet implanted and on Pytalon themselves. In Jessica's mind, that equated to twenty men who were not yet zombies, outside of the rebel organization she was now a part of. While Jessica wanted to ask Ben and Tim just how many there were in their group besides the professor, she dared not, because Lisa wasn't truly accepted as one of them yet.

As they approached the spectacular view of Albuquerque, New Mexico, Jessica heard another interesting tidbit of chatter on the channels she monitored. It seemed these remaining twenty Feds were now looking to acquire their own EE women. Slowly an idea formed in her mind. She hated what

Peter Delius had done to her lover, Ben. Yes, she dared think that word now; love was a concept foreign to her implant-enforced behavior, for this was real emotion, not fake. "Ouch." She responded to a jolt of pain in her right foot.

Lisa giggled, "We're making progress. See how much your toes bend now."

"Yes, but I can't bend them half as much as you are bending them," Jessica countered.

"We're getting there, but I'm stopping to watch the scenery. This sure beats the hills of Missouri. It's really spectacular around here, isn't it?" Lisa commented.

From the front, Tim called out, "We're going to have to stop in Albuquerque. The bus needs a recharge of its EM engines. It'll probably take an hour if we can find a service station. Ben, we'll have to go out in the public view, damn it."

"You'll do fine, dear," Amanda insisted. "Let Jessica and me do the talking if possible. Tell us what we need to ask and do for this recharge thing. Sorry, I don't know anything about it."

Relieved, he proceeded to give her explicit instructions. Meanwhile, Jessica checked over her appearance and that of Lisa, before assisting Ben. She also slipped on her new heels.

"Do I dare wear my flats outside, Jessica? I mean I still feel a little compelled to look my best," Lisa asked, growing more worried by the minute. She wasn't wearing nylons so she could use her toes effectively.

"Sure, why not, Lisa. If you get a bad headache, you can always come back on the bus and slip on your heels. We've found whenever you finally start obeying the implant, the headaches vanish pretty rapidly," Jessica advised her.

The view of the mountains was spectacular from this service station site on the eastern edge of the sprawling city. The women opened a back panel and brought out a long, thick electric cable. While Ben and Tim struggled to get it over to the hookup plug, Amanda used her ID card to pay for the service. Two other much smaller EMAC vehicles were just finishing their servicing. A fast food mart beckoned from beneath a thin metal canopy, and several others were just walking out carrying bags of snacks. All looked quite peaceful, and Amanda decided they could venture a trip to the mart. A little chocolate would taste good about now.

With the re-charging beginning, the five EE women began making their relatively slow way to the nearby mart. The afternoon was sunny and warm. The air was a little thin, but crisp at this higher elevation. They had gone about three hundred feet, halfway, when four relatively grubby looking men in their late twenties came around the side of the mart and spotted the team of five. At once, Amanda noticed something was wrong. Men on Pytalon virtually never really looked at her or paid much attention to her, but these four were eyeing them and talking about them. Nods and fingers pointed towards the women. Amanda was certain something was amiss when the four men changed course and headed directly towards them.

They had come too far to turn around and head back to the bus. In their heels, they would be overtaken long before they got to the safety of the bus. Amanda felt a surge of panic, something she hadn't felt for some time. She'd been off Pytalon long enough now that her long dead emotions had become quite active, Jessica's too. "Shit!" Ben whispered.

"Let us do the talking," Jessica whispered to Ben and Tim, who felt miserable. Ordinarily, they'd have moved in front of the women and tried to protect them. Now their roles were reversed.

"What do we have here, boys? Five EE women for sure," one man exclaimed. His body was trembling, and he didn't look well.

"Are you sure? I see fairies or butterflies, Don," a second man uttered, blinking madly.

"Must be EE women. Monster knockers, but they look like they are bleeding or something, Don. You sure they are women? Maybe we're still seeing things," the third man added.

The fourth man was exceedingly nervous, glancing around in all directions. Occasionally, he swatted the air with his hands, as if beating off some flying insect. "Maybe we can get laid. God damn bugs! How come there are so many bugs around this place, Don? I thought you said there was food here. We're the food for these bugs. They look like women, sort of. Should have brought our horses. Do we even have horses anymore? Maybe that was when I was a kid. Suppose so. My prick is getting hard so they must be women."

"Aye, five of them, at least I think so. Don't see their men around," Don said, rubbing his crotch as if he had an itch. "Going to get me a piece of tail. Can't remember when I last had it, boys. Them's EE women all right, supposed to please men." He called out to Amanda, "Woman, you're supposed to please men, so come please me. I need please'n badly. Been so long, I cain't remember. Don't be bashful; we'll do you all." He reached out to grab Amanda's arm, but his aim was totally off, and he snatched at air instead. She hadn't moved.

"Damn your bugs, Henry. They are interfering with me," Don explained his wild miss of Amanda. "Come here, lady; do your thing with me."

"Hello boys," Amanda finally chose to speak. She spoke in a very pleasant voice, but did not flirt. "I'm sorry, but we all have sponsors. We aren't allowed to pleasure anyone but our sponsors. It is in our contract. Sorry." She rightly guessed they were coming off Pytalon, probably four more cases of badly made pills. Their electronic monitoring indicated such was occurring at most major manufacturing plants.

"Don't matter to us. Don't see any sponsors around. What they don't see won't hurt 'em none. Henry, keep your damn bugs to yourself!" Don growled angrily and swatted several non-existent bugs that were supposedly flying around his head.

"I see dozens of sponsors over yonder," Henry pointed off towards the rocky mountainside, up ahead on the right. Everyone glanced that way, but saw nothing besides the pretty scenery and several billboards with Insanity warnings.

"I only see butterflies, Henry. You're imagining again," another replied. "Tail, I need some tail now. Come on you EE women; earn your keep. I'm ready."

The four moved in closer and were about to take them by force. Just as Don was about to grab Amanda roughly, Lisa sprang into action. Still wearing her flats, she swung her right leg in a broad arc, landing a karate kick on Don's head, knocking him to the ground. Two others tried to land wild punches on Lisa's body. Repeatedly, she leapt and swung her legs, extending them at the last instant, landing solid blows on the advancing men. The fourth man got distracted and began calling Lisa a pretty butterfly. She ignored him.

Don got to his feet and shook his head, shaking off the force of the blow. He drew out a wicked looking knife. Just as he was about to use it on Lisa, a strange contraption came flying into the group, running smack into Don, knocking him to the ground. He lost his knife as he fell. "Yahoo," the teen yelled as his contraption struck Don. He continued driving the strange four-wheeled machine around, moving it closer to the other three men, who flailed their arms about, as if fending off some fire-breathing dragon.

During the commotion, Don got to his feet. He yelled, "Dragons! Run for your lives!"

"I see a huge butterfly. It's going to eat you Don! Run, run!" another yelled. All four turned and ran rather crazily back the way that they had come.

"And don't come back," the teen yelled, parking his vehicle and stepping off in front of the five astonished women. He was the same age as Lisa, Amanda estimated, just out of high school, with short brown hair and blue eyes. He wore western style clothing with button snaps on his plaid shirt and muttered, "Sanity is doing a good job." Then he turned back and spoke normally, "Wow, five EE women in one place. You're EE women, aren't you?" Lisa nodded.

"Pretty amazing foot work, miss. You really are the most exotic young woman I've ever laid eyes on, most pretty, but I really liked the way you fended them off. Been a plague of it around town. Some say it's because of a bad batch of Pytalon, but who can say for sure. Our AP-cops have their hands full. There are too many crazies around for them to handle. I say, so what if they arrest them, then what are they going to do? Pump them full of more bad Pytalon? World's gone a bit wacky. Name's Greg Whitehorse. I was going to be an inventor, but now they want me to become a doorman. What a waste. See my invention here? Last year before they upped my Pytalon, I invented a miniaturized EM motor. It powers my four-wheeler here, you see. It isn't safe for you to be outside around Albuquerque anymore. Things are a bit crazy. Is that your big EMAC bus there? I've never seen one quite so big." He finally ran down, muttering softly, "Sanity is helping others."

"Yes, we are. I'm Lisa. You invented this little vehicle yourself? That's amazing. Thank you for helping us. Those men are having withdrawal symptoms from some bad Pytalon." She guessed he was dealing with the drug much as she had. All seniors got a slightly larger dose of Pytalon, only she always managed to spit out the pills before they affected her too much.

"Very pleased to meet you, Miss Lisa. Say, you heading to the mart? If so, I'll tag along and make sure those fellows don't try to mess with you again."

"Thanks, we were after some chocolate bars," Lisa replied. "I probably could have taken him even with his knife, but I might have gotten cut. You're pretty inventive." They continued their slow walk towards the mart, but Amanda kept a keen eye out for the men.

"Well, I was when I was a junior, you see," Greg continued to chat, "but that ended last year when they upped my dose. I invented the miniaturized EM motor in my junior year. It could really be a most useful invention, powering all sorts of smaller vehicles to help others get around more easily. Why take a big EMAC to the grocery store when you only need a gallon of milk? What a waste, you see. I was going to become an engineer and inventor when I graduated, but then they told me I was to be a stupid doorman. Then, all this Pytalon mess began, and they've rather forgotten about me. I wish I could run away to somewhere that's safe where I can invent more things and make my miniaturized EM motor power lots of things."

"I know what you mean," Lisa chatted gaily. "I was planning to become a physical therapist and help people recover, but then, they got to me and turned me into an EE woman, though I surely don't know why. These women came to my rescue, because they mostly botched the implant thing. Anyway, I believe I know how I can help get folks safely off Pytalon too. That's what I'm going to try to do very soon."

"Way cool, Lisa. I'd sure like to get off that stuff. It's making me feel sort of stupid." He added softly, "Sanity is taking your meds daily." Then he snapped out of it and added, "Well, I know why they probably chose you to become an EE woman; you are incredibly pretty and exotic." Greg smiled.

Lisa grinned and said, "Ah, that's just a birth defect."

"Doesn't make you any less pretty, though, Lisa. Say, I bet I could make you a four-wheeler that you could drive around too. You know, put in foot controls. I'll see if I can, that is, if I can ever get out of here so they don't make me into that stupid doorman. So where are you five going? Must be somewhere important, since you're EE women and all that. Everyone knows that EE women only are with the most important of men, you know."

Lisa flushed a little. She really wanted to have Greg hold her and kiss her, but then she wondered if that was just her implant speaking. Then again, she did like her strange rescuer and inventor. Oh, how she wished she had more EE training, then she'd know what to do. "I suppose we're on an important mission. If I can really safely get people off Pytalon, then that would be a very important thing." She wanted to say "Kiss me," but dared not. Her face felt red hot. Lisa suddenly realized she was becoming highly aroused by Greg and felt even more awkward and embarrassed. Was it her implant or were her feelings genuine?

Amanda sensed Lisa's emotions, though she was surprised that she was able to do so. Her own eight years of being wholly under the influence of her EE implant had nearly destroyed her intuition. "So Greg, you're an inventor and want to get to a safe place where you can pursue them and not be on Pytalon? What do your parent's think about this?" They entered the mart and headed for the candy bar isle.

"Folks are zombies and don't even know me anymore. Yes, I'd give anything to just be allowed to work on my inventions and things. Why?" He again betrayed the fact that he was still a bit under the influence of Pytalon, muttering, "Sanity is following orders and doing what you are told." He seemed embarrassed about this, before changing the subject. "Say, aren't EE women supposed to be accompanying the bigwigs? Where are your men? They should've been here to protect you. It's not safe around town anymore."

After picking out several bars and using her ID card to pay for the lot, Amanda wanted to ask Tim if there was any chance that they could offer to bring Greg along with them. In her mind, having more *good people* like inventors might well be a very good thing. However, they were in public, and she knew both Ben and Tim were terrified of opening their mouths and being discovered. She was able to avoid answering him for a minute while she handled their purchases. Greg automatically took hold of Lisa's bar, opening it for her and holding it for her to take a nibble. Amanda smiled. The fellow was still observant and helpful—she gave him that much, but what to do? How to answer him? Should she lie? Or should she thank him and leave him here?

As the six stepped out into the fresh air amid the splendid view of the mountains and gorges, Tim spoke up, rather startling Greg, who heard a man's voice coming from one of the EE women. "Well, Greg, Ben and I are their sponsors, only we ran into a whole lot of trouble with the Feds, who drugged us and turned us into EE women, more or less. Rather embarrassing for us, you see. Are you really serious about fleeing to a safe place where you can be yourself, invent things to help others, and stay off Pytalon?"

"What? You sound like a man but look like an EE woman. I don't understand. The Feds? Gosh, those are really, really bad men. We had two here in Albuquerque, but thank the gods, they were implanted and put on Pytalon two weeks ago. Now they mostly help the IP-AP-cops out. Yes, yes, I would love to get somewhere safe, but my EM motor can only run my four-wheeler about an hour out of town before it needs a re-charge. It's only a miniaturized EM motor, after all, not a real EMAC, which can go thousands of miles on a charge," Greg replied honestly and sincerely, though a bit confused about Tim's sex.

"Yes, we're quite a mess, half-woman, but still men where it matters. Damn Feds anyway. Greg, we're heading to Phoenix and a safe house there where Lisa can see if she can get folks safely off Pytalon. After that, we're heading to New York City to see if we can get our boobs back to normal and such, so we don't look like EE women anymore."

"But they are all implanted, aren't they? You can't do that, can you? Sanity is having a good implant. We had that drilled into our heads in school. No one can disobey an implant, can they? I don't understand, but then I'm just an inventor. Probably I'm not supposed to understand all this Insanity," Greg admitted.

"Son, no one can understand Insanity. That's what it means: insanity, incomprehensible, makes no sense. Anyway, are you really serious about fleeing here?"

"Yes, more than anything. I want out of here. Who wants to be a doorman for the rest of their lives? I want to invent things. Can I possibly come along with you?" he pleaded, suddenly realizing these people might be his salvation.

"Okay then, Greg. We have at least another forty-five minutes to wait on our re-charge. Go fetch whatever you want to bring along. Don't tell a soul about us or you leaving. If you aren't back here in forty-five minutes, we're leaving you behind. Got it?" Tim told him.

"Whoopee! Thank you, thank you, thank you. I'll be back in a flash. Say, can I bring along my four-wheeler too?" Greg effused.

Tim grinned, "Sure thing son. It'll fit in our lower cargo bay. Now hurry up; I'll hold Lisa's candy bar for her." He handed Tim the half-eaten bar, winked at Lisa, and dashed off to his vehicle. A moment later, Greg zoomed out of the huge lot, heading into the town.

To the others, Tim explained, as they finally approached their bus, "He's an inventor. We could use his miniature EM motor. Besides, he looks like a very promising young man. I can't stand by and watch a promising young man be implanted into being a doorman—incredible waste of a person."

"Thanks Tim. I really do like him," Lisa commented, her face still warm. Sheepishly, she added, "He can sleep with me, since there are only three beds in the bus."

While Tim and Amanda headed to the rear to check on the re-charge process, Lisa whispered to Jessica, "I really like him, but I don't know what to do next. What do I do? Should I just kiss him? I want to feel his arms around me and all that."

Jessica smiled, but inwardly cursed the psychs of St. Louis who implanted her but failed utterly to give her the subsequent training so she would know what she needed to do to perform what the implant drove her to do or in this case, what she really felt like doing. "When you're alone, you might start off by giving him a kiss and see where that leads. If he responds, let your bodily urges guide you, Lisa. They won't fail you."

"Really? Okay, I'll try it tonight. I do want him to like me. He seems to think I'm pretty, but with these monster boobs, I don't think so. Should I wear my heels now? Should I put on some makeup too? I should look my best," she asked.

"See if you can keep your headaches at bay and not do those things. If you can't, let us know, and we'll fix you up. He's seen you like you are now and thinks you're pretty, so you're looking your best, don't you think?" Jessica attempted to weasel around the wording of the teen's implant commands. It worked and Lisa relaxed a little.

Greg returned with two duffle bags on the back of his four-wheeler in less than a half hour. "Hi all. I couldn't bring all my shop tools, but I suppose I can borrow some in Phoenix. I'm ready. Hi Lisa. You look even prettier than before."

She flashed him a smile. Jessica had only brushed Lisa's hair, but still Greg noticed. "Thanks, Greg. Come on; let's get your things stowed. Tim, where do we put his four-wheeler?"

Tim, Ben, and Greg got the heavy vehicle stowed in the lower storage bay, but not without a good deal of trouble. In their heels, the two men had a most difficult time and relied upon Greg's strength to get it safely in. Then, Greg carried his two bags into the bus following Lisa, who gaily chatted and gave him a tour, showing him where to put his things. "You'll have to sleep in my bed since there are only three beds on the bus. I hope you don't mind."

Greg flushed, "Oh not at all, Miss Lisa! Maybe I can help you with things."

Before long, they were back on the road. Greg was impressed with the bus, and Lisa made a good tour guide. Finally settling down on a seat beside Lisa and opposite of Jessica and Ben, who returned to their monitoring operations, Greg asked, "You know, I've been thinking. Why are you going to Phoenix? There's nothing there anymore, not since the Iran War a hundred and fifty years ago."

Up front, Amanda overheard him. "You're right, Greg. My major was history. They fired a neutron bomb at Phoenix to kill our president. He was the only president in history to be killed in a battle in a war on US soil. Of course, the Israelis, Egyptians, Saudis, and Indians launched a massive counterstrike and wiped Iran off the map. Greg's right, Tim. Phoenix is deserted. No one lives there anymore. It's supposed to be a radiation death zone. I should have remembered all this long ago. Sorry. I'm still having some after-effects of Pytalon."

Tim chuckled. "You're both partially right. The radiation levels are back to normal—have been for some twenty years now, but only we renegades live there now. It is the only safe town-like place in the world right now. The zombies in charge have long ago forgotten about Phoenix. Last time we were there, some hundred men, women, and children were living there, but that was several years ago. There might be more there now. The neutron bomb killed all living things, but left everything else intact, such as the houses and even the MTE. It's pretty amazing."

Chapter 9—Phoenix

The bus pulled into the outskirts of the desolate city some two days after picking up Greg, and was forced to halt at a roadblock barricade. Several men with handguns stepped out in front and walked to the bus door. Tim opened it and briefly introduced the party.

"I've always wanted to meet Weasel and Wart, but you're both not how I imagined you would look! Anyway, welcome to Phoenix, home of the free. I'm Bill Smyth, with a 'Y.'" Neither Tim nor Ben remembered seeing Bill when they were here several years ago. "By the way, I'm now the Mayor of New Phoenix," Bill said in a very serious tone of voice.

Ben laughed, "This is not how I imagine myself looking either. We got caught by the Feds back in St. Louis."

Bill commented, "We heard. The professor's here and told us all about you. How the devil are you able to operate after receiving the EE implants, fellows? Are you also on Pytalon? Sorry, but I have to ask these questions for safety reasons." He was thirty-five, Amanda guessed, well-muscled with a domineering sort of personality. Worse, she caught him giving her a good looking over. Even though she was merely sitting next to Tim, she was definitely aroused Bill. *Well,* she justified, *I am an EE woman, and I am supposed to rouse men.* That didn't make her feel any more comfortable, however.

"Yes, we got implanted, but they forgot to give us Pytalon, we think. Jessica back there—she has figured out how to desensitize the EE implants. If it weren't for her, we wouldn't be here today. Instead, we'd be quite insane. We owe her and Amanda our lives actually. Don't get caught by the Feds; they can be downright nasty," Tim briefly explained, hoping this was enough detail to satisfy Bill and let them go into the city.

"Well, your story jives with what the professor told us. You're cleared to enter. Follow that EMAC. It'll take you to temporary housing. The professor is there and wants to speak to all of you immediately. Things are brewing now, that's for sure! They're cleared," he called out to three other men, who pulled the barricade back, revealing a small EMAC. Since Bill stepped back, Tim closed the bus door, and drove slowly towards the EMAC, which also began to move into the sprawling city.

They didn't have far to go and soon stopped at what had once been an expansive country club. Amanda pointed out that the vast, overgrown lands around this very large complex might have once been a golf course. She'd read about them in her history books, though no one had any idea why men and women would want to hit a tiny ball all over the landscape. After they stopped, the EMAC pulled out, heading back to the barrier.

As Tim opened the bus door, the professor stepped out of the large double doors of the clubhouse. He was wearing a yellow tee shirt and blue shorts with flip-flops. He'd grown a beard since the two women had last seen him. Amanda and Jessica both noticed this detail. "Welcome to Phoenix. Come on inside; take a load off your feet, mates. Sure is good to see you again. Wow, fellows, you weren't kidding about the EE implants! Jessica, Amanda, it's good to see you both. You're looking vastly better than when you came knocking on my door. Bloody good. Come on in. This is supposed to be your place while you're here. It has every amenity you can possibly imagine, pool, sauna, the works. I, for one, am in love with the pool table. You fellows ever shoot pool?" the professor chatted away as if nothing had ever happened since the women had first met him months ago.

"Oh, I have your history book to return to you, professor. It was highly educational for us, perfect timing. How did you know?" Jessica asked. As soon as she'd heard Bill mention that the professor was here, she dug out the book from her bags. As she carefully stepped down the three steps to the ground, she handed him back his book.

"My pleasure, my dear. I'm glad you enjoyed it. I have a knack for such things. My, you are no longer wearing your ballet boots, Miss Jessica," he replied with a kindly smile.

She grinned. "Thanks to our physical therapist here, Lisa. She's been able to get my feet somewhat fixed up. I can wear regular heels now, but only for a short while. It's been getting better though. She really thinks she can get Pytalon out of a person's system. We're going to be her first test subjects, along with Greg here. Oh, Greg Whitehorse, this is the professor. He came to our rescue in Albuquerque. He's an inventor and made a miniaturized EM motor. I hope it's alright if we brought him here," she added growing slightly worried it might not have been such a wise move to bring him along. After all, they knew almost nothing about him, except that he and Lisa were becoming romantically involved.

"An inventor, eh? Great. We can use all sorts of new things. Society has been dead for too darn long now. Come on. I'll show you around this place. It's very luxurious indeed. I feel like one of you EE women living in a penthouse suite," he teased. Jessica smiled, knowing what he meant. In this screwed up society, the EE women had the best luxury accommodations, except those few who were *normal* and leaders.

The next day, Lisa began her big experiment. Her idea came from ancient history a couple centuries ago, in which toxins that were stored in the body could be sweated out. She needed a sauna and plenty of vitamins, along with cold showers, sea salt, and potassium. This much she already had worked out. The actual process was wholly experimental. No one had done such a thing for several hundred years. Still, the teen was eager to try, and she had no shortage of volunteers. Namely, Greg, Jessica, and Amanda were eager to do anything to get the residual toxin effects out of their bodies. While Greg was suffering the most from his recent withdrawal from the lower doses of Pytalon, the two women had taken adult doses for over eight years and still had intermittent bouts of the drug's effects on them. Additionally, both Tim and Ben had recently undergone the psych's PDH implants, and the heavy drug used in that process was still lingering in their systems.

"Okay, you've all taken your vitamins. Now we exercise a little to get the blood flowing and then we hit the sauna to sweat all the toxins out," Lisa explained.

"But we don't have any bikinis to wear," Jessica interrupted her.

After some checking, none could be found. Phoenix was mostly a ghost town. The only commodities here were those that were brought in by those who came. So the group decided to simply wear their underpants. "Heck, we all have the same mammoth boobs, except Greg here," Tim suggested. Greg soon got over his embarrassment being surrounded in the sauna by so many humongous breasts.

That first day, all five tasted, smelled, and felt the toxins beginning to be sweated out of their bodies. They found it grueling to be in the sauna sweating profusely for five hours, breaking only when they overheated or needed more salts. Lisa kept accurate records of their progress, but it was very apparent from the first day of the sauna treatment that her plan would work. The only detail was how long it would take to get the lingering Pytalon and other toxins out of their bodies. As it turned out, this was highly variable. Tim and Ben had the least amount of drugs in their bodies, since they only had one exposure during their PDH implanting.

Lisa had a bit more, but not much. She had always managed to spit the stuff out, thanks to her second birth defect, the pocket in her gum lines. Greg took longer, as he'd been subjected to low doses of Pytalon for much of his youth. While Greg finished in ten days, Jessica and Amanda took twenty days of sweating to rid their bodies of accumulated toxins. Eight years of daily doses had built up a substantial residue within their bodies.

Everyone felt fantastic when they finally finished Lisa's program. Their emotions were present. Lingering aftereffects had vanished. They could think well and were alert, which greatly pleased Greg, who now had more ideas for new inventions that would help others. After their initial success, dozens of others wanted their chance to be cleansed. Lisa stayed in New Phoenix and began a long career as a physical therapist, helping many others get safely off Pytalon and other drugs. Of course, Greg stayed there with her.

While the two women were finishing up, the professor and Bill had several lengthy talks with Ben and Tim. Two situations were critical. First, the twenty remaining Feds now controlled the whole world and were rapidly becoming tyrants with selfish behavior patterns. Second, the "factory goofs" allowed bad Pytalon pills to be widely distributed with the terrible side effects that came from a sudden withdrawal from the mind-altering drug. Already the AP-cops and the Feds-turned AP-cops were overwhelmed with rounding up the newly created Insane, that is, those coming off Pytalon. Worse, there was no guarantee the new Pytalon pills they were subsequently given actually had the drug in them. Many were resorting to the tried and true PHD implant methods to get these Insane individuals back to being Sane once more, overloading the psychs, who were now mere zombies themselves.

The professor also wanted Jessica to brief him and several others on her method of desensitizing an implant. Ben correctly pointed out that to do so, one needed the precise words the psych had spoken to the individual when the person was actually being PDH implanted. That proved not to be a problem. Weasel was able to quickly hack into the psych's database and download all the hundreds of "scripts" they normally used. He also pointed out that sometimes the psychs used additional verbiage, as had been done in his case with his wearing of ballet boots. Still, armed with these scripts and Jessica's methods, the professor and colleagues thought they had a chance of helping to get the implants desensitized.

"Look, desensitized doesn't mean the implant's effects are wholly gone," Ben explained. "Tim and I still have these uncontrollable urges from time to time. It's still there, only we do have a good deal of flexibility in whether to follow the implanted commands or not. It's not a panacea, professor. It just allows us to get by," Ben explained.

"I see, Ben. Duly noted. That brings up something else I wanted to discuss with you both before you head to New York City. If you go ahead and get your knockers back to normal so that you look like men once more, what's going to happen with your implants? Won't you find yourselves at their mercy to some extent? I mean you'll not be able to act out the EE women's role at all. Mates, that's been bothering me since we first discussed the possibility of having your boobs returned to normal," the professor said gravely. "Frankly, it has worried me considerably. I almost regret having found that zombie doctor in New York City for you."

"We worry about that too, professor, but what choice do we have? We're just plain screwed. We look like EE women until we speak, then the charade is instantly over," Ben replied. He sighed and added, "The only positive thing is that Jessica doesn't mind my looking like this. Her implant forced her to pleasure both men and women, so my appearance isn't disturbing her. We want to get married. So does Tim and Amanda."

Tim spoke up, "That's true. Also, professor, we've had quite some time now to study the two women and how they're doing. Regrettably, we all know that at times they're still being adversely affected by their own implants, even though Jessica has tried her desensitizing approach on them. While there was some improvement, there are still moments when they have to deal with the mental aftereffects and have a rough time with it. Still, professor, what other choice do we have? We're in a sort of limbo-land, half male, half female."

"Thank you fellows for being honest with me. I rather suspected as much, so I bloody well did a bit more research. I've found another doctor and clinic where they can complete the sex change, making you both female. That would at least alleviate part of your untenable situation, but perhaps that is not such a good idea any longer, since you both want to marry the two women," the professor sighed, running his hands through his beard for a moment. "Well, here's the data anyway. It's your decision, fellows. Blimey, I can't begin to tell you which option you should choose. Damn that Peter Delius to Hell!" He sighed again and then perked up, "Say, if you're serious about getting married, there is a non-denominational pastor here at Phoenix who can officially marry you."

"Hey, that part sounds terrific! We'll talk to the ladies when they finish their sauna sweating tonight," Ben replied, finally hearing something good for a change.

"So our real options are rather limited. There's no going back on an implant, is there? We're damned no matter what route we choose," Tim replied to the professor's earlier suggestion. "If we do nothing, simply put, we're freaks,. If we get the boobs removed, then we'll be normal men again, but suffer all manner of problems from the implants, which could really be debilitating, considering how awful the headaches can be when we don't follow the commands. If we take this third choice, we'd end up with our sex changed and be real women, but then there goes our marriage, to say nothing of being women in this insane world. We have no way to weasel out of this mess, do we?" Ben chuckled at the jest, and the professor smiled, but sadly shook his head no.

"No matter your choice, fellows, Bill wants you to take along several stun guns for your protection. Keep them handy when you're out of your bus or safe houses," the professor added. "Me, I don't care for such things, but in your case, you had best follow his advice, if only to protect Amanda and Jessica."

That evening the four sat down for a discussion. Tim and Ben outlined what the professor had told them earlier, especially the part about being able to get married. "Oh, let's do get married!" Jessica exclaimed, extremely happy over this unexpected news.

Amanda added, "But please, let's wait until this sweating thing is over. We're exhausted each night, but I'll give all credit to Lisa. Her process is working well."

"Agreed. Yet, what happens if we take the professor's offer and get the rest of the surgery done so we're no longer stuck halfway between sexes?" Ben asked what he felt was the key question.

Jessica replied, "I know our implants are still affecting us, though nowhere near what they used to be. My goodness, no. We're a million times better, but still, the implants are there. Amanda and I weren't going to say anything about you fellows going to New York City and getting this thing undone so you would be all male once more, but," she paused, still uncertain whether to bring this up.

"But?" Ben prodded gently.

"But if you become male again, the implants are still there. They will still be forcing themselves on you from time to time, though obviously not like they were those first few days," Jessica pointed out. "I wouldn't wish these migraines on anyone, except maybe Peter Delius. Honestly, guys, we're really worried about that. We have been thinking a lot about what might happen to you if you became all male once more. The third option is a real possibility; we certainly wouldn't mind all that much if you chose it and became all woman. After all, that would mesh well with all four of our implants, causing the least conflict in any of us. On the other hand, you'd be giving up an awful lot if you went that safe route. Considering the implants are involved, we've decided to leave the choice up to you. We'll marry you no matter what route you decide to follow. We love you, not your bodies," Jessica explained more fully.

Ben laughed. "Well, that's good to hear, but doesn't help us decide which route to take."

Amanda countered, "You can't expect us to decide that for you. My God, Ben, with one route you'd be losing your male body, and with another, you could well suffer debilitating migraines from time to time for the rest of your life. Doing nothing and staying as you are is likely to get you into trouble out there in this crazy world. Honestly, men see you first as EE women. When they find out the truth, they might get violent, especially if they are only partially off Pytalon."

"I know, I know. It has to be our decision, but I can't decide," Tim complained. "Except I don't want to stay the way I am now. This is a bloody nightmare. I sound like the professor," he lamented.

"Take all the time you want, love. Getting married to you is all I really want right now. I want you," Amanda answered him. The four grinned and headed for their beds in adjoining rooms.

The next day, they told the professor they would get married as soon as the women finished ridding their bodies of the Pytalon toxins. Ben added, "One thing is certain, we don't want to remain as we are: half and half." The older man, the professor, smiled and agreed with both points.

Ben looked again at the second address the professor had given them. It was for a clinic in Los Angeles. *Well, that would certainly be closer than New York City.*

Several days later, the two couples were married in a simple ceremony. Much to the men's dismay and embarrassment, several dozen showed up to watch. The professor soothed their feelings a bit by saying, "Look, couples getting married for love and not being ordered to do so by Total Care is such a rare thing. You bloody well wouldn't want them to be denied this chance to share your joy with you, now would you?" Both grumbled, but accepted his explanation.

However, Ben knew he had to do something about their mess and soon. It was driving him mad. Stuck in limbo was interfering with their lives in a major way. Besides, he and Tim hadn't spent much time on the rebel cause these past couple of months, and he felt guilty about that. So many others were dependent upon Weasel and Wart. One way or the other, they had to deal with their mess and soon. *Well, not on our wedding night*, he added to himself.

***

A week later, their bus fully recharged and re-supplied, the four headed off to check out the clinic in Los Angeles. As they came down from Victorville, the scenery was most impressive, and Tim kept their speed down so they could enjoy the view longer. Los Angeles and its many adjoining cities was still as large as it had historically had been. Nearly all available land, save the most dangerous hillsides, had been converted into homes, businesses, and apartments, forming a solid mass of humanity. Of course, all were on Pytalon and a large percentage had been implanted. Once known for its gangs and crime, now all was peaceful and docile. Here, only the Feds leader was not under the influence, they presumed. However, the fiasco over badly made Pytalon had not yet made its appearance in LA.

As they finally entered the greater LA valley, Tim had no choice but to keep their EMAC bus on autopilot. Once the home of ancient freeways, now the air space was filled with EMAC vehicles, while extensive MTE escalators often followed the

120

paths the antique automobiles used to travel, which were called Interstates back then. "Incredible! Look at all the EMACs!" Jessica exclaimed, her eyes wide with wonder. None of the four had ever seen so many in one place. Chicago had quite a lot of them, but not like this!

An hour later, the four walked into Ocean View Clinic and asked for Doctor Grimshine. They had ignored the doorman who opened the door for them along with a whisper, "Sanity is doing a good job." His eyes were glazed and vacant. Likewise, so were the others, they soon discovered.

After explaining what they were interested in discussing, the doctor, a middle-aged man with a receding hairline, led them into a private conference room. In a dull monotone, he began discussing, "Yes, I can see you have already had a good deal of work done. So all that remains is to alter your vocal cords and the replacement of your male organs with female ones. As EE women, you would expect the female organs to work properly, correct?"

"Er, yes," Ben replied. Clearly the man was both implanted and on Pytalon. *Do we dare trust this man with a knife?*

"This type of surgery is done here on a fairly regular basis," he drawled on. Ben didn't believe it. If everyone was on Pytalon, they'd have no need, desire, or thought for such things, he reasoned. The doctor continued, "You see, here in LA, some job opportunities are for women only, and there are more males needing employment than there are positions. Total Care often sends men here for a sex change so they can be gainfully employed. Sanity demands no unemployment. Here is a brochure on the procedures. In your case, we could get you in on Monday at the earliest. The surgery is fully automated and guaranteed, of course. It is a completely safe procedure. Our modern medical machines handle the entire procedure, so nothing at all can go wrong. Plan to spend a week in recovery, though your bodies will be healed within two days. We allow the extra days for the person to get used to the changes in their bodies. Since you have already had your EE work done, perhaps the recovery time would be shortened." He continued to talk about the process, but always in a bored, monotone. Finally, he asked, "Any questions?"

"Just one. Doctor, will the female organs be the real thing? I mean could we get pregnant and bear children?" Ben asked, unable to think of any other way to ask the question.

121

"Oh, yes, yes, your body would be indistinguishable from any other woman's body with two exceptions. You have an extra rib and your hips are narrower. For an additional fee, that rib could also be removed, and I would recommend having it removed if you're planning to bear children," he continued his un-emotional explanation.

"Okay then. We'll talk it over with our wives and let you know," Ben replied.

"Perfectly so. Sanity is doing the right thing. If you decide to have it done, see Betty at the reception desk. She'll give you the many forms to fill out and arrange your surgery date. If you will excuse me, I must make my rounds. Ten are in recovery now. They are being employed next week as nurses. We're always short of qualified nurses, you see." The doctor abruptly departed, leaving the four alone.

"Well?" Jessica asked.

"I don't see we have any real choice," Ben sighed. "We can't stay like we are. If we're to continue our work, we can't put up with migraine headaches all the time. On the other hand, I just learned something I didn't know before. Men are being forced to have their sex changed just to get a job. Can you imagine that? Not only are they drugged and implanted into being zombies, they are being ordered to get their sex changed. This society is far worse than I ever believed!"

Jessica flashed him a smile and pointed out, "Dear, now they don't have any more gangs and crimes out here, according to the history book. Some would say that is a good thing." He flinched, and she quickly added, "I'm just teasing you. This is a horror I never imagined possible. It has to stop."

They headed to the reception desk to get the forms. As they filled them out, the two noticed a special feature. Did they want to have their sperm saved in the sperm bank to be later used to impregnate their wives, should they marry? Both men checked this one, pleasing Amanda and Jessica.

A week later, the four checked out of the clinic. The first day after the surgery had been a particularly painful one, but by the next day, the pain had miraculously vanished. Both had been issued new ID cards: Beth Snells and Tilly Hickory. Neither had wanted to change their names, but Ben and Tim didn't match their bodies any longer. These were the closest they could come and still keep their names short.

On September 1, the four hit the road once more. This time, the rhythmic sounds of the medieval song Ungaresca was blasting through the bus. Jessica grinned broadly. At last, Ben, or Beth rather, was back to her old self. She thought, *Finally, the world is as right as it can be under the circumstances.* Both Beth and Tilly seemed very relaxed now that the awful burden had been lifted from them, and they threw themselves into the tasks at hand. The first of which was to get rid of these last twenty *normal* men, the Feds.

Chapter 10—Revenge

Driving out of LA, Beth said, "Jessica dear, pull up the surveillance video from our old safe house in East Peoria. Run the detection program against it to see if it's now safe for us to return there. I sure do like this ancient music."

"I know dearest. I've become partial to this music too. I'm on it," Jessica replied, immediately setting to work on the challenge. During these past weeks, she'd been a fast learner, particularly now that her implant wasn't affecting her quite as much and that the Pytalon residues were out of her body. She felt alive, more alive than she could ever remember and madly in love too. She rubbed the wedding ring Beth had given her, smiling at being in love. They had matching rings, just as Tilly and Amanda had. Officially in the EE women's registry, the four were now flagged as two married couples, which she hoped would help keep male requests for the four's escort services down to none. Essentially, with the EE women, marriage was tantamount to a retirement from the service. All four hoped that would continue to be the rule.

As the detection program began running, Jessica checked over the other spying connections. Finding them all in operation, she sat back to observe her lover. Jessica's mind drifted back onto the source of her mate's situation, Peter Delius, the scheming sadist and leader of the Chicago Feds. She wanted payback for what he'd done to Ben and Tim. It was one thing to force an eighteen-year-old girl into being an EE woman as a career, but it was an entirely different proposition to do what Peter had done to the two adult men. No, Jessica wanted revenge, and slowly a plan began to formulate in her mind. She was an EE woman, fully trained, and very experienced at it. Further, she and Amanda knew how their organization worked. Amanda had put that knowledge to good use back in St. Louis, saving them all.

Now, Jessica decided to put her knowledge to work. She realized she too had become something of a weasel, taking after her lover. She smiled, as her plan began to solidify. An Internet search finally yielded the one missing piece. She grinned once more. Just then, Beth jovially called out, typing sure is a bitch with these nails, but they make good head scratchers."

"And other more intimate uses," Jessica teased back. Beth turned back, lovingly ginning at her.

"Boobs get in the way too," Beth added. Jessica laughed and began making some arrangements on the Internet. She opened a new tab and checked on her and Amanda's old apartment complex in the skyscraper in Chicago. It seemed as if they had fled there years ago, but in fact, it had only been a few months. Their old apartment was still rented to them, and their rent was paid up through next March. Perfect, she thought, and submitted the first of her many orders.

That done, she glanced at the detection program. Video images were flying by at a very high rate of speed, but the overall image of their old quarters remained nearly stationary. Nothing was changing. The detection program would alert her if suddenly the Feds, AP-cops, or anyone else were caught on the video feed wandering around the old abandoned factory. An hour later, the program ended. She called out, "Your safe house in East Peoria checks out as still safe. No signs of anyone being around there since the Feds searched it looking for us."

"Great going. I'll punch in those coordinates," Tilly called back, and then correcting herself with a grin, "rather, Amanda will be punching them in. It will be good to be back home again. I'm very partial to that place, though I wonder if I can manage to continue my sneaking around now. Can't sneak much in these heels." Amanda giggled. That was an understatement. Even entering the bus, she and Tilly needed to help each other with the steps. Well, she'd always depended on either Jessica or Bill for walking assistance for eight years and now she was depending on Tim or Tilly.

"Dear, once we get settled in at the warehouse in East Peoria, can we make a quick trip to Chicago?" Jessica asked Beth. "I'd like to get a few of my things from our old apartment and show you where we lived. Besides, our rent is paid up until next March, so we should use it."

"Sure, I don't know why not. I'd love to see where you and Amanda used to live. I bet it sure is a swank place," Beth replied.

"Yes, it's small but very nice. I think we left it in a bit of a mess when we fled," Jessica admitted, hoping it was not a complete disaster. She trembled slightly, recalling how they were fighting Pytalon withdrawal symptoms at the time.

Two days later, the bus pulled inside the old warehouse in East Peoria. At least this time the Feds couldn't track their bus. Back in Phoenix while waiting on their wives to finish their sweating therapy in the sauna, Ben had tinkered with the geo-nav box, disabling the location transponder. While this in no way affected how the unit performed, it completely blocked anyone from pinging the unit to obtain the location of the vehicle in the warehouse.

In fact, Beth and Tilly felt anything but secure at this time. They had lived twenty-five years as men. Forced into becoming women, neither man felt comfortable with their new and unwanted situation. They hadn't ever had any such desire to have their sex changed, but that had been the only viable option for them. Their wives took it in stride and slowly educated them into the ways and mysteries of being women, but neither felt confident. Yet, it was worse, because they were officially EE women and supposedly the most erotic and sought after women in the world. Both were very content in quietly resuming their lives in their secret safe house in the basement of the abandoned warehouse. Tucked away here from the public eye, they felt and hoped a tiny measure of normalcy would return to them.

It was worse for Wart, who was used to going off alone on spying missions, while Weasel only very rarely left the basement of the warehouse. Tilly bit her lip, wondering if she even dared to go off alone on missions again. The stun gun in her purse gave her little comfort. She also knew if it weren't for the stabilizing effects of Amanda and Jessica, resulting in falling in love, she'd probably have ended her life sometime back. Thus, both Beth and Tilly were very excited about finally being back in their old haunt, where they could avoid the public eye, and perhaps relax and come to grips with what had happened to them.

"It's just as we left it," Beth pointed out, after carefully stepping down the steps of the bus. She felt a great deal of relief. She added, "I know, dear, take small steps and be sure to make more trips to unload our stuff." Jessica smiled in reply.

They spent the rest of the day unloading their things from the bus and cleaning up the place. When they left, they had stored their valuable electronic equipment behind a secret panel hiding a small storage room. All four pitched in to unpack the computers, sound systems, video systems, and so on, placing them back into their original locations, so they were operational. Amanda also spent time in the kitchen getting it back into its serviceable condition. While in Phoenix, she received some cooking lessons from one of the women and finally felt a little more at home around pots and pans. Her life as an EE woman had never included cooking. Instead, with her sponsor, she was always taken out to fancy diners, or if alone with Jessica, they ordered in. Now she felt it was her responsibility at least to cook for her mate, though Jessica volunteered to help her. Fixing supper, Amanda paused to smile. Beth finally got her stereo system up and running. The familiar ancient music began echoing in the basement. *Now it feels like home again.*

The next morning that comfortable feeling vanished for everybody. "Oh, we have a text message on our EE women's cell numbers," Jessica called out from her post amid the many electronic monitoring devices.

"Check ours for us, will you?" Amanda asked.

"Oh shit! Double shit! No, make that quadruple shit!" Jessica swore loudly above the music in the background. The others slowly came over, looking over her shoulders at the monitor. She had four windows open, displaying the text messages sent to each of the four women's registered EE cell numbers.

"Oh my God, no!" Amanda gushed, as she read them. All four were identical:

> Please log in to your account. Your services are demanded at a party in Chicago hosted by Peter Delius. Full details on your account.

Four stomachs knotted tightly. Carefully, Jessica typed in the address and logged in. There was one new message waiting for her and as promised in full detail. Hastily, she logged into the other three accounts, bringing up their personal accounts on the worldwide EE women's exchange. "Oh my God, no!" she whispered, as the others gasped. All four read their own identical message.

> Your services are required at a party sponsored by the Feds leader Mr. Peter Delius to be held in his office in Chicago on Thanksgiving Day. The party begins promptly at six p.m. He has paid your fee in full. Ten thousand credits have already been deposited into your account.
>
> Most noteworthy, similar parties are being held in the twenty other Feds offices worldwide. This marks

the largest EE sponsored affair in recent memory! Congratulations on being among the select EE women of the world to attend one of these historical parties!

Mr. Delius has made some specific requirements on your appearance at the party. It will be a fetish party.

Click here for your appearance details.
Click here to see all the attendees at this party.
Click here to see all the parties worldwide.

One by one, Jessica carefully clicked on their appearance details. She and Beth were required to wear their ballet boots. All four were required to wear outer corsets that matched the colors of their dresses. All four were required to have their nails be at least four inches long, but nail extensions were acceptable. Further, as an added incentive, Mr. Delius was providing each attendee with her own, very expensive earrings, to be delivered to the local EE branch office by October 1 and worn to the gala event by the attendee. The last line of each message requested the woman arrive at the EE apparel store no later than the second of October to pick up their new outfit, heels, and of course the earrings.

"Damn, there is no link to take to decline this request," Beth exclaimed.

"Of course not, love. An EE woman is obligated by law to do these things. It's part of your contract; it's what EE women are to do, you see," Jessica replied, trying to sound as calm as possible. She was anything but calm inside. She had endured significant pain in her feet just getting them bent enough to wear the usual EE woman's heels, and now she was being forced to backtrack and wear the nasty ballet boots once more.

"But I couldn't even walk in them," Beth wailed, completely panicking.

"We'll practice, my love. With nearly two months lead-time, we should be able to get your feet strengthened enough to handle one evening in them. Trust me, we can do this," Jessica kept her voice low and soft, hoping her trembling was masked.

Amanda whispered, "Out of the lion's den and straight into the lion's mouth."

"I wish we had real guns and not these stun guns. I'll kill him," Tilly swore under her breath, her fists clenched.

Jessica calmed down. *I have to stay cool. Wait, this is even better than what I was planning.* "Gang, trust me. This will work out in our favor. Trust me. I have a plan, but in case something goes wrong, I don't want you to know about it so you can't be punished for it."

Of course, all three began hounding her with questions. What plan? What was she going to do? How would this work out in their favor? Jessica held her ground. "Gang, give me time to finish my details. This is something I want to do on my own—something I have to do myself. I have to earn back my own self-respect. I have to do this myself. Please, please let me do this one thing for us, please," she begged.

The self-respect button worked on all three. Beth and Tilly's self-respect was at an all-time low. Having lived with Jessica for so long, Amanda knew Jessica really meant what she was saying. All that Jessica would say was, "Beth, make sure you have all the gadgets you need in your purse to extract whatever information we may want from the Feds main computer system." That was completely enough to occupy Beth's mind for days! She was suddenly very excited, a golden opportunity to gain total access to the largest and most important database in the world. Jessica knew Beth very well, and inwardly smiled at her manipulation of her mate.

"Do you like me as a red head, a brunette, or as a raven haired beauty," Beth teased Jessica.

Weeks had passed, and the group was now in Chicago at the EE Women's Apparel store on Lake Shore Drive. This exclusive store only catered to the needs of such women. The four found the promised apparel for the party was waiting for them along with their earrings. Additionally, the four women took this opportunity to do some long overdue shopping, especially Beth and Tilly, who had very few outfits. Plus, it was time to get them new wigs. Even though the two wanted their own hair to grow, it would take years for their hair to be an acceptable length for EE women. They needed new, human hair wigs. The colored wig's tresses were at least three feet long.

Jessica giggled. "Dear, I don't know. Why not get all three, and we can see which one looks the best on you?" Beth laughed and did just that, trying to imagine herself as a red head. Beth and Tilly each picked up ten more outfits and matching heels, while Amanda and Jessica added three more outfits to their growing collection.

The EE saleswoman, Sally, was exuberant over this incredible party the Feds were holding. She talked on and on, outlining how this gala was ground breaking. "Imagine, we EE women are attending the finest parties in the world. My, I do wish that I was in your heels, dears." Jessica bit her lip. She wanted to say Sally was more than welcome to go in her place, but dared not say anything for that would be out of character for an EE woman.

"Oh, we are so honored, Sally, so honored," she replied.

"Oh, I almost forgot. I'm to check on your nails. The specifications were most specific, four inches long," Sally said very business-like. "Sanity is looking our very best always."

She carefully measured each of the women's nails. "Naturally, you will all need to get nail extensions. Would you like to schedule that now? We can squeeze you four in today, if you'd like. Anything for you four, very special EE women," Sally poured out her genuine-felt admiration for the four chosen Chicago women.

Two hours later, the four had their nails done. "Boy do we ever have claws now," Beth whispered. "How are we going to manage doing anything with these?" she whispered to Jessica.

"Hush, not now, love. Oh Sally, could you please have a deliveryman bring all our things to our apartment for us? We don't want to scratch our nails," Jessica said demurely to the clerk, who readily agreed. The four spent several thousand dollars in her shop already. To Beth, she whispered, "We can talk at our old apartment."

An hour later, the four entered Jessica and Amanda's old apartment penthouse. "Well, for once, I'm grateful for all of those menial jobs: doormen and deliverymen. We would have never been able to cart all these packages here by ourselves," Beth commented. Indeed, from the store to their apartment, over a dozen Pytalon drugged zombies had assisted them at every step of the way. To Beth's amazement and peace of mind, not one man had paid attention to her. They were glassy-eyed zombies, but most helpful, she thought.

"Wow, love! What a view!" Beth looked out of their north windows onto the beach and Lake Michigan.

"I know. We loved it here. Come on. I'll show you around. Then I need your help with these packages," Jessica replied.

"You two lived a life of utter luxury!" Tilly commented to Amanda, as she was shown around the small, but luxurious apartment suite.

"Don't mind the mess, dearest. It may be luxurious, but I love more where we live now," Amanda replied. "Luxury is nothing compared to freedom. I'll take freedom anytime." Tilly smiled, so true, but only a handful of people in the world could even say such things, certainly not the billions of zombies.

A few minutes later, all four sat down on their couch and watched as Jessica struggled to get the special delivery packages opened with her long nails. They had arrived many days ago. All three were quite curious about just what was inside Jessica's mysterious boxes. "Well, we're really going to need to get used to these nails. Ah, here we are." She pulled out a wine bottle and held it up.

"But wait, Jessica," Amanda burst out, "we can't drink alcohol. You know that! If you're on Pytalon, drinking alcohol will kill you, after it has made you so sick that you pass out. Oh, I see, we aren't on Pytalon anymore," she hastily corrected herself.

Jessica giggled. "No love, this isn't for us; it's for all the Feds at the twenty parties worldwide. It's some very old, quite expensive wine, which is almost impossible to find anymore. It's rare to find a place that still makes alcoholic beverages. Only those who aren't on Pytalon can drink it. I bought this case for the men at the party. Now these other packages go with these wine bottles." Again, she struggled to get the next two packages opened.

One box held a syringe with a set of very long needles. The other box held a small vial of some pale colored liquid. "Okay, what we need to do is to inject four ccs of this into each of the twenty-four bottles, being careful to leave no trace of the puncture."

"What is it that you are injecting, my brainy love?" Beth asked.

"Best that you don't know, dearest. I wish you hadn't even seen these bottles, but you have, so that's that," Jessica replied.

"Well, I'll look up this stuff on the Net as soon as we get back," Beth teased his wife.

She giggled, "Okay, okay, it is a potent knockout drug. One sip of this wine and Mr. Delius will be out like a light. Now don't ask me any more about it, please. If it fails, I don't want

131

you three being involved."

"But silly, we are involved; we're a team and married too," Beth countered. Jessica giggled; he was right.

"Oh okay. I'm going to get all the last remaining Feds leaders knocked out at their own parties. You'll then get your chance to infiltrate their huge computer systems, love. So you have to be prepared." Beth laughed and promised she would be.

Two hours later, they had injected the drug into all two dozen bottles and had repackaged the box for shipment. Jessica then sat down at the old computer in their study and typed a secret message. "Wow, Beth, typing now is a real bitch," she commented. She used her hacking skills to enter a new order into the EE women's computer system. It took her ten times longer than it should have because of her shiny, red talons. She sat back, reviewed her message, and then hit the Send button.

"Now we must wait for the deliveryman to pick up this box. Meanwhile, we should have someone carry all these packages down to our EMAC for us," Jessica declared. She got no complaints from the others.

That night in bed back in their safe house in East Peoria, Beth asked, "So my love, what was in your message anyway?"

She giggled. "I used my new-found hacking skills, dear. I had the EE Women's Association thinking they are sending a complimentary bottle of the extremely fine wine to each of the Feds leaders as a thank-you present for their party. I doubt any of those men will be able to resist at least tasting such an expensive gift. One sip and they'll be out like a light. I'm not saying any more, not just yet." Beth couldn't get Jessica to say more about her plan.

The next day, Beth forgot entirely about the plan. Instead, all four now had to learn to live with such long nails. In addition, Beth had to practice walking in her new ballet boots. Jessica only needed a little practice before her old ability to walk in them had returned, along with the pain and cramps in her feet. The outfits they were to wear were identical in color: sky blue satin gowns with matching outer corsets. Their new earrings were put through every electronic test Beth could devise. She suspected they had tracking devices, eavesdropping microphones, video cameras, geo-locators—all manner of diabolical devices could've been inserted into these monster earrings. All were identical and quite long, reaching down onto their shoulders. Beth finally determined they were loaded with precious stones and gold. She couldn't find any electronic devices in them. Frustrated, she then magnified the gems and retrieved the microscopically engraved serial numbers, which she looked up on the Gem Stones Registry.

"Well, they are genuine. They were made many years ago in Amsterdam. Being a set of four matching pairs at a cost of fifteen grand a pair, I'd guess Delius stole them," Beth reported. "They are real."

"Beth, let's get you used to walking in these boots," Jessica replied. "It's going to take all the endurance you can muster, but dearest, you have to be able to get by in them just this one night. You can't crawl before Mr. Delius. I won't let you deface yourself in that way. You simply must walk in these boots. Besides, love, you look terribly sexy in them. They are supposed to be bedroom boots, you know."

The many weeks passed quickly for the four. At the beginning, they discovered everything took much longer to accomplish because of their overly long fingernails. Beth's feet ached each night when she finally went to bed, but as Jessica had promised, she knew when the night of the party came she could walk semi-gracefully in them for several hours. Beth had already sworn to herself that she wouldn't let Jessica down, since Jessica was planning to get her total access to the most important database in the world. Enduring foot pain and awkwardness was the very least Beth could do for Jessica.

Three days before Thanksgiving, Jessica decided to see who else was going to Delius' party. "Well, look at this, gang. He has invited two other top EE women to the party besides us. Ilse Kunegunther of Hamburg is coming along with Erika Bjork of Amsterdam. Those two are the top fetish fashion EE women of Europe! Come look at their pictures," Jessica called out. The three soon joined her, looking over her shoulders.

"Wow, now those are two really gorgeous young women!" Beth exclaimed.

"Incredible looking women," Tilly added, gaping at the two models. "Look, they are also wearing ballet boots. You two will have company. Thank God Delius isn't making Amanda and me wear them too."

"Prettier than me?" Jessica teased Beth, who flushed. Jessica giggled, adding, "I know, they are the top models of all Europe. I find them sexy too, dear. Remember, we service men and women," she emphasized the latter sex. All four laughed. After packing what they would need, the four left their safe house and drove back to Chicago to their penthouse suite.

Thanksgiving Day came, and the four focused on getting ready for the party, allowing extra time. Mid-afternoon, another EE woman came to their door and handed Jessica a special envelope. She said, "This just came in. Special orders. See, your name is on the front of it along with instructions. Bye. Have a wonderful time at this monumental party. All of us Chicago EE women are so jealous of you four! We even heard that Europe's top models are coming. Amazing and historic. Sanity is doing a good job. Please Mr. Delius, my dears." She nodded and left.

"What's it say?" Beth asked, growing more curious than normal.

"To be opened only if Mr. Delius passes out. That's what it says. I guess we will have to wait and see," Jessica said coyly. "Now back to getting ready, my love."

"But my ears are being pulled off," Beth complained.

"Honey, you are wearing fifteen thousand worth of earrings. Besides, you look good in them," Jessica replied with a wry smile.

With her vast experience in getting around in her boots, Jessica timed their arrival at the Feds' headquarters perfectly. Amanda was supporting Beth, while Tilly helped Jessica, as the four walked into the building ignoring the zombie doorman. Just inside, another zombie guard asked for their names and then directed them to the elevators, telling them to push the penthouse suite button. Just as they turned to walk to the elevator, Ilse and Erika entered. The four waited for the two to join them. Both were wearing similar sky blue gowns with matching corsets and black knee-high ballet boots. From the way they were walking, Jessica knew they had been wearing nothing but them for many years, just as she had done the past eight years. They walked gracefully and confidently towards the four.

"Hallo. I be Ilsa von Hamburg," the gorgeous young woman called out politely with a definite German accent. "Dis be Erika von Amsterdam. We be so happy to be in the States."

"Hello. I'm Jessica. This is my mate, Beth. My friend Amanda and her mate, Tilly. You both look stunning. Sanity is providing pleasure for men and women. Shall we provide that now?" she asked demurely.

"Ya, ve should not keep Mr. Delius vating. Such gorgeous earrings you are wearing. Ve should perhaps complain dat ve did not get some," Ilse exclaimed, praising them indirectly.

As the six headed to the elevators, Jessica paid close attention to the two model's words. Something began to bother her, but she couldn't put a finger on it. "We just arrived stateside yesterday," Erika said. Her English was better, but she had a definite foreign accent too. "We hope to see more of the States before we go back home."

"Ya, ve vant to see de mountains rocky and the canyon grand, if ve canst," Ilse added.

"Perhaps you can get Mr. Delius to take you on a sightseeing trip tomorrow," Jessica suggested. "I wish we looked better than we do. Sanity is always looking our best. You both look so much better than we do."

"Ya, ve be'st the top fashion EE models of Europe. Danke. You look good though," Ilse replied. Jessica's mind strained to put a finger on what was bothering her about the two women, but couldn't. The door opened, and now it was party time. Into the lion's mouth, she thought. Her companions had quite different thoughts. Beth, for one, felt panic striking her. It was all that Amanda could do to keep Beth from falling down as they stepped out of the elevator into the plush, luxurious penthouse.

"Ah, right on time. Let the party begin," the cold voice of Peter Delius called out to the six women. "Come on in and let's see how you all look. I do hope you're all looking your best as I ordered."

"Ah yes, ve do always look our vest. I be Ilse Kunegunther of Hamburg. Dis ve my dear friend, Erika Bjork of Amsterdam. Ve be so glad to be in States. So much to see. Danke, danke, Mr. Delius."

Peter eyed each woman, verifying they indeed wore what he had ordered. "Ah, Ben or rather Beth now. I see that you are looking so much better than when we last met." Beth detected a coldness in his voice. She resisted the temptation to curse him. That would give them all away as no longer being under the heavy influence of their implants and Pytalon.

Instead, Beth forced herself to say, "Sanity is giving pleasure to men and women. So good of you to invite us to your party."

Peter's eyes seemed satisfied with Beth, and they moved over to Jessica. "Ah, Miss Jessica. You are looking fit as well. I do hope you four are enjoying wearing those fantastic earrings. They're worth a fortune, you know. Ah, Tim or Tilly is it? Yes, you also look good. Adapting nicely, I see. Ilse, Erika, the pleasure is all mine to have this wonderful opportunity to have you over for a visit." He led them into the living room, beckoning them to sit on his expensive, leather couch, while he took a seat in a matching sofa across from the six beauties, admiring each in turn, but mostly avoiding both Beth and Tilly. Jessica sensed he would have little to do with those two. He still believed their bodies were males. She felt a tad more confident.

"Thank you for coming to my Thanksgiving party. We're celebrating and giving thanks to the fact I'm now the sole ruler of the Midwest. We twenty men now control the entire world, so you, my gorgeous EE women are here to help me celebrate the culmination of my life. I'm now the God of the Midwest and perhaps even more soon," he boasted.

"But come. Let's party." He spoke a command word and some dance music began playing in the background. "Ilse, you ravishing beauty, come here, and give me pleasure. Erika, you and Jessica dance for me. Come, come. Let's have Tilly and Beth also dance. Ah, my dear Jessica, you get to dance by yourself."

"Mr. Delius, don't you know our dancing is very much limited by our boots?" Erika protested slightly. Again, Jessica's mind was aroused, but she still couldn't say why.

"Ah, yes, yes, but just wiggle and do your best, my lovely Dutch woman. Ilse, pleasure me. Then, I have more surprises for you all. A little light bondage should enliven our party even more, don't you think, Beth?"

Beth fought hard against reacting. Quietly, she replied, "We are here to give you pleasure, sir." Her eyes spotted six handcuffs and some O-rings on leather straps lying on a nearby table. Inwardly, she grimaced, but kept on smiling like a zombie. Oh, how she wished this night was over!

While they attempted to wiggle seductively to the dance music, Ilse pleasured Peter, which didn't take long to accomplish. She was highly skilled and worked her magic swiftly. However, Jessica also spotted her noticing the bondage devices on the table. Again, her intuition was aroused, but she still couldn't say why.

"Oh look. A vottle," Ilse suddenly spotted the wine bottle and fancy wine goblet on the table.

"Wait. Don't drink any of that, my wonderful women. It would kill you. It is wine, you see, a gift from your EE association, a thank-you present to help me further enjoy this fine evening. It is a rare wine, so very hard to acquire these days, but alas my pretty women, it isn't for you. It doesn't mix with your Pytalon. So please, don't touch it," Peter warned them. *At least, he's warning us about it*, Jessica thought to herself.

"Vut Veter, I can call you Veter, can't I?" Isle said demurely, batting her long lashes and smiling broadly, her thick red lips seeming so enticing. "You should have some now since you've been pleasured. Men should drink after sex so you can come again." That her English improved also struck Jessica as rather strange.

"Well, of course. But first, let's add to the flavor of our good times. A little light bondage my gorgeous young women. Come over to the table and allow me to add to your breathtaking beauty this fine evening," he said coyly. All four had a very uneasy feeling about this. Was he planning to kidnap them or something worse, Jessica wondered? None of the six had any choice. As EE women, they were supposedly implanted to please their sponsors. Peter was their sponsor at the moment. Dutifully, all six moved over to the table, but Amanda kept a hold of Beth, while Tilly aided Jessica, and Erika and Ilse held onto each other. Jessica thought those two seemed very familiar with each other. Again, she felt that something was wrong, but couldn't say what.

"I will cuff each of you at your elbows. That way, you will still have the freedom of your lower arms and long nails. You don't need to speak any longer, so these rings will prevent any unnecessary chatter, but leave you free to fulfill your pleasuring duties for me," Peter explained.

Beth found her arms being forced together tightly behind her back at her elbows. She heard the clicks of the handcuffs. She could move her lower arms towards her front a little. He raised the O-ring gag, and she dutifully opened her mouth to accept it, inwardly reeling. It took all her willpower to stand still and allow Peter to do this to her. *No matter what happens, I will not give us away to him!* She thought repeatedly.

Within minutes, all six had their arms bound and were gagged. "Ah there now, isn't this so much better?" he asked. Ilse made a gurgling noise, which made him smile. "Okay, back to the couch and dance for me once more. Oh, Erika, this time you get to please me, while I sit and sip this fine wine." He poured the tall crystal goblet full and headed back to his sofa. Very carefully, the six women followed him and attempted to fulfill his wishes. Jessica thought, *At least, he showed us where the key is at, in his breast pocket. Maybe this will work out as planned anyway.*

Poor Erika, she nearly fell trying to get down on her knees before him. She had to turn her body in order to rake her long talons over his body before she had him ready for her tongue. Meanwhile the others attempted to wiggle to the music. Jessica watched him sip his wine. *Good,* she thought, *he has taken a very large amount swiftly. All we need now is some time.*

He moaned slightly as Erika did her best to please him, much as Ilse had done. Then he went wholly limp; his eyes closed. Erika sat back and made gurgling noises. She was suddenly alarmed and struggled to get to her feet, wobbling wildly. Now Jessica knew she had to act. Carefully, she moved over to the unconscious Peter. It took her several minutes to retrieve the key to the handcuffs. As soon as Beth saw what she was trying to do, she too came over to help, followed shortly by Tilly and Amanda.

For nearly twenty minutes, they attempted to get one handcuff unlocked before achieving success. With an arm free, Beth quickly removed her gag and remaining cuff. Then, she undid Jessica, who spoke up, "I received a note I'm to open should our sponsor fall asleep. I'll get it while you un-cuff the others, Beth." She purposely played along with her own ruse, since she still didn't trust Ilse and Erika. It took Beth another ten minutes to get the others free, primarily because of her long nails.

"Vat's going on here?" asked Ilse, whom Beth had just freed from her bindings.

"I received this envelope that says only to open it if our sponsor falls asleep or goes unconscious. I shall open it now. He seems to be in some trouble. Perhaps this will tell us what to do," Jessica said calmly. She knew what was inside. She'd sent these to all twenty parties. All the arrangements had been made in advance.

Jessica read the note aloud. "I, Peter Delius, am unconscious now. It is my wish you have my body transported to the local implant building. I have already left instructions there for the psych man to follow. Thank you ladies for a most wonderful party. Please transport my body secretly. I don't want others interfering with my plans. You may keep the earrings, ladies."

"What? He vants to ve implanted?" Ilse exclaimed, somewhat out of character, Jessica thought.

"Yes, that's what his note says. We must always do what our sponsors tell us to do. Right?" Jessica said.

"Oh yes, yes, we must do what our sponsor wishes," Beth played along, now seeing the larger picture. Immense pride in her wife swelled within her.

"Yes, we must always do what our sponsor desires," Amanda added, also playing along just as a perfect EE woman would respond.

"Yes we should," Tilly added, trying hard to keep a straight face, as she too now grasped Jessica's entire plan.

"Vut, vut," Ilsa protested slightly and out of character. "Vell, I suppose dat ve must do as he vishes," she went along with Jessica too. "Vut how do ve do dis?"

"You five look around this place and see if you can find a cart of some kind. I'll see if I can waken him first before we take him," Jessica ordered. She retrieved the wine bottle and poured more of it into Peter. She wanted no chance he would awaken prematurely. Beth took this opportunity to install all her computer-monitoring devices. Further, she uploaded a hack that would permit her remote access anytime she desired. Her pride in her mate grew rapidly. Jessica was more than worthy of being Weasel's mate.

Amanda returned with a food cart, having removed all the various plates and dishes from it. "He was planning to feed us a royal feast it seems. I don't think one man could possibly have eaten all the food that was on it. I'll go find a bed sheet to cover him, Jessica."

It took all six of them to get Peter's body onto the bottom of the cart. Amanda covered it well. "Now let's order an EMAC to take us there," Jessica suggested.

"Dis is so strange—not vat ve expected," Ilse commented, but continued to go along with Jessica's wishes. Soon, they joined forces to push the cart over to the elevator. In their ballet boots, the four could only push marginally while Tilly and Amanda in their heels helped to push a little more. They reached an unspoken agreement to all push or pull the cart.

No one stopped them or even questioned them as they pushed the cart out of the Feds headquarters. The EMAC driver, also glassy-eyed, readily helped them get Peter's body into the vehicle. A half hour later, he helped them get him out again and back onto the cart. The doorman at the implant station came to their assistance, pushing the cart inside for them. Again, Jessica had thought of everything. Earlier this evening, the local psych had received a special communication from the Feds ordering him to return to prepare for another special implant this evening, so he was expecting someone.

"We've brought him here per his request, sir," Jessica explained to the glassy-eyed psych man. "Do you have your orders for Mr. Peter Delius?"

"Ah, let me see. Why, yes, here they are. Yes, they are very explicit. I will get it done right now. Will you be waiting to take him with you?" he asked.

"No, he will need some recovery time, right?" Jessica replied.

"Ah, yes, yes, three days at least. If you'll excuse me, I have work to do on him now. The doorman will show you the way out. Sanity is doing a perfect implant," he said in a monotone, turned and left, pushing the cart with Peter's body ahead of him. The six dutifully followed the doorman and carefully climbed back into the waiting EMAC.

"Destination?" the glassy-eyed driver asked as the door closed.

Jessica turned to ask Ilse where she would like to be taken. To her utter shock and surprise, Ilse had pulled a stun gun out of her purse and was pointing it at her. Likewise, Erika held another gun. Between them, all four were covered. Ilse called out to the driver, "New O'Hare please." To the four, she added, "You are coming with us now. Ve vill not hesitate to shoot. You will come willingly or not."

Chapter 11—Kidnaped

"What's going on?" Tilly whispered, not daring to attract the driver's attention.

"You're coming with us, one way or the other," Erika answered just as quietly. "Don't make a scene. We won't hesitate to shoot you. Shut up. We'll be there soon."

Ilse added softly, "Well Weasel or Ben or Beth, whatever, I admit you're not quite what we anticipated. Yes, I was faking my German accent. Erika and I speak English rather well. Now sit back and don't give us any reason to shoot you."

Suddenly, all the little things about these two women that had been bothering Jessica came into sharp focus. She realized they too were somehow off Pytalon and probably exercising a good measure of control over their EE implants. She chastised herself for not having recognized all the signs earlier, but wisely said nothing now.

Twenty minutes later, the EMAC pulled into New O'Hare, stopping before a nearly deserted building. "Danke," Ilse said to their driver. "We get out here. Come on, move," she added, waving her gun a little.

As they got out, Beth and Tilly weighed their chances of being able to retrieve their stun guns and shoot the two before they were shot. Both realized with their overly long nails, such would be fruitless; they'd never manage a "quick draw." *Best bide our time,* Beth thought.

They walked slowly through the empty terminal, where a lone doorman did open the main entrance for them. As before, Amanda held onto Beth, while Tilly supported Jessica. Ilse and Erika held each other's hand for support, while keeping their guns at the ready in their other hands. After passing through the terminal, they stepped outside where an Air Liner was waiting.

"Okay, single file, up the stairs and into the liner, easy does it. I don't want you to take a tumble. Go right once you're inside. There are comfortable seats waiting you," Ilse ordered.

Several minutes later, the four took a seat and waited for an explanation. The seats were leather and plush. Both Jessica and Beth greatly appreciated sitting down, particularly Beth, whose feet were now beginning to throb. The two women entered and spoke to the pilot. As the door closed, they walked back to their captives, guns still drawn. "Pour yourselves a drink. Hope you like fruit punch. We do. It's a long flight, so relax and enjoy the punch. We'll have sandwiches later on," Ilse commanded. "Come on; drink the punch."

Jessica figured the punch was doped, and she was right. A few minutes after drinking it as ordered, she drifted into a deep sleep. Nearby, the others did too, as the Air Liner headed across the Atlantic Ocean on its way back to Amsterdam. "Well, that didn't go quite as we planned," Ilse commented.

"No, we just didn't count on Delius wanting to end it all. Well, good riddance I say. One less of the Feds to have meddling in our affairs. Weasel sure isn't what we expected," Erika replied. "Is Weasel a he or she?"

Ilse lifted up Beth's gown and peeked inside her panties. "A she. So's Tilly. Strange. We were led to believe that Weasel was male. Ah well, so much for intelligence."

"Yes, but if Weasel is a she, will we still be able to get her to do what we want? I mean if Weasel was male, I'm sure our charms would work on him. Worse, she's married to Jessica. Tilly and Amanda too," Erika replied softly, also confused.

Ilse bit her lip. "You know, if they are married, then Weasel must be attracted to women. Therefore, I think our charms may still work on her. We have to try. If not, then we can threaten to harm her mate and the others. The real question is: are they on Pytalon or not. I rather thought so at first, but seeing Jessica taking charge when Delius passed out, she simply can't be. She's too aware."

"I agree. All four seem too alive and too alert to be drugged up. Let's take no chances and assume they're not on Pytalon. We need to lose these ridiculously long nails soon. I almost couldn't operate the gun," Erika commented. The two busied themselves removing their nail extensions and re-polishing their usual two-inch nails. That done, they removed their restrictive corsets, slipped out of their ballet boots, and sat back to relax and enjoy the return trip home.

As they neared Amsterdam, the two women struggled to get the four bodies stuffed into four large shipping crates. Finally, they sat back again and smiled. "We'll be landing in five minutes," their pilot called out. Hastily, they donned their boots and checked their appearance.

Once on the ground, the baggage handlers commented about the heavy weight of their four crates. "We took advantage of our trip to the States to buy some of their fancy clothing and heels," Ilse replied coyly. *Strange,* she thought, *the baggage handlers are just a bit too nosey. Perhaps, they are spies too.* Her paranoia escalated once more. Still, nothing happened, and an hour later, the building attendants finished depositing their crates and bags in their penthouse suite. The two smiled and thanked the men, but they were mostly unaware of such things, replying, "Sanity is doing a good job."

Quickly, the two opened the crates and dragged each woman out, leaving them lying on the floor for the moment. "Well, I didn't really think we'd get this far, Erika, but here we are. Now what are we to do with the extras?"

"We should drag them into the spare bedroom and tie them up, don't you think? We can't handle all four of them at once," Erika replied. "Come on; let's drag them. Sure is hard though." While one pulled, the other pushed and eventually got the three into the bedroom. They locked the door and returned to Beth or Weasel. She was still unconscious, so the two cleaned up the area, storing the crates and their dirty clothes. Then, they sat on their couch until she woke up.

An hour later, Beth finally stirred. "Oh my head. What happened? Oh!" She suddenly came alert, recalling their kidnaping. She looked up and saw the two gorgeous women, her captors, sitting demurely on a very fine quality couch.

"Ah, she's awake at last," Ilse spoke first. "Well, Weasel, just so you know, you're now in Amsterdam. Your three companions are locked in our spare bedroom. You're in our exclusive penthouse suite on the top floor of what many years ago was called the Playboy Building, whatever that meant."

"Why are you doing this? What do you want?" Beth replied, adjusting her wig and rubbing her head as well. She felt a little groggy, but the room was finally in focus.

"It is simple, Weasel. We want, no, we demand you do three things for us. After that, you and your companions are free to go," Erika said calmly.

"What three things?" Beth asked, finally managing to sit up. No way was she going to try to stand. These two women were obviously experts with ballet boots. She wasn't about to make a fool of herself. *Why am I even thinking such thoughts?* Beth wondered.

"First, you're going to locate our two missing sisters.

143

Second, you're going to rescue them. Third, you're going to get all four of us into the States and give us new identities, ones that can't be traced. We want to disappear from Europe forever," Erika answered him.

Beth thought swiftly. She could smuggle them into the States easily enough. Arranging new identities was one of her specialties, but what was all this about missing sisters? "Why me?" she finally asked.

"Because you're Weasel. Your reputation here in Europe is legendary. You're, frankly, the best. We're the best EE women, so we chose only the best to help us find our sisters," Ilse answered him in near perfect English. *Now isn't the time for any misunderstandings,* she thought.

"Well, thanks for the vote of confidence. Damn it, Ilse, Erika, why didn't you just ask me for my help? I'd of gladly given it to you," Beth retorted a bit annoyed. "You didn't have to kidnap us."

"Yes we did. You don't understand. We're being constantly watched and spied upon wherever we go. Spies are all around us; we've seen them. Our communications are being monitored all the time. We didn't dare get in touch with you by any normal means. Besides, they were kidnaped over here in Hamburg and Amsterdam, so you need to be here. We brought you here in those four crates, disguised as stuff we bought in the States. This way, no one knows you are here with us," Ilse pointed out.

"But your Air Liner pilot saw us getting onboard," Beth countered.

"No, he couldn't see the entrance from his seat. He was ordered to remain in his seat while we boarded," Erika answered this one. "Now will you help us or do we have to harm your three companions to make you? We're prepared to do that, starting with your wife or mate or whatever you call her." She began rubbing her forehead.

Beth realized what was happening with these two women. They were obviously still suffering aftereffects of Pytalon withdrawal, delusions to be precise, and their EE implants were kicking in again. Erika was in need of pleasuring and was obviously developing a migraine. *How long has it been since Erika last had her sexual needs satisfied,* she wondered. *Probably quite some time. It must be daytime. The sun is shining in their big windows.*

144

"Look, Erika, Ilse, if you let my three companions out and let us work together, I give you my word we'll do as you ask of us. Four heads are better than one. Besides, you have the guns, and where am I going to find the equipment I need anyway? Everything is likely written in Dutch or German, and I can't read those."

She saw the two wavering a little. "Look, we'll help you, but you have to treat us right." She decided to level a bit more with these two. "I need my wife, Jessica. She is my right hand in such things. After all, she was the one who arranged to abduct and implant Delius and the other remaining Feds leaders. By now, they are implanted, thanks to Jessica. Come on; you have the guns."

"What? Jessica planned that whole thing? But how? He went unconscious after drinking the wine. Oh, she drugged him just as we drugged you four," Ilse replied. From her twisted facial expression, Beth suspected she was also getting a headache. They all heard the others pounding on the locked door.

"Come on. A little trust will go a long way," Beth suggested. She saw Erika wavering, and she looked at Ilse.

"Well, okay then, but don't try anything. Ve will shoot, you know," Ilse finally consented. She rose and walked to the spare bedroom door and soon returned with the other three.

"Beth! Are you okay, dear?" Jessica called out, seeing her sitting in the middle of the floor where she'd awaken.

"Groggy, but otherwise fine. And you?"

"Fuzzy headed, but okay. What do they want?"

"Sit down. We'll tell you. Try anything and ve will shoot you," Ilse tried to sound as if she meant it, but her head was now throbbing.

Erika repeated their three demands, and Beth added, "I agreed we would help them, Jessica. I promised you would all help too and not do anything foolish. They're convinced they're being spied upon everywhere they go."

"Okay then, let's do it; let's find their missing sisters. Say, can we get out of these things and get more comfortable?" Jessica suggested. "Besides, typing on the computer is a bitch with these extensions. I see you've already removed yours."

"Well, okay, but don't try anything. We will shoot," Ilse agreed, though she rubbed her head seriously.

Jessica also realized both their captors were getting migraines and correctly guessed why. She suggested, "Why don't you let us go back into that bedroom and get ourselves fixed up. Meanwhile, you two can satisfy your needs. You can lock the door on us." Erika was very glad to oblige. Just as soon as the four were alone, they removed their outer corsets. The two dug their heels out of their purses and swapped them with their ballet boots. Next, Jessica and Amanda removed the nail extensions from Beth and Tilly, before doing themselves. That took several hours.

By then, they were hungry. When Ilse and Erika opened the door letting them out, both young women looked greatly relieved. Erika explained, "We've ordered pizza. Hope you like it. Oh! You don't have to always wear ballet boots?" Erika asked, quite surprised to see both women wearing normal EE women's heels.

"I used to for eight years, Erika, but then with some rather painful physical therapy, I'm now able to wear normal heels most of the time, thank goodness," Jessica replied.

"Did you really arrange to get the remaining Feds implanted, like Beth said?" Ilse asked.

"Yes, I arranged it. I wanted revenge for what Peter did to Ben and Tim. Now he gets a taste of his own sadism," Jessica replied. Suddenly, Beth and Tilly knew what kind of implant she'd ordered up for Peter. She added, "The other Feds are now likely doormen." She grinned mischievously, adding, "Never mess with Weasel's wife." All six laughed, breaking the ice further.

"Well, we best get started on finding your sisters. We'll take notes, and you tell us about it," Beth finally got the conversation back onto the only track that would allow them to return home. While they were waiting on the pizza, Ilse began her tale. Strangely, both women's story was nearly the same, only happening in two different countries.

"My sister is Elke Kunegunther. She would be twenty-three now; I'm twenty-seven. I was looking out for her all through high school. Our parents were nothing more than a pair of zombies. We would have starved if I hadn't cooked and cared for us. Then when I graduated, they turned me into an EE woman. Poor Elke was left to fend for herself. Then last year, something went wrong with our Pytalon stuff. It sort of stopped working and still isn't working much at all. We started becoming aware of things again and remembered my sister. I looked her up on the computer and found that she'd been abducted by the Geheime Politie, the G.P., the secret police. We can't find her at all," Ilse related her sad tale.

Erika's story was nearly the same. Her sister was Fjola Bjork and would be twenty-three if she were still alive. Both Erika and Ilse had been together since they were implanted as EE women, some nine years ago. Both were still suffering from their implants if they didn't obey the commands sufficiently. Both women had now amassed a small fortune as the top EE women in Europe, but having come off Pytalon, they were still having some delusions and paranoia. Together, they had acquired a computer and had tried to find their younger sisters. Both had met a dead end with the G.P. Still, the two were used to having only the finest of everything: clothes, food, restaurants, shoes, and so on. Having heard from the underground that Weasel was the best, they'd made their plans. It had been a simple matter of an email to Peter Delius, suggesting they be invited to his party.

Over pizza, Beth and Jessica had the two women show them what little they had discovered about their sisters. "Darn, I can't read anything on either page," Beth complained.

"Neither can I," Jessica admitted.

Their captors laughed, and Ilse said, "Just like Americans." Then they read the two pages back for the four.

"Well, that gives me something to think about. Let me ponder this problem overnight," Beth suggested. "In the morning, I'll see what I can find out. There hasn't been a computer system yet Weasel can't penetrate."

"Okay, you must be in need of pleasuring yourselves by now," Erika agreed and hinted.

"We're just tired. We no longer suffer the effects of our EE implants all that much," Beth felt obligated to explain. "Jessica found a way to desensitize them. Now they're just an occasional annoyance, and a friend of ours found a way to also get the residual Pytalon toxins out of our bodies, so we feel really good."

"Vat? Dis is possible?" Ilse exclaimed. She was taken by complete surprise. "Ve didn't know such dings vas possible." She was so shocked that her English faltered a little. They chatted about both for a while before retiring.

The next morning, while their captors struggled to fix breakfast, Beth and Jessica got to work on the problem. "First, let's assume they aren't delusional, and that they're being spied upon. So Jessica, while I take their computer apart, you take the portable devices from my purse and go over everything software-wise. Let's make darn sure this computer is secure before we go snooping."

"Aye, aye, Weasel," Jessica teased her. Both smiled and set to work.

"Nothing inside, all clear here."

"Not so here. Take a look, I've detected six spy-wares already, and I'm not done with all the tests! Someone is watching what they do," Jessica whispered, as if someone might overhear her.

"So their delusions aren't delusions after all, incredible. Okay, dear, send each the signal that the computer has been turned off. That'll silence them for a time," Beth suggested, though she need not have, Jessica was already doing just that, one by one.

"Hey, there is another that's sending out spy data in real time and from this place," Jessica said, becoming rather alarmed. Beth double checked her work and took out another small device from her purse. It was a signal detector and locator. After tuning it to the frequency being used, Beth then traced the outgoing signal to a repeater box whose wires were embedded within the plate glass of their huge windows that faced the sea.

"Well, this one is a bitch to disable without the listeners knowing about it," Beth replied. "But nothing Weasel can't handle." She grinned. A few minutes later, the capture program itself was captured and now sending out Web surfing information that indicated the user was looking at EE outfits online.

"Now we can get down to work," Beth exclaimed. "While I'm checking on some things, please go report what we've found to Erika and Ilse, and see what's holding up breakfast." She left to do just that, while Beth set to work. No way was she going to stay on European pages. She couldn't read them. No, the answers would be just as easily found on stateside networks. After a time, Jessica returned with tea and rolls, a continental breakfast. Neither was particularly happy with breakfast.

Around ten, she stopped and joined the others. Ilse and Erika looked up anxiously. "Well, I'm getting somewhere, just not sure where yet. Say, would one of you take this device in your hand, but conceal it, and walk outside your main door to the elevator. Pause a second, as if you forgot something, and then come back," Beth asked.

Erika rose and did as she asked, while Beth admired how easily Erika walked in her exotic boots. Jessica saw her and gave her a teasing poke in her ribs. Both grinned. "I can't help it; she's one gorgeous woman, dear." Both giggled. Before long, Erika walked back inside and handed the small device to Beth.

"Ah ha. Just as I suspected. There is a spy camera watching your door. Interesting. I wonder why someone is so darn interested in your comings and goings," Beth pointed out.

"Vell, ve are top EE women, so I suppose they want to vake sure that ve are safe?" Ilse suggested nervously, though she didn't believe what she was saying. That was obvious to all.

"Well, I'm going to find out who is on the other end of this one. My handy-dandy homemade detector will give me some clues. Back to work, Jessica." The two rose and headed back to the den with the computer. "Wish we had a real setup and not this toy computer to work with."

"Can we reroute it through yours back in East Peoria?" Jessica suggested.

"I think we can safely manage that trick. Still, one small monitor? How can they do anything on it? Oh, they're EE women and aren't expected to," she answered her own question.

A half hour later, Beth found the recipients of both the video signal and the wireless broadcasting emanating from their computer: the Geheime Politie! Annoyed, she carefully piggybacked onto her main system back in East Peoria and began digging for clues, hitting database after database. She focused on the year the two teens had been abducted. At last, she found the entries buried away in a forgotten database of the Pytalon Corporation, having been copied to the stateside network from their European system as an offsite backup copy. Now she began to study the reports.

They ordered in for lunch, and Beth ate mechanically, her mind miles away. Jessica also studied what Beth was reading, hoping to learn more, but was frankly stymied. It seemed as if the Geheime Politie had abducted both women in early June just after they graduated. It was also the time of the year when the governing powers, Total Care Europe, would be dictating each graduate's new career, usually implanting and upping their Pytalon dosage to that of an adult, rendering them mindless zombies.

"There is something very curious and odd about these two abductions, Jessica, my love. Can you spot what I'm seeing?" Beth asked and challenged her. She added, "It would be easier to see this if we had two monitors side by side, as we usually have. Still, have a look see."

"Let me see," Erika said urgently. She'd overheard them and came as quickly as she could to see too, looking over Jessica's shoulders while resting her arm on them to steady herself.

Ilse joined them. "Ya, the G.P. took her sister," she declared. "You see it right there. I can read English too, some."

"Yes, that would be its appearance, Ilse, but look closer. Something isn't adding up. Something is not quite right in these entries. Admittedly, this is a copy of the European records, and we'll have to hack into those next. I'm afraid I'll need you to translate a bit, Erika," Beth admitted.

"I don't see it. I admit defeat, love," Jessica finally admitted her failure.

"Don't fret it. I'm sure you would have spotted it if we were home with our many monitors side by side," Beth replied diplomatically.

"So vat is it?" asked Ilse, growing a bit impatient and annoyed.

"Look at what is missing here. No, first look at this entry here and then look down at Fjola's entry. Come on. You can do it," Beth hinted.

"Well, what's missing is where they took her. In the first one, they clearly indicate they took her to someplace called Dordrecht, wherever that is," Jessica replied.

"Precisely, dear."

"Dordrecht is just south of here, on the outskirts of Rotterdam," Erika explained.

"In all the other G.P. entries, they always provided a location. With Fjola's they omitted it. Curious, isn't it?" Beth replied.

"I don't understand," Erika cried.

"Neither do I yet, but Weasel is just getting started, my lovely dear. Now let's see if the original here in the Netherlands contains the same entry or if some of it has been deleted from the US copy," Beth suggested. She switched to the local copy and had Erika read back the full entry very carefully. "Ah ha. See, it's the same: omitted location. Curious isn't it? I wonder if there are others like this one. I'm going to set up a detailed search on my home system. It'll take a while to run, so let's go relax or something."

"Ya, but vat about my sister, Elke?" Ilse asked.

"Her entry is similar to Fjola's, a missing location. Let my search do its thing, please. After all, you hired only the best in detectors," she teased the two women.

Both looked at her as if she were nuts. Then, Ilse realized Beth had made a joke, and she laughed, explaining it to Erika, who also giggled.

While they were waiting, Beth asked the two just what the Geheime Politie were. Erika tried to explain. "Over a century ago, I think they were our elite police force, but then the Feds came in and took over, but I'm not very sure of history. I got bad grades in those classes," she admitted.

"Ya, now they are under the Feds here in Europe," Ilse added what little she knew of them. Nevertheless, Beth didn't like the sound of their name, secret police. An hour later, the computer beeped, and Beth returned to see the results of her search.

"Now this is getting more curious. Look, during that same year, there were four similar anomalies all around the same period. The students were just graduating. Further, during June in the year before, there were four similar cases. In the year after your sisters went missing, there were again only four similar cases. Yet, there are hundreds and hundreds who have their locations present in the listings," Beth explained.

"Ya, but what does dis mean?" asked Ilse.

"It can't be written off as a clerical error. One or two random ones, yes, but this is a predictable pattern of four just-graduating teens going missing each year and only in June. This isn't random clerical errors. Something else is going on, and Weasel is about to dig deeper!" Beth replied, growing quite excited. She loved a good mystery, and now she had just uncovered a big one. Jessica and Tilly knew there would be no stopping Beth. She would work at it for years, if necessary, until she discovered the truth.

Tilly took the two aside so as not to disturb Beth. "Look, she's on to something. I've been with him or her rather for many, many years. See that look in her eyes? Well, when she gets that look, there's no stopping her. She'll find the answer, even if it takes years. She's like a bloodhound that has just picked up the scent of the fox. Nothing is going to stop Weasel now." Tilly grinned, proud of her dear friend.

"Ya, but vat is with you two? You keep goofing and saying him, but she's a woman. We peeked while we were on de

Air Liner," Ilse finally asked what had been bothering her for some time.

"Yes, what's going on?" Erika added.

"Long and nasty story," Amanda broke in. "Let's make some tea, and I'll tell you about it." Tilly gave her a grateful look; she felt relieved not to have to tell her own, highly embarrassing story.

A while later, Ilse commented, "Now it makes sense. We could see we were, how do you say, exciting them, but we figured they must be happy women, no that's not the right word."

"Lesbians?" Amanda suggested.

"Ya, that's it."

"Yes, they both are highly aroused by you two," Amanda admitted, with a wry grin.

"Well, of course, but that's so sad that this happened. It is criminal, I think," Erika added seriously. They chatted a while longer over hot tea.

Beth and Jessica continued their cyber-sleuthing long into the evening. Around nine that night, Beth snapped her fingers. "Bingo."

"Yes, I concur. That's them. Well done, my love. Shall I get Ilse and Erika now?" Jessica asked. Beth nodded. Moments later, the two came as fast as they could in their boots.

Beth explained, "You see what most people don't know is that whenever something gets posted to the Internet, it never, ever goes away. It gets stored somewhere on someone's server. All you need to do is find that server. Of course, the server varies; it's not always the same one. I was able to track the IP address of the poster of those anomalous entries. Tracing backwards led me to a server registered under phony names. But I dug deeper and found that a group called the Freiheitskampfer, whatever that means, was paying the bills."

"Freedom fighters. That's what the word means; it's German," Ilse pointed out.

"After more digging, I found more data on them and some of their members. Then, I came across a manifest and dug a little deeper. I found many destinations to be around some place in Germany called Berchtesgaden."

"Ah, yes, that is a park, heavily forested near the Alps, picturesque but most remote," Ilse added.

"Makes sense."

Jessica grew a little impatient. "Dear, stop stalling; show them the pictures!"

Beth grinned, "Okay, okay, dear. Would you look at these two images and see if you recognize them?" She switched to another window in which she had pasted two ID card images side by side.

"That's Eike!" Ilse exclaimed.

"That's my Fjola! I'd know her anywhere!" Erika gushed.

"I know. They didn't even bother to change their names. They just changed ID card numbers. Well, probably for most purposes that's good enough, but not if they really wanted to hide. Anyway, they live and work at a hotel down there, just outside a place called Faselburg, on a dead end side road," Beth finished up, adding, "Ta da! Weasel strikes again."

"Danke! Danke! Danke!" Ilse exclaimed, forgetting all about English. She was highly excited and shaking slightly.

"We need to go there soon!" Erika added. "But how? We are being watched by the G.P."

"Oh no. This time of year, there is snow everywhere down there," Ilse said, speaking slower and remembering her English. "We can't really walk in the snow in our boots."

Amanda laughed, "Heck, we can hardly walk in the snow in these heels either."

"Well, somehow I have to go see my sister," Erika ignored the protests.

Chapter 12—The Geheime Politie and the Freiheitskampfer

"Have you considered your sisters might not want to be found or rescued?" Tilly cautioned the two women. "They could well be members of your local freedom fighters, whoever they are."

"But I have to talk with her," Erika continued to insist. "I know we can't even walk in the snow, but somehow, I have to talk with her. Please, you promised to help us rescue them. She might be in danger."

"Hey, it's been how many years since you last saw her? Any real danger has long past," Tilly countered, but she knew they had to get them to their sisters. "I admit I'm wholly unfamiliar with the scene here in Europe, but stateside, I know what's going on. Let me see if I can help Ben, er Beth, on this one." She left and joined Beth in the den.

"You know they're insisting on visiting their sisters," Tilly said rather seriously.

"Figures. It was part of what they wanted us to do for them. I've been trying to figure out just what the Geheime Politie is," Beth answered.

"But we're hampered by the language barrier," Jessica finished the thought for her. "We keep copying bits into the translator program, rather crude, but it is giving us a better idea."

"Well, we know they're running a pretty sophisticated spying operation on these two women. Assuming those men are actually on Pytalon as they're supposed to be, there must be something terribly important about these two EE women that we're not seeing yet," Tilly began working her magic.

"Good assumption. I believe the Geheime Politie are on Pytalon, from all that we've seen so far," Beth agreed. "So where does that lead us? We could use your advice about now."

"Well, either they're protecting them or they're trying to gather evidence to arrest them, hoping they will lead them to others in the underground movement here in Europe. Obviously, the two women are off Pytalon and have been for some time. With all the spying, surely the Geheime Politie already know this fact, even if they're mentally more like zombies. Jessica here spotted that fact on our first meeting. So for my money, it's one of those choices or even a combination," Tilly argued.

"Okay. The best line of attack will be to find out the motives of the Geheime Politie. Give us a few minutes here. I have a way to get into the Geheime Politie server in Amsterdam. A friend of mine owes me a favor," Beth replied and typed a coded message, sending it to the "Wolf." The Wolf was a hacker acquaintance in Amsterdam somewhere or so Weasel thought.

Before long, a reply came. It read: Weasel! Wow! Cool, man. Heard you had a bit of trouble a while back. Glad to see you're still in operation. A pair of coded numbers followed, which Beth copied and pasted into another browser window. Presto, she was into the database. She then thanked the Wolf, promising to tell him what this was about later on.

"Okay, while you are working on that, I'm going to catch up on the local news around here, since we're obviously going to have to do some traveling," Tilly suggested. "The girls tell me they watch a lot of the BBC News to practice their English, so it shouldn't raise any red flags."

An hour later, Tilly rejoined them. "Gang, not so good. The streets are simply not safe to walk anymore. Too many are coming off Pytalon, and it's insanity city out there. Some are mugging others, stealing trivial things. One man was beaten to death for his worn out shoes! Some were stabbed by men insisting they were devils or strange beasts. Hallucination city. Getting around is going to be risky."

"Not so good for us then. Well, you are right as usual, Tilly. The Geheime Politie is spying on the women. Apparently, these two women are on their number one watch list in Amsterdam and in Hamburg, when they're there. The signs are confusing though. They're supposed to be ensuring the safety of the women, but they hope the women will lead them to others who are sabotaging production lines around Europe. Quite why they believe these women know anything about that, I haven't been able to unravel. Not sure if it's worth digging that out."

She continued, "In addition, it looks as if these two women are scheduled to become mothers in December. They're scheduled to get a drug change so they can get pregnant. Two men who will be the fathers have been chosen and are already on their changed meds so they can sexually perform. I wonder if they know this. I suppose we should tell them. Why don't you,

Tilly? Jessica and I want to keep on this trail. I think Jessica might have a way we can safely get them to their sisters."

A bit later, Beth heard a pair of shrieks followed by gasps coming from the living room. "We don't want to have some stranger make us pregnant! You *have* to get us to the States before that happens, please, please, Tilly," Erika cried.

Beth didn't hear what Tilly answered, but guessed she promised they would. *This mess is gradually growing worse,* she thought.

A short while later, each woman's cell phone beeped. They had a new text message from the professor. Haven't heard from u. R u all right? Did u survive the encounter with Delius? We r worried here. Beth sent back a short reply indicating that they were okay but dealing with another emergency. She purposely didn't elaborate just yet.

Walking stately in her boots, Erika came into the den holding her phone. "Excuse me; we have just gotten another EE assignment. I need to check my EE account to see what it is about."

Jessica grinned. "Here have a peak." She already had Erika's account up, displaying the new message.

"Oh! This is good news. They want us to go on an extended tour and visit the States for Christmas! Will this help us get to our sisters? The town of Berchtesgaden is only a few miles north of where my sister is at," Erika gushed excitedly.

"We know. I just arranged that tour," Jessica replied with a wry grin. "I have a knack for 'arranging' EE events. See, we have a way to get you both Stateside, before they try to get you knocked up. If you will also notice the fine print, you're bringing along four of your US EE fans—us! Now all we have to do is to work out the traveling details. We suspect the Geheime Politie will want to have a say in this too."

"Right dear. A message has just been posted on the Geheime Politie site notifying them the two women have another EE tour. I think there'll be a flurry of new messages. The big two I'm watching for are, one, will they want to have a hand in the travel arrangements and, two, will they postpone the impregnating until they return or push it ahead," Beth explained, still watching the screen.

"Oh no! They can't push it up sooner, can they?" Erika asked, almost wailing. A normal EE woman would have little or no reaction to the news she was chosen to become pregnant.

However, off Pytalon, it was a different story entirely. Erika and Ilse now had real emotions and feelings again. The thought of intercourse with an unknown man just to get pregnant was repugnant to both women. Did the Geheime Politie already know that detail, Beth wondered?

The next day, Beth herself sent a message to the Geheime Politie, claiming to be a medical doctor. Yes, they were weighing the option of pushing the impregnation ahead, getting it done before the women left for the States. Beth sent in a message that said absolutely no. The drug needed at least a month before it would be effective. Trying to impregnate them earlier was guaranteed to fail. She hoped her fake message would help alter the course of events. In the end, it did. The following day, the impregnation was postponed until the EE women returned from Christmas in the States.

"Okay, here is how this is going to work. Tomorrow, you're scheduled to meet the Air Liner when it lands around noon. We four will be there, and you'll meet us, your US fans. We don't have any coats or clothes with us, because you have offered to take us on a big shopping spree the minute we get here. After we get the shopping done, we'll be staying here with you one night, and then we six will be driven down to this town close to your sisters. However, the Geheime Politie are planning to accompany you from the moment you leave your apartment here tomorrow all the way through going Stateside," Tilly explained, going over it a couple times to make sure the two women had it memorized.

"But how will you get out of here and to the Air Liner?" asked Erika. "The spy camera is there."

Beth chuckled. "It'll go blank for a minute when we leave."

The next morning around eleven, an EMAC drew up to the backside of the tall apartment building. The four stepped out of the rear door and into the waiting vehicle. All had gone as planned so far. Beth's device nicely blocked the spy camera, and they made a hasty exit going down the back service elevator. Beth had been meticulous, making sure nothing of theirs remained in the women's penthouse suite. She anticipated the Geheime Politie might sneak in and look the place over while the women were off picking up the four arrivals. As it turned out, she was right.

They waited for some time at the Air Liner port. The weather was chilly, and the four were extremely pleased to see the women arrive in their EMAC. All were shivering, unprepared for the winter season. Tilly did discretely point out the Geheime Politie EMAC that was shadowing the two women. All six put on a good show for the unseen eyes, making it look quite real—excited fans from the States. Their shadow followed them to the EE Shop. For a minute, they were almost glad of their escort. Several insane men jumped out of a side street and started pounding on the EMAC, yelling this was a devil's beast coming to kill them. The escort vehicle sped up and chased them off. This surprised the two women, however.

Tilly commented, "Our perfect society is coming unraveled." She meant it as a sarcastic criticism, but the two women took it as the truth.

They spent four hours shopping, purchasing four new outfits each. Both hostesses insisted they get one fetish style outfit and a heavy winter coat. Again, the six mostly ignored the helpers and doormen, who continued to say things like, "Sanity is doing a good job." Although the four didn't speak Dutch, they had a good idea what these men said. From the corner of her eye, Tilly spotted the Geheime Politie, and she relaxed. If trouble came, help would be nearby. *Funny,* she thought, *the police are helping us. How strange.*

When they arrived at the penthouse suite, Erika noticed their bottle of Pytalon wasn't where she had left it. Upon closer inspection, she thought there were fewer pills in it when they had left this morning. "The Geheime Politie must have been in here and are making sure you have enough," Tilly suggested, while Beth and Jessica quickly checked to see if there were any new spy devices in place. Thankfully, there wasn't.

The six busied themselves with preparing for the next day's journey to the south and the Alps of southern Germany. They all dressed warmly, wearing long skirts and knee-high boots, whose spiked heel was the same six inches as the normal EE woman's heel. The two hostesses had no choice but to wear their ballet boots, thigh high this time to protect their knees if they should fall. Walking in the snow was treacherous for any EE woman, these two, even more so. Tilly and Amanda walked on either side of Ilse, supporting her, while Beth and Jessica supported Erika. That was their plan, along with a half-dozen large bags. The four managed to get all their new things into two of these bags, leaving each of the two fleeing women a pair of bags for whatever they desired to take with them. Sadly, they had few personal items. After being implanted, they'd lost all track of such sentimental things, and now had only a few mementoes and a lot of fancy clothing.

The next day, they summoned a baggage handler who carted their six bags down to the waiting EMAC. Again, the four chatted as if they were both visitors and wholly impressed with the two hostesses. Once inside the vehicle, Beth quietly checked for spying devices and pointed to one, which was pointed towards them. "Oh this is such a **good** trip, and we're **so** honored to be chosen to come with you, Miss Ilse, Miss Erika. We EE women in the US **always** look to you to help us pick out the best dresses. We must always look our very best, and you two are so beautiful," Beth said, faking it. The others caught on and continued conversations that would be appropriate. It wasn't hard; the two began pointing out the sights of Amsterdam and later the countryside.

Jessica had planned well. Upon their arrival in Berchtesgaden, a glassy-eyed photographer was present, and the six posed for photographs. However, snow covered the ground, and the six had a precarious time covering the twenty feet into the chalet-hotel, A-frame in shape and very picturesque. The countryside and the not too distant mountains were spectacular. The six took a few minutes to view them before making their treacherous way inside, where the photographer took a few more shots. Jessica had also arranged for several of the photos to be subsequently uploaded to the women's EE pages, adding to the believability of this excursion. Much later, Beth did some checking and discovered it had been a good thing that Jessica had thought of all aspects.

Once in their room, Beth again checked for spy devices and found none this time. Instead, she spotted several men keeping watch near the main entrance. So far so good. They were within a few miles of the women's sisters. Now for the difficult part—how to elude the police, how to get to where the sisters worked, and then get back without causing a big scene, which could well curtail their planned escape to the US.

Once again, Jessica had been thorough. As they checked in, the hotel manager greeted them. She'd used him as their "sponsor," even though he was probably on Pytalon if not implanted himself and would fail to be aroused by six EE women. He was tall, thin, with a perfect black moustache. "Welcome to Chalet Berchtesgaden. I'm your host and sponsor, Bardulf Beringer. I do hope my English is not too bad." Bardulf was rather handsome, but Jessica immediately saw he was very much in control of any implant he may have had and was not glassy-eyed. For a moment, she was taken by complete surprise, having anticipated a zombie host who wouldn't ask any questions. Suddenly the whole game changed!

"So pleased you're sponsoring us. I'm Ilse and this is Erika, as you probably already know. These are our visiting fans from the States. I'm sure we'll be able to please you most vell." Her English slipped slightly, as she too realized he wasn't a zombie, but was well aware of everything.

He is going along with the charade, Jessica thought. *He could have exposed us right this instant, but he isn't. Does he want sex? Damn.* She spoke up, "Danka. I have learned at least one word of German, Mr. Beringer. I do hope we look our best for you. We wanted to wear something more appropriate, but Ilse said it was very cold here."

"Oh, you look just fine to me. Yes, it is winter here in the mountains. It's wise to dress warmly. I have reserved our best suite for us. If you'll follow me, I'll show you to our suite." He pointed to a glassy-eyed man, who picked up their bags and followed after them, muttering something that Jessica assumed was sanity is doing a good job or something akin to that. She began sweating. *What does this man have in mind? Why is he going along with our masquerade?*

Their suite was magnificent, smelling of pine. A crackling fire had already made the room toasty, and the six quickly removed their heavy coats. There were only two bedrooms, each with king-sized beds. Mr. Beringer poured himself a glass of wine and studied the beautiful women before him. "Well, this is a terrific pleasure, no doubt, Ilse, Erika. You're the most famous of all EE women in Europe, and I'm well aware of the both of you, though I admit I know nothing about your fans from the States. Your Geheime Politie bodyguards are down at the front doors and will remain there. Therefore, you can cease pretending, ladies. Why have you arranged this meeting with me? Why Berchtesgaden? We don't take kindly to having the Geheime Politie in our town."

Ilse and Erika gasped, taken by surprise. Neither knew just what to say. Jessica took the initiative. "Mr. Beringer, this is my doing. We wanted to see the Alps, and with their constant police guards, I couldn't think of any other way, but to pick someone at random and have them sponsor our short trip and us. I'm sorry if we are upsetting you."

160

"Hum, I see. I see quite a lot. None of you is currently on Pytalon, are you? You are EE women. That much can't be faked, but none of you is acting like the EE women I've met before. What's going on here? Why Berchtesgaden?" he asked.

While they were talking, Beth quietly turned aside and got out her cell phone. Hastily, she sent a text message to the Wolf. Help. Who is Mr. Bardulf Berringer of Berchtesgaden Hotel? He has us in a bind right now! She hit send. Just as the manager asked his question, his cell phone began beeping.

"Think of your answers carefully, ladies." After glancing at the notification that he had a text message from Weasel, he said, "I have to take this." He pressed a button and read the message, then looked up very much surprised. Beth, hearing the almost immediate beep of Mr. Berringer's phone, turned to look at him. She saw the surprise on his face. "What is going on here? What are you six up to?" Then, his mouth broke into a huge grin. "Weasel?" His eyes glanced from woman to woman.

Beth flushed and said hesitantly, "Wolf?"

"Well, damn! Yes. Weasel? You are **not** as I pictured you! An EE woman? Good lord! The famous Weasel is an EE woman! Wonders of all wonders." He was both excited and very much impressed. "I never dreamed you were here in Germany or that I'd ever actually be able to meet you. I'm truly honored."

"Nah, I'm the one who is honored finally to meet you, Wolf, or Mr. Beringer," Beth grinned, shaking his hand, forgetting for a moment she wasn't a man any longer.

"Damn. Weasel, an EE woman. I would never ever have guessed your identity. Sit down, all of you. Please, what is this all about? I admit I was very curious when suddenly I became the sponsor of our top EE models in Europe. What is going on? Mind you, many are going to be very upset with you for bringing the Geheime Politie here. We're trying to avoid their attention."

"Long story. I guess I owe you an explanation. I was a man, and so was Tilly here, Wart." Of course, the Wolf knew all about Wart too, and the explanation was delayed while the Wolf formally greeted her as well.

"My goodness, both Weasel and Wart. Incredible, incredible."

Beth continued with a brief description of what Peter Delius had done to them, Jessica and Amanda's rescue, and their subsequent decision to complete the change of sex. "Aye, you both were probably very wise to do it. Those hideous implants just never go away; they are truly evil!" the Wolf commented and backed their decision.

She went on to describe how Jessica had managed to get to Peter Delius and all the remaining Feds, eliminating them. "So that's what happened! Let me just say that here we were stunned when we heard our number one criminal had been implanted at Thanksgiving. Jessica, what's your handle?" Mr. Beringer asked. "Weasel-2 perhaps?"

She giggled, "No, Shifty Eyes." Everyone laughed and Beth continued.

"Just as we were taking out Peter Delius, these two fine EE women here kidnaped us and snuck us into Amsterdam! We'll never ever live this one down—kidnaped by EE women. Please, Wolf, keep this bit to yourself. Instead, say we're here on a mercy mission or something," Beth asked, flushing. Wolf simply laughed and eyed the two women once again.

"They wanted us to find their long ago kidnaped sisters, which Weasel and Shifty Eyes did. It is a most intriguing story, and I honestly don't know the players. Perhaps you can fill in the missing pieces for us," Beth said. She went on to describe their research, and what they found. "They were actually taken by the Freiheitskampfer, whatever they are, and are living not far from here in a place called Faselburg, on a dead end side road. Jessica arranged for this trip so these two can meet with their sisters. Also, when we finish that, we're taking them to the States where they will disappear into the underground and get our new therapies."

The Wolf roared, "Freiheitskampfer!" He laughed again. "That's us, silly Weasel. That's our organization. We snatch promising teens before they are implanted and drugged out of their minds. We modeled our program on yours, thanks to the professor. Plus one for Wolf, minus one for Weasel." Both laughed.

"Well, I can see we need to communicate across the Atlantic much more. Thanks to Jessica here and another teen we rescued, Lisa, we now have a way to desensitize implants and to rid our bodies of the toxins from Pytalon. Let me tell you, Wolf, we four feel a thousand times more alive and are much healthier after going through the programs," Beth pointed out.

"Please, you must share this with everyone else. Lord knows we can use both therapies. Well done, Miss Shifty Eyes."

"Mrs. Shifty Eyes. Beth and I are married. So are Tilly and Amanda," Jessica pointed out.

"I'm sorry. Didn't know. Congratulations! This is the best news in a long time. Perhaps, there is some hope after all. Things are really degenerating, you know. Insanity rises," he pointed out the obvious.

"Anyway, Wolf, we need to arrange a meeting with their sisters without the Geheime Politie getting any notion of it," Beth said. "Any help would be greatly appreciated."

"You got it. I'll see if I can get them secretly here tonight. However, you must help me maintain the ruse for the Geheime Politie. You're supposed to be EE women, and I'm your sponsor. I'm afraid I must insist we continue that game."

"Of course, Wolf. Everything depends on this whole trip going as planned. We want to get home too. We don't speak German or Dutch and have been mostly floundering these past few days," Beth replied.

Both chuckled. He commented wryly, "You Americans." Now they all laughed.

"Well, we've been up here too long. The Geheime Politie might be getting a tad suspicious of us. Come. Let's go down to the main quarters, and socialize some for them. Erika, Ilse, if you will take my arm," he offered. Both did so eagerly, planting a kiss on each cheek and whispering a thank you in his ear. Besides, they were used to having an arm supporting them, as they made their relatively slow walk beside him. The others followed behind them, pretending to be awed by the women as well.

As the afternoon passed by, Jessica kept an eye on the Geheime Politie spies. Both were exceedingly bored, and she knew their ruse was working to perfection. After a very nice meal, they headed back up to their suite. Mr. Beringer continued to be attached to Ilse and Erika, as befitting their sponsor. Truly, he was enjoying this immensely, perhaps too much, Beth thought, growing slightly jealous of him. The two were the most beautiful women she'd ever seen. Later, two younger women in maid's outfits went up the stairs, but the spies didn't even notice them.

"Fjola! It is you! I can't believe it!" Erika gushed, moving as quickly as she could to hug her long lost sister, who had tears in her eyes.

"I thought I'd never see you again, Erika. I've been following you on your EE web page, but how can this be? You're an EE woman, but you don't act like one," Fjola asked. Nearby, Elke and Ilse where hugging and saying nearly the same things.

Beth and her group, along with the Wolf, moved over to the far corner of the suite to give the sisters some privacy. However, Fjola squeaked, "Weasel? The real Weasel? Here?"

Beth cringed. *Not again*, she thought. Then, she had no choice but to accept the adulation and praise heaped on them by Fjola and Elke. *It seems everyone knows about the Weasel*, she thought, and was glad to retreat once again, allowing the sisters a chance to talk privately.

Beth and Jessica took this opportunity to relay some of the details about how to desensitize an implant and how the sauna treatment rid bodies of the toxins. "But doesn't knowingly repeating the implant words bring the pain and unconsciousness back in on the person?" Bardulf asked. "We've seen that happen many times. That's why we avoid bringing implanted people into our folds."

"Yes, it most certainly does, but the trick is to persevere and keep on doing it. If you keep doing it one sentence or phrase repeatedly for hours, it does eventually desensitize that sentence. Mind you, it doesn't erase it; it's still there, but nowhere near as powerful as before," Jessica explained.

"So you're saying you, Weasel, and the others are still bothered by the EE implants? Subject to their effects on you?" he asked, confused a little.

"Yes, but the effects are relatively mild, and we can mostly ignore them, especially if we make sure to pleasure each other at night and when we get up," she explained.

"My god, Wolf, if Jessica hadn't done that on me, I'd be dead by now," Beth added.

"I see, but how did you ever come up with this treatment, Jessica?" he asked.

"Necessity, I guess. I was about to lose the only man I have ever loved, really loved, and I knew from my own eight years that the implants weaken with time. So I tried it and it worked," she tried to explain her reasoning at the time, but really couldn't state it any clearer. For her, it had been an emotional thing; she was caught with it, when her own emotions began to turn on full for the first time in eight years.

Fjola and Elke interrupted them. Although their sisters were now crying, they weren't. Fjola said, "Thank you, Weasel, Shifty Eyes, all of you. This is the best Christmas present ever. Please take good care of them in America."

"Ya, danka, danka," Elke added, but her emotions got the better of her, and she stopped to wipe her eyes. "You best go now. Don't vant to draw G.P. suspicions to us or you." One by one, the two gave each of the four a hug, followed by a long hug with their sisters. After wiping their eyes and adjusting their dresses, they marched out, as if they'd finished their work. From the corner of her eye, Elke noticed the spies paid no attention to them as they left, heading for the kitchen where they had left their coats. Both younger sisters felt relieved they hadn't drawn attention to themselves.

After their emotions settled a little, Bardulf commented, "Ilse, Erika, you're picking an opportune time to get out of the EE business."

"Why?" asked Erika.

"Because with the demise of the last twenty Feds, there are no 'legal' sponsors left for you. I expect gradually your association will be assigning you to permanent husbands, who are mostly zombies," he explained.

"Perhaps that's what was intended. I just discovered they were scheduled to become pregnant in December, but this trip to the States got it nicely postponed," Beth explained. Both women were very eager to leave Europe and disappear in America.

"You know, the psychs never could *cure* insanity, but they managed to leave a legacy of having almost caused an entire planet to become insane," Bardulf philosophized. "Right now, there are only a few little pockets of normal folks left in the entire world. If they don't get that Pytalon mess straightened out, millions will come off it and very likely become insane for a while. The world might not survive the coming wave of pure lunacy caused by their *curing* drug. Grim."

"Oh maybe it won't be so bad," Beth countered. "If we all continue to do our part, if we keep on extracting the brightest youngsters, and if we can undo the effects on others, maybe we have a chance, Bardulf. I hope so anyway."

He laughed. "Well, best let you get some sleep after you get some pleasure," he teased the two women, who grinned. He added, "Later on, if you want to become mothers, I know someone who would gladly become the father. Me." Both women smiled.

The next morning, Mr. Beringer again played the perfect sponsor, escorting both models to their waiting EMAC. Both made sure he had goodly traces of lipstick on his person so the spies would spot it, adding to the illusion. Once the vehicle began moving, by prearranged agreements, they chatted about how lovely the coming Christmas party would be and how much pleasure they could give their host this time. Hopefully, Beth thought, that would keep their eavesdropping spies happy and content.

At noon, the six boarded the Air Liner, Dutch Airways, along with twenty other passengers, mostly businessmen in their suits. Not one even noticed the EE women; they were perfect zombies. However, Beth did note two men did watch them carefully and concluded those two were Geheime Politie. Most of the passengers got off in New York City, but the six continued on to Chicago along with those two men, confirming their status, as far as the six were concerned.

Near dark, the six walked slowly into Jessica and Amanda's penthouse suite overlooking Lake Michigan. It was snowing hard now, the Lake Effect, Amanda explained in detail to her two guests. They ordered Chinese and ate lightly. They spent the next few days doing some real shopping, since the two wanted to wear stateside apparel, as Erika put it. Slowly, the days passed. They couldn't *disappear* until the Christmas party.

Christmas Eve, Beth had their untraceable EMAC loaded with their things, though they left a change of outfits in the apartment, giving the appearance they would be returning here from the party, just in case the Geheime Politie somehow got inside to look for the missing women. Right on time, they took a public EMAC over to the Feds building. Arm in arm, they walked in. Again, they weren't stopped; they were expected. No one mentioned Peter Delius hadn't been seen for some time. In fact, none really knew he was absent. Zombie life moved on following the same, century-worn patterns.

Beth spotted the two men entering, just as they reached the elevators. Hence, she knew they would see them go up to the top floor. Perfect. Once they got off on the top floor where they had been at Thanksgiving, all six walked over to the freight elevator and descended to the ground level. It opened in the back of the building, totally out of sight of the front entrance area. No one was even there. Quietly, the six slipped outside into the snowy night.

"Oh no, snow! We can hardly walk on it!" Erika whispered, extremely worried, holding tighter to Beth and Jessica's arms.

"We only have to go a half block to the covered MTE. Easy does it; one step at a time," Beth whispered. The snow was already four inches deep and very slippery. Twice each group slipped and fell. Actually, Erika and Ilse slipped, but pulled their two helpers down with them. Their extreme heels and the snow didn't mix. All were very glad to step onto the covered MTE. As they rode the escalators, they glanced up at the snow-covered roof overhead. It was transparent plastic and made for an interesting look. Soon, they arrived back at the apartment skyscraper and headed directly for their EMAC. Five minutes later, Tilly and Amanda drove it out, while Amanda punched in the coordinates for their East Peoria safe house.

Around ten Christmas eve, they pulled into their safe house. Once inside, they relaxed, held their own celebration, and headed for bed. Early the next morning, while Amanda cooked breakfast, Beth and Jessica made new ID cards for the two women. "Look, we don't want anyone discovering your new identities easily. So your names are going to be changed too. You'll be Erica Whitehall, and you'll be Lisa Swan. Later on, you can change them again if you like. This way, the Geheime Politie will not be able to track you via your ID cards, which I have just destroyed, nor will they be able to trace your names. Jessica has added you to the Flagstaff EE association, since that city is closer to where you will be staying, Phoenix. Again, all this can easily be altered later on, as your plans change. For example, if you never want to appear in public again outside of Phoenix, you could be dropped completely off the EE women's listings. Just remember, if anyone actually sees you, outside of Phoenix that is, they will know you are an EE woman and may well ask for your registration."

Both were satisfied. After Amanda's good breakfast of bacon, eggs, toast, and tea, the six hit the road once more, arriving in Phoenix two days later. After introducing them to the others there, they chatted with Lisa, who gaily chatted away. "Hey, I have twenty people doing my sauna sweating process now. Been keeping busy. I'll get you two started today, once you get settled in." She saw the two newcomers staring at her, and Lisa added in her usual way, "Birth defect. Just ignore it; everyone does."

"Vut you are an EE woman too?" Isle asked, rather shocked at Lisa's appearance.

"Yes, got rescued by these four and saved. Now I'm doing my part to save others. Come on. I'll show you your new quarters. See you four later on sometime. Busy, busy, busy. Say, do you also want to be able to stop wearing those awful boots?" she asked of Ilse and Erika.

The four grinned and waved goodbye for now. The professor wasn't here, so they hastily headed back home. Weeks of work had mounded up in their long, unexpected absence. Jessica mused during the drive home, "You know, perhaps one day soon, we should remove ourselves from the EE women registry. If things get as bad as the Wolf was suggesting, might we be in trouble, dear?"

"No, we four are officially married. I believe we're safe enough for now," Beth replied.

From the front, Tilly called out, "Hey, I wouldn't be too certain of that, Beth. The way things are crumbling, we could be in big trouble. Have you given any thought to moving your main base of operations from East Peoria to Phoenix?"

"What a hassle. No, not really."

"I think you should, Beth. I really do." She would be proven right and soon.

Chapter 13—Pickle Barrel

"I need to be able to do my work. This is getting to be ridiculous," Tilly grumbled. The four were back in their safe house in the abandoned warehouse on the west side of East Peoria. They'd left the two beauties in Phoenix last week and now had their place in full operation. That was the trouble. Tim or rather Tilly was used to taking off on his or her *trips* for the underground, gathering intelligence.

"I know love, but it is just too dangerous for a woman, especially an EE woman to be out there now. The insanity is growing, and I'm scared for you," Amanda pleaded. She loved Tilly more than she'd ever imagined was possible, though her implant still gave her some troubles with her emotions.

"Yes, but a trapped butterfly is not free," Tilly grumbled.

"Look, you don't have to wear these expensive fancy gowns and heels. Let's see what you look like dressed plainly. I don't think we can disguise your boobs, though," Amanda volunteered. The butterfly analogy got to her. She felt Tilly's anguish for what it was. *Maybe I can love too much*, she thought. Together, they tried different clothes.

"Well, my body is still mostly the same as it was," Tilly observed, pulling on his old jeans, "except for the boobs. Honestly, I prefer your delicious curves, dear." Amanda grinned.

"It's curious that you have female organs, but not a real woman's body. Your buns are not big enough and your waist isn't small enough, if the truth were told. Then again, your muscles are bigger than one might expect. I really hadn't noticed these details before now. I wonder why?" Amanda replied.

Tilly laughed. "What's worse is that I was highly attracted to Erika and Ilse, but I felt no attraction at all towards the various men we met. God, whatever would I do if a man made a real advance towards me? I'd be repulsed, except I'd get a headache from the damned implant."

"Interesting. So even with the implant saying to pleasure men and women, you aren't attracted to men?" Amanda asked.

169

"No, repulsed might be a better way of saying it. I love women, you in particular. Guess I'm not gay, but then this is all so strange, isn't it."

"Yes, but look what that's saying about the psych's implants. They can't truly alter a behavior pattern to be *completely* the opposite of what it was originally," Amanda suggested.

"Keep in mind I'm desensitized to it. I suspect others might not have so much freewill left. I think we're mostly anomalies now, thanks to Jessica. Well, if I don't wear the wig, my hair isn't long at all. Doesn't look too bad, except for the boobs. Wearing a parka rather disguises them. I think I can pass fairly well now. Thank you, my love." Tilly breathed a deep sigh of relief. While not perfect or remotely what he used to look like, she felt she could go about the world and not attract undue attention.

"Well, I'm off. Back by suppertime."

"Got your cell?" Amanda asked. She waved it, and they shared a goodbye, passionate kiss. Amanda hated to see her go off alone, but knew Tilly had to do this. She then busied herself with other chores around the warehouse. She began thinking about how she could help Tilly more. While she too could slip into jeans, her feet wouldn't allow wearing anything but the EE women's tall stilettos. Amanda realized the one thing she had to do was get her feet able to wear flats once more. She had to undo her eight years of constantly wearing the taller heels. That gave her a plan of action.

Jessica and Beth continued to monitor the communication channels. What occupied most of their attention were the alarming rates of people going temporarily insane and causing no end of problems in the society beyond their safe house. "It's an epidemic," Jessica commented, and Beth nodded.

That's what was bothering Tilly. She had now traveled around sufficiently to see an epidemic was precisely the term. In every major city, the outbreaks of temporary insanity due to bad Pytalon were in the thousands. She and the professor had years ago predicted something like this would happen. That much was true, Tilly thought as she roamed the downtown streets near Main and Adams streets. Eventually, someone directly involved in the manufacture of the drug would suffer sufficiently from Pytalon that they would dope off and allow the goof to occur. That conclusion, Tilly still held. However, such goofs wouldn't be limited to the manufacturing of the drug. Similar goofs should occur in nearly every occupation. The bad Pytalon was the far-reaching ramifications of the error.

No, what continued to bother Tilly was the epidemic scope of the manufacturing failure. Today, she looked around for corresponding failures in other areas of the society and in Peoria in particular. The more she looked, the more frustrated she became. She watched, as the AP-cops picked up a woman who was shrieking wildly about rats eating her legs. A number of passers-by seemed unsettled by her wild antics. Fortunately, the AP-cops were very efficient in their handling of her. Meanwhile, Tilly watched another man jump from the long abandoned river bridge that once carried land vehicles across the river. With the invention of the EMACs and the MTEs, the bridge had been left to rot, being far too expensive to tear down. The man hit the ice in the river and disappeared. Two AP-cops saw him jump, shook their heads, and ignored him, content to worry about the living insane, not the dead.

"That's the anomaly!" Tilly whispered to herself. "No corresponding increase of errors in other types of workers. She stepped back into an alleyway and dialed Amanda. "Hi, up for some calculations?"

A few minutes later, Amanda called out, "Beth, Jessica, Tilly wants you to get operational blueprints for some of the Pytalon manufacturing lines, detailed ones, how the machinery is to operate with emphasis on what role humans have it the production line."

"Why does he, er she, want that?" Beth fired back. "She knows nothing about chemistry and manufacturing."

"Dunno, she's given me some nasty equations to solve." Amanda felt very pleased. She too had a purpose again.

Tilly returned home around noon, bringing hot chicken, potatoes, gravy, and cold slaw for everyone. "Miss me? Well, that was interesting. I'm able to get by without attracting too much attention. How are the calculations coming? Beth, you find me those plans yet?"

"Well, I had to do some digging behind the company's firewall, but I got what you asked for. What the devil do you want with those plans anyway?" Beth replied, snatching a breast and large scoop of the potatoes.

"Not sure what I'm looking for just yet. Lot depends on Amanda's calculations," Tilly replied. She was more interested in looking over her mate's results than the chicken she'd brought back. "Damn, this is far worse than I expected. Are you sure about these percentages?"

"Yes, dear. Triple checked them. What do they mean anyway?" Amanda asked, helping herself to a pile of the cold slaw.

"If the goof-ups in the manufacturing lines of Pytalon are caused by the long-term use of the drug by the assembly line workers, then there is a ninety-nine percent chance that we should see similar errors in all other goods being manufactured. However, we're seeing around a tenth of a percent of errors in such goods. Your chicken dinners are just fine, for example. We should be seeing uncooked chicken, spoiled cold slaw, moldy gravy—things like that. Obviously, we aren't seeing the degeneration that the professor and I predicted many years ago. No, gang, we're looking at some entirely different phenomenon! The final number is what I'm really after, Amanda. She's calculated that there is a ninety-nine percent chance someone is directly causing these faulty pills! Gang, we have a saboteur who is operating worldwide."

"Ah, so someone is trying to destroy the world?" Amanda asked, a little confused.

"Probably trying to bring down the drugged society. Whoever is behind this is definitely *not* in our underground movement, but I'll check further, in case I've missed something. Lord knows, I've been mostly out of touch for the last six months. Still, I don't believe the professor would have stood for it. The sheer number of those coming off Pytalon and going temporarily insane is threatening to destroy civilization completely, if left unchecked. This isn't the path to recovery of our world. It's total anarchy and barbarism."

"Each some chicken, love, and let's look over those plans," Amanda suggested. Tilly's conclusions bothered her more than she cared to admit. Someone was behind this, and because of their sabotage, she and Jessica had come off Pytalon.

Tilly sent a detailed text to the professor first, before sitting down at her computer and bringing up the pdf files containing the plans for the San Francisco plant and the Detroit plant. "What are we looking for?" Amanda asked, looking over her shoulders.

"I am zeroing in on where something could go wrong, omitting the Pytalon from the pill base. Look here. As the base pills come down the line, these injectors are to inject a hundred pills simultaneously. A worker sits there and presses a button to cause the injection to occur. Now if that person failed to do his job, no drug would be in those pills," Tilly explained.

"But what's that thing there," Amanda pointed a long red nail to a side view.

"Well, I'll be! That red button isn't needed and doesn't do a darn thing anymore. Let me magnify the writing. Ah, yes, the button was used a hundred years ago to inject the drug into the base pills, but was completely replaced by an automatic robot system. However, with all the implanted personnel whose job was to sit there and press the button, they retained the job, but the button does nothing at all. It says to begin phasing out new Technician Fourth Class positions. I guess they're the button pushers. Now this is interesting! The critical part of the operation is computer and robotics controlled so nothing can go wrong," Tilly explained.

"And yet it must have gone horribly wrong everywhere, even in Chicago, or Jessica and I wouldn't be here," Amanda pointed out.

"Sabotage! That can be the only answer. I have to relay these findings to the professor. He can relay them on up the lines. We have to stop this sabotaging fast!" Tilly replied, excitedly texting away. "I need to get into one of those plants and see if I can find what is being damaged."

"Hey, why didn't you say that's what you were looking for?" Beth countered. "Electronics, computers, robots—those are my things."

"And mine," Jessica added with a wry grin. "Come on, dear. Let's see where we could most easily sabotage the process." The two took their plates over to their bank of computers and brought up the plans that Tilly had been studying. Within a few minutes, each had reached the same conclusion.

"Have a look here, Tilly, Amanda. Jessica and I agree. If we were secretly going to sabotage the manufacturing process and allow placebo pills to come out and not be discovered and not have the plant destroyed like Ben did in Chicago, then the absolute easiest way would be to put a clamp on this small plastic tube that carries the Pytalon liquid from the holding tanks to the hundred tiny needles here. One clamp and the flow is stopped, and no one is the wiser. Some Pytalon-drugged nincompoop must have thought up this modification. There should be a flow monitor in this tube, setting off an alarm and shutting the line down when not enough liquid is flowing. They didn't, so the designer must not have been in his or her right mind, that is, on Pytalon themselves."

"What would it take to stop that flow by crimping the tube?" Tilly asked.

"A nipple clamp," Jessica replied, inadvertently using one of her EE devices as an example. That was the first thing that came to mind. "Doesn't need a whole lot of force to clamp it shut. You could pinch it shut with your fingers."

"That's good work, you two. I need to get into some of these plants and see if I can find such a clamp. If so, maybe the perpetrator left some fingerprints I can lift. If I find some, we can alert all the manufacturing plants to look for them in their assembly lines," Tilly replied.

"Now how the heck are you going to get inside and tear apart their machinery to look for clamps?" Jessica countered.

"That's your jobs," Tilly replied quite seriously. "Find me a way in there. Best try St. Louis, since Chicago is not fully back on line after that Air Liner destroyed the middle of their building. What is more troubling is the subsequent distribution of the bogus pills. Someone knows just which batches are placebos and are controlling their distribution. Obviously, they are making sure those people in the food processing industry are not getting them, just those people who are disposable and not in more sensitive or critical work. This is a carefully planned operation."

That afternoon, the professor, Bill Smyth, and Tilly fired text messages back and forth, discussing the massive ramifications of her findings. Suddenly, the chaos of the last six months made sense. It wasn't the slow degeneration the professor and Tim had predicted years ago; rather, it was a deliberate attempt to destroy the entire world. What scared these three was that a person or persons unknown to them was doing this. There was another secret organization at work that they knew nothing about, let alone it even existed! This frightened all three. Tilly felt real fear for the first time. They had a powerful and unknown enemy out there. If left unchecked, they would surely destroy the whole world and soon, the way things were going.

By early evening, the three agreed Tilly should try to prove her theory by visiting one of the plants and seeing if she could find the blockage. If so, they would begin a campaign to alert all the many other plant managers to the source of their problems.

"I need the layout of the St. Louis Pytalon manufacturing facility, Beth. I'm going there to see if I can find their blockage," Tilly reported.

"We'll come with you," Amanda suggested.

"No, best if I go alone. If I get caught, then you three can come rescue me," Tilly countered. "This is my area of expertise, breaking and entering, and gathering data. Wart, you see, is going into action again. Don't worry, love. I've done similar things a hundred times or more. I'll go in late at night when no one is around. Be in and out in no time, as long as I have an accurate set of floor plans."

"But I want to help, Tilly. I can come, drive the EMAC, be there in case of trouble, and be your lookout," Amanda protested and Tilly agreed. Having a backup might be a good thing in this situation.

"Okay, plans are up on your computer," Beth called out. While the two began studying the layout, Beth and Jessica chatted.

Later, armed with the plans on her cell phone and all her tools of the trade, Tilly and Amanda headed off to St. Louis. First stop, snatch an EMAC that wouldn't be missed for a few days. That was easy enough to do. Tilly had *borrowed* a Caterpillar Company vehicle on numerous other occasions. Most sat idle on top of their company headquarters in downtown Peoria. An hour later, with the geo-tracking turned off, the two sped towards St. Louis at top speed. They planned to be there before midnight and scout the place out first. If all were well, Tilly would break in around two in the morning.

"I don't like this. I've a bad feeling about them," Jessica admitted her fears to Beth. Their two friends had been gone only an hour.

"Me either. I hate dealing with unknown people. Come on. Let's do some more sleuthing. Someone has had to have access to this part of the robotic system in order to block the flow. It began about six months ago. You check when all the trouble started in, say, ten other big cities. Something had to have changed just before all the outbreaks of insanity happened because of bad Pytalon. Let's see what clues we can find, love," Beth suggested. She knew having something to do would help take Jessica's mind off what their friends were about to do.

Several hours passed swiftly. Between the two, they finally found a solid lead. Just before one of the ten plants began producing bad Pytalon pills, their robotics inspector had died and was replaced with a new man. "That has to be the connection we're looking for," Beth pointed out. "They killed the old inspector, replacing him with their own man, who then proceeded to sabotage the plant while presumably doing a routine inspection. Clever and no one is the wiser! These are diabolical fellows we're dealing with."

"And murders too. This sounds very dangerous. I'm texting Amanda with our findings. So far, there are ten of these bogus inspectors out there and probably many more, one for each plant in the world," Jessica concluded, typing away.

"I'm sending this to the professor and Bill too," Beth added, also typing out a lengthy text message on her secure, disposable phone.

***

Tilly and Amanda parked their EMAC a block from the plant. It was a ten-story building with attached warehouse. Three floors were dedicated to production, each a separate unit. "I only need to inspect one. If I find the blockage, I'll undo it and get out. If it is free of obstructions, then I'll try the next one up," Tilly whispered.

"How will you get in?" she asked.

"Through the sewer lines. We're parked over one entrance now. I'll be back in less than an hour. Send a blank text if trouble comes." They shared a brief, passionate kiss, before Tilly, dressed all in black in men's clothing, slipped out of the vehicle, lifted the manhole cover, and disappeared from sight. Amanda set her cell's alarm for one hour and began her nervous wait.

Tilly turned on her flashlight, brought up the plans on her cell, and headed off. Before long, she stopped to pick an old, rusty lock, and then entered the basement of the factory. Knowing the location and coverage of the security cameras, she used one of Beth's handy devices to scramble the signals before she passed them. On up three flights of stairs, Tilly scampered, wholly unchallenged by the night watchmen. *Child's play,* she thought to herself. Soon, she entered the factory room, which occupied the whole floor. Again pausing to consult the plans, she soon found the right spot to begin her search. She undid two thumbscrews and lifted a cover, exposing the plastic tubing that carried the liquid Pytalon from overhead vats down to the hundred injection syringes. Even by flashlight, she could see the small metal clamps on the hoses. One by one, she carefully unscrewed them, slipping them into a plastic bag. She wore gloves so she wouldn't confuse any possible fingerprints that may be on them.

Ten minutes elapsed since she entered the room. For a moment, she toyed with the notion of going ahead and inspecting the other floors and their facilities, but then thought better of it. The plant managers would need to find them for themselves, if she were to be believed. Stowing the bag, she got out her cell and sent a short text to Amanda, Beth, and the professor saying that indeed she had found clamps shutting off the flow to the injectors. That done, she slipped her cell into a pocket and turned to leave.

She found herself facing a man dressed all in black just as she was. He had a ski mask covering his face. He wore soft deerskin moccasins, and hence, he had easily been able to slip up behind her while she was working. What got her instant attention was the barrel of a gun pointed at her face. "Damn!" she whispered, unable to keep quiet. She knew he couldn't be a guard, not in that outfit. Instinctively, she raised her hands, flashlight pointing to the ceiling, temporarily hiding him from a clear view of her. She wished she hadn't had that immediate reaction to a gun pointed at her head. Too late. She felt a slight stabbing pain in her neck. Her legs felt like mush; her head began swimming. She collapsed, but the man caught her, lifted her up, and carried her out of the room, going back down the stairs she'd come up minutes before. Her last thought was, *Somehow, they knew I was coming here.*

Outside, Amanda glanced at her cell once more. She'd received Tilly's message and relaxed a little. They had been right. Someone had deliberately sabotaged the plant with the result of causing hundreds of people unwillingly and unknowingly to suffer the awful withdrawal symptoms when they came instantly off Pytalon. Further, Tilly was ahead of schedule, and that gave her a better feeling about the whole night. Soon, she'd be back here, and they'd be on their way home.

Just then, a man dressed all in black with a ski mask over his face stepped up to her window and pointed a gun at her head! "Step out of the vehicle or I'll shoot you." Panic struck instantly. She dropped her cell and fumbled for it as she tried to comply. If only she had another instant to send Tilly that blank text. Trembling, she managed to send the text while getting out. Elsewhere, Tilly's phone silently vibrated, but she was unconscious and unaware of it.

"What's going on?" she asked. Her voice sounded strange and shaky, she thought. The man didn't answer. Instead, she too felt a little stabbing pain in her neck and almost at once blacked out. The man picked her up and carried her to a waiting EMAC, tossing her inside, where Tilly also lay unconscious. He climbed in behind the other man in black, and they sped away from the building at a rapid rate.

Back in East Peoria, Beth and Jessica relaxed after receiving the brief text. "Tilly was spot on. Someone has been deliberately blocking the production of Pytalon pills," Beth exclaimed. "He's or rather she's not called Wart for nothing. In record time too; damn, she's fast. Now we need to get this to all the Pytalon manufacturing companies around the world. I'm sending that to the professor now. Let him figure out how to do it. No sense in risking our necks on that one. He's better equipped to deal with them anyway."

"Hey, I just got a blank text from Amanda. What does that mean?" Jessica interrupted him. She texted back asking what was happening, but got no reply at all. Now both began to worry.

Hastily, Beth hacked into the factory's security system. "Darn, nothing unusual is going on there. The guards haven't noticed anything. What the devil is going on down there?"

"Dunno, but I'm getting worried. It's not like Amanda to ignore her cell, unless she's in big trouble," Jessica replied, growing more and more worried.

An hour passed; both women's worries only escalated. They were certain something had happened to the pair. Even hacking into the AP-cops system there in St. Louis yielded no information. All was quiet. Nothing.

"Nothing is worse than knowing," Jessica said nervously. "Should we go down there and see?"

"Take us a couple of hours to get there. By then, they might be back here," Beth countered. She hated leaving the safety of her warehouse.

Just then, both their cells beeped. "Oh, it's a text from Amanda," Jessica exclaimed, relieved and excited.

"From Tilly," Beth added. Both looked at their messages. "Shit!" Hers read, If you want to ever see them alive, do precisely as we ask. Are you Weasel? Both showed each other the terrible message; they were identical. Beth replied, Yes. Both waited.

Another message came within a minute, one to each phone. What city are you in or close to? Both replied East Peoria. After an even longer wait, another message finally came. One hour, be at the corner of Main and Jefferson streets. Bring no one else. Alert no one. We're monitoring you. If you do, you'll not see them alive again.

"What do we do?" Jessica asked, fighting down her growing panic.

"We lock up here, equip ourselves for the unknown, and do as asked. Maybe we will find out who is behind this. Maybe they will listen to reason," Beth replied, her voice rather shaky. She didn't believe a word of what she'd said, but said it to try to keep Jessica calm. Both hastily set to work, shutting everything down. Then, they went their separate ways, grabbing this and that, which they thought might be useful, including two stun guns. After walking a short way from their safe house, they hopped onto the MTE and rode to the designated location with several minutes to spare.

It was around four in the morning, and the streets were deserted. Only the streetlights were lit, along with a few dim store signs. Beneath the clear plastic V-shaped canopy over the MTE escalators, they could see light snow falling, deflecting off the steep sides of the canopy. The street cleaners would have some snow to remove in the morning, Beth thought.

As they approached the intersection, two black clad men with wearing black ski masks stepped out of the shadows. One said only, "This way." Both were pointing guns at the two in their parkas. A short distance away, they saw a waiting EMAC with more men inside. "Get in," the gruff voice ordered when they were close to the door. As they bent over to climb in, each felt a light stabbing pain in their necks. Once seated, both passed out and didn't see the other two men join them or the vehicle speeding away at top speed.

***

Some awful smell aroused Tilly. A man moved on to the next woman, waving a vial beneath her nose, waking her. Tilly still wore her winter parka, but her hands were handcuffed together over her head. She was hanging from a meat hook, and her feet didn't touch the ground; her wrists throbbed. A rag gag was tied around her mouth. Three strangers stood before her, as she twisted her head to the right to see the others. When she

179

saw all four of them had been captured, she groaned and wondered how they had gotten to Beth and Jessica. She felt like a pickle caught in some barrel with no way out.

"Vell, vell, you are now all awake I see. Weasel and Wart, together at last. You have *no* idea how much trouble you two have caused me over these past years. And I had no idea whatsoever you were *women*, EE women to be precise. Unglaublich! Incredible! No one would ever have predicted that, sehr gut, sehr gut. I had the *best* tortures imaginable arranged for you, but alas, you're not men at all. So as they say, the best laid plans have to be laid aside. I vill not torture women. We draw the line at that. Fulch! I so wanted to torture Weasel and Wart. Alas, it is not to be." The man appeared to be in his middle fifties, with a moustache and goatee. His hair was black and cut short. From his accent, he was of German birth. This much Tilly guessed. He wore a soldier's uniform with many medals pinned on its front.

"Forgive me; we haven't been properly introduced." For a moment, it looked as if he were somehow thinking about just who he was or perhaps listening to some unheard voice. Then he came to and barked grandly, "I am Grand Field Marshal Hans Gudrunda, *the* supreme leader of the Free World of Earth, the FWE. I am the best trained, most brilliant minded, keenest strategist ever to walk this earth!" For an instant, Tilly thought that he was repeating the words of some implant.

In an angry tone, he snapped out of that and said, "You have interfered with my plans for the last time! While I vill not hesitate to shoot you if you should try to escape, as long as you're here, you'll be under my protection—that means for the rest of your lives." He seemed to relax now, adding, "Further, I'm told you're married to each other. Hence, I'll respect that and not allow my men to rape you, unless as EE women you desire their company. Oh ya, you're at an abandoned army base several miles north of Sandpoint, Idaho, in the Rocky Mountains. Quite pretty here, reminds me of the Alps, but right now you're in our meat locker where my men deposited you. They were expecting to be able to torture you here. Alas, they will be disappointed."

He turned to the other man and said, "Have you removed all their cursed electronics, Gruber?"

"Ya, got them all, Grandest Field Marshal. Electronics are bad, bad, bad things to have." He also sounded more like some recording. He pointed to the small pile of their cell phones and other devices lying on the floor near his feet.

"Gut. You know what to do mit them," he barked.

At once, Gruber ignited a blowtorch and incinerated or melted the entire pile of their phones and devices. He seemed extremely excited about the destruction, though. In fact, Hans and Helene also smiled appreciatively. Tilly again thought this was rather bizarre behavior, but felt her last hopes of rescue going up in smoke. No cell phones.

"Okay then. I'm officially turning your care over to our own EE woman here, Keeper Helene Troys. As long as you do vat she says und vhen she says, you vill be vell treated. Disobey her or cause her trouble and you vill pay dearly. There is," he paused, "how do you say, ah yes, a limit to vat I vill tolerate in women anywhere. So you four behave and do as Keeper Helene tells you and you vill stay alive. Disobey und vell, I still have those tortures available. Verstehen sie mich? Understand me?" he hastily corrected himself. Tilly nodded her head; the others did so as well.

"Lower them for Helene, Gruber," Hans ordered. He did a perfect military pivot in place and marched out of the meat locker room as though accompanied by some unheard military marching band. Gruber walked over to a switch and pressed it. Slowly, the hooks holding them up off the floor lowered. Tilly was never so glad to have her feet on the ground. The aching in her arms began to subside, as she finally was able to lower them. She glanced at the frightened faces of her mate and friends and saw they too were relieved to be on the ground again.

Keeper Helene spoke in a deep alto voice, "You will follow me now." She turned and the four followed her, while Gruber watched them with a close eye. He had a revolver strapped to his side, Tilly noted. Outside the meat locker, they found themselves in the out of doors. Cold air hit them. A low porch ran the length of this very long set of barracks, protecting them from the snow. It was mid-morning, and they could see the rugged mountains some distance away along with many feet of snow just beyond the porch. Small walking paths had been shoveled across the open areas, like a maze of cris-crossing lines. Tilly thought, *We are really in one fine pickle this time. I don't see any easy way out of here.* She had no idea how right her analysis was, but she soon would have.

Chapter 14—Prisoners

Grand Field Marshal Hans Gudrunda paced the floor of his field office at the abandoned army base just north of Sandpoint, Idaho. His Supreme Plan for World Domination, his SPWD—he loved acronyms—was going better than expected. The news coverage reported the ever-growing outbreaks of temporary insanity in all the major cities. It wouldn't be long before the despised civilization of earth would collapse, and he, Grand Field Marshal Hans Gudrunda, would step in with his mighty force, the FWE, the Free World of Earth, and take over. A voice inside his head said, "You are the Grand Field Marshal, *the* supreme leader of the Free World of Earth. You are the best trained, most brilliant minded, keenest strategist ever to walk this earth!"

He barked to the walls, "Of course, I am!"

Just then, his electronics man, Gruber Dichts, who was six years younger than he was, came rushing in, forgetting to salute. Hans quickly corrected this breakdown in protocol. After a proper salute, his longtime companion spoke hastily, "Grand Field Marshal, someone is asking for the plans to the Pytalon factories and the injection robotics."

"Vell, don't just stand there, electronics man. Go find out who this is?" Hans barked. He hated electronics and everything to do with such things. Here on this base, he'd outlawed all such things, retaining only the TV and one electronics station run by Gruber. For communications worldwide, he and his men used ancient radio sets, which in the modern world were highly unlikely to be intercepted. No one used such things anymore, not for a century. Gruber dashed off to comply.

Hans never explicitly said why he demanded there be no electronics in his vast organization, he just insisted upon such and did not allow anyone to possess modern electronics. Many speculated it was because Hans had been implanted by the psychs who used electronics in the process. At last, he headed to the only room on the entire base that had computers, networks, and other electronics. He became worried.

Gruber muttered to himself, "Electronics are bad, but I am their master." When Hans entered, he remembered to salute this time. "Grand Field Marshal, I have traced this inquiry to Wart and his accomplice in malice, Weasel. They are on to your plan to disrupt the Pytalon production lines. I think they know how you are doing it. This is bad, is it not?" he reported and asked.

"Fulch! Very bad, Gruber, very, very bad. They're interfering yet again. Ve cannot let them disrupt de SPWD, de master plan! Find out what they are up to. Where are they now? What are they planning to do? Find the answers, electronics man. I need answers now. I vill go arrange an attack force to stop them." Hans turned and left Gruber to his cyber-sleuthing for a time.

"Captain Henry, it seems the notorious Wart and Weasel are attempting to disrupt our SPWD. They have somehow figured out what our *inspectors* have really been doing at the Pytalon plants. They must be stopped, captured alive if possible, and brought here. I'm going to have fun torturing them."

"Aye, sir. I'll get my squad ready to fly as soon as you tell us where and when. We will not fail you, sir! Consider them captured and get your tortures ready!" the young captain replied, saluting his leader. He turned and ran back to the barracks to get his squad ready.

A little later, Gruber reported they had the plans for the St. Louis factory. Hans made an executive decision and ordered Captain Henry and his men to head directly there at top speed. "Ve vill let you know if there is any change in their targets. Ve vill try to give you some idea of vhen they vill strike the factory, captain. Bring these vile men back to me. I'll have the torture chambers ready and waiting. Ve have been waiting for years to get our hands on these slippery electronic demons. Now ist our chance."

"Aye sir! We will not fail!" Captain Henry jumped to attention, saluted, pivoted perfectly, and marched down the narrow path through the three-feet of snow to their waiting EMAC. Two vehicles took off at once. Hans walked briskly to the room he'd designated as his torture chamber. It was also his pleasure chamber, for Hans loved young men. Often, he would have his soldiers round up a young lad and bring him here for Hans to *play with*. The play was rather rough. If the lad survived, he was given a chance to join the FWE army. If he refused or didn't survive, he conveniently *died*.

"I shall begin with the old Chinese method of pulling off their fingernails and toe nails. That should wake them up sufficiently. Then, we take off their fingers, one by one. Must make sure they regain consciousness for each one—that's twenty of them. Oh, this vill be my finest torture ever!"

The voice inside his head said, "You are the Grand Field Marshal, *the* supreme leader of the Free World of Earth. You are the best trained, most brilliant minded, keenest strategist ever to walk this earth!" Once more, Hans muttered, "Of course, I am that and much, much more." With his tools ready, he returned to the single electronics room to see if Gruber had made any more progress in his spying.

"Ya, dis is why ve do not vant any of dis electronics stuff on the base, except here. It has led to the downfall Wart and Weasel. They depend wholly on such things, and ve do not, Gruber. Electronics are bad, bad, bad things."

"Yes sir! Very bad. I think they're going to hit the factory in the middle of the night," Gruber reported.

"Excellent, excellent, Gruber. Use the radio to let Captain Henry know that. I vill be in my torture chamber awaiting the arrival of our special guests! Oh, tonight vill be sehr gut, sehr gut! Ve vill eliminate the last of our rivals. Ve vill be the supreme rulers of all earth now. Nothing can stop us any longer."

Shortly after two in the morning, Captain Henry called in. "Grand Field Marshal, we have captured Wart and his companion. Weasel was not with him, but I have a plan to net Weasel and his companion as well. Permission to use their captured cell phones, sir," he requested. Hans agreed. Henry then reported, "Sir, there is one small problem. Wart and companion are both women, EE women to be most precise. How is this possible? EE women?"

"Vat? EE women? Unheard of!" Hans replied angrily. All of his plans for torture evaporated. "Are you sure?"

"Monster boobs, sir. Long nails, thick lips. Must be. Have Gruber check these names on his computer to verify, sir," Captain Henry suggested. He rather hated to make such a request, but he needed confirmation, and this would give Hans time to adjust his torture schemes. Perhaps the Grand Field Marshal would let him have some fun with the women. One was extremely attractive.

After a series of radio exchanges and Gruber's Internet searches, Hans sighed. All four were EE women. His hopes for

184

torturing the infamous Wart and Weasel were dashed completely. The voice in his head ordered, "You are to protect women and small children."

Hans muttered to himself, "I know, I know. You don't have to remind me. Still, I can shoot them if they attempt to escape. I vill give them over to our Keeper Helene. She'll know what best to do to them." He marched off to find her.

"Keeper Helene, you vill soon have four more EE women under your care. These are the infamous criminals Wart und Weasel. They are married, so I vill respect that if they obey you. You may shoot them if they try to escape." She was forty-nine and an EE woman herself, but she was bundled up against the cold of the base right now. She had long brown hair and a burly disposition, a no-nonsense woman. Sometimes, Hans wondered if she even had had an implant.

Like Gruber, Helene followed Hans to the States years ago. She had always been one of his faithful followers and true believer in the SPWD, the master plan. Helene's position as Keeper was to see that the ten EE women were always properly prepared to service the men of the base, excepting Hans, whom she knew preferred young teenaged boys.

"Vhat am I allowed to do mit them?" she asked, a bit perplexed. "Married? To each other?"

"Ya, each other. Zwei couples. Let them do each other, but honor their marriage. No one else touches them, unless they ask for it. However, Helene, do your best to hobble them so they cannot escape. Ve are to protect our women, you know, so I would rather not have to shoot them as they escape."

"Yes, Herr Grand Field Marshal! You can count on Keeper Helene. I vill make sure dat they cannot physically escape here," Helene replied with a broad grin. She loved this aspect of her work down through the years.

Midmorning, Captain Henry's two EMACs landed. Quickly, he and his men took the handcuffed women to the designated area, the meat locker and hung them from four meat hooks, suspending their feet off the floor. Finally, they tied crude cloth gags over their mouths. Captain Henry dismissed his men and headed to report to his leader.

"Danka, danka, Captain, sehr gut indeed! You may go get some much-needed sleep. There vill be a promotion in this for you and your men. Such field initiative—you have apprehended our archenemies! Sehr gut!" Henry saluted, turned, and left. Hans left to fetch Gruber and Helene. Soon all three walked into the meat locker to inspect the freshly delivered meat. Helene quickly inspected all four and pronounced them EE women, satisfying Hans completely. "Okay, wake them up, Gruber. Dis is our finest hour. Da Wart and da Weasel are ours now. No more interruptions with our grand SPWD!" Gruber took out the vial of smelling salts and moved to Tilly body, waving it under her nose.

It was at this point that some awful smell roused Tilly, who saw a man moving on to the next woman, waving a vial beneath their nose, awaking them. She still wore her winter parka, but her hands were handcuffed together over her head. She was hanging from a meat hook and her feet didn't touch the ground; her wrists throbbed. A rag gag was tied around her mouth. Three strangers stood before her, as she twisted her head to the right to see the others. She groaned as she saw all four of them had been captured and wondered how they had gotten to Beth and Jessica.

"Vell, vell, you are now all awake I see. Weasel and Wart, together at last," Grand Field Marshal Hans Gudrunda barked his opening lines. They watched as their cell phones and other electronics were destroyed and listened to his speech, explaining they would be shot if they tried to escape, but otherwise would be under the care of his own EE woman, Keeper Helene Troys.

After being lowered and untied, Keeper Helene spoke in a deep alto voice, "You will follow me now." She turned, and the four followed her, while Gruber watched them with a close eye. He had a revolver strapped to his side. Outside the meat locker, they found themselves in the out of doors. Cold air hit them. A low porch ran the length of this very long set of barracks, protecting them from the snow. It was mid-morning, and they could see the rugged mountains some distance away along with many feet of snow just beyond the porch. Small walking paths had been shoveled across the open areas, a maze of cris-crossing lines.

She also saw two EMACs sitting out on the field and suspected they had been brought here in them. *Now if there only is a way to get to them*, Tilly thought, *then we could fly away from here.* Helene led them into a room. The sign over the doorway said Women's Latrine. Tilly hoped it wasn't as crude as the sign implied. She wasn't disappointed. Inside, she found they were in a very nice bathroom with showers.

Helene uncuffed each woman rather awkwardly using one hand. In her other hand, she held her revolver at the ready. "You vill now undress fully and take a shower. I vant to see vhat kind of EE women you are. I've seen your web pictures and am most distressed over your appearances. Now shower or I shoot." Quickly, the four obeyed, though Tilly constantly continued to estimate whether she could overpower this rather overweight EE woman, past her prime. She decided one gunshot would bring an army of soldiers down on them, and they'd never get to the EMACs before being shot. The four did as asked and took a shower.

When they dried off and stood in a line before Keeper Helene, the older woman looked positively disgusted with them. "You four are a disgrace to all EE women in the world! Two of you have overeaten so much so that your waistline is monstrous! Dressed as a man, shame on you, Tilly. Well, this ends right here!"

She began talking rapidly first to Tilly and then the others, figuring the four had probably forgotten them. "Your body is hypersensitive to sensual touches. Your body needs sexual sensations and stimulations several times each day. You exist to provide elegant and sensual experiences to men and women of power. You are an exotic escort. You must look your very best at all times. You must be ready to flirt at any time. You must be ready to engage and satisfy the sexual fantasies and satisfactions of both men and women at any time. You are a super-sexual, hypersensitive woman. You must wear only the finest and exotic gowns and heels. You must look perfect at all times. You will repeat these words to yourself several times each day. You must not forget these words."

Once she repeated it four times, she stepped back and added, "The Grand Field Marshal has said you're married to each other. Is this hideousness true?" The four nodded. "Ah well, it must be so. You'll not be housed with the other EE women, and, as long as you obey me and our few rules, no one vill bother you, but you must then be satisfied with pleasuring each other. Do I make myself clear?" All four nodded grateful for this small kindness, particularly so for Tilly and Beth.

"Gut! Now then, I vill correct all these despicable omissions on your part. Dis way," she explained, leading them through a side door into a spacious dressing room. A wood burning fireplace crackled, and the room was warm, thankfully. Several other elegantly dressed EE women were also present.

187

They looked up at the four newcomers and smiled.

"Ladies, you know what must be done. These two must have their awful looking waists reduced, severely, I might add. Dress them and then ve'll do their nails. Ve vill use the four-inch extensions on them. Dat vill make escaping even more difficult for them," Helene ordered. She added, "It gets chilly in these old barracks, so ve vill be dressing you warmly. Don't worry on that account. First, put the O-ring gags on them. Ve don't want to hear their pathetic protests—such a shameful lot of EE women. They disgrace us all!" Before any of the four could say anything, the women forced their mouths open, inserting the large O-ring, strapping the head harness securely. Without undoing the several straps, Tilly knew they couldn't get out of them.

"These vill be removed at meal times so you can eat, unless you start talking, in which case they vill not be removed, and you can lick up your meals," Helene explained. Next, several women helped each other to put heavy corsets around Tilly and Beth's waists, tightening them mercilessly. It took three women on each one to get it sufficiently tight. Amanda and Jessica were lucky and felt bad for their spouses, who could now scarcely breathe. After the usual garter belts were put on along with the fine nylons, panties were slipped onto each woman. Then, each had a fine white silk full slip put on her, followed by a white silk blouse. Next, they were told to sit and a heavy leather hobble skirt was put on them and laced up. These went from their waists down to their ankles and only allowed them to move their feet and ankles a foot at most, perhaps less. To Tilly and Amanda's dismay, they were then fitted with knee-high ballet boots, as were Beth and Jessica. Now the other two felt badly for Tilly and Amanda, who had never worn them and would be in for a horrid time. Both tried to complain, but Helene ignored their gurgling protests. Tilly and Beth had long hair wigs put on them, covering their still rather short hair.

Another couple of hours passed while they each received nail care. All four cringed as they saw the length of the extensions being added, making their nails nearly six inches long. While the red polish dried, the women applied the usual and rather overdone EE women's makeup. That done, they were told to put their arms behind their backs. The women slipped a leather single arm binder onto each woman, buckling the straps crisscrossed over their shoulders. There was no way for them to slip the binders off, thus freeing their arms. A strap held the bottom snugly against their waists, preventing even lateral movement of their arms. Helene then spoke up, "These vill be removed at meal times. You vill wear them at all other times, including while you sleep. You have tongues, so use them to pleasure your spouses. Are you warm enough? Nod your heads." They nodded that they were.

At Helene's signal, several of the women held up mirrors so the four could see how they now looked. "You see, this is how EE women are supposed to look, of course minus the restraints needed to keep you prisoners here. No escape is possible, so don't even think about such silliness. Now up you go. We'll take you to your rooms now. Ladies, I think you'll have to support those two. Honestly, they can't even stand in these, the most exotic of our footwear," she chastised Tilly and Amanda. "Well, that will soon change. Now you are all proper looking EE women.

As they were slowly escorted out of the dressing room, Helene again chanted, "Remember, your body is hypersensitive to sensual touches." She rattled on the implant words, ending with, "Now you look like proper EE women should look." After a pause, she added, "And do try not to drool all over your silk blouses. Ah, here comes our Grand Field Marshal. Sir, do they meet with your approval now? No escape is possible."

"Keeper Helene, you have outdone yourself this time. Yes, they look like perfect EE women now. No escape is possible, Weasel, Wart. You'll remain here until you die, never again thwarting my mighty plans. Take them to their rooms." He saluted Helene, who beamed with pride.

Their room was spacious but chilly even though a wood burning fireplace was going. There was a single couch and two beds on opposite sides of the room. The four headed for the couch and struggled to sit down without falling. Helene and one of the women who had been dressing them entered behind them. "This is Sally. She vill be with you to help you with your needs. If you need to use the bathroom, nod your head, and she'll escort you there. Remember, escape is impossible, so sit back, and relax. Enjoy yourselves." She turned and left them.

Sally sat on the edge of one bed. She wore an elegant, but heavier satin gown, dark blue, which had a narrow walking slit in its back. Thus, her legs were kept warm. She merely sat there staring off into space, hands folded in her lap. Except for her vacant stare, she looked like a normal EE woman.

Tilly wanted to cry, so did the others. Suddenly, life had become unbearable. Constrained as they were, there was little any of the four could do except sit there on the couch, but Tilly and Amanda dreaded having to walk. Unused to these boots, their feet cramped and throbbed already. Beth and Jessica wanted to offer advice to the others and let them know that even they found walking in these leather hobble skirts almost impossible, but of course, they couldn't do more than look at each other.

In a rush of self-chastising thoughts, Tilly began to blame herself for all of this. *If I hadn't been in such a damned rush to go prove my theory, we'd all be safe at home! It's all my fault.* More such thoughts came for a while. Then, her mind drifted onto a more fruitful path, pondering just how they had been discovered. She reflected on all she had done. Nowhere could she see anyway she'd given them away, but of course, she didn't know who all was in this insane organization anyway. Maybe they had spies among their group in Phoenix.

Time slipped by. Now her thoughts drifted to their situation. At last, she began to realize it could have been far worse. This Hans fellow could have had them all killed outright. He could have maimed them permanently. He or his men could have raped them and used them as kept play toys, which they probably were with the poor young woman who merely sat there on the bed gazing at nothing at all. They could have been beaten, their arms, legs, and ribs broken. Her mind raced with various ideas of painful torture, even being put on heavy doses of Pytalon and turned into unfeeling, unthinking, glassy-eyed zombies.

No, he was honoring her marriage, their marriages, and restraining his men from using them as sex toys. *How strange,* she thought. *Still,* Tilly reasoned, *we aren't actually being physically harmed, just hobbled, and immobilized. Our minds are clear. Minds.* Suddenly she realized that was all she had left, the only remaining resource she could use, her mind. She had somehow gotten her friends and mate into this mess; she had to get them safely out of it by using her mind.

Tilly had no way of knowing what thoughts Amanda, Beth, or Jessica had running through their heads. Going down that route was pointless right now. *Use your brains,* she thought. In fact, the other three had rushes of various similar thoughts as she had, and all eventually reached the same conclusion that she had. *Sit back, behave, and use your mind and powers of observation.*

Darkness came early this far north in early January, but it also brought the sound of a dinner gong, alerting everyone that supper was being served in the mess hall. That finally brought Sally out of her daze. Another two women soon came, and they helped the four to their feet. "This way to the mess hall. You must look your best," Sally said softly, adding, "The men will be watching you."

Jessica and Beth were able to manage walking, if awkwardly, but Tilly and Amanda could barely stand. Hence, the three women held securely on to the two, leaving Jessica and Beth to manage on their own. Slowly, they walked out of their quarters and out into the cold Idaho evening. *At least, we are beneath the shelter of the overhanging porch,* Tilly thought. They walked past ten other doors before entering the large mess hall. Now all four paid attention, as much as they could spare while trying to walk and not take a spill.

Tilly lost count, somewhere around fifty men were present and a dozen women, mostly EE women, she noted. Some had helped dress them; she recognized their faces. They were led to the front of the room where Grand Field Marshal Hans was sitting. His table looked out onto several rows on which the others currently sat. Most had already gone through the buffet line and were devouring their meal. However, all eyes turned to gaze at the four.

As the three women helped the four to get seated, Hans rose and announced, "Here before us tonight ve are honored to have our archenemies die Weasel and die Wart joining us. They will be joining us every night from now on, men. No longer vill they be a thorn in my grand plan for us and earth." A hearty round of applause followed his brief announcement.

Helene came up to them and one by one removed their O-ring gags and then unfastened their arm binders. All four exercised their jaws and rubbed their cramped arms. They were careful not to speak, remembering the warning they had been given. "Okay, there is the buffet line, go get yourselves a tray and what food you desire. Bring the tray back to your seats and eat."

This time, Tilly found she was on her own; her helpers didn't hold on to her. She and Amanda stumped rather precariously towards the line. Jessica and Beth were right behind them faring only a bit better. All prayed that they wouldn't fall down. They'd had enough humiliation for a lifetime already. From Tilly's point of view, by some miracle she managed to get through the line and to her seat without taking a tumble, spilling her tray, but she was gasping for breath from the overly tight corset. Beth was likewise struggling to keep from fainting.

Once seated, they discovered having such long nails made eating far more difficult that it should have been, but that was more of a minor inconvenience and annoyance, far more readily born. By the time they finished, most of the men had already left. All wore soldier's uniforms, Tilly noted, concluding this was a paramilitary encampment.

As Helene came up to bind them back up, Tilly decided to make a plea. "Please, Helene, we agree, there is no way we can escape. Please, don't put those gags back on us. Our mouths are drying out. Our mouths won't help us escape, not really. Besides, where would we go? At least, let us be able to cheer each other up." She saw that she wasn't getting anywhere; the woman felt no sympathy for her arguments. In a flash, she saw another approach. "Look, Helene, we're EE women, after all. We must look our best at all times. We can't look our best ever with those rings in our mouths forcing them open. Our lips and faces look awful, not like an EE woman is supposed to look."

Helene mechanically repeated, "You must look your very best at all times. You must be ready to flirt at any time. You must be ready to engage and satisfy the sexual fantasies and satisfactions of both men and women at any time." She blinked, as if coming to the present time. "Yes, that is quite true. You do not look your best at all. Very well. If you vill promise to continue to be well-behaved women and not try anything, I vill leave them off, and we'll see."

"Thank you, Helene. Now we can look our very best," Tilly replied meekly. A few minutes later, all four arm binders were secured and they made their long precarious walk back to their barracks room. The three women removed their hobble skirts and pulled down their bedding. Dutifully, the women obeyed and mostly fell on to the beds. Kindly, the three women helped tuck them in, pulling up the covers. Sally whispered, "Call out if you need something during the night. The night guard will alert one of us." She turned out their lights and left the four alone.

"Thank you, Tilly," whispered Amanda. Beth and Jessica whispered theirs too.

"We have to use our brains," Tilly whispered back.

"Keep your voices low. How did you three get captured?" Hastily, they exchanged brief stories. "Okay, here's the plan. Obey the rules, but stay alert and observe everything we can. Tomorrow, Amanda and I have to somehow learn to walk in these boots or we can never escape."

"We can't get far with our arms bound," Beth whispered back.

"With our teeth, we can undo each other when the time comes, but Amanda and I have to be able to walk then. Be patient with us. My feet are killing me now, and I can barely breathe," Tilly whispered back. "Hush, I hear the guard outside. Moan in pleasure a little. Four sexy moans followed, and they heard the guard snicker and move off. She then had the final word for the night, "We now know who our real enemy is so before we escape, we need to learn as much about them as possible. Observe, everyone, observe."

The next morning, Helene and her three helpers came to get them up and dressed again. After making a trip to the bathroom, they returned to their quarters. Once more, Helene began reciting the EE litany, not varying a word from her previous recitations. As she did so, the others did their makeup so when the four appeared in the mess hall, they would *look their best*.

As Helene recited her almost chant, Jessica began to understand Helene better. Helene was acting more like the psych man who was giving Jessica her implant than herself when she underwent it. There was something backwards with Helene's EE implant, Jessica reasoned. True, Helene had the overly thick lips that all had. She boasted the monster breasts— the one giant size fits all that they had seen repeatedly. She wore elegant gowns and the usual six-inch heels, but she was very much in control of herself, unlike Sally for example. Several times now, Jessica had heard Sally whispering the implanted words to herself, just as she had done years ago, as well as Beth, Tilly, and Lisa had. No, there was something fundamentally different with Helene.

Again, the four were humiliated, having to struggle to walk solo through the buffet line, bringing their trays to their tables. All the while, the various soldiers whistled and catcalled after them. Beth and Tilly were again gasping for breath and nearly fainted. Once more, they were the last ones out of the mess hall, which they took as a good omen. The lecherous men wouldn't have to see them make their pathetic long walk back to their room.

However, during the meal, Jessica again had the opportunity to observe Hans. Buried amongst his other chat, were the same lines he had used before, namely: "Yes, I am Grand Field Marshal Hans Gudrunda, *the* supreme leader of the Free World of Earth, the FWE. You are right. I am the best trained, most brilliant minded, keenest strategist ever to walk this earth!" Observant Jessica found this both interesting and quite backwards. He seemed to be responding to some unheard voice, agreeing with it. How very strange. Yet, he was definitely manic in nature.

She had no doubt he was a good leader. Obviously, he was. His entire army had remained unknown and hidden all these years. Her companions never suspected he existed. Moreover, he had cleverly drastically altered the production of Pytalon worldwide. No, here was a man to be reckoned with, and yet he was acting as if he too heard voices in his head. Had he been implanted? If so, his was backwards, just as Helene's was.

After Helene bound their arms once again, Tilly decided to take a small gamble. "Miss Helene, Amanda and I have never worn these boots before. May we be allowed to practice walking some in them during the day? Like up and down from here to our room? If not, may we at least walk around the small room? We would like to be able to walk elegantly in them, like EE women are supposed to do, so we can look our best before all these men."

Again, Tilly played to Helene's implant and it worked. "Why yes, that would be most satisfactory Tilly. You really do need to learn to walk gracefully in them. Honestly, you do; you must always look your best when out in the world. Sally vill accompany you."

Despite the excruciating pain in their feet, Tilly and Amanda did as much walking each day as they could manage. While it was freezing outside and they were given no coats, they endured it for brief periods. The outings gave Beth and Jessica time to observe this army base, since being rather used to these boots, they could put more attention on their surroundings. For days, their routine was virtually identical. Still they were getting more and more information on their captors and Grand Field Marshal Hans Gudrunda.

After a week of captivity, Jessica managed to have a brief conversation with Major Henry, who had been promoted from captain because of his highly successful capture of the four. While out practicing their walking, he came nearby and Jessica spoke up, "Congratulations on your promotion to major, sir."

He stopped and beamed. "Well, thank you, miss. Yes, I'm a brilliant field soldier. I'm exceedingly bright and highly intelligent. I'm superior in field tactics." He spoke in a rather maniac tone, as if repeating something he'd been told. From the slight glaze in his eyes, Jessica knew it was his implant talking, not Henry. His eyes cleared, "Yes that is why I was able to capture all of you so easily. I'm brilliant in the field. One day, I'll be the field marshal's right hand man, maybe more."

"Oh, I'm sure you'll be even more than that, Major Henry. I've not seen a soldier as brilliant as you are, sir," Jessica poured it on rather thick, but he continued to puff up and beam. He bowed and continued on his way. Finally, a working theory formed in her mind, confirmed by Major Henry's behavior.

Later that night when they were alone in their room and tucked in for the night, Jessica whispered her theory. "Gang, I think we are looking at failed psych implants. The ones, which have caused all the damage, like with us, for example, all used the pronoun 'I,' as in 'I must always look my best.' With these, I think that someone goofed and used 'you.' 'You must always look your best.' Can you see the difference the pronoun is making here?"

"Er not exactly," Beth whispered back.

"If you have something in your mind saying to you, 'You must always look your best,' it's rather like a demon voice telling you this. You're not it, but it is giving you advice, you see. When it says 'I must look my best,' then it is confused with yourself; you believe this is you talking and saying that you must look your best."

"Take Helene, for example. She keeps going around telling others they have to look their best, while she isn't under the pressure to do so herself, excepting for the EE woman's role that she has. With us, our implants were forcing us to flirt, but with Helene, her implant tells her to tell others to flirt, not herself. It's like a voice inside her head telling her those words, which she recites to others and are not directly applicable to herself," Jessica attempted to explain her theory better.

"With Hans, he has obviously had an implant too, but again, I believe the psych goofed and said something like 'You are the best trained, most brilliant strategist ever to walk this earth,' instead of saying 'I am the best trained, most brilliant minded, keenest strategist ever to walk this earth.'"

"But I don't see the logical difference," Beth complained.

"When the implant uses the word 'I,' the implant forces the behavior onto you personally, but when the implant used the word 'you,' the implant talks to you, like some really close friend might. In that case, the words tend to re-enforce your own beliefs about yourself, as in the maniac behavior of Hans and Henry, or it can become what you tell others, as in Helene's case."

"Say, I remember reading something about this in that history book the professor lent me," Amanda whispered, suddenly making sense of Jessica's theory. "She's right. In the very beginning, the psychs used 'you' and got terrible results. Behavior patterns were not really altered as they had intended. Then, they figured it out and began using 'I.' After that, they were able to alter the behavior patterns of the person."

"Great. So what we're looking at here are a bunch of failed implant cases," Beth concluded. "Probably they have all gone off the grid, so to speak. From the age of the failed cases, that must have happened some time ago, maybe thirty years or so, with some more recent exceptions, like Henry."

"Some of the young soldiers look like high school recruits," Amanda suggested. "Joining his army probably appeals to some who don't want to get implanted and drugged up. Honestly, I might have considered it too if I had even known about them and what the implant would do to me."

"This explains why they have remained unknown to us, not to mention their abhorrence of all things electronic," Beth said with a sigh.

***

By February, the four women were getting extremely bored! Used to a high level of action, they'd endured nearly a month of exactly the opposite. Outside, the deep snow was only barely beginning to melt. Worse, it had been cloudy nearly every day, adding to everyone's cabin fever.

At lunch, Grand Field Marshal Hans Gudrunda was highly upset. "You four have really set back our grand plan. You know that? Oh, you can talk." He added, seeing the four merely looking at him.

"We don't understand how?" Tilly ventured to pump him for more information, excitement growing within her. *Perhaps this hasn't been in vain after all.*

"All the damned, cursed Pytalon factories have removed the blockages that took us years to get into place. Worse, they fired all our inspectors who did the work. All plants are back to full production, and the necessary riots have ended. The world is back at peace once more, a world of mindless zombies doing the same thing every day. Hideous. You've set us back at least a year, damn you anyway." He was mad, that much they could tell, but would he take his anger out on them? Tilly was weighing the odds he would just do that!

Jessica decided to see if her theory was right about him. She said, "Oh Grand Field Marshal Hans, "You are the best trained, most brilliant strategist ever to walk this earth. I am sure *someone* of your caliber can come up with an even *better* strategy."

His anger subsided. "Well, that's true. I am the *best* ever. I should be able to invent an even better action to bring down this *insane world*. Yes, that is what I *must* do now. Life is full of bumps. You four have merely given me a minor bump. That plan did have its flaws. I need an even better one." Jessica smiled, her theory confirmed. She now had an idea of how she could manipulate Hans, if only in a minor way.

Later that night, Jessica asked, "Do you suppose we could manipulate Hans into joining us or is his maniac behavior beyond control?"

"Beyond control, I'm afraid," Tilly replied. "Good work today at lunch, Jessica. I was impressed. We need to get free and get these rebels under some kind of control before they do even more irreparable damage to the world." None disagreed, but could see no way out of their prison.

"I wish I was at my computer so I could research Hans and see if I can identify other members of his worldwide organization," Beth lamented. "I'm going stark raving mad doing nothing at all but sitting."

"Start inventing a way for us to get out of here," Jessica suggested. Beth sighed; escape was impossible.

The next day, Jessica had another idea. Poor Sally was just a young teen, probably only recently having had her EE woman's implant. As usual, she merely sat on their bed staring into space, though frequently repeating the words of her implant like a slave. True, if they needed to use the bathroom, she would pull out of it and assist them, but she did little else.

"Sally, I'm going to help you get over the crippling effects of your recent implant. I want you to say aloud, 'I must look my best at all times.' Come on; say it," Jessica coaxed her. Soon, she did so, but quickly, Sally complained her head was aching. "That is to be expected. You must be brave and endure it. Keep on repeating it, and I promise your headache will go away. Come on, Sally; you can do it." Jessica continued pushing the teen along, but with compassion and sympathy. After all, the four of them had been through this themselves.

By suppertime, this one sentence had been destimulated significantly. Both Sally and Jessica were quite pleased with this first step. During the ensuing next three weeks, the two continued to work on the various phrases and sentences they guessed the psych man had installed in Sally's implant. At the end of that period, Sally finally had a good measure of control over herself. No longer was she staring off into space; no longer was she reciting endlessly the words as her implant had ordered her to do. "Thank you, Jessica. I feel so much better now," Sally whispered, unwilling to have the other EE women of Hans' group know she was back in control of herself, unlike most of the others.

This, of course, now created more problems for Sally. She had been picked up as a sex doll for the soldiers here, along with the other dozen EE women. Now, however, she didn't want to be a sex doll or even flirt with most of the soldiers. In her mind, she was being raped nearly every night! However, Sally did her best to not display any outward signs to the men, for that would get her into serious trouble. She did spill her emotions and feelings to Jessica when they were alone during the daytime hours.

"Is there at least one man here you rather like?" Jessica asked the sobbing teen, late one afternoon.

"Well, I do have some feelings for Major Henry. He is at least kind and considerate of me," Sally suggested.

"Okay, then why don't you see if you can talk with him? Perhaps, he can single you out as his, and he could be your sponsor, which is rather like being married. Then, you would only have him taking you to bed," Jessica suggested. Sally brightened up some and said she would try.

Two days later, Sally was all smiles. Indeed, Major Henry really did like her and was very eager to make her his private EE woman. More interesting from Tilly's point of view,

Major Henry began telling Sally the plans they were making. In turn, Sally began relaying them to Jessica.

The new grand plan called for using explosives to blow up all the Pytalon manufacturing lines worldwide! Already, Grand Field Marshal Hans' men had been raiding some of the Feds' supply houses, building up their supply of explosives. They were being stored here on the base! Major Henry's task was to construct satchel bombs with timers on each. When the time was right, the field marshal's agents would drop them off at the various plants, putting them into position on the right floors of the buildings. Because of their earlier project of clamping the liquid Pytalon flow lines, they knew the location of all the plants and each plant's floor layout. Placing the satchel bombs could be easily done. A simple midnight break-in would be all that was needed! Boom. At dawn, worldwide production of the debilitating anti-psychotic would be ended. Recovery time was estimated to be many months, by which time, everyone in the world would be off the drug. That was the plan.

The four knew it had a fatal flaw. While the world's population would suddenly be off Pytalon, the consequences would be devastating. Many would commit suicide. Many would have bad hallucinations and delusions and, as a result, murder or harm a huge number of others. In short, the entire economy of the world would suddenly cease. No more goods would be made at the other factories. No more crops grown, harvested, and shipped to the grocery stores. No more fresh meat. No more repairs of broken equipment. The world would be plunged into a chaos from which virtually no one would survive.

Tilly knew she had to do something to prevent this. But what? At last, in March, she had an excellent opportunity and took it. Major Henry had brought Sally a bouquet of early spring flowers. While Sally began putting them into a makeshift vase, Tilly took a long shot gamble.

"Major Henry, I didn't know you were planning to become a farmer and raise all of your own food, but I don't think I could actually butcher a cow or pig and then dry the meat. More power to you. I'm sure Sally will help you with canning and such," she said in a somewhat flirting manner.

"What? I've never grown anything in my life, miss. Whatever are you talking about?" he asked, somewhat confused by her notions.

"Well, forgive me, but I overheard you and Sally talking one day about blowing up or somehow destroying all the Pytalon plants at one time. So naturally then, I assumed you and everyone else here were planning to grow your own food and do your own butchering and canning. I'm sorry if I got it all wrong, major. No one really tells us anything. All we do is sit here all day, dreaming. So our minds think of strange notions. I take it you're not going to blow up all the Pytalon plants."

"What? Well, yes, you don't have anything to do but sit and dream. I can see that. You are partially right. I guess it won't hurt to let you know what is coming soon. The Grand Field Marshal's new plan is indeed to blow up all the Pytalon plants in the world and at the same time, ending once and for all the manufacturing of that wicked psych drug," he replied.

"Oh my. Then, you *are* planning to become a farmer and do your own butchering and canning," Tilly stated with a wry grin. "So I was right; you're going to become farmers."

"What? No, Tilly, we aren't going to do any such thing. We're going to free all the billions of drugged zombies," he countered.

That gave Tilly the opening she so greatly wanted. "But the consequences, major, will be hideous. Look what happened in all the major cities when you effectively ended Pytalon production by clamping off the liquid. The withdrawal symptoms were just awful. Look at how many people killed themselves. Look at how many went insane and killed, raped, or severely beat other people. If everyone undergoes this, who will be left to continue to make, process, and deliver your food? Who will be left to make new consumer goods? Who will be left to repair things? Fix the MTEs when they break? Who will continue to do their old, critical jobs? No one. The whole world's economy will end all at once. So naturally, I figured your soldiers would step in to maintain law and order, but soon, there would be no more food. That's why I assumed you were planning to become farmers and make your own food." She continued to elaborate, punching in her image of the resulting worldwide chaos.

Major Henry was stunned. He sat there saying nothing for some time. At last, he whispered, "Perhaps you're right. I must think about this. I must talk with the Grand Field Marshal." He rose, kissed Sally, and left them. Finally, Tilly saw a light at the end of their imprisonment. They'd been held captive for eleven weeks.

Chapter 15—Chaos Strikes

Grand Field Marshal Hans Gudrunda had more problems than he could handle during January and February. He had underestimated the Feds and their resourcefulness. True, they were now all zombie-like on Pytalon, but that didn't detract entirely from their training and principles, just their ability to think and their intelligence. Yes, the Feds were slow in responding and seeking out the perpetrators, but they were like bloodhounds on the trail of a critter. During January, they began methodically tracking back the *inspectors* who had performed the sabotage on the many Pytalon plants. Eventually, these many dozens of trails began to lead back to the field marshal and his expansive band.

Of course, the precise location of the field marshal remained unknown to the Feds, but now they knew their *enemy*. Worldwide, the Feds continued plodding along in their investigations. While they now took some twenty times longer, they still got their jobs done, no thanks to the Pytalon drug. After all, the Feds was an organization devoted solely to the eradication of rebels to the world society. Thus, through January and February, they plodded along, always getting closer to the field marshal.

However, in late February, explosives, detonators, and timers began vanishing from their extensive stores all around the world. Hans anticipated they wouldn't notice the disappearance of such at any one location, since he had purposely spread the thefts around a dozen Feds locations. He didn't count on the methodical, if zombie-like, Feds. The thefts were noted within days and countermeasures taken. Security was tightened at the remaining depots, and several further attempts to steal explosives were thwarted, much to the field marshal's dismay.

As March rolled around bringing the first hints of the spring thaws, the Feds were closing in on the field marshal's location in Idaho. They had traced the worldwide shipments of the explosives to a four state area: Idaho, Montana, Washington, or Wyoming. Certainly, the encampment was in the Rocky Mountains, of that they were certain. Diligent, if somewhat moronically, the Feds continued their relentless searching for Grand Field Marshal Hans Gudrunda's base of operations. Hans was keenly aware of their search and had even anticipated how long they had until they were discovered here north of Sandpoint. Thus, during March, he issued orders to get the satchel bombs finished, and he prepared evacuation plans, should the Feds finally locate this base.

Relocating was not much of a problem for Hans. This base here was the twentieth new center for his operations. Paranoid, he tended to relocate his operations at least once a year. "Never give them a stationary target was his motto. It had served him well for some thirty years now. In addition, the numbers in his *army* of volunteers had grown steadily, now numbering close to one thousand, scattered widely around the world. An EMAC train would handle relocation..

Crossing the vastness of the western lands with goods and supplies had always been done by large, diesel trains. Those had been replaced over a century and a half ago by the huge EMAC trains, which like all EMACs, floated above the terrain, eliminating the need for rail lines and their costly maintenance and construction, to say nothing about the total elimination of fossil fuels and going "green." Rail lines, roads, and the vast Interstate highways of some two centuries ago were simply left to be reclaimed by Mother Earth, though some Garbage Collectors Twentieth Class had once been involved in recycling the metal rails. Hans had his evacuation EMAC train parked out of sight at the northernmost edge of the abandoned military base.

During the middle of March, his men began the tedious task of loading all their supplies and goods onto the train cars. Because of the danger of the explosives and because Major Henry had not yet finished his construction of the satchel bombs, these were being left for the last minute before the evacuation commenced. The field marshal expected the bombs would be divided and sent on their way by his many agents, around the time he would issue the evacuation order. If not, they would be hastily loaded onto the train and sent on their way later. Hans felt he'd covered all the possibilities, secure in his notions that by April at the latest, all Pytalon production would cease. By June, he anticipated being the leader of the entire world.

At suppertime on March 21, Grand Field Marshal Hans Gudrunda made a formal announcement. "Soldiers, it is time that ve move to our new base of operations. The satchel bombs are ready to be loaded and distributed. In mere days now, the world vill be rid of Pytalon, and ve, my fine soldiers, ve vill be the sole rulers of the whole world! Tomorrow, ve begin formal evacuation." A loud round of applause drowned out him out, and he stopped and basked in their show of appreciation.

He turned to the four women. "And you, my fine looking enemies, you'll not be forgotten. You'll be evacuated as well. An EMAC will be standing by to transport you to our new base of operations, since our train is already full. I must say you four have been model prisoners. However, tomorrow because of all the hustle, bustle, and confusions, I must insist you wear your gags once more, until ve get you safely to our new base. Helene, you vill see they are gagged after breakfast. Ve must be out of here by noon. Soon, ve vill be the world's new leaders. A New Age ist coming und soon!" More applause, but the four groaned. That first day wearing the O-ring gags had been sufficient for them!

At breakfast, everyone was encouraged to eat well, since their next meal might not be until suppertime. As always, the four were the last to finish eating. Helene hovered over them, attempting to hurry them up. "Come on; ve don't vant to be late," she chided them. "I have to see to the other women too, you know." Soon all four again sported the O-ring gags. "There now. No confusion from you four. Sally, you lead them to the EMAC, one by one. I vill see to the other women now. Time is precious."

Tilly rose, intent upon being first into the waiting EMAC. Somehow, she was determined to make their escape in this vehicle. With Sally's arms around her, she made her slow, cautious walk to the waiting vehicle, located in the middle of the grounds. Tilly did note it was directly opposite the building where the satchel bombs were stored. In her hobble skirt, Tilly couldn't negotiate the three steps up into the EMAC. Sally had her stand there while she headed off to get help. Before long, she returned with Major Henry, who lifted her up and into the vehicle.

"When you get the others here, Sally, come get me, and I'll lift the three others in for you, dear," Major Henry suggested. Sally grinned and gave him a passionate kiss. He headed back to the bombs, while she headed back to the three waiting women in the mess hall. It took five minutes per woman to make the hobbled, perilous walk to the EMAC. However, as Sally brought Jessica, the last woman, chaos erupted, beginning with gunfire!

The Feds finally found the base. A dozen EMAC vehicles swooped down, emitting fire from their onboard gunnery. Defenders raced here and there, retrieving their own weapons, while sergeants yelled orders. Above the din, Grand Field Marshal yelled, "To the train! Delaying fire, men. Get the bombs onboard now!"

Major Henry, seeing the arrival of the Feds and now seeing several landing with heavily armed and protected men dashing out, their guns blazing, made an instant decision. Although he had been pondering it for days, the reality of the gunfire and Feds' assault reached him. He ran towards Sally, lifting Jessica, the last of the four women, into the EMAC. "Dear, this is for us," he said and pressed a button on the small device that he held in his hand.

A huge explosion followed. The entire building with all the bombs disintegrated in a massive fireball, sending a sonic concussion wave outward, along with deadly debris. Shrapnel from the remains of the building struck Major Henry and Sally, nearly cutting their bodies in half. The EMAC vehicle rocked from side to side, knocking Jessica to the floor. Mass pandemonium erupted after that.

During the past fifteen minutes, Tilly had not been idle. Instead of taking her seat, as soon as Sally disappeared, she made her way to the driver's seat, utterly determined somehow to fly them all to safety! By the time of the explosion, she'd managed to get the EM motor running. She looked back and saw Jessica was finally onboard. When the explosion occurred, she watched in horror as bits of flying boards from the barracks killed Major Henry and Sally. She acted, pressing the Close Door button with her nose. Now they were securely inside, if only she could somehow operate the vehicle with her feet and head.

She pushed the acceleration pedal to the floor, and the vehicle lurched forward, wildly out of control, smashing into a couple of the Feds' vehicles and then part of the roof of one of the buildings. Tilly struggled with her head to get control of the steering wheel and finally pulled it back with her chin, narrowly avoiding a collision with a landing EMAC. Their vehicle swooped up steeply, climbing at its maximum speed, her boot pressing the pedal to the floor.

The flight of the EMAC was a wild one, swerving this way and that, as if a crazy person was in control. With each swerve, Tilly nearly lost all control of the steering wheel, struggling madly to regain her almost non-existent control of its path. In the passenger compartment, Jessica rolled helplessly back and forth across the floor, while Beth and Amanda struggled mightily to stay in their seats. Adrenaline flowed; they were making their escape!

After some ten minutes, Tilly finally managed to get the vehicle flying level. She yelled to the others, but only gurgling sounds echoed around the inside of the EMAC. Now that their wild lurching had ceased, Jessica wiggled and got herself to a sitting position on the floor, looking up at the white faces of Beth and Amanda. By using head gestures, Jessica finally got Amanda to lean her head down towards her.

Jessica was determined somehow to get Amanda's O-ring gag undone. If they could get their mouths free, they could use their teeth to get the cursed arm binders off themselves, freeing their hands. After many tries, Jessica finally got the leather strap wedged between her ring and teeth. A gentle tug and the strap unbuckled. One down, three to go. A few minutes later, Amanda spit her gag out.

"My gag is out. Keep it steady, Tilly. Way to go getting us out of there!" she yelled and quickly began using her teeth to undo Jessica's four head buckles. Within minutes, the three were free of the O-rings. Now they set to work on the leather straps that held their arm binders secure. Fifteen minutes later, the four were free of them at last as well. Now they carefully undid the cords that kept the lower portions of their leather hobble skirts tight, giving them much more freedom of motion. As soon as Amanda was free, she made her way carefully to the front.

She punched in autopilot, but the vehicle still had the original base as its coordinates. Thus, it began to circle around and head back. "Don't worry, we can alter course as soon as I get you freed," Amanda said to a worried Tilly. Ten minutes later, Amanda turned off the autopilot, and Tilly turned them around once more. "Where to?" Amanda asked. "Home?"

"Absolutely!" Tilly replied. "I told you I'd find a way to get us out of there. Sorry it took so long. Those were Feds back there. How the devil did the Feds find them?"

"Damn, doing anything with these overly long nails is a royal pain!" Amanda grumbled, but finally found using her knuckles worked better than trying to use the tips of her nails. "Something is not working here," she called out, panicking slightly. "It's not taking any input anymore."

"I'm losing control here too," Tilly's frightened voice added to everyone's panic. "I think the EMAC suffered some damage in the explosion."

"We're trailing smoke!" Beth yelled from the passenger's compartment. "That isn't good, is it? EMACs don't smoke." She realized that was a rather silly comment on her part. She was shook up right now. Their escape was threatening to unravel just as they had finally gotten their freedom back. Already she'd looked around the compartment for any phones or other electronic devices, but found none. Hans refused to have such things anywhere except in the hands of his trusted Gruber. She yelled to Amanda to see if there were any up front.

Amanda gave up trying to get coordinates into the geo-navigator and began looking for phones or anything that they could use to signal for help. She found none, which only added to her panic.

Tilly had been more or less flying south by east as she fled Sandpoint. Below her was nothing but rugged mountains, still snow-covered. If they crash-landed here, she'd not give much for their survival. "Amanda, look down there for some place where we can put down without crashing into the mountainside or trees or—well, you know what I mean. I think I'm going to need some help holding the wheel—slowly losing power. Damn, so close and yet so far."

"I'm looking. See if you can follow that line, whatever it is. It looks sort of flat," Amanda replied nervously. "She glanced at the geo-navigator. At least, it continued to record their position. "Hey, I think it's that ancient road, I90 on the map. Those things are supposed to be flat, aren't they?" She'd never actually been on one before, but from her history lessons, she knew at one time humans traveled by vehicles that had to run over the ground, hence roads.

"Okay, I'm turning to line up with it. Hope we can stay up long enough to clear the Rockies," Tilly said, hoping against what she'd been observing, and that they'd make it to flatter lands. In her favor was the fact that at the start, she'd been unable to control the EMAC much at all, and as a result, she'd gained quite a lot of altitude above the mountains. As the power slowly drained away, she was gliding downwards. The electro-magnetic effects still kept their descent somewhat controlled instead of plummeting like a rock.

Soon the reality they were going to crash land hit Beth and Jessica. Out of their windows, they saw the landscape rushing past them, the ground growing dangerously close to the vehicle! As fast as their long nails permitted them, they fastened themselves in with their restraining belts. Up front, Amanda secured Tilly and then herself.

"I wish I could lose some of this speed," Tilly whispered. She thought a hundred miles per hour was too fast to crash land, but she had no experience on which to base her thought. With the EM engines now totally out, there was no way to decrease their air speed, at least none she knew about. "Brace yourselves. We're going to crash soon," she yelled.

Wham! The EMAC struck the grass-covered ancient concrete road. Enormous sparks followed in their wake, as the metal belly of the craft skidded along. Like sandpaper, the concrete ate through the hull as though it were made of wood. Fortunately, there was nothing onboard an EMAC that would ignite and explode, excepting the interior and themselves that is. The jar of the collision threw them all forward. One by one, they blacked out from the concussion of the crash. Their EMAC skidded along for nearly five hundred feet before coming to rest. Smoke rose from the abraded metal hull, followed by the hissing sound of melting snowflakes. The late winter blizzard chose this moment to begin in these parts of western Montana.

Chapter 16—Juan Carlos

Twenty-six year old Juan Carlos was a hunter by nature. When he was in his teens, his parents had finally been taken by the psychs in Missoula, implanted, and dosed with Pytalon, turned into *useful members* of society, a doorman and a maid. Juan rebelled and lit out for the safety of the rugged mountains of the Lolo National Forest and Clearwater National Forest. For several years, he lived a hearty mountain man style of life, learning to be wholly independent and off the grid. Some five years ago, he'd moved back into the abandoned ranch home in which he'd grown up. The psychs and the authorities had long ago forgotten he even existed, much to his pleasure.

Then one day not long after he reappeared at his old home, an Englishman dropped by, altering his life. The man called himself the professor and made him an offer he couldn't refuse. More than anything, Juan wanted to stop the psych men from ruining the lives of others, though at this point, he couldn't have found lives to save anymore. All those isolated farms had years ago been converted. Still he wanted to do what he could, and he became the professor's eyes in and around Missoula. It was just after noon, and he sat on a sofa, awaiting the promised blizzard. While smoking his pipe and occasionally sipping his strong black tea, Juan reflected on just how successful he'd been. He'd managed to get twenty of the brighter young teens out of Missoula and into the safety of the professor. Juan really didn't know where the teens had been taken, only that they were safe.

Suddenly, he heard a banging noise followed by a hideous scraping sound. True, it was soft, but nothing besides the crackling of his wood burning stove broke the stillness of his ranch. He quickly put on his heavy fur coat and hat, donned his gloves, and headed outside for a look-see. Far to the south, he saw faint tendrils of smoke drifting among the snowflakes that had begun descending. "Must be down by the old road. No one ever goes there. I wonder what has crashed there. Guess I'll go see." He saddled up his horse and galloped due south down the long dirt lane that led from the ranch house down to the old weed-covered Interstate road.

He reined in and rapidly dismounted. "My god, it's an EMAC!" He looked around but saw no one. Believing someone was inside, he pried the damaged door open and peered inside. To his utter amazement, he saw four EE women. None had any coats, and they wore strange looking apparel, he thought, but then he'd never actually seen one of these exotic women personally, only pictures on the Internet once in a while. All were unconscious, faint trails of blood lined several cheeks. He backed out, looked around, and decided he had to help these women. However, the blizzard would soon be on them, and they had no warm coats to wear. Thus, he remounted and galloped back to his ranch.

Hastily, he hitched his horse up to his small wagon, loaded it with several blankets, and headed back to the crash site. When he returned, the blizzard had picked up steam, but the women were still unconscious. One by one, he picked each woman up and carried her to his wagon. There, he covered them up. Five minutes later, as visibility began to shrink noticeably, he headed back to his ranch house, about a mile further north, cradled against the sharply rising mountains.

Once there, he carried each woman into his ranch house. He decided to put them all on his parent's old bed. It was large, and there he could tend to their wounds. Five minutes later, they were lying side by side. Juan then handled his horse, making sure she had enough hay to ride out the blizzard snug in the dilapidated barn. Once inside the ranch house, he heated up some water and gathered what medical supplies he had. "I hope they're not seriously injured," he muttered to himself. "In this blizzard, I can't get them into Missoula and the hospital." Carefully, he began wiping the blood off Tilly's forehead. She'd taken a nasty knock to her head when the EMAC first hit the ground. Amanda, likewise.

As he did so, Tilly stirred. "Oh my head. Oh! Who are you? Where are we? We crashed." Her hands went up to her head, but she felt something warm. Pulling her right hand back, she saw red.

"Nasty knock on your head, miss. Are you all right otherwise?" Juan said rather meekly. He had seldom been around women and none his own age, not for years now.

Tilly felt herself a bit. "Yes, sore, but only my head. I think I'm all right." She noticed the others lying beside her. "Are they okay?" she whispered.

"Don't know. You were all unconscious when I found the wrecked EMAC. Here, hold this cloth to your head until the bleeding stops, and I'll check on the next one," Juan suggested. She did so, rolling slightly to see Amanda who was lying next to her. She was also bleeding from a head wound. As Juan wiped her forehead off, Amanda groaned and came too. Again, he asked her to hold the cloth while he moved around the bed to get to Beth next. Fortunately, Beth and Jessica were only knocked out. Their safety harness had protected them from serious injury, but they were a bit sore.

"So where are we? Who are you? We crashed," Tilly asked him, as soon as Jessica revived and appeared otherwise okay.

"Juan, Juan Carlos, miss. I heard your crash and found the four of you unconscious. There's a blizzard going, so there is no way to get you to the hospital in Missoula. I brought you here to my ranch house in my horse-drawn wagon. You landed on the ancient Interstate road just south of here, about twenty some miles west of Missoula, Montana."

"Oh. Okay. Thank you sir," Tilly replied, still somewhat dazed. She tried to sit up, but her head throbbed.

"Take it easy for a while. No one is going anywhere probably for a couple of days, miss. Why did your EMAC crash? Who are you anyway? Heading to Missoula? Helena, perhaps?" Juan asked and suggested.

"It got caught in an explosion and damaged, but we were able to escape in it. We're just trying to escape. We've been held prisoners for months," Tilly explained, still holding the cloth to her head. "I'm Tilly Hickory, my wife, Amanda Wales Hickory. Our best friends, Beth Snells and her wife, Jessica Walsh Snells."

"Holy crap! You're the ones we've been looking for—for months now! Unreal! The professor has been having everyone search high and low for you four! Wow! I looked all over this whole area and didn't find you. I have to let the professor know you're safe here with me. Incredible! Hang on. I'll get my cell!" A very animated Juan dashed out of the bedroom, returning shortly, already talking with the professor. "Yes! Yes, I found them. They crashed landed an EMAC just south of my ranch and in a blizzard, sir. Okay, I'll put Beth on."

He looked slightly confused, "Er, which one of you is Beth? I don't have your names straight yet. Sorry. All this has me slightly befuddled."

Beth grinned and took the cell. "Professor? Yes, we're alive and well, we think. Very long story and a bad one. We've overlooked another renegade band who were behind the Pytalon sabotage, and worse, they were about to bomb all the plants worldwide. The Feds found them and us at an abandoned army base north of Sandpoint, Idaho, we think. No, don't panic yet. During the Feds' raid, we got one of the rebel men to blow up the bombs, so no immediate threat." She put the phone on speaker.

The professor replied, "Thank god you four are alive and well! Bloody hell, I have had every person I could find out looking for you these past months. No one found the slightest trace. We began to believe you were murdered and your bodies dumped somewhere. So what's with all this Feds' action? What the devil happened to you in the first place?"

Beth sighed. "Long story. I'll let Tilly tell you." She handed the phone carefully to Tilly.

"We were successful in locating the clamps on the liquid Pytalon lines there in St. Louis," she began. She talked for nearly twenty minutes, outlining the key things that had happened and that they had observed, making sure he had the names of the key personnel. "Yes, he is running a manic trigger, calls himself Grand Field Marshal Hans Gudrunda," she carefully explained, spelling out the German name. "Yes, he doesn't want anything to do with anything electronic in nature. He's completely off the grid, but he does have one electronics man, Gruber Dichts." She continued her lengthy explanation.

"Yes, professor, we were incredibly lucky this time. Hans thinks nothing of torturing and murdering men, but he has this thing about women and married women. That alone saved us, but," she began relating how they had been treated, hobbled and constrained for months.

When she finished, the professor said, "Okay, you rest up and hunker down there. As soon as this blizzard passes, I'll send an EMAC for you. I'll have our medical staff at the ready to check you out. We can discuss this new radical group more completely when you get here. Put Juan back on, please." She handed the phone to Juan, nearly dropping it, for her nails had grown some these past months. Theirs were now approaching seven inches, making most everything rather awkward to do.

"Yes, I'm here professor," Juan spoke up.

"I want you to take the very best care of those four. Guard them with your life. They're the most valuable four mates in our whole group. I'll be sending an EMAC as soon as the weather clears, but that is likely to be a couple of days. Lord knows, this bloody insane field marshal might come looking for his prisoners. Do not let them fall back into his hands, son. I'm assigning you to be their personal bodyguard from now on. Well done on rescuing them."

"Yes, professor, I will." He hung up and looked at the four. "You're that important? Aren't you some of those exotic escort women? I don't understand, but I will guard you with my life."

"Yes, we are officially EE women, but we're married and no longer in that trade. I guess I can tell you a bit more," Tilly replied. "I am called Wart and Beth is Weasel, Jessica is Shifty Eyes."

"No! You're teasing me now, right?" Juan looked somewhat bewildered. "You can't be Weasel and Wart. They're the most famous of all us in the resistance movement!"

"Sorry to disappoint you, but that's who we are," Tilly replied, growing a little testy. "You expected men, right?"

"Well, now that you said so, yes. I've always heard they were men, not women, and certainly not exotic escorts," Juan readily admitted. "That's what everyone has always said, that they were fellows."

Tilly sighed. Beth decided to break the ice some. "We were, Juan. Tilly and I. We were Tim and Ben, but we were caught and implanted by the Feds as EE women, even though we still had our manhood intact. We were left in limbo land—half and half. We didn't really have much of a choice except to get the sex change completed. While we looked female outwardly, the moment we spoke, our voices sounded deep and male, giving us away. Honestly, we didn't have much choice."

"Incredible. I'm sorry. I didn't mean any offense. Shoot, you're the most important people in the professor's whole group. You're famous. Everyone knows of your exploits. Truly, I'm sorry. I didn't mean any disrespect, misses. Trust me. I'll guard you with my life, but nothing is going to be happening until this blizzard passes. It's a whiteout outside."

"Thanks, Juan. We appreciate everything you've done for us. Right now, we'd rather like to take a long hot bath and get out of these awful clothes," Beth thanked him and suggested what she most wanted to do just now. Her corset was binding her, and she desperately wanted out of the leather hobble skirt and ballet boots, which she'd been forced to wear for nearly twelve weeks now.

"Well, like I said, I'm off the grid, but I can heat up the wood water heater. There will be enough for one tub full in about a half hour. Will that do? Do you have clothes and women's things with you? I admit that I didn't search your EMAC. If so, I'll go back and see if I can find the vehicle in the blizzard and bring you your things," Juan replied.

"No, we've nothing. They took our purses and destroyed our cells when we were captured. We've only got these horrid clothes," Beth lamented. "No chance of getting into Missoula and finding a women's clothing store that is open is there?"

Juan grinned, "Afraid not. Look out the window. It's early afternoon, but you can't see anything at all. Blizzard is raging. I'll see what I can find of my shirts and pants that'll fit you. Honestly, misses, I've never been around women much, so I really don't know what all you might need. I guess you'll have to ask, and I'll see if I have them. While the water is heating, would you like a dark chocolate bar? I have plenty. I'm sort of a chocolate freak," he grinned sheepishly. They did, and he was pleased they seemed to enjoy them as much as he did.

They helped each other to their feet. "How can you possibly walk in those?" Juan asked, lending an arm as well.

"Very carefully and slowly," Jessica answered. "Once you get used to them and your feet and leg muscles strengthen, they aren't so bad on smooth, level surfaces. I had to wear them for eight years a while back. It took forever and a whole lot of pain to get my feet adjusted to wearing normal EE women's heels. Now thanks to Hans, I'm probably back to square one and have to endure it all once more. Thanks for your steadying hand. They are supposed to be the sexiest heels for bedrooms only."

"Well, they certainly are that," Juan agreed with her.

When the tub was full of steaming, hot water, all five crowded into the small bathroom. "Juan, this is embarrassing, but could you please undress us?" Jessica asked. He did so, but was floored by the sheer size of their breasts. "Go ahead and look at them, Juan. It's all right. They are huge. With the EE women, apparently one size fits all. We've noticed all EE women have the same sized breasts, humongous, but we find them rather sexy too," she flirted a little with Juan.

Juan laughed a little. "Well, from what little I know, you exotic escort women are supposed to be the sexiest and prettiest women in our insane society. You're certainly that and then some. Very pretty. I'll leave you to your bath and see if I can find some shirts and jeans that might fit you. Socks too. Maybe some of my boots will fit as well," he suggested hopefully. They thanked him and took turns in the tub, with those outside the tub assisting them.

"Damn and double damn," Amanda said, finally able to examine her feet. For the past several months, she'd had to wear the boot constantly, even while sleeping. Now she could look them over carefully and was shocked. The others, seeing her feet, began a close inspection of their own. Something was terribly wrong with them, their toes seemed all bunched up and didn't move at all. "I'll never be able to get my feet flat or even into regular heels," Amanda moaned. All four had a sickening feeling, but got on with their baths, hoping the warm water soaking would do their feet some good. Their hair needed a washing as well, including the two wigs worn by Tilly and Beth. Their own hair was now shoulder length and both decided to stop wearing the uncomfortable wigs from now on. They reasoned their hair looked presentable.

When they had all finished their long, soaking baths and had pat-dried their hair, Juan reappeared, loaded with clothing. "Will you help us dress, Juan? We will have a hard time with our nails, you see," Jessica flirted with him a little.

"Sure. I rather figured you might like some help. These are all I could find. Need to dress warmly; this ranch is rather drafty." He helped each woman into one of his tee shirts, but their overly large bosoms only seemed to be greatly magnified in them. Rather than wear their dirty panties, they opted to take his suggestion and don some of his underpants.

"I never thought that I'd be wearing these again," Beth joked, as Juan slipped them on her. He grinned. The heavy cotton long sleeve shirts fit fairly well, but the jeans were made for a man's body, not theirs. With a belt, they at least stayed up and were warm.

"Now for your feet, misses," Juan said. "I brought some heavy cotton socks for you and some of my boots for you to try, but your feet—they look strange. Are they broken? I mean your toes."

"Ah, maybe that's what happened to them," Jessica realized. "We can't bend them in the slightest. It's like they are frozen en pointe," she explained, but had to explain the term. "I had ballet lessons when I was a young girl." Juan tried to flex her toes, but came to the same conclusion. "I'm afraid we're going to have to put those damnable boots back on, but let's wear these nice warm socks, gang."

Now clean and dressed, they were hungry and followed Juan on a brief tour of his old ranch house. "I'll rustle up some grub," he suggested. "Flapjacks, bacon, eggs do for you? All I have to drink is tea. I carry that with me when I'm in the back country."

"Sure, we're hungry and will eat most anything. Want us to help?" Tilly volunteered.

"Can you get around enough?" he asked, looking at the four standing on their toes.

"Well enough on flat surfaces. We'll set the table," Amanda suggested. "Use those dishes?" She pointed a long nail at the old corner cabinet.

Juan laughed. "Sure. Those used to be mom's dishes, before they took her away, implanted, and drugged her. I've not used them, since it is only me that is ever here. We should use them to celebrate your escape." She grinned. Slowly and carefully, the four set about setting the table for five.

"Don't you have a girlfriend, Juan?" Amanda asked, after finishing and sitting down.

"Nah, I don't want one of them zombies around. Besides, I spend most of my time out in the forest. At one time, I was going to be a park ranger, that is, when I was in high school. I'm a darn good hunter and gatherer. This bacon comes from a wild pig I shot and butchered last year. Excellent bacon, if I do say so myself."

"So you're an independent, self-sufficient man? You do everything for yourself?" Amanda asked, becoming curious about him.

"Yes, sort of a backwoodsman. Like I said, I'm off the grid. The professor gave me this cell phone, but I don't use it much. I have to sneak into Missoula from time to time to find an outlet to charge the darn thing. Avoid detection. I sure as hell don't want to get implanted and drugged into a mindless zombie. No way. I'll fight to the death to prevent that and to prevent others from getting it done to them as well." He was quite vocal about this point.

The meal turned out to be excellent. All four women complimented Juan on his cooking. "If you come live with us, we'll make you our permanent cook," Amanda teased him.

"Well, the professor said I'm to be your bodyguard from now on. I suppose he means for me to accompany you wherever you go. I don't mind cooking, especially for four gorgeous young women, famous ones at that," he teased her back. She grinned.

"Darn, I hate to do this to you, Juan, but with our nails, we can't easily help you wash the dishes," Beth spoke up, as they rose from the table. She had wanted to contribute something.

"Well, if you can manage to walk them into the kitchen, I'll wash them up while the tea kettle is coming to a boil. Perhaps you can make our tea?" he suggested.

A half hour later, the five returned to his spacious front room, the four sitting beside each other on the couch. From here, they could hear the wind howling outside and even felt some drafts coming in. All were thankful for the warm clothing. Juan sat in a wooden chair across the room, his teacup beside him on the floor. He spoke up, "Misses, I hope that you don't mind, but usually around now after supper, I play a little." All four shook their heads no, but wondered just what he meant by that!

He picked up a long hollow tube with holes in it and began to blow into it. The sound was mellow in the alto range. Suddenly, Beth spoke up! "That's La Follia by a guy called Arcangelo Corelli! Extremely ancient music, right?"

Juan stopped playing and stared at her in amazement. "Why yes, that's what it says on the music paper. I found a pile of discarded music and these things, recorders I think they are called, in a dumpster in Missoula. The psych men dumped out all the contents of the library there, making it their Implant Station some years back. I salvaged some and sort of figured out how to play these. I have two, this one and a smaller one. I didn't think that anyone knows music any longer; it's been dead for a century or more."

"Well, I certainly do, Juan! I have a huge collection of ancient music at my place, but I prefer even older music. Medieval, I believe it's called. Go on, please, please play some more of that!" Beth exclaimed. Then she asked, "I've never seen a real musician before. Is it hard to learn how to play?"

"Nope, real easy like. Fingers cover the holes. I bet you can play some, even with your long nails—well maybe not the real high notes because you have to kind of cover the bottom hole half-way, sort of. I'll play some and then you can try it, Beth. I've never met anyone who knew anything about music. I thought that it was as dead as our insane society out there,"

Juan suggested.

Later, while Beth tried her hand on the recorder, Juan added, "I found some other musical instruments over the years, rummaging in the trash in Missoula. I have this one, which I think is called a violin, but I have never been able to figure this one out, so I stick to what I can play. When you are all alone like I am, a little music is really nice."

For several hours, Juan played some of the songs he knew, and Beth continued to practice with the smaller recorder. Eventually, she was able to pick out a simple early music tune. "This is super cool, Juan! Thank you, thank you. Make darn sure that you bring all these with you if you are tagging along with us!" Beth gushed. She couldn't recall even being quite this happy about music. "I can actually play it a little, me, Beth, me play music! Incredible!"

Amanda yawned. "We should get some sleep. It's been a very hectic day for us all. Where are we to sleep, Juan?"

He led them to his parents' bedroom. "I've got this room with the big bed and my room. I suppose I can sleep on the floor and let you use my bed too," he volunteered.

"You'll do no such thing, Juan. The floor is cold. My toes tell me that much. No, we four can squeeze into this one. You sleep in your bed, please," Beth insisted. Juan helped the four out of their jeans and long shirts, but suggested they sleep with their tee shirts on. None disagreed, for it was chilly in the room, especially with the blizzard howling outside. He also helped them out of their boots and tucked the four into bed. He left a lantern burning as a nightlight for them and retired to his own room.

Tilly commented, "My head hurts a little." None of the four realized fully what their slight headaches were indicative of—not yet.

They awoke to the smell of breakfast cooking. The room was quite chilly. The fire had gone out during the night, and Juan had relit it, but the cold was still present. Hastily, the four dressed themselves, helping each other into the shirts, jeans, and finally their boots. "Morning, Juan," Beth called out, as she made her careful way into the kitchen. She definitely liked this man, perhaps because he was able to make music and the kind she loved.

"Morning Beth. The snow has let up some, but the wind is still blowing strong. There will be rather large drifts, I expect. We'll be housebound today for sure. Maybe tomorrow it will let up. Tea is ready there if you can manage it."

"I can. We're not helpless, Juan, just have to go slow, easy, and careful like. Thanks for fixing breakfast. I'll take some more lessons on the recorder, if you don't mind," she suggested, hoping that he would agree.

He turned and smiled, "You bet!"

As they ate, he asked, "Since we're all cooped up here today, do you all play cards?"

"What's that?" Amanda asked.

"Another ancient relic I found in a Missoula dumpster." Later, he taught them a card game called Canasta. The four found they really did enjoy playing a game.

"You know," Amanda said between deals, "I've never played a game since I was a very little girl and then it was only dolls having a tea party. This is great fun. I wonder how many other fun things have been lost in our society out there. I'm going to have to ask the professor when I see him next if he has some more history books on games."

As they turned in for the night, Beth said, "Juan, thank you. I have never in my life had as much pure fun as I have had today! Incredible what we've all been missing. Of course, you don't know you're missing it if you've never had it—these games and music and all. Thanks."

Juan looked very pleased. "I haven't had so much fun ever. So thank you too, Beth." He grinned, and she leaned over and gave him a kiss on his cheek. He flushed. Once more, the four retired for the night with a slight headache.

After breakfast, Juan's cell rang. After he hung up, he explained, "The EMAC will be here in about two hours. That was the professor. I'm to pack what I want and follow you four wherever you go. Oh yes, and bring all my guns," he chuckled. The four helped him pack his things into four large duffle bags. One contained guns, knives, and related items, impressing the four.

The EMAC arrived right on time. Juan had just finished phoning a friend to check on his horse occasionally when the EMAC touched down. The four couldn't walk in the deep snow, and Juan carried them to the waiting vehicle, where two men with guns were waiting. Then, he loaded his bags and waved farewell to his ranch house.

A few hours later, the EMAC landed in Phoenix, where the weather was a balmy seventy degrees, most welcome by the four. As Juan lifted them down the three steps, the professor came running out to greet them. "Blimey, you four are sure a sight for these eyes! I had almost given up hope you were even alive! I've had a hundred men out looking for you all over the world." He hugged each woman tightly in turn. "Come on in. I see Juan's clothes look appealing on you," he managed a little tease.

"Warm and comfy," Beth teased him back with a wry wink, but that low-grade headache had returned.

"Aye, let's get your feet tended to first, then we need to sit down with the others and have a very long talk," he ordered.

An hour later, the resident doctor looked at the eight x-rays and shook his head sadly. "This is a disaster, women. Look, you can see the damage for yourselves," he suggested. Even the professor looked at them too. It was as Jessica had suspected. Subjected to the constant wearing under those tortured conditions, the bones in their toes had broken in several places and had now more or less fused together, nicely healed, but . . ."

"So what can you do for them?" the professor asked.

The doctor shook his head. "Nothing, I'm afraid. Well, we could amputate their toes, but would that really help them? Then they really would be hobbled up, I'm afraid. We'd have to take too much of the other bones as well. Unless they simply can't get by wearing their boots, I wouldn't recommend amputation. Save that as a very last resort."

"It's okay, doctor. We can manage. We have done so for months. Besides, I did for eight years. I'd rather wear these boots than lose my feet," Jessica replied. The other three nodded, but didn't try to say anything; their emotions were too close to grief.

Heading off to the big meeting and briefing allowed them to focus on something other than their own feet, thankfully. As promised, Juan accompanied them wherever they went, including sitting in on their lengthy meeting, which lasted far into the night. During the long meeting, all four women's headaches returned, but they still didn't know why.

"So when we get back, we're going to research these men in depth. In addition, we'll start monitoring all possible abandoned military bases, see if we can locate them, and then keep an eye on them. We simply can't allow them to blow up all the Pytalon manufacturing sites," Beth summed up.

"I'll work on gathering men to go after them," Bill Smyth promised. "We've recently acquired a supply of guns, so those won't be a problem for us now. You find them, and we'll see if we can handle them."

"Right. And I hope you four don't mind, but I insist that Juan here accompany you from now on. He is to be your bodyguard and helper. I insist," the professor demanded.

"Oh, that's perfect with me," Beth shocked him. He'd expected the women to protest rather significantly, and he was prepared to outline a dozen reasons why they should accept him as their bodyguard. Instead, he shook his head, somewhat bewildered. Beth didn't explain. *Best to leave him a little mystery,* she thought.

When the meeting ended, Lisa arrived along with Greg, who had his arm lovingly around her waist. She was as bubbly as ever. "Oh hi everyone! I am so glad to see you four again. Everyone has been looking for you, and some thought you had been killed, but I told them nothing could stop Weasel and Wart. Gee, what happened to your clothes? You are wearing men's."

One by one, the four gave her a big hug, but she interjected, "Oh, you have to hug Greg too. We're married now. I was going to hold off and have you four be my bridesmaids, but I couldn't wait." After congratulations, they gave Greg a hug as well.

Lisa continued to chat furiously, "You should see the four-wheeler that Greg fixed up for me. I can drive it now. One foot controls the acceleration and braking, while the other steers it. He lowered the steering mechanism too. I need it because I have twenty saunas all over Phoenix going now—lots of patients are lined up to become toxin-free. Of course, there is a whole world of Pytalon infected patients out there, and I don't see how I can handle every one of them though, but I keep very busy at it. Greg's doing all sorts of inventing too. When you all disappeared and no one could find you, he set to work on figuring out a way always to be able to find you. Tell them about your RFI tag thing, please. I don't quite know how it works."

Greg fumbled a little and then tried to explain, "In ancient times, the doctors who look after pets, such as dogs and cats, had these tiny chips they would insert painlessly into a pet. The little chip contained things as the pet's name, their owner, and address. That way, if the pet was lost, anyone with a bar reader could pass it over the RFI chip and read out the information."

He continued, growing more animated. "So I took it one step further. We couldn't find you to come and help you because we didn't know where you were located. I devised a tiny geo-locator beacon. It can be inserted into say your shoulders where no one can see it. If you go missing again, I can send out a signal to the many geo-synch satellites up there and that will activate that tiny transmitter, and we'll know where on earth you're located to within five feet." Greg smiled confidently and added, "The only drawback is its tiny battery life is only a few hours, so we'll have to be quick about it or turn it off frequently."

The professor spoke up, "Ladies, I wish you would consider having these put in your shoulders. We don't want a repeat of this bloody mess happening again. Please."

Tilly sensed he was near to begging them. "Well, it does sound highly practical. Since I'm out and about the most, I should take advantage of this, don't you think?" She was thinking along other lines, though. In the future, she could purposely be captured and thus lead their men straight to their captors. "But how close to me do you need to be to activate it, assuming that I get kidnaped again, Greg?"

"Not a problem really. The signal is sent from one of the communication satellites. Although one of them only covers a portion of the world, it would only take a few tries to have sent the activation signal to all corners of the world. It is really fool proof, as long as the battery holds out."

"Okay then, let's do it. I think this is a wise precaution to take, all things considered," Tilly declared, rubbing her forehead again. Her headache was growing slightly.

"Great! Maybe Lisa can take you to the store and you can get some dresses and things while I make the preparations," Greg suggested.

"Okay sounds great. Oh!" Tilly exclaimed, suddenly realizing the true source of her headaches. "Gang, our headaches are coming from our implants. Wearing men's clothes violates the dictates of the implants! Duh! How stupid of us not to have spotted this before."

"But I thought you said you weren't bothered by them," Juan asked, slightly confused. "I thought the darn implants were a permanent thing. So I guess they are?"

"Well, permanent for most," Jessica relaxed. Tilly was right. This was the source of her low-grade headache. "My technique desensitizes them drastically, but it doesn't get rid of them entirely. EE women are implanted to always look their very best at all times, you see. We've not been following that dictate for what, three days now. So that's why we've had these mild headaches; the implant is trying to force us to conform. Juan, if we were fully under the effects of the EE implant, we would never have been able to wear your jeans and shirts for ten minutes. We would have gotten total migraine headaches and simply had to change clothes."

"I think I see. A mild headache isn't so bad then, I guess. And Lisa is an EE woman too? You look so different," Juan replied.

"Oh, that. Birth defect, nothing more. I just use my feet. Come on; let's do some shopping. By the way, Erika and Ilse said for me to say hi for them. They are running the saunas for me right now. When they finish up, they'll try to join us, that is, if you're still here," Lisa chatted away.

"Before you ladies get involved in your shopping," the professor spoke up, "be prepared to leave for East Peoria just after supper. We're taking no chances. We're going to EMAC you back. They'll go at top speed and travel during the night hours, just in case this field marshal fellow is somehow on to your location right now."

"Okay, makes sense. We'll hurry up," Tilly replied.

As the five headed off to go shopping, Lisa commented, "Darn. I was so hoping you were able to wear men's clothes. I've tried wearing some of Greg's cool shirts and jeans too. They are far more comfortable and certainly practical, but I kept getting headaches until I changed back. I guess that's still not going to happen, darn." All five chuckled.

An hour later, as promised, Ilse and Erika joined them. After exchanging warm welcoming hugs and kisses, they chatted furiously, trying to make up for lost time. A little later, Erika said, "Well, Tilly, I agree, you do look much better wearing the corset beneath your dresses. You too, Beth." The two had been experimenting with them. After three months of wearing them, both women had grown used to them and didn't like their lack of proper curves when not wearing them. In the end, both women decided to continue wearing them to keep up the disguise.

"You should get a good supply of the boots, though. We heard about your feet. News travels fast here in Phoenix, especially when it concerns you four," Ilse explained. "You should get only the ones that have a solid steel shank and heel. They are covered in leather, so of course the metal isn't visible. It's just the steel heels almost never break on you. They come in colors to match your gowns too. I think you would look good in a light blue, Beth. Let's see." The group continued shopping. By the time they finished, they had each picked out another half dozen dresses and a dozen different boots, some to match gowns they had back at their safe house in East Peoria.

They returned just in time for supper, which they ate hurriedly. The professor was most insistent they get underway by eight. All were now properly dressed in satin gowns with matching boots. Ilse and Erika had also applied a bit of makeup to each, and their headaches had vanished entirely. Of course, Juan was rather shocked when he first saw them returning. "Holy cow! You look—well, fabulous, gorgeous. Wow," Juan exclaimed, almost speechless. The four grinned, flirting with him slightly.

As they finished eating, Greg arrived and gave each a small *shot* in their left shoulder, injecting the tiny microchip. "There you go. Now if you get kidnaped again, we can find you very fast." He felt very proud of his contribution, and the four gave him a hug and kiss, causing him to blush rather pronouncedly. Lisa giggled.

After saying their farewells and watching Juan and the two drivers loading their new purchases onto the EMAC, they made their slow way to it, allowing the men to lift them up and into the vehicle. After waving one final time, they took their seats, and Juan strapped the safety harnesses for them before doing his. Slowly, the EMAC rose silently into the nighttime sky and then rapidly accelerated to its maximum speed, heading directly for East Peoria. The five dozed; they wouldn't arrive until around five in the morning.

Chapter 17—Threats

The EMAC rose into the still dark morning skies, though the first hints of twilight had appeared in the eastern skies over Peoria. The five and their many bags were standing just inside the abandoned warehouse. Rusting junk lay all around this apparently tattered ruins, slightly dismaying Juan. "Come on, Juan. It's this way. Like our disguise?" Tilly asked with a wry grin. She'd noted his confused face.

They walked to an apparently blank wall, confusing the young man even more. Then, Tilly presses a hidden button, and the wall slid open, revealing a stairs that led to their underground safe house. "This is the stairs, but let's take the elevator today. Too much stuff and going down stairs is now way too hard for us." The elevator was next to the stairs, and they loaded their many bags into it. "Over there hidden beneath the tarp is our EMAC bus," she added.

"Wow, this place is huge. Look at all the computer things!" Juan exclaimed. He'd just walked into their main computer center, off which side rooms held their bedrooms, kitchen, bath, and Tilly's workroom.

"We left it all on standby mode," Beth explained. "As soon as we store these things and show you around, Jessica and I have tons of monitoring to catch up on—duh, like three months of it!"

"This is Amanda's and my room," Tilly continued showing Juan around. "This is Beth's and Jessica's room. The bath, the kitchen, and panty. That's Amanda's and my workroom. Gang, we have a problem! Where are we going to put Juan? We're out of rooms!"

"Hey, we can give up our playroom back of the kitchen. Perhaps, Juan can clean it out and make that his space," Beth suggested, thinking fast. She almost said Juan could sleep with her and Jessica, but flushed and thought better of that idea, wondering what was coming over her anyway.

"Sure, any old place is fine for me. I've lived in far, far cruder places than this. This place is more like a heaven to me. After I get it fixed up, can I lend any of you a hand? I just can't sit around doing nothing," Juan replied.

"Are you any good with math?" Tilly asked.

"Er, not too good."

"Okay, oh, say, you're a hunter. You can help Amanda and me. We have to work out some prediction equations on Grand Field Marshal Hans Gudrunda and his associates quickly. Given them, we can then try to predict his next moves and could use your hunter instincts in the study," Tilly suggested, and Juan agreed. They all set to work as Beth proudly got her music files playing once more. Juan grinned, tapping his hands together in time with the ancient music. Beth flashed him a smile as well.

On one monitor, Jessica replayed the last three months of surveillance video at a high speed, using the motion detector program. If someone came wandering into view of the cameras, the program would detect the image changes and alert her. By evening, she announced their place remained undisturbed during their three-month absence, comforting to all. Beth had a ton of messages waiting for her and many she had to handle. The Wolf had sent her a goodly number; even he was trying to locate her. She sent him a lengthy reply.

Mid-day, Juan and Tilly left to get groceries. All theirs had long spoiled. Juan merely dumped them on their ever-growing garbage pile in the back of the warehouse. This also gave Tilly the opportunity to show Juan around the city. "Usually, I'm out wandering at night, but we'll get you used to the city first. I'm glad you're with us, Juan. In these boots, I'm severely limited now, so I hope you don't mind if I lean on you for support."

"Of course not," he replied. "I'm doing something very useful for the cause. It beats wandering around the national forests." Tilly couldn't imagine why anyone would want to do that, but wisely said nothing.

At suppertime, they compared notes. "We've got a basic set of formulas worked out for Hans, but they'll need refining before they'll be useful," Amanda explained. "Give us a few more days work on them, and then we'll bounce them off Juan. How about you two?"

"Got caught up on the many messages. All has been rather quiet, except for the Feds. I've just begun to go through their latest message database. They've been focusing all their efforts on tracking down those responsible for the sabotaging of the Pytalon plants worldwide. As far as I can tell, they have arrested ten men, but are hunting for another twenty or so. Give me a few more days too, and I'll know more."

Jessica spoke up, "I've been searching for other abandoned military bases in the country. I've pulled up dozens of them, scattered all over the place. Somehow, we've got to find a way to monitor all them in hopes of finding Hans and his army."

"Any casualty lists for the Feds raid on the base where we were at?" Amanda asked.

"Not yet, I'll look into that first thing tomorrow," Beth replied. "How about a relaxing card game, everyone?"

The next day, Beth reported Hans and most of his men had escaped the Feds' assault, but fifteen men and one woman had been killed. That provided more impetus for Tilly and Amanda to get their prediction equations worked out. Later that day, they found Juan's insights invaluable in refining their basic formulas. He was a hunter and so was Hans, though he was now on the run from the Feds, if only briefly.

With Beth's help, Jessica set up an automatic image retrieval program that captured satellite images of the various bases she had on her watch list. Several times each day, when the satellite was in position, it relayed a copy of the ground images to Jessica's computer. Now all she had to do was to study them, looking for signs of activity.

Later on, Beth discovered the Feds too were monitoring abandoned military bases similar to the one north of Sandpoint, Idaho. That factor was then input into Tilly's prediction formulas. At supper, Tilly explained their preliminary results. "There's a fifty percent chance Hans has gone into hiding for the time being. There's a fifty percent chance he has sent out agents to steal more explosives. There's also a fifty percent chance he is searching for us, gang. I don't like that last one much. I've had all of Hans I care to have. Oh, there's also a thirty-four percent chance he is stepping up his recruitment to replace his lost men, but there's only a ten percent chance he is really on the run. He is too well organized to let one Feds' raid trouble him much."

Juan spoke up, "Tilly, we had best take care and avoid the public eye in this city. If he is after you, he knows Beth and Jessica were somewhere in the Peoria area and probably assumes you and Amanda also live here as well. If he is looking for you, he probably has agents out there in the city looking for you."

"Damn!" she replied, knowing he was quite right.

"Say," Beth continued her reporting, "on the EE Women's site, they have put up an announcement saying the EE women are now being married off. You were right. With there being no *normal* men to hire their services, they're now accepting marriage offers. Plus, any man can request his wife become an EE woman to serve him better. Fat chance that will amount to much. The zombies hardly even notice their wives."

"Yes, but who is this Petra Delius?" Jessica asked. "She has been sending us a lot of messages. I've not had time to check on her. Is she perhaps related to the Feds Peter Delius?"

"What? Let me check on her right now," Beth said. Shortly, she had pulled the woman's official photo off the Chicago EE women's web site. "Oh my god, it's him, er her, Jessica!" All four stared at the image. There was no mistaking her identity.

"Who is Peter Delius?" Juan asked.

"He was the head of the Chicago Feds and who tried to take over control of the world. He is the one who had Beth and Tilly implanted as EE women when they were still men. I got him back and had him implanted as an EE woman, just as he did to Ben and Tim," Jessica explained, relating more of the story for Juan's benefit.

"So she's back. I bet anything she's after revenge," Tilly remarked.

"That's just great. Now we have two enemies that are after us," Beth grumbled. Just then, her cell phone vibrated. "Hang on, got to take this—a text from the Wolf." A moment later, she added, "Make that three enemies after us. The Wolf just sent me a head's up warning. He's learned that agents of the European assassin known only as Persephone have been making inquiries about Weasel and Wart. Plus, this past week, they've added Shifty Eyes to the search."

"Just great. Who the devil is this Persephone?" Jessica asked, frustrated. She'd never had enemies before and now had three after her.

"Don't know. I've never heard of her before," Tilly answered.

"I'll research her now," Beth said, rising carefully to her toes and moving in her usual carefully placed steps to her computer array. An hour later, she reported, "Awful woman. She's on the German Feds most wanted criminal list, Persephone, the Assassin. Apparently, she is responsible for the assassination of twenty men and women—people in power, it seems. No one knows her identity, where she lives, or how to contact her. Somehow, she has been building up a network of spies, according to the German Feds' site, but they don't know the actual numbers, only a collection of rumors. Why put rumors up as facts? I surely don't know, but that's the Feds."

"So this assassin is after us too? What on earth for?" Jessica asked.

"Well, her name is appropriate. Persephone means human killer," Amanda spoke up. "Learned that in one of my history books in high school."

"I've no idea why a German assassin is after us," Beth replied, "unless she has been hired by either the Grand Field Marshal or Petra Delius. I'm inclined to suspect the latter, since as a top Feds, Peter Delius obviously knew about this German Persephone assassin."

"I guess the professor was wise in asking me to be your bodyguard," Juan spoke up. The four women smiled and agreed with his assessment.

Then Beth sent a text to Ilse Kunegunther asking her if she had ever heard of this Persephone assassin. She hadn't, but had once met an EE woman named Persephone, obviously not the person Beth was interested in discovering. With no other leads, Beth had to set the matter of the female assassin aside for now.

The next day, Beth got another tip from the Wolf. She followed the Internet link he sent her, and then gasped. "Oh no, big trouble is coming! Shades of hacking past!" As quickly as they could, the others joined her, looking over her shoulders and resting their hands there as well to help maintain their balance.

For the benefit of Amanda, Jessica, and Juan, Beth elaborated. "This was my first major hacking assignment for the professor, some seven years ago now. Back then, one of the Feds got this bright idea to implant an ID computer chip in everyone. His proposal would allow the Feds, via any geo-tracker, to pinpoint the precise location of any person in the world, as well as identify who they were. Of course, the zombies had no opinion on it whatsoever, but all those who weren't implanted and on Pytalon saw this as the worst possible threat. If that program ever got off the ground, the entire game would be over quickly. Thanks to my hacking, I convinced them that no one had the skills to invent this new microchip. All the chip designers were on Pytalon or so I claimed, pretending to be an authority. It worked, and the whole project got shelved."

"But apparently, it didn't completely go away. It has taken the zombie chip designers seven years to invent the necessary microchip prototype. A company in Germany has finally come up with it and is asking the Feds for financial backing and support. At least, the zombie Feds are stalling. I suspect they have forgotten all about it and are having to rethink that project. This is super critical, gang. I'm going to have to closely monitor the Feds' discussion on this and maybe even do a little hacking. Jessica, contact the professor by cell and tell him this really bad news," Beth asked. She turned and saw four pale faces. They knew as well as she that if this program were actually implemented, it would mark the end of everything. No one could ever hide from the Feds or whoever had the remote sensing devices. Well, with the field marshal, that might be a good thing, she thought. Still, if it was truly implemented worldwide, all resistance would effectively be ended, and the population of the world would forever more remain in their zombie state. Grim.

Juan suggested, "Hey, if this really happens, you four are welcome to come back to Montana with me and disappear off the grid completely."

Beth stayed up late that night writing up a formal response. The device must be extensively field-tested, she wrote, thinking that would slow things down a bit. We don't have any significant problems with the people who have been implanted and/or are on Pytalon. What's the use of wasting time and effort and credits on them? None that I can see. The people in whom we want this microchip are the rebels. If we can't find them in the first place, then how are we going to get these microchips in them? Yes, after we capture them, we could insert the microchips, but why? We just send them to the local psych men for implanting and a goodly dose of Pytalon and they are handled, that is, if we don't shoot them in the first place. I can't see the value of this project, but only a great waste of our resources.

There, she thought, that should give them something to ponder. After reviewing it, she hacked into the Feds' email system and sent a copy to all the major section heads, pretending that the sender was one of their own. That man would have a little explaining to do, she thought. But then again, if her message was taken seriously, he might not. She then sent a private copy to the Wolf and the professor before turning in herself.

In the ensuing days, Juan continued to explore the city as well as bringing back needed groceries. In addition, he picked up packages at the Peoria Drop Box containing the new electronic devices Beth ordered to replace those that they lost when the field marshal's men kidnaped them. A hunter by nature, he kept his eyes alert for trouble. Although he was in a city, prey was prey, only in reversed roles—the women he was sworn to protect were the prey. More than once, he spotted men who were covertly watching the various zombie women as they walked on the streets. While EE women were rather rare, whenever one did appear, he noticed these men paid extremely close attention to her. Their actions left no doubt in his mind they were looking for the four women, but were these the field marshal's men or were these Persephone the Assassin's men or perhaps were they Petra Delius' men? He couldn't tell which.

For a while, he toyed with the idea of confronting one of them and prying it out of the man. He rejected this because he would then have to kill the man to prevent becoming a target himself, being watched, or killed. No, protect the women was his charge. All he could do was watch and wait as the days led into April.

The passing weeks added more data to Tilly's behavioral model of Hans Gudrunda. She and Amanda raised the chance that Hans had gone into hiding up to seventy percent, while lowering the chance to steal more explosives down to thirty percent because none had been reported stolen. It was the no-data data that altered the percentages. However, they had to raise the chance he was searching for them up to eighty-five percent. She'd have to wait for more data from the professor to revise the recruitment percentages, though. She couldn't go out into the cities and look for herself, not with three threats against her.

By the second week in April, Tilly had to revise the chance he was searching for them to one hundred percent. Beth finally got in a new supply of her spy vid-cams. She pinned one onto Juan's coat before he took his daily stroll around the city. When he spotted the men who he'd earlier observed watching for EE women, he pointed the camera at them, giving the four a good look at the men's face. They recognized one of the soldiers that had been dining in the mess hall with them. Now there was no uncertainty left. For whatever reason, Grand Field Marshal Hans Gudrunda desperately wanted these women back. "Maybe they'll eventually give up and leave the city," Beth suggested hopefully, watching the man on her screen.

"I wouldn't hold your breath," Tilly groaned. "I feel like a rat in a cage, which is my own home. Oh now what?" she exclaimed as her cell phone vibrated. She dropped it, misjudging it with her overly long nails. She cursed and squatted down to pick it up, an even more awkward movement for her or the others for that matter. "I've about had it with these nails, pleasure, or no pleasure." Amanda gave her a rather dirty look, though.

"Well crap. It's that darn assassin again. Now she has my EE cell number."

"What's she say?" Amanda asked, suddenly growing worried. Even Beth and Jessica stopped what they were doing to listen to Tilly's reply.

"She sent a text. Reads: Tilly. PLEASE—all in upper case letters. My god, she doesn't have to scream at me," the highly annoyed woman grumbled before continuing. Please answer my calls. *Well, Persephone, I sure as hell am not going to answer them!*

Her phone vibrated again. "Crap. This woman doesn't give up. Now she says, You have something of mine and I want them back. Answer me. What does that mean?" Tilly exclaimed, shrugging her shoulders.

While the others began to discuss what they could possibly have that belonged to this notorious assassin, her phone vibrated yet again. "Now she says, 'Look, I am an assassin. If you do not pick up and answer me right now, I will most assuredly come and assassinate you and then pick up what is mine that you have!' Crap. I suppose it won't hurt to at least talk to this crazy woman," Tilly sighed, resigned to hearing what she had to say.

"Put her on speaker phone and keep her talking while I trace her location," Beth advised, cranking up her tracing program.

Tilly complied. "Okay, okay, Persephone or whatever your real name is. This is Tilly. What do you want?" she growled into her phone.

"Well it's about time. Now then, you and your wife and friends have some things that belong to me, and I want them back," a woman's rather mellow voice echoed in the room.

"Duh, I don't think so, lady. We've never met you, so I don't see how we could possibly have anything that belongs to you," Tilly retorted.

"You do. You got them last Thanksgiving from a Feds leader called Peter Delius. I believe he gave them to you around that time. Didn't he give you each a set of long, dangling diamond earrings, very expensive ones?"

Tilly actually blushed. "Oh, well, yes, he did. We each got a pair. Why? How do you know that?"

"Damn bastard stole them from me in October. He left a note saying he would return them in December. Nope, the thief certainly didn't. He's totally disappeared! It's taken me a damn long time to trace what happened to them. The trail leads to you and your wife and friends. Now don't you tell me you don't have them and have sold them? I've been monitoring the jewelry markets, and they've not appeared anywhere in the world. Earrings this expensive have to be validated through the Amsterdam Jewelry Exchange, and they haven't. So I want my earrings back."

"Okay, okay, he did give them to us. We still have them, but we don't wear them. They are so heavy they nearly pull our ears off," Tilly replied, exaggerating slightly. Persephone seemed to calm down, as far as Beth could tell. She seemed relieved to hear what Tilly was saying.

"Good. As long as you return them to me, I won't have to kill you."

Beth signaled Tilly that she had a lock on Persephone's location. On the monitor, she could see Amsterdam and watched as Beth's program rapidly zooming in on the phone's exact location. What the four didn't know was at that same instant as Beth precisely located her, she had precisely located them.

"I'll arrange for a courier to pick them up from you. The courier will arrive and say to you: 'Flowers bloom in the spring.' You are to reply: 'Tulips are best.' Then, you hand the courier a pouch with the four pairs of earrings in them. No questions asked and no problems. The courier will arrive around noon day after tomorrow. Thank you and goodbye." Persephone hung up.

"What? How does she know where to send the courier? I didn't give her our location," Tilly complained. "Bet she has to call back for it."

"Oh crap!" Beth exclaimed.

"Oh no, she traced your call like we did hers!" Jessica gushed with a sudden realization. "She knows where we are—

right here!"

Beth typed away and turned, "Yes, tomorrow noon will give her just enough time to get here from Amsterdam. Damn, damn, damn. Our safe house cover is blown and to a known assassin too!"

"We could go to our Chicago penthouse. We should be safe there," Jessica suggested.

Chapter 18—Confluences

Peter Delius, the head of the Chicago Feds and recently the head of the entire Central US, lay on a soft bed with satin sheets. His body felt very strange, but his mind was quite foggy. For a moment, he tried not to move. The steeled, veteran combat man struggled to remember where he'd last been. A vague image appeared. Yes, now he remembered; he had the two top EE models from Europe and his four meddling EE women. Yes, it was his sadistic party. There they were, totally bound and helpless, plying their wiles on him. He was sipping a fine wine.

Wham! The implant kicked in. Pain, drugs, and words. His mind replayed the words precisely. "My body is hypersensitive to sensual touches." On it ran playing out the usual EE woman wording, finally ending with, "I must not forget these words. If I fail, I will get an intense migraine headache."

Helpless to avoid it, Peter found himself repeating these words, over and over. His mind was a grey fog. *How long have I lain here?* He finally collected his will power and tried to move. *Oh, the satin sheets! How sensuous they feel. What's this?* His hands felt his now enormous breasts, as were all EE women's breasts—the convenient one size fits all. He poked himself accidentally with his now two-inch, bright red, painted nails. He screamed, but immediately began reciting the litany once more, shocking himself further. He could not stop himself! "My body is hypersensitive to sensual touches." The words just came out of his mouth!

His screams brought an EE woman scurrying into the room. "Hello Peter. I'm your temporary nurse and educator. Your conversion has gone perfectly as they all do. All is just right, according to your specifications. Now just relax. It does take some healing and recovery time. I'll have you up on your feet in a few days, and then we can get you looking just perfect. Here, take this," she explained, forcing a couple of aspirin-sedatives down his throat. Soon, Peter dozed, but had an awful nightmare. He was a half-woman creature struggling to live.

He awoke to find the nightmare had become reality! Again, he involuntarily repeated his litany. The strange, but beautiful woman reappeared. He felt an uncontrollable urge of passion for her and tried his best to pull her down into bed with him. "There, there, we can have some fun later, Peter, but first we have to get you looking your best."

"Oh! Yes, I simply *must* look my best. Please, I don't know how," Peter found himself saying, but couldn't stop himself. He watched helplessly, as the delicious woman dressed him in a silken slip, a garter belt, black seamed nylons, silk panties, a slippery red satin gown that came down only to his knees. He wanted to protest, as she began slipping the black knee-high ballet boots on his feet, but found his head seemed to split as he tried. He fought hard from having an awful migraine headache. As he relaxed a little and stopped protesting, the migraine vanished as suddenly as it had appeared! Next, she glued a long, black human hair wig on his head and brushed it out. Finally, she applied the usual somewhat overdone makeup most EE women wore.

"There you go, Peter. Now, you look perfect, stunning, if I do say so myself. We EE women must always look our very best at all times. Now, we can hug," she declared, rubbing him sensually with her hands. Most willingly, he responded.

"Now we need to get you up and about. Don't worry. It does take quite some time to get used to walking on your toes, but a good EE woman learns to manage it," she explained. Thus began weeks of torture for Peter Delius.

In his few lucid periods of sanity, he tried to fight against his conversion, but always such efforts ended in splitting migraines. His feet throbbed, ached, and cramped mercilessly, but he found he had no choice but to bear it and continue walking in them. After two weeks, he was able to get around barely, but was able to handle his own dressing and makeup, which he attempted to keep to a minimum.

"Lenora, I can't live like this," he tried to explain to his EE nurse and educator three weeks after his implant. "My voice gives me away. I'm a freak! I don't dare go out in public."

"Well, yes, I was afraid this might happen, Peter. Most that get this sex alteration implant get it fully done, not partially, as you requested. I'm not even sure why they allowed you to go only halfway."

"But I want it undone," he pleaded, fighting off another instantly arising migraine.

"Silly, the implant won't allow it. Some have tried, but they eventually killed themselves. Their headaches were just too debilitating. I would recommend visiting the clinic and getting the rest of your body converted." Peter was shocked to hear her saying this—lose his manhood—lose it forever, becoming a woman? Horrors beyond horrors, and to be an EE woman as well! Even this mental reaction brought on another splitting migraine, and he had to sit down fast. After another day of this, Peter realized Lenora was right. He couldn't get the operation undone; the implant would literally kill him. He had only one choice open, the clinic. Lenora, kindly, made the arrangements for him and even helped him to the clinic, since he was still only barely able to walk by himself.

***

On January 1, the start of the new year 2271, Petra Delius took very slow, carefully measured steps into her old apartment building. Several delivery zombies followed behind her, carrying all her new clothing and supplies. Lenora had been kind enough to assist her in purchasing a satisfactory new wardrobe. The clinic had officially changed her ID card to Petra Delius, and she still had access to her vast fortune, less the conversion fees the clinic charged her and the EE store, whose bill equaled that of the clinic, much to her amazement. Until now, she had no idea how expensive it was to be an EE woman. Well, we have to look our best always, she justified irrationally and involuntarily.

Once in her own apartment, she collapsed onto her sofa, her feet throbbing from such a long walk here. Dozens of packages lay piled on the floor, left there by the deliverymen, who continually muttered, "Sanity is doing a good job."

Right from the second day, she'd managed to stop taking Pytalon, which was the only redeeming feature she had. At least, she wasn't a mindless zombie, endlessly repeating those words, she thought. "No, I repeat even worse things," she said to her walls in disgust.

Disgust. That was what she felt when men looked at her. She was supposed to flirt with men and women. Well, she loved women, especially beautiful women, but men utterly disgusted her. Yet, her implant drove her to behave just the opposite! It was nearly driving her nuts.

During the next few days, she pitched all her men's clothes, though not before trying to wear them, only to get a splitting headache when she did. At last, she realized because of the implant, there really was no going back to her former life as a man and a powerful one at that. She was stuck being an EE woman for the rest of her life—all thanks to that damned EE woman, Jessica!

Jessica! Oh, how she hated that woman for what she'd done to him, the most powerful man in the US! She focused on her alone because of the six women he had at his Thanksgiving party, she was the last one he remembered seeing. Her face was up close to his just before he blacked out. Then, he remembered Ben and Tim and that he'd done this very thing to them! Hatred swelled in her.

"How could that bitch do this to me—to me!" she shrieked. For days, she fumed and even went so far as to bring up Jessica's EE woman's page to stare at the reviled face of the woman who had done this despicable thing to her. After a time, she realized Jessica was officially married to Ben, who now was being called Beth. The other EE woman, Amanda, was married to Tim, now called Tilly. Petra sank back in her chair. She realized she had done this very same thing to Ben and Tim, the wives of the woman who in turn had done it to him.

It finally dawned on Petra that Jessica had done this to her for revenge. She imagined Jessica sitting back reveling in her victory over Peter. "How sweet her revenge must be to her," she whispered solemnly. Unfortunately, Petra found herself once more repeating her implant litany to herself. When she finished, she again swore vengeance against the woman who had done this to her.

During January, she lived as a hermit in her fancy apartment in downtown Chicago, overlooking the frozen Lake Michigan shoreline. Each day, she fought against the almost overpowering urge to go out on the streets and hook up with anyone, man or woman. The only temporary relief she had was to excite her own body with her fingers or her woman's toys, a parting gift from Lenora. It dawned on her she was supposed to be out there in the world making her sponsor sexually pleased. This, she couldn't stomach, unless her sponsor was female. During that month, Petra only had a tenuous hold on her life, miserable as it was.

By February, Petra had longer lucid periods where she could think somewhat, though she was forever repeating her implant litany, much to her continual dismay. No matter what she tried, she simply couldn't stop herself from periodically reciting the words she'd come to detest. Still, during the clearer portions of the day, she began to realize the sheer magnitude of what she'd lost. She or rather he had been the sole leader of the

Central US with plans to take over the other two thirds from their top Feds leaders. Now that was gone. Even her robust body had been undergoing subtle changes. Though at first she tried to exercise to keep her strong arm muscles, that soon failed. Migraines always forced her to stop. Gone, gone forever—the finality sunk into her very being by mid-February. Petra cried for a long time; her grief seemed endless.

She stared for hours at the images of those who had done this to her. Finally, hostility replaced her grief. "I must get revenge on her, on them. Wait! They've gone missing? What? They can't just disappear on me, not until I get back at them!" she called out angrily to her computer monitor. Again, she was overwhelmed by her implant, watched herself reciting the damnable litany once again, and then dealt with her perceived heightened sexual needs.

A while later, Petra's mind calmed once more. "Don't get excited. I think that brings it on or aggravates it," she cautioned herself. "I still have all my knowledge and clearances." She logged into Peter's account and rapidly searched for information on the four women. A half hour later and a dozen variations on search parameters, she finally found one tiny entry. An agent had reported various men were searching everywhere for the four. That was all she found. She cursed the Feds.

However, she had come across many entries on the sabotaging of the numerous Pytalon plants worldwide. At last, this caught her attention, and she dug into the voluminous reports. After some digging, she came across the initial entry that had triggered all the action. The underground renegade known as Wart had put them on to the fact that rebels were blocking the plastic flow pipes that fed liquid Pytalon into the injectors. Further, this Wart suggested the renegades had murdered the original inspectors and substituted their own men, who had then done the sabotage. Subsequent memos outlined the truth of his assertion. Each plant was inspected and the clamps found and removed. "So this Wart fellow was on our side, how interesting. I thought that he was an enemy of the state. Hum."

Next, she read dozens of memos concerning the *fake* inspectors. A dozen had been captured. Intense interrogation failed to reveal much, except for one name, Grand Field Marshal Hans Gudrunda. Here Petra paused and did a parallel search on the man, but discovered little about him. He'd gone off the grid after a failed implanting session over thirty years ago. Back to the trail of memos, she went, curiously following the trail left by the men she once led.

"At least, they're still able to do their jobs, though implanted and drugged; albeit they're terribly slow at it," she whispered. She continued to read, noting the Feds had launched a worldwide search for this field marshal. Unfortunately, they had no real leads yet. She did note the captured renegades were subsequently re-implanted and put on heavy doses of Pytalon.

Petra's curiosity was pricked, and she continued to monitor the progress the Feds were making on locating the insane rebel Gudrunda. She noted they had properly placed three squads of heavily armed Feds on alert for instant deployment when the rebel's location was uncovered. "Good. Kill them all," she swore at her monitor. "Patience, Petra; they're just terribly slow because of the Pytalon. Crap, I was the one who got them on the drug in the first place. This is my fault they're taking forever to track this traitor down. Shit."

For a time, she felt humbled by the far-reaching effects of what she'd done. "Well, we didn't know he existed back then," she justified her actions, but it didn't set well with her.

Then came the pivotal day. The Feds had discovered their location at an abandoned army base north of Sandpoint, Idaho! She hacked into the video feed coming from the field units as they deployed, wishing with all her might that she could have been there with them, flak vest and heavy weapons at hand. Just imagining herself there brought on an instant migraine, and she stopped that quickly and began pleasuring herself, which turned the headache off almost as fast as it had turned on. She whispered another curse and contented herself to watching the live video feed.

As the EMAC vehicles approached the complex, she became engrossed in the operation. "By the book, guys, by the book," she called out to the screen as if she were right there giving them their marching orders. She ignored the re-growing headache. Gunfire erupted and the chaos of battle commenced. As the vehicle she was monitoring landed, she spotted another EMAC sitting in the middle of the open area surrounded by the barracks.

"Wait! Look there, isn't that one of the women? I recognize her! There they are. Oh my God, they were being held there, prisoners. Look at their condition. Ballet boots, hobble skirt. Their arms, oh—somehow tied in that thing—they're helpless. Oh, I do like those gags, though. Serves them right. Wait, I see, this Gudrunda fellow is taking the women away with him! You can't do that; they are mine to torture!"

The massive explosion startled her, and she blinked several times. The screen went blank for a time. Petra fiddled with her computer, but it was working. The video feed had been temporarily knocked out. After a frustrating few minutes, the video returned. She saw the EMAC with the women taking off in a wild, crazy motion. The furry of the battle was focused elsewhere towards the northern edge of the base where an EMAC train was just departing. "Damn! He's getting away. Show me the vehicle with my women!" she yelled at her monitor.

Finally, she got a faint view of the dizzying distant path the vehicle was making as it left the area. The Feds didn't pay it much attention, focusing on the train, securing the facility, and rounding up stragglers. "Well, they got away, damn, damn, damn."

She calmed down and watched until the feed was terminated. If she wanted to learn more, she'd have to wait for all the after-action reports to be filed. Instead, after saving key parts of the video on her computer, she pondered what she had learned. Bringing up the images of the three women standing beside the vehicle, she smirked. "Now that is good bondage. Serves them all right for what they've done to me. Bitches." Her head throbbed, and she backed off, taking a deep breath and slowly letting it out. "Don't get emotional," she whispered to herself. Unfortunately, she then found herself reciting her implant litany once more.

When she was back in control of her thoughts again, she admired the three hobbled women. "What does this rebel want with my women?" she wondered. "Why should this man who is off the grid want to capture and torture them? Have they pissed him off too?" The more she pondered this mystery, the less it all made sense. Clearly, he was going out of his way to take them with him as he evacuated just ahead of the Feds' assault, but why? She had no answer.

As she studied the after-action reports the next day, she again cursed. Both the vehicle with the women and the train had eluded them. Their location was now unknown once again. "Well, if I'd been there, this wouldn't have happened," she spat at her monitor and just as quickly regretted her emotional outburst. Her head began throbbing mercilessly, and it took her a few minutes to get back in control.

Time passed. Then, she discovered somehow the four women were back, freed from their captivity. "How? How? How?" she cried out. "Their arms were bound; they were wearing these awful boots and a hobble skirt no less. They were gagged nicely. How in heaven's name did they get out of there? Oh!" She suddenly put the crazy, wild path the vehicle had taken together with the fact they'd escaped. Now their erratic flight made sense to her, although she hadn't the faintest idea how they could possibly have flown the EMAC the way they were bound.

Out of curiosity, she began sending them email messages using their EE women's page addresses. She didn't expect to hear back though, but immense pleasure flooded over her by just letting the four know she was still alive and after them once again.

Not long after that, she got another scare. She received a message from the EE Women's Association. Because there were no *normal men* left to be their sponsors, the remaining registered, unmarried EE women were going to be married off. Petra panicked at the thought of being forced to marry some man. She found even such thoughts repugnant and fought her ever-increasing migraine as it turned on. "Now what the hell do I do?" she muttered, holding her head from the pain.

She pondered her fate for the next few days. At last, the only solution she could tolerate or even desire would be to marry another EE woman, if she could find one who was willing to enter such a marriage. Ordinary women would not, of course, she reasoned, unless by some accident she could find a lesbian. How to find someone occupied her thoughts for days.

Then Petra realized she had put Ben and Tim in this same exact position: men turned into EE women, who in all likelihood found men disgusting as sex partners. She cringed at what she'd done to them. Now that she faced it herself, she felt humbled for the first time. Sympathy for her two victims was an entirely new emotion for Petra, and for a time, she didn't know how to handle it. Part of her wanted to get even with Jessica and the others for what they'd done to her, but at the same time, they'd merely done to her what she'd done to their men, ruined their lives utterly! Somehow, her own desires for revenge seemed terribly petty to her right now. Emotions. Petra was flooded with emotions, most she'd never felt before. "What is happening to me?" she cried out, frustrated beyond belief.

***

It was May Day. She'd not been out of her apartment since she first returned her after her surgery in January. She was too afraid to go out; she could just barely walk. Again, she checked her EE Women's email site to see if there was any help coming. She'd already received four offers of marriage to unknown men. These, she hadn't even bothered to answer. "Oh my God!"

A new email had arrived from Grand Field Marshal Hans Gudrunda himself, but perhaps one of his cronies had posted it, she thought. It read: Miss Petra, I have an opening in my organization for an EE woman such as you. My men will satisfy your every need and then some. Room and board is free. Looking forward to having you join our staff. Hans. She shrieked, and then calmed down.

"Here is the very man that we, er I mean the Feds, are looking high and low for, and he wants me to become a prostitute for his soldiers! How utterly disgusting! Wait! What should I do about this email? Should I let the Feds know about this? Maybe we can lay a trap for him and apprehend the insane criminal. Crap, the Feds. If I go to them, I don't think I can bear the utter humiliation when they see what I've become! Oh God! What do I do? He can find my address here, come, and kidnap me if I refuse him. Oh no!" Petra felt sheer panic sweeping over her entire body. She shivered and tried to take calming breaths. Then she realized if Hans had any powers of observation, he would realize that from her facial features she had been Peter Delius, the top Feds. He'd surely torture her; she'd be prime enemy number one, ignoring her sex change. He would likely show her no mercy whatsoever!

As fast as she could, which was pathetically slow, she gathered up all of her various guns and knives, placing them at strategic locations around her apartment. Finally satisfied she could get to one quickly enough, she relaxed a little, but fastened one onto her waist anyway. As she caught her breath, she realized guns would do her no good if they broke in during the night while she slept! Her panic returned.

Hobbled by the boots she had to wear, she couldn't run from them; she could barely walk and then only slowly and carefully. No longer could she put up much of a physical fight, but would have to rely upon her guns. "Ah, I can sleep in a closet. I need to make some booby traps that'll alert me to an intruder," she declared and set about inventing them. By suppertime, the traps were set, but she broke down into another emotional fit of crying. "I'm not even safe in my own home."

Her own words hit her like a solid slap in the face. "Good God! I—the head of the most powerful soldiers on the planet, the Feds—I can't believe I'm not safe in my own home! This is utterly ridiculous, but it isn't, is it? Women aren't safe from the ravages of men, are they? Damn, damn, damn. She found herself starting to recite her implant litany again and forced herself to say sarcastically, "No, we're supposed to look our best, to look pretty, all the time. Crap. But that's what I've become! I won't be helpless, I won't. She tried to stand up defiantly, but nearly lost her balance on her toes. "Hell, I sure as hell am that and then some!" She sat down instead.

It struck her she'd done this very thing to Ben and Tim, turned them into relatively helpless women. For the first time in her life, Petra felt the pangs of real guilt for what she'd done. "What have I done to those two men? I take it back. I take it back. I didn't mean it, not really," she wailed.

After a moment, she calmed down and explained to her walls, "Well, I did mean it actually. I don't know why I did it, but at the time, I did mean it. It's just I didn't really understand what I was really doing to them. It does serve me right, Jessica. I, I forgive you for doing this to me."

"Oh get a grip on yourself, Peter, er Petra," she talked to herself. "Well, I would make it right with those two men, but that's not possible. Implants are permanent. They are just as screwed as I am. No, I'm screwed worse. They're married to a pair of beautiful EE women. They aren't facing being married off to some unknown man." Again, Petra felt sorry for herself.

Sometime later, she again looked at the video cam's images of the three standing beside that EMAC there in Sandpoint, Idaho. "My god, they were abused by this Hans fellow. It's horrible to have to wear these toe boots all the time, but they had their arms bound and wore gags too. And those hobble skirts. Hans shouldn't have done that to them, not to any EE woman. Oh, not to any woman, period. If he's looking to find them again, there's no telling what Hans would do to them this time or me, if he comes after me, and he will, if I answer him and tell him no. I just know he will. Doomed. We're all doomed." She sat back and sighed, again a feeling of hopelessness swept over her, filling her with an emotion she'd never felt as Peter.

Again unwillingly, she found herself reciting her litany. Once she finished, she felt a little better. Protect and serve. Suddenly for no apparent reason part of the oath Peter had sworn some thirteen years ago when he was sworn into the Feds came into her mind. She chuckled sarcastically, "Well, I sure failed at that, didn't I. Power corrupts. I was corrupted. No, that's not right either. I did it to myself. I might as well be honest with myself. I had a taste of power, got carried away with it, and screwed up big time. How did I miss detecting someone as awful as this field marshal fellow?" She had no answer for that question and soon gave up thinking about it.

A novel idea struck her, "You know, there are no checks and balances. As the top leader for the Central US, I could and did any darn thing I wanted to do. There was no one else to answer to. Now that is an interesting thought. No checks and balances are anywhere in our world, nowhere. The top person can do as they please. Somehow, that's not right. Everyone should have some check on their powers. Interesting notion, but useless now, Petra. Get back to the serious problems at hand," she chided herself.

Still, she couldn't get her mind off the four women. Something continued to gnaw at her. Then, it struck her. If the women had escaped from Hans and since he really wanted them prisoners for some unknown reason, then certainly he would try to recapture them. Perhaps he already had, she mused, since she hadn't received any answers to her many emails to the women. No, if she were Jessica, she'd not even deign to reply. "She's justified in ignoring me," she sighed. Still in her fragile mind-state, Petra began to believe the four women were in serious danger from Hans, just as she was, and this began to eat at her.

Since the hour was getting late, she double-checked all her guns, made her pathetically slow way into her bedroom, and then crawled into her clothes closet, pulling a blanket over her, hiding her from view. She took out her pistol and kept it in her lap. If they broke in, she'd not go down without a fight. Her headache rose, but she ignored it this time. She slept ill.

In the morning, Petra once more had to order in some breakfast. Now she began to worry. What if this Hans fellow substituted one of his henchmen to bring her breakfast, disguised as the deliveryman? When the Pytalon drugged man arrived, whispering, "Sanity is doing a good job," she had her gun in one hand ready to shoot if necessary. The deliveryman didn't even perceive her gun, however.

As she ate, she decided she was being paranoid now. She wasn't going to let this rebel Hans dictate her life for her. "I have to take a stand. If this Hans kills me, then so be it. At least, I'll be done with this nightmare of mine. Hell, maybe I can kill him first. I am or was a Feds. Heck, I've not abdicated my position, not really. This world will be a far better place with this Hans eliminated, that's for sure." She ignored the beginnings of a migraine as she said this.

"I'll take one bag with me, along with my purse. Let's see how many guns I can secret away in this space. They might find one gun in my purse, so I must have others where I can get to them." With a steeled purpose in mind now, Petra began packing a bag with some of her clothing and two pairs of her boots. She found she could easily conceal a revolver in each of her boots. That made four. Another she wrapped up in a dress, laying it on top of the boots at the bottom of the bag. Before long, she had what she thought she would need for at least a week. After that, either they were laundered or perhaps Hans would provide her with a new wardrobe. After stowing yet another gun in her purse, she felt ready to face him.

She sat down at her computer and finally replied to his offer of employment, stipulating she had to bring along one bag of clothing. Would he provide more? She sat back, took a deep breath, and hit the send button. Now all she could do was wait. As far as she was concerned, this Hans fellow was as good as dead. It would be him or her, she thought, but this nightmare had to end soon. She couldn't take much more of it.

"Apparently, he or someone in his employ is monitoring the email system," she said softly. A new email had just been posted to her account, and she saw the sender was the same. It read: Excellent! Bring your bags. I'll have my man pick you up at your place at noon? He'll provide lunch for you during your short trip to my barracks.

"Well, he is all business." She sent back an acknowledgment and then realized she had been right all along! He had not asked for her address. Thus, he knew where she lived and could have kidnaped her any time he desired! She shivered a little, and then sighed. "Well, perhaps it'll play out better if it looks as if I'm doing this willingly instead of being kidnaped." She hoped this would be the case. Petra triple checked her things and then sent off a new email. Satisfied, she sat patiently waiting for noon to arrive.

Precisely at noon, a well-dressed soldier arrived at her door. "Miss Petra Delius?" he said formally and politely when she opened the door. She said so. "Very good. Grand Field Marshal Hans Gudrunda sent me to bring you to him. I have lunch prepared on the EMAC."

"Excellent, sir. There is my bag, but I'm afraid I'll need your arm to walk. These boots make walking most difficult, sir," she smiled at him and wondered why she did that. She couldn't flirt with men. Women, most assuredly, but not men. She or he never found men remotely attractive to her or him. She was momentarily confused sexually. After picking up her bag, he put his other arm around her, steadying her. Despite her misgivings, she found walking much easier with his support, but hoped they didn't have far to go.

His vehicle was parked just outside the front entrance of the skyscraper in the passenger pickup zone. He politely helped her up the three steps, where another woman sat waiting. "Hello, Miss Petra Delius. I am Helene. Grand Field Marshal Hans has sent me along to keep you company and help you with anything you might need on the short trip to his barracks. I have prepared a delicious lunch for you. Please, sit, and help yourself. The fruit punch is most excellent," she explained.

Petra noticed she had traces of a German accent. Still she was an EE woman, though she must be in her fifties, Petra thought. After being seated, she smiled, and sipped the offered punch. "My, it's quite delicious," she replied. "I do hope I'm not inconveniencing you too much. Hans needn't have sent you. I'm sure the driver..." She felt woozy, a little light headed. Then, all went dark. Petra passed out.

Helene caught her head, preventing it from landing in the middle of the food on the small table in the passenger compartment. The driver stepped back and quickly dumped the food into a garbage bag and got out their needed equipment and supplies. Once Helene declared all was ready, he followed her orders, as they prepared Miss Petra Delius. All the while, the EMAC drove on, following the previously laid in autopilot course.

***

Lady Persephone Briton was thirty-one, extremely fit, agile, very intelligent, and very, very dangerous. Her alias

Persephone, the Assassin, was well known throughout Europe, as was her trademark, the Ace of Diamonds card, which was always found lying on her victims. From her point of view, she claimed no one paid any attention to just who her targets had been. She considered herself Persephone, Righteous Vigilant. Well, someone had to be in these insane times, she reasoned.

Lady Persephone was the great-great-granddaughter of Lord Briton, who had made a vast fortune nearly two centuries ago by making the electro-magnetic motor commercially viable on a worldwide scale, revolutionizing travel. Something of an historian, he had built a replica of an ancient Welsh castle on his estate in southwest Sussex, England, just outside East Horsley. Within the stone walls, he had also amassed thousands of books, music CDs, and movie DVDs, at the time when they were being discarded wholesale at the beginning of the psych implanting and Pytalon era.

As the only child of Lord and Lady Briton, Persephone spent her childhood immersed in these relics of antiquity. Later, they moved to Amsterdam, or rather her father Lord Briton was ordered to go there. She was too young to realize just why they had moved there, but she was all too keenly aware of her parents after that. Both had gotten implants, and Lady Briton had become an EE woman that much she knew. Lady Persephone got a quick education into the horrid effects of this psych duo on people, her parents. She swore never to take awful drug and to avoid being implanted herself. This she managed to do until she was twelve.

When she learned Lord and Lady Briton had given their zombie consent to have Persephone converted, the twelve year old managed to flee Amsterdam, taking up residence at her family's castle in Sussex. There, the castle stewards, Jones and Eliza Edwards, zombies themselves, took care of her basic needs.

Enamored with the antiquities stored in the many studies of the one hundred-room castle, she began training herself, using the old ninja and martial arts movies as her substitute teachers. Seeing these men and women apparently flying and defying gravity, as they launched their spectacular attacks, she was determined to learn how to do these as well. She had no knowledge that these were stunts done with nearly invisible wires supporting them. Rather she assumed with enough practice and skill, she too could execute them.

Thus, during her teen years, she spent hours practicing her martial arts, ignoring the bruises that came with it. She became expert with the pair of Japanese swords, whose names she didn't know. Persephone also spent hours studying normal subjects as well. From her years in Amsterdam, she was fluent in German, Dutch, and French, as well as her native English. Her skills also included sleight of hand. By eighteen, she was a master of disguises, the bag lady being her favorite. That is, she would don the clothing and appearance of a fifty-year-old Garbage Collector Twentieth Class, the lowest of the lowest in their society. No one ever paid the slightest attention to those men and women who roamed the back alleys of the cities scrounging the garbage for useful items that could be salvaged and taking them to the recycling centers.

At eighteen, she adopted her Persephone, the Assassin, the Righteous Vigilante, role. Why? The Edwards had been lucky enough to be granted the right to have one child, a girl Mary Beth. While she was rather uncomely, she had a bright mind. When Mary Beth was twelve, a *normal* executive of the local Pytalon plant had her abducted, and then he raped her repeatedly, satisfying his lust for young girls. When Mary Beth was finally returned to the Edwards, she was a different person entirely, withdrawn and even suicidal. The psychs quickly implanted her and heavily doped her up on Pytalon, turning her into a mindless maid. The Edwards were devastated by all this, never recovering, eternally in the lowest throws of apathy.

Lady Persephone waited for the Feds to arrest and implant the perpetrator. It never happened, and at last, she took matters into her own hands. Using her many skills, she stole into the Pytalon plant and slit the throat of the man who had done this to defenseless Mary Beth, leaving the first of her Ace of Diamond cards on the man's chest. Thus, she began her long career as the Righteous Vigilant, though the rest of the world knew her only as Persephone, the Assassin. Until now, no one in the world knew the identity of this assassin, but she was greatly feared and on the European Feds' most wanted list.

If Lady Persephone had any vices, it was her love of diamonds. Her great-great-grandfather had left her a vast collection of some of the world's finest pieces, including the four sets of matching earrings. Back then, Lord Briton had made a web site displaying many of his finest pieces. In October, Peter Delius came across that page while searching for suitable, exciting EE women for his planned party at

Thanksgiving. After seeing these huge earrings, he sent a formal request to Lady Persephone requesting he be loaned the four pairs for his very special occasion. To avoid blowing her cover, Lady Persephone had no choice but to loan them to him. He promised to return them by December 1. However, the date came and went. No earrings were returned.

Fuming, Lady Persephone sent numerous emails to Peter, all of which went unanswered. At last, she began researching him. One way or another, she would get her earrings back, and he would be the next recipient of an Ace of Diamonds, she so swore.

Unfortunately, her computer hacking skills were definitely second-rate. Nevertheless, she spent hours trying to find out what had happened to Peter Delius. She did learn he'd vanished right after his Thanksgiving party. How curious, she thought and kept on it. Then, she got a lucky break while searching on "Delius." She found an EE woman's web page of one Petra Delius. Related, she wondered. She was a master of disguises, and at once saw she was indeed Peter! For a moment, she was shocked. Although she had heard some men were given sex changes along with their implants and Pytalon doses to help fill vacancies in women-only jobs, that a Feds leader would have this done was shocking to her. Was he mentally unsound? Did he have a secret wish? No, she recalled her conversations with the man when he wanted to *borrow* her priceless earrings. If anything, she pegged him as a womanizer at best and suspected even worse of him back then.

She dug further and several days later began to believe that Peter had been abducted and given a forced sex change. Lady Persephone had a good laugh over this discovery. "Serves the womanizer right," she roared, before continuing. Somehow, she had to get her earrings back from him. Yet, if he had been abducted, who now had the earrings? She concluded four of the six women he had invited to his special party had likely worn them at that time. Could they have the earrings?

She was familiar with the two gorgeous European EE women Peter had flown over for his party, Ilse Kunegunther and Erika Bjork. She tried contacting these two first, since in her mind, these two women would be the most likely to have worn such priceless earrings, being top fetish EE models in Europe. However, they too weren't responding to her emails to their EE women's site. Frustrated, she sent out a Persephone, the Assassin, alert to some of the contacts she sometimes used around the world, asking them for information on all these six women, plus Peter or Petra Delius. She wanted her earrings back.

Finally, she received a message from Petra Delius, explaining she didn't know what happened to the earrings, but the four US women had been wearing them before they drugged him unconscious. Armed with this information, she began emailing each of the four EE women, as well as searching everywhere for detailed information about them. *Just who are these four?*

Soon, two checked out, more or less. Jessica and Amanda had well documented histories. They seemed on the up and up, as far as Lady Persephone could tell. Just why they had married the other two EE women bothered her some, but then they were EE women, she justified.

However, the other two remained something of a mystery to her, defying all her futile attempts to uncover their history and past. What she found most curious was the undeniable fact that two years ago, they didn't exist. She'd accidentally discovered that fact when she inadvertently gotten into the EE women's archives. This only fueled her suspicions these four had absconded with her earrings. She continued to email them, while she directed her network of informants to try to find the location of said four women.

During the late winter, she discovered all four had gone missing for several months. This, she found most curious, but was unable to ascertain more about it. Then, mysteriously, the four had once more surfaced. She found several messages to that effect. Once more, she emailed them every few days, demanding an answer.

In May, she finally got a response. She breathed a huge sigh of relief. They had her precious earrings, and her clever cell phone program pinpointed their exact location. True, she had to keep the woman talking long enough for her program to zero in on her location, but she got it, on the west side of East Peoria, Illinois, USA. Hastily, she estimated how long it would take her special EMAC to get there and arranged to pick them up at noon. She said to Tilly, "I will arrange for a courier to pick them up from you. The courier will arrive and say to you: 'Flowers bloom in the spring.' You're to reply: 'Tulips are best.' Then, you hand the courier a pouch with the four pairs of earrings in them. No questions asked and no problems. The courier will arrive around noon day after tomorrow. Thank you and goodbye." Lady Persephone hung up, finally satisfied.

Hastily, she made her preparations. She always kept a complete arsenal of weapons in her EMAC, as well as numerous disguises. She changed into her bag lady outfit and stepped into her vehicle. It was a very old one, built by her great-great-grandfather. Thus, it didn't have the latest geo-tracking chips in it. No one could ever follow her vehicle. She punched in the coordinates she'd gotten from the cell phone trap program and settled back for the long trip across the Big Pond, her name for the Atlantic Ocean.

Around ten the next morning, she finished putting on her makeup, completing her bag lady disguise. An hour later, she approached her destination. She first cased the area from a thousand feet above. Suspecting traps was second nature to her. Lady Persephone was about to land when two other EMACs caught her attention. She zoomed her binoculars on them. Men were scrambling out, and they had guns in their hands! "Crap! What is going on here? I want my goddamn earrings."

She set her ship down some distance away and proceeded to walk a block to the abandoned warehouse. Perfect, she thought, no one would pay any heed to a bag lady roaming inside this place. Perfect. She crept inside but saw nothing but piles of rusting junk machinery and all manner of discarded debris. She pretended to be poking around and moved closer to the designated meeting point as shown on her small, handheld geo-locator. She got into position, but still couldn't see the four women anywhere around, but the men were certainly close, probably also moving into position just outside. What had she stumbled into? Who were these four? Why were armed men after them? She felt for her Japanese sword, feeling its comforting sheath just beneath her baggy, filthy, patched dress.

Just then, she heard a grating noise and came instantly to alert. She spotted the four women wearing exotic boots moving carefully out of a concealed door, led by an armed man. *Well, let's get this over in a hurry,* she thought and stepped forward. The man spotted her and came to attention, pointing her out to the women. She said softly, but unmistakably, "Flowers bloom in the spring." She had her fingers crossed. *Will they give the reply?* Just at that instant, two men appeared entering the abandoned warehouse from the opposite end, close to the others.

***

A guard alerted Grand Field Marshal Hans Gudrunda that several incoming Feds EMACs had been spotted coming to Sandpoint, Idaho. "Okay, delay them long enough to get the bombs loaded. Get the prisoners into the EMAC. I'll man the train. Move. We haven't much time," he barked his orders, feeling the adrenaline starting to flow. He lived for this incredible high feeling! He manned his own fifty caliber machine gun mounted in a top turret of the specially modified EMAC train. As the Feds vehicles landed, he opened fire, knowing his rapid fire, large caliber, armor piercing rounds would damage those vehicles. His task was simple: prevent these vehicles from following them, once the bombs were loaded.

The acrid smell of gunpowder filled his nostrils, though his earplugs dampened some of the steady concussions of his rapid firing gun. The continuous vibration in his hands and arms felt wonderful. He was *alive*! One vehicle would never fly again, he noted, as its EM motor smoked and shut down. He grinned and continued firing. The EE women prisoners were nearly loaded. If only they'd get those bombs to the train. He continued pouring out deadly fire, downing several Feds.

A massive explosion shook the train, temporarily halting all gunfire from both sides. It took only seconds for Hans to grasp he'd just lost all his bombs. One of the Feds must have accidentally triggered one of them, perhaps by an errant rifle shot, he assumed. "Retreat. Train leaves in one minute," he screamed above the din of the battle as it resumed. He continued providing covering fire, as his remaining men retreated to the train. He saw the EE women's vehicle taking off, but rather erratic in its motion. For a moment, he panicked, believing it was certain to crash. Relief came as the vehicle pulled steeply up at the last instant before slamming into the mountainside.

The last man scrambled aboard, and he gave the order, quickly relayed to the driver. The huge train gave a violent lurch, as it too took off, heading steeply upwards, trying to avoid incoming fire from the Feds on the ground. It worked. They failed to hit the large, fast moving target. A minute later, the train left Sandpoint, Idaho far behind them. From the rear observation deck, a soldier reported no signs of the Feds following them. Grand Field Marshal Hans finally relaxed and climbed down from his gun turret, motioning for another soldier to take his position, just in case.

A few minutes later, he entered his private car where Helene and Gruber were waiting his arrival. "Ve lost the bombs," Gruber reported solemnly.

"Ya, ve did. Feds got a luck shot. How many men were lost, Gruber?" Hans asked.

"Only ten, Major Henry died with the bombs, though."

Hans cursed. Major Henry was his most promising soldier. "Make contact with the other EMAC. Make sure our four EE women prisoners aren't hurt," he ordered.

The Electronics Man groaned. He hated to have to give Hans this bit of news. "No answer. None at all."

"Vat? How can dis be?" Hans exclaimed in a sudden burst of anger.

Gruber shook his shoulders. Helene offered, "Hans, perhaps the women are flying it themselves. Lord, I don't know how they can, but that's the only thing left. The driver knows he has to report to you as soon as he is clear of the valley. How else will he know where to go? Ve should have taken more precautions with the women, brought them along with us on the train."

Hans cursed again. "Vell, ve vill just have to capture them once more. That's simple, but virst, ve must get to our new headquarters and get setup. Gruber, start figuring out where ve can steal more explosives to replace the lost bombs. I'm taking a rest break." He laid down and closed his eyes, wishing the battle hadn't been so short. His adrenaline rush had vanished, leaving him feeling quite tired.

Many hours later, the EMAC train set down in an isolated area of the Ardennes in the south of Belgium. His new headquarters was an abandoned Belgium military base a few miles northwest of the small town of Lavacherie, surrounded by dense forest. A month ago, he'd sent an advance team of ten here to get the place ready for his main force. This site was perfect. No one could get close to the base without hiking through the dense forest and getting lost. Of course, coming in via EMAC would give them plenty of advance warning, especially since the advance team had set up two radar dishes to provide additional security.

The first few days, Hans busied himself with issuing the needed orders to get the camp in proper order. Finally, he had to tackle the missing vehicle with his four EE women. Why? Gruber was unable to locate any new Feds bases where they could steal explosives! "Grand Field Marshal," Gruber moaned, "the Feds have moved them all to some secret site. I can't find out where that is." He half expected to be slapped by Hans, whose temper would surely explode with this setback news. To Gruber's amazement, he didn't.

"Vell, I expected such a move. The Feds aren't wholly stupid zombies. Ve need to find our missing EE women. Beth, in particular. She can hack into anything. Ve'll just have to get her to find us that new location. So how are you doing on finding them?"

"Nicht so gut. Vanished. No trace, but they're alive. I've found messages from others who are saying they have been found," Gruber reported the little he'd found out.

"Well, ve have to find them. Get on it Gruber. I'll lend you a hand with my superior intellect," Hans ordered. After some thinking, Hans said, "Look, ve picked up Beth and Jessica in that small mid-western town of Peoria. They must be living somewhere in that city. So I vill send a number of spies there. Eventually, they'll spot the women and ve'll snatch them, but I must work out a new way to coerce Beth into helping us. Dis would be so much easier if she was a man; ve could torture her into helping, but they're women and married too, so no easy way to do that. I must come up with a better plan, Gruber. You keep in contact with the spies."

Hans grew frustrated. No word came from any of his agents in the field. It was now late April and still no word on the women's location. However, Gruber did find something. "Field Marshal, ve aren't the only ones looking for the women. Look here, Persephone, the Assassin, is also looking for them. We just ran into one of her spies and exchanged some information. Ve didn't give anything away, but she is looking hard for them."

"Persephone, the Assassin! Mein Gott! If she gets to them before ve do, they're as gut as dead! Ve must get to them first, Gruber! Ve must get Beth to find where the explosives are being kept. Keep everyone you can spare watching for the assassin. She may find them before ve do, and ve must be ready to react when she does, before she kills them. Ve are now doing the four women a favor, saving their lives. Dis assassin is formidable." He was so excited that his English slipped.

Early May, they got a distinct break: a cell phone lock lasted just long enough for Gruber to get a location fix. "Ya, dis assassin hast led us to die vier women! Just like I thought," Hans exclaimed, filled with a great satisfaction. Once more, he'd proven to his men that he truly was the Grand Field Marshal. "Now ve must get there before the assassin does. I vill send Helene und vier men at once."

Around eleven thirty the following morning, Helene met up with their spies in Peoria. They took the two EMAC vehicles to the designated location, parking as close as they dared. "Vat is dis?" Helene exclaimed as she stepped down. One of the local scouts told her it was an abandoned warehouse. "Sehr gut! Sehr gut! Ve can take them easily. Shoot any men guards that might be with them first. Don't ask questions. Just shoot men on sight. Use the tasers, ve don't vant to kill innocent men by accident. Let's go get them." She, of course, followed at a safe distance behind the group of men, several of whom fanned out to cover the area and to prevent any possible escape. Two men walked slowly into the abandoned warehouse.

At first, they saw no one, and then spotted a Garbage Collector Twentieth Class, but wholly ignored the pitiful woman. Just then, they heard a grating sound and moved towards it. One armed man stepped out, followed by the four women. The Garbage Collector said something, but the men didn't hear what and could care less. Without warning, they fired their Tasers. The guard dove, avoiding one shot, but the second shot hit him, knocking him out cold.

"You will come with us. Grand Field Marshal Hans Gudrunda wants to see you most urgently. We will shoot if you resist," one man ordered.

Shocked by the sudden changing events, Jessica first saw the bag woman, who she ignored for a moment, looking around for the courier. Then, the woman spoke, "Flowers bloom in the spring." Recognition struck Jessica, but at that instant, she heard others to her left. Turning, she and the others saw two men firing guns at Juan, who ducked and rolled, but was struck by the second shot. He lay motionless on the ground. All four were temporarily shocked. In their boots, they couldn't do much of anything and stood there listening to the man, a horrible sinking feeling in their stomachs. Hans was once more kidnaping them!

Tilly said bravely, "Looks as if we don't have a choice." Slowly and carefully, she began moving towards the two men. Jessica flashed a glance over her shoulder at the bag lady. She held the bag of earrings in her hand behind her back. As she too began to move towards the two men, she cleverly dropped the bag, hoping the courier would see it fall and retrieve the valuable earrings.

As they exited the side of the warehouse, they saw two waiting EMACs and Helene, who was grinning broadly. "Ve meet once more. Grand Field Marshal Hans Gudrunda has been missing you very much. Now he vill be most pleased you rejoin him. He did say there was no escaping from him, not ever. Come, into dis vehicle." She led the way.

The men lifted each woman up the three steps to speed them along. However, as they reached the top, another man injected them with a syringe. The knockout drug took affect almost instantly. He caught each woman before she fell, sitting her on one of the passenger seats. Three minutes later, Helene and her prizes were airborne. Now she and her helpers began to implement the latest ideas Hans had to coerce Beth, in particular, into helping him find where the Feds had moved their explosives.

Chapter 19—Allies

As soon as the group departed, Lady Persephone moved quickly to the fallen man. She felt for a pulse. *He's alive, just stunned, could be worse.* Next, she quickly picked up the bag the Jessica had dropped. She looked inside and smiled. Her four pairs of huge dangling earrings studded with diamonds were there in perfect condition. She smiled and tucked them into her cleavage where they would be safe for the moment. She turned to the man and knew she had a decision to make, several in fact.

This field marshal fellow had to be stopped. That was a given. He'd just taken these four women for the second time. Although she didn't know them, they had honored her request for the return of her earrings and hadn't asked any questions or asked for a reward, which she was half-inclined to have paid. In fact, the one called Jessica had gone out of her way to make sure her earrings hadn't fallen into the hands of their kidnapers. Lady Persephone felt obligated to help the four women.

She looked at the man once more. He was rather handsome, strong muscles, a fighter, she assumed. "I can't leave you here. Lord knows what might happen to you if I do. There are probably many rats around here. Okay, fellow, you're coming with me. I have to leave now, if I'm to track them," she whispered, knowing he couldn't hear her. She dragged him to her waiting EMAC, dumped him in the passenger compartment, and moved on up to the driver's seat. A minute later, she was airborne as well. She guided her vehicle upwards at an angle as steep as it could safely handle. Before long, she leveled off and turned on her radar system. She ignored several distant pings, focusing on the bright one not too far ahead of her. That had to be them. She was several thousand feet above them and decided to rise a bit higher to make sure she was not detected, continuing to remain several miles behind them as well.

Satisfied with her position for the moment, she began to do her pre-flight checks. All was perfect, except for one thing: the remaining charge for the EM motors. She'd used up three-quarters of the charge coming across the Big Pond without

257

stopping. She had to—in order to get here as quickly as she had promised. Now, she mused how right that had been. A day later and she'd not have retrieved her earrings. The real question in her mind was the destination of the kidnapers. If they were stateside, she'd probably have enough charge to follow them to wherever they were taking the four women. If they crossed the Big Pond, she simply had to stop for a re-charge. While she was pondering her options, the man moaned, regaining consciousness.

"What the hell? Where am I? Beth? Who are you? The bag lady courier?" Juan's head spun. Questions flooded his mind, which mechanically vocalized them, as he got his bearings. He had been diving out of the way of a Taser shot before he blacked out from a direct hit. He rubbed his sore shoulder. Now he felt motion and smelled the EMAC. He knew at once that he was airborne. The raggedly dressed woman he'd glimpsed was driving. It didn't make sense.

"Lady Persephone Briton here. I'm following the men who kidnaped the four women you were with. I take it you were their bodyguard. I couldn't leave you lying there in that rubbish. Rats might have had dinner."

"Er, thanks. Yes, I was supposed to protect them. Rather failed this time. We were expecting your courier and were taken by surprise. Looks like Grand Field Marshal Hans Gudrunda has found their safe house here and kidnaped them again. Last time, he tortured them, forcing them to wear those awful boots all the time. Their toes broke and fused, healing wrong. Now they can't wear anything but them. Nasty fellow this Hans. I need to make a phone call," he said, realizing he needed to alert the professor to have them send the activation signal so they could locate the women.

"As long as you aren't calling the Feds, go ahead. I'm following them from a safe distance where they won't see me, unless they have installed a radar system on their EMAC, which I seriously doubt," she replied. "By the way, who are you?"

"Juan Carlos, miss. Your disguise fooled us all." He then speed dialed the professor. In a low voice, he said, "Hans kidnaped the four again. I'm on their trail. More later."

"Mind if I come up front?" Juan asked politely.

Lady Persephone thought about that for a moment. "Well, okay, come on up, but I warn you don't try anything. I guarantee you'll regret it." He nodded and made his way to the second driver's seat.

"Thanks for bringing me along and a big thank you for following those evil men," Juan said politely. His keen eyes began looking her over. She seemed anything but a bag lady or courier. *No, she is a fighter too*, he thought. Then the thought struck him. *Can she be the assassin Persephone? If so, is she planning to find the women so that she can kill them?*

She sensed his eyes on her and picked up his sudden unease. "What?" she said insinuatingly.

"Well, we were trying to find out if this assassin who has the same first name as you was out to kill us, er, I mean the four women," Juan tried to put this as nicely as he could. "This Persephone, the Assassin, had the four rather scared. We figured we had the Feds, this Hans fellow, another ex-Feds Petra Delius, and this assassin all after the four of them. Fairly scary."

Lady Persephone laughed. "Well, for four EE women, they certainly have made a whole lot of very nasty enemies, Juan. However, I assure you Persephone, the Assassin, is not after them. Rather she is trying hard to help them, though she isn't sure just why yet."

"You? Her?" Juan put it together.

She laughed, "I prefer Persephone, the Righteous Vigilante. Someone has to look out for those who cannot in this insane world, which has gone completely off its rockers. I admit it is refreshing to meet and talk with a man who is not implanted and/or on Pytalon. Don't worry. I've never killed anyone who didn't deserve it in spades. My card." She handed him an Ace of Diamonds. "I was going to flip it on the ground where Jessica dropped the bag of earrings, but took care of you instead. You can keep it as a token."

"Well met, Lady Persephone Briton. Say, what's with the lady title thing?" Juan asked.

She sighed. "I come from a royal English lineage. My title is hereditary. My parents are bloody zombies and no longer count, so I'm the new Lady of our castle in Sussex."

"Castle? Huh? I saw a picture once of great ancient stone works. Is that what you mean?"

"Right, only mine isn't ancient. My great-great-grandfather built it with all the modern conveniences you could possibly want," she replied rather proudly. Then, her expression changed altogether. "Damn! They are heading back across the Big Pond! Crap!"

"What?"

"They're going to cross the Atlantic Ocean. I used up almost all my EM charge coming across to pick up the earrings. We're almost out of charge. I won't be able to continue to shadow them. We have no choice but to stop for a re-charge."

She then smirked, "Oh, you can't escape the assassin this easily, fellows. Juan, fasten your seat belt. You're in for a bit of excitement before we land to re-charge. I'll not abandon this chase!" She glanced to see he was secure. Then, she pressed a switch and a red light changed to green. "Hang on," she said grimly. The vehicle sped up and arced far to the right of the vehicle they were shadowing. She then pushed the throttle to maximum speed.

"Are you going to ram them?" Juan called out, growing terrified Persephone was going to try to crash into the other EMAC forcing it to land. She didn't answer, but focused all her senses, grasping the flight wheel tightly. There was no room for error. Her ship flew directly at the side of the unsuspecting enemy EMAC. At the last instant, she pulled up slightly, narrowly missing the other ship. At that last moment before she pulled up, she flipped the toggle switch.

"There, the light is blinking. Success. Time for a re-charge," she said calmly as if nothing had happened.

"Were you trying to hit them or something?" Juan asked, wiping the sweat from his forehead.

"No, distract them so they weren't aware of my magnetic sensor hitting the side of their ship and latching on to it. Tracking beacon. After we re-charge, we can pick up their trail easily. I'll not lose those women. I want this Hans fellow. I aim to give him one of my cards," she said rather grimly. Juan smiled, greatly relieved.

"Lady Persephone, you're something else. Excellent move, excellent thinking. I'm a hunter-trapper, and that was the slickest move I've ever seen one of these vehicles do."

She grinned. "You haven't seen anything yet, big boy. You're with Persephone, the Assassin. Come on. Let's get this thing re-charged. I'll land us at a station in D.C., and you can handle it, while I change my clothes. A bag lady shouldn't be flying an EMAC." He grinned.

After she landed, Juan stepped out and used his ID card to pay for the re-charge. After hooking up the cable, they had little to do for several hours. When he stepped back aboard, Lady Persephone looked like a royal lady, dressed in a while silk gown and low matching heels. "There, do I look the part now?"

she asked coyly, unable to refrain from teasing him a little. After all, she wasn't worried about her cover. If he turned out to be on the wrong side, she'd merely eliminate him. End of blown cover. Besides, she found herself rather enjoying his company. He wasn't a dope.

"Care to join me for dinner?" she asked. Already, she'd microwaved two meals and set her small table. He climbed inside, thanking her. She turned on her computer, and a symphony began playing in the background.

The reaction she received from Juan was not what she'd anticipated. Rare was the person who even knew about such things as music, not in this Pytalon-crazy world. All that had been lost nearly two centuries ago. "Oh my goodness! Music! You have music too! So does Beth. I have some of the printed music and play two recorders. Beth has just got to hear your music too." He was genuinely excited, and Persephone was surprised herself.

"Beth has music too? You actually can make music?" she asked, her eyes looking Juan over as if she'd never seen him before.

"Yes, My Lady. She has many songs, but she likes what she calls Ancient Music, many centuries old. I found some discarded printed music and several instruments in a trash bin outside the Missoula Library. I managed to teach myself how to play the two recorders some, but haven't figured out the violin yet. That one is very difficult. I can't find the notes, since there appears to be an infinity of frequencies it can make. Please, once we rescue Beth, she'll want to hear your music, My Lady," Juan insisted.

Lady Persephone laughed. "Do you realize how long that will take her? I have thousands of what were called CDs but now I have most of them on my main computer."

"She has hers on her computer too. What's this one called?"

"Symphony Number 9 by a fellow called Beethoven. It's many centuries old too. It is my favorite. Let's eat. We're not likely to have time for such later on."

Two hours later, she determined she had sufficiently re-charged the system to get her to any location in Europe. If they went beyond that continent, she'd have to stop again. She would rather not spend another two hours to get it fully re-charged, not with the four women's lives at stake. After undoing the cables, they were airborne once more, almost at once out over the Atlantic Ocean heading towards Europe. Lady Persephone left her music playing, much to Juan's delight.

Meanwhile, she punched in the commands for her navigator to follow the signal beacon, which was still operating perfectly. While she was occupied, Juan's cell vibrated, and he accepted the professor's text message. It read: Tracking working. Over Europe. Contacting Wolf for aid. He smiled. One way or another, he was going to get to the four women and quickly this time.

The two dozed during the long flight over the ocean, though periodically, she roused to check on their progress and to make sure her signaling device was still functioning. At dawn, they were just coming over England, and she had Juan watch the controls while she rustled up some breakfast of sandwiches she had prepared for her own return journey, storing them in her small fridge. She did at least brew some strong black tea, which to her amazement, Juan loved. "I have tea all the time. No time to fiddle with coffee when you are out in the forests." He then explained some of his duties he had been doing back in Montana.

"Well, they've landed. Unfortunately, I would have preferred a nighttime landing. It looks as if they're somewhere in the Ardennes. I don't trust this field marshal fellow. If he has a military mind, then I would anticipate all manner of traps lie waiting for us. Surely, they would be able to detect us approaching. The Feds, after all, are hounding him," she explained.

"Well, if you can land us a safe distance away, once I know the precise location, I can get us there," Juan suggested.

"Through the dense forest?" she asked in disbelief. One could easily get lost in the Ardennes.

"You bet I can. I just need to know their location. I have a compass. If I know where we land and where they are, it's a simple matter of walking there," he tried to explain, but couldn't find the right words for something as simple as navigating through dense forests. He'd done it all his life.

Suddenly, she swerved hard to the left. "Just got a faint radar ping," she said grimly. "I don't want to take any chances on getting detected. I'm going to find us a good place to set down. I'll hold you to your woodsman skills, Juan. Don't let me down," she threatened.

A bit later, she landed her vehicle in a small clearing smack in the middle of the forest. "Here, you can take all the readings you want. I have to change and prepare for the overland journey," she ordered, disappearing into the passenger section. Juan studied the geo-navigator screen, memorizing their position, the position of the enemy vehicle, and then estimating the distances involved. They would have to hike some twenty miles through the forest, but there were a couple of ancient roads that might make travel easier. He discarded these. Surely, Hans would have such easy paths watched night and day. Take no chances was his motto, not with the women's lives at stake.

Juan almost didn't recognize her when she returned ready to go. She wore an all-black outfit with matching mask. She had two swords strapped across her back and all manner of other wicked-looking, sharp spiked disks strapped to her chest belt. He had no idea what they were. A set of binoculars and a pair of night-vision goggles were around her neck. She also had a pack with some food, water, and rope in it along with a first-aid kit. "Are you ready, Juan?"

"Sure, but don't you want a gun or something?" he asked.

"Never use them if I can avoid them. Silent, but most deadly, is Persephone, the Assassin. Let's get going. I'd like to be there by dark, if possible. I've some food and water for later on."

"Okay, but the forest might provide for us, though it is still early May. This way," he said. She wore sturdy boots, much like his. Thus, he relaxed a little. *She should be able to keep up with me.* The forest floor was rocky and rugged; the trees were dense here, but varied as they hiked along. Juan went in a straight line, as much as possible.

"I hope you know where you are going," she whispered. "I'm lost already. Well, not really, I always have my pocket locating device on me, so I could find my way. Stay alert for outlying sentries. I'm certain a military man would post them," she whispered.

After covering ten miles, they spotted their first sentry. "I'll take him out on our return trip. If we take him out now, then Hans could well be alerted long before we get to him." Juan agreed and led them safely around the bored soldier and his rifle. They dodged another four sentries before reaching a rise from which they could see the abandoned army base below them.

Silently, Juan began pointing out the posted sentries. Here, they counted ten scattered around the edges of the large complex of buildings. Their EMAC train was hidden beneath camouflaged tarps. She took out her binoculars and began studying the layout. Suddenly, she inhaled sharply. "Oh my God!" she whispered, then handed him the binoculars and pointed. Shortly afterwards, he too gasped. They'd found the four women, but they were in an awful shape. As he watched, they seemed to be being led from a mess hall to sleeping quarters, which he noted carefully. Smoke curled from the kitchen next to the mess hall.

"We need to know their strength before we attack," she whispered. "We must watch them a while and make darn sure there'll be no surprises when we attack."

"True, considering the condition they're in, there's no way we could make a nighttime attack, which is what I would prefer," Lady Persephone whispered, more to herself. "We're going to have to secure the site, and one of us will have to bring the EMAC here to pick them up. The ground will be impassable for them in their boots, even if we can free them from the rest of it. Hans is mine!" she added dramatically.

"Probably we should hit them in the morning, as they come out from the mess hall at breakfast," Juan suggested. "That would give us time to pick off the sentries and move in close before they come out.

"Agreed. I like all those trees close to the mess hall. That will aid me," she added. Juan didn't see how, unless she would use them for cover from the gunfire. "Count men. We need to have a good idea how many there are. Look. They're taking the women into that barracks, three doors down from the mess hall. Crap, there are other women down there!" She used her binoculars once more and added, "EE women. They must not be prisoners; they look like normal exotic women, possible prostitutes, do you suppose?"

"Either that or kept women who have no other choice," Juan refused to believe women would stoop to that level. They watched and counted, but time seemed to move interminably slowly as far as he was concerned. Lady Persephone, on the other hand, seemed content to be as patient as she needed be.

Late in the afternoon, another EMAC landed, causing both spies to perk up and pay close attention. Another much older EE woman disembarked carefully, followed by another man who lifted another woman down. "Oh no, they've got another EE woman bound just as our four!" Lady Persephone whispered. "Say that's Petra Delius, the ex-Feds leader! What's she doing here? Why is she bound like the others? What am I missing here?" she whispered, growing more worried by the moment.

He borrowed the binoculars and took a good look. Hans stepped out to greet the new arrivals, giving the older woman a hug first. They were too far away to hear what was said. A second man disembarked, carrying a purse and a bag. Hans waved him to the same barracks the four were kept in—Juan saw that much. He watched as the poor woman struggled mightily even to walk to the barracks and then disappeared inside.

"Right. Does this mean the Feds are closing in? Petra used to be Peter, the leader of the Chicago Feds. He's the one who had Ben and Tim implanted as EE women, forcing them ultimately to get the rest of their sex changed," he explained.

"What? I didn't know that. Tell me more," she whispered back.

"I'm not sure how much of this I should be telling you. It's not my place. Just know Petra is no friend of our four women," Juan replied, wishing that he'd kept his mouth shut.

"Okay. At least, we know Petra is or was with the Feds. What does this field marshal want with her? A bargaining chip with the Feds? No, I doubt that," Lady Persephone whispered to herself. "The Feds probably want nothing to do with Petra now; she's been implanted and good for nothing except being a sex doll. So why would he want her? She's being treated like our four. What's the connection? I don't get this at all. We should keep a close watch on them," she added.

Juan's phone vibrated, and he quietly peered at the text message. It was from Wolf and read: Be there by morning with a force of twenty. He texted back Petra Delius was also now a captive and being treated as badly as the four, but he didn't reveal just what their physical condition actually was. A subsequent text read: Damn. Am checking on the local Feds. Hold off attack until sure Feds are not on their way. He replied with a "k."

As the sun sank, Juan watched helplessly as the five women made their painstakingly slow and wobbling way from their barracks in a single file towards the mess hall. He swore more curses than he ever had in his life. Silently, Lady Persephone did likewise, steeling herself for the butchering she knew she would do come morning. Later, they watched the poor women struggling mightily to make it back to their room. Juan felt rather sick. *How could anyone do these things to a woman, no less? The man is as insane as those on Pytalon are!*

During the night, they took turns dozing while the other kept watch, noting the coming and goings of the sentries. At dawn, they compared notes. A dozen men marched out at sunrise to replace the night crew. After they disappeared into the dense forest surrounding the base, Persephone said, "Now, move out. You guard and protect the women; leave me free to do my thing."

"Hold a second." Juan's cell phone vibrated, and he saw the Wolf was texting again. He read: Feds r on their way. Expect them to arrive by ten at the latest. We r 20 miles south of you now. Advise. He whispered, "We have some help twenty miles south of us. Feds will be here by ten."

Lady Persephone gave him a funny look and thought for a second. "Tell them to take out the sentries and come straight to the barracks. Come on. We need to get into position now while the sentries are eating." She gave him a moment to send the text, and then she moved silently down the slope using all available cover. Juan was impressed. She was not only a silent hunter, but nearly invisible because of her black pants, shirt, and hood. He followed her, moving just as silently, but making for the women's barracks, while she headed for the further side of the mess hall. Juan didn't know what she had planned, but intended to do his duty and protect the women as they came out of the mess hall.

***

When Beth awoke, she felt stiff and uncomfortable, and she tried to rub her head with her hands. They didn't move. Brief panic brought her fully alert. Her arms were crossed above her upper back, her fingers near the opposite sides of her torso. She glanced at Jessica sitting beside her and saw her arms were in a similar position, lower arms against each other across her upper back. They were fully encased in what appeared to be a plaster cast similar to one you would get for a broken leg or arm. She couldn't move her arms at all, except to lift the whole cast slightly off her back. Even most of her fingers were encased in this wicked cast. Further, she had that awful O-

266

ring gag in her mouth, but she also tasted rubber. It was filling the hole in the ring. Again, she glanced at Jessica and saw a large rubber fitting totally filled her O-ring hole, but there was a small tube sticking a half inch out of a hole in the very center of the rubber plug. As she wiggled a little to relieve the cramps in her legs, she saw she was once again wearing the awful leather hobble skirt that only allowed her a few inches to move her feet.

Jessica stirred, and Beth saw the momentary panic in her eyes too. She looked over to Beth and began to grasp her bondage as well. Then, the other two stirred. One by one, the four suspected that the professor had gotten their homing microchips activated. Surely, he and Greg knew where the women were located, and a rescue would soon be coming. That alone kept the four from an utter panic.

Beth also smelled the perfume Helene always wore and assumed she was onboard the EMAC with them. Probably she had a hand in their bindings. Silently, Beth thanked Greg repeatedly for his thoughtful and now lifesaving invention of his microchip. This time, Beth knew they would be unable to free themselves without help. Her arms were completely immobilized within the diabolical cast.

Just then, Helene stepped into their view probably from the second driver's seat, Beth guessed. "Vell, awake at last. The Grand Field Marshal did tell you dat there vas no escape. This time, you'll not get the slightest chance of escaping. He hast devised these new arm casts that vill remain on you at all times. That little tube sticking out of your rubber ring plugs is your feeding tube. At mealtimes, a long tube will be slipped over it, and you are to suck up your food and tea. You're on a total liquid diet now, naturally. Brilliant, isn't he? Oh, yes, don't even bother trying to push the rubber plugs out; they can't be. They have an inner layer that is wider than the O-ring. So no pushing them out. Magnificent, eh? Sit back and relax. Ve vill be arriving in an hour." She turned and walked back up front.

She was accurate. Beth felt the ship descending and then landing, but where she wondered. As the door opened, she smelled a forest and saw rough ground with many trees, dense at the edges of the weed-covered area beside the vehicle. One by one, the four were lifted down. They could see they were in another abandoned army barracks, but where? The field marshal in his resplendent uniform came strutting out to greet them. Beth sighed.

"Ah, here you are at last. My, ve thought ve hast lost you when the Feds attacked us, but no matter; you're safely back with us. I do hope you like your new bindings. The arm casts are my latest invention. See, I don't torture or harm women; that would be a terrible sin. Now then, here ist the deal. I'll release you from your arm casts and O-rings, *after* Beth here agrees to hack into the Feds computer system and locate where they have taken all their explosives. The Feds blew up our painstakingly made satchel bombs, so now they have to be replaced. Beth here is the key to your partial freedom. When she agrees and accomplishes it, then I vill have your casts and O-rings removed. Now then, it's time for lunch. If you vill follow Helene, she vill lead you to the mess hall and insert your feeding tubes. I do hope you enjoy the liquid food. Ve have to—how do you say this, liquefy your meals—quite an annoyance so my cook says. Beth, when you decide to cooperate with me, nod your head vigorously up and down. Until then, enjoy your stay with us here in the Ardennes. Yes, you're in Europe now, far from your home stateside." He turned and marched off to the mess hall.

"Follow me ladies," Helene barked. That was easier said than done. The ground at the base in Idaho was at least smooth and level. Here, the ground was rocky and uneven, to say nothing of the tall grasses and weeds that had long ago broken through cracks in the pavement below. Walking on their toes was a nightmare, especially without the slightest help from their arms. It was all the four could do to walk the hundred feet to the mess hall.

As promised, Helene then stuck a long tube into their rubber gags. A bowl of a yellowish liquid and a cup of tea sat on the table in front of them. They had no choice but to move their heads about, get the other end of the tube into the bowl, and then try to suck up the food. They were hungry and did appreciate the tea. After that nightmare, the four were walked back to their new barracks room. Over the rough ground, walking was exceedingly treacherous. This time, their captivity was going to be hideous, but all four knew a rescue was soon to come, thanks to Greg and his foresight. It couldn't come too soon!

***

Petra awoke to a dizzying headache and tried to rub her head. Her arms didn't move. Panic struck. She suddenly remembered getting into an EMAC and then passing out. Her arms seemed pinned behind her back, her lower arms horizontal across her middle back. Again, she tried to move them. Nothing. Twisting, she saw what looked like the start of a cast. Now her jaws ached too, and she felt her mouth was forced open but somehow blocked.

"Ah, you are awake, Miss Petra," Helene spoke from across the aisle in her slight German accent. Petra's terror filled eyes met her cold, penetrating eyes. "Don't bother struggling. Your arms are in a full cast across your back, including your hands. You won't ve able to move them in the slightest, Hans' latest genius idea. You see, he believes it's a cardinal sin to harm a woman, so you're not being harmed, just constrained. Oh yes, you have a leather hobble skirt on over your gown, so no taking large steps any more for you. You're gagged with an O-ring plus a rubber plug with a tube hole in the center. When it's time to eat, I'll insert a rubber tube over the plug, and you can suck up your liquid meals and tea. No need to speak and thank us. In fact, you're never going to speak again, much less escape. Escape is impossible now. You'll spend the rest of your life as Hans' special prisoner. Soon, you'll be joining four others who are dolled up just as you are. Oh yes, don't worry; no one vill rape or molest you. Hans doesn't believe in that. One final note, when you need to go to the bathroom, just nod your head. That's all you need to be able to communicate to us forever more. Now sit back and relax. It vill be sometime before ve arrive." Helene seemed particularly pleased with her handiwork on Petra.

Well, I won't be able to kill Hans. Thank God I alerted the Feds. Soon, this Hans fellow is going down, Petra thought to herself, trying hard to stem her escalating panic. It didn't work. She began shaking and trembling, fighting against her restraints until she fatigued from the effort. Only then did she finally settle down a little.

Of course, when they landed, her panic leaped to the forefront once more. *I can't move. I can't even stand up by myself. Oh God!* Her legs trembled so badly that Helene had to support her to keep her upright. However, she gave Petra a push, and the woman had no choice but to try to take the tiny steps to the door. At least, a man was there with his arms up ready to lift her down. Once on the rough ground, she again was in trouble, wobbling wildly about trying to take her usual somewhat large steps only to meet the immovable restraint of the leather hobble skirt. If the man hadn't watched her carefully and caught her, she would have fallen down four times before reaching the more level ground close to these strange buildings.

Just then, a man wearing a splendid military uniform came out. He had a huge grin on his face and very cold eyes. "Welcome Petra Delius alias Peter Delius, the head of the Central US Feds. I'm so glad you accepted my offer. I do hope you find your bindings to your liking." Petra shook her head violently no, but he only laughed. "What's that you are saying? Sorry, I can't understand you, but it doesn't matter at all. Women have nothing useful to say anyway, especially EE women like you. As I had Gruber say in the email, your room and board vill be free for the rest of your life. Yes, you vill be just as you are now. You'll have to get used to sucking up liquid food, I'm afraid, but it all gets mixed up in our stomachs anyway. By the way, I give you my word no one vill rape, molest, or harm you in anyway."

Petra relaxed slightly; this was some slight comfort. She couldn't have endured any more. Hans then laughed coldly. "Now then, if you want to get out of the arm cast and gag, you only need to do one small thing for me. It seems the Feds have moved all their explosives to some new location. You give me that location, and after we retrieve the explosives, then no more gag and arm cast. Simple. You do me a favor, and I do you a favor. When you're ready to cooperate and do this small thing for me, just nod your head up and down. Sideways nodding means you need to use the bathroom. So, Miss Petra Delius, are you ready to cooperate right now and do this small favor for me?" He leered at her. Petra shook her head no.

Even if I did know that I'd never give the location away to the likes of you, she thought to herself. *I was right. This man needs to be killed. If only I could get free and get to one of my guns, I'd do it in a blink! Damn this sadist anyway. Oh shit, I'm supposed to walk again.* Hans motioned for Helene to lead her to join the other four women. Once more, she moved most precariously, needing a balancing hand several times to avoid falling down.

As she stepped carefully into the room, she saw the other four women sitting in a line on a couch. A king-sized bed and a smaller one lined two walls. They were bound just as she was. She met their eyes, one by one. Helene pushed her in, and she nearly fell. She was ordered to sit in a chair that faced the four women. Helene smirked, "Vell, ladies, we'll see who breaks first: Petra Delius here or Beth Snells." She turned and left.

Oh how Petra wanted to talk to them, especially Jessica. In her mind, she thought, *I forgive you, Jessica, really I do. It was all my fault. I came to kill Hans, but I can't. Don't worry, the Feds should find us soon, I hope.* The only thing she could do was shake her head no, hoping Beth would interpret the gesture as meaning she would never help Hans find the explosives. After sitting a few minutes, she began to cry. This was going completely wrong. What if the Feds ignored her message? She'd be stuck like this forever.

Just thinking that, her implant kicked in strongly. How long had she gone now without pleasuring? Her implant dictated she receive it at least three times a day. Petra guessed it had been more like two entire days without it. Her head ached, trying to force her to obey, but she couldn't move. All she could do was wiggle slightly and cry.

Eating diner was another nightmare. Sucking up the liquid food was immensely challenging for her, just as it was for the other four, but she had to eat; her stomach demanded it. Misery upon misery. Finally, a woman put them to bed, clothes and all. She lay beside Jessica, but was helpless to say or do anything but cry softly to herself.

Beth was shocked to see Petra Delius captured as well. Now she grasped his plans more fully. Either she or Petra would eventually break down and find the Feds new location for him. Even if she didn't have the locator microchip in her shoulder, Beth knew she would never help Hans, but would Petra break? Would she give up and do it? She hoped and prayed she wouldn't. *Damn, she will break. Peter was a wimp, really. Given this kind of torture, I'm sure she will break down. She's crying even now. Crap, I hope we're rescued before she gives Hans the location!*

The next morning came and no rescue yet. Several of the other EE women came, got the five women up, and helped them to the lavatory, one room north of their barracks room. They heard the many footsteps of the soldiers passing by on their way to the mess hall where they would soon be heading. The handling of the five women was slow and painstaking. Some of the soldiers were just finishing up, as the five women and escorts came out of restroom facilities, making their way south to the mess hall. All were dreading another liquefied breakfast.

From the corner of her eye, Tilly spotted movement off to her right. She hazarded a glance, hoping not to take a bad tumble. She spotted Juan for an instant, before he ducked behind a tree. Her heart leaped. Rescue. If Juan was here, others must also be nearby. Oh, how she wanted to tell the others.

Beth, struggling to keep from falling, spotted something black up ahead, closing on the entrance to the mess hall. Two men stood guard on either side of the door, but they were watching the five women and their escorts, smirks on their faces. In a flash of moving black and steel, their heads mysteriously fell off their bodies! Beth blinked and saw a black clad figure standing between the two falling bodies. The figure kicked the door to the mess hall open and backed off to one side.

A sentry far to the south yelled, but Juan fired twice, dropping the man. As mass chaos erupted, the women stopped moving. Another two sentries appeared, one to the south and one behind them. Juan dropped both of them, though one got off an errant rifle shot, striking the side of a barracks. Soldiers charged out of the mess hall, and the real fight began.

To the amazement of the five women, the black clad figure seemed to run up the side of the mess hall front wall, her body horizontal to the ground! Twin blades whirled, slicing heads, necks, and gun arms, severing many. Now the figure, nearly ten feet above the ground, back flipped out over the fallen bodies. Two more soldiers came out, and the whirling blades cut them down, while the figure was halfway through the back flip!

As her feet touched the ground, Persephone, the Assassin, lunged northward. A hail of gunfire came from inside the mess hall, sending a rain of splinted boards and bullet fragments flying all across the front side of the mess hall. The noise was deafening, and soon a portion of the door and surrounding front wall was little more than a shell of vertical struts with bits of horizontal boards hanging on by a nail or two.

At this point, they heard the voice of Grand Field Marshal Hans. "Charge! Kill the bastards!" Several dozen men charged out of the splintered walls, pushing and shoving their way through the remnants of what had been a rather flimsy door and wall. Once more, the black clad figure sped into action, twin blades nearly invisible so quickly they moved! The figure moved with lightning speed, but not on the ground! Again, she walked up the sides of a supporting strut, back flipping over the mass of men, blades whirling. Bodies piled up on top of one another.

In the midst of this incredible display of martial art skills, four sentries came running up from the south, two from the north. Juan fired repeatedly, downing the two northern ones. Beth spotted the Wolf and several of his men appearing behind the four southern sentries, who were trying to get a bead on the fast moving black figure. The Wolf fired, as did his men, dropping the four with several bullets into their backs. The Wolf signaled Juan with his hand, indicating he had his back now.

Juan ran up to the women and began unfastening the straps on their gags. "Thanks Juan," Beth exclaimed. "She's Petra Delius, the Feds leader!"

"We know. Hold still. I'm cutting the cords of your skirt so you can walk better. She's Persephone, the Assassin, in case you are curious."

By the time he had the five gags removed and their leather skirts' cords cut, some forty soldiers lay dead in a massive, bloody pile before the mess hall. Only Hans remained inside. The Wolf and a dozen of his men had now fanned out and had the rest of the base covered, picking off the occasional sentry who came running back to the base from their forward positions.

As soon as Juan removed Petra's gag, she gushed, "Jessica, I forgive you! I deserved it. I came to kill Hans and rescue you, but was ensnared too. However, the Feds should be coming too. I swallowed a locator beacon and sent the Feds word that I would be leading them to Grand Field Marshal Hans Gudrunda. Unfortunately, the beacon is in the latrine now. Who is that? Who are you?" she asked Juan, as he cut the ropes of her hobble skirt.

He didn't get a chance to answer. Grand Field Marshal Hans Gudrunda, his voice shaking, felt a fear he'd never known! He hollered, "Who—who are you?"

A breathless female voice said softly, "You should know. Persephone, the Assassin. I've come for you, Hans Gudrunda." He fired wildly, as she rushed into the mess hall, dodging his bullets. A throwing star stuck into his gun arm's shoulder. Paralyzed, his hand dropped the gun. Wham. Another struck his other shoulder. Persephone then walked upright and slowly towards the now helpless field marshal. He wet his pants, but still tried to get his arms to work, trying to pull out his long knife. She stood before the general and spat on his face. Then one of her swords flashed in a lightening swift motion, splitting his head in half down to his lower jar. She leaned over and stuck an Ace of Diamonds in the bloody crack. She turned and headed back outside, dropping another couple of cards on the large pile of dead soldiers.

"You all right?" she called out to Juan and the women, glancing at Wolf and his men, making sure they were friendly before lowering her guard.

"Yes, several near misses. Are you injured?" Juan asked.

"Slight scratch from a nail. I take it these are Wolf's men?" she asked, pointing to the others just to the south of them. Juan replied they were. "Good. We need to get them out of here quickly."

The Wolf spoke up hastily, "Well we meet again, Beth, Jessica, Tilly, Amanda. We have thirty minutes at most before the Feds swarm this place. We've taken out the southern sentries. Juan, we should take them to my place. I've located a podiatrist who believes that he can heal their feet." He turned to Lady Persephone and added, "Bardulf Berringer of Berchtesgaden Hotel, ma'am."

"Lady Persephone Briton. Thanks for your timely arrival. I've summoned my EMAC. What should we do with this woman and the other EE women?" she asked, pointing at a horrified Helene and a dozen EE women. Now that the gunfire had ceased, they ventured out of their barracks rooms.

"The Feds will take care of them, but please take me with you, I beg you," Petra cried out, panicking over the thought she would be left behind, completely helpless.

"You can't do this!" Helene screamed, drawing a pistol from her purse and aiming it at Lady Persephone. "I won't let you." She pulled the trigger. Blam. Unfortunately for her, three actions occurred nearly simultaneously. First, Juan's hand came down hard on her hand. The bullet hit the ground and ricocheted nearly striking Petra in the back. Second, the Wolf's gun fired, striking her in the chest. Third a throwing dagger from Lady Persephone struck her in her forehead, right between her eyes, followed by yet another Ace of Diamonds card.

Just then, they heard the soft sound of an EMAC descending. "Mine," Lady Persephone called out, relieving their fears that the Feds had come early. "Come on. Let's get the women aboard fast, and get out of here. Bring Petra. Bardulf, you are with us; send your men back to their vehicles at top speed." She took charge, as she was always wont to do. Juan and Bardulf grinned and obeyed.

Each picked up a woman, tossing them like sacks of potatoes over their shoulders. Two of the Wolf's men joined them, carrying the five women into the passenger compartment of Lady Persephone's EMAC. After setting Beth down, she moved to the driver's seat and called out, "Bardulf, you are up here with me. Hurry, we don't want to get caught by the Feds, and I need the coordinates."

Shortly, he complied, but not until he saw his men making a sprint back into the forest south of the base from which they had come. As he sat down beside her, he said, "Can we make sure my men get safely away?" She nodded and gained some altitude, turning on her radar.

"Damn, Petra was right. Here come the Feds in force!" she called out loudly so the Petra could hear the news. Ten EMACs were small blips on her screen. She added, "They will be landing in about five minutes. This is cutting it a tad close for my liking. Where to, Bardulf?"

He punched in the coordinates and watched, as his two EMACs got airborne as well. Only then did he relax. "Okay, they are up and away. Burn the juice," he called out. She grinned and did so. An hour later, they descended onto a small grassy knoll just behind his A-frame hotel.

Chapter 20—Explanations and Decisions

"Well, we have one big security breach, namely Petra Delius," Lady Persephone pronounced as she landed her vehicle. "Yet, I couldn't just leave her, not bound like this."

"Quite true," Bardulf replied, returning to the passenger compartment. He looked at Petra and explained, "Petra, we couldn't leave you back there. That would have been inhumane, and we're not animals. Unfortunately, you now know too much about us for your own good.

"Please, I came to kill Hans and rescue them too. I brought seven guns with me, but I was drugged right after they picked me up. However, I did bring the Feds who would have rescued us all. I won't ever say anything. Please, I forgive Jessica. I deserved what I got, but I'm a different person now. I've changed, please. If you don't believe me, please go ahead and kill me right now. I can't take this headache any longer," she pleaded.

Lady Persephone, who had made her way back to the passenger compartment, heard Petra's speech. She replied, "For now, we'll take you at your word, Petra. However," she said sternly, "if you ever betray us, I have an Ace of Diamonds with your name on it." In a friendlier tone, she added, "Okay, so how do we get them out of these casts, Bardulf?"

"I have Doctor Gugenheimer waiting inside. He can be trusted. I anticipated some casualties, but thanks to your incredible skills, Lady Persephone, we have none. He is that podiatrist I mentioned. Come on. Let's get them carried inside and out of their restraints. Then, we can talk more fully. I have many questions that need answers," Wolf replied.

The doctor was a balding man of fifty-five with a rotund face matching his belly. "Ah, most relieved. I'm a foot doctor not a trauma doctor—so glad there are no wounds to handle," he said, as Wolf and the others brought the five women into the hotel lobby where he was waiting. Emergency medical supplies lay piled on one couch. Vat ist dis anyway?" he added, seeing the strange casts on the women, shocking him some. "Sit, sit, ve vill get dem off soon. Nothing broken?" he asked.

Beth replied, "I don't think so. He began with Beth. While she leaned forward and Lady Persephone held her hair back, Doctor Gugenheimer began making exploratory cuts with his small saw. It took him nearly fifteen minutes to free her, primarily because he had never seen such a cast before and went slowly to avoid cutting her arms in the process. The others went far more quickly. Meanwhile, Bardulf manned his observation post in the basement to make sure the Feds weren't on their trail. Finally satisfied they weren't followed, he returned to the lobby where the doctor was just finishing freeing the last woman.

"Sehr gut. We weren't followed. The Feds are cleaning up the mess. I believe we've made a clean get away. I see you're free now. Baths and then let's talk," he suggested. Beth grinned; that was perfect for her.

An hour later, the five women joined Lady Persephone, Juan, and Bardulf in his tall-ceiling dining room, whose giant windows looked out upon the Alps, quite picturesque. This was a resort hotel, after all, though hardly anyone ever visited such places—not for over a century, only the occasional wealthy corporate executive. His business had virtually dried up since they too were now Pytalon zombies.

"So how did you find us?" Beth began after sitting down at the table. She glanced at Lady Persephone, who also had bathed and now wore her elegant white gown as befitting the Lady that she was. Juan began, but almost at once yielded to Lady Persephone, who outlined their part. The Wolf then explained the professor and Greg had activated the four women's locator beacons and gotten a precise fix on their location in the Ardennes. At that point, the professor called him, and Wolf rounded up his forces, arriving just as the rescue had begun.

Even before her bath, Petra desperately pleasured herself, so very long overdue. Finally, her migraine vanished. She listened quietly, but keenly. When they finished their lengthy explanations, she was a far wiser ex-Feds. "May I ask a few questions," she said in a lull in the conversation. "You're Persephone, the Assassin?"

Lady Persephone laughed, "I prefer the Righteous Vigilante. I only kill those who deserve death, but yes, I am she, Europe's most wanted villain, it seems." The others grinned.

"And you're what the Europeans call the Wolf?" she asked, looking at Bardulf.

"Yes, I'm the head of the Freiheitskampfer, the freedom fighters of Europe. Remember, if you ever divulge this, you're a dead woman," he added quite seriously.

"I'll never tell," Petra added quickly. "Honestly, I would never have told Hans the location where the Feds are storing their explosives, not ever." She then turned her attention to Tilly. "And you, Tilly, are you also called Wart?" Tilly nodded; she hated to have her secret identity divulged, but the cat was completely out of the bag as far as she was concerned.

"Then you aren't the enemy the Feds always believed. It was you who discovered Hans' plot to sabotage the Pytalon factories and gave that information to the Feds?"

"Yes, but I was kidnaped by Hans as a result. We spent months as his prisoners as a result and had our feet mutilated too," she added, grimacing.

Petra sighed. "Everything is so backwards! The Feds believed you were our enemies, when in fact you were trying to help the world, but I know why I and the Feds all believed so. You see, we top Feds leaders have no one to answer to, excepting ourselves. I corrupted myself with all that power. I'm truly sorry. I realized for over a century, maybe more, there have been no checks upon the power of the top leaders of the world. We could and did just what we wanted to do, much to the detriment of our world, I might add. I truly am sorry, but I can't undo what I've done, especially with the implants. Maybe somehow I can help make it right, though."

She elaborated, "You see, right now, there is no one running the world. It is all on automatic, what with everyone, who was leading, now implanted and on Pytalon too. We need new leaders, but leaders who have some checks on their powers. I don't quite know how to say this properly. Let's say I was leading the Chicago Feds. I really should be enforcing the laws—what is right and proper for the world. There should be someone else who determines what these rules or laws are, not me, as I used to do. Plus, there should be someone else who oversees the laws and can invalidate those they believe aren't sound and wise rules. See what I mean? Each of us needs some measure of checks and balances on our powers. Ultimate power corrupts. I know, having corrupted myself with all that power. I've done some awful things, but now I want to help make things better somehow, even if I'm reduced to a sex doll. There must be some way we can make things better somehow. Lord knows how many more Grand Field Marshals there are out there still. We never even knew about him until Tilly broke the news to us."

"Well, I accept your apology, Petra" Tilly sighed. She knew what it took this woman to admit what she'd done. It felt like the right thing to do. "What is done, unfortunately for the three of us, is done. No matter how hard we want to go back, we can't. Implants prevent it, period. Petra does have a valid point. Right now, there's no one running the world, let alone any of the countries. It's as she says, all sort of on Pytalon automatic pilot. Need I add this isn't very good? While I don't have accurate figures on this, it's a near certainty even larger disasters are coming for the world at large. Zombies can hardly run a whole world, not for long. She's right. We need new leaders and quickly."

"If Beth forgives you," Jessica sighed, "then I do too." Beth sighed, and forgave Petra.

"But shouldn't the professor be involved with these kinds of decisions?" Jessica hinted by way of a question.

"Absolutely. Of course, this moves our timetable for the salvaging of our world up faster than he and I predicted," Tilly replied. "Dialing him." She outlined what had happened with their rescue and their current discussion.

"Put me on speaker phone, mate," he then requested, and she did so. "Greetings from across the Big Pond," he teased, and Lady Persephone smiled. Here was another Englishman. "Look, this is an extremely significant breakthrough. I'll be joining you in two days. Petra, please stick around. Tilly and I always predicted that one day the world would find itself effectively leaderless, just not this seven stand that thoughtoon. I have some ideas to discuss with all of you, including you, My Lady. I do hope you'll remain as well."

She smiled. "Yes, I must meet the professor. We English must bloody well stick together," Lady Persephone teased him back.

"Good, carry on. I must make some arrangements and get on my way. See you soon." He hung up.

"But how could you and this man have predicted all this?" Petra asked, somewhat taken aback by the sudden change of viewpoints.

Tilly explained, "My specialty is behavioral prediction based on firm mathematical formulas. It is a statistically valid process, but does require accurate input variables to obtain accurate percentage predictions. Amanda has been assisting me with the number crunching. Nearly any kind of behavioral patterns can be mathematically modeled, you see."

Petra didn't see, but accepted her reply. She wasn't good at math and knew it. "So you kind of know or can predict what will happen next?" She couldn't hide her somewhat perplexed look.

"Yes, she can," Amanda spoke up. "You see, we knew weeks ago there was a fifty percent chance Hans would try to find us after we escaped from him when the Feds raided Sandpoint. As we obtained more data, we were able to up the chance of this happening to ninety percent and then to one hundred percent, but that was after Juan got us the images of some of his men who were looking for us around the city.

"Oh. But then you must have known I was after you too, seeking revenge," Petra mused. "Thank God, I came to my senses and did the right thing," she added quickly.

Tilly grinned. "Right. At one point, we believed all three of you were after us. Now I really have to do some extensive research. If we missed Hans and his crew, then how many other threats are we not seeing? Frankly, I'm worried. We really do need to protect our world and the zombies until we are ready to begin bringing them safely out of it."

"What do you mean by bringing them out of it? Implants are permanent, and no one can safely come off Pytalon. Lord knows I've seen how horrible that is. Insanity in spades," Petra replied.

Beth laughed a little before replying, "Yes, implants are permanent, but, Petra, Jessica here has found a way to desensitize them sufficiently so we can get by fairly well, unfortunately just not good enough to try to undo the sex change. One of our friends has a good handle on getting people safely off Pytalon, getting the toxins out of their bodies."

Bardulf spoke up, adding more credence to what Beth revealed, "She's right. We've begun implementing Lisa's program here, and thus far, it does look most promising, though it is extremely time consuming."

"Wait! Are you saying there is a safe way to get someone off Pytalon and back to some semblance of the way they were before going onto that drug?" Lady Persephone asked. They nodded, and she exclaimed, "This is monumental news! Then, there is hope the world's billions can be saved. I thought the only future lay with the children and keeping them off it, allowing the zombie generation to die off."

"Yes, I put that into my calculations years ago, Lady Persephone. That was our very first plan, though I admit we've been more or less following that both in the States and here in Europe," Tilly replied. "However, with Lisa's startling discovery and process, Amanda and Jessica have rid their bodies of that awful toxin and with a great recovery of their well-being, I might add. It does work, but it takes an awful lot of time and work."

"We need to get this program going in a major way," Lady Persephone concluded. "Count me in. I'll help in any way I can."

"Me too, I want to help get people off Pytalon too," Petra added. "I know I'm almost useless. I can barely function with my EE implant, but I'll do my best to help. I don't know how you two can do all you do," she looked at Beth and Tilly. "It's all I can do to have a few lucid times during the day."

"Excuse me, but do you still vant me to examine their feet?" Doctor Gugenheimer broke in. "If not, I should be going home." That ended the discussion for the time being. All four wanted him to see if he could do anything for their feet. However, none held out any real hope; their doctor in Phoenix was clear in his diagnosis.

He undid Beth's boots first, and everyone stared at her now malformed toes and foot. "Ya, dis ist as I expected. Best take another set of x-rays, miss." He wheeled in his portable machine and did just that. Soon, the images appeared on his viewing screen, and everyone gathered around to see for themselves. The doctor began to point out the salient points, as if he were teaching a bunch of young interns. "Ya, Bardulf, it ist as I suspected."

"But can you do anything about them?" Beth asked. "We don't want our toes amputated. That would only make things worse."

"Aye that it would. No, I've seen these breaks before, but usually in young children who work too hard with their ballet lessons. Feet are my specialty, you see. Reconstructive surgery is needed, and you would need to be off your feet for two weeks. Plus, you would need to be in casts for another six to eight weeks after that," he explained.

"Right now, we can't afford to be immobile for over two months," Tilly commented. "There is far more at stake here than our feet. Let's wait and see what the professor has to say before we make any firm decision." The others agreed, and the doctor left.

281

Juan finally spoke up, "Beth, while we are waiting on the professor, Lady Persephone has a huge collection of ancient music too. We listened to a symphony while we were traveling. I told her you have a large collection. So how about hearing some?" The three spent a very enjoyable time, listening and chatting about the old music. Even Petra began to enjoy the marvelous sounds.

"I never knew this existed. It's beautiful," she commented. "Why am I so emotional? Oh God, not now," she complained, but began involuntarily whispering her EE implant litany. When she finished, she looked very embarrassed. She realized she'd not heard any of the other four women ever repeating the words of their nearly identical implants. Petra fought to keep from crying. Hastily, she changed the subject. "They're ordering us EE women to get married to total strangers, now that there are no more sponsors around. I can't look at men that way, even though my head seems to be splitting, trying to make me. I'm attracted only to women. You four are so lucky to have each other. I really am a basket case, but I'll still do all I can to help everyone."

That night, as Beth and Jessica lay in their warm bed, Jessica whispered, "I suppose I should work some with Petra and get her some relief from her implant."

"Well, she seems to be a changed person, and she did try to come to our rescue," Beth whispered back. "It's the only decent thing to do, but do you want me to do it?"

"No, I did it to her. It was my plan, my revenge, not yours, my love. I should be the one to do it for her. I'll work with her in the morning while you, Juan, and Lady Persephone listen to your old music," Jessica replied. "Amazing, people can change."

"Yes, but in this case, I think the sex change was the driving force behind her total change of heart and outlook. Maybe, dear, it was a good thing for her. Otherwise, she or he would still be an obnoxious and dangerous man to have controlling the Feds," Beth suggested.

The next day, Juan, Lady Persephone, and Beth spent hours in her EMAC listening to and discussing her selections of the ancient classical music. They made plans to share their mp3 files soon. They only stopped because the professor arrived.

Meanwhile, Jessica and Petra met in Petra's room in the A-frame hotel, compliments of the Wolf. "Can I ask you something personal, before we begin?" Petra asked, almost pleadingly. Jessica nodded, and Petra took a deep breath. "This is so embarrassing, but I still have a man's outlook. I mean I'm still male mentally, but now I have this female body. I'm not and never have been attracted to men, only women, pretty ones I must admit. I have to keep fighting the implant, which is driving me to have sex with men, but I can't even stand that thought. So I end up with these migraines all the time. Do Beth and Tilly have the same problem? Is there no hope but to somehow endure it? The EE Women's website told us we're all to get married now, since there are no more sponsors, but I can't possibly marry a man. I'd rather just die and get this nightmare over, but then I'm sworn to serve and protect our people. I can't just quit, not really."

Jessica smiled and wondered where to begin. "Well, yes, Beth and Tilly are in a similar mess. They are attracted to women too, and frankly are mostly revolted by the thought of going to bed with a man. In our case, Ben and I were in love, as were Amanda and Tim before all this happened to them. So they really have lucked out, unlike yourself, Petra. However, once we have your implant desensitized some, you'll be in far more control over your life. My own personal advice, Petra, is to marry someone out of a deep, long lasting love. Perhaps, there are other EE women with somewhat similar feelings. You might try making a worldwide posting of your desires and see what comes of it. Now then, let's get started."

Petra sighed, "Thank you, thank you Jessica. I promise to do all I can to help save our world and people."

"You'd better. Now then, let's start with the phrase 'I have to repeat these words.' I want you to say that aloud and with feeling, as if you really mean it."

"Yes, but that will pull in these awful headaches," she protested.

"Of course it will, but we just keep doing it, and you'll see what happens. Come on, say it." Thus began the long process of desensitizing Petra's PDH EE implant. By the time the professor arrived, Petra no longer felt the urge, drive, or need to repeat her implanted mantra, much to her relief.

"Well met again everyone. Lady Persephone Briton, I'm honored to make your acquaintance. Bardulf, good to see you. Petra," the professor called out, stepping down from his EMAC around suppertime. "Ah, the air is so fresh here, pines?"

"Welcome to Berchtesgaden, professor. This way, I have the dining room waiting for us. Hardly any business any longer, which suits us just fine," Bardulf replied, shaking his hand and leading the way.

Inside the elegant A-frame hotel, Lady Persephone had what she called a boom box playing a series of ancient galliards and pavans. She'd explained to Beth and Juan that the musicians were playing them on instruments called shawms. Further, she had two examples of shawms in her collection, though she had no idea how they were played.

As the professor walked into the room, Beth on his arm for support, he commented, "Ah, it sounds as if I'm entering Weasel's den once again." She laughed, as did Lady Persephone and Juan. After taking their seats and pouring themselves some fruit punch, the professor got down to business.

"Okay, Wart and I predicted one day the world would indeed find itself leaderless and running on a Pytalon automatic. Bloody hell, it wasn't supposed to happen for another quarter century though! Need we discuss the consequences of this?" he began, looking from face to face, finally lighting on Petra's.

She replied, "No, it's as if the world is walking along the edge of a sheer cliff. One slight misstep and down it all goes. Right?" she looked at the bearded Englishman for confirmation.

"Right, Petra. Succinctly stated. Wart and I had some long-range plans for this eventuality. However, coming so soon, we haven't yet gotten the personnel found and rehabilitated. Thus, the question before us is what do we do now? Petra, would you mind restating what you worked out about needing a balance of powers?"

Petra looked a little surprised, but went ahead and explained, "Yes, if you think this is important. When I joined the Feds, I swore an oath to protect and serve our people. Well, I sure failed at that, didn't I? Power corrupts. At first, I said I was corrupted. Then, I realized that wasn't quite right. I did it to myself. I had a taste of power, was carried away with it, and screwed up big time. I still don't know how I missed detecting someone as awful as the field marshal was. At this point, I realized something else. There are no checks and balances. As the top leader for the Central US, I could and did any darn thing I wanted to do. There was no one else to answer to. There are no checks and balances anywhere in our world—nowhere. The top person can do as they please. That's not right. Everyone should have some check on their powers."

"Right, Petra. If history is our guide, in ancient times, they did have checks and balances in the governing processes. One group made the laws, another group executed the laws, while a third group adjudicated the laws, striking down those that were not in the best interests of their people, or something like that. There was also something about the members of these three groups being elected, but in our world, that is out of the question," the professor explained.

Tilly countered, "So what're we to do? We don't have the people ready to step in and take over."

"Mates, we're going to have to step up and take over the stewardship of the world. We have no other satisfactory option, I'm afraid," the professor answered with a sigh. "Bloody hell, I never wanted to be in this position, but we are, ladies, gentlemen. The question is what do we do about this power vacuum? I would suggest we take Petra's comments literally. There must be checks and balances on the power positions we're going to take. Otherwise, as Petra says, eventually, ultimate power tends to corrupt, to lead one astray, no matter their intentions."

He went on, "We need to lead by making those decisions that will ultimately provide the most good and benefits for the majority of the people, who at this time are incapable of making such decisions, thanks to the psychs and drug manufacturers. The most good for the most should be our guiding principle. Any objections to this starting point?" He looked around and found none.

"This is all well and good," Lady Persephone said calmly in her mellow voice, "but just what are you proposing we do? The real question remains before us. How are we to accomplish this lofty goal?"

"One step at a time, My Lady. The Feds operate worldwide and are the topmost enforcement bureau everywhere. Hence, we need to install one of us as their top leader," he proposed, looking around the room at the many faces.

He then suggested, "I would like to suggest Miss Petra take that post. She is still a Feds, technically. She hasn't resigned her commission, and from all data at hand, the Chicago branch still considers Delius to be their leader, as witnessed by the Feds' response to Petra's message to them about using herself to locate Hans Gudrunda."

"Me? But I'm an EE woman now. They'll not respect me, will they?" Petra gasped. She'd never thought about returning to her former position.

"You can always say you recognized the Grand Field Marshal as being the most serious threat to world safety in a century. With the Feds being unable to locate him, you took a devious route to entrap him, by turning yourself into an EE woman so you could infiltrate his group. In a way, you did just that," the professor pointed out.

"Well, I suppose that would fly," Petra hesitantly admitted, seeing enough elements of truth in the explanation. "But me, back in the Feds and controlling the worldwide operations of the Feds? Isn't that ultimate power once again?"

"Indeed, so we need checks and balances. I propose Bardulf and our organization provide the 'laws' so to speak. We know how to recover a person from the implant-Pytalon mess that he or she is in. No one else is in a better position to provide the guiding light, so to speak. Beth and Jessica can continue to monitor the world and search out threats as always. Thus, Petra, you would be answerable to us. However, both of us need some checks and balances on our actions, so I propose Lady Persephone becomes our 'court of law.' That is, she looks over our shoulders and over Petra's, and can veto any move we make she deems inappropriate. Any two of the three branches can overrule the other one. This way, each of us can be held accountable for our decisions and actions. What do you think?" he ended his carefully planned move. Would they accept this additional responsibility? He wasn't sure they would.

"Oh my, professor. You're asking a lot of us—the whole world!" Lady Persephone replied, biting her lip. "Okay, I'm game. The Righteous Vigilante will do her part, if Petra will do hers. I'm concerned she'll be unable to perform adequately. She has been implanted," she pointed out the weak link in his proposed scheme.

"I know. I face a great deal of humiliation and probably worse," Petra sighed, "but I'll do my very best. I simply must help make things right somehow."

"I'm becoming more certain she will. However, she'll first need to get that implant desensitized," the professor backed Petra.

"We've been fighting the good fight here in Europe," Bardulf spoke up. "Now it seems we finally have a chance, a fighting chance at that. Count the Freiheitskampfer in on this deal. It will be sehr gut not to be hunted any longer, no question of that!" Several smiled and nodded their agreement with his sentiments.

"Good, bloody good! Then as I see it, we have two details to work out immediately. First, we need to help Petra get herself established as the worldwide Feds leader. Second, we need to get a real plan of attack on our rehabilitation project. Lisa can only detoxify so many people at one time. We need to setup detoxification centers around the world, staff them, and train them, along with therapists who can desensitize the PDH implants as well."

Beth spoke up, "Add a third. We all missed Hans and his group. I bet there are many other groups similar to his out there that are trying to undermine things. We need to get a handle on what it is that we don't know."

The professor laughed. "Beth, Jessica, may we leave this third one in your capable hands for now?" She laughed as well and agreed. The group then focused on the two major details. As a group, they prepared a lengthy memo, outlining the basic reasoning behind Peter Delius' rather drastic action to become an EE woman so she could infiltrate and ultimately destroy the Grand Field Marshal. That accomplished, she intended first to return to her position as the Chicago Feds leader. However, since the other top leaders were now gone, having become implanted doormen, someone had to oversee the entire worldwide Feds operations. She appointed herself to that position, backed by the excellent success she had destroying the diabolical threat of Hans Gudrunda and his band of saboteurs. Once everyone agreed on the proper wording, using Petra's email account, she sent it to the many branch offices of the Feds.

The professor then said, "As far as the next step, I suggest before Petra returns to her office, she should spend a couple of weeks with Jessica until she gets the EE implant under control." Everyone readily accepted this suggestion.

Lady Persephone added, "Everyone, you are invited to come to my castle for those couple of weeks." She and Beth wanted to exchange ancient music, and Juan wanted to see the ancient instruments as well.

"Fine, now about the second detail. We need physical therapists and saunas and vitamins," the professor began outlining his ideas to get the rehabilitation project going on a larger scale than their tiny pilot project in Phoenix and here in

Berchtesgaden. Both groups decided to train up a pair of therapists and to fire them off to open a new rehabilitation centers—one in Berlin and one in Chicago.

Petra spoke up, "I should issue orders that these rehabilitation centers must be heavily protected by the Feds and that no one should be ordered to get any more implants. Plus any who accidentally come off Pytalon should be sent at once to one of these rehab centers." All agreed with her, and she wrote up the orders, but had everyone verify she'd written them properly.

"Say Beth, once I'm back in my Chicago office, would you like to have an office there too, complete with all the electronics you desire and need?" Petra volunteered. "There are plenty of plush apartments close by."

The offer took Beth by surprise. "Well, let me think about it, Petra. We have time."

The professor countered, "Unless Beth and Jessica want to do so, I would advise they stay in their secret location. That way, if trouble comes to you, Petra, then Beth and Jessica wouldn't also be compromised. If someone comes after you, we would still have our best sleuths available to help find you. Still, it might prove useful if they did have an office there in your building for part of the time. One can argue both ways. It's up to Beth and Jessica."

"Could Tilly and Amanda also have an office there too?" Jessica asked. "We've never been parted since we became EE women, Amanda and me that is."

"Sure I don't see why not. I'll arrange it when I get there and find you a nice penthouse suite," Petra replied.

"We still have an apartment there," Amanda spoke up. "It is not too far from the Feds building, I think. I know it's a bit small, but it's been home for Jessica and me for eight years."

"Okay. That's great then. I'll see about two offices close together. We don't walk all that well in these boots," Petra replied, pleased she was able to do a little something for the four women. Jessica sensed Petra desperately didn't want to be alone in Chicago. She understood why too.

"Say, is there any possibility that Ilse and Erika might return here? I know their sisters would dearly love to have them," Bardulf asked.

"They are both now nearly done being trained as physical therapists. When they finish, I'll relay your suggestion," the professor replied. "Of course, we'll miss having the two top models with us." He and Bardulf chuckled, and Beth and Tilly grinned.

"Have you four made any decision about having your feet done?" Bardulf asked.

"We're going to wait a while," Beth answered for them. "We're really worried there are others like Hans Gudrunda out there waiting for a chance to cause more sabotage. I really do want to do a super-thorough search as soon as possible. We can always get them done later on when things quiet down."

"Professor, can I ask you a question?" Petra spoke up. Something fundamental was still troubling her. He nodded, and she did so. "Are the Feds men really going to take me seriously? I mean when I was Peter Delius, I never took any EE woman seriously, believing them to be nothing more than sex dolls. Is this really going to work?"

"You aren't wrong, Petra. I have traveled widely. Most all EE women are sex dolls—that was their purpose in the first place. However, not all of them are sex dolls, as you have discovered for yourself. In your case, the men you'll be leading are themselves implanted and on Pytalon. They'll have no sex drive and will in all likelihood focus solely and only on 'doing their job,' as a zombie would. So yes, I wouldn't have suggested you take this post if I didn't think it would work out for you."

Petra breathed a sigh of relief, though she still had her own doubts. After all, she had lusted for the EE women when she was still male, recalling her ill-fated Thanksgiving party. *I've certainly changed since then. Now, if we can only change this messed up world.*

Vic Broquard

Part II Organization

Chapter 21—Adjustments

"I'm really nervous about this," Petra admitted to her new five friends. "What if. . ."

June had come to Chicago, and the six had just returned from their stay in Lady Persephone's castle in Sussex. Beth had traded several hundred ancient music files with her. She and Juan had thoroughly enjoyed their mini-vacation at the picturesque castle, to say nothing of admiring her immense collection of ancient music disks and other electronic equipment her great-grandfather had painstakingly acquired.

They had returned to Chicago, since Jessica had finally finished desensitizing Petra's EE implant, much to everyone's relief, though none more so than Petra herself. Finally, she felt human again. While the implant was still there, she now could exert significant control over it. Gone were her constant migraine headaches, and she could think well again without constant interference from her implant. The six were in an EMAC on their way to the main Feds skyscraper overlooking Lake Michigan on Lake Shore Drive. This would be her first day back as the top leader of not only the Chicago Feds but also as the supreme leader of the Feds worldwide.

"Take a deep breath and relax, Petra. It'll be just fine," Jessica interrupted her "what if's." Remember, they're all on Pytalon and mostly zombies themselves." Privately, she hoped this would be the case. They were taking a big gamble on this aspect. Quickly, she glanced at everyone's appearance. Their nails were trimmed to their usual length, about two inches, per the normal guidelines for EE women. All still wore their knee-high ballet boots, since the four weren't yet willing to spend the six weeks recovery time off their feet. There was just too much pressing business at hand to squander a month and a half. All wore respectable satin gowns and looked completely presentable as EE women.

The vehicle halted before the main entrance, and the driver calmly announced, "Feds building." In a lower voice, he added, "Sanity is delivering my passengers to their destination and on time." This last, the six ignored, as Juan opened the passenger door. One by one, he lent his arm to steady each of the five women as they carefully stepped down to the pavement.

Many others were passing by on the street, but none even looked at the small group. Each was lost within their own world, thanks to the effects of Pytalon, though some obviously also had implants. Those muttered their litany to themselves as they walked glassy-eyed down the street.

Petra spotted the usual window washer and doorman on duty at the front of the Feds building, just as they had for as long as she could remember. As they made their slow, careful way to the main doors, the doorman spoke up, "Good day. Welcome to the Feds Building." He opened the door for them, whispering to himself, "Sanity is doing a good job of opening the doors." Petra had always ignored the doorman all these years, but today, she flinched. The reality of just how awful society had become thanks to the psych drug hit home to her. Inwardly, she gave thanks that her new friends had worked out a way to get people off this nightmare drug.

Just inside the bulletproof glass doors, a large reception desk loomed. Two security guards were on-duty. Their glassy-eyed stares took in the new arrivals. Petra walked nervously up to the desk, the others following along behind her. "Petra Delius and party. I need to get clearance badges for these five guests of mine."

"Yes, we have been informed of your arrival. Sign here and write down the names of those in your party," one replied in a monotone. Then, showing a slight change, he added, "Good to have you back. You look different somehow, Peter, Petra."

"Thank you. People do change. There, all signed in, sir." She'd never gotten the man's name before. *How strange to have passed by this guard for years and never taken the time to get his name. Well, I was power-crazy back then.* "By the way, what is your name?"

"Felix Rausch, ma'am. Here are their badges." He then whispered, "Sanity is doing a proper check-in."

After affixing the badges to their dresses, Petra said, "This way to the elevators. Walking is more treacherous on this plush carpeting though. Watch your steps." *God, I hope I don't take a tumble in front of everybody!*

They rode the elevator to the top floor where Peter's old office had been. Memories flooded back to five of the six. Beth, Jessica, Tilly, and Amanda cringed a little. Their memories weren't the best. Juan merely took in the new surroundings. When the doors opened, Lech was there waiting on them. For a moment, Petra panicked. What if her old second in command refused to allow her access to the office? What if he refused to have an EE woman in charge? Only men were Feds operatives.

His eyes were also glazed over. "Welcome back boss. It has been far too long. I've done my best to keep things going, as you would have wanted them done. We've recovered seven of your handguns from that military base in the Ardennes. Excellent work, boss," he said, again in the distinctive monotone, devoid of any real emotion. On Pytalon, he was incapable of feeling or displaying any emotion at all.

Lech then added, "On behalf of all the Feds here, we want to thank you for taking such drastic measures to discover the hideout of our most wanted criminal, Hans Gudrunda, and for taking so many of his men out before our forces arrived. We had very little to do there," he continued in his monotone. Then, his eyes cleared for a brief moment and he added, "You really did do it. You do look like an EE woman, boss." Just as swiftly, his eyes glazed back over again.

"Lech Smith, these are our new operatives who'll be having the two offices on the floor below this one," Petra began the formal introductions, unsure of how to respond to Lech's comments. Mechanically, Lech shook each person's hand in turn. Beth could sense he was trying hard to remember which name went with which person.

That done, Lech continued his reports. "I have left the most recent memos on your desk."

"Excellent work, Lech. Are there any current emergencies that need handling right away?" Petra asked, thinking it would be good to get the conversation onto proper Feds business.

"Well, yes, as a matter of fact, boss. Top memo. We could use your insight on this one. I'll be in my office if you need me," Lech replied. Petra nodded and he left.

"See, all is going along perfectly," Jessica validated Petra, who breathed a huge sigh of relief.

"They wouldn't normally have accepted me, except they're on Pytalon now. Okay, we should get you to your new offices. Lech is efficient. Here are your official ID badges," she picked the five up from her desk. After handing them out to the others, she led them back to the elevator. After walking down a long corridor with many side offices, they arrived at two adjacent ones, each with a placard on them. Beth and Jessica Snells. Tilly and Amanda Hickory. "If you need anything, buzz me on the intercom." Petra turned and headed back to her office, while the four examined their new offices, leaving Juan to stand guard.

As arranged beforehand, all four women began a careful search for electronic bugs and other surveillance devices. They didn't trust the Feds, but they found none. "Okay, first thing, change all our passwords on these systems," Beth ordered. "Gosh, we have a superb setup here. I'll give them that!"

Jessica smiled. "So are we going to make our own hook into this system so we can get to here from back home? That's what I would do."

"Precisely, my love. Where have you been all my life," Beth teased her.

"Right here, waiting for you to find me," Jessica teased her back.

Meanwhile, Petra glanced at the emergency memo, and then reread it twice more before pressing the intercom button buzzing Tilly. "Hi, me here. I hate to do this to you, but can you and Amanda come up? This new emergency is frankly so strange that I'm not certain what to do about it."

Five minutes later, the two very bored women walked slowly into Petra's office, eager for anything to break their monotony. Neither could really do much work at all until they were back in their safe house in East Peoria. "What's up?" Tilly asked. All three women sat on the large couch, and Petra handed them the memo printout.

It read: Fifteen civilians were gunned down in Kroger's Grocery Store around 10 a.m. on May 21. No surveillance cameras caught the culprit, but a street cam recorded a single man armed with a 9mm gun exiting the store around the same time. Victims included ten women shopping and five store personnel, including the manager, stock boy, and three clerks. No witnesses. All present in the store were slain by one or more shots to the head. See Video File 112436 and 112437. Referred to Feds by responding AP-cops, 21 May.

"Cue up the video files, will you. How very strange indeed. Ordinary women shopping for groceries, weird indeed," Tilly mused, biting her lip.

"Do we have any formulas for something like this? Why would anyone murder everyone in a grocery store for heaven's sake?" Amanda asked.

"Clueless," Petra remarked, rising carefully and retrieving her handheld video controller. She chastised herself.

I should've brought this with the memo. It looks as though I'm not prepared. Equally carefully and slowly, she returned to her seat and sat down. After entering some codes, the first of the two videos appeared on her giant flat screen monitor on the wall. This one showed the aftermath, as the Feds shot the scene before the bodies were sent to the morgue. The second one showed a man wearing a hooded, grey jacket leaving the store. The gun was clearly visible in his right hand, though he stuck it in his belt shortly thereafter.

"May I?" Amanda asked, pointing to the controller. Petra handed it to her, and she backed the video up some. Then, she replayed it in slow motion and finally stopping. "There, you can see his eyes. They aren't glazed over, so he isn't on Pytalon. He's not heavily drugged up at this point in time."

Petra exclaimed, "You have keen eyes, Amanda! I missed that detail. You're right; he isn't a zombie. Too bad the image of his face isn't complete enough to put through our facial recognition software. He's wearing gloves, so no chance for fingerprints. No DNA is likely either. He is a mystery man at this moment. So any recommendations on a course to follow?"

Tilly ran her hands through her hair a moment before answering. "From my perspective, I need more data. Specifically, has this sort of mass murder of civilians occurred before? If so where, how many were killed, etcetera? If this is an isolated event, that's one thing. If not, it's quite another. The behavior prediction formulas vary between the two scenarios."

"Okay, I'll get our people looking into that aspect. For now, Lech has distributed a copy of the man from the video to the AP-cops in hopes someone might spot him," Petra explained.

"We'll get both formulas ready to plug and chug. Let us know the results as soon as you get them," Tilly explained. She and Amanda then returned to their office. Tilly grumbled, "I need my own computer. I doubt I can remember the actual formulas."

Amanda suggested, "Maybe we'll be able to return there soon."

Tilly sighed and smiled.

Once Petra sent off her orders, she checked her EE Women's website to see if she had any new replies to her email requesting a lesbian companion. Petra wanted out of being forced to marry some unknown man. Already, she had gotten a half dozen men offering to marry her. She had received two replies from other EE women, but both women were in their fifties, far too old for her, but kept them on the back burner as a last resort.

To her surprise, she had one new email. It was from a Cho Lin in Peking, China. The last name sounded familiar, though Petra couldn't place it. China, she thought, Lin. Then it came to her. Tao Lin was the Feds leader there in Peking, but he, like all the other leaders, had been implanted and put on a heavy dosage of Pytalon. She opened it and read:

Dear Miss Petra Delius,

Please help me. I am prisoner in dad's office. He was Tao Lin, Feds leader here Peking. I wanted to marry my lover, Mei Bing, but Tao would not let me. Says I bring shame on Lin ancestors. Must marry man, not woman, but Mei and I loved each other. I no marry man. Dad and I argue long over this. He very angry with me, but I not give in. Love Mei. He cuts off my fingers one at a time until I give in and marry man he chooses. I still not give in, but should have, maybe. Hands infected, now have only stumps. I still not give in. Mei Bing now dead. He had her murdered. Still I no marry man. Man no wants me like this. He orders me to spend all my days in his office and hires caretaker to dress me and bring me here each day. Take me home at night. Now dad is gone, but his orders still stand. No one listens to me. I trapped here. Please come get me. I can't open doors, but I can still give you much pleasure. I marry you. I see your pictures on EE site and read your email. I very willing to marry you, but I need lots of help, but I give you good love, best pleasure. I type slow with pen in mouth. Please help me. See my old picture on my EE page.

Cho Lin

"Good god!" Petra exclaimed and reread her email for the third time. Then, she opened a new browser tab and went in search of Cho Lin's web page. "Oh, you're a beauty, Cho!" She stared at her image. Cho had a round face and was very attractive with very long, straight black hair that fell to her knees. She read the old description, noticing she too always wore ballet boots from her beginnings as an EE woman. She checked on Cho's age; it was the same as hers: thirty-one. Her eyes looked utterly captivating and Petra found herself highly attracted to Cho. "Oh!" she exclaimed, realizing her viewpoint of Peter Delius was totally influencing her view of Cho. As Peter, he would have tried his best to "sponsor" Cho. Failing that, he would have invited her to his parties.

Petra decided to act. She typed a response and sent it. "I've got preparations to make now!" She ordered an Air Liner to standby and then paid a visit to her five friends. "Look, I have to make an emergency trip to Peking, China. An EE woman there is in dire need."

"Great. We're done here. We'll return to East Peoria now and get to work on your murder situation," Tilly suggested, extremely glad to have found an opening allowing them to leave Chicago for home.

"Yes, I've got everything here all set, Petra. Jessica and I can access everything from home. We've left you our contact info so you can reach us at any time, night or day," Beth added. She too wanted the comfort of her own place. The Feds office, while spotless, was sterile from her point of view. Everyone was relieved. Petra was free to go rescue Cho Lin, and the five were free to return home.

"Thank you for helping and being so understanding," Petra replied. "I'll be sending you anything my Feds come up with on other mass murders, just as soon as I get them. Do I send Lady Persephone a message I'm making this trip to China?"

"Yes, we're all supposed to keep her posted on our movements," Beth replied. "I'm sending her word now that we're on our way to East Peoria. I'll add you're on your way to China and that everything is working out perfectly. It's wise we have one central person keeping track of all our whereabouts, though I've had more than enough kidnaping to last me for the rest of my life."

"Oh thank you, Beth. Yes, perfect. Mind you, I don't know why I was so darn nervous about this. Well, yes I do know," Petra declared, biting her lip a little.

Amanda replied, "We all do. If the men here weren't Pytalon zombies, you wouldn't be taken seriously nor would you have been allowed to resume your post." Petra smiled, knowing Amanda was precisely correct. As Peter, she never took any EE woman seriously, nor any woman for that matter.

Yet, women were just as able to lead as men, perhaps more so, she mused.

"Yes, it was a man's world," Petra admitted. "I'm afraid I'm guilty of that as the next man. Well, I have certainly changed my viewpoint," she hazarded a slight tease. Amanda smiled.

An hour later, the five headed home to East Peoria, Tilly driving, and Amanda co-piloting as usual. Beth said, "I suppose after we get things under control, we should consider taking the two months to get our feet fixed up."

"If we get things under control!" Jessica teased her mate. "Ever since I met you, it's been one exciting event after the other. I've certainly not been bored, but I admit I'd like a little quite time."

"Oh no! Then I would be extremely bored," Juan teased her back. "Whatever would I do then?" All three laughed and relaxed. Soon they dozed off. Late afternoon, they were back in their subterranean safe house. An hour later, Juan brought them dinner, and they had their systems up and running once more.

As they ate, Tilly pointed out, "Okay, Amanda and I have to get going on these murders, but we need data."

"Jessica can go over all the recordings made while we were gone, and I'll look into your murders for you," Beth suggested.

A short while later, Amanda and Tilly began working up the complex equations that would help them make predictions about their murderer, while Beth began searching for similar murder events. Before long, Weasel hacked into the Chicago AP-cops database, chasing down more details.

Around ten that night, she sat back and let out a long sigh. "What's up? Find anything?" Tilly looked over at her and asked.

"More like an epidemic of wonton murder sprees. It is not limited to Chicago either. Detroit has had them, as do New York City, LA, and New Orleans. Those are the ones I've looked at so far. You aren't going to have to work hard on your predictions, though. Here, I'm sending you my summary from these cities, going back one year now. I can't decide if I need to examine all large cities or if I need to go back beyond one year. After you analyze these, let me know how you want me to proceed. I'm pooped. How about you, Jessica? Ready for bed?"

"After bit, I'm following a lead right now. Surveillance all checks out. No new catastrophes have been reported at the national level, so I began following two ideas. First, I wondered how many other Hans' are out there. That is, folks whose implants were done wrong. So far, I've found none, but I need your help hacking into the psych's national database and their worldwide one too. Second, I wondered if there were other anti-government groups out there who have web pages advertising themselves and for recruitment. I've found two of those so far: the National Citizens' Rights and the Coalition for Human Rights. We should probably look into these two groups, but I've only just begun. God, I hope none of these are as insane as the field marshal's group!"

"So much for a nice, peaceful summer," Juan groaned. "I'm going to bed. Just thinking about more such wild groups is making my head ache," he teased. "Next, you will be finding whole pockets of people who have been completely overlooked and are neither implanted nor on Pytalon."

"Damn, we never thought about that point!" Tilly exclaimed. "We have to look into that one, Juan. Good thinking!" He groaned; he was only jesting, but now realized if some had been overlooked, they could well be a major problem too. "That would make sense, you know. There are many isolated places on Earth that could have easily been overlooked. You know, the wilds of western China, tiny South Pacific islands, the Amazon Jungles, the Congo. There could be lots of people who have never been a part of the 'Sane World Program' of the psychs or the various Total Care programs."

This made sense to everyone, but Beth wondered how she could possibly find out about them since they wouldn't likely have any electronic presence in the world. The more she thought about this aspect, the more worried she became. "Tilly, what are the odds there are small groups of people who somehow were overlooked and are neither implanted nor on Pytalon?"

"Actually quite high in all likelihood. The professor and I once speculated on just this detail. I did come up with some figures, but they lacked any real physical data so they were mere speculation, and we dropped it back then. Certainly after all these years, such people would have to be living under the radar, so to speak, though that is very easy to do nowadays. Zombies aren't observant. Still, we should take another look,"

Tilly answered, running her hands through her hair. *So much to do.*

The next day, sleep had done wonders for Tilly and Amanda. Fresh ideas sprouted over breakfast. "Beth, Amanda and I have been thinking, and we have some work for you and Jessica to do—you too, Juan. We reason this way. If there are overlooked pockets of people who have somehow managed to avoid the psychs' program, then of necessity, they must be off the grid. That means they can't be using their own ID cards to purchase their necessities. Heck, they might not even have a Universal ID Card. Like Juan, they could be living in more remote areas, but they could also be living in the cities as well, where they could easily hide among the masses."

"Makes sense, but what are we to look for?" Beth protested slightly. She didn't see any way to track people who had no identification whatsoever. There would be no database records to find.

"They have to live and that means they need cash and food and shelter. While there are some like the Wolf and us who have managed to play the game and remain 'hidden' in the society, I would expect most weren't so able. Hence, start looking for discrepancies. Look for grocery stores that have significant 'missing' inventories. I would suspect many people are simply stealing what they need, but on a small level so as not to draw attention to themselves."

"Say, that makes sense! You got it," Beth exclaimed, suddenly catching on to Tilly's argument.

Amanda added, "It's as if we're now moving into a new era. The professor and the Phoenix group are working on salvaging people, and now we're searching for normal people who have somehow eluded the psychs and their worldwide program." She added, "Though I suppose at any moment we could be back dealing with more of the Han's ilk."

"Me too, but what do you want me to do?" Juan asked.

"Get more familiar with our city and its surroundings. Search out likely places where those who are off the grid might be hiding out or living. Abandoned structures like ours here would be fruitful places to search, but by all means take your weapons with you," Tilly suggested. "I would expect these people to be armed and highly protective of their hideouts, just as we are here."

"Ah some fun at last," Juan teased her.

Juan had been gone an hour when Beth called out, "You're on to something, Tilly. I've hacked into our local grocery store and been examining their books. I've compiled three columns here. Here is what they ordered from their distribution centers, here is what they claim to have sold, and I added this column, what appears to have 'disappeared' from their inventory. Of course, this isn't conclusive; some could've been damaged, spoiled, or simply misplaced. Still, there's a substantial loss of inventory each month going back a year or so."

Jessica added, "And I'm writing a program to search out other stores' data in all major cities, working from corporate headquarters downward. Of course, it may take days to run, but it should give us a feel for how widespread this phenomenon actually is. Gosh, it feels so good to be back to normal living again." The others flashed her a big grin; they were thinking the same thing; no more living under threats. Now they could do their investigations without fears or worries.

"Gang, Amanda had a bright idea," Tilly changed the topic to their researches. "Compare the bullets from the different mass murders and see if the same guns were used in them. Brilliant. I'm going to test our supposedly newfound connections now. Keep your fingers crossed." She dialed Lech Smith.

"Yes, Tilly here. We have more information on the mass murders. Yes, plural," she explained what they'd uncovered so far. "What we'd like done is to have the CSI department compare the bullets recovered from each of the last dozen mass murder sites. This will either point to a single set of guns being used each time or completely different guns. What will this prove?" she asked, responding to his complaint. "Are we looking for one group of murderers or are we looking for a dozen different groups of murderers?" she explained in simple terms the Pytalon-drugged man could easily grasp. "Good. Text me the results when you have them. We're checking into this phenomenon further. It's also happening in other cities as well. More later, thanks, Lech." She looked up and smiled. "He's going to get it done, but it'll take a while to get the evidence from the previous murders, which were never reported to the Feds by the AP-cops. I guess we do have some Feds pull now." All four grinned broadly.

"Now this is something I would never have predicted," Beth added.

Later, Jessica launched her research program to search many databases in hopes of discovering just how widespread this "missing inventory" situation actually was. Of course, it would take days to run. With time on her hands, she decided to research implants, specifically these PDH implants, which she was able to desensitize, given a couple of weeks and a lot of determination on her part and her patient's. Just who invented them, she wondered, as she began her web searching. The Pytalon drug was merely an advancement on the supposed anti-psychotic drugs prevalent in the US way back in the early 2000's, though at the time, few realized the hideous consequences those earlier drugs had on those who took them. Suicides were far more common than the psychs and drug manufacturers ever acknowledged, which in part fueled their research into better ones, leading to Pytalon.

However, just who invented the PDH implanting procedure, she wondered. In the 2000's psychiatrists were being attacked wholesale in the US because their barbaric practices had never cured anyone, only making the person totally subdued or a vegetable, assuming they survived their electric and insulin shocks and brain surgeries. Faced with jail terms and monstrous fines, many fled the US to China, where they were welcomed with open arms. Back then, China was well on its way to becoming the industrial giant that it was today.

There, they were able to continue their "experiments" on human beings because in a land of billions with a severe overpopulation problem, the value of a human life was virtually nothing at all—so a man or woman died. There were tens of thousands ready to take their place, Jessica read on the website of the Coalition for Human Rights. Fascinated, she read more. History had always fascinated her, now even more so. Two brothers, Bo Bin Lin and Han Lin had worked together to bring about the first PDH implanting devices. Bo Bin, the psych, and Han, the engineer, had brought electronics and drugs together. However, their initial successes were dubious. Their goal was to implant workers so they would perform as well as robotic machines.

Electro-mechanical robots were needed in most all new Chinese factories, but they were terribly expensive. A human-bot was cheap and, when worn out, could easily be replaced. That was the original goal and thinking, Jessica read. In time, the technology proved successful, in that zombies could cheaply run the manufacturing lines in China. Then came Pytalon and the two technologies joined, as the whole world needed a "cure" for insanity, which had become widespread. No one correlated this uprising of insanity with the anti-psychotic drugs then in use. Instead, the psychs were given more money and authority to "deal" with the rising levels of insanity. Jessica sat back, absorbing what she'd read.

Something bothered her, though. *If the Lin's invented it, why would they stop their research at that point? I mean if I were on to something potentially as huge as this, then I wouldn't just stop experimenting. Well, it did go into mass production worldwide, but still, I wouldn't stop because of that. Of course, those brothers are long dead, but their associates certainly would continue their work. I sure would have. I wonder what came after that or is coming. Now how am I going to figure that out?* She bit her lip a little before an idea came. The two brothers had formed the Lin Foundation for further research, according to the Coalition for Human Rights. She found the company's web site and found it was now being led by co-CEOs: Bo Bin Lin and Han Lin.

Strange, she thought. *Same last names. Wait, same names as the founders! Could those two still be alive after all these years?* "That would make them over two hundred years old!" she exclaimed.

"Who is that old?" Beth asked, her interest pricked.

"Oh, the founders of the Lin Foundation—the men who invented PDH implanting machines almost two centuries ago," Jessica explained. "They're still listed as the current CEOs of the company, but they can't be two hundred; no one lives that long."

"Check their faces; that'll proved they're different men," Beth suggested. "Let me help a bit." A few minutes later, the two had four images up on the monitor. "See, the ones on the left are the original founders and the ones on the right are the current leaders. They don't even look remotely related, but then they're Chinese, and I'm not so good with their facial features."

"I can see that, but why the same names? What are the odds two hundred years later, two men with the exact same names as the founders are running the company?" Jessica asked.

Overhearing their conversation, Tilly spoke up nonchalantly, "Thousands to one against it, probably higher."

"Interesting. Let's see what we can dig up on these two fellows," Beth suggested. She and Jessica began doing more research. "Remember, nothing that gets posted on the Internet is ever really gone."

Jessica chuckled, "Yes, I know, you told me it's on somebody's server somewhere."

Four hours later, the two hit pay dirt on an obscure Swedish archival site. For reasons unknown to the two, this site had taken periodic snapshots of the Lin Foundation's web site during the last two hundred years. An hour later, the two stared dumbfounded at what they'd uncovered. The company's CEOs had always had the same names: Bo Bin Lin and Han Lin. When the original founders grew old, two new younger men replaced them, but they had the same names. "How very strange!" Beth exclaimed.

"Goofy, if you ask me. Why? I've heard of very strange things, but this takes the cake," Jessica replied. None of the many men who had the same names looked remotely alike. "Perhaps Lin is a common name in China." Jessica theorized.

"Might be, but this can't be a coincidence, love, not with identical names each time. I wonder what's going on." Beth replied. "Perhaps these new replacement CEOs have had to change their names to match those of the founders. That I could sort of see."

"I wonder what the Lin men's bank accounts look like," Jessica asked, being drawn even more into this most unusual mystery.

"Well now, that's something we can find out," Beth replied with a mischievous grin. A half hour later, with Jessica looking over her shoulder, she stared in disbelief at what she'd found in the bank records she'd just hacked. "Their personal accounts have been active for two hundred six years, continuously! What the devil is going on here?"

"Well, maybe they leave their accounts for their replacements?" Jessica suggested. "But that's weird, isn't it?"

"This gets weirder by the minute. Look at this, the first replacement Lins only lived for three years before they were replaced. These current ones have been at it for twenty-five years now," Beth pointed out.

"Yes, each successive pair seem to last longer than their predecessors, excepting the original founders, that is," Jessica observed.

"I wonder what they are doing or inventing now," Beth asked. "From these snapshots of their company web site, they were very active in getting PDH implant technology in worldwide use. After that, nothing new appears on their pages. Could they have just stopped inventing their brainwashing technologies?"

"I suppose so, if they too got implanted or on Pytalon like everyone else," Jessica suggested the only reasonable answer. Still that they wouldn't try to refine or further their technology for over a hundred plus years bothered her, and she bit her lip, once more baffled and perplexed. The mystery surrounding this company was simply not unraveling as it ought to.

Chapter 22—A Nightmare

Petra Delius made a quick stop at her apartment to pack an overnight bag. The trip to Peking would take nearly twenty hours one-way. Her own estimate was this would be a three-day trip: one each getting there and back, and one day to rescue Cho Lin and get her things onto the Air Liner. Already she had sent the Peking Feds office a short email stating she would be arriving for an inspection. Petra didn't anticipate any real trouble, but she strapped on her 9mm gun and her backup piece as well. It wasn't that she felt particularly vulnerable as an EE woman; rather it was a simple matter of having to wear the ballet boots. Those made walking treacherous and slow. That yielded vulnerability in her mind.

At last, she carefully climbed up the steps into the Feds Air Liner and closed the passenger door. Her hands moving along the sides of the hall for support, she moved up to the driver's seat and sat down. It took her about ten minutes to punch in the destination coordinates and obtain the necessary international flight clearances. Finally, she pressed the Execute Program button, and the large EM driven ship rose silently into the air and then slowly accelerated to cruising speed, all under the control of the navigational system. She smiled, reflecting on just how easy international travel really was. Press a button, sit back, and relax; the system was foolproof.

If anything did go wrong, a loud alert siren would sound, along with flashing red lights, impossible to miss, even if one were sleeping at the time. Still, Petra couldn't recall when any such emergency had happened in her lifetime, though she knew from history lessons in high school, there had been some a hundred years ago. She was confident all the "bugs" had been worked out of their many navigation systems. Now she had some twenty hours to kill and spent a good deal of it sleeping or dozing, though she mechanically pleasured herself periodically to keep her implant satisfied.

As she approached China, Petra ate a quick breakfast, changed her dress, and put her long hair wig back over her own hair. Hers was now about four inches long, wholly unacceptable for an EE woman. No, she mused, she would have to be wearing wigs for at least another year, as uncomfortable as they were.

After checking her minimalist makeup, she strapped her two guns on and returned slowly to the driver's seat. She was in time to watch her descent onto Peking and shortly thereafter, the Feds' airfield, not far from their main headquarters building. She noticed they had an MTE that connected the field to their twenty-story building and breathed a sigh of relief. She wouldn't have to do much walking to get there.

Once landed, she took a deep breath and rose, carefully making her way back to the passenger compartment and opened the doors. No one was there to greet her. "This isn't starting off on the right foot," she whispered. Her stomach tensed slightly. She took another deep breath and carefully descended the three steps to the ground. After closing the door and securing it with her ID card, she headed towards the nearest MTE with carefully measured steps. The last thing she wanted was to take a tumble. Surely the Pytalon drugged Feds were probably watching her from the windows above, but she dare not take her eyes off the ground. Walking in her boots was treacherous without a strong arm to help her with her balance.

Several minutes later, she stepped into the lobby and made her slow way to the central desk. "Supreme Feds Commander Petra Delius," she said clearly, presenting her ID card to the glassy-eyed guard, who checked her in without a word. "So which elevator do I take to get to the top office?" The guard, she discovered, spoke no English, and he didn't send for anyone to escort her up either. Both should have caused her more worry, but she sloughed it off. Petra was determined to rescue Cho Lin. Unless the previous Peking Feds leader was weird, his office should be on the top floor. She spotted the elevators herself and headed towards them.

Once inside, she passed her ID card over the code reader and pressed the top floor's button. As expected, her card allowed her access, and the elevator began moving upwards. *Well, so far so good. What can go wrong?* If she took the time to reason the answer out, she might have played this game a different way, but she didn't. *Undoubtedly, they're waiting for me in the top office. That would make sense.* Her mind filled in the inexplicable gaps.

When the doors opened, she saw a dozen Feds standing just inside the plush office, obviously waiting her arrival. *This is more like it.* "Hello, I'm the Supreme Feds Commander, Petra Delius," she said officially, looking from face to face.

Several men began talking in Chinese, but she didn't understand a word they said and regretted not having brought along a translator. Their tone didn't sound hopeful; rather she swore they were angry. Why? She had no idea. She introduced herself again and asked if anyone here spoke English. More angry but unknown words were exchanged among the men. At last, one thin man spoke up, much to her relief.

"I speak English. In Peking, China, we don't allow women into the Feds organization. The men aren't taking this very well. They're angry, especially since you're an implanted EE woman. Oh, he is saying perhaps the Feds in Chicago are imbeciles, allowing you to be a Feds and a leader. Here in Peking, we're too smart to allow such blasphemy, if that's the right word. They say you're not going to be tolerated here. Such a thing is unthinkable. You're to turn around and go home at once or else," the man said nervously. Petra suspected his opinion was somewhat different from the others, but had no way of knowing for sure.

"Well, tell them I'm recognized worldwide as the Supreme Feds Commander; they'll just have to accept that," Petra refused to budge, but grew a bit more nervous, fingering her gun in its holster. She listened as the translator hastily said something in their language. From the other men's reactions, she suspected they didn't like her response. *Well, they had better get used to it.*

Several men talked quickly, but the translator man merely listened first to one and then another. At last, he turned to her and explained. "I am to tell you that you are in China. Here, women have no rights. They obey the men in their lives, if that's the right way to say it in English. Certainly, here a woman can't hold any position of real power. Your presence here—they find it to be the worst insult imaginable. You must go."

"I will go, but not before I take Cho Lin with me," Petra replied. "Tell them to bring Cho Lin to me, and I'll leave with her. However, they haven't heard the last of this. I guarantee you I'll be returning to put this house and all other Feds in China in order. Disrespect for your Supreme Commander will not be tolerated."

He hastily translated her message. She didn't expect these men to like what she'd said, but they should at least comply and bring her Cho Lin. Already, she was making plans to return with a dozen armed Feds and put this office on the proper path. Were all the other Feds offices here in China following similar prejudices?

The men talked fast and furiously for several minutes. The translator didn't bother to tell her what was being said, but from their tone, it probably wasn't pleasant. At last, the translator turned to her and said nervously, "I'm sorry, Supreme Commander, but I'm told to tell you this is your last chance. Leave now, at once. Cho Lin must stay here, per legal orders left by her father, our recently departed leader. Go now, ma'am, please." He seemed terribly sympathetic to her, almost as if he regretted having to relay their message to her.

"Look, I came here for Cho Lin. I'm not leaving without her. Tell them to bring her to me, and we'll leave at once," Petra replied forcefully. The translator turned and gave the men her reply. She saw one of the men give a small head nod. What was that about, she wondered, but sensed someone coming up behind her. Before she could turn around, she felt a pin prick on her neck. As she tried to turn around to face this new threat, the world turned black. The Feds man injected her with a powerful knockout drug and caught her body as it fell towards the floor within seconds of receiving his injection.

Strong arms carried her into the elevator and down to the lobby, where they headed to the back door. Two other men were there, dressed as emergency medical attendants. They had a stretcher with them, obviously prepared for this eventuality. Once on the stretcher, she was carried out to an unmarked EMAC emergency vehicle and taken aboard. Three minutes after having been injected with the drug, Petra was moving through the skies of Peking.

Forty-year-old Bo Bin Lin and forty-three-year-old Han Lin were waiting at the side entrance to their Lin Foundation when the EMAC arrived. Both smiled as they saw it arrive. "This will be rewarding, Han," Bo Bin said mildly excited.

Yesterday, he'd received a frantic call for help from the Feds in Peking. He'd willingly volunteered to help them with their slight problem. "It is always good to have the Feds watching our backs," he'd explained to Han.

"Well, we've the perfect solution. Mei Bei can finally have her contract terminated. I bet she'll be elated to have her own body back," Han replied.

Bo Bin laughed snidely. "We've kept her for thirteen years, but her contract was only for five years. She'll be more than elated. Just make sure she is re-implanted and given a heavy dose of Pytalon. That way, she won't be able to remember much of the past thirteen years. Still, we must honor our deal with her. Place five thousand credits into her account, will you? I'll go give her the good news."

Bo Bin walked down into the basement where the living quarters were located for their "experiments," of which Mei Bei was not the only resident. He passed by Tao Lin, who had been recently implanted and dosed on Pytalon, turned into a doorknob polisher. Still, no one knew exactly how this had come about, but the Feds were suspected, the Chicago Feds, that is. This was his new body now, a much younger man, but he was still heavily under the influence of both. As Bo Bin passed by Tao, he greeted his great-great-grandson. "Morning Tao Lin."

"Sanity is doing a good job. Doorknobs need polishing," the glassy-eyed man replied, continuing to polish a doorknob that certainly didn't need it. His original body was being kept in a special room above this basement living quarters. Bo Bin hoped in time Tao would recover. Perhaps then they could learn how this awful thing had come about. He passed several others and finally spotted Mei Bei who was sitting on a couch watching the others.

"Good morning, Mei. How are you doing this morning?" Bo Bin made polite conversation.

"Miserable as always," she replied. The body she occupied was thirty-one years old, and she knew her contract had only been for five years. However, with this body, she could do nothing about it except occasionally to plead for her release.

"Good news, Mei. Tomorrow your contract is up. You'll be returned to your own body. Five thousand credits will be in your bank account as well. Thank you so much for your invaluable help with our research project."

"What? Oh, thank god! It's been just horrid like this. Thank you, thank you," Mei gasped, becoming animated and flushed. *I'm going to be released!* More importantly, she would have five thousand hard-earned credits, which was why she had signed up to be a research guinea pig for the Lin Foundation. No other way could she have earned such a sum. While she wanted to ask why she hadn't received additional compensation for the extra eight years, she dared not say anything. Bo Bin might not release her! Instead, she continued to smile, repeatedly thanking him, as he turned and left her.

When they received word Petra Delius was coming in the EMAC, Bo Bin returned to fetch Mei Bei. He kept his arms around her to help steady her walk and keep her balance. After taking the elevator up one floor, he guided her to a lab and helped her lay down on a work bed. He fastened several electrodes to her head. "This won't take but a few minutes, Mei Bei. Again, we thank you for your assistance in our research." In the next room, her original body lay unconscious on a similar table, also hooked up to this same machine. He then set a number of controls and activated the machine, sending a strong current into both heads. She saw a brilliant white light and couldn't help but stare at it. After a time, the light began to fade.

Their newest implanting device was not really implanting, but a Transference Machine. This, the two brothers had invented nearly one hundred seventy-five years ago. However, only in the last century had they really perfected it. Mei would wake up to find herself back in her own body, though it had also aged thirteen years. What she didn't know was that she would undergo another EE implant and be heavily dosed with Pytalon. The end result of this would be her near total loss of memory. Thus, she could not divulge what had happened to her these past thirteen years. If she ever did, Bo Bin wouldn't hesitate to have her meet with an untimely accident. Such had happened dozens of times already, but these days the implants and Pytalon had nearly reduced such things to near zero.

Transference. That had been the process the two brothers were after. Via transference, they had become immortal. When their bodies got ill or sick or in danger of dying, they merely found a new younger man, kidnaped him, and ran their Transference Machine. The kidnaped person awoke to find themselves in the old body, while Bo Bin and Han awoke to find themselves in possession of a new body, ready to continue with their research and work. In the early years, it had been necessary to do this frequently, for the process only barely worked at first. Initially, the biggest problem they had to overcome was the original person eventually found their original body and tried to take it over again. Being a psych, Bo Bin had no idea that he was dealing with spiritual beings, he believed he was transferring minds only. Han had developed the electronics necessary to force the physical transference.

These days, the transference lasted as long as they desired, thirteen years in the case of Mei Bei.

Mei's original body was kept alive in a sort of vegetative state under the control of various medical devices on the floor above the basement. Their current research centered on keeping these vegetative bodies in good condition, which was one reason they had greatly extended Mei's contract, as well as many others for that matter. However, there were also secondary reasons. Many of the "new bodies" were specially designed for special needs, typically imprisonment, one way, or another. Bo Bin's great idea was to take troublemakers and criminals and transfer them into physically handicapped bodies, which could no longer be used to cause trouble or commit crimes. Mei's body for the last thirteen years was one of these.

Of course, the brothers had kept this transference research secret. The men and women who worked here in their foundation were heavily doped on Pytalon and implanted to service the needs of the special "bodies" under their care. None of these personnel could possibly ever reveal the true nature of their research, which had been wholly secret for nearly two hundred years now.

Assistants carried Mei Bei's body into the recovery room, where Han was waiting, ready to redo her EE woman's implant. Ten minutes later, he injected a goodly dose of Pytalon and summoned her caretaker. "She's ready to be dressed and sent on her way. When she wakes up, get her presentable as a perfect EE woman, and summon me when she's ready to go." The glassy-eyed woman nodded, saying something about sanity is doing a good job, which he ignored and headed to help Bo Bin with the secondary transference.

Han found Bo Bin was about ready to perform the operation. The electrodes were still attached to the thirty-one year old Chinese woman. Bo Bin had already gotten Petra Delius prepared. "Ah, you are back. Any complications with Mei?" he asked.

"None. A perfect implant session. She's in recovery now—probably wake up in an hour or two. When she's ready to leave us, we'll be summoned for a last minute check on Mei. How's our new guinea pig?" Han asked, mildly interested. This was the first westerner they had worked on, but he didn't expect there would be any differences.

"All set. This time, we're using our Transference Machine for what it was intended to do—handle troublemakers. Petra Delius is just that. Honestly, a woman Supreme Commander of the Feds? Rubbish! According to the Feds, she came here to rescue Cho Lin, Tao's daughter. I believe she intended to take her back to America and perhaps marry her. EE women! Well, once we have her transferred and stable, we're to return her to the Feds building. There, they're going to put her in the care of Cho Lin, giving her something to do," Bo Bin explained.

"Well, this will be a great test of our procedures. However, if something goes wrong out there, how will we know about it?" Han asked, a little worried.

"Nothing happened for thirteen years with Mei, Han. Relax. Nothing will happen at all, except the Petra woman won't be able to do anything and will be causing the Feds no more problems. Let's get on with it. Han, this is a magnificent day. For the first time, we're using our invention for what we intended it for, outside of making us immortal—that is, to handle troublemakers. I feel fantastic. Soon, Han, we'll have many more such requests from the Feds. Mark my words." He gloated over their success.

"Ah, then we should begin to kidnap men and women and have the necessary operations performed on them at once," the ever practical Han replied.

Bo Bin grinned and nodded. "We'll hold a meeting to discuss the initial numbers we anticipate needing after we get Petra Delius on her way back to the Feds. Would you like the honors?"

Han grinned and activated the machine. It took only a few minutes for the machine to do its work, transferring Petra into the new body, leaving her original body in a vegetative state. Next, they wheeled the comatose body into the special wing and hooked it up to their complex life support equipment, where the body would continue to live until it grew old and died or they found some other use for it. Han suggested they perform surgery on it and reuse it to imprison other female troublemakers. Bo Bin agreed, though the body looked somewhat strange with narrow hips.

They then wheeled Petra's new body back down to the living quarters. Carefully, they lifted her up and sat her on the couch that Mei had always used. "Ah, Lian, here is your new charge. She is called Petra Delius. She'll be waking soon and will be under your care, just as Mei Bei was. Do you understand me?" Bo Bin asked of the EE woman, who was heavily dosed on Pytalon.

The fifty-year-old woman nodded, "Yes, I look after Petra now—when she wakes, just like Mei. Sanity is doing a good job."

"Good, Lian," Bo Bin replied, retrieving some smelling salts from his pocket. He passed it under her nose several times before Petra roused.

Petra came to with a splitting headache. She raised her arms to her head, but nothing happened. She felt nothing; worse, her breathing was difficult. She opened her eyes and blinked. "Where am I? What happened to me?" she mumbled and again tried to rub her forehead and temples. Nothing happened. She felt nothing. She tried to take a deep breath, but couldn't. Panicking, she was barely able to inhale shallowly. Petra jerked alert. She was sitting perfectly erect, her ballet boots squarely on the floor, but her arms weren't there. Again, she tried to breathe and couldn't. She fainted.

Bo Bin brought her awake a second time. Again, Petra tried to rub her head, but her body had no arms. She was only barely able to breathe. As she tried to grasp what was happening to her, she noticed she was wearing a Chinese silk gown, not her own red satin. This one was yellow with red dragons on it.

Bo Bin said calmly, "Take shallow, short breaths. You're wearing a very tight corset, Miss Petra Delius."

She did as asked, gulping for breath, her heart racing. *What has happened to me?*

The voice said, "Lian will be looking after you for a while. Lian, please bring the mirror over so Miss Petra can see her new body."

Still gasping and fighting to keep from fainting, Petra watched the Chinese EE woman bringing a foot-square mirror over to her.

"Can see? You look just perfect, Miss Petra," Lian suggested.

"What? This isn't me!" Petra gasped at the reflection in the mirror. "I'm not Chinese."

"You are now. Take shallow breaths, yes, like that. You'll soon get used to it. Right now, this must all seem very strange to you, but I assure you this is very real," Bo Bin said rather calmly. Mei had undergone similar reactions some thirteen years ago when she took over this body, which was only eighteen back then. *My how time has gone by!*

Petra stared and made a funny face, trying to convince herself what she was seeing was real. She had a female Chinese woman's body, an EE woman for sure. The thick lips and monster breasts gave that away. Her dress was strapless, and she could see that her shoulders were empty. Her arms had been removed from their sockets, but the surgery had been nicely done. Very little scaring was visible. Her waist was incredibly tiny, magnifying the pronounced curves of the body. Her hair was black and very thick, draped over one shoulder down her front, but the ends were out of sight, perhaps on the floor.

"This can't be real. I'm hallucinating. You've drugged me or something. Maybe this is all just a very bad nightmare, and I'll soon wake up," Petra muttered, shocked beyond all rational thinking.

"Miss Petra, I assure you this is very real. We have your body in a vegetative state for now. We'll take very good care of it, until we need to use it for another troublemaker. Let me introduce myself. I'm Bo Bin Lin, the great-great-great-grandfather of Miss Cho Lin. Tao Lin, the previous Feds leader here in Peking, is my great-great-grandson. He is in his new body over there," he pointed to a strange man who was polishing the doorknobs once more.

"I—I don't understand. Where am I?" Petra tried to get a mental grasp on reality.

"You're in the living quarters of the Lin Foundation, which my brother, Han, and I formed nearly two centuries ago. After we invented the PDH implant technology and got it in widespread use, we continued our work. Han and I have perfected the Transference Machine, which allows us to move a person's mind into another body. Don't worry; the original person who had this body has been dead for thirteen years. Mei Bei was a volunteer for us, and she has occupied your body here for the last thirteen years. We only take volunteers and pay them well. Her contract is up, so we've put her back into her own body now, and she's on her way home as we speak."

"But I don't understand? You can't be two hundred years old," Petra exclaimed. "This has to be a nightmare."

"Oh, yes Han and I certainly are that old. Each time our bodies get too ill or old, we simply transfer ourselves into a new, youthful body."

"But that would make you immortal," Petra protested. She'd never heard of any such thing. People grew old and died. That was the way life was.

"Yes, we are that. With our latest invention, we will never die. We invented the Transference Machine for entirely different reasons, though, and you, Petra, are truly the first to validate our original goals. You see, the world was and still is full of troublemakers and criminals. In your case, you're a troublemaker. Honestly, women in China have no rights at all and certainly couldn't ever be a Feds, let alone their boss. You caused our Feds to lose face when you came here, so we've transferred you to this new body. As you can see, you're completely helpless now. No longer can you cause the slightest trouble to anyone. Here, I'll put your ID card on a chain for you, since you can't pick it up anymore, let alone hold on to it." He leaned over, slipping it around her neck.

"You'll remain in this new body until it dies of old age. However, we aren't heartless. The Feds monitored Cho Lin's pleas for help via email. They know you came here to rescue her and possibly to marry her. So after you're fully recovered from the transference, you'll be taken to Cho Lin. Together, you will spend your days alongside of her in her father's office, though at night, her mother will take you both home and tend to your evening and morning needs, returning you to the office by nine each morning. See, you and your girlfriend will be spending your time together, just as you planned, well mostly. There's no way for you to return to your original body unless we perform another transference, which we'll not do because you are a troublemaker, you see."

He went on rather pompously, "Our grand plan to rid the world of all troublemakers and criminals is now bearing fruit! After we rid China of those, we'll naturally be expanding our operations worldwide. Yes, the Lin Brothers strike yet another major blow to insanity! We are saving the world from the likes of you and other far more dangerous criminal elements, but then as a Feds, you must know about the criminals. You see, this is a wholly humane way to deal with troublemakers and criminals. Locking them up in prisons never worked; it only made them worse, for the most part, to say nothing of the cost drain on the government. Well, I'll admit here in China, we merely shoot them, wasting valuable ammunition. Implanting them and putting them on Pytalon isn't very efficient either. The world doesn't need any more

Garbage Collectors Twentieth Class. Besides, they're still a drain on Total Care Program. Now we've a humane way to keep the likes of you from causing trouble or committing crimes. You're physically incapable of any such thing now, and it provides a worthwhile job for your caretaker. Isn't this a spectacularly beautiful solution to the world's problems?" he asked.

"But I'm helpless like this. I probably can't even walk now without falling down," Petra fought hard to keep from becoming hysterical and passing out again.

"Helpless is the whole point, Miss Petra, and yes, you can walk. Mei, who occupied your body for the last thirteen years, kept your body in good shape. She was able to walk just fine, as you'll soon discover, once you get used to your new body.

"But I can't do anything like this," Petra complained bitterly.

"Of course you can't, Miss Petra. That's why Lian, your care taker, will be here to help you with your needs, until you are comfortable with your new body. After that, Cho Lin will take over her duties."

"But Cho Lin has no hands," Petra struggled to find a way out of this mess.

"No she doesn't, but I'm sure she'll find a way to manage. She's been able to care for her needs during the day, so I'm sure she can help you."

"If I promise to leave China at once, can you put me back in my own body? Please, this is utter hell! Please, I beg you; don't leave me like this," Petra tried the last thing she could think of.

Bo Bin laughed, "Of course I'll do no such thing! You are as you are now until you grow old and die of natural causes. That, I estimate, will be perhaps another forty years, maybe more."

"Then shoot me. Put me out of my misery. I can't live like this. No one can," Petra wailed, nearly fainting again.

"Oh don't be silly. Mei Bei lived very nicely for thirteen years. She got along well with this body, so I'm sure you will too, only you'll be unable to cause any more trouble for anyone. Now then, you should get up and practice walking. You don't want to keep Cho Lin waiting for days, do you? Lian will assist you. I've many more things to do. Good day, Miss Petra Delius. Enjoy your new body." He rose and walked out of the room.

Lian stepped to her side by the couch. "You should get up and walk around now, Petra. Be careful of your luxurious hair. It's so long. It touches your ankles when you rise. All of us here are envious of your marvelous hair, so thick and long. Oh, yes, Mei always makes sure it's draped over her chest, as it is now. That way, she doesn't sit on it." In a low whisper, she added, "Sanity is doing a good job helping other EE women." Petra noticed her glassy eyes and knew she was also heavily doped on Pytalon.

"But I can't. I have no arms to keep my balance," Petra protested.

"Mei didn't either, but she managed just fine. I'm sure all you need is some practice. Up you go," Lian ordered, giving her a slight push. Petra tried to stand, but found she had to lunge with her whole body to get to her feet. She flailed her non-existent arms wildly, trying to keep her balance. Lian came to her rescue, steadying her before she fell. "There you go. Let's walk around the whole living quarters, and I can show you where everything's at." Bravely, Petra did as ordered, terrified and gasping for breath. If only she wasn't wearing such a horribly tight corset, things might be a bit easier, she thought and then laughed at her own silliness. Nothing would ever make this easier, at least not significantly.

Her hair did fall to her ankles, she noted, trying to remember to keep it in front of her body where she could keep from stepping on it or sitting on it.

"I feel rather faint," she gasped a little.

Lian merely told her to keep breathing short, little breaths. Slowly and carefully, the two walked around the living quarters, which Petra decided must be at least five hundred feet square. Many small bedrooms lined one side, while a dining room and bathrooms lined the opposite walls. There were no windows, and Lian explained they were underground.

She noticed a one armed woman making a puzzle at a small table. Several men were also as armless as she was. However, she counted five others whose bodies were still intact. Lian whispered to her as they walked. Three men were blind, as were two other EE women, but they still had their arms. She was panting heavily when they finally returned the couch.

After sitting down, she did notice her new legs were much stronger than her original body's legs. Petra theorized Mei had strengthened them by walking a lot, but how she could do so and still breathe remained a mystery to her. By the time she caught her breath again, it was lunchtime, and she had to rise again and be led to the dining room, where the others had already gathered. Lian proceeded to feed her while feeding herself. Several other helpers were assisting the other armless men and women as well.

Only when Lian helped her into bed and turned out the lights was Petra finally alone. Lian had also pleasured her so that was handled, though such thoughts were the last thing on her mind. At last, she broke down and began crying softly to herself. She was living a horrid nightmare, far worse than anything she'd ever imagined possible. Gasping for breath, she had to calm herself down. Lian told her the only time the corset would come off would be during her weekly bath. She'd also said during those times, Mei had complained her back was quite weak, and Lian had to support her quite a lot. Again, recalling this brought another round of sheer panic to Petra. She fainted and quietly fell asleep.

The next day was spent in walking endlessly around the spacious living quarters. Lian seemed to know just how much walking she could do before she had to stop to catch her breath for a few minutes. Petra soon realized Lian must know all about this body, since she'd been assisting this Mei, whoever she was, for the last thirteen years. She vowed to pay attention to Lian and quickly learn just what her new body could handle. One thing, her legs and knees were quite strong. Miraculously, her feet didn't ache as they often had with her original body. Further, if she just relaxed, her body seemed to have a knack for keeping its balance, much to her relief.

Three days into her new body, Bo Bin came to her just after breakfast. "Well, Lian says that you have adapted to your new body well, so it's time you're taken to your lover, Cho Lin. If you will follow me, I'll take you to the waiting EMAC."

Sensing this was her last chance, Petra again begged, "Please don't do this to me, Bo Bin. Have mercy on me. Put me back in my own body, and I will leave at once. You can't do this to me."

"Oh don't be silly, Miss Petra. I'll do no such thing. You're the first troublemaker to be handled by our new methods. We will study you and make such changes as are necessary for the next troublemaker to come our way. Besides, I have already transferred you. Come on. The EMAC and Cho Lin are waiting for you." Petra had no choice but to rise carefully and follow him, struggling mightily not to fall down. If nothing else, she refused to give him that pleasure.

They took the elevator up one floor. "On this floor, we keep the empty bodies in a sort of vegetative state until they are needed. Follow me; we can take a quick peek at your previous body," he sneered.

Petra reasoned, *I'll bet this is to convince me this is real and that I have to behave or they'll kill my real body.* Carefully, she followed Bo Bin, wishing he would slow down some. They passed by numerous small rooms, each with a body hooked up to various machines, but he stopped before the window of a particular room. Petra finally reached him and looked through the window. She gasped. There was her body lying on a soft bed with many tubes and electrodes attached to it. That was not why she gasped. She saw heavy bandages over its shoulders. Her arms were missing.

"Yes, as I said, we've prepared your body for the next troublemaker who comes along. So you see, Miss Petra, there's no going back. Now, I bet you're dying to see our incredible Transference Machine before you leave to join Cho Lin." Petra did, actually. She fought the urge to vomit, struggled for breath, but carefully turned to follow this beast of a man.

As she measured each step, she thought, this man and his brother simply have to be stopped. The Feds in her rose to the forefront. *With no checks and balances, this is precisely what can happen. Well, I'm not dead yet. Bo Bin, your days are numbered. Somehow, you're going down big time, invention or no invention!* Distracted by her thoughts, she stumbled and wildly wiggled to keep her balance. *Damn, focus on the present, Petra!*

"Oh, it does take time for you to adjust. Mei Bei complained she kept trying to use her arms for several months when she first entered your new body thirteen years ago. She and I began to call them ghost arms. You'll get used to your body soon enough, I assure you. From our point of view, you'll be unable ever to create troubles for anyone now. I'm a true genius, you know. One day, I'll be as famous as Leonardo da Vinci!"

Not if I can help it! She stared at her body through the window. She couldn't see if they had harmed it in any other way. *I suppose he's really showing me this so I won't want to go back to my real body since it'll be as helpless as this Chinese one is. He has a point. While that body underwent a sex change operation, it still doesn't quite look like a real woman's body. Maybe this Chinese woman's body will be better for me; at least it has always been female,* she mused.

She was breathing rapidly, but shallowly, when they reached the elevator. They got off on the third floor where the brothers had their Transference Machine set up. She saw two beds and a whole lot of wires and electrodes before she saw the machine with many dials and switches. The Feds in her rose, "So how does it work? Is it complicated to operate?" *Play to his ego, Petra; listen and learn.*

That she expressed an interest in his invention pricked Bo Bin's interest. He began outlining how the machine worked. "The beds are labeled 'A' and 'B.' The transfer normally goes from 'A' to 'B,' but this switch, if flipped, causes it to go the opposite way." He continued to explain how his machine worked. Although just how it worked eluded her, its operational controls were so simple she could operate it. *Oops, if only I had my hands,* she corrected her thinking. Petra paid close attention to his explanation. In the back of her mind, she envisioned one day that she might be able to use this machine to get herself into a normal body once more.

After spending a half hour here mostly standing in one spot, Petra's feet cramped. Thankfully, Bo Bin ended and led her back to the elevator. On the top floor, a Feds EMAC was there waiting for her arrival. The driver looked somewhat annoyed at having to wait for so long. "Oh sorry, we got delayed. Here is Miss Petra Delius in her new body, all ready for you. Glad to be of service," Bo Bin hastily apologized. "She's all yours now."

The driver nodded and said, "Get in, Petra."

"Aren't you going to help me up the steps?" Petra complained. She stared at the three steps. In her boots, taking them was treacherous, but she'd always had the use of her arms on the supporting rail. She panicked a little.

"No, you get yourself inside," he grumbled.

Her legs trembled a little, but Petra refused to give him any satisfaction. She moved slowly to the steps, noticing her hair was down to her ankles. She tossed her head to one side, watching her tresses slip off to the right, slightly out of the way. As she very carefully took each step, to her amazement, Petra discovered her legs were much stronger than her own had been. Silently, she praised the unknown Mei Bei for having strengthened these legs. Panting a little, she finally sat down, and the driver buckled her safety belt. As he proceeded to take his position and prepare to take off, Petra realized she needed to know where this Lin Foundation was located with respect to the Feds building so she could later find it again. Thus, as they took off and during the brief fight, Petra paid close attention, committing the directions to memory.

As the EMAC settled on top of the Peking Feds building, she saw her own large Air Liner still parked on the airfield, just where she'd left it. That was a comforting sight, though just now, she couldn't have said why. Now she faced going down the steps, far more difficult than going up. She took her time and kept her panic at bay, but was never so glad to be on a rooftop before. Panting shallowly, she followed the driver, who led her into the building.

When the elevator doors opened on the floor below the rooftop EMAC landing area, she saw the same faces of the Feds whom she'd met several days before. Several began speaking, but as before, she couldn't understand them. Suddenly, she realized Lian and Bo Bin had spoken English to her. Curious, she thought. Then the young translator spoke to her.

"I'm to welcome you back, Petra Delius. Cho Lin is expecting you and will be helping you with whatever you need. At five, someone will let you out of her father's office and escort you to the front doors. Cho Lin will lead you to her home, where her mother will help you with your evening meal and so on. After breakfast, you're to be back at our front doors by nine each morning. I'm to tell you this will be the schedule every day for the rest of your life."

He flushed a little, "I'm to tell you if you wish sex, just let the men know, they'll be glad to provide it for you. I'm sorry, Miss Petra. I wish you had just left when I asked you to. Follow me and I will lead you to the office where Cho Lin resides. Lunch and tea will be brought to you around noon each day." The dozen men moved aside, revealing a large set of glass doors, which opened into the late Tao Lin's office suite that occupied nearly all the top floor. She followed the translator into the spacious outer room. The huge desk sat vacant. Off to the left were his private suites. "She is in there. We keep those outer doors locked at all times, so you'll not be bothered by anyone. I'll be back at noon with your lunch." He turned and left. Petra heard him locking the doors, as she continued moving towards the side suite of rooms.

Just inside the very plush office, she saw the woman she'd come to rescue, Cho Lin, who had heard voices and risen from a brown leather couch. She looked just like her photographs on her EE Woman's web page. Dressed in a light green silk gown, Cho Lin had an oval face, with black eyes and rich, mid-thigh length black hair. Of course, she also wore ballet boots. She was indeed a very attractive young woman, Petra noted, very curvaceous, as were all EE women. The first thing Petra observed was her outstretched arm stumps. Indeed, her hands were entirely missing, but it was obvious Cho Lin had also been crying recently.

"Oh! You don't look like your pictures at all. What have they done to you? I'm so, so sorry. It's all my fault. I feel horrible," Cho Lin spoke up hastily, her eyes looking Petra over from top to bottom.

"I've got to sit down and catch my breath. You look even prettier than your pictures, Cho Lin. Yes, it's me. Long and strange story," Petra said, breathing rapidly and shallowly. Cho motioned for her to sit on the couch, and Petra carefully moved over to it. Before sitting down, she noticed some of her hair had slipped onto her back. "Please, can you kind of push my hair out of the way? I can't do much of anything anymore. Sorry to be such a burden for you, Cho Lin."

Cho moved equally carefully over to her and used her arms to arrange Petra's hair out of the way. After sitting down rather awkwardly, Petra said, "Look, Cho Lin, none of this is your fault. It's really me, but somehow I'm in this Chinese woman's body now. Let me explain." Petra then outlined what she knew had happened to her in as much detail as she could. While she saw Cho Lin moved in and out of her EE implant, Petra's explanation was more to help solidify her own observations of what had happened to herself. The Feds in her demanded no less. If she ever got free, she would need to relay this accurately. Besides, what the two brothers had invented had monstrous potential, both for good and for ill. She could attest to the evil side.

When she finished up, Cho Lin was speechless. At last, she said, "We always heard stories that Bo Bin Lin was our great-great-great-grandfather, and Han Lin, our uncle, but who could believe such a thing. Now I wonder if all I heard was true." Before she could continue her reply, she hastily muttered, "I must look my best at all times." She pushed her hair a little with her stumps, arranging it more over her shoulders. Petra kept silent, wisely.

"Why would they want to implant me? Oh, so I could be like mom, an EE woman, but no, that doesn't work quite right either. They wanted me to marry a man, that's why dad had it done. I wish Bo Bin had never invented that awful machine. I can't stop saying all those words, Petra. I hope you don't mind, but I suppose you have to stop and recite them often too." Her eyes glazed a little, and she recited her implant litany after which her eyes cleared once more.

"Petra, you are really very beautiful. I promise always to be here to help you. Somehow, I will be your arms. I can still give you good pleasure; just tell me when you need it. I just love your thick, long hair, so sexy, so becoming. I wish mine would grow longer too. It is, but slowly. Did they put panties on you? Mom never does put them on me. That way I can manage to lift up my dress to go to the bathroom by myself. Don't look for any of the men to help us, not ever, even if we should fall down. I did once and waited for hours, but no one came to help me. We're on our own. They bring me lunch, so I suppose they'll bring enough for both of us. I have to eat it like a dog from a bowl, but I can drink my tea fairly well. I'll help you always, Petra. You're the most beautiful woman in the world. I'm so honored you are with me."

"Well, Cho Lin, I'll admit I'm highly attracted to you. I think you are extremely beautiful. You look so good in your light green gown. I love your hair too. I've never seen anyone with such rich, long black hair before. How do you brush it? How the devil am I supposed to brush mine, come to think of it?"

Cho giggled. "I can do it with my stumps, but it takes me a very long time—many fumbles. I do yours; you'll see. Somehow, Petra, we'll get by. I'll always do my very best for you, as if we were married. I promise you, but I'm so sorry I have ruined your life."

"Look, Bo Bin ruined it, along with the Feds here, not you, my dear. Stop blaming yourself. You couldn't know they were monitoring your emails. You only wanted to get free of this imprisonment. Let's hear no more of that. Rather, I'm to blame for coming here half-cocked. I sometimes forget I'm not Peter Delius any longer. I should've studied up on the culture here in China. I brought this on myself, Cho Lin. My foolishness got me into trouble. I give you my word; somehow, I'll bring the

Feds here to justice, as well as Bo Bin and Han Lin. Even if they are your distant relatives, they must pay for their many crimes against humanity and us. Crap, I have to go to the bathroom. I'm so utterly helpless like this, Cho Lin. I'll be nothing but a burden for you." Petra fought hard to keep from breaking down again. *I have to be strong,* she told herself mentally. *But how? Like this, I truly am dependent on her!*

Cho Lin led her to the luxurious bathroom complete with a Jacuzzi, which they couldn't make any use of, not without help undressing and re-dressing. Soon, Petra saw Cho Lin could manage to help her with this. She was able to use her stumps to get her gown raised. Both were thankful she wore no panties, but Cho Lin did say she could also manage them, only that it took her a very long time to get them down and back up. The sink faucet had an arm Cho Lin could manipulate well with her stumps. Thus, she could wash her off and make use of the towels as well.

"You manage very well, Cho Lin. Thank you. I really do appreciate your help," Petra validated her, pleasing the young Chinese woman considerably. They chatted until the translator man brought in their lunch tray containing foot-long subway type sandwiches and tea. He placed the tray on the table, turned, and left them to deal with eating. While Cho Lin could rise easily from the couch using her stumps to push off, Petra could not. She was forced to lunge her body up. After Cho Lin pulled a chair out for her, Petra sat down rather hard.

Cho Lin slid one sandwich off the plate and over before Petra and then moved one in front of herself. "I am sorry, but this is the only way I have found to eat." She leaned over and began chewing on it. Petra emulated her, discovering she was quite hungry after all. At least they had straws for their tea.

That done, they returned to the couch and chatted, sharing more of their lives with each other. Finally, Cho Lin whispered, "I do so want to pleasure you. I have been waiting to kiss and caress you ever since you said you were coming. Please, may I?"

Petra grinned and nodded. "Somehow, I must find a way to satisfy you, lovely Cho Lin," she whispered back. Their lips met ever so gently, before their passions kicked in. Later, they continued to tell each other about their lives. Cho Lin was fascinated to hear what she'd done as Peter Delius. Finally, as it grew darker, the translator returned to let them out. Cho Lin put a steadying arm around Petra and led her out of the building.

As they stood outside the Feds building, both breathed in the fresh air for a moment. Then, Petra noticed her Air Liner was still where she'd left it and an idea began forming in her mind.

"It's a long walk to our house. I'll support you as best I can. This way," Cho Lin explained. Petra was never as glad for a MTE as she was just now. However, out in the open, she noticed her legs and knees were quite strong. She faired far better than she would have if she had her own body doing the walking. Several miles later, they arrived at a very nice home, single story, where she lived with her mother, Xia Lin, sixty-three years old.

The first thing Petra observed was that Xia was also an EE woman, but heavily doped up on Pytalon, just barely functioning. Still, she was able to feed the two and care for their immediate needs, particularly undressing them for bed. However, she didn't remove Petra's corset. At last, Petra got a good look at her legs, as did Cho. They were very muscular and well defined, far more than Cho Lin's legs were. Now Petra understood why she was able to walk better than she had with her original body. Somehow, the unknown Mei Bei had really strengthened up her legs and knees. For that, Petra was thankful.

Xia's home was luxurious, as befitting the wife of the top Feds leader, but it lacked any real emotions and love. Petra wasn't even sure if Xia really recognized Cho was her daughter! The older woman merely went about her chores and dealing with their many needs rather mechanically. Still, Petra didn't complain.

In the morning, when they began their long walk back to the Feds building, she asked, "So what happens if we don't get there on time?"

"I tried that twice. I must look my best at all times," she muttered, distracted before she regained clarity of mind. "They came and got me, but still forced me to walk there on my own."

Petra bit her lip. *Well, we can't just sleep in. So think. How are you going to get out of here, Petra?* The morning was a bit brisk; she began to enjoy the walk, as long as they went slow enough so she didn't get out of breath. As they approached the Feds building, again she noticed her Air Liner parked on the airfield just a few hundred feet away. An idea took form. "Do they follow us all the way to your home at night?"

"Oh no. They forget about me as soon as I leave their front doors. Once I got lost and had an awful time finding my way home," Cho Lin admitted, adding, "I was very young then." Petra began to see a way to get out of here and back home.

They were met at the door, escorted to the top floor, and locked inside. Cho Lin explained this was what happened every day without any variations. "Well, we'll just have to see about this," Petra grumbled, rather annoyed to have to wait until five to put her plan to work. *Cho Lin can use her stumps to manipulate an ID card. Well, heck, I can too, if I can get it between my teeth. The real problem is punching in the coordinates. I've a tongue. I'll manage somehow.*

The hours drifted by, but again Petra used them to share more of their lives with each other. Cho Lin's was dreadfully short, having spent so many years cooped up here in this office, but she wondered what her teenage love, Mei, looked like. She had no idea she now closely resembled her, only that Cho was definitely in love with her. *Well, I'm rather mad about her too,* she thought, recalling how good their last passionate kiss had been.

She dared not mention anything about her plans to escape. Probably, the Feds were listening in on their chatting. She hadn't revealed anything that wasn't already known within the Feds, at least those in Chicago. Petra was careful not to mention her set of new friends or their grand plans for the future of the world. *No, I volunteered to enforce the laws, and arms or no arms, I'll do what I said I would do. If I don't, I can't live with myself, not after what I did to Ben and Tim. I gave them my word and they accepted it.* She bit her lip for a moment.

Finally five o'clock came. As expected, the translator man opened the doors and escorted them out of the building. Again, he apologized to Petra, who took note of him. He seemed to be a fish out of water among the other men here in Peking. As in the previous evening, Cho Lin began to lead them towards her distant home. However, once out of sight of the Feds building, Petra asked her to stop.

"Do you need to catch your breath?" Cho Lin asked anxiously, obviously worried she had set too fast a pace.

"No, we're going to make our escape now. Do you recall seeing that Air Liner parked on their airfield?" Cho nodded, but looked rather bewildered. Petra sighed, thinking, *well, she is under the heavy influence of her EE implant.* "That is my Air Liner. Only my ID card will unlock the doors. Come on. We're going to see if we can get to it without the Feds catching us. If so, I need to pass my ID card across the scanner beside the doors. If you can get it into my mouth, I think I can do it."

"I will try my best. Do I look my best now? If we're escaping, I must look my very best," she muttered, flushing with embarrassment. She'd noted Petra almost never recited any part of her EE implant litany, but she wasn't able to control hers. Somewhere in the back of her mind, she wondered about having first said the word "best" and if that somehow triggered her involuntary recitation.

"You look beautiful, Cho. Come on," Petra replied, stepping carefully onto the MTE escalator that ran back the way they had come. A few minutes later, they stepped off at the edge of the airfield. Petra estimated they were some three hundred feet from the door of the vehicle. At her slow pace, if someone spotted them now, they could never reach it before they were apprehended. She hoped Cho Lin was right—that they never paid any attention to her after she left. "Come on, Cho Lin. This is our one chance at freedom." Carefully, she began to take her measured steps towards the beckoning vehicle. She knew if she stumbled and fell, in all likelihood, she couldn't get herself up and doubted Cho Lin would be able to help her up. Hence, she took each step cautiously. By the time they reached the door, she was panting for breath, inwardly cursing the overly tight corset.

"Okay, see if you can get my ID card into my mouth," she asked. Cho Lin fumbled with her stumps and managed to hold it well enough to lift it up to Petra's open mouth. She bit down on it. She was unable to bend enough to get the card to the sensor. However, she was able to bend her knees. Beep. Click. She heard the acknowledging signal, and the door unlocked.

"Quick. Press that button," she ordered, gasping more than before. Adrenaline was flowing now, if only she could breathe right. The door opened, revealing the three steps that looked more like mountains to the armless woman. Wobbling wildly, Petra raised one foot up. Once more, she felt her stronger than normal muscles working well. Balance was her main problem she realized, that and her overly long hair, which she stepped on, causing her to flinch. A minute later, she was inside and hoped Cho Lin could manage on her own. "Holler when you get inside and I'll shut the door. I'm heading to the driver's seat up front."

Cho Lin used her arms to help her maintain her balance as she too carefully ascended the steps. "I'm inside. Shut the doors. I think someone might be coming. A man is running this way." Petra pushed her nose into the button, and the doors automatically shut and sealed. She pushed the activation button, and the navigation system came online. This meant no attempts to open the doors from the outside would be accepted by the craft.

"I'm coming, my dearest," Cho Lin called out. She was still using her arms against the sides of the hallway to help her along. "How can we fly this? I don't know how," she added worriedly.

"Good. You made it. Have a seat. See if you can find a way to punch some numbers into that keypad there. Damn, I can't even point to it," Petra replied, growing more annoyed at the terrible restrictions on her actions. She nodded towards it with her head. Already her hair had gotten tangled in the controls, and she was sitting on part of it. This she ignored, because everything depended upon getting airborne as soon as possible.

Cho Lin was inventive. She picked up a pen between her teeth and nodded. Hastily, Petra called out the sequence, and Cho Lin pushed them with the pen. At last, with their destination locked into the guidance system, Petra leaned forward and pushed the autopilot button with her nose. "Okay, well done. We're now on our way! I think we're going to make it, Cho Lin."

Unfortunately, at that moment, Cho Lin began to recite her implant litany once more, embarrassing her even more. Petra never seemed to have to say hers, even when under such stress as this. Cho Lin felt really badly that she did, hoping Petra didn't need her to do something while she wasted precious seconds spouting the words. After she finished, she whispered forlornly, "I'm sorry. It comes over me, and I have no choice but to say all that."

"It's not your fault, love. There is nothing to be ashamed of. Once we get to safety, I know someone who can help you to get control over your EE implant. Once we get to the right altitude and level off, see if you can do anything about my hair. I feel so darn helpless, Cho Lin. I'm not worthy of you. You deserve better than a helpless woman," Petra admitted what she had been thinking about for some time now.

"But you're not helpless. You're rescuing us, flying this huge Air Liner. I could never do this. You are very smart, my love. Besides, I promised you that I would always be here for you. I—I love you too, Petra. I've been staring at your pictures for days, but now with this body you look like the most beautiful woman in the world. It is I who am honored to be with you," Cho Lin countered. Petra sighed. She added, "Are we safe now?"

"Not yet. They could still shoot us down since we're in Chinese airspace. Once we hit the international airspace, then we'll be safe, I hope. Two more minutes, Cho Lin. Come on, ship. Move!" Petra called out, watching the console before her. A blinking blip indicated their current position on the tiny world map. A faint ping sounded as they finally reached the international airspace.

"Whew! Now I believe we're safe, Cho Lin. International airspace. Okay, we're flying level now. See if you can get my hair out of my way. I need to find some way to call for help." Cho Lin visibly relaxed, rose, and did her best to get Petra's magnificent locks untangled from the ship's controls.

Chapter 23—Countermoves

"What's with Petra? She's not answering my texts, and my calls are going to her voice mail," Tilly complained. Now that she and Amanda had a good handle on the murder sprees, she had been unsuccessfully trying to relay the data to Petra.

"Don't know," Beth replied. "She's not answering mine either. At least Lech is. He has the Chicago CSIs looking into a bullet rifling comparison between the last six murder scenes. They are happening monthly, how strange. One would think the culprit is a werewolf, only coming out with the full moon or something. Plus, the store thefts definitely are following a pattern. Juan has found four people here in Peoria who are living off the grid. Of course, they are on their way to Phoenix now, but still, Petra needs to have her Feds begin to look into this in all the major cities. Do we have the authority to ask Lech to do it in Chicago or elsewhere?"

Tilly shrugged her shoulders. Jessica spoke up, "Worse, I sent her several lengthy emails about the strange things surrounding that Lin Foundation in Peking, asking her to take a day or so to investigate it for us. She's not replied to any of them either."

"Hey, that's not like Petra. I'm getting a bit worried about her. She's been gone five days now. It doesn't take that long to go there and bring back someone," Tilly concluded. "I'm texting Lech and asking him if he has heard from her. If not, can he trace the location of her Air Liner?" The others agreed with her, and Beth even texted Lady Persephone to see if she had heard anything from Petra. She hadn't and replied that she too was growing a little alarmed at her uncommon silence.

An hour later, Lech reported that her Air Liner was on the Peking airfield, but when he asked the Feds there about her, they claimed she went missing shortly after arriving. Now he too was worried, especially because of what he thought were evasive answers to his questions. He added he did get the Feds there to begin conducting a search for her.

"Okay, that does it. Do we have anyway of locating her?" Tilly asked. "I wish she'd had time to get one of Greg's locator chips in her shoulder as we have."

"Well, I've got her Air Liner under surveillance now, thanks to Lech," Beth replied. "I piggy backed onto his electronic checking and have the vehicle's ID number. Jessica is getting periodic images from the geo-satellites. It's parked right where they told Lech. No action, just parked. I can try to hack into the Peking Feds surveillance videos, if you think we should."

Tilly bit her lip, thinking hard. It wasn't like Petra to go rogue and not answer their messages. She seemed sincere about really helping everyone. Could that have been a mere excuse? Was she up to some devious mischief or worse now? "First, hack into Petra's email and see if we can figure out why she went to Peking, China in the first place."

"You got it," Beth replied. "Weasel strikes again. Okay, I'm in. She really should use a more secure password. Say, come look at this. She's trying to rescue a Chinese EE woman named Cho Lin. Ah, the late Tao's daughter. Oh crap, she's been victimized horribly. I can see why Petra headed off to Peking so quickly!" The others gathered around her monitor and read the various emails, while Beth opened another window and proceeded to bring up Cho Lin's EE woman's web page. She added, "At least she's cute."

Tilly bit her lip again. "Lech didn't say the Feds there said anything about Cho Lin being held prisoner in her dad's office. Could they be holding Petra prisoner there too?"

"Well, there's one thing I can try. I've got clearance to access the Feds' databases. Let me see if I can latch onto some surveillance videos from the Peking Feds building. Let's see. What date should she have arrived there? Crap, the International Dateline messes things up a little," Beth suggested, but became annoyed at having to deal with the date switch. Jessica watched carefully just how her mate pulled this one off, grinning at each step.

A half hour later, Weasel struck again. "Ta-da. There she is walking up to the security guard in the lobby! So she did arrive there," Beth declared with certainty.

"Yes, but Lech reported the Peking Feds did say she arrived. She disappeared after that. Can you see if she is seen leaving the building? Any other views within the building?" Tilly asked, coming over to see for herself.

"There's one on the roof where they keep their EMACs, and there's one over the desk of their leader, Tao's office. Let me see what I can see. Lots of video to go through," Beth replied. A little while later, Beth said, "Look at this. The Feds are carrying someone out to an EMAC, but I can't tell who it is. The image is too fuzzy. It's only a security cam, after all."

After several hours of fast forwarding through many video files, Beth was no closer to finding an answer. As they ate supper, she summarized what she'd found out. "Definitely I can see this Cho Lin woman entering and leaving her father's office. I can see clearly she has no hands, but there's no trace of Petra leaving the building, unless that one fuzzy image was her being carried out by the Feds and put into that EMAC. I can't tell whose EMAC it was, because the image is too poor. I'm running the image through an enhancement program while we eat. Maybe I'll be able to tell more in a while."

They chatted about the possibility Petra could be being held in some other room or even a prison cell in the building, if there were cells there. No one had any reasonable theories, only that Petra was definitely missing and very likely in trouble. While Juan washed the dishes, Beth headed back to examine the modified image.

"Hey everyone, come here. I have something. Look, you can just make out the feet. Those look like ballet boots to me. Is that Petra being carried out? Unconscious?" Beth called out. The others came to look and agreed with her theory.

"But who is taking her? How did they get away with this kidnaping right there in the Feds headquarters?" Jessica asked.

"Something smells rotten here," Tilly replied. "Can you figure out whose EMAC that is? Maybe that would give us some clue about who took her and thus why."

"Now that it's enhanced, let me capture that company logo and run a trace on it," Beth answered. Using her mouse, she highlighted the foreign logo and saved it as an image. Then she reentered the Feds database and launched a comparison with known company logos. "I like this Feds program. It allows me to easily compare images," she added. A few minutes later, she had her answer: the Lin Foundation.

Tilly chuckled. "Well, I did ask her to check out that foundation for Jessica."

"Yes, but why are they kidnaping Petra? How did they do it right there in the Feds own building? Are the Chinese Feds working for this weird foundation?" Jessica asked, growing more perplexed by the minute. Nothing was making sense. "Could they have executed a scam, sort of like we did with Peter Delius? I suppose so, but why take Petra?"

Beth shrugged her shoulders. Tilly answered, "If we knew that, we would be closer to resolving this mess. I don't suppose there's anyway to track that EMAC and see where it went, is there?"

"Not without knowing its ID number. Sorry. Jessica and I can bring up the geo-satellite images of Peking and see if we can spot it, but there are probably lots of EMACs flying around a city that large," Beth replied with a sigh. "Let me sleep on it and see if I can come up with a bright idea. Tomorrow, I'll relay what we've found to Lech, though it's not likely he can do anything about it, drugged as he is.

Jessica called out, "Well, I'm going bleary-eyed looking at all these videos, but here's something that's weird too. Look, today, a new Chinese woman has joined Cho Lin in her father's office. Definitely Chinese, look at her face." The others gathered around to peek at the image on her monitor.

"Good god, she doesn't have any arms!" Beth cried.

"Definitely an EE woman. Look at those boobs and that curvaceous silhouette," Tilly commented. "Well, at least it isn't Petra. That's for sure. She's definitely of Chinese birth. Wonder who the poor woman is anyway?" All shrugged and headed for bed, all except Juan, who continued to view that short video. He waited a little longer and got a second view when the two women were leaving the office. He spotted an ID card hanging from a chain around the new woman's neck. The image quality was too poor to see more. Still, he froze the image, intending to ask Beth to enhance it in the morning.

Noon the next day, Beth finally got around to enhancing the image for Juan. They had been checking up on everything else during the morning, but found nothing new at all. Lech reported hearing nothing and was growing alarmed at Petra's mysterious disappearance. "Now this is only getting weirder by the minute! Juan, everyone, come look at what Juan found— Petra's ID card!"

"What? Yes, that's her ID card and image on it," Tilly confirmed Beth's observation. "My god, this new Chinese EE woman is absolutely stunning! She's in the same league as Erika and Ilse, a top model for sure! Wow!" Amanda poked Tilly in her rump and they all laughed. "Well, she is gorgeous," Tilly added.

"Agreed, she is quite attractive, but she's also terribly handicapped, far worse that Lisa," Amanda stated factually. "But that doesn't answer the question. How the heck does she end up wearing Petra's ID card around her neck? She certainly isn't Petra, and the ID card is definitely not jewelry, not remotely. What in heaven's name is going on there? Where's Petra anyway?"

Lech texted Tilly, saying the Peking Feds still had found no trace of Petra. They merely said their building was huge and that it might be possible for someone to kidnap a woman there without their knowledge. They asked Lech if Petra had any known enemies. The investigation was going nowhere at all, frustrating Beth.

Jessica then began fast-forwarding through days of geo-sat images of the Lin Foundation. "Darn, that EMAC that took the woman in ballet boots certainly didn't land at the Lin Foundation. In fact, none has landed there or taken off from there for seven days at least! So where did the Lin Foundation EMAC take Petra? This is becoming screwier by the minute! Nothing about any of this is making any sense at all!"

Although the four spent the rest of the day trying to unravel the mysterious disappearance of Petra Delius, by supper, they knew no more. All were frustrated and quite annoyed. Juan suggested, "Something will turn up. Be patient. It always does. Petra has a good head on her shoulders. She doesn't panic easily, not without good cause."

Tilly's cell phone rang. She picked it up and said, "It's Petra's cell! Hello, Petra?"

She heard a stranger's voice on the phone. "Yes, it's me and I'm in deep trouble. Can you put me on speaker phone and somehow record this?"

Tilly did as asked. Beth hastily hooked up a microphone and began recording the conversation. Everyone gathered around Tilly's phone. "Okay. We are all here and recording. Go ahead, but mind you, we know this isn't Petra's voice," she added sternly. Whoever was making this call on Petra's phone, she wanted them to know she knew it wasn't Petra.

"Yes, it's me. I'm now in a Chinese EE woman's body, one that has no arms. I've rescued Cho Lin, who has no hands. She is with me. We're in my Air Liner and have reached International Waters. I need help badly, but in case we get shot down, it's absolutely vital you hear what happened to me and take appropriate actions. This is unbelievably critical, Tilly," Petra began. She started with the reception she met when she walked into the former leader's office. She then explained in total detail all she remembered and had heard, including a full description of the Transference Machine's operational controls. An hour later, she finished up by telling them how they had escaped. "So far, they haven't shot us down. I'm hoping they don't want to do that because we're in International Waters, but with these psychos, who knows."

"Okay, Petra, we have all this recorded, but it sounds fantastic—transferring one person into another person's body? That's hard to believe," Tilly countered.

"I remember my whole life, all my secret codes, you guys, everything. Okay, I can see how this must sound. I'll prove it," Petra sighed. She began reciting what had happened to them all in Europe and their time spent in Sussex with Lady Persephone. She presented enough details that Tilly found it hard to believe this strange sounding woman wasn't Petra. One thing was certain, Petra would never have voluntarily divulged this much detail of their group—at least she hoped so.

Jessica spoke up, explaining what she'd discovered about the Lin Foundation. "At least, some of what we've found here is now starting to make sense, that is, if you believe this Bo Bin and Han Lin were somehow able to get new bodies during the last two hundred years."

"I'm glad some of this is making sense. You just have to see this for yourselves. I was shocked to see my old body lying there comatose with all the tubes and electrodes attached to it. Gut wrenching actually," Petra added.

"Yes, but there is one flaw," Beth countered, still not truly believing this strange woman on the phone. "We captured an image of a woman wearing boots similar to Petra's being kidnaped and put into a Lin Foundation EMAC."

"I was unconscious. I can't vouch for that, Beth. Sorry."

"Yes, well the problem with your story is that we have been monitoring the Lin Foundation for days and haven't seen a single EMAC either arriving or departing from the foundation grounds."

"Well, they said it was the Lin Foundation. With all that I saw, it had to be. I can't explain that discrepancy, Beth, but I memorized the route they flew from there to get me back to the Feds building. I can retrace my path to where it's at," Petra explained. "Please, whether or not you believe me, Cho Lin and I are desperate. We need help. I'm almost totally helpless like this."

While the others were talking, Tilly was guessing at probabilities. Surely, this wasn't Petra, but someone impersonating her and doing a superlative job with it. Still, if the woman was the one they'd seen on the video, she was armless and trying to fly a huge Air Liner. If Cho Lin were with her, she had no hands and was almost as helpless as this other woman was. Tilly dared not risk the Air Liner making a crash landing in some city, harming perhaps hundreds on the ground. Images of the damage done to the Chicago Pytalon skyscraper hit by the Air Liner came to mind.

Tilly spoke up, "So what coordinates have you punched into the geo-navigator?"

"The Chicago New O'Hare airfield. Is that all right? If not, Cho Lin can use the pen to punch in an alternative destination. I can't fly it and Cho Lin doesn't know how. We are stuck with the autopilot. I don't know of any other way," Petra replied rather calmly. At least her friends were listening to her, though she began to doubt that they believed her.

Thinking fast, Tilly replied, "Look, since you admit you can't fly it, landing at New O'Hare is risky. If something goes wrong, the area is too heavily populated. Collateral damage is unacceptable. Enter these coordinates," she said, calling out the numbers slowly.

"Okay, Cho Lin is doing her best, but she's only gotten the first digit entered. Can you repeat them very slowly?" Petra asked.

It took them five minutes to enter the coordinates though it should have taken mere seconds, Tilly observed, adding credence to the notion that the physical condition of the women were as stated.

"Where are we landing?"

"At the Peoria airfield, far more open lands surround it in case of trouble. We'll be there to watch you land. In fact, Beth is now tracking your flight. How much charge is left in your cell phone? Can you possibly call us using the Air Liner's phone system?" she asked.

"Only one bar, not much. Needs charging, but there's no way I can get it plugged in, and I doubt Cho Lin could do it either. Thank god for speed dial. I had Cho Lin press the one digit to get to you. To use the craft's phone system, I have to get the head phones on my head. Crap. How the devil am I going to do that? Okay, I'll call you back in a while, one way, or the other. Tilly, if we get shot down, promise me you'll bring an army over here and put Bo Bin out of business before he causes more damage." Tilly gave a hesitant agreement and Petra hung up.

"I don't believe a word of what that woman said! Transferring one person into another person's body? Get real!" Tilly spoke up.

"True, but if these two men, Bo Bin and Han, who invented the whole damnable PDH implanting thing, are really them, then there's no telling what else they could have invented in two centuries of experimentation," Jessica countered. "Besides, what she said makes what we have found out about the Lin Foundation make some kind of sense. Before, it made none at all."

"What I'd like to know is how an armless woman is able to fly one of those huge aircraft?" Juan asked.

"Oh, there is a fancy navigational system on them, foolproof," Beth explained. "All you really have to do is enter the precise coordinates of your destination. Once activated, the system automatically flies you there, taking all manner of precautions. The whole air travel system is fully automated. Pilots are only needed if an emergency arises."

Tilly's phone rang, but had no caller-id this time. "Ah, it's Petra again." She put it on speaker phone once more.

"We managed to get the head phones on me. Now we can talk unlimited. That's a relief. I still don't see anyone coming after us. It's possible we haven't been missed yet. I need to get a hold of Lech and arrange a raid on the Lin Foundation before they abscond with their machines and prisoner-volunteers. If you can see my body lying there, that will speak louder than all the words I can say," Petra admitted. "I thought I was having a bad nightmare or something, until I saw my own comatose body lying there. That was a real convincer."

"Okay, Petra. We'll go along with you. Beth is sending the lengthy recording to Lech as we speak," Tilly advised. "After he hears it, I'll teleconference him into our connection here. Will that be satisfactory?"

It was. Petra continued to chat. Just hearing the voices of her friends gave her back some confidence that perhaps this wasn't the end of everything.

An hour later, a much subdued and confused Lech joined the conversation. After some pleasantries and verification codes were exchanged, Petra ordered, "Lech, this is a Category One emergency. Open file number 1A, read it, but keep this line open."

"Yes boss. Category One emergency. 1A. On it," he replied in his Pytalon-induced monotone. Again, Petra wished she'd never ordered her men onto the damnable drug. *Whatever was I thinking when I did it? Hell, I knew what I was thinking. Unrestrained power. Yes, that's precisely what Bo Bin and Han Lin are doing, but they're true psychopaths and sadists.*

Presently, his voice returned. "Boss, are you sure about this?" Tilly detected some slight emotion in his voice.

"Absolutely, Lech. You can fire me if I'm wrong about this. I take full responsibility for calling this one. Will you execute those orders at once?" Petra asked. She would have kept her fingers crossed if she had them. She crossed her boots instead.

"Yes, boss. On it." After a minute, he asked, "Rendezvous over Hawaii sound about right?"

"Oh. So quickly? Wow. Yes, then we won't be wasting so much time. Tilly, Lech will be meeting me halfway across the Pacific with a heavily armed escort. We'll be raiding the Lin Foundation in force as well as executing a holding pattern on the Peking Feds, until we verify what I've seen. Change of plans. Is there any way you can have your people can join up with Lech and meet me in Hawaii? God, I sure could use your help on this one."

Tilly bit her lip again. She was going out on a limb with this one. "Okay, we'll see what we can do. Stay on the line while we see what can be done." She switched to a private line with Lech. "Lech, is there any way to board an Air Liner while it is in flight? I would rather not risk her trying to land the craft when she can't actually control it. If something should go wrong, she couldn't deal with it."

Lech thought about it for a minute. Un-drugged, he'd have replied almost at once. He fought hard to bring that information back into his conscious mind. "Well, there is an emergency boarding protocol. It can be done."

"Okay, then where should we meet up with you? We don't have access to an Air Liner," Tilly replied. The two arranged to merge at the giant airfield in Los Angeles. She then contacted the professor and played the lengthy recording for him.

"My god, Tilly. If this is true, Petra has stumbled into the find of the century! She's right. If this technology is as she reports, it's not only being abused, but it represents another terrible strike against our world, perhaps worse than the PDH implanting. Come to Phoenix at once and pick me up. I'm going to go with you on this one!"

"Thanks professor. I really could use your viewpoint on this one. It sounds utterly fantastic, way beyond all belief, but if it is real, my god, one could live forever by stealing other people's bodies! They have to be stopped," Tilly replied.

An hour later, the five were in their EMAC flying at top speed towards Phoenix. Beth brought along a small geo-tracker so that she could continue to see where Petra's craft was located. Tilly called Petra back on their EMAC's phone and relayed the news that the professor was joining them. "We are going to try an emergency boarding protocol. According to Lech, there's a way for one of us to get onboard to help you. Hang in there. We're going to meet you over Hawaii."

"Thank god. I can't believe Bo Bin intends to transfer some other woman into my body later on. This is all so unreal, but yet it's more than really real. I feel so utterly helpless. Well, I promised to do all I could, and I aim to live up to my promise, Tilly, no matter what," she added bravely.

Hours passed. Once they picked up the professor, he began chatting in depth with Petra, having her go over the details of the Transference Machine again. He kept pulling on his beard all the while, deep in thought and reflection. "So Bo Bin can somehow transfer a person out of their body and into another body. I wonder how he gets rid of the person. I mean, say he wants to take over person A's body. Does he kill A? No, then the body would be dead. If he transfers the person out of person A's body so he can take it over, then he must put that person back into his own dying body. I wonder if he can transfer a person out of a body and leave them there—sort of in a 'no body' state. That would be murder in my book, though."

"He claims he would transfer the person into his dying body and then kill them. With the supposed 'volunteers' he has for their experiments, he keeps their vacated body in a sort of comatose state, but where did the original person who had the body I have go? That's what bothers me. He must have somehow transferred them out and killed them," Petra tried to follow his line of reasoning. "That part wasn't too clear to me. I wish I had thought to ask him that question. Perhaps when we capture him, we can place that question before him." The two continued to chat for some time.

When their EMAC landed in Los Angeles, they had only a short wait, before a giant Air Liner landed nearby, and Lech stepped out, waving to them. The six headed over to the huge ship, slowly of course. As they walked, Tilly began to feel sorry for Petra or whoever the woman was. She needed her arms to help keep her balance, and this Chinese woman had none, assuming she was the same woman they saw in the enhanced image from the surveillance video of Tao Lin's office.

Onboard, they took comfortable passenger seats, but also saw twenty well-armed Feds in the rear seats, who merely nodded to the newcomers. Soon they were airborne once more. While Beth continued to track Petra's craft, Lech did the same with the onboard system. Then, he took Juan aside and began to show him how to execute the emergency boarding protocol. "It can only be done by someone who isn't implanted and not on Pytalon. Your reaction times have to be spot on," Lech explained in his usual monotone.

While Juan was occupied, Beth noticed six other large Air Liners were trailing theirs. She pointed this out to the others. "Petra is launching a major raid!" Tilly exclaimed. "I hope she knows what she's doing and that this isn't a trap for us all."

"I feel lots safer with this many Feds tagging along. I bet she's got at least a hundred Feds on this raid," Beth added. "I don't think we'll be in much danger, not with this kind of fire power behind us."

Tilly smiled; she couldn't agree more.

Hours later, the group of seven liners spotted Petra's, and Lech turned his around and laid in a course to parallel hers but just above her ship. Looking out of their windows, they saw Juan dangling from a rope just above Petra's ship. All watched rather worried. "He has a harness on," Lech explained. "Safety first."

As they watched, Juan maneuvered his body until he was above a ceiling hatch. "He is punching in the override code now," Lech continued his emotionless explanation. "Ah, it was accepted. Now he is descending inside their craft." A loud beep announced Juan had disconnected the cable, and they saw it being rapidly retracted. Juan was safely inside. Then, the ceiling hatch closed, and they could see no more, but Lech at least turned the speaker volume up enough so they could hear the conversation he was having with Juan.

"Onboard, safe and sound. Remember, I don't know how to fly this thing," Juan spoke up. "Petra is the woman you captured in the enhanced video image, Beth, only she is even more striking in person. Okay, down to business. How do I turn this thing around?"

Petra's voice told him. "We should lay in the coordinates for the Lin Foundation. Lech, were you able to find them?"

"Yes, boss. Relaying them to Juan now," he replied, again showing no emotion whatsoever. As they watched, Petra's ship turned around, heading back the way she'd come. Lech turned the autopilot back on and sat back, relaxing. "Be there about dawn. Sleep if you can or eat." He dozed off, as if nothing exciting was happening. Tilly just shook her head.

Onboard Petra's liner, after Juan reset the navigator and verified their ship was turning, Petra said, "Whew, what a relief. Thank you for helping out, Juan. As you can see, I really do need the help, Cho Lin too. Oh, Cho Lin, this is a good friend of mine, Juan Carlos."

"If you really are Petra Delius, then all I can say is you have a knockout body. I think you're more attractive than Erika and Ilse, and that's saying something," he admitted.

"I haven't gotten too good a look at myself yet. While it may be a sexy looking body, Juan, I'm almost completely helpless like this. Worse, I can barely breathe in this damnable corset, but apparently, the body requires it. Weak back or something. Have to worry about that later on. The main thing is to capture Bo Bin and Han and their Transference Machine. I don't know if we can make things right for many of those they have in their so-called living quarters, but I have to try. Can you imagine being knocked out and waking to find yourself in an entirely different body? That is spooky and scary, to say the least."

"Can we somehow put you back in your own body?" Juan asked.

"We could, but Bo Bin amputated its arms already, so there's nothing to be gained by doing so, I suppose. We'll have to see if it is even alive when we get there. Say, we're starving. Any chance you could fix us something to eat? Of course, I'll need a little help with it."

"Come on. Let's get your hair untangled, and we'll go back to the passenger compartment and rustle up something," Juan replied.

Hours later as the sun rose, the seven Air Liners hovered over the Lin Foundation. Beth recognized it from the aerial geo-sat images. "We've arrived. Looking for a good place to set down," Lech's voice came over the radio. Juan was valiantly and slavishly following Petra's voice commands, holding their ship steady. The sprawling, huge city lay below them, just awakening to a new day.

"So down there in that building is this Transference Machine," the professor commented.

"If Petra's right," Tilly added, still not wholly convinced. It was far too much to believe.

As Petra gazed out the window, she spotted the Feds building in the distance. Something wasn't right. "Wait, Lech. Hold on a minute. Something doesn't feel right. The sun is in the east, and we're way south of the Feds building. I don't think this is the right place. Lech, humor me. You hold here and let us go over to the Feds building. I'm going to retrace the route we followed when they returned me back to the Feds building from where they were keeping me."

"Right boss; holding positions," Lech replied.

"Okay, you have the controls, Juan, easy does it. Pull back slightly; right, point it towards the Feds building."

"Which one?" he asked.

"Crap, I can't even point it out to you. Okay that one there," she began trying to find some way to describe it to him. Eventually, he got the right one and eased the huge ship closer to it. "Okay, now make a forty-five degree left turn. Easy. Right, this seems right." She continued to give him directions, as she gazed at landmarks on the ground, comparing them to her memory of them that morning. Finally, she spotted it. "There! That's the place. See the EMAC on the roof? Lech, this is the place. Bring everyone here."

"Yes boss. Captains, on my mark," Lech relayed. Soon the other seven ships hovered close to Petra's liner.

"But this isn't the Lin Foundation," Beth pointed out.

Tilly laughed. "Oh, these fellows are clever! They have a secret laboratory, which is the real foundation. The public one we found is simple camouflage for the real one! Clever fellows."

One by one, Lech got the large ships landed, using available open space where they could find it. Actually, that worked well, as the Feds ended up having the whole area surrounded. While the Feds then began unloading their heavy equipment, the professor helped the four women down to the ground. Together, they made their careful way over to Petra's ship, where Juan was just lifting Petra down. He'd already lifted Cho Lin to the ground. All around them, the early-rising townsfolk were rapidly evacuating the whole area as if they sensed trouble coming and wanted no part of it.

"Wow, Petra, Juan is right, your Chinese body is a real knockout, a top model for sure," Jessica offered some support to Petra. She couldn't even imagine how awful this was for her. Even when held captive by Hans Gudrunda, they knew their helplessness wouldn't be permanent, that they'd eventually be rescued. Petra had no rescue to give her hope, hence Jessica's attempts to make the best of it. Still, she was not lying; she was every bit as attractive as Erika and Ilse, perhaps even more so.

"I'd rather be ugly and have my arms back, if it's all the same to you. Thanks anyway. Where's Lech? We have a battle to wage here. I noticed six heavily armed security guards when I was inside this place," she replied. Jessica could tell Petra's mind was now wholly on the capture of this installation and the men responsible for the wholesale destruction of the entire cultures of the world.

Lech came running up, along with four other men. "Petra?" he asked, looking at the gathered women.

"Here, Lech. Well done, expect a nasty fight," she replied.

He moved over to her, fastening a Blue Tooth communications device on her ear. "There, boss. Now you are in constant touch with the seven captains. Got seventy men with full gear."

"Thanks, Captain Lech. Yes, I just promoted you. Take charge of our Chicago men. Okay, Captains, listen up. I know there are at least six heavily armed security guards inside, but there could well be more. Take them out anyway possible. There'll also be two Chinese men in their fifties inside. Those must be taken alive, shoot to cripple, not kill," Petra barked her orders.

"Captain Jose of LA here. There are Category Five Blast Doors at the main entrance. Your orders, Supreme Commander?"

"Use the EM dozers," Petra replied without hesitation.

"Okay boss, let's get you and your party behind this transparent blast shield," Lech ordered. The four men with him moved in front of the group. They carried a six-foot tall transparent wall of some kind. "Bullets and shrapnel can't break through this," Lech explained for the benefit of the others. Okay, move towards those blast doors." Slowly, the party began their slow walk of about one block.

"Snipers are in position, Supreme Commander. Captain Roberto of San Francisco here."

"Excellent. Stay alert. No one is to escape this assault. One company, stay alert for the Peking Feds who may well attack our backs. Most of them are in league with these traitors inside here," Petra ordered. Another captain pulled his squad back and began watching their backside.

As they approached the stainless steel entrance doors, Tilly could see this building was only three stories tall, but according to Petra, much was beneath the ground. However, what caught her attention wasn't the heavily armored Feds, but the strange looking EM-powered dozer moving slowly on tracks towards the blast doors. As it approached, someone began firing rifle shots from the roof of the building, where the EMAC was parked. Bullets ricocheted off the dozer and the driver's armor. The Feds return fire was enormous! They watched as the sniper's body fell off the roof, dead long before he smashed into several trash bins.

When the dozer reached the nearly impregnable blast doors, the driver increased its EM power, and it punched through the doors as if they were made of butter. Concrete and supporting metal beams crumbled, forming a momentary grey dust cloud. Lech commented in his monotone, "Good call, Commander. Without the dozer, we'd have a very hard time breeching those doors. Probably have to use explosives, planted charges."

"Right, but that might harm the innocents inside and damage this valuable machinery," Petra replied. Secretly, she was glad she had made this call, forcing the Feds to use their highest priority equipment and armor. Gunfire erupted from the gaping hole, and two Feds squads returned it in kind. Several bullets bounced off their protective, transparent wall, much to Tilly's relief. Juan merely looked amused. With the impregnable blast walls gone, the battle was now wholly one-sided. After a couple of minutes, the gunfire ceased coming from the building, and a squad of Feds rushed in. Over her headset, Petra heard various voices calling, "Clear! Dead guard."

"Okay, entrance is clear. Awaiting your arrival, Supreme Commander," a captain spoke up. The small group began moving cautiously towards the entrance. Juan kept his arm securely around Petra's waist, steadying her, though not distracting her attention from the battle at hand. The voice added, "We count six guards killed." Petra relaxed a little, since that jived with her count, but there could well be more lying in wait.

As Petra very carefully stepped over the rubble at the entrance, the voice called out through the headset, "Got two older men here with a white flag. They say they want to parley. Orders?"

"Hold them. We're on our way. Search them; make sure they aren't armed or have a bomb detonator on them," Petra ordered, trying to think of all the diabolical tricks these two men might be attempting to pull.

A few minutes later, Petra and her group met up with the captain, his squad, and the two Lin brothers. Bo Bin was still holding a white cloth. When he saw Petra, he grimaced. Petra smiled. "Well, Bo Bin Lin, Han, we meet again. I believe I'm still causing you troubles, perhaps far more than you bargained for. You both are under arrest for massive crimes."

"You! How did you—but you're helpless! Captain, surely you aren't following the orders of this pathetic EE helpless woman, are you?" Bo Bin pleaded with the ranking man.

Captain Jose merely slapped him across his face rather hard. "Don't be disrespectful to the Supreme Feds Commander." He flinched and shut up. Just then, more voices came through on her head set, as one by one the other captains reported in. The building was secure, but the Peking Feds were on their way here.

"Okay, leave Captain Lech and his squad here with me. Get the others into position to counter the Peking Feds," she ordered. Captain Jose, flashed a brief smile, turned, signaled his men, and moved back towards the destroyed entrance.

"What is the meaning of this? Why have you attacked us? We've done nothing wrong," Bo Bin spoke up again. "Here in China, women have no value, except to raise sons for men. Surely you know that."

"How many men have died so that you two could have their bodies when yours grew old or ill?" Petra countered.

"But there are billions of bodies here in China. You can buy anyone you want for a penny," Bo Bin justified instead.

"And that gives you the right to steal their lives, destroy their games?" she replied.

"Of course. They were pitiful peasants with no future. Your beautiful body was a mere farm girl, destined to slop the pigs all her life. See, we have put her out of her misery and provided you with her most attractive body," Bo Bin countered.

"So it's just fine to murder peasants, is it?" she asked.

"But of course, there are billions of peasants here in China. We're true geniuses. They are nothing. They gave their lives so we can continue our vital work," Bo Bin replied. "We have saved the world with our inventions. There is almost no crime anywhere any longer. Surely you know of all this?"

"I certainly do know. Now then, you're going to give my friends here a guided tour of your facility. Show them everything, Bo Bin!" Petra ordered. He bowed slightly. Thus began an eye opening tour! First, the two brothers proudly showed them their Transference Machine. Then, they went to the first underground floor, where the comatose bodies were kept. Petra couldn't help grimacing when she again saw her body lying there.

"My god, Petra! It's your body, just like you said!" Beth exclaimed.

The professor pulled hard on his beard. "If I hadn't seen this with my own eyes, I wouldn't have believed it. Petra, I believe you fully now. This is a remarkable discovery and invention of theirs. But Bo Bin, why have her arms been amputated?"

"So that we have another body waiting for the next troublemaker. Our idea was to be humane and not kill the troublemakers, but to put them into a body in which they can no longer cause trouble for the world. Surely you can see this is so much better than killing them or wasting valuable resources imprisoning them," Bo Bin justified once more. The professor didn't answer him. He added, "Perhaps, we can make a deal to provide you all with a new body when yours gets too old?" No one replied to that suggestion. It was just too wild a notion.

They next visited the living quarters in the bottom level. This shocked them further. Here they discovered three men and two EE women who were armless. Two other men and a woman were blind. Additionally, six others were their caretakers. Bo Bin explained that the six had volunteered for this job and that their bodies were upstairs in the comatose preservation state, along with six others who also volunteered to run these rather helpless bodies. "Those two men will be our next bodies in just a few more years," Han pointed out two of the young male assistants.

Bo Bin added, "You see, we are prepared to handle a number of troublemakers. Please, we will transfer any number of your American troublemakers, Miss Petra. Just bring them to us anytime." He continued to play for leverage. Surely, he thought, these people would now see reason and the immense value of their work. The blast doors could be repaired and new guards hired. He added, "We were going to announce our discovery to the world very soon and begin to create many more helpless bodies to house all the troublemakers that still plague our world. Our implants aren't wholly effective on the worst ones, you see. This way, they'll be helpless and cause no further troubles."

"First, you are going to return all the volunteers to their own bodies and send them on their way," the professor took charge at last. He'd seen enough. "We will watch your every move, so don't try anything stupid."

"But who will then take care of our helpless bodies?" Bo Bin asked.

"We'll see to that detail later on; let's get to work. You've a lot to set to rights," he replied. The two men assembled their working staff of five and began to undo the various volunteer contracted men and women. Meanwhile, the professor sent word of all this to Lady Persephone.

Captain Jose reported in that six of the local Feds had been killed and the others surrendered. With Juan helping her, she excused herself from the proceedings to deal with the Peking office. A half hour later, she found the young translator was alive and well. The man had refused to fire his weapon and had surrendered. To his utter surprise, she appointed him the new Captain of the Peking Feds. "Now go and find suitable men or women to man up your department."

With a big grin, he saluted her and headed of to comply. The other five men Petra ordered to be taken to the implant station to become door polishers. Of course, they cursed her mercilessly. She only smiled back at them.

"Kind of severe," Juan whispered, as he helped her back into the building where the others were paying very close attention to the operation of the Transference Machine.

"True, but this way they won't be a problem in the future. Come on; let's see how the recovery operation is going," she replied. "Never mess with Petra Delius!" she added with a wry smile. "Well, now it's going to be very easy to mess with me, Juan. About all I can do is walk. Crap. Worse, there's no value in having them transfer me back to my original body, is there? I'm better off with this one, whose legs have really strengthened up considerably. I bet my original shoulders are really aching now, but maybe it can't feel the pain. I wonder if those unconscious bodies feel anything. This is so weird isn't it?"

"Now that's an understatement, Petra. As he said, if we hadn't seen it with our own eyes, we'd never have believed this was possible. Thank god you discovered this mess before they went worldwide with it."

"Yes, but I've paid a pretty steep price to stop them," Petra countered. "Still, I'm living up to my promise to Jessica, Persephone, and the professor. I'll do my very best."

"That you have, Petra. That you have," Juan agreed with her.

Around suppertime, the two brothers finished up with the last transfer, sending her on her way. Repeatedly, Bo Bin promised each of the volunteers that their promised credits were in their bank accounts. However, Beth verified that indeed the funds were there; she didn't trust either man. The more helpless and comatose bodies were now resting on the floor, while the large group dined in the living quarters. While they were eating, Lady Persephone arrived from her castle in Sussex. After commenting upon how Petra now looked, she was given a tour of the facilities. The professor didn't explain to the two men that it would be Lady Persephone who decided their fates.

After the hour-long tour, Lady Persephone met privately with the professor and Petra. "I must admit, Petra, at first, I didn't believe a word of your report that Beth forwarded to me. The whole thing is mind boggling, but now it is only too real. My god, there lies your body! I can't imagine what our world would have become if these men had gotten this into broad application. Using the deaths of others, they have become effectively immortal. Lord knows who else would have done anything to continue to live beyond their body's life span."

"I know, shocking. They don't value human life over here, at least these two and their Feds associates," Petra replied.

"Well, the first thing is what to do for you, Petra," Lady Persephone began her official duties as the judiciary portion of their triangle of checks and balances. "I can see your point.

There is nothing to be gained by having Bo Bin put you back into your old body. Actually, this Chinese one is amazingly pretty."

"I agree. Nothing to be gained and perhaps much to be lost."

"Have you considered taking one of the fit male bodies they were going to use for their new bodies?" she asked.

"Yes, but that won't work either, not with my EE implant. There is no going back to being male, not unless I want to endure continuous migraine headaches. That I can do without," Petra replied with a sigh. "Too bad, though. That would've been a great solution."

"Right, I believe that is also a wise choice too, Petra. I'm sure you don't want one of the two armless EE women's bodies either." Petra chuckled. "What about finding another woman who is willing to die so you could have her body?"

"Oh don't be ridiculous, Lady Persephone! While I would love to be whole again and not utterly helpless, that's not the way to do it. I'd be no better than those two. No, I must be thankful that this body is strong and healthy. I suppose that it's rather sexy will help some too. However, don't get me wrong, Lady Persephone. I'm not backing out of my promise to all of you. I'll still do my very best for the cause," she added hastily, worried that Lady Persephone would get the wrong idea about her.

Lady Persephone smiled, "Sorry, just testing you, Petra. I know you will hold to your promise. Perhaps one day down the line something will turn up to help. So the question we're left with is what to do about the two inventors, the two sadistic psychopaths?"

"My men will gladly execute them, but that's too good for them," Petra gave her the usual option expected from the Feds.

Lady Persephone pursed her lips slightly, deep in thought. "Look, it is justice that we desire. While killing them is more than warranted, they will not have learned anything before they die. I'd like to teach them something before that happens. Professor, do you know enough to operate their machine now?"

"I believe so, My Lady. I helped them with the last three volunteers," he replied.

"Okay, then my judgment is that Bo Bin Lin and Han Lin be transferred into the two armless EE women's bodies and their current bodies put to death. No going back for them. I'll take them back to Sussex with me and see they have someone to care for their needs until they die of natural causes, which isn't likely for another fifty years or so, if I can judge those Chinese women's ages correctly. Let's knock them out before you make the transference, just as they did to Petra. Of course, both will need an EE woman's implant before they regain consciousness. I'll see to that as well, using their own implant machine. That's my final judgment in this matter. Oh yes, this place must be dismantled, and the equipment brought to my castle for storage and study. It may be a useful tool in the future, who can say?"

"I'll order my men to begin taking the place apart as soon as you both have finished with the two men," Petra replied. "I do like your justice, My Lady," she grinned, "a real taste of what they have been inflicting upon others. Love it."

The professor prepared the knockout drug, and the two unsuspecting men drank it willingly, as they sipped their after-dinner tea. He and Juan carried the men up one floor and laid them on the table-like beds. An hour later, Bo Bin was in the first woman's body, and Juan wheeled her into the adjoining room, where Lady Persephone was preparing the EE woman's implant. An hour later, he wheeled Han into the room, just as she finished up with Bo Bin.

"Okay, wheel her into the living quarters where she will eventually wake up on her own," she requested. An hour later, Juan wheeled Han down to join Bo Bin. She accompanied him. "Well, they'll need new names," she grinned mischievously.

Two hours later, both began to stir and everyone gathered around them. Lady Persephone waved some smelling salts before their noses, rousing both women. Bo Bin regained consciousness. "What happened to me?" he said in a soprano voice. He tried to rub his head at the same time. Suddenly, the woman's eyes opened wide as Bo Bin realized he was now transferred into one of the armless EE women's bodies, complete with ballet boots. She screamed wildly, as did Han who also awoke quite shocked. "What have you done?" Bo Bin shrieked.

Lady Persephone calmly said, "We're making good use of your transference project by putting troublemakers into bodies that'll be unable to cause more troubles. These are quite young female bodies, so you can live another good fifty years, maybe more." Both women screamed wildly, but were helpless

351

to do much else. She added, "Yes, your old bodies have passed away and are being buried with the others who died here today, so there is no going back for you two."

Both ceased screaming and began reciting their EE woman's implant litany, much to their utter humiliation. They had no choice but to recite it, just as no EE woman had, thanks to their implant machines. "Now let's get you two to bed. We have a lot of traveling to do tomorrow, and you want to look your best, don't you?" Lady Persephone explained. Both women nodded, in spite of their desires not to. She forced them to get to their feet and walk to a bedroom.

As Petra watched them wobbling wildly and frantically, she smiled, knowing precisely what was going through their minds. "Pity that they never considered how the women felt about all this," she said to Juan. "If they had, they might have followed a different path."

"True," the professor spoke up. "However, this whole transference thing has got me thinking. Perhaps there is far more to all this than their simpleton explanation that they're moving a person's mind from body to body. I'll need to do some extensive research, I'm afraid. I think Petra has stumbled onto something that is bloody important for us all! Well done, Petra."

"Thank you professor. I sure do hope it's worth the price I'm paying for the discovery," she replied. "I best go see how Cho Lin is faring. She is still heavily under the influence of her implant. Jessica, I could use your help in desensitizing her somewhat, if you don't mind."

"Sure thing," Jessica replied.

"Petra, I think you should return to Phoenix with us and have our doctors look over your body to make sure it's healthy and that there's nothing that can be done for you," the professor suggested. "Besides, that will give Jessica time to work with Cho Lin."

"Okay, I have some serious problems to handle now, if I'm to remain as the Feds Supreme Commander. How am I going to do anything? Maybe Lisa can offer some suggestions," Petra replied, though she didn't hold out much hope Lisa would have any workable ideas. She couldn't use her feet the way that Lisa could.

The next morning, Petra complimented her captains on a job well done. After that, she headed back to the States with Lech and her friends. Only the professor and two teams of Feds remained behind to see to the dismantling and transport of the equipment.

A couple of days later, Petra was given a clean bill of health by the doctors in Phoenix. Her feet, however, were another matter. Her toes had become more like small nubbins, far worse than Beth and the other women's toes. She suspected not even the lengthy surgery by the German podiatrist would help her, but didn't mention it. Her back muscles had atrophied, and she was put on a regime of strengthening exercises. By the time Jessica had finished desensitizing Cho Lin, some two weeks after their arrival in Phoenix, Petra was strong enough to avoid wearing the overly tight corset, which pleased her significantly.

However, Beth provided the best assistance for her continued survival as the Supreme Commander. "Look, make good use of all the doormen. As long as you stay in the city, there're always doormen around. Now what you need is voice-activated software on your computer. You speak the commands and dictate, instead of typing and using the mouse. You should be able to run your entire business this way. I'll get it all setup for you."

"Really? Now that is good news. Yes, if somehow the computer could respond to voice commands, I'd be all set to continue running the Feds. Unfortunately, it can't feed me or help me use the bathroom or get dressed. Cho Lin will have to help me with those things. If not, I guess I can hire a personal assistant to be my hands when needed. The main thing is that I can continue being the Supreme Commander and fulfill my promises to you," Petra replied a bit stoically.

Jessica validated her, "You're the bravest woman I've ever met."

Petra laughed, "What choice do I have? Really, life is almost impossible for me. Being brave is about all that's left for me—that and my looks and hair. I do love my hair; it's amazingly long and so full. Lisa wanted me to get it cut short, no way." She laughed at the small bit of vanity that remained to her. "Oh yes, and my legs are much stronger than they were on my dead body," she added. "That sure does sound strange, doesn't it?" Jessica smiled; that it did, but so many things were strange these days.

The first of July, Beth had Petra's office fixed up for her. Her laptop computer, her large desktop computer, and the Feds server were now fully voice-controlled. She had Petra speak the one hundred voice-recognition words, and the fancy program stored them, fabricating a huge series of now-known commands. Beth printed them out in triplicate, fastening a set on Petra's desk, on the coffee table in her lounge, and in the top drawer, as a backup. She also emailed herself a copy in case these were lost or damaged. "Okay, everything is all setup. Are you sure you don't want us to stick around a while longer?" Beth asked.

I wish you'd stay with me always! Petra thought, feeling the rise of panic in her stomach. Bravely, she replied, "No, you have your work to do. I've promised to do mine, and my place is here, running the Feds' offices worldwide. Cho Lin and I will be all right. We can go in and out of my office suite now, what with the automatic doors. The doorman has been alerted to watch for us. We'll be okay. If not, I can always hire an assistant." *There, I've cut the cord, and I'll be on my own again. God, I hope I can handle this!*

Beth gave her a hug and a nod to Cho Lin. Taking her carefully measured steps out of the fancy suite, she stopped to pick up the others from their new Feds offices before heading back to East Peoria.

Chapter 24—Of Thefts and Murders

"Dial Tilly," Petra spoke into her headset. The warm late-July sun flooded her Feds office suite. "Tilly, Petra here. The CSI lab results have just come back. You guys were right. The last six murder sprees here in Chicago were all done with the same set of two guns! I've ordered the Chicago branch to search through the AP-cops' database and see if there are more of these senseless killings and if they're also linked. Either one person is using two guns or there are two shooters. I have alerted the AP-cops to be on the lookout for more serial killings like these. We can see no pattern in the stores that were hit, but if there were more shooting that haven't yet been identified as associated with these, we might find a pattern. I'm having the other US captains search their local AP-cops databases for similar murder sprees. Haven't heard back from them yet. Does this help you?"

"Yes, it does. In a way, this simplifies things," Tilly replied. "I'll get back to you with some suggestions within a day or so. Amanda and I need to work up the prediction formulas. Oh, Beth wants me to tell you the store thefts situation is beginning to resolve into a clearer picture. She believes there are people who have been overlooked by the Pytalon and implant programs and that they are likely robbing the stores to survive. She'll know more later on. Thanks for the update. How's everything working out for you?"

I can't tell her the truth—that my life is a nightmare. Instead, Petra said, "We're getting by. It's hard, but we are managing somehow." Pretending to have an incoming call so she could hang up quickly, Petra fought hard to keep from crying. She dared not let Tilly know how awful life had become. She couldn't face that. "Got to run, another call. Bye." Once she saw the connection broken, Petra allowed her tears to come.

Cho Lin rose, got her balance, and came over to her. Using a handkerchief between her stumps, she wiped Petra's eyes for her. "It'll be okay, my love," she whispered. "We're surviving."

"I know, dearest Cho, but it's so hard for me. Thanks. I'm in control again. Hearing her voice rather set me off. Sorry to make you have to wipe my eyes."

"That is what I can do to help. I'm not bright like you," Cho Lin explained for the hundredth time. "So I do what I can to help you." She put her arms around Petra and gave her a gentle, loving squeeze.

In fact, things hadn't been going very well for the two, who had somehow managed to get by the first couple of weeks. True, once dressed and on their way to her Feds office, things went fairly well for the two of them, thanks to the ever-present doormen and the voice-activated office software. Still, eating lunch was a nightmare. Going home after work was the worst part of the day. Once back in her apartment, their difficulties crescendoed.

"I think we're simply going to have to hire us a live-in personal assistant. I'm tired of eating out all the time, to say nothing of the embarrassment of having to eat like a dog in public. It takes you and me hours to get dressed each morning. We simply have to admit we need help, Cho Lin. I'm going to place an ad for a helper for us right now," Petra said determinedly, but not without many reservations. She had always been fiercely independent, even as Peter Delius. Now she found herself wholly the opposite. She had a very hard time swallowing her pride, but life was unspeakably unbearable now.

Meanwhile, Jessica and Beth were continuing their exhaustive investigation of inventory discrepancies, focusing on both Peoria and Chicago for starters. Juan had pretty much solved the Peoria situation, having located several families who were living off the grid because they didn't know how to do otherwise. They had no birth certificates or other identifications, and thus the "system" failed to recognize them. Left to their own means, they kept a low profile, taking only what they needed to survive. Now they were on their way to Phoenix where they could be trained and given useful, productive lives.

The Chicago scene didn't resolve so readily. Tilly refused to send Juan there alone; it was far too dangerous. Chicago was huge, and with the mass murders, quite deadly. Armed with the latest information from Petra, she and Amanda began to rework their prediction equations. Until now, she'd assumed different groups committed each mass murder. With ballistics telling a different story, the formulas had to be reworked and current numbers inserted and solved.

Jessica first spotted the definitive correlation between the Chicago mass murders and the "missing inventory."

Looking over their summary lists for some Chicago stores, she asked, "Say, Tilly, what were those dates of the mass murders?" Tilly called them off. "Well, isn't this strange. A large number of the missing inventory went missing on those same dates! How strange is that?"

"What? Same date?" Tilly looked up, suddenly very interested in Jessica's data. "Times, let's compare times and locations." She brought her summary pages over to Jessica's monitors. Together, they began comparing one to the other. "Well, the dates and times match, but not the locations," Tilly pointed out. "Still, this may have a bearing on the problem."

"What if the murders were carried out to distract the AP-cops from the thefts?" Jessica speculated.

"Brilliant, Jessica! Positively brilliant!" Tilly exclaimed. "That would explain everything. The mass murders, which seem to be utterly pointless and random, could well be nothing more than a distraction while the perpetrators raid another store. I think we're getting lots closer to solving this one. Back to my calculations. I wonder if we can predict when they will strike again."

"Well, it's never the same day of the month, though it looks like they strike once every month," Jessica pointed out. "I'll look at it further."

She had more data than Tilly had. Their database scrubbing program had gone back an entire year, not just six months. Still, looking over the largest of the "missing inventory" each month, she saw what seemed to be random dates. Jessica didn't like random events, especially something this awful. *There just has to be a pattern here, only I'm not seeing it. What's so important about the 16th? Think outside the box. I've heard that line before, but what's the box that I'm in? Oh well, I'll keep looking.*

Later on, she pulled up the computer's calendar for one of the months and stared at it. Then she saw the four little circles and asked Beth, "What are these little circles on my calendar here?"

Beth rolled her chair over to her monitor and looked. With a little laugh, she said, "The moon. Those are the phases of the moon. The hollow one is the new moon, the solid one is the full moon."

"Oh! Thanks. I should've known that one. Silly me. Wait a second. One of the murders occurred on the full moon. I wonder," she said, bringing up the previous month and checking the date. "Oh my." She continued backtracking and then called out, "Tilly, I found it. The murder dates aren't random. They occur whenever there's a full moon."

"What? Exactly? All six of them?" Tilly answered, rather surprised at such a silly correlation. "Are we dealing with werewolves or something?" she jested.

"What's a werewolf?" asked Amanda.

"All six occurred when the calendar shows a full moon. I'm looking back further to see when some of the other larger 'missing inventories' occurred," Jessica replied, bringing up the next previous month.

A while later, she added, "Yes, all major ones occurred when there was a full moon. It isn't random after all," she added proudly.

"Well, Jessica, you may have just cracked this one for us. We don't need my behavior prediction calculations to guess when they'll strike again. When is the next full moon?" Tilly asked.

Jessica had to readjust her computer calendar. A minute later, she called out, "In three days. Do you think there'll be another mass murder then?"

"If what we are observing holds true, then yes. I'll send all this to Petra. I bet she'll be very pleased to know this murder spree is solvable. She can get her Feds on it; there's still time to go, three days," Tilly replied. Beth gave Jessica a loving smile.

***

Across town in what was now called Old Town, Philo Dailey paced around his dilapidated apartment in Housing Unit X, a ten story brick building in sore need of countless repairs. Surrounded by a dozen similar units, they had been scheduled for demolition fifty years ago. However, that had not happened and would not as long as no one paid any attention to these five blocks. The many Garbage Collector Twentieth Class men and women and their families occupied a large percentage of the units, and they were wholly shunned by nearly everyone— though forgotten by everyone might be a better viewpoint, a viewpoint exploited for years by the fifty-five year old Philo.

Here in Old Town, he was known as King Philo. He ruled these housing units with an iron fist. Yet for forty years, he provided for his many subjects so well that they swore undying loyalty to King Philo. Outside of Old Town, Philo did not exist, as far as any Feds or AP-cops databases were concerned. On the other hand, his influence certainly did, though not directly.

His loyal Duke Leo handled the AP-cops for him. New clothes, fancy chocolate bars, rich coffee, along with many other commodities reserved for the wealthy ended up in certain AP-cops' hands in exchange for looking the other way or simply ignoring certain situations. One such situation occurred every month, on the average, and that was the wholesale acquisition of their "supplies."

Duke Leo, a twenty-five year old Garbage Collector Twentieth Class, knocked on King Philo's door before entering. "Duke Leo. Welcome. News?" Philo greeted his second in command.

"It's as you suspected, my king. The Feds have definitely discovered the 'buried shootings.' Our contact said the Feds took all the evidence from the last six months. Does this mean the Feds are on to us? What do we do now?" Duke Leo was worried, in as much as Pytalon allowed him to worry.

"This is no good, my loyal duke. Leave me now. I must consult with the gods to see what we must do," Philo replied. Duke Leo bowed and left the ramshackle of a room. The gods Philo referred to were the constant voices inside his head that told him what to do, the voices of the psych who had given him his implant, another psych man, and a nurse. Yes, he was a "botched PHD implant," though of course, he had no way of knowing that.

He was barely eighteen when he was taken by the psychs. In high school, he was something of a bully, so much so that most other teens avoided him at all costs. Even his teachers wanted nothing to do with him. He was strong, arrogant, and quite often angry. Several times, he got detention for striking one of his teachers. Hence, when he was taken, the psych was ordered to make him into a Garbage Collector Twentieth Class.

Philo was given the usual knockout drug, subjected to the intense electronically generated pain, followed by the psych reading the prepared script that would thereafter force Philo to be a Garbage Collector Twentieth Class. However, having finished the script, a fellow psych dropped by for a chat. The psych didn't realize all that was about to be said would also become part of Philo's implanted behavior.

"I see you're being God again," his friend joked.

"Yes, you and I are gods, kings of the world out there," the psych replied.

The friend chuckled, "Ah, king of the Garbage Collector Twentieth Class I see by his chart."

"Yes, king of the Garbage Collector Twentieth Class." He poured out some fine wine for his friend. Noticing his friend eying the wine, he added, "Well, we deserve only the best, don't we?"

"Yes, we certainly do. We're making the world a safe place to live. We get rid of the scum bags anyway we can," his friend replied.

"In a way, you and I are literally kings these days. We have the responsibility of everyone around us on our shoulders, don't we?"

"Yes, that we do. We have to look out for everyone and the well-being of our whole society, which has gone to the dumps these days. Insanity is everywhere," his friend replied, sipping some wine. He added, "Is it Full Moon?" He meant the brand name of the wine, some of the best wine still available, but extremely rare these days, since it didn't mix with Pytalon.

"Yes, Full Moon is the best," he replied. "We deserve the best that life has to offer for what we do for everyone else. I wish they would see that too. If it weren't for us, the whole world would become insane. We must be smart and on top of everything. Listen to me, my friend. Mark my words, one day we will be honored by everyone for what all we do to eliminate the world's insanity, giving everyone what they justly deserve."

"Aye, there's no doubting that, my friend. We're brilliant, intelligent, and wise. Everyone rightly listens to us now. That's as it should be. There isn't anything you and I can't figure out. We just need time to think," his friend pointed out.

"So true, but there are times when I think we should just kill them. You know, the really bad ones. Why even waste time and resources on them? Give the goods to those who need it."

"You have a point. Killing them is a good solution, but could we get away with it? Probably not. Say, nurse, what do you think?" his friend asked the Pytalon drugged nurse.

She'd only been barely able to follow what the two men had been saying. Somewhat confused, she replied, "I can use the goods. It seems like there is never enough to go around." She was thinking of her medical supplies that were running low once more. Was this what the men were discussing, she wondered within her drug-daze? "Sanity is always doing a good job," she added. Both psychs chuckled a little.

All of that was added to Philo's implanted behavior. The "you" referred to himself and thus acted as the voices, which then talked to him inside his head. As Philo continued to pace around his room, the voices told him, "You and I are gods." Philo agreed; he was hearing the voices of the gods. "You're king of the world out there, king of the Garbage Collector Twentieth Class," the voices said to him.

Philo muttered, "Yes, I am their king. I know that, but what do I do now? The Feds are getting too close to us."

The voices continued, saying, "You're brilliant, intelligent, and wise. There isn't anything you and I can't figure out."

Philo agreed. "Yes, there isn't anything we can't figure out."

The voices said, "We just need time to think." Philo agreed and strained his mind, trying to "think."

His voices said, "Kill them—the really bad ones. Why even waste time and resources on them? Killing them is a good solution."

Philo replied, "You have a point. Kill them. The really bad Feds. But what about the evidence? I know. Kill the really bad ones again and use that to cover stealing the goods, the evidence! Thank you, my gods! Duke Leo, Duke Leo?" he called out, heading out of his throne room looking for his second.

"Yes, my king?" Duke Leo came running up to his liege.

"The gods have spoken. First, we'll steal all the remaining evidence from the AP-cops. So we need to arrange another shooting to distract everyone while we break into their evidence room and take everything else the Feds might want. We should do that soon. When is the next full moon?"

"Tomorrow. See the calendar there shows a big round circle moon," Duke Leo answered.

"Good, make it so, my duke. Second, I need you to find out who is the leader of the Feds here in Chicago. The gods have said the solution is simple: kill them," King Philo explained.

"On it, my king," Duke Leo smiled and scampered out to make some arrangements and to make some inquiries.

***

Lady Persephone hadn't been idle since returning to her castle in Sussex, along with the Lin brother's equipment. She and the professor spent several days setting up the equipment.

He returned to Phoenix after that. Quite why she wanted their equipment operational, she couldn't say. "Call it a gut feeling, professor," she'd answered his serious query.

"Okay. I have one too and that is there's far more to this Transference Machine than those two sadistic psychs know. I've a lot of research of my own to do. I'll keep you informed, My Lady," the professor explained before he left.

She hired a helper woman to assist her two "EE women," namely the Lin brothers. Currently, she had them in a private room on the ground floor. For the first few days, the two cried a lot in between rattling off their implant litany, but Lady Persephone had no sympathy for the two. They had invented the latest PDH implant machine and procedure that had nearly destroyed the entire world. No, the two sadists were getting a taste of what they'd unleashed on the entire world, as well as the poor women and men in their laboratory, to say nothing of Petra. However, she also wanted them nearby if she needed to use the Transference Machine or the life support pods.

Tonight, she chose to dine with them. It was time they chose new names. Lady Persephone sent word to Sally to bring the two women to the formal dining room. She always dined in elegance, complete with golden chandeliers and table candlesticks in a manner suited to proper British aristocracy. Sally brought the two into the elegant, spacious room, both talking frantically about not falling down. She thought they walked more like a pair of storks. Sally seated them across the table from her. "That will be all for now, Sally. I'll take care of them and call you when we finish. Thank you."

"Yes, My Lady," Sally replied properly and left, eager to get her own supper with the two caretakers of the castle.

"Do I look my best, please?" Bo Bin asked her. "I must look my best. How could you have done this to me? My head is splitting! Don't you know EE women must be pleasured at least three times a day?"

"He's right. We must. You're torturing us. Do I look my best? I must, you know," Han added.

"You both look just fine. Tonight, we dine on chicken breasts, rice, and mixed vegetables. Bon appétit, ladies. Oh yes, you must pick proper women's names tonight," she added.

"But surely you'll feed us?" Bo Bin looked helplessly at the delicious food on the plate before her.

"Don't be silly. You can help yourselves. Bend over and eat, ladies."

"But we won't look our best," Han complained.

"I don't mind this once," Lady Persephone replied. The two had no choice but to lean over and gobble at the food on their plates.

"This is inhumane," Bo Bin spoke up, food dripping from her chin.

"What did you expect? How do you think poor Petra manages or any of the others you mistreated?"

"But, but, we had assistants for them—to help them with every need," Han countered.

"Yes, but what if their assistants aren't always there? How did you expect them to get by?" Both looked rather startled, but their hunger got the best of them. Later, she wiped their faces off and put a straw into their teacups for them. "Now then, what names do you desire? Bo and Han will never do; you're EE women now."

Begrudgingly, Bo Bin decided to be called Bao Lin, while Han chose to be Huan Lin.

"Now then, Bao and Huan, tell me about how new bodies can be acquired. You see, I would like to help Petra Delius out of the terrible body you two put her into, but I certainly don't want to kill another woman just to get her body. Ideas, ladies?"

"We'll help you, but you must help us. We can't live like this," Bao answered, a gleam of hope in her eyes. "Damn, not again." She began reciting her implant litany. Her recitation triggered Huan to do the same thing. A few minutes later, Bao finally was lucid again for a short while. "You're making it terribly difficult to obtain new bodies, but still there is a way."

"Do go on," Lady Persephone suddenly perked up, becoming very curious.

"Well, sometimes the PDH implants aren't successful and the person dies, well sort of."

"Precisely what do you mean? I thought everyone survived the implant process."

"They do over here in the West, but in China, our land is so huge, and they wanted to save money. Many of the more remote areas are still using the Model I version," Bao explained.

"So?" Lady Persephone nudged her.

"With that early model, sometimes the person is given a bit too much electrical pain. Centuries ago, we just thought they died from it, but now we know better. While we remedied that difficulty in the Model II, our researches into the Transference Machine led us to an entirely different conclusion."

"Yes," Huan picked up where Bao left off, as she again had to recite her litany. "We now believe the charge was simply too great, and the personality fled the body, after which the body slowly succumbed, though it remained alive for quite some time in a comatose state. If you can put one of those bodies into one of our stasis pods, you can keep the body alive indefinitely. Please, we've helped you. Now you must help us. We can't live like this."

"Thank you. I'll help you, but of course, you can live like this. You had Mei Bei living like this for thirteen years before you put Petra into that body. So don't be silly. You are both doing fine. I'll see if I can find you your own home and caretaker. Now it is time for you to return to your room." She summoned Sally.

"But we need to be pleasured," Bao complained.

"You silly women. You're supposed to pleasure each other when you don't have a man around to do it with." Both looked rather stunned. When Sally entered, Lady Persephone told her their names. Until now, she had been calling them simply "miss."

An idea began to form in Lady Persephone's mind. From what she'd seen of Petra and now these two women, she knew Petra's life was a living horror, whether or not Petra would admit it to her and the others. "Well, if I know Petra, she'll not admit how awful her life is—too independent, too man-ish to own up to it. Plus, she is continuing to do as she promised to do. Most would have given up by now, but she's back at her job leading the Feds once more. Brave woman. So I need to find out about these old Model I machines and where they're still being used. Time for some computer work."

Several hours later, she found what she desired. Diaoezhen was a rural town in the mountains north and east of Peking, rugged terrain. Here they used one of the ancient Model I's for their implanting, just as Bao and Huan had told her. Further searching yielded two other towns close to this one. She smiled and began working on her extensive preparations. However, she did purchase a small home and a second helper for the two women, keeping her promise to them.

Two days later, she had her EMAC loaded with several of the medical pods and a substantial amount of food, prepared for an extended stay in that area of China. Lady Persephone made another stop though. She hired a translator, Marne Best, who spoke fluent Chinese. She was an implanted translator who often worked for a firm in London. That she was also on Pytalon helped, she would ask no questions and do as she was asked. A long day later, Lady Persephone and Marne landed at Diaoezhen and headed straight for the local psych.

After explaining what she wanted, the Pytalon-drugged psych agreed to let her know when an "accident" occurred. After visiting several other nearby towns, she and Marne played the role of visitors on a vacation. To her complete amazement, five days later, the psych man summoned her.

Via Marne, he explained, "Alas, we have had another accident. Pity, Chan was going to be a very beautiful EE woman, made to order for our mayor. But alas, our equipment failed, and as you can see, Chan has passed away." Lady Persephone hastily checked on the eighteen-year-old woman. She was breathing; she had a strong pulse, but she was comatose. Now she understood what Bo Bin and Han had told her about this older model. While the psych man believed Chan had died, in fact, Chan merely abandoned her body forever, because the voltage had been too much for her to tolerate. Quite where she had gone, no one knew. He asked, "Shall I go ahead now and administer a lethal dose?"

"Oh no. I'll take over from here," Lady Persephone replied. Shortly, she rolled a pod into the room. With his help, she got the lifeless woman into the pod and hooked up the life support mechanisms. After thanking the man, she and Marne left, pushing the pod into the EMAC. A day later, they arrived back in London, where Marne departed with a thousand credits added to her bank account.

Later, back in Sussex, Lady Persephone wheeled the pod into her castle and into the room that contained all the machinery. "Perfect. Job well done. This will be a pleasant and welcome surprise and reward for Petra," she commented to herself. "The Righteous Vigilante strikes again, making things right in the world."

***

"Hi Petra. We've worked it out, and Jessica actually solved the whole mystery," Tilly began to explain their findings to Petra. "The murder spree always occurs on a full moon, but those are used to cover up a burglary and theft of goods from another store on the other side of the city or at least many miles away. There's a full moon in two days. Expect another murder

365

spree, and, while all the AP-cops and rescue personnel are there handling the gruesome scene, the perpetrators will be robbing some other store far from the scene. Ta da. Solved. Pretty amazing, right?"

"Wow! Yes, amazing and nasty too. Thank you; thank Jessica for me and everyone else! I'll get the Feds onto it today. By golly, it'll be good to end this long murdering spree and bring them to justice! Thank you ever so much, Tilly!" They chatted a bit more and then Petra hung up. She now had to make plans for the predicted event and summoned Lech to her office.

After explaining the results Tilly and the others had discovered, she said, "So there's a full moon in two days. We should expect they will once again launch a murdering spree somewhere in Chicago. However, when the AP-cops and the emergency response teams get there, the perpetrators will be striking at another, more distant location. Somehow, we need to nail these bastards. Have all your men on standby. Monitor the AP-cops. I'm sure you'll hear of yet another bunch of innocent people being murdered some place. Do not send your men there. The perpetrators will be striking elsewhere. Your job is to figure out where they're striking and capture or kill them."

"We can take the EMACs and hover over the city some miles from the murder site, once we know where that is. We'll get them, boss," Lech replied in his usual monotone, but Petra detected a slight trace of excitement and smiled. He saluted and headed off to begin making preparations. Chicago was huge, and Lech decided to call in all the Feds from the surrounding areas, including from as far away as St. Louis. Petra monitored Lech's orders, satisfied he was doing everything that was possible to be able to locate where the next theft would occur once they knew where the murders occurred.

Around five, the security guard at the front desk paged Petra. "Supreme Commander, there's a young woman here, a Betsy Small, who says she's supposed to meet you here at five."

"Right. Tell her we're on our way down now. Thank you," Petra replied. To Cho, she added, "Our possible nighttime personal assistant is here. Come on; let's go meet her, and if she is satisfactory, she can come home with us. Finally, we'll have some much needed help."

"Okay, I do hope she is fine. We need help. Thank you, my love," Cho Lin replied. She helped Petra to her feet, and together, they headed for the office suite's doors, where a doorman was always on duty until they left each night. He doubled as a janitor and glass washer as well.

"Good evening. Sanity is a job well done; doors opened on time; windows cleaned."

"Thank you," Petra replied mechanically, doubting the man actually received her thanks. A bit later, they met the eighteen-year-old high school girl, who had answered her ad.

"Oh my! I can see why you need so much help! I'm Betsy Small, miss," she exclaimed, her eyes opening wide as she saw the physical condition of the two EE women. After a brief chat, Betsy was more than willing to be their nighttime assistant, and she joined them on their walk to Petra's apartment. I say walk, but really they did very little actual walking. The MTE escalators ran nearly everywhere here in the heart of the sprawling city. After barely twenty careful steps, they stepped onto the MTE proper and continued to chat. Sally stood behind the two EE women, ready to catch them if they should stumble.

"Is that them?" whispered one hooded man.

Duke Leo whispered back, "Yes, the armless one is the prime target. Take the handless one too, if we can. Don't harm the other woman following along behind them. We don't want to kill anyone but the Feds leader—king's orders. Get ready; here they come."

"Yes, we could definitely use a good cook. We've been forced to eat out every night. It is so embarrassing to eat. . ." Petra was explaining to Betsy. Just then, several shots rang out. One hit Petra, ending her words mid-sentence. Both Petra and Cho Lin took several gunshots in rapid succession. Betsy screamed wildly, shaking her head no. She saw the two hooded men dash off and continued to scream at the top of her lungs. Of course, in a Pytalon-drugged society, no one paid any attention to her, save one AP-cop who made his way over to the bloody scene.

"Miss, what happened here?" he asked in a monotone, dispassionate voice, temporarily halting the MTE.

"She's the Feds Supreme Commander. Two men shot her and her companion," Betsy finally managed to calm down enough to reply. Fortunately, the AP-cop hearing the word Feds, decided to phone this one into the Feds. Lech and several others came running out of the building, guns drawn, but of course saw no one. When Lech arrived beside Petra, the AP-cop had temporarily stopped the MTE to examine the two victims.

"This one's dead, sir," the AP-cop said. "This one is still breathing, but barely. Probably won't make it." Lech took charge, sent for an ambulance EMAC, and then tried to question the hysterical Betsy, whose description was merely two hooded men. Lech then found Petra's cell phone in the purse that she carried around her neck along with her ID card.

"Tilly? Lech here. Bad news. Petra and Cho Lin have just been shot. They were on their way home from work. Two men in hooded sweatshirts. Petra is still alive, barely. Doesn't look good though. Cho Lin is dead. What do you want us to do besides get her to the hospital?"

"We're on our way, Lech! Thanks for the news. Let us know which hospital," Tilly replied. "Gang! Petra's been shot! Cho Lin is dead. That was Lech. Petra's in a bad way. Come on; we are going to Chicago as fast as we can!"

"Oh my god!" Beth exclaimed. The others had similar reactions. While Juan rushed outside to get the EMAC powered up, the four made their slow, careful way outside, securing their facility as usual. "Thanks, Juan," a white-faced Beth added, as he helped her onboard, then the other three.

While Juan drove, Tilly and Beth began phoning everyone else with the awful news. While Tilly relayed the news to the professor, Beth phoned Lady Persephone. "Yes, Petra was shot and Lech is taking her to the emergency room. I'll keep you posted My Lady."

"Wait, Beth. If she is not expected to live, you simply have to keep her on life support long enough to get her over here to my castle! I've just gotten back from China with a new body for her, one that's in mint condition." She explained what she'd done. "Yes, they're still using the first implant model, which sometimes kills the patient. I was there; the poor young woman was officially dead, but yes, you might call me a body snatcher, and just in time too, it seems. Keep me posted!"

Juan pushed every ounce of speed out of the EMAC, reaching Chicago in near record time. Lech kept them posted on which hospital, and they went directly to St. John's, where Lech was waiting for them, ashen faced.

"I thought you predicted the mass murders would occur tomorrow," Lech protested.

"This wasn't a mass murder, not like the other six, Lech. Someone wanted Petra dead, but who?" Tilly countered.

"Oh. Yes, I see—not a mass murder. Who would want the Supreme Commander dead?" he asked rhetorically. No one had an answer.

"If she isn't going to make it, we're supposed to keep her on life support and get her over to Sussex where Lady Persephone believes she can work a miracle for Petra," Tilly advised.

"In that case, I best have an Air Liner standing by. It doesn't look too good for her, poor thing. Took two in her chest and one in her head," Lech explained and then began making phone calls.

Tilly got the attention of a nurse and issued her order to keep Petra on life support if needed. An hour later, the doctor came out to consult with them. His eyes were glazed, and Tilly cringed; a Pytalon zombie operating on Petra rubbed her raw! "I've followed your orders and put her on life support. There is really no hope for her recovery," he said trying hard to muster the tones of sympathy, which of course he didn't feel. He had no emotions at all.

"Okay, then bring her out in the life support unit. We'll be flying her elsewhere," Tilly ordered. Lech nodded and the doctor complied. A half hour later, the five lifted off from New O'Hare along with the stasis unit from the hospital that was keeping Petra's body alive a little longer. Lech's last words to them as they left were, "I swear I'll find those two men and make them pay for this." His voice displayed an unusual amount of emotion for a person on Pytalon. Tilly knew this had affected the Feds man rather severely. Well, it had done so to all them.

"Keep hoping and praying," Tilly consoled the others as they flew through the night sky. "Lady Persephone has a new body waiting for her."

"But there are a whole lot of if's," Beth countered. "Will Petra survive until we get there? Her body is with us, but is she? Can Lady Persephone really operate the Transference Machine? Will it even work on Petra? Damn. She should have been given a constant bodyguard."

Juan smiled. He had long had the same thought. He called out, "Hey, don't forget that Petra was Peter and Peter would never have consented to having a bodyguard, just as I would never accept one or Lady Persephone, for that matter."

Vic Broquard

"So she endured all this stoically? Isn't that just like a man?" Jessica commented snidely. Juan laughed, breaking the tensions a little.

Chapter 25—Experiments and Changes

The Air Liner landed on the rolling estate of Lady Persephone in the morning hours. She was there to greet them and urged them to make haste. She and Juan carried the stasis unit into the castle, while the four women held on to each other and made their precarious way across the grasslands into the building. Already Lady Persephone had the Transference Machine set up and ready to go. The young Chinese teen was hooked up, and the two placed Petra's body alongside of her. Carefully, Lady Persephone made the necessary electrode connections to Petra, while the others watched. Jessica kept her fingers crossed. Tilly watched carefully, but Beth was more interested in the machine's operation. Amanda leaned on Juan, fighting to keep from crying.

"Okay, here goes nothing or everything," she called out and activated the machine, which ran through its programmed cycle. They saw both bodies jerk slightly as the electricity began to flow through their heads. Once the cycle finished a couple of minutes later, Lady Persephone unfastened the many electrodes from the Chinese teen. "Now we wait. Perhaps I should try to rouse her. Bo Bin didn't tell us whether to do that or not."

"Go ahead and try," Juan suggested. She found some smelling salts and waved it beneath the teen's nose. She jerked and gasped for air. A shrill, high-pitched scream followed. She sat up on the cot and looked around.

"Petra?" Lady Persephone whispered.

"I'm shot? What's happened to me? I have arms? Is this some terrible nightmare again? Cho Lin? Of course, I'm Petra. Who else would I be? Oh!" She became silent as she realized something major had happened to her.

"Yes, you were shot and were about to die, so we had you put on life support. We brought you to Lady Persephone," Tilly explained. "She's found a new body for you. I'm so sorry, but Cho Lin didn't make it. She died at the scene. Lech swears he will find the two men and make them pay. Is it really you, Petra?"

"Oh! Damn, I have the worst headache imaginable! Yes, it's me. We were walking home when these two men began firing at us. I remember feeling something hitting my head and then a wave of pain. Then, I saw this brilliant, white light, the most beautiful thing I've ever seen. I couldn't help myself, and I rather followed it, not wanting it to fade away. Now I'm sitting here with a smashing headache. Poor Cho Lin, damn. Oh, that's me there!" She now saw her nearly dead body lying next to her, its head heavily bandaged as well as her chest.

After a moment, Petra looked at Lady Persephone and gasped, "You've saved me! I'm really still alive!"

"You bet. We bloody well can't have our Supreme Commander dead, now can we? However, considering what I had to do to get this body for you, let's not make a practice of getting yourself all shot up like that, okay?" she teased her a little bit.

Petra began feeling herself. "Got big boobs. EE woman?" she asked.

"Yes, she was an eighteen year old Chinese woman who was undergoing the EE woman's implant when she perished. Bo Bin actually helped us with this. Apparently, in the smaller towns in China, the psychs are still using their flawed original model implant machine. Sometimes, the patient dies, and that's what happened to her. I was right there, got her body into one of these stasis pods, and kept it alive, though the teen was long gone. Of course, all this raises more questions than I have answers for. Wish the professor was here," she added.

"Thank you. I have arms again and my feet—they're perfectly normal! Yahoo. Now if this horrid headache would go away, I'd be just fine. Oh, I'm hungry too. What do I look like?" Petra asked, her thoughts coming almost faster than she could chat.

She was covered with only a thin sheet. "Don't look, Juan," she teased as Lady Persephone helped her up and held a mirror for her to see her new body. "Eighteen? Wow. I just lost thirteen years. Oh, not bad. I'm rather pretty still. Ah, the same thick, long black hair. Love it. Monster boobs, well, that's to be expected. Best thing, hands and feet! Thank you, Lady Persephone. I owe you more than I can ever repay you for this. I wish Cho Lin were here." Her eyes watered; already she missed her. Petra began to feel a rush of emotions, far more than she ever had before, but didn't quite know what to make of it and was glad when Lady Persephone spoke up.

"Just keep on being our Supreme Commander, Petra. We need you," she replied.

"I keep my promises, but do you have anything for this headache of mine? And some clothes? I'm freezing." That brought chuckles all around.

While Lady Persephone handled her requests, Tilly texted the professor and Lech with the incredibly good news. "Hey, the professor is on his way here," Tilly called out. "Expect him for supper."

"Well how do I look now?" Petra asked, doing a slight twirl. She wore a white cotton day dress of Lady Persephone's that didn't fit her massive bosom, but otherwise covered her. While the four women looked at her, she added, "I know, it doesn't fit well and isn't appropriate for us EE women, but at least I'm not naked, just really tired. Any word from Lech? I'm not sure what day it is, but he was supposed to be on the anticipated mass murder situation."

"He said he's on it, Petra," Tilly answered. "You look good, but tired. Why don't you get some sleep?"

"I think you're right. I seem to be a cat with nine lives, thanks to Lady Persephone. Can you wake me if Lech calls and needs help?" They promised to do so, and she followed her host to a guest bedroom.

When Lady Persephone returned, she said, "Incredible. The moment she laid down, she was asleep. My god, she's undergone an enormous amount of trauma and loss in the last half-day or so. She's taking it rather well though. Perhaps while she is sleeping, you could visit our local EE women's store and get her something more appropriate to wear. I can give you a good guess on her measurements. I had a devil of a time finding anything that would fit over her bosom."

Tilly giggled, "We know. One size fits all, monsters. You're right. We should get her something appropriate to wear. No sense in aggravating her EE implant. You know, that was incredible foresight on your part—getting a hold of that teen's body. You must have been planning this for some time."

"Caught!" Lady Persephone grinned. "Yes, I had it in the back of my mind since we first saw her armless body and the Transference Machine. Mind you, I would never have gotten one for her if it involved killing the host person. No, the idea took fruit when I learned from Bo Bin that some of the Chinese psych men in rural areas were still using the barbaric Model I machine, which, according to Bo Bin, occasionally killed the person being implanted. So I took a gamble and it paid off, rather timely if I do say so myself. Of course, now that it has proven successful, I wonder if I should 'procure' more bodies, keeping them alive in the stasis pods of Bo Bin and Han. What happens if we lose one of you or the professor or others who are important? Do we dare lose the very ones who stand a chance at salvaging the world from brink of destruction? Bo Bin and Han were playing God, being immortal for two centuries, causing in part the annihilation of the world's cultures. Shouldn't we play God and stay alive long enough to put things right again?"

She went on, "Petra has proven to be a valuable ally. She alone of us has control of the Feds worldwide, and for the first time in my life I'm not hiding from the Feds."

"Neither are we," Tilly replied. "We no longer fear and hide from the Feds. I agree, if we lose Petra, it's doubtful the Feds will continue to assist us in saving the world. They're all hooked on Pytalon now, just as are the vast majority of the people. I know I'd like nothing more than to have my male body back—Beth and Petra too—but with our EE implants, that would only cause us one continuous migraine. Yet, I can see the wisdom in somehow staying alive so we can somehow salvage the world. Without anyone of us, the chances for Lisa and the professor to work their magic are lowered. Yet, who can say they would be unable to save the world if one of us should die? Playing God—that's a good way of putting it, Lady Persephone. I just wonder if there are unanticipated side effects that we don't know about as yet."

She shrugged her shoulders. "We can keep a sharp eye on Petra and see how she does this time. You were closer to her before. Any unwanted side effects with her and Cho Lin?"

"None that we saw, beyond the lifestyle she was forced to be living," Tilly replied. "Well, if I have a vote, I would like to be able to continue helping save the world. So if I get shot or something, I'd take a new body if one were available and if you didn't have to kill the person who had it. I guess that limits us to Chinese women and men, though. However, we should get the professor's input on this one."

Around five, Tilly roused Petra. "Wake up dear. It's suppertime and the professor has just arrived. We found you a proper outfit in town. Come on. I'll help you get dressed."

Petra sat up, rubbed her eyes, and then began crying. "You can't imagine how wonderful it is to be able to wipe my eyes again! God, living in that other body was a horrid nightmare. Thanks for getting the dress. My headache is nearly gone. Wow, I can finally brush my own hair again. Simple things. Tilly, you can't imagine how much these simple things of life are so important to me now."

"Yes I can. Remember, we were held captive by the field marshal for nearly four months," Tilly replied. A half hour later, Petra looked like a young EE woman once more, wearing a light blue satin gown with matching pumps. She took Tilly's arm out of habit.

"Thanks, it is easier to walk in these boots with someone supporting me."

Petra laughed. "Tell me about it. Honestly, these heels are almost as bad. Somehow, I did get used to wearing the boots. Isn't that just crazy?"

Tilly laughed, "And sexy." Both laughed.

"Well, I must say I'm bloody well glad to see you again, Petra! I thought we'd lost you for good," the professor exclaimed, when Petra and Tilly joined them in the large, elegant dining room. "Your new body looks very attractive."

"And young. Eighteen, she told me. Good to see you again, professor. Say, why did we get shot?" she asked sitting down next to him. "I mean in our Pytalon society, crime is almost extinct. No one harms anyone any longer; they can't. Well, I guess a handful can, but why us? Why shoot Cho Lin and me? Random violence? I can't get my head around this one. I know I've made some enemies, but they're all handled, one way or another. I don't understand why we were shot."

"None of us understand it either," he replied. "None of Tilly and my predictions would suggest such things happening just yet. Of course, when many people come off the drug without supervision, then yes, random acts of violence are predicted and expected. However, from all we've heard, this was a targeted execution, not some random act by some hallucinating man. We don't understand it yet, either."

"However, as we dine, may I ask you some probative questions, Petra? If not, I can wait until after we dine."

Lady Persephone suggested they dine first. A half hour later as the group sipped the tea from expensive china cups, the professor began his interrogation of Petra. "Now then, dear, you've undergone this transference process twice. I want you to think hard and try to give us some clues about what happened to you during the procedure. Anything you can recall might be important. I know it's likely very painful to remember, but I believe it's important. Please, Petra."

"Okay then. Cho Lin and I were walking home from the office. Oh, yes, I had just hired a young teen in high school to come and spend her nights with us as our personal assistant. We were chatting when these two hooded men rose up and pointed guns at us. I heard popping sounds and felt a sharp pain in my head. Everything went black after that. No wait. I felt some impacts in my lower chest. I don't recall hitting the ground though. Nothing after that."

"Right. You were transported to an emergency room and underwent surgery. Then, you were put on life support and brought here," the professor explained, though he wondered if even telling her this much was a good idea. "Think hard; can you recall anything about the transference process itself?"

Petra bit her lip and closed her eyes. She was silent for quite some time; the others waited patiently, though concerned. "You know I do recall something," she said very slowly. "I saw something very brilliant, white, so incredibly beautiful. No, that's not quite the right word. Pretty, gorgeous—no, not those either. You know when you look at something or someone who is incredibly beautiful, you get this certain feeling. Aesthetic! Yes, that's the right word. I saw this incredibly aesthetic light. Somehow, I was attracted to it. I couldn't help myself, not really. It was so beautiful, so fantastic, so wonderful feeling. I followed it, not wanting to let go of it, as it seemed to be dimming down. Then I woke up in this body."

"Now this is interesting, Petra," the professor replied enthusiastically. "Now think back to when Bo Bin transferred you into the armless woman's body. Was that aesthetic light there too?"

She thought hard, trying to remember. "I was standing there looking at the Feds. I felt a sting in my neck, and then the world went grey and black. I felt my legs giving out, but I don't remember hitting the floor. All is black and sort of foggy." Again, she went silent for several minutes. Then she said slowly, "Yes, I see this white brilliant light, so pretty, yes, aesthetic light, so enticing. I'm attracted to it, and it seems to be moving a little bit. When it is gone, I wake up in the armless Chinese woman's body." She opened her eyes. "Yes, it was there both times. I couldn't help myself. I just had to follow it. It was so beautiful, and I didn't want to lose it."

"Fascinating. Well done, Petra. I have been doing a lot of research, reading ancient texts these past weeks. I'm now convinced the psychs have this all wrong. Bo Bin claims he is merely moving a person's mind from body to body. I think he has accidentally proven man is a spiritual being, who has a mind, and for a time lives within a physical body. The ancient Buddhists believed man was an immortal spiritual being, who has a mind, and inhabits a body. When the body dies, he acquires a new baby body. It is a cycle. The ancient Vedic Hymns also suggest this cycle of birth, growth, decay, and death repeating endlessly. The Buddhists believed man could and should end this cycle and remain exterior to these bodies, if my understanding of this is remotely on track. Yes, this ties into the ancient religions of Earth, now of course, long dead and abandoned in this Pytalon and implant age."

"Still, I think Bo Bin has proven we are immortal spiritual beings with minds that for a time inhabit a physical body. What their Transference Machine is doing is somehow moving the spirit, the personality if you prefer, and the mind from one physical body to another, using the one thing that is powerful enough to do this: aesthetics. What's more important is that, Petra, you have stopped those two men before they took this any farther. If they had been allowed to continue their experiments, they could well have enslaved the whole world by aesthetics. No one would be immune from such things."

"But is this procedure of theirs—this transference process—is it safe to use?" Lady Persephone asked, barely following the professor, who was now highly animated.

"Well, who can say for sure? Petra, did you have any bad side effects from the process when you were in the other body—other than the physical limitations that body imposed upon you?" he probed.

"No, the limitations were monumental. Between them and trying to do my job, I didn't notice anything amiss. What kind of side effects might there be?" she asked. "I feel fine right now. My headache is mostly gone."

"Well, I was terribly worried at some point you might sort of slip back into your original body, the one they kept in their stasis pods and amputated its arms. You didn't feel any kind of pull back into it, did you?" he asked.

"Well, no. It was pointless even to think about going back to it, not after I saw it lying there, its arms gone. I mean, my new body had far stronger legs, and I was able to walk much better in the boots. Going back into my original body, I would be just as helpless, maybe more since my legs weren't as strong. Besides, I figured it would be in intense pain from the surgery. I wasn't even remotely tempted to think such thoughts. Right now, my previous Chinese body is dead, I think. Besides, I wouldn't ever want to go back into that armless body again." She shuddered a little.

"Wait," she suddenly had a horrid thought, "are you suggesting at some point in time, I might slip out of this body back into my previous one?"

"Yes, that has been a major concern of mine from the beginning. Just how permanent is this transference process? Their lab notes were all in Chinese, and I have been having a bloody hard time trying to understand them. However, initially, they experienced that sort of thing—a transferred person slipping back to their former body. Apparently, that problem was solved, since Mei Bei was in your armless body for thirteen years without mishap. Still, it bothers me. What if your previous body was in perfect health with all its parts and you were stuck in one of the armless ones? Wouldn't you desperately want to get out of this one and back into the old, perfect one? That was my reasoning."

"Yes, but wasn't Mei and the others being paid for staying in those bodies as volunteers? Even though life was awful for them, they knew when their contract was up, they would be returned to their own bodies and be well paid," Lady Persephone countered.

"Yes, point taken. Still, I'm worried about it," he admitted.

Lady Persephone changed the topic. "Well, there's something else everyone should know, Petra in particular. I checked on the stasis pod holding her wounded body. Guess what? The body is definitely recovering! It seems there are some remarkable healing capabilities in these life-sustaining pods of Bo Bin and Han Lin. Perhaps it's just time doing the healing since the pods keep pumping needed nutrients into the bodies. I'm not a doctor, but I can tell when a wound is healing. Her three wounds are most definitely healing up. Amazing."

"How can you tell this?" Petra asked, rather taken aback by this news. Everyone had thought the body was beyond saving. That's what the doctor had told them in the emergency room.

"Well, before supper was served, I checked up on how it was doing, figuring I'd at least change the bandages. It's only humane to do that much for her or it. All three wounds are definitely on the mend. Come and see for yourselves. I've left the two abdomen wounds open to the air to speed their healing." Everyone headed off to inspect Petra's former body, which was still in the room with the Transference Machine.

Beneath the sealed glass canopy, her two lower chest wounds were most definitely healing up. "What does this mean?" Beth asked.

"It means instead of dying, her body is actually on the mend, I think," Lady Persephone replied. "Of course, with the head wound, there is no telling yet how well the recovery might be."

"So is it still alive?" Petra asked.

"So far it hasn't died as the doctor told us," Tilly answered.

"What do we do with it? I mean, if it fully recovers," Petra asked, looking at her former self.

"Well, let's see if it does actually recover," the professor suggested, and they accepted his suggestion.

They returned to the dining room where a fresh pot of tea was waiting. As they sat down, Tilly's cell phone rang. After answering it, she put it on speaker phone. "Lech has a report to give to Petra and us. Good news, I think. Go ahead, Lech. She's all ears."

His monotone voice came through loud and clear. "Boss, Lech here. You and your associates were right. Another mass murder occurred around ten in the morning of the full moon, just as predicted." Tilly and Jessica smiled and nodded to each other. He continued, "As ordered, I kept the Feds in the skies over Chicago and far from the scene of the murders, where fifteen women shoppers were gunned down. An hour later, we intercepted a frantic call from the guard on duty at the AP-cops evidence room downtown, about five miles from the scene of the murders. Dozens of men raided the place and killed the guard on duty. They set fire to the building, but we got there enforce and killed or captured the lot of them. Unfortunately, we couldn't save the building or the evidence stored there."

"Very well done, Lech! So who were these men?" Petra asked.

"We are still sorting the crazy scene out, but some refer to one of the leaders as Duke Leo and the other as King Philo Dailey, who is supposed to be a Garbage Collector Twentieth Class, but we have no record of him, and he has no ID card. Leo has a record of assaulting people, but he vanished before being apprehended several years ago. From what little we do know about them, this King Philo fellow lives in Old Town in those condemned housing units. We're still investigating and gathering evidence. We did recover two nine mm guns, similar caliber to the guns used to shoot you and kill Cho Lin. CSI is on ballistics now. Will keep you posted."

"Again, very well done, Lech! With luck, you have apprehended those who have been on a murdering campaign for at least a year, possibly far longer," Petra validated him.

"Are you doing okay? When you left here, I thought that you were as good as dead."

"Doing well, thanks, Lech."

"Good. Say, if ballistics proves out, then we have the men who shot you and killed Cho. If so, it makes sense. They must have figured you were on to them and were trying to stop your investigation, boss."

"That would make sense. Until now, it seemed like a random act of violence, which we almost never see in Chicago. Keep me posted. Good job," Petra replied.

After he hung up, she added, "Whew, I feel so much better with that explanation for the shooting. I was having a hard time with being the victim of a random act of violence. It feels much better to know they were after me because I was after them. Of course, the question is how did they know I was on to their schemes?"

"And how come this King Philo isn't in your databases? That is even more important, I think," Beth countered with her own questions.

"And why did he want to destroy all the evidence in the AP-cops building? Was he behind every crime in Chicago?" Tilly asked her own questions.

Petra laughed. "We all have our questions, don't we?"

After breakfast, they checked on how Petra's old body was doing and found that it was breathing on its own and resting well. The unit's sensors monitoring the bodily functions had shut down several of the life sustaining functions, as they were no longer needed. The primary connections to intravenous feeding and catheter were still working, however. As they stared at the body through the glass cover, its eyes flickered and opened.

"Well, now we do have a conundrum here. Obviously, the body is quite alive and from the sensors, doing well enough to be off life support, save feeding. It is awake. What the devil do we do now?" asked Lady Persephone. "I guess it is my mistake. I did program the stasis unit to preserve the body, as Bo Bin did with all his 'patients' or 'volunteers.' Suggestions?"

"Hum, yes, I believe that I do," the professor spoke up. "Look, we need to know how stable Petra is with her new body and whether she can be pulled back into her old body. Oh, this is getting too difficult to manage. What was the teen's name who had her current body, My Lady?"

She replied, "Chan Fang of Diaoezhen."

"Okay, we will call this one Chan and that one Mei, since it was Mei who had it for thirteen years before Petra took it. Now what I am saying is Mei is obviously alive. Is there any chance Petra can be pulled back into her Mei body from her Chan body without having to use the Transference Machine? That is key here. Besides, Mei is alive and I am unwilling to just kill her," the professor explained.

"Hey, I don't want to kill Mei either, but I see what you are driving at, professor," Lady Persephone countered. "Will she be stable in her Chan body or not? Okay, what do we do?"

"Well, let's see if we can get the Mei body up and eating. She's probably sore and hungry at this point," he suggested. While Petra and the others watched, the two opened the canopy and removed the IV and catheter. Mei was still wearing her boots, hose, and garter belt. The rest of her dress and undergarments had been cut away in the emergency room. Together, they slipped an arm around Mei's back and raised her up to a sitting position.

Petra watched her previous body being roused. Its eyes were open now. *Well, I did like that body. It is extremely pretty—helpless, but gorgeous. I really do like it.* Suddenly, she was also seeing out of its eyes. She gasped, but both the Chan and Mei bodies gasped. "Oh my!" Petra exclaimed, "I'm seeing double."

Everyone stood there shocked! Both Mei and Chan had uttered the precise same words at the precise same instant, only each voice had its own timbre. Chan's was a little higher than Mei's. "I'm looking out of Mei's eyes and Chan's too," both bodies continued to speak simultaneously. "Oh, this is really weird! I am seeing myself each way! Oh my! Freaky! Cool, though. Oh, Mei is very hungry and her belly hurts some still. Head too, a little."

The professor recovered from the shock first. "Mei-Petra, can you move your feet? Can you turn your head? With a head injury, there can be some lingering aftereffects, I'm told."

Mei-Petra turned her head and made other motions with it, though slowly, since it still hurt. She wiggled her feet and then leaned forwards some.

Both voices spoke, "Other than a sore belly and a headache, it seems fine to me. Can we feed me?"

"Okay, let's see if Mei-Petra can stand. If so, let's see if she can be walked to the dining room," Lady Persephone suggested.

While everyone wanted to put a helping arm around Mei-Petra, Chan-Petra, said, "Let me take one side of her, please. It's less confusing to me this way, because I'm seeing about the same thing from each pair of eyes." The professor took one side and Chan-Petra, the other. Slowly, they moved across the room. "It's working well. I'm able to walk, but my legs feel like mush, very weak. I don't think I could walk on my own just yet," both voices said in unison. The others dashed ahead to scrounge up something for her to eat from their leftovers.

After getting Mei-Petra seated, Chan-Petra sat beside her and began to feed her. Lady Persephone dashed off and returned with a hairbrush and a bowl of water and towels. While Jessica began laboriously handling her somewhat tangled hair, Persephone gave her a sponge bath. Meanwhile, Tilly rounded up a dress she hoped would more or less fit her. Both women spoke together, "I feel like a pampered cow." Everyone chuckled at Mei-Petra's first attempt at a little humor after her ordeal.

Once fed, cleaned, and dressed, the professor poured Mei-Petra some tea and inserted a straw, setting it such that she could easily reach it. "Doing okay now, Mei-Petra?" he asked.

"Yes, much. Thank you, everyone. This is so strange, but I'm getting accustomed to it. I think I can control which one is speaking now," Mei-Petra said. Chan-Petra was silent, startling them all.

"Excellent," the professor cleared his throat. "We're now in wholly unexplored territory."

"No kidding! I have two bodies. Oh, I see. I really do have some affinity for Mei. Honestly, even though life was or is awful in her body, I rather loved other aspects of her, my body, that is. So when I saw her being raised up by you two, I sort of slipped into her again. I seem to be able to control which one I am using at the moment." She focused her attention slightly and the Chan-Petra added, "Now I am more in Chan's. It seems I'm wholly aware of both bodies, but if I focus my attention a little bit, I can control each one independently of the other. Does this help us?" she asked.

"Yes, very much so," he replied.

Just then, Tilly's cell phone rang and again she put it on speaker phone. "Lech here, boss. It's night here. I'm about to head home, but I wanted to bring you up to date. Ballistics are back. They're a perfect match to the slugs taken out of Cho Lin, the latest murdered women, and they match the six previous murder sprees. So yes, boss, we got the murderers. Also, the raid on the housing project yielded more information. As you probably know, only the lowest, poorest live there, but we found all manner of very expensive food items, apparel, and home fixtures there. Apparently, King Philo was robbing stores and doling out the goods to the others in the housing project. Strange behavior. We still can't find any record of him in our databases. Still working on that one. At least you can relax now. We positively got your shooters."

"Excellent work, Lech. Thanks for the update," Chan-Petra replied.

A bit later, they got back to the huge problem at hand. "So what do we do now?" Chan-Petra asked. "I don't want to just kill my Mei body. I'm very pretty and sexy, even though I'm mostly helpless in it, except for giving voice commands and walking that is, thanks to Beth. With my Chan body, I'm whole again and can perform normally. I don't want to kill Chan either. Am I going to have to decide which one dies?"

"Oh good lord no!" Lady Persephone declared. "This isn't the backwaters of China, where life is worthless. Professor, can't she keep them both? If not, I suppose that I could chat with Bo Bin and put one back into a comatose stasis like he had the others there in Peking."

"Of course we aren't going to kill one of her bodies. I'd rather not put one into a comatose state either, not unless we have to for Petra's sake," he replied, thinking hard. "It all comes down to whether or not Petra can learn to operate both bodies without difficulties. At least that's how I see it. We are immortal spiritual beings with minds, if we believe the ancient religions. Thus, we are seeing Petra, the being with her mind, now controlling two different bodies. There can be no other explanation. This is positively smashing! Bloody hell, Petra has just proved what the ancient religionists were always trying to prove. Incredible. Okay, back to earth, professor. What now? Well, I would suggest that Mei-Petra not overdo it; she's been damn close to death. Give her body time to recover."

He went on, "Petra, you need to work on being able to control one or the other body at will and not get confused or such. For example, can you take the Chan body with Tilly and Beth and go do some shopping for clothes for the Chan and Mei bodies, leaving your Mei body here resting? Or will there be a range or distance factor that comes into play here? It could well be that she has to be close to both of them," he explained in response to the funny look that Tilly gave him. "What happens to the Mei body when she is far away from it? Will it still respond to stimuli or will it just sit there like a zombie? We have many questions that need answers."

"Another one, when Chan-Petra is away shopping, what happens to Chan-Petra if we can somehow get Mei-Petra talking or moving a little? You see, there could be all manner of potential problems here. It may take us days to sort this one out."

"Well, I do need more clothes and so does Mei," Chan-Petra acknowledged. "Okay, take me to the EE store and I can get us more outfits. While I am gone, professor, conduct your experiments on Mei-me. I admit this is confusing, but I can control two of them when I am close and neither are doing much of anything. However, if this isn't possible, I obviously want to keep my Chan body, but I don't really want to harm my Mei body either."

Lady Persephone, Tilly, and Amanda headed off with Chan-Petra to do some serious shopping. Meanwhile, the professor, Beth, Jessica, and Juan looked after her Mei body. They gave the women time to get into downtown London before they began to work with Mei. "Petra, can you hear me and respond to me?" the professor asked her.

"Oh! You took me by surprise. Yes, I can. I'm picking out a dress right now."

"Good. Okay then, we're going to get you up and walking to the living room. Let us know if you have problems there," he explained. Juan and he helped her rise to her feet.

"Oh, thanks guys. I didn't have to lunge myself up. Rather confusing. It takes my attention away from here a little bit. Doing okay as long as you hold onto me," she replied. "I keep shifting back and forth between the two bodies as needed." Slowly the professor and Juan conducted more experiments with Mei.

A half hour later, the experiments were put on hold. They were in London's fashionable EE women's shop. Already Petra had picked out two new outfits for her Chan body and three for her Mei body. Additionally, the other women couldn't help but pick up a new outfit for themselves. As they were chatting and comparing dresses, a young EE woman of Chinese ancestry and wearing the typical ballet boots came up to Chan.

"Chan Fang! It is you! It's me, Yan Wen!" she exclaimed, overjoyed, taking Petra off guard.

"I'm sorry, do I know you?" Petra replied, looking confused. Something about this young woman seemed very familiar, intimately familiar, but Petra swore that she had never seen her before.

"It's me, Yan Wen from Diaoezhen. We lived across the street from each other. Remember? We were lovers during high school, that's why our fathers insisted we become EE women. Don't you remember, Chan?"

Strange intimate feelings came over Petra. "I've only recently become an EE woman, Yan. Just a couple of days ago in fact. I'm only now buying my gowns."

"Oh! That explains it. Yes, I'm two years older. They took me when I was eighteen too. I couldn't remember much of anything after I was implanted either. My sponsor brought me to London right away, but he died a month ago, and now I'm trying to figure out what I should do," Yan chatted gaily, before stopping to recite her litany briefly and checking her makeup in her compact.

"It's a little more complicated with me, Yan," Petra began to try to explain. "You see, I didn't make it through the implant."

"Oh dear! Well, they said I nearly died too, but you look really sexy, Chan, gorgeous, in fact."

"It's a bit worse than that. Chan did die during the implant, but thanks to others, they were able to save Chan's body and now I have it. I'm Petra, Petra Delius, but I have these very strong feelings towards you, Yan, even though I've never met you."

"Died? But you are very much alive. Oh, maybe the Lin Foundation in Peking can help you. I've heard they help some of us, but I don't know how," Yan replied, somewhat confused.

"Well, actually, the Lin Foundation did help save me and somehow put me into Chan's body."

"Oh that is good then. I have never forgotten you, Chan. You look all grownup now and really quite beautiful, just like I was always telling you, my sweet. I always wanted us to get married one day. When they were taking me away to become an EE woman, I remember you telling me that you would always love me too. I'm so sorry I didn't remember you until I saw you in the store here. The implants do strange things to your memory, but now we can be together at last, if you still feel the same. I can help you with everything, since you are newly implanted," Yan suggested. "Besides, I really don't know what to do now that my sponsor has died. I'm rather lost, really lost, if I'm honest with you, my love. I don't really know anyone in London. My sponsor kept me on a short leash. Now they are kicking me out of his estate, and I don't know where I'm to go. No one tells me anything, but then I'm only an EE woman."

Petra felt a strong bond with this young woman, whom she guessed was twenty now. "My situation is more complicated, but even though I'm not the Chan you knew and loved, with this body, I still feel that physical connection you both had, as strange as that sounds. I feel—or rather I'm feeling my body feel it. Lady Persephone, I can't just leave Yan here alone and lost. I would like to bring her back with us, at least until we can sort things out a bit more. Would that be acceptable with you?"

"Is she your sponsor?" Yan asked, looking up, a bit of hope returning to her eyes.

"Well, sort of, that would be one way of looking at it, I suppose, but it's more complicated than that."

"Sure, we can't just abandon her. It's not humane or civilized, but do be careful, Petra," she advised.

"I'm an experienced EE woman. I give good pleasure, madam sponsor. I have always loved Chan since we were little girls back in Diaoezhen. We promised we would one day marry each other. Thank you so much. I'm lost right now, nowhere to turn. Thank you so much," Yan said to Persephone, alternating between flirting with her and flirting with Chan, but also being sympathetic and grateful, as well as showing signs of relief. "I'm so glad I recognized you, Chan. I was so lost. Now I'm found again." She quickly recited her implant script, though softly to herself.

Chan waited until Yan's eyes returned to the present and replied, "Good, Yan. It's still more complicated, but I think you'll have to see for yourself what I mean. Come on; I've picked out enough gowns. If I stay longer, I might buy the store out."

Lady Persephone chuckled, but shook her head at the final cost Petra paid at the checkout counter. EE women's clothing didn't come cheap, she thought once again. She drove them back in her EMAC, but not before notifying the others that they were bringing Yan Wen along with them.

"You are both women?" Yan asked quite confused. She had entered the fabulous castle, very much impressed with Chan's sponsor. Then, came the many introductions, which left her rather confused, so many new faces and strange names. At last, Chan-Petra introduced her to her Mei-Petra self, trying to explain she was both women. This totally confused poor Yan, who still was fairly heavily under the influence of her own EE implant and two years of near isolation from the world, living wholly within her old sponsor's estate.

Chan sat down beside Mei, pulling Yan with her. "Let me tell you more about this mess. You see, not even this was my original self, my first body. I got captured by the Lin Foundation brothers, and they used their new Transference Machine to pull me out of my own body and into this one here."

"But why? She has no arms. How can she be a proper EE woman? I don't understand," Yan complained, fighting a headache coming on.

"Because I caused the Chinese Feds and the Lin Foundation big troubles."

Yan brightened up considerably! "Oh, now I get it. Yes, you and I, we always caused the villagers many problems, didn't we? So why this one?"

"Because she is nearly helpless and that way I couldn't cause them any more troubles."

"Oh, I do see it clearly now, but that is a bad thing to do to an EE woman. However did you manage?"

"It was very hard, Yan, but I caused them more trouble than they ever could have imagined. I put the Lin Foundation out of the business of harming others and got rid of all the bad Feds men. Then a few days ago, I was about to put some other bad men out of the picture in Chicago—that's where I live. They shot me and killed my dear friend, Cho Lin. I was very nearly dead, but My Lady here had thought ahead and had gone over to our home village, Diaoezhen, and when Chan died during the psych PDH implant, she brought this body back here and used the Lin Foundation machine to save me from dying by putting me into Chan's body, but then my other body got well. Now I have two bodies."

"Thank you for saving my Chan for me, My Lady. You live in the States? Big city?" she asked.

"Yes, very big city."

"I would love to come and live with you again, Chan. I promise to help care for your other body too, that is, if your My Lady sponsor will allow it," Yan offered.

"I'd like that, Yan, very much."

"But what does your sponsor say to all this?" Yan asked, again growing a little confused.

"I'm my own sponsor, Yan. I'm the head of the Feds worldwide. I can do what I want, as long as I don't harm others, of course. Lady Persephone and these others are my dear, dear friends, just like us."

"Oh, friends, not sponsor. You are, how they say, big cheese, then?" she asked in broken English.

"Yes, a very big cheese, Yan. If I say you can come with me, you can come. No one will stop us. Right now, however, we are trying to figure out how I'm to be able to control and run both bodies here. So we're staying here a few more days."

"Okay, I'll give you much pleasure, dearest Chan, to make up for missing two years. Together, we'll make other Chan happy too. You will see. Yan is very good, perhaps Yan is still better than Chan with giving pleasure," she teased Chan a little. Both Petra's smiled back at Yan, but Yan then recited her implant litany once more.

"Now then, I have to talk with the professor here." Yan nodded. "So what did you find out while we were gone?" she asked.

"Actually, quite a lot, Petra. It seems as long as Mei-Petra doesn't do a whole lot, she doesn't interfere with you in the slightest. Lady Persephone kept me appraised via text messages. If Mei does relatively simple things, the distraction to Chan-Petra is noticeable, but not in any major way. We didn't get to test it further. I'd rather not risk it until her wounds heal more fully. However, as you might expect, I now have ideas for a many more tests. I think this is going to work out for you, but we'll need to discover for you just what your limits are and that sort of thing. I'm at least hopeful, Petra. This is certainly the wildest situation I've ever encountered."

"Thanks for helping me, professor. I don't want either one to die. I know the Lin brothers wouldn't care, but I do."

"We all do, Petra," he replied. "Now why don't you take your packages to your room along with Mei and Yan and take care of your needs? My Lady's steward told me the dinner will be at six, so you have almost two hours to get ready."

Around six, the three women made their way back into the dining room. All three faces looked rather flushed, but they were wearing new gowns and their hair nicely done. Mei was between the two and Chan sat on Mei's right. "I'll feed Mei since I know what I need. That's one benefit I've got now," she explained.

Later over tea, she brought up another new detail. "Professor, I have some of Chan's memories. When Yan and I were indulging ourselves, I suddenly began seeing memory images. They aren't mine, but Chan's of when Yan and Chan shared themselves intimately. Isn't that strange how I can have some of Chan's memories?" He asked her to elaborate a little more about the quality of the memories. She added, "Well, they're not exactly like my real memories, but are much smaller, fainter, and not so detailed, I suppose. Nevertheless, they were there and I saw them."

"Have you seen any of Mei's memories?" he asked.

"No, but then I didn't know to look for them. If I can find them, I'll let you know."

The ensuing days were extremely happy ones for Petra, who had never really known such true enjoyment. She and Yan and her two bodies worked very well together, especially satisfying for the Mei-Petra body. She began to have everyone address her in the Chan body as Chan, but as Petra in the Mei body. "After all, everyone is totally used to calling me Petra, not Chan's body. I think it will be simpler this way." Indeed, she was right about that point.

When Petra's wounded body was completely healed, the professor put Petra through tests that were more difficult. They found when Petra had to walk anywhere on her own, she needed to pay close attention to each step, as did all the women who wore these boots. At those times, Chan was effectively stopped. That is, she remained motionless or if she had been talking, she stopped speaking, since her attention was definitely elsewhere.

Beyond that, the many hours of training and practice these experiments took allowed Petra to become fully adjusted to her unique situation of running both women's bodies. At last, Petra reached a decision about them. "Look, my Feds office is all setup for this body, and all the Feds know this body as Petra. It will only confuse them if I use the Chan body as the working Petra body. Chan and Yan can come with me and be sort of my personal assistants. However, if I need to take some more serious actions, I'll use Chan-Petra, knowing the Yan will watch over Mei-Petra for me. Does this make sense?" It did.

During these days, Jessica quietly worked on desensitizing Yan's EE woman's implant. When they were finally ready to head back to Chicago, Yan exclaimed, "Jessica! Thank you! You have given me back my life! I can actually think about what I want to think about, not just how to pleasure someone. I feel so alive now and I promise to help Chan and Petra with everything. I'm able to do it, thanks to you. How can I ever thank you?"

"Just help Petra. She needs it and deserves it," Jessica replied with a wry smile. She'd seen just how alive all three women had become these past couple of weeks. Already on the quiet, Beth had used Lady Persephone's computers to check up on Yan Wen and found she was just what she seemed to be. Petra's friends then relaxed and fully welcomed the young newcomer into Petra's life.

Two days before they left for home, while studying the Lin brother's Transference Machine and their PDH implant machine, Beth made a curious discovery. The implant machine had a built-in recorder that activated when the machine was operating. She played back the last recordings and listened to Lady Persephone's dialog as she handled the Lin brothers. At the end of the recording, she noticed the machine attempting to make a wireless Internet connection. In this case, it failed to find the Lin's wireless router half a world away from Sussex.

"Now why would the machine want to connect to the Internet?" she asked herself. After pondering this anomaly for an hour, she went to Lady Persephone and asked for permission to question the Lin brothers, well sisters now they had been altered into EE women. After explaining why she wanted to talk with them, she agreed, and together with Lady Persephone supporting Beth, they walked across the expansive lawn and gardens of her castle estate to a small cottage that bordered her property. Here was where she kept the two EE women.

She knocked and the hired teen caretaker answered the door and unlocked it for them. "My Lady, so nice to see you again," she formally addressed her employer. After brief introductions, she led the two into the living room where the two miserable women were sitting on a couch watching TV. Beth turned it down and sat in a chair across from the two.

"Well, I see you two are adapting nicely," Beth began. "You are Bao and you are Huan? Or is it the other way around?"

"I'm Bao. This is utterly humiliating! You can't do this to us. Put us back to rights immediately," she exclaimed, but then found herself repeating her implant litany. She'd gotten too emotional and it triggered again. She calmed down and added, "We're miserable. We can't pleasure ourselves and have migraines all the time. You're torturing us, can't you see that?"

Beth wanted to say, "Just as you were torturing all those others," but calmed her own emotions. Getting into an arguing match wouldn't help her. "Perhaps something can be done about that. I was examining your PDH implant machine and noticed two curious things. First, the machine seems to record every implant session. Second, the machine wants to make an Internet wireless connection."

"Well, what of it?" Bao retorted, but regretted it; her head throbbed.

"Why make the recordings? Do all the implant machines make similar recordings? Why the Internet connection?" Beth asked.

"Tit for tat," Huan spoke up, trying to remain calm so her implant wouldn't kick in as it had for Bao.

Beth thought for a moment and then smiled. "Acceptable. I know a way to relieve your headaches. You tell me all about these recordings and I'll do what I can in return."

Bao grumbled but agreed. "Look, I'm a psychiatrist. We document everything. Spotless records. Every implant unit ever made has the recording unit. It records every implant session. When it is completed, the unit uploads the recording to the PWDB, the Psych Worldwide Database. We have the precise record of every implant ever done. Spotless data collection, perfectly preserved for posterity."

Huan grumbled, "Yes, but you never do anything with those records, Bao."

"Ah, but the true scientist always records his data, brother," Bao countered.

"How interesting. How does one get access to those recordings?" Beth asked.

"Classified. Only we psychs have access to them. What would you want with them anyway?" Bao became suspicious, but her head began throbbing again.

"Curious. Okay then, give me your access login and password, and I'll see what I can do about your headaches," Beth concluded.

"But that's confidential," Bao protested.

Huan complained, "Oh for Tao's sake, tell her and let her get rid of these hideous migraines, Bao!"

Bao had no choice. Faced with a chance to be rid of the debilitating headaches, she spat out what Beth wanted to know. "All right ladies. Don't go anywhere. I have an errand to run to get you what you need to reduce your headaches. I'll be back shortly as I promised."

Lady Persephone gave her a quizzical look, but followed her out of the cottage, making sure the caretaker locked the door after they were outside. She did. "Take me to the EE women's store. I need to make a couple of special purchases for those two."

A half hour later, Lady Persephone began laughing wildly, seeing what Beth just purchased for the two women: double dildo panties. She could scarcely contain her mirth when they returned to the cottage and Beth helped the caretaker slip them onto the two women. "See, I keep my word. All you have to do now is to get up and walk around and you will be highly pleasured. Besides, you'll also learn to walk better in your really sexy boots," she added. Poor Lady Persephone— she had to step outside where she laughed so hard that tears flooded her eyes.

As she helped Beth walk back across the lawn to the castle, Beth said, "Now I can find out the precise wording of anyone's implant. Since Lech could find no record of this King Philo character, the psych's database might have his session recorded. We'll just have to see, but that's going to have to wait until I get home to my computer systems."

***

The day before they were scheduled to return to the States, Lady Persephone and the professor held a private discussion. "You can see the value of this now, professor. It's a miracle that Mei-Petra survived; the doctors in the emergency room pronounced her all but dead. She probably would have died there in the Chicago hospital, if I had not acquired the Chan body and then put her Mei body in the Lin's stasis unit. You and I both know we bloody well can't afford to lose any one of us key leaders. What if that field marshal fellow had killed Tilly or Beth or both? We'd lose the two best that we have. If we should lose you, dear countryman, who would be able to provide the steady guidance we need? It seems to me we have been handed powerful sword with this Transference Machine of theirs. We should make more use of the technology they provided for us."

"Ah, My Lady, it's but a two-edged sword. Are we to play God now as well?" he countered.

"Saving key personnel's lives is not evil. The spiritual being who had the Chan body perished during the implant. The psych man was about to terminate the physical body when I stepped in and took it. We've seen no sign that that spiritual being is around or even remotely connected to Chan-Petra now, not for these past several weeks," she countered his resistance.

"Ah, but spiritual beings can't be killed. We're immortal," he corrected her.

"I'll accept that as true, though I can neither prove nor disprove that. However, if the person abandons their body as no longer capable of supporting their life and takes off to get another one, again assuming that is what happens, what's the harm in our making use of that body? We're keeping it alive and giving it new purpose and direction instead of allowing the psychs to terminate it and bury it. Surely there is no comparison to our doing that versus what the Lin brothers were doing to those poor men and women or what they had in mind for the use of their machine."

"Granted, there is no comparison between the two purposes, My Lady. I give you that point. Mutilating the body and then forcing another being into it so they can then be controlled is a bloody abomination by all human standards. God, they could have severed the body's spine making the body a paraplegic or even a quadriplegic before they forced the person into it from their own body. There is no end to the potential damage that Transference Machine can do to us humans," he pointed out.

"You'll get no argument from me on that point. Yet, I can see much potential good that can come from the machine's use as well," she argued.

"I will concede that point, My Lady, but we both know the immense power the Transference Machine offers may well lead to our own corruption," he pointed out.

"Then, perhaps we should utilize Petra's arguments that power must have checks and balances on its use," she suggested, unwilling to concede her point.

He pulled on his beard in thought. "I can see where you're coming from, My Lady. I had hoped that one day Tim or rather Tilly now would be able to take over for me. I'm not getting any younger. Okay, checks and balances. Shall we say it takes two out of three to have it done?"

"Agreed, as long as there are still two able to vote. If say Petra and I get into trouble, then there would only be one vote possible, yours."

"Accepted. How many bodies were you planning on stockpiling then?" he asked, with a sigh. He knew he couldn't talk her out of this, not when she'd barely managed to save Petra, even though it turned out rather differently than she'd planned.

"One for each of the key personnel. Most of us are now only able to handle a woman's body. I won't put the EE women into a male body—that would not only be inhumane, but very likely counterproductive, what with their bloody implants. Probably it would be wise to have most of the women bodies also be EE women, if possible, less disruption of their lives. Shall we say six female and three male bodies?" she suggested.

"Wish they wouldn't all be Chinese born, but here in the West, the psychs are using the latest models of the PDH implanting machines to avoid the occasional accidents. Still, I'll agree with six and three. Just make bloody sure they really are dead," he replied sternly and then laughed. "That's silly. If the bodies were dead, they would be of no use to us. Make sure the psych is about to terminate the bodies before you snatch them, and keep the damned machine secure. I don't trust those Lin brothers. I know they are practically helpless now, but then so was Petra and look what she's become." Both chuckled.

"Agreed. Have you helped her work out how she's going to explain having two bodies to Lech and the other Feds?" she asked. "That's a dilly."

"I'm leaving that one up to her. She knows her Feds and how to handle them. However, if she asks for help with it, then I'll see what I can invent. Honestly, if I were her, I'd have left that bloody messed up body go, but then I'm not her," he replied.

Lady Persephone grinned, "But you aren't a woman. Beauty is one thing we women treasure and appreciate. Mei is ravishingly stunning, despite her obvious handicap. I think Petra had second thoughts when she discovered Chan was perfectly normal. She could then afford to keep Mei, whose handicap isn't such horrible liability any longer. Besides, women, not on Pytalon that is, tend to nurture life, not destroy it." She laughed a little, adding, "The Righteous Vigilante is an exception." Both chuckled.

***

August 1st, Petra finally returned to work at her office in the Feds building in Chicago. Chan and Yan had their arms around her on either side, supporting her all the way from her fancy penthouse suite to the Feds skyscraper. As they walked in, Petra introduced the two new women to the front desk security guard, who already, compliments of Lech, had their ID cards prepared. When they subsequently stepped out of the elevator on the twentieth floor just outside her huge office suite, all three were taken by surprise. There stood Lech and nearly all of his Feds men. Spontaneously, they all began clapping!

"Welcome back, Supreme Commander Petra Delius!" Lech shouted above the clapping. "We all wanted to express our gratitude for your miraculous recovery and your incredible work bringing down King Philo and his band of mass murderers and thieves." Mei-Petra's face flushed and a wide smile formed on her face. Her forehead did show a small scar from the head wound.

"I don't know what to say men, but thanks. Sanity is doing the very best at keeping Chicago and the world safe. I was just doing my sworn duty, as you all have done too. Thank you."

"Yes, but you took three bullets and were even pronounced dead, boss," Lech added.

"I know and now, thanks to the miracles of the Lin Brothers, I have fully recovered and have a backup body. This is Chan-Petra; she is me too. Just as we all carry a backup gun, I now carry a backup body. Cool, eh? Now it'll take a whole lot more to bring down us Feds!" Mei-Petra explained, thinking swiftly, using this opportunity to explain the nearly unbelievable fact that she had two bodies. She counted on the fact they were all on Pytalon, which would make nearly anything she said sound reasonable or at least they wouldn't protest or raise objections or ask too many questions.

"Backup body? Incredibly cool, boss," Lech replied, just as she anticipated. These men depended upon their backup guns, and thus it seemed acceptable to have a backup body. Strange how little reasoning powers those on Pytalon actually had, she thought as she watched the whole group agree wholeheartedly with Lech. She relaxed considerably; all would work out well.

"Okay men, we best get back to work. I have weeks of intelligence to catch up on. What's been done with King Philo and Duke Leo?" she asked.

Lech flushed, showing a rare trickle of emotion. "Boss, we can't outright execute them, though Lord knows they deserve it. They surrendered. We wish they had continued the shootout so we could have killed them. There are no prisons anymore. So I had them re-implanted, put onto a heavy dose of Pytalon, and sent back to their home in the Old Town complex."

"What? They are back out there?" Petra's ire rose slightly.

"Well, sort of. I took guidance from what happened to you a while back, boss. I had them changed and implanted into EE women with the same fancy boots that you and Yan are always wearing. Now they can at least provide pleasurable experiences for those in their so called kingdom," Lech replied, his face slightly red.

Petra grasped the whole picture and began laughing. "Well done, Lech, well done indeed. That combination is nearly unbreakable. We won't have any further trouble from those two now. Good thinking, but personally I wish we were allowed to execute murderers, but we aren't, so we do the best we can. Well done Lech. Well done all of you," she validated them, and the Feds seemed pleased, as much as she could tell from their glassy-eyed stares.

A bit later as she sat down at her big desk and voice activated her many computers, she no longer felt helpless in her Mei body. Chan and Yan were right here with her, and Chan, being herself, always provided instant help when needed. "This is going to be perfect," she said.

As Chan, she added, "More than perfect."

Yan smiled, "Oh yes. Most perfect indeed, but what can I do to help, Chan?"

Chapter 26—Tracking the Failures

Back home in their East Peoria safe house, Beth began her new project, while Jessica handled their routine catch up surveillance. Specifically, she was extremely curious about this hitherto for unknown database the psychs maintained of all their implant sessions. She thought if Bao was right and every implant that any psych had ever done during the last couple of centuries had been recorded for posterity, then that database must be humongous. Beth was not disappointed. Once logged into their private system, the sheer size nearly blew her mind.

The first action she took was to search out how it was organized. Having a rather scientific mind herself, she was appalled at what she found. The highest-level index was by city or town. Beneath that, everything was stored by date of implant. She groaned, "Those psychs are complete imbeciles! The way this is setup, one can't find anything at all! Idiots! Well, if Bao is right, no one ever looks at all this data anyway, so I suppose they don't really care. Okay, Chicago. Good grief, two hundred plus years to search. Idiots! What if you don't know the date of the implant, but only the person's name or perhaps you want to review all EE woman implants? You'll never find anything. Grr," she exclaimed, very annoyed.

"Can you write a search engine program?" Jessica suggested. "I can, if you want."

"Thanks, love. I can do it. Sorry about getting so worked up, but I should've expected something like this. They're psychs after all," Beth grumbled. She set to work. An hour later, she had a nice interface built. She entered the name Philo Dailey and the city, Chicago, hoping the city was correct. Then, she turned her worm loose on the database and sat back listening to her ancient music. After an hour of patient waiting, she gave up and began to work on other things for Amanda and Tilly. Jessica continued her mundane reviews of their ongoing surveillance systems, but found nothing out of the ordinary, at least here in East Peoria or Chicago.

She had left the thefts program running when they'd rushed off to the emergency room in Chicago when Petra had been shot. It finished and she began to sort out the voluminous reports. In nearly all major cities, inventory discrepancies were rampant. This she took as an indicator there were more people living off the grid than anyone had suspected before now.

Tilly glanced at the sheer size of the report Jessica was creating for her and commented, "Well, I can see in a city of millions how easy it would be for the powers that be to overlook some of the people living there. I'm going to have to lower my percent coverage in all the prediction formulas. I can see that much already. Thanks, Jessica." She smiled and continued to work on a concise way to organize the results.

Beth's search program finally retrieved the recording of Philo's implanting session. It was stored in a very compact format, and she had to run it through the psych's un-compactor program to turn it into a playable file format. At last, she sat back and listened to the session. At first, it followed the precise script for anyone being turned into a Garbage Collector Twentieth Class. She had the script up on her display, comparing it to what she was hearing from the actual session. Then to her amazement, other voices entered and she heard the whole conversation between the two psychs and the nurse!

"Gang, come here. You simply have to hear this session! No wonder Philo acted as he did all these years! The psychs are even dumber than we give them credit for!" The others gathered around and she replayed the session. When it finished, everyone roared with laughter at just how stupid the psychs had been, not at the destruction that Philo had acted out according to what had been implanted into his mind. Later, she phoned Petra, told her about it, and sent the playable recording so she could hear it as well. So much of Philo's seemingly erratic and wild behavior was perfectly clear. She also sent the results to the professor.

An hour later, the professor called her, joining in a conference call with Petra. "Excellent work, Beth," he complimented her.

"Yes, now Philo's behavior makes complete sense," Petra added. "Thank you. Now my shooting and Cho Lin's death has closure, but. . ."

The professor broke in, "But now we know the root cause of Philo's behavior—destructive to the society. So we need to know the names and locations of any others whose PDH implants have been, shall we say, bloody well messed up."

"Right," Petra took control once more. "Start with Chicago. We need to know all the currently living others who are a threat to others. Later on, perhaps we can deal with those who are a threat only to themselves. Right now, we need to know about all the other potential 'Philo's' that are in our city. My Feds will check each and every one of them out. If this proves successful, then I need it done for all the other major cities. Later on, we can work downwards to the smaller towns and outlying areas."

"Weasel, I don't know how you come up with these things sometimes, but bloody good on this one!" the professor complimented her again. "Impressive. Petra's request takes top priority. We don't want some other lunatic taking shots at her. One assassination attempt is entirely sufficient."

Beth groaned. "You don't know what you're asking! The psych's database is a nightmare of disorganization! Okay, okay, I can take a hint. This is important. I'll get on it, but look, this is going to take quite some time."

"We have lots of time, as long as things stay quiet here," Petra replied. "By the way, things are working out well for me now. Thanks for everything."

"What did they want?" Tilly asked when Beth hung up her cell. Beth rolled her eyes around and then explained the urgent request. Tilly laughed, "That'll keep Weasel busy for ages." Beth groaned again.

Jessica volunteered to help her mate. "Come on. We have to find a way to automate this thing. At least we can easily focus on one city. What we need is a way to automatically detect deviations from the standard script for a given type of implant."

"Okay, I can make a script that will start at a certain date and pull each successive recording. The program can then run the un-compactor program. I sure don't want to sit here and listen to each one and manually compare them to the scripts that we have," Beth began.

"We don't have to, love. We could record each script or better yet, use your voice-controls software to convert the recording to a text document and then run a comparison analysis on the two," Jessica suggested.

"That's feasible. Each recording has the type of implant in its title along with the date, so we can extract the title. A little tweaking and that can be turned into a filename to compare to—yes, it's doable. Come on. We have a whole lot of programming to do, dear," Beth replied, regaining her enthusiasm.

Because of the extremely long time the program would be running, they had it spit out the discrepancies as soon as they were detected, saving the sound-to-script file and the comparison results, using a filename that included the person's name and date of implant. After testing to get the glitches out of it, Beth turned it loose.

"We'll probably have to fine tune it some," Beth declared. "It's going to catch the use of the word 'you' instead of the word 'I' and similar goofs as well as the ones that we are looking for, but this beats listening to all them."

"We can make a list of the wrong pronoun implants for later use. Those would only create behavior patterns like Helene's, where she was telling us that we had to look our best. Those create mania behavior patterns. Still, Hans' was also like that, so we're going to have to check them too. I wonder how many were wholly screwed up like Philo's was," Jessica asked.

Beth shrugged her shoulders. They could only wait and begin to examine the results as the long running program began spitting them out.

As the first ones appeared, Jessica had another thought. "You know, the psychs might have realized they made a mistake on someone's implant and then redid it at a later date. We're going to have to check for that too. We don't want to give Petra's men wrong information." Beth groaned, but knew she was right.

Their search began sixty years in the past and slowly worked its way towards the present date. With millions of implants to search, the process was an excruciatingly slow one, but quite thorough, as long as the psychs actually recorded their sessions. Beth had no way of knowing if that was the case, but had to presume it was, since in recent times, even the psychs were on Pytalon and merely going through their dictated motions.

Before long, results began appearing. The first one that caught their interest was Betsy Rhimes, who was being implanted as a maid. Right in the middle of the session, the psych made a blunder. He then said, "Damn. I am always goofing up." He then repeated the script sentence properly. Both Beth and Jessica laughed. "I bet that she frequently makes mistakes or has accidents," Beth predicted. She decided to have Petra check this one out just to see if they were on the right track, in that what was being said to the patient undergoing the PDH implant would subsequently influence their behavior.

Two days later, Petra reported the older woman was still a maid, but that she frequently made all manner of "goofs" and had been demoted many times. "You're on the right track. This is great news, Beth!" Petra reported.

As the results began to come in, Beth and Jessica began to see a pattern emerging and divided them into two groups. In one group, the "goofs" would yield a manic type of behavior in the person or so they believed. In the second group, the errors that were made may well be causing the person to wish to harm or damage others or property or even the system. Those in this second group were fired off to Petra as soon as they were identified.

The project took two weeks to scrub the database just for Chicago. They identified fifty men and women who could possibly be causing serious trouble; those were in the second group. However, the first group of manic behavior patterns numbered closer to nearly a thousand! Each one of these had to be tracked down and examined by the Feds.

When the first of the fifty in the second group appeared, Beth emailed the data to Petra. "Ah, now we are making progress," Petra said as she commanded the computer so open the attached document. She still insisted on using the Mei-Petra body for the official work, knowing that she could use her Chan body at any instant when she needed something. "Ah ha. She's found a dilly here. Call Lech," she commanded. A moment later, he picked up the intercom. "I have an assignment for us. Beth has found a potential troublemaker, a William Townsend."

Shortly, the doorman opened the door, and he walked up to her large desk filled mostly with monitors. "Come around here, Lech, and read this one. I'd turn the monitor around, but I can't do that. Sorry." He barely smiled and did so. The psych had added two extra sentences to the AP-cop's implant script. He'd added, "You are a fast runner. You can beat anyone." Beth and Petra interpreted the words literally, meaning he could beat up anyone he wanted to. Hence, the red flag.

"I agree. Possible suspect," he said in his monotone voice. "We will investigate him today."

"I should tag along in case of trouble," she added.

For once, Lech took a stand. On Pytalon, this was no small feat for him. "No boss. You don't go anywhere without two guards. I'm not risking your life a second time. Let us do the groundwork. You're the Supreme Commander now."

Somewhat startled, Petra replied, "I suppose you're right, Lech. I always was out in the field before, but now I'm a liability if trouble arises. You win, but do keep me posted."

Again, she detected a slight smile on his face, if only briefly. "Oh, and be careful, Lech."

After he left, Petra bit her lip and lowered her head a little, unable to do much else physically, but Chan pounded her fist on the table, taking out her frustrations. "Chan? What's the matter?" Yan asked, growing worried about her dear friend.

"Ouch that hurt. Frustrated. I should be out there—in the field—in the city going after the bad guys. I swore an oath to serve and protect the people of Chicago. When I was Peter, I did just that, well sometimes. I was a power hungry man, but still I protected. Now with the body they recognize as me, Petra, I'm a total liability if I went with them. About all I can do is walk and only slowly and very carefully. If we're interpreting this man's goofed up implant right, he could well try to beat them up. He has a manic command that only adds to his strength and total loss of control. Hell, if he came after me, I couldn't even get out of his way. Lech is right. I know it, but that doesn't mean I have to like it."

A couple of hours Lech returned to report. He had several bruises on his face. "Got him, boss. You were right. He's had a long record of abusing his authority as an AP-cop. He regularly beats suspects rather severely when he arrests them. He tried to resist, but we got him. The real question now is what do we do with him? You get to decide. I'll give you a full report by morning, boss. Well done on spotting him. Your program is starting to pay off." He nodded and left as the doorman whispered something about doing a good job opening the door for him.

"Incredible. We are on the right path now. Computer: dial Beth. Hi Beth, you were right on the AP-cop, Townsend. He was regularly severely beating up some of those whom he arrested. He gave some of my Feds some punches when they arrested him. Whatever you are doing, keep it up. It's successful," Petra reported.

"Excellent. I have another one for you, but since it is getting late, I will send it and any others that come up during the night to you first thing in the morning. Say, what are you going to do about the man now you've arrested him?" Beth asked, curiously.

"Don't know. I'm going to phone Lady Persephone and ask for her advice. After all, justice is supposed to be her arena. Thanks again." After the phone disconnected, she ordered the computer to call Lady Persephone. After outlining what the situation was, she asked, "Okay, so what are we to do with these people we arrest? They are only dramatizing and acting out their implanted behavior. Are they really to blame for their bad actions? We have to do something with them. This guy has severely beaten dozens of people over the years, including my men when they arrested him."

"Good question, Petra. I've been giving that some thought. We have no prisons any longer, not for at least a century, so we can't lock them up. We have no technology to undo what has been done to them by the PDH implants of the psychs. In the past, many were just given new implants, but that is only going to cover up the original one. Lord knows when the old one will resurface again, forcing them to commit more crimes or harm others. I hate to say this, but perhaps the best thing we can do is make a bid for time. Implant them again into a very docile type of job and see they're given a large daily dose of Pytalon. I know, make them into zombies. It's either that or kill them, and I'd rather not kill them if possible. Perhaps one day someone will invent a way to undo all the mental damage the psychs have done, and then they can be salvaged. I'd like to think that's possible, don't you?" she replied.

"Yes, think positively. Okay, I'll arrange it. Thanks. Say, what is that noise in the background? Chinese?" Petra asked.

Persephone laughed. "Yes, I'm in China acquiring more dead but alive bodies just in case someone else gets mortally wounded. We can't afford to lose you or any of the others in our group. Far too much is at stake now. So Beth's plan is working?"

"To perfection. Weasel and Shifty Eyes are amazing. She has more uncovered already. I expect a busy day tomorrow. By the way, Lech has assigned two guards to accompany us to and from our apartment now. I guess I have to get used to having bodyguards."

Persephone chuckled, "Yes, you do. We need you, Petra, if you didn't already know that. We are counting on you. Oh, the professor is calling. Have to run. Chat later."

Petra reflected a moment and then commanded, "Computer: new document to Lech regarding the disposition of Mr. Townsend. He is to be taken to be re-implanted as a doorman and then put on a heavy dose of Pytalon. However, have someone check up on him periodically to make sure he isn't reverting to beating others. Petra. Computer: end document. Computer: send to Lech. There, that's done. Yan, I think it's time to head for home."

During the course of two weeks, the possibilities continued to flow from Beth. With each one, Petra reviewed the data and then agreed, handing them over to Lech and his men to handle. Everyone turned out to be a trouble case, including one man who even shot one of the arresting Feds before they returned fire, killing him. Most involved men and women either harming others, such as beating them, or sabotaging factory production lines in some way by causing "accidents." Until now, none had even been suspected as the cause behind things going wrong at the various plants around the city.

After three weeks, all those on Beth's critical list had been handled, one way or another. Next came the nearly one thousand, where the psych man's goof had been to use the wrong pronouns, which could possibly create a manic behavior pattern. Each one of these people had to be tracked down and observed. Lech rubbed his head. "So many, boss. This is going to take us some time."

She smiled, "You won't be bored, Captain Lech." He nodded and left to begin working down the list. Some of these were mostly benign, such as the EE woman who had been given the erroneous wording, "You should always wear the sexy ballet boots." She now ran one of the EE women's apparel stores in Chicago, and she constantly extolled the EE women shoppers who entered her store to wear sexy ballet boots, if they weren't already doing so. After some three months of leg work, Lech and his men wrapped up the complete list. Only five on it were deemed problems, sent for re-implanting, and put on Pytalon.

Petra then dictated a very extensive outline of the program and how it was being implemented successfully in Chicago. She sent it to all the many Feds captains in the other major cities of the world, along with Beth's best guess when she would have the lists prepared for that city. "Damn, it's going to take years to get through all the major cities," Petra grumbled, wishing it could go faster.

As if reading her mind, Beth called her, "Jessica and I have worked out a way that we can automate this and send the results as they come up directly to the Feds in the city being handled by our program. We need a list of email addresses for your Feds in the cities we're doing."

"Terrific! This needs to go faster because it is being very successful. I'll get them to you soon."

"Yes, but don't get too overconfident, Petra. These are only the known anomalies. There could well be many others that we don't know about or who are off the grid entirely," Beth cautioned her.

"Well, it would have flagged the Grand Field Marshal. That's something," Petra replied. "But what others would be off the grid?" she asked.

"This is Amanda's idea really. You see, Tilly and the professor have been thinking that perhaps this spring, the graduating seniors for high school should not be allowed to become implanted or put on Pytalon. Rather, they want them to begin making the gradual evolution out of this mess of psych caused insanity. Apparently, that got Amanda thinking about the seniors, and she wondered if in the past some of those kids disappeared out of the system to avoid getting implanted or put on Pytalon. Jessica has been looking into that some and has found hints that this has been happening for many years. We'll have more on this later on," Beth explained.

"Well, now that Amanda suggests it, it does make sense. If I knew I was about to be implanted and turned into a zombie working on a job I didn't want, I might run away too," Petra replied, catching on. "Say, I bet there are a lot of those kids out there who have done just that. Wonder how we can find them?"

"First, we need to ascertain their numbers. I mean if there are only a few, it probably is no big thing," Beth suggested. "We'll keep you posted."

Later that day, the professor called. "Petra, good job on rounding up the psych goofs. Tilly and I believe that we stand a good chance of success if we begin to release normal high school seniors into society without having them undergo implants and Pytalon."

"That's interesting, but what about a test pilot group first? I mean if you do this with all high school graduating seniors worldwide and if it doesn't pan out, we have a larger problem than we have Feds to handle them. We could be swamped cleaning it up, if it doesn't work out," Petra countered.

"We agree on this. We'd like to try it in two test areas this spring, Chicago and a rural area. We've not decided on the rural area yet, but perhaps you can suggest one. Plus, Petra, the reason I've called you is that we would like you to make a visit to the various Chicago high schools and give an assembly to the student bodies."

"What?"

"Yes, tell them what is going on and why. Assure them those who wish to undergo the usual graduating implants, Pytalon doses, and job assignments may continue to do so, but that those who wish a choice may have it. Of course, you'll need to stress that those with a choice must not belittle or lash out or bully or pick on the zombies, just because they aren't that way. They'll be expected to begin to rebuild the world, Chicago in this case. Perhaps you can also make a plea for some of them to join the Feds there as well."

"Oh, me? Talk?"

"I'm sure you can do it. Perhaps hold a question and answer period after your speech. Some might like you to visit their classes and talk more one on one with them. It's time we see if we can't get the mostly un-impacted youth to start helping straighten out this messed up world of ours. It this works out in Chicago, then next year, we'll implement it broadly around the world," the professor explained, trying to sound as upbeat as possible about this change.

Although Petra had many reservations, none the least being that she was an EE woman, the professor convinced her to do it. Again using her voice commands, her computer showed her the fifteen high schools in the greater Chicago area and the email addresses of their principles. After composing a lengthy letter outlining the new procedures to be followed with the spring graduating seniors, she asked to hold an assembly meeting with the seniors. She also suggested she could meet afterwards with individual classes if they desired a more personal discussion. Satisfied, she sent the fifteen emails.

Soon she began receiving replies and suggested dates. Petra sighed, sat back, and made use of her Chan body to deal with the scheduling, arranging the dates on her calendar. The first one up would be New Lincoln Park, rather close to the Feds building. Petra felt a little anxious as she got all the dates arranged. She had two weeks to get her speech prepared!

October 12th came at last. Two security guards escorted Petra, Chan, and Yan to the sprawling high school. She insisted everyone stay backstage though, while she alone met with the students. Petra had never felt as nervous in her life as she stood backstage listening to Principle Marks make some opening remarks to some two hundred seniors lounging in the chairs of the auditorium. "Miss Petra Delius, the Supreme Commander of the Feds, is here today to discuss some very significant changes that will impact your lives and decisions about the future come graduation day this spring. Let's give a warm welcome to her, Miss Petra Delius." The seniors clapped dutifully, but without the slightest enthusiasm. All were on low dosages of Pytalon.

Petra took a deep breath and carefully walked out onto the stage before the microphone center stage. She saw a bunch of rather bored students, who were glad to be out of classes for a while. However, when they saw her, many gasped, and whispers flew right and left. She had anticipated this, though. An armless EE woman definitely brought reactions from those not implanted and on Pytalon.

"Hello, I'm Supreme Commander Petra Delius. Yes, I control all the Feds worldwide; they all answer to me, and yes, I have an EE woman's body that has lost its arms. That hasn't stopped me from doing my job of serving and protecting the people of the world. Now then, first let me tell you a bit about the massive changes in the way that we are governing the world." She noticed several suddenly paying more attention.

"Yes, in the past, I corrupted myself with unrestrained power. Thank goodness I've learned my lessons. Absolute power that had been placed in the Feds organization is now a thing of the past. Now, the world is ruled by three different groups, any two of which can override or veto what the other group is doing or planning. I run and oversee the Feds. Our job is to enforce the laws and keep the world and Chicago safe and crime free so everyone can live their lives in peace. Another group is making the laws, and a third is handling justice when needed."

"If you haven't noticed, our world is doomed. Nearly all adults are basically zombies, glassy-eyed, unthinking, unfeeling, no emotion people, who do their jobs and nothing more. For two hundred plus years, the world has stagnated; nothing new has appeared. Everything continues as it always has, good or bad. Some of you have probably wanted to rebel, seeing your parents as zombies. Rightly so. Our society is fundamentally insane. Goofy. Nuts. Crazy. Why?"

"The psych men with their PDH implanting and the drug manufacturers with their Pytalon are responsible for the world being as it is today. While some of us believe these men are evil and ought to be destroyed, let us withhold such judgments until later. What is critical now is to find a path back to sanity for us all, before it is too late. We've seen the utter chaos that ensues when the adults fail to get their Pytalon. Hence, we have discovered a safe way to get a person off that vicious, mind altering drug, but the process is a long and tough one both for us and the person trying to undo his or her zombie-like state. Believe me, it isn't fun. Also, we have found a way to desensitize the implants of the psychs. No, we can't wholly get rid of the behavior and attitudes they implanted in us, but we're able to control them significantly. Otherwise, as an EE woman, I couldn't possibly do my job."

"Already, some of us are beginning pilot programs to begin to bring adults off Pytalon and desensitize their implants, giving them back their lives. Yet, considering the billions of people on this planet and that we didn't get this way overnight—try more like two centuries—it will be a very long process. Still, those whom we have rescued sing praises. They have their lives back once more."

"Change isn't going to occur overnight, probably not even within my own lifetime. However, if we all work together towards that goal, in time, we can restore earth to a vastly more prosperous and happy world. To that end, those who make the laws are changing Senior Graduation Assignments. No longer will you be forced into a job or position that you do not want to have. No one will be forced to get a PDH implant. No one will be forced to take Pytalon." This created quite a buzz among the students, and she allowed them a moment to absorb this news.

One of their teachers interrupted. "But what about the Total Care program, which promises them steady employment, food, housing, clothing, and healthcare for their lives? If they don't participate in the Total Care Choosing, will they still be eligible for the Total Care package that safeguards them? Healthcare alone can financially ruin anyone if they aren't part of the program. It only takes one accident."

Suddenly, Petra realized no one had yet looked into this bigger picture! She replied, "I'll look into this shortly. I believe for the time being, everyone will be covered in the Total Care program. That said, we do recognize some of you would like to be implanted following in the footsteps of your parents or your own goals. This will still be allowed. Those of you, who don't want to have either done, will not be forced or compelled to have it done. So on Assignment Day, you get to choose your path. Those of you, who choose not to be implanted or go onto Pytalon, will be shouldering a much *larger* responsibility to everyone else who does. On your shoulders rests the fate of the entire world. You'll be held to higher standards than those on Pytalon or who have been implanted, since you have the ability to think and act in the best interests of everyone."

"On Assignment Day, we'll provide you with a listing of the most crucially needed jobs that need filling. I would also like to encourage you to consider joining the Feds; we take both men and women. Look, if I can make it to the very top, so can some of you young women."

"I've taken up too much of your time. However, I'm ready to answer some of your questions. Also, I can come to your classes and meet with you in smaller groups, if you so desire. Let your teachers know if you want me to drop by for a chat before I go today. So questions?"

"Sorry, I can't point. Go ahead," Petra responded to a fellow who raised his hand.

"Is this choice on Assignment Day going to happen everywhere?"

"This year, no. It is being offered to all seniors here in Chicago and a small high school in southern Illinois. We are piloting this new program. If it works out well for you and everyone else, then the following spring, it will be offered to all seniors in every high school in the world."

"Are you still a sex doll? You look like one, but how can you do anything?" one girl asked. Many whispers followed and Petra guessed rightly that question was on lots of their minds.

"What? Do my monster breasts give me away?" she teased them. The students roared with laughter. When they quieted down, she explained further. "Yes, originally I was, and it was not what I wanted. However, thank heavens Jessica volunteered to work her magic on me and desensitized my EE implant. Yes, it's still there. I have to dress as I am or I get headaches, but I'm in control of it for the most part. Yes, it's difficult or impossible for me to do some things. Yet, it hasn't stopped me nor should it stop you. Life is within us. We should live life to the fullest—help others as we can, and make this crazy world a better place for our children and grandchildren."

She fielded several more mundane questions about how much choice they would really have in choosing their jobs after graduating. With no more questions, she thanked them and the assembly ended. Once backstage, she said, "I need to get off my feet for a bit." Yan and Chan took hold of her and led her to a chair. As planned, they stayed around to discuss how the choosing of jobs would be done with the various councilors.

Finally, Principle Marks came to find her. "One class has asked to meet with you, if you have the time, Miss Delius." She did and he led the way, though Chan and Yan held on to her until they reached the classroom. They and the two security guards remained outside, while she entered alone. Their teacher, a glassy-eyed middle-aged woman, had a stool up front and she made for that, grateful to be allowed to sit down.

"Hi everyone. So you have more questions for me. Shoot. I'll nod at you. Yes," she nodded to a boy.

"Some of us like to invent things. Are we going to be allowed to do that?"

"Absolutely. I know a perfect place where you can go and invent things to your heart's desire. Our society hasn't had a new invention for over two hundred years. It's about time new things get invented." She fielded numerous other related questions.

One girl then asked, "This is really the best news ever, Miss Delius. My boyfriend and I want to get married, once he has a job. If we aren't on Pytalon, can we raise a family, have kids and all that?"

"Of course you can have all the children you desire; just make sure you're financially sound and can afford them. That's another benefit of not being on Pytalon. As long as you both aren't on that awful drug, neither of you will need to take the special additional drug so you could have intercourse and children."

"What if I wanted to become an EE woman for my husband? Just not on Pytalon though—that stuff is awful! My parents are zombies and hardly ever even notice me. If I did become one, we'd have great sex, wouldn't we?"

"You can have great sex without becoming an EE woman, but yes, if you desired it, you would be allowed to do so," Petra replied.

After fielding a few more questions, she carefully rose to leave. As she was making her slow, careful way to the door, one young teen whispered, "You should check out the Southend Mission." She nodded to the teen.

Once outside, she asked her security guards if they knew where the Southend Mission was located and what it was. They didn't. Back in her office an hour later, she used voice commands and her computer to look up the Southend Mission. The only data in the computer database beyond its address was the phrase: Get Help Here.

"How very strange. What is this place? Okay, let's check it out yet today," Petra decided. Again, she summoned her two security guards and had them ready the EMAC that was parked on the roof. By the time the three reached it, the guards had it ready to go. She gave them the address. With Chan and Yan helping her, Petra got into the vehicle without mishap. Twenty minutes later, the vehicle came to rest in a rundown part of Chicago, the far south. The security guards didn't like the looks of the area and took up shielding positions, guns drawn, as the three made their way carefully down the three steps to the ground. Petra looked up at the dingy, single story brick and metal building. A sign over the automatic door read: Southend Mission: Get Help Here.

"Okay, let's see what this place is," Petra whispered. The three headed for the door. Unlike the many other buildings in Chicago, there was no doorman here to open it for them. However, a sensor triggered as they approached it and it opened automatically. They stepped inside and discovered a completely new, unknown, and unsuspected world!

"Oh my god!" Taken by surprised, Petra whispered using both her voices. They had entered a large sitting room of some kind. Men and women sat on secondhand, worn-out chairs, sofas, and couches. However, that wasn't what shocked them; rather it was the physical condition of the twenty-five people here. Some were missing hands, others, arms, others a leg or two. Some appeared to be blind.

A one-armed man came up to them. "Oh my. Another one. Hello, I'm Phillip Stormbeak. Welcome to my Southend Mission. Yes, here you can get help, miss. We take in anyone who is in need, providing a place to live, the care needed, and two square meals each day."

"Oh my god! What happened to all these men and women?" Petra asked. "Oh. I'm Petra Delius. My companions, Chan and Yan."

"Well, misfortune has happened to us. I lost my arm in a construction accident some twenty years ago. As you know, in our society, there is no place for these others or me, but then you're acutely aware of that, Miss Petra. Sally there lost her hands in an accident, and her sponsor dumped her out on the street." He pointed to an EE woman in her thirties. "Bill there lost both legs while working for the sanitation department. I've fixed up that board with rollers so he can get around some. John lost his eyes when a coworker goofed up and splashed sulfuric acid in his face. Betsy lost her lower arms in a milling machine while trying to save another coworker who got herself caught in the machine. The coworker died anyway. On it goes, story after story. Sad really. Here, they can still have a way to live and survive, though not on that awful Pytalon. We don't allow that to be taken here. The Total Care Program's assistance to these people isn't enough for them to live on. Anyway, I'm sure you'll find many here who will be very willing to help you with your needs, Miss Petra. In turn, all I ask is you help others as you can. You have eyes and John needs someone to guide him, as does Len there and Alice over there. I am sure you'll be very comfortable here."

"Oh my God, I never knew there were people in such conditions!" Petra exclaimed, still trying to grasp the whole picture. "Don't they have some place where they can be cared for? Doesn't Total Care help them? I don't understand."

Phillip laughed, "Not in our drugged society. Hell, no one will even pay the slightest attention to them. Zombies can't see anything. Without a job to earn credits, where could they live, let alone get the assistance they need? The Total Care's subsidy for us is pathetic. No one could live on that allowance. Sally's sponsor didn't want to take care of a helpless EE woman. Betsy's husband didn't even realize she lost her lower arms and she is almost as helpless as you are. There simply is no place in our 'great society' for people like us, except here at the Southend Mission. Yes, Total Care provides them with the barest minimum of assistance, just enough for us to keep them alive, but barely."

"I had no idea! Well, this has to change! Oh, I'm Petra Delius, Supreme Commander of the Feds. I give you my word this will be changed just as fast as I can arrange it. Good lord. This is unbelievable, but now that I see it, I can understand it. Zombies make mistakes, and they and others pay dearly for it."

"What? The Feds? You? I don't understand. You're all three EE women. There are no women in the Feds, certainly not armless ones," Phillip countered growing a little angry with her.

Just then, the door opened and the young teen, who had whispered the name of this place to her as she was leaving her high school class, entered. "Oh, it's you again. You came. You actually did come! Amazing. Phillip, she's the head of the Feds, no less. She just gave a long assembly speech to our class a while ago. How's mom doing?"

"Just fine, Linn. Wait—she really is with the Feds, Linn? She's an armless EE woman for heaven's sake," Phillip protested.

"Yes, she's making big changes. We don't have to get implanted anymore or take Pytalon when we graduate in the spring. We even get to choose our own jobs now! Isn't that the best news ever? Maybe I can make enough to get an apartment and hire someone to look after mom so she can have a real life again," Linn replied enthusiastically.

Phillip's face reddened slightly. "I'm sorry. I mistook you for—well you know what I mean. The Feds have women in them now? I don't understand. Our kids are getting choices? Not implanting? No Pytalon? What's going on anyway?" He looked as confused as he sounded.

"Don't worry. I'm the only woman in the Feds so far. Yes, we're now making changes, starting here in Chicago. Ultimately, we want no more PDH implants done and everyone off Pytalon, but honestly it took two hundred years to get where we are. It won't happen overnight, but yes, bit by bit, we are trying to undo this awful mess of a world," Petra explained. "Linn, may I meet your mother? Did you bring her here?"

"Sure. She's bright and alert now, after the awful withdrawal symptoms went away. Yes, dad didn't even know she lost her lower arms. I had to do something, and I heard about this place. Phillip has saved us. Mom likes it here, but I know she would rather live with me, but there is no one to watch her while I'm at school. Come on," Linn said, happily leading Petra over to Betsy.

"Mom, this is Miss Petra Delius, the Supreme Commander of the Feds no less. She's making many changes. I won't have to get implanted or go onto Pytalon when I graduate! I can pick my own job so we can get an apartment and someone to help us. Oh, Petra, this is my mom, Betsy Linsley."

"Pleased to meet you, Betsy. Sorry I can't even hug you," Petra said with a smile.

Betsy rose and smiled back. "Well, I can sort of hug." She put her upper arms on Petra's shoulders. "Isn't my Linn here a bright, young student?"

"Yes she certainly is that and much more," Petra praised her daughter. After tossing her hair a little to the front, she sat down on a chair Linn hastily scooted over for her. The three began to chat a little. Before long, Phillip joined them, dragging up a chair for himself.

"So how do you manage to pay for all this, Phillip?" Petra asked, already suspecting his answer.

"Total Care provides a tiny amount—mostly through volunteers and what little donations I can raise. It's just barely enough to be able to make them two meals a day. Why?"

"Well, it is time for a change, Phillip. Tomorrow, I'm sending a couple of Feds here to take you shopping. First, get all new furniture. Second, lay in a large stock of food. You all deserve three *good* meals a day. The Feds will put ten thousand credits into your account when they come, that should get things rolling. When the seniors graduate in the spring, I'll see that a new job opportunity is posted. That way, I'll get you some teens to work here and help with everything, paid for by the Feds, of course. Plus, Phillip, get a new sign at least twice as large as your current one," Petra explained, watching his jaw drop.

"I—I don't know what to say, except thank you, thank you! On behalf of all of us, thank you, Miss Delius."

"Petra, just Petra. I'll drop by in a couple of days to see how things are coming along. I'm rather booked with giving assemblies for the other high schools until then. Between now and then, Phillip, think about what each of these people could possibly do. While I lack arms, that isn't stopping me from contributing what help I can. Surely, we can put our heads together and find something productive for these people to do. It will do wonders for their self-respect. I know. I've been there, done that."

"Incredible. Yes, you would be surprised at what some can do, but no one wants to hire them," he replied.

"That's about to change, Phillip. We need all those who aren't zombies to pitch in and help us restore the world to what it ought to be."

"Petra, may I ask you a personal question?" She nodded and Phillip asked, "You are an EE woman, right, and your companions too?" She nodded again. "But you are thinking clearly, brilliantly. I've not heard you complaining about not looking your best and such as poor Sally does all the time."

"Yes, one of my friends has found a way to desensitize the PDH implants. While they aren't gone, mind you, I'm now very much in control of my life and thoughts. I'll see if I can find someone to help Sally and Betsy get desensitized too. Then they can be far more productive and alive too."

"You'll do that for mom? That would be a miracle for her. She is so frustrated all the time, unable to run the milling machines as her implant keeps on dictating to her," Linn replied, very much impressed.

"Sally really does want to help me run the mission here, but she is always stopped by her implant. She keeps repeating the words, you know," Phillip explained. "I'd like to marry her, but I haven't been able to get her attention off her implant long enough to really hold meaningful conversations. Is it really possible Sally could be more like you, Petra?"

"Absolutely. I'll try to get someone to come by as soon as possible. We have one person who has been trained to desensitize implants who has recently come to Chicago to help. I'll see if I can get these two into her schedule as soon as feasible, Phillip. Say, it's getting late. I best be going. Don't forget, the Feds will come by tomorrow with credits and will be helping you get all new furnishings and food for this place."

"Thank you, thank you. Everyone, a huge round of appreciation for Miss Petra Delius, our shining savior," Phillip called out. The group thanked her and applauded, each in their own way, though some were able to clap.

On her way out, Petra said, "Linn, after your mom gets desensitized, bring her to see me at the Feds building, top floor. I believe I have a job for her that she could do well. We'll see."

"A real job? Oh thank you, thank you, Miss Delius, thank you," Linn gushed.

That evening after making the necessary arrangements, Petra dictated a lengthy email and sent it off to Tilly, Beth, the professor, and Lady Persephone. Undoubtedly, in other cities there were many other people in similar straits as those she'd met today. Zombies were accident-prone. The society had no means to provide for those who suffered such serious accidents, save the Total Care Program, which certainly wasn't providing much for these people. She did know prosthetic limbs used to exist some two hundred years ago, but not now. One had to learn to adapt to a loss of a limb. She gave thanks to Phillip who had taken the initiative to help these less fortunate of Chicago and wondered how many more were out there, probably dying for lack of care. She made a mental note to look far deeper into the Total Care system, but events kept her from doing that immediately, rather unfortunately though.

416

Chapter 27—Escape

Bao and Huan began to have relief from their migraines thanks to the special panties that Beth put on them. Finally, the two began to have a few lucid moments in which to think. While none of their long range planning ever included precisely what had happened to them, they had all manner of backup plans set up and ready to be executed. With their monumental discoveries and inventions, they knew that eventually someone would uncover their Transference Machine. They had expected the Feds would find out and raid their foundation to steal the machine for themselves.

Well, part of their expectations had come true. The Feds had raided their hidden foundation and taken their machine. However, they hadn't anticipated being put into these helpless bodies and given EE implants. Thus, it took them some time to get used to their predicament. As their lucid periods increased, they were at last able to think a little, despite the Pytalon's effects.

Centuries ago, the Chinese mafia, the Triads, and the Japanese mafia, the Yakuza, had finally settled their long standing differences, about the time the Feds grew in power and worldwide domination. In a rare act of self-preservation, they'd merged their organizations to counter the Feds, forming the Trikuza. As the PDH implanting began to become commonplace as well as the massive usage of Pytalon, they had no choice but to dive deep underground within the world society. Recruiting at the high school level became the only way that they could acquire new, unaltered members, but they had to pick candidates wisely.

These were given extensive martial arts training at a very rigorous level. Those that failed were summarily executed. Those that passed were given the special tattoo, a triangle with a dagger through its middle, usually placed on their right upper arms. These men and women were then given training in how to fake being a zombie. That is, they were able to pass as Pytalon drugged members of society, but ready to carry out any orders they were given.

Even the very existence of their organization was no longer even suspected by the Feds, who believed they'd been wiped out a century or more ago. Their only real difficulty was recruitment, which in the last hundred years had fallen off rather sharply. They couldn't use blatant force and intimidation any longer. That would raise red flags with the Feds. At this time, the Trikuza had fewer than five hundred members worldwide.

Ten of these worked and lived in the Chinese quarters of London proper. More importantly, the Lin brothers had a deal with Master Lao Bing, the head of the Trikuza in China. When the mafia leader's body was close to death, the Lin brothers promised him a new body via their Transference Machine. In return, the Trikuza were to help the brothers if they ever got into trouble with the Feds. Unfortunately, when Petra launched her raid, the two men had no idea that it was coming and thus were unable to send for Trikuza fighters to help defend their hidden laboratory and workshop.

Bao and Han were far too wise to have only one Ace up their sleeves. While the official Lin Foundation building was a mere "museum" of their earlier machines, they did most of their research at the hidden one that Petra raided. However, they also had a second backup site, fully equipped—almost a duplicate of the one that was raided, including many bodies in stasis machines as well as "volunteers" running their test bodies, rather similar to what Petra and the others had already found. The two brothers alternated their time between these two secret facilities. In addition, they had a third backup site which only held their inventions—no bodies or volunteers, just copies of their equipment. At this second site, they had two more male bodies ready for their use, since their current bodies were in their fifties when Petra raided their foundation. "Always be prepared" had kept them alive and active for over two centuries now and wholly unknown to the rest of the world, save a very few individuals, such as Master Lao Bing.

Speaking in Chinese so the teenage girl couldn't understand them, they discussed their escape plans during the few lucid moments they had during the daytime hours. Bao said, "We have prepared for this, Han. We need to get to Backup Station Two in Peking."

"Yes, but we can't use the bodies we prepared for ourselves. These EE implants are driving me nuts. Oh hell!" Han involuntarily began reciting the implanted script once more. After that, she struggled to her feet and walked around some until the dildo panties had worked its miracle for her.

"Ah, that's better. What women do we have there? I don't recall."

"They are all like us, as planned. Crap. We will just have to steal two of the volunteer women's bodies, that's all. Oh no, not again!" It was Bao's turn to recite her litany involuntarily. She took a hint from Huan and walked around for a time afterwards. Pleasured enough, she sat back down. "The zombie technicians can fasten the electrodes to us, but we must watch them carefully. They make numerous mistakes."

"But the machine? How will we run it?" Huan asked.

"I think I can set all the controls using my teeth. It's our only way out of this mess," Bao replied. "We can use Cai Cheng here in London to get us out of England and safely to Peking and our second base."

"Right. He'll do it for us, though he might have to check with Master Lao Bing first. One major problem. How are we to get out of this house and find Cai Cheng? She keeps the door locked. Have you forgotten we're helpless like this?"

"No, I'm working on it. Between the two of us, I think we can knock her to the ground and then knock her out. She keeps the key in her pocket though. I haven't worked out how to get it out of there or how to use it to open the door."

"Big barrier, Bao. How do we turn the knob? I think we need a different route out of here. Let me think. I'm going to walk more and see about something." Huan threw herself forward, getting to her feet, wobbling a good deal to regain her balance. She then began walking or stumping rather around the room, staying close to the walls this time, though enjoying the sensations caused by her special panties. She had to stop for a time, recovering from the pantie's effects. At last, she sat down and caught her breath, during which time, she again had to recite her litany.

"We go out through a window. Smash it with our steel heels. Get back up and sort of fall outside. Get up and make our way to the nearest MTE," Huan proposed. Unfortunately, Bao didn't hear much, as she found herself reciting the litany, so Huan repeated it when she recovered and became somewhat more lucid again.

"When do we make our break?" Bao asked.

"Tonight after supper, when she is getting ready to undress us for bed. We need the cover of darkness to make our escape," Huan suggested. "Besides, who knows when our next meal will come?"

As the unsuspecting young teen prepared to get them into their nightgowns, Bao suddenly lunged into her, falling onto her. Both ended up falling to the ground. At once, Huan fell down sharply on the teen, knocking her senseless. Then both banged her again. Satisfied she was out cold or dead, the two struggled mightily to get to their feet from the floor, no small feat in itself. Then, they made their slow, careful walk to the front window. Huan carefully got herself on the floor and then wiggled her legs into position and began kicking at the glass pane. It shattered. She then rolled out of the way and struggled to get back up onto her boots.

Meanwhile, Bao managed to fall out the window and rolled a little ways away before spending a couple of minutes desperately trying to get to her feet on the soft lawn. Huan came tumbling out, knocking them both back onto the ground. Five minutes later and a whole lot of struggling, both were on their feet. "Which way to the MTE?" Huan asked.

It was dark and the ground, soft, a perilous combination for the two EE women in their boots. More than once, one or the other mis-stepped and tumbled to the grass, requiring many precious minutes to regain her feet. After what seemed an eternity to the two women, they finally reached the MTE and carefully stepped onto the moving escalator. "All we have to do is follow the directions to London," Huan whispered.

"And hope no one catches us or tries to rape us," Bao added.

Around midnight, they stepped off the MTE in the Little Chinatown part of London. "Now what do we do? How are we going to find one of the ten men in all Chinatown?" Huan whispered. "I have to pee and I'm soaking wet. I can't take much more of this walking."

"Here, let's sit down on these steps. Careful, our feet can't take much more. Damn," Bao fell down hard, but could do little about it except bear it. After involuntarily reciting her litany once more, she added, "We wait. Someone will find us. They're always watching."

Sure enough after a half hour, a man ambled up to the two EE women who looked as miserable as they felt. Their gowns were dirty and soaked from the light misty fog from earlier in the evening. Their hair was somewhat tangled up. The man was of Chinese origin in his mid-twenties and he spoke in his native tongue, "Well, well, what do we have here?

Incredible. A pair of most unusual EE women. Out for a night on the town? I can use some company about now."

Bao smiled, "Excellent. You're Trikuza. Take us to your leader. Have him call Master Lao Bing. This is going to be the most important call you'll ever make to your master, believe me," Bao replied in her native tongue as well. "We know Master Lao Bing, and he'll reward you for rescuing us, whether or not you believe me, he will. Damn!" She found herself reciting her litany once more.

Huan hastily spoke up, "Indeed he will. Just please make the call. As you can see, we're unable to do so. Please, for your own sake do this."

"How do you know of Trikuza?" he inquired.

"Because it's late at night, you're not a Pytalon zombie, and this is Little Chinatown. You patrol the area. Need I go on? You've a tattoo of a dagger piercing a triangle on the upper part of your right arm beneath your shirt. Shit!" Huan found herself reciting her implant words now, triggered in part by her mention of his arm and beneath his shirt.

He eyed the two women with unmoving, heartless eyes, but backed off and pulled out his cell. The two women couldn't hear what he was saying, but soon he motioned for the two to get up. "Please, can you help us up? It is a bitch getting up without assistance," Bao asked. At least the man did as she asked, but no more. He led the way on down the street and into an alley where they waited for a few minutes.

Another man ten years older appeared silently behind them. "What is it that you wish of Master Lao Bing, EE women, the strangest I've ever seen?" he asked coldly.

"You call Master Lao Bing and tell him you have Bo Bin and Han Lin with you, and they desperately need to talk to him on the phone. He'll want to talk to us," Bao replied.

"But you're not Bo Bin nor is he Han. You're helpless EE women. What do you take me for? A fool?" he said argumentatively.

"Looks can be deceiving. Make the call and I promise you that you will please Master Lao Bing exceedingly well," Bo Bin answered calmly.

The man stared hard at Bao for a minute. "I'll make the call. If this is a hoax or the master is displeased, I'll not hesitate to cut your throats!" He pulled out his cell phone and made the call. "Master, most humble apologies for calling you, but we've got two armless EE women here who have asked us to call you for them. They claim to be two men, a Bo Bin and Han Lin, but these are definitely two armless EE women, master."

"He said to put you on; here, I will hold it for you," he said, somewhat interested. The master didn't berate him as he had expected.

Bo Bin said, "Aldebaran. Yes, the Feds raided us. They took the machine and used it on us. Yes, they transferred us into two of our special women and were keeping us locked up. We've escaped, but we need to be returned to our second place at once. Yes, our deal still stands. Yes, we'll perform it as soon as we get ourselves fixed up. Yes, thank you Master Lao Bing, thank you. He wants to talk to you," Bao said.

The man took the cell back. His eyes opened wide, as he listened to his new orders. "Yes master! Yes, at once. We will leave within the hour. Most kind of you, master, thank you." He hung up and stared at the two disheveled, helpless women.

"I don't know who you are, but the master does. We're to treat you with the greatest of kindness and to bring you to him immediately. Chan, get an Air Liner ready to go within the hour. I'll take them to HQ and have them attended to now. This way, ladies." He led them further down the darkened alley and then into a building, but both women had to pause several times to allow the sensations created by their special panties to die down, rather annoying them and their guide.

Both blinked at the brighter lights. They were in some kind of nightclub, but only a few others were present. "Fang, Dai, take these two women and see to their needs. They are going to see the master so make them presentable." Fang was an EE woman herself, but Dai was a Pytalon zombie.

"Oh my, yes, you must look your best. Please, let us help you," Fang began fawning over the two, leading them to the women's restroom. By the time they were refreshed and their hair brushed out, it was time to head to Heathrow, where the liner was waiting. At least the men now helped them into the EMAC and then later into the Air Liner. On board, they were fed, and then they laid back and slept for the many hours of the flight.

It was evening when they were lifted to the ground at a remote airfield outside Peking. Master Lao Bing was there himself, but they also saw at least fifty other men in the shadows, his protection squad. "My, you both have gotten yourselves into a mess this time. Welcome Bo Bin, Han, but I can't tell which is which." He signaled a man who handed a sack of credits to the men who had brought them here. They returned to the Air Liner and departed, even as they walked slowly to his waiting EMAC.

"Yes, long story, Master Lao Bing. We need your help to get our revenge on those who did this to us, but first we need to get ourselves into new bodies, and we'll take care of our agreement with you as well. We were almost undone by the Feds raid, but we're geniuses still, even if we're now implanted," Bo Bin replied. Unfortunately, she had to recite her litany again, though she barely whispered it.

Han hastily took up the slack. "Miserable bitches did this to us, but we're too smart for them. Give us a little time to fix ourselves up, and we'll make sure you're handled properly."

"We heard about the Feds raid, but there was nothing we could do. By the time we knew of the raid, it was all over. I have had eyes out looking for you both, but we had no idea you were in London of all places," Master Lao Bing explained. "I can't lose my future, now can I?" he smiled at Huan. Unfortunately for Huan, that triggered her involuntary recitation of her own implant words again.

"Yes, I wish to push the transfer to my new body up as soon as you are able to do it," Master Lao Bing continued. He saw the condition of his two associates and doubted how long they would remain sane enough to perform the transfer. Besides, if the Feds raided them once, they may well do so again, and he could lose his chance at immortality. Hence, he was eager to assist the two and to get his new body some ten or more years sooner than he had planned.

A half hour later, the EMAC landed on top of their second secret foundation building, wholly unmarked with no distinguishing features that would indicate what was inside. In this facility, everything was underground. The first floor appeared to be mostly an empty warehouse but with an EMAC inside. After his men lifted the two women down to the floor, Master Lao Bing asked, "Do you need further assistance or should I await your call?"

"We can manage from this point. Thank you, Master Lao Bing. We owe you for this rescue. As soon as we get ourselves handled, we'll make sure everything is prepared for you and call. Thank you." Both women bowed slightly, and he did so as well, before turning and leaving the two women standing inside their warehouse.

A minute later, they stood before the elevator, and Bo Bin used her nose to push the buttons. A few minutes later, they stepped out into their underground facilities and two of their zombie helpers came up to them. "Show us the stasis pods, Lian," Bo Bin took charge.

Shortly, they gazed sadly at the two comatose male bodies that they had set aside for their next reincarnations. Both knew with their EE implants, they simply couldn't use them. Instead, they looked at the women volunteers who were currently in stasis pods. Currently, they were occupying the EE women's bodies in the living quarters two floors beneath this one. Neither hesitated a moment to steal these volunteers' bodies. Each picked one that suited their tastes and had Lian and his helper move them to the Transference Machine room. The stasis pods were there long before they managed to get themselves there.

While Huan oversaw Lian attaching the various electrodes to the volunteer comatose woman, Bao worked on setting the dials, using her mouth and teeth. No way would either Lin trust Lian to make these settings. One goof and they would perish or worse. That done, she had Lian help her lie down on the second table. Again, Huan oversaw the connection of the many electrodes to her head. Satisfied, Huan then used her nose to push the Activate Program button. Now all she had to do was watch and wait. The entire process was done automatically.

When the program completed, Huan asked Lian to rouse Bo Bin. "Oh my head," she said. "Thank god I have hands again," she added, sitting up and rubbing her head. "Give me a minute, Han."

An hour later, Han was sitting up rubbing her head, complaining of a headache as well. Both of their previous armless bodies were now put into the stasis pods for future use. "Thank you Lian. We had best find some clothes and eat some solid food. Meanwhile, bring the stasis pod marked Bing up here and take these two back down to the preservation room," Bo Bin ordered.

As the two nearly naked EE women walked back to their old offices, Bo Bin grumbled, "I guess I'll still have to get used to being called Bao and you, Huan. Crap!" She began to recite her litany once more, and Huan followed suit, spitting out a curse of her own.

"Thank heavens we're off Pytalon now. These bodies are free of it," Huan added. "I almost lost my mind there in that house. Another couple of weeks, Bao, and I wouldn't have been able to think clearly any longer. It's a good thing they wanted our minds halfway clear. The fools thought we would tell them more about our inventions. Ha. Just enough so we could get what we needed to escape."

Bao finished her litany and added, "Huan, I never would have believed our salvation depended upon getting those dildo panties, but it did. The EE implant we invented centuries ago certainly works very well—almost too well. At least we're somewhat stable now; we have arms again and can do our work, but we can barely walk in these exotic boots. Somehow, we have to work around these constant recitations of the implant words."

"Agreed, remember, after a year or so, the EE women are no longer reciting the words so frequently. I don't think taking a non-EE woman's body will help us, do you?" Huan asked.

Bao bit her lip, "No, you have a point there. Our implant demands a hypersensitive body. If we take a normal woman's body, I fear we'll be fighting headaches that cannot be ended without another transference into an EE woman's body. We're stuck with these. Damn, all this talk is driving me nuts again." She had to sit down and handle her body's sexual needs, repeating the litany once more. Huan joined her.

Satisfied and lucid once more, they made sure Lian had the right body brought to the Transference Machine room. Then, Bao called Master Lao Bing to set up the appointment for early the next morning.

"Master Lao Bing, remember, you'll wake up and find yourself in this new youthful body. However, the physical skills you possess, your martial arts, will not be there. This body will need to be trained, but we both suspect that, since you know martial arts, it will be a simple matter of training this body's reflexes. We can't guarantee that such will be easy," Bao cautioned him.

"Yes, that's the liability I face. Yet, to be immortal, it is a small price to pay. My trusted men will take me to a secure facility once the process is finished, but I must make sure this body is dead once I'm in my new body. That was part of the agreement," he said solemnly.

"But of course. We don't want someone else going around impersonating you with it. It shall die by your own hands, Master Lao Bing," Bao replied. "Are you ready then?"

"May I make another request?" Master Lao Bing asked politely. Bao nodded, knowing any last minute changes would only benefit themselves. "I've become fondly attached to my EE woman, Juan Wu. I would like her to get a new youthful body at the same time as I do."

"Not a problem, we have many from which she may choose," Huan answered, again seeing the wisdom in keeping so many here ready for such eventualities as this.

Master Lao Bing grinned mischievously. "I have already chosen the one. I would like her to have the body that you just had, Bo Bin, er Bao, the armless EE woman's body. She will be more appealing to me that way."

Bao chuckled, "Does she know? About getting a new youthful body, I mean?"

"Yes, I talked to her last night. She was most distressed that I will be young again while she will be old. I promised her that she could join me. Consider your recent debt to me paid in full with this change in plans."

Bao smiled greatly relieved over this unexpected stroke of luck. "Thank you, Master Lao Bing. Yet, there is another detail Huan and I wish to discuss. It's the small matter of obtaining our revenge upon those who have attempted to destroy us and our great works."

Master Lao Bing looked up with cold eyes. "Do go on."

"We're most embarrassed by this, but six women, five of them EE women, have brought all this down upon us! EE women! We're disgraced beyond all words. True, they used the men in the Feds to do the initial assault, but these women were the masterminds behind the raid and our subsequent disgrace. Now we find ourselves in a position from which we can't easily obtain our necessary revenge, unless we cease all our valuable research projects for quite some time. Even then, we don't know that in our present circumstances we can capture these women."

"Ah I can see your circumstances most clearly. Nor do I wish you two to cease your incredibly valuable researches and works. If you will give me the names and such information as you have on these six women, I'll see they're brought to you so you may regain your honor," he replied coyly, seeing at once what Bao was after.

"Most excellent, Master Lao Bing. In that case, we're prepared to extend a second long term contract to you. We'll have another youthful male body and a female one always at hand for your later use when this new one grows old. As a safeguard, we'll keep it stored at our third backup facility. Will that balance our obligations to you, Master Lao Bing?" Bao inquired politely.

Master Lao Bing bowed, "Indeed, that would balance quite nicely. Give me the details and consider it done. Make your preparations to receive your honor back."

Hastily, Bao wrote out the six names and what little information they had about them. Master Lao Bing then handed it to his right hand man, who bowed and stuffed it in his pocket. He then brought Juan Wu down from the EMAC, where she was anxiously waiting word that she too would be given a new youthful body. As she made her way to Master Lao Bing's side, her smile told everyone just how pleased she was for this great honor.

She bowed before him and said, "It has been my great honor to have pleasured Master Lao Bing for thirty years. I am so humbled that I will be granted the opportunity to continue to please Master Lao Bing for so many more years to come. I promise to always do my very best to please you, Most Honorable Master Lao Bing." Juan Wu bowed low.

"Yes, Juan Wu, you have always been the best. I have arranged for you to have a new youthful EE woman's body so you may continue pleasing me. I have arranged for your new body to be even more pleasing to me, Juan. I do hope you'll also find it more pleasing than yours is now."

She smiled, flirting with him. "I'm sure if you find it even more pleasing than I am now, then I will be most pleased with it as well."

"Excellent, Juan Wu. Remember when you wake up in your new, young body, that I have chosen it specifically for you and that I find it much more pleasing than your current body," he installed a subtle suggestion. Bao recognized what he was attempting to do. Master Bing was a quick learner, Bao noted once again, while Juan quietly repeated Master Bing words to herself several times, looking very pleased.

An hour later, the two transference processes were complete. The first actions Master Yao Bing took were to flex his arms and hands and then to strangle his old, now comatose, body. Meantime, Boa finished the transference of Juan Wu.

Yes, Juan Wu was quite shocked when she awoke, but Master Lao Bing was right beside her, repeating his words to her.

Quickly, she calmed down. Remembering them, she looked very pleased indeed. "I remember, my dearest honeybee. I am still me, and I am even more pleasing to you now. How strange it seems. You look different." Juan Wu was still a little confused, but quietly recited her implant words, giving her some comfort.

With his arm securely around her waist, the two eighteen year olds, accompanied by several bodyguards and his number two man, left the secret foundation. "Well, that went better than anticipated," Bao said, as she and Huan hastily sat down to pleasure themselves. All this flirting between Juan Wu and Master Bing had triggered their own implants, which they had to satisfy or face migraines once more.

"Come, we have many preparations to make. We want to be ready to regain our honor when Master Lao Bing brings us our six women," Bao suggested. "We don't have enough EE women's bodies here, even if we count the volunteers."

"We could simply alter their existing bodies. Surgery is always an option," Huan suggested.

"They would experience great pain and would be bedridden for some time. No, Huan, we must have their new bodies prepared for them in advance. We have much work to do," Bao countered, but then had to stop to recite her litany once more.

Chapter 28—Becoming Aware of the Dropouts

Jessica was the first to discover the discrepancies between high school enrollments versus graduation numbers. For over two hundred years, graduation from high school was mandatory for all teens, no exceptions, part of the Total Care Package, From the Cradle to the Grave. Anyone trying to "drop out" was eventually rounded up by the AP-cops and sent to the psychs for handling, usually by implant and Pytalon. Thus, when she decided to look at the figures of graduating seniors for Petra and her many school assembly visits, she came across the slight difference in figures.

High school in the twenty-third century was vastly different than in ancient times, when there were sports, football games, cheerleaders, bands, and then numerous colleges and universities for advanced education. With the construction of the "sane society" came corresponding changes in the education of children. Yes, in the lower grades, they were taught the usual reading, writing, and math skills, along with basic science. However, when they entered high school, each year they took placement tests, which were used by the councilors to help place them in the appropriate classes. Primarily, the teens learned the necessary vocational skills that corresponded to the future jobs they were best suited for or that were deemed necessary to fill, compliments of Total Care.

The many no-so-bright students were placed in positions such as Garbage Collectors and similar positions where thinking skills were minimally needed. Brighter students were prepared for positions on assembly lines at the various manufacturing companies. The rare bright student, if lucky, entered the upper management of a company and wasn't implanted, though he or she was dosed heavily with Pytalon. One might say the education achieved from colleges and universities had been pushed down into high school classes, at least on the technical side. There were no arts, humanities, social sciences, performing arts, and similar things. Those no longer existed, save for some ballet training for young girls. Some still believed ballet training was useful preparation for future EE women. So much so, that those girls who had ballet training were often later scheduled to become EE women at the time of their Choosing.

Graduation from high school meant the teen was fully trained for some position within the "sane society." Trained, of course, was a relative term, considering most then underwent an implant suited to their new position and were given large doses of Pytalon, becoming zombies mechanically performing their assigned jobs every day without the slightest change of routine.

As Jessica began to study the statistical numbers from the Chicago high schools, she noticed that every year a few of the seniors simply vanished. They didn't report to school on their Total Care Assignment Day or thereafter. Of course, their Pytalon drugged parents knew nothing about them, only barely aware they had a child or two. As far as the system was concerned, those students had vanished. True, the AP-cops began searching for them. Occasionally, they discovered the run-away students, who were then implanted and drugged appropriately. Thus, Jessica had to correlate the AP-cops arrests with those who had turned up missing on Assignment Day.

As Beth's long running program continued to spit out possible "goofs" in the implanting processes, Jessica continued to satisfy her curiosity regarding the small number of dropouts from high school. After a private chat with the professor, she knew he was behind the disappearance of some of the brighter students from high schools around the country. He was recruiting for his Phoenix group each year. She recalled how they had done the same thing with Greg, the inventor and now Lisa's husband. Some of those who vanished were now in the "underground," helping.

She decided to correlate their grades with the disappearances there in Chicago. After spending a few hours at it, she couldn't see any real pattern. Some students who had gone missing were bright, but others were not. At last unable to make further headway, she shared her results with Beth, Tilly, Amanda, and Petra, hoping they would have some suggestions for her to follow.

"You're going to have to visit the high schools and observe," Tilly answered her pleas for help. "Nothing beats direct observation, Jessica. That's what Wart always does or rather used to do. Perhaps we should pay some of the Chicago high schools a quiet visit and see what we can discover."

Cleverly, Tilly was suggesting a trip outside into the field, something she truly was now missing. "Well," she justified, "Juan can come along as our bodyguard."

Just then, all four received a page to join a conference call. "What's up?" Beth asked, as she and the others quickly joined the professor, Petra, and Lady Persephone.

"Terrible news, bloody terrible," Lady Persephone answered. "Bo Bin and Han Lin have escaped! Yes, I find that incredible, but they have. They knocked the teen to the floor when she was getting them ready for bed, and they knocked her out. She didn't wake until late the next morning and has a concussion. She'll be all right though."

"But the house was locked," Beth protested.

"They smashed the front window out and must have fallen out of it. Bloody hell, when I get my hands on those two, they will regret their escape!" she said vehemently. She calmed down. "I have search parties out now looking for them. They couldn't have gotten far. We'll soon have them back in custody. Don't worry."

They chatted a bit more, but Beth was worried. Those two were psychopaths. While she had thought they were completely helpless, now she wasn't so sure. They had managed to escape by themselves. Her opinion of their resourcefulness rose considerably, and she didn't share Lady Persephone's confidence that the two women would soon be found and recaptured.

***

Late October, Petra had only one more high school to visit and deliver her assembly message. Still Lady Persephone had sent no word of the capture of the two women. It had been weeks since their escape. Somehow, the women had simply vanished without a trace. Lady Persephone was now operating on the theory that someone had found the two helpless women and had either captured them or were holding them for their own pleasure or amusement, though she didn't discount entirely that someone had taken them in, giving them sanctuary and the help they needed.

With their long running program scouring the psych database automatically and sending email warnings of the discovered "goofs" performing nicely and without any intervention on their part, Beth and Jessica were extremely bored. Tilly and Amanda also wanted to get out, tired of being cooped up in their safe house. Winter would soon come, and all four knew they'd be more or less stuck inside until spring. Hence, they decided to tag along with Petra as she made her last high school appearance. There, they could look into Jessica's mysterious "disappearance" of a few seniors each year.

Juan packed his many guns and knives and drove them to Chicago, where they joined Petra, Chan, and Yan in her office. After some light chat, they plus Petra's two Feds bodyguards headed up to the roof and the waiting EMAC.

"We're going up north to New Saint Patricks," Petra explained, as the small group took the relatively short trip to the school. While Chan, Petra, and Yan handled the senior assembly, the other four met with the four women job councilors.

"Well, yes, you're quite right, Jessica. Each year there are always a couple of seniors who miss their placement date. Sometimes, they're too ill to make it and take a rain check, but yes, some never do show up," a woman named Phyllis explained.

"So what do you do with them?" Tilly asked.

"We forward all information about them to the AP-cops, who then track them down," the glassy-eyed woman replied.

"I see. And do they always find them?" Tilly probed.

"Well, not always, as I understand it. Why?" Phyllis asked, struggling hard to maintain a proper conversation with these EE women. She always had to struggle to maintain conversations that did not relate directly to students and their future jobs.

They chatted a bit more, but Tilly was not getting anything useful from her or the other three. Jessica tried another approach, sensing how difficult the four women found discussing matters not strictly within their implanted behavior patterns. "So how do the students learn about potential job opportunities?" she asked.

The instant relief that Phyllis and the others felt was plainly obvious to the four. "Well, that we can answer. You see, during their senior year, following the Total Care Program, companies send in their people, who look over the student records, and request to meet with those that appear to be likely candidates for their available employment needs." She chatted a good deal about how successful this was in matching students with appropriate jobs when they graduated.

"Yes, the company representatives have to be registered with the school. I can give you a list of those who are allowed to send their personnel here to meet with the students," Phyllis was happy to make a suggestion she could handle. Shortly, she emailed the listing to Jessica. "There, my dear, the list of companies is on its way to your computer. I hope this helps you some. I do hate to lose even one student, you know. Sanity is doing a good job, but I can't do a good job if they don't show up for their appointments. How sad," she added. She also handed Jessica a printout of the companies.

Tilly and Jessica browsed the list, while they waited patiently for Petra to finish her speech and question and answer period. "Well, most of these companies I recognize," Tilly commented. "Wait a second, there are three here I've never heard of. Beth, have you any way of finding out about these three?"

"Sure, I have a virtually transparent computer sitting on my lap right now," she said rather sarcastically. All four looked at her lap and broke out into a hearty laugh. Smiling, she said, "Sure, I'll get on to it as soon as we get home, Tilly. Maybe sooner, if I can get to one of Petra's computers or ours in our Feds office. Let's see what Petra wants to do next."

As the large group stepped outside the sprawling school, the late afternoon sun was quite bright. Tilly felt invigorated being active even this little. She missed her "fieldwork" times.

Petra was rather fired up, on an adrenaline high from her talk. "This has been quite an experience for me and so productive. I just know we're on the right track, getting a new generation out of the psych's hands. The students are welcoming this with a great deal of enthusiasm. Incredible!"

The group moved slowly towards their EMAC in the staff lot. Juan spotted a dozen Chinese men milling around not far from their vehicle. "Trouble ahead! Watch yourselves!" he called out, calling everyone's attention to the men. Instinctively, Petra reached for her gun, but found nothing happening. No arms, no gun around her waist. She stumbled slightly, causing Chan and Yan to grab her to keep her from taking a spill. Just as Juan pulled out his gun, the ten men, who appeared to be in their twenties, rushed the group, firing Tasers at them.

Juan fired two rounds, downing one man. The much slower security guards had only gotten their weapons drawn, when the rushing men reached them. To Juan's amazement, they attacked using martial arts skills, much as Lady Persephone used. One knocked his gun from his hand, and the fight began in earnest. Beside him, the security guards were greatly outclassed, but one somehow managed to get in a blow that knocked one of their attackers to the ground.

Not to be left out, Petra stabbed at the man's head with her steel spike. While she did manage to kill him, she also fell onto the pavement rather hard, pulling Chan and Yan down with her. Juan got another attacker with his knife before taking a Taser in his back. A minute later, Tasers struck all the others. Jessica, Amanda, Beth, Tilly, and Petra blacked out. Beside them, Chan, Yan, Juan, and the two security guards lay unconscious as well. None heard the AP-cops' whistle or the siren sounds of the coming emergency vehicles.

"Oh my head! The women!" Juan exclaimed, rousing. He was sitting up, an emergency responder was squatting before him, dabbing at a bleeding wound on his forehead. He jumped up to see what the situation was. Three of their attackers were covered up. Nearby, others were helping rouse Chan and Yan, while the security men were still being tended to, being raised onto stretchers with broken limbs, he assumed from the care the responders were using. "Where are the other five women?" Juan yelled loudly.

"Sir calm down. These are all that we found when we arrived. You have a possible concussion," an AP-cop answered him.

"No, they have kidnaped the Supreme Commander of the Feds and four others. Phone, I need a phone to call the Feds immediately!" Juan fairly screamed. At the mention of the Feds, the AP-cop's face whitened a little, and he hastily handed Juan his cell phone.

"Lech! Get down here immediately! They've kidnaped Petra, Beth, Jessica, Tilly, and Amanda. Yes, your two security guards are alive, but probably have some broken bones. Yes, I got two and Petra and a guard killed another. Get down here at once!" Juan fairly screamed into the phone before calming down.

By the time Lech and a squad of Feds arrived, Juan was back to battery. Lech found him going from attacker's body to attacker's body, taking a picture of each and examining them. "Any news?" Lech said, his voice displaying some slight worry, so unusual for one on Pytalon.

Chan was holding her heard. "I can't see anything from Petra's body. I think it is unconscious, Lech. I stabbed that one with my heel—Petra's heel that is. Who the hell were these Chinese men?"

"Looking into that now," Lech replied. One of his men was using the portable fingerprint machine, sampling the three dead men. "You all right, Juan?"

"More or less. We could have all be killed, but it seems they were after the five women for some reason. They must have wanted them alive or they would have simply gunned us all down," Juan theorized. "Say, look at these tattoos on their right upper arms. Have you ever seen them before?"

Lech looked, but shook his head. "I'll run them in the Feds system and see if there is a hit on them. These men aren't in the system—no fingerprints on file, but then so few are anymore. I best get a hotline setup in case they're being held for ransom."

"I don't think ransom is why they were taken, but that can't hurt," Juan replied, rubbing his head. "Chan, let's get you and Yan back to Petra's office and see if we can find out anything about these tattoos. That's the only clue we have right now. I also need to make some phone calls." He gathered up the many purses, while Chan and Yan, holding on to each other, made their way to the EMAC.

Some twenty minutes later, the three headed down the elevator from the rooftop of the Feds building. "Chan, you see what you can find out about these tattoos. All three men had them. I'll notify the others of the kidnaping," Juan requested.

"On it. Give me the phone with the photos you took. Here, use mine to make your calls while I download the photos. Yan, fix us something to drink, juice is fine," Chan took charge. She was, after all, Petra.

Juan notified Lady Persephone and the professor of the abductions, relating what little he knew thus far. After he hung up, he called out, "Greg is activating their locator beacons for a brief minute to get a fix on where the five of them are at and will let us know."

"Excellent. Say, this is weird. Come take a look," Chan called out, rather surprised at what she'd found. Juan came around to look at her monitor. "That's the tattoo used to mark members of the Trikuza mafia. They were thought to be extinct, but I guess not. The last known entry in our Feds database is at least fifty years old. It says Master Lao Bing might be the head of the organization, but there is no real certainty on that rumor. We have no idea how large or powerful this mafia actually is, Juan. We thought they were extinct. I guess not. They operate mainly out of China, if these old records are still true."

"China? Why doesn't that surprise me? You don't suppose that somehow the Lin brothers managed to get back there from London, do you? Armless EE women?" Juan looked at Chan in complete disbelief over what he was suggesting. Yet, there was the connection: China."

Chan bit her lip, as Petra was wont to do. "You know, the Lins did have Chinese EE women's bodies. If they somehow managed to find some Trikuza members in London, they could well have taken them back to China. It is possible, Juan, but where would they have taken the women and why?"

"Revenge," Juan answered. "Those Lins were geniuses and psychopaths too. They did swear to get revenge on those who captured them. I best give Lady Persephone an update. She could well be in danger of being attacked as well."

A bit later, Lady Persephone replied to Juan's warning. "Yes, I'm already aware of that. My stewards have told me there have been two suspicious Chinese men hanging around my estate in Sussex. I'm not there, best not say where I am, but keep me posted, especially if you get a location them." She refused to say more, and Juan got the sense she was extremely angry.

The professor called back a half-hour later with the news they were in transit, somewhere just off the coast of California, heading westwards. Juan decided all signs pointed to China and began to prepare to go after them. Lech joined them, and Chan explained what she and Juan had found out thus far.

When he saw confirmation of the tattoos tying these men to the Trikuza, Lech collapsed into a chair! "What's the matter, Lech?" Chan asked.

"Boss, we don't stand a chance in hell of dealing with Trikuza, not since we all were forced onto Pytalon. Before that, we might have had some outside chance with those killing machines, but not as we are now. It's a miracle the two guards are still alive!" Lech displayed far more emotion than he ever had before, which Chan correctly interpreted as meaning Lech was extremely worried about this unexpected situation. "We don't stand a ghost of a chance against them," he muttered, sinking into apathy.

"I know. We all thought they were extinct some fifty years ago. I guess they've been very successful at hiding underground all these years," Chan replied. "Well, I'm going to throw the entire Feds at them, just as soon as we have a fix on their location! What I can't understand is why would the Trikuza want to kidnap these five women? Makes no sense. We didn't see any connections between the Lin brothers and the Trikuza. How strange this is!"

Juan asked, "Could the Lin brothers have hired the Trikuza to kidnap the women? Is that feasible?"

"Well, that's feasible, but it probably cost the Lins a very high price. Besides, we have frozen their bank accounts—well, at least the ones we know about, that is," she amended herself. "Still, that's the only explanation that makes any sense. I'm sending an alert to all the Feds in the world. I intend to hit them with everything that we have!"

***

Petra came to, rather startling Chan, who closed her eyes and began paying close attention to her kidnaped body. She'd known something was happening to it hours before; she'd gotten an excruciating headache. It was dark, very black, and she assumed it must be nighttime and that she was underground perhaps. No blindfold. She couldn't feel anything around her head, but she was sitting up. She wiggled a little, felt a strange sensation, and realized she must be wearing those erotic panties that Beth had shown her. Where was she? She strained her ears and heard soft, distant voices and the sounds of labored breathing close to her. She leaned a little and felt a body next to hers. It moaned a little.

Then some awful smelling odor struck her nose, and she jerked back from it. "Stop. What is that? Where am I?" she called out. "Turn on the lights for God's sake!" Next to her, she heard four others being awakened. The voices sounded strange, they were not those of her companions. Who were they?

"Ah, awake at last!" she heard the voice of Bao and then Huan. They must be sitting close to her. "Welcome Petra, Beth, Jessica, Tilly, and Amanda. While we're lacking only Persephone Briton to make this little sextet complete, you five will have to do for now until she joins you. Yes, it is us, Bao and Huan or Bo Bin and Han if you prefer. You didn't think you had stopped us, did you? Ha. We are geniuses." Both women laughed sarcastically for a bit.

"Oh, I didn't answer your question, Miss Petra. Yes, the lights are on fully. However, the nice green glass eyes of yours cannot see any light. All five of you are blind, though you have identical green glass eyes, and your four companions sitting beside you also have no arms and have nice young Chinese EE women's bodies as well. We've taken the liberty to refresh your wonderful EE implants, but don't fret, thanks to Beth here, we know how you may satisfactorily pleasure yourselves, now that you cannot see. If one dildo is good, think of how delightful two are going to be?" Both women again broke into a hideous round of laughter.

Huan added, "All you have to do is to walk around a bit." She roared with laughter.

"I decided to be humane and not make you have to suffer the pain and lengthy healing process in your shoulders. This way, you four may more fully and readily appreciate your capture and new bodies. We put your four companions into already prepared bodies. I do hope you enjoy them. By the way, there is no going back for the four of you. Already your old bodies have been prepared for the next batch of troublemakers. Their arms and eyes have already been removed, you see. Oh, you can't see. So sorry." Again, the two women laughed sarcastically.

Bao continued, "You Petra have taught us a very valuable lesson. While we thought that merely lacking arms would be sufficient to keep one out of creating more troubles, we now know that is not true. However, by being blinded as well, that should do the trick nicely. Hence we're now fully prepared for all future troublemakers, what with your four new bodies in the stasis pods, healing up." Once more the two women laughed.

Petra couldn't see her four dear friends, but accepted what Bao was saying as the truth. She took a gamble and asked, "Now that you have us, could you answer a few questions we have? We know how you escaped the Sussex cottage, but how did you get away? Where are we? Have you rebuilt your old laboratory?"

Huan couldn't withhold herself. Laughing, she said, "We have many powerful friends. The Trikuza make great allies. Where are you? Why, you are right there sitting on a couch. We haven't had time to rebuild our former laboratory. Always be prepared, Petra, just as you five obviously were not. We're using our second backup facility, and we have more." She laughed again.

"So what are you going to do with us?" Petra asked, fighting off her headache.

"Why, we're going to do nothing for you. You five are in a living quarters, which are much like those in the facility that you raided and destroyed. Here you will stay and live out your long lives, though we have one young teen here who will feed you and assist you with dressing and such. Otherwise, you're free to wander all over the facility and see it all for yourselves. Oh, I'm sorry. I guess you won't be able actually to see it." Huan laughed heartily once more, amused by her own taunts.

Bao's voice then said, "If your heads are throbbing, then I suggest you rise and walk around some to pleasure yourselves. We found that always gets rid of these EE women's headaches. Feel free to recite your litanies at any time. We have work to do now. See you around sometime. Oh, I keep forgetting, you can't see anymore!" Bao now laughed rather hysterically. Petra heard the two women rising and moving away from them, still laughing. Shortly, though, their laughs ceased, and the five heard them quietly reciting their litany.

That triggered their own renewed implants. All five found themselves unable to avoid reciting their own new PDH implanted words. In the back of her mind, Jessica noted the wording hadn't changed. She knew in time she could get these new implants desensitized. Once they finished, all five knew they had to pleasure themselves. Their migraines were throbbing. One by one, they tried to lunge forward, recalling how Petra had done it before she had Chan and Yan there to help her rise gracefully. Unable to see, they all wobbled wildly, trying to get their balance on their toes.

Waves of terror swept over all five. They took the tiniest of steps, wiggling their torsos to keep their balance. Even these slight physical motions had the desired effect with their special panties. Shortly, they had to sit back down, falling onto the couch. "I can't live this way!" Beth whispered. The others echoed her words, but were utterly helpless to do anything at all but sit.

Later, they guessed it must be suppertime; their stomachs were growling. "Is our helper going to lead us to the table?" Jessica whispered, her voice shaking from the terror she felt.

"God, I hope so. We don't have any idea where it's at. If we fall, what will we smash into?" Tilly added, trying hard to suppress her ever-swelling fear.

At last, someone was close to them. Unfortunately, she was speaking in Chinese, and none of the five understood her. At last, Petra felt an arm trying to urge her to rise. "I think she wants us to get up," she whispered and gave a mighty lunge.

She overdid it and would have fallen hard, but the unseen woman caught her just in time. Standing there in total darkness, Petra felt frozen to the spot, but she heard their helper getting the others up. Eventually, she felt a slight push on her back and attempted to take a very tiny step in that direction.

By the time they were finally allowed to sit down, their panties were soaked. They performed their function very well. All five felt utterly drained, but starving. One by one, their unseen helper did feed them, but it was awful. They were forced to wait for the touch of something on their lips before they opened their mouths. To say that they were humiliated would be a gross understatement.

Sometime later, when they were lying in a bed, Beth whispered, "It's all my fault. I gave them the panties that allowed them to get the needed pleasure. If I hadn't done that, they would never have been able to escape. I'm so sorry everyone."

"It isn't your fault," Petra whispered back sternly. "It's the fault of Bo Bin and Han. We have to hang on somehow until help arises. Don't lose hope. Remember Chan." She dared not say more because Bo Bin or Han might be watching them or listening in to their conversations. She had no way of knowing they weren't, rather they were off fighting their own implants.

***

"Has Greg got a fix on their location yet?" Juan asked the professor. He'd called him when Chan began to appear "elsewhere." He suspected Petra needed all her attention on her kidnaped body right now. Yan looked scared for Chan, though.

"Yes, they're in Peking, China again. He's emailing you their coordinates now. Hold on. He says they're moving once more. He'll send along a revised set shortly when they stop moving. Lady Persephone is already getting close to their location. The Wolf is on his way with a dozen of his men as well. Has Chan really mobilized the entire Feds force worldwide?"

"Aye, that she has. They are planning to meet as a group in LA and in Singapore. From there, they'll rendezvous over the coordinates and make a massive sweep. We're to leave here shortly, that is, if Chan can be moved. Wait, she is rousing. I'll call you right back," Juan said hastily, moving to Chan's side. She was sitting behind the large desk filled with monitors and microphones.

440

"Oh dear God! It's far worse than we've imagined. She's been blinded too. The other four are in new armless Chinese bodies and blind as well. They've all been re-implanted as well. As long as I stay focused on this body, the implant isn't bothering me too badly, but when Petra has to move, it takes all my attention. God, this is horrid! We have to get to them at once."

"Okay, it's time to leave. Lech has the Air Liner loaded and ready. We're rendezvousing with all the US Feds in LA. Come on; let's get topside to the EMAC before Petra there needs your attention again," Juan encouraged her. Soon, they were airborne on their way to LA.

***

Lady Persephone had spent the past many weeks in China, traveling from remote town to remote town, looking for more EE women who died while being implanted. Already she'd recovered five such women, but had been unable to save another six. During this time, she'd also made an observation. Here only the prettiest young eighteen-year-old teens were selected to become EE women. Hence, if she ever needed to transfer any of her friends into one of these, they wouldn't lack for beauty at least. She'd only recovered one male body, however. Those were harder to acquire, but she didn't know why, but perhaps it had something to do with the different electrical resistance of the male and female bodies. Already, she'd discovered that female bodies had a significantly lower resistance to electricity. Did that mean females were more susceptible to the electrical currents being shot through their heads during the implant? She didn't know.

When she heard the shocking news of the Lin brother's escape from her teen caretaker, Lady Persephone fumed, cursing herself for her obviously failed belief that the men or women were helpless. "I should've known they weren't as helpless as it might seem. Just look at Petra. Damn, damn, damn. Now I have to put this to rights somehow. It's my fault."

Later on, Juan relayed the awful news that the Trikuza had been involved. After a quick database search on her part, Lady Persephone sat back shocked. If the Feds alone attempted to fight these martial arts killers, the Feds would be wiped out! "Bloody Hell, they'd be wiped out even if they weren't Pytalon zombies! How much worse can this get? They're supposed to be extinct!"

After that, she learned Chan had called up every man in the Feds worldwide organization! She knew these fanatical murderers, these Trikuza men, would butcher them all. "I have to act first or they are all dead men! Greg, send me coordinates please," she yelled to the window of her EMAC. The longer she had to wait, the more anxious she became. At last, she took a deep breath and began to focus her energies. She changed into her all black vigilante outfit and armed herself with every weapon she'd brought along with her.

Finally, Greg sent the coordinates, and she fired up her EMAC, heading there at top speed. She was only about a hundred miles away from the heart of Peking. Soon, she told herself, soon. Then came Greg's second call. They had been moved again, new coordinates. "Well, they aren't too far from where they were at," she said to her window. She sat her EMAC down some distance from the last known location. It was nighttime and she passed along the deserted streets, a mere shadow in the night. She knew if Trikuza were about, they would detect her anyway. She'd face that when it came. Right now, she wanted to find the location where they were being held.

At last, her handheld geo-locator indicated she was within three feet of the women. "This can't be right! There is nothing here but an alleyway with some dumpsters. Oh my God, have they all been murdered and their bodies dumped here?" she whispered, her anger seething. She quietly opened the nearest one to the coordinates Greg had sent. She used a small pen light to peer into the dark container. She gasped. There lay a jumble of arms! A lone rat was dining on one. Focusing to prevent gagging, she carefully counted them. Eight arms. That meant all four women were definitely in a very bad way.

Quietly, she moved back to her EMAC and entered the original set of coordinates. That location was some six blocks further way from the dumpsters. She sent a quick text message saying the current coordinates only yielded the four women's arms. They had been amputated and now there was no way to locate where they were being held, unless that first location was still valid. Lady Persephone had to know. Quietly, she exited her EMAC and headed off to inspect the original location Greg had sent her.

When she came within two blocks, she halted, spotting a dark cloaked man watching the street. Her senses heightened.

Observe, she thought. Soon, she spotted another man further on down the street. She backtracked and approached from a different direction. Again, she spotted a lookout about two blocks from the target location, which she still couldn't see. She backed away to think.

From the last set of messages, she estimated the Feds were at least a day away, maybe more. *Do I dare do this one alone? I've never backed down from what is right. One at a time, they will fall. Send these Trikuza a message before the Feds come. Right.* Resolved, she began her first move in the grand game.

The lookout was being lackadaisical about his duties, she noted. He left a drainpipe unwatched. Foolish man. Silently, she began climbing up the pipe. Simple matter really. Then stealthily, like a cat stalking a bird, she crept across the rooftop. Positioning her body above his, the cat pounced, her feet landing on the backside of the top of his head. A soft cracking sound told all, as the cat landed, back flipped, and drew her blade. There was no need; the body slumped to the ground, already dead. The cat sprang back into the shadows as silently as she'd come, leaving an Ace of Diamonds marking her prey.

Thrice more, the cat stalked and struck, before she stood before what appeared to be a single story warehouse of no importance whatsoever. Yet, she knew this was where her friends had once been, before having their arms removed. The cat chose not to enter, for a cat and a box do not mix well. Instead, the cat chose to expand her message. Only this once would the mice fail to be on their highest guard. She took out another six Trikuza, leaving her calling card with each. However, on the last card, she left an additional message. It said simply: Call This Number.

Minutes later, the cat entered her lair and secured its door. Nearly silently the EM motors kicked in, lifting the vehicle up into the sky and away from this location. Lady Persephone set the autopilot to hover and put the disposable cell phone out on her passenger table and sipped a strong black tea. She was patient, but she knew she had to pull this one off. If not, the Feds were doomed.

Around dawn, the phone rang. She picked it up on the second ring. "Glad you chose to call," she spoke confidently.

"Ten. Impressive, Persephone, the Assassin. Compliments. What message are you sending? I'm listening," a voice said calmly in her ear.

"You are interfering in a matter that will cause you immense grief. Check the skies nearby. You might wish to slip away, at least in part. Already what was hidden has been uncovered. Alas, the cat cannot be put back into the bag. Yet, much may be saved if right choices are made," she replied, carefully choosing her words and speaking both slowly and clearly.

"Cats are hard to bag, but then what of agreements of value?" the voice replied.

"Agreements are only as strong as the makers and live just as long," she countered, now grasping his meaning and intent.

"A wise man looks before he acts. I shall look." He hung up. She knew better than to try a back trace on the caller. He'd be using a throwaway phone, just as she did. She dropped the phone onto the floor and crushed it with her boot.

After sipping more tea, she whispered to herself, "Well, I have either saved the Feds or doomed the Feds, but then they were doomed already. Sleep time for this cat." She set her system's communications to sound a loud beep on any incoming calls and retired.

***

"Damned impressive, Lech," Juan exclaimed. Twenty-four hours had passed and the giant fleet of thirty Air Liners hovered over Peking, awaiting the arrival of Lady Persephone and her EMAC. It was nine o'clock in the morning.

"Yes, this time, they shall not escape us," Lech replied, a slight hint of enthusiasm in his otherwise monotone. "Ah, an EMAC is descending towards us now."

"Lady Persephone calling Chan-Petra or Lech," her voice sounded over the comm speakers.

Lech looked at Chan. "Okay, as Supreme Commander, I should take this, but put it on speaker phone." He flipped a switched and nodded. "Go ahead. Chan-Petra here. The Feds are ready to land. What news?"

"Okay then. We need to check out that apparently abandoned warehouse directly below me—at the original coordinates Greg sent us. The Trikuza were there in force last night, guarding the place. Our prey hasn't left by surface means that my sensors could detect. Tell Lech and the other Feds captains these Trikuza are extremely competent fighters and more than a match for themselves, even if they weren't severely hindered by Pytalon."

Lech flinched; he already knew that, but hearing it from another only added to his worry. She continued, "I took the liberty of sending a very clear message to the Trikuza last night. If they heeded my warning, you may find only a few token Trikuza there to save face, but more than willing to kill as many Feds as they can before they're slain. If they didn't heed my warning, there's sure to be a blood bath. In that case, I'll help as I can. When do we strike?"

Chan replied, "Now is a good time. Petra is sitting on a couch and doesn't need my attention. Let's do it. Lech, order everyone to set down on the streets surrounding this warehouse. Approach it with extreme caution and use the dozer on the entrance."

"You won't need the dozer on the entrance," Lady Persephone hastily interrupted. "Once inside, you might. The facility must be underground."

"Got it. Okay, let's do this!" Chan said enthusiastically. Lech issued the orders, and the thirty Air Liners descended onto the streets, causing widespread panic among the men and women in the crowded streets and damaging the MTE system all around this zone. That couldn't be helped in this circumstance, Chan noted.

Lady Persephone joined Chan, Juan, and Yan, along with Lech and his Chicago squad. Slowly, they advanced towards the warehouse. Lady Persephone noticed the dead Trikuza bodies were nowhere to be seen. Further, they met no resistance as the approximately two hundred fifty men approached the only entrance of the single story structure. She whispered to Lech, "Warn them to stay alert once they enter the building. That's where you're likely to find any remaining Trikuza." He did so, notifying the various captains.

One captain led his squad through the doors. All at once, gunfire erupted, and Chan spotted flashes of bright steel. "Swords," Lady Persephone called out. Another squad raced inside, and then another and then another. Finally, one captain called out, "Clear! We got them!" When they finally entered, they found five dead Trikuza men, all older men. Lady Persephone noted quickly and thought to herself, "Sacrifices." Twenty Feds were dead or severely wounded though. Medics were tending to the wounded Feds.

"Four to one, holy crap!" Lech exclaimed, overcoming his Pytalon daze. He was shocked. "Damn, blast doors again, bring in the dozers," he yelled. Ten minutes later, the wounded had been evacuated and on their way to a local hospital, and two dozers approached the blast doors, navigating around an EMAC parked in the center of the empty warehouse. Five minutes later, the blast doors were rubble. Captains with their squads poured through the breach. Some took the elevator while others charged down the stairs. Within minutes, some twenty-eight squads were charging through the four underground floors, calling out what they were finding. Lady Persephone kept her fingers crossed, hoping and praying there were no Trikuza lurking below ground.

Only when the last squad called in "Clear" did she relax and her group entered the secured building. She had a sinking feeling about what they would find. Chan already had a good idea from what her Petra body had heard and felt.

The Wolf hastily rushed over to join them. "Four to one. God, these Trikuza are a nasty bunch. I think Jessica has found some of her high school dropouts. Any word on our people yet?"

Chan whispered, "Wolf, it's really bad this time. Brace yourself." To the others, she said, "Okay, into the lion's den we go. We have to find Bao and Huan in this menagerie, so trust no one."

Chapter 29—Now What Do We Do?

"Just who is who? This is one god-awful mess," Lech declared. He and the many Feds finished an exhaustive search of the underground foundation, rounding up every person found. All were gathered in the basement living quarters, where Chan and the others now had to sort out what was what. Adding to the confusion, Bao and Huan insisted that a couple of their helper men were Bo Bin and Han and that they were just hired helpers. Of course, the men said the opposite.

Chan, Juan, Lady Persephone, and the Wolf found their five friends nervously sitting upright on a couch. "Juan? Is that you? I'm really, really scared! I can't see and I can't do anything and oh no!" Beth called out approximately where she heard his voice, but then began reciting the cursed EE Woman's implant script once again.

"Yes, Beth I'm here, the Wolf, Lady Persephone, Chan, Yan, we're all here. The place is secured now. We have one big mess this time. You five just sit tight while we sort it out," Juan said trying to sound as calm and confident as he could, but he was anything but calm.

Lady Persephone recognized the women's terror at once. She added quickly, "Beth, Tilly, Amanda, Jessica. Don't worry. No matter what you're feeling right now, I will be able to set things right. I need time. You'll only have to endure this awful plight for a little while longer. I promise you."

"Thanks, My Lady. I've never ever been so scared in my life," Beth admitted. "We've been implanted again too, making it so much worse. I can hardly think straight."

"We know. You just relax a while," she said softly.

Beth and the others heard a confusion of voices around them. "What's happening?" she asked.

"You handle things. I'll explain what's going on to them," the Wolf volunteered, wholly out of his league. Never had he seen such a situation and frankly was more than overwhelmed by what he was seeing.

"Beth, the Feds have rounded up everyone and have ushered them here in this living room area, where we are. There are four men and four women who appear to be whole. I mean they have their arms and eyes. Some are wearing white uniforms. Right now, they are trying to figure out which of those eight are Bo Bin and Han. It is crazy. They are all claiming not to be the two but pointing to others as being them. Some of the women are pointing to the men, saying they are the Lin brothers, but the men are denying it, pointing to some of the women saying they are them. What a mess."

He went on, "Then, there are six armless men and three other armless women besides you five. All nine have their eyes still, but two of the women are screaming that two of the women with arms have stolen their bodies. They are in rather a panic state if you ask me."

Petra spoke up, "Tell Chan that we can recognize Bao and Huan. They're women still, not men. We can recognize them from their voices."

"That will help a lot," Chan called out from an indeterminate distance away. Beth just could not tell how far. "Okay, you four women, over here. Stand before these five." Beth heard footsteps approaching her. "Good. Now then what do you want them to say, Petra?"

"By the way, there is no going back for the four of you. Have them each say that sentence, one by one," she replied.

Chan tried to get the first one to comply, but the woman apparently didn't speak English nor understand what was wanted of her. The other three followed suit. "Apparently these four don't speak English, Chan explained, growing more frustrated by the minute.

Petra fumed. She suspected two of these women were her tormentors. She said loudly and with authority, "Okay. Then, Chan, I order you to take all four of these women and shoot them in their heads. Kill all four of them!"

Chan knew what she was doing and watched the reactions of the four women. Two continued to look fearful, but with forced smiles. They simply didn't understand what was being said. Two others visibly flinched and one started to protest. "Ah, these two. They are Bao and Huan! Tie them up and get them out of my sight for now!" Chan ordered. Two Feds did as asked.

"You fiends! You can't do this to us. You'll all be slain mercilessly soon. Help is on the way, you'll see!" Bao fairly screamed at them.

"Excuse me, Supreme Commander." Petra recognized that Chinese voice. He was the Feds translator she'd put in charge of the Peking Feds after the previous raid. Of course,

Chan now knew this too. He continued, "Those two armless EE women over there claim that those two women you've just identified as Bao and Huan have stolen their bodies. They say they're volunteer workers here, and those two bodies are theirs and were supposed to be in a stasis pod until their contract was up, at which point they would get them back. They're most distressed their bodies have been stolen and that they are stuck in these bodies. Does this make even the remotest sense, Supreme Commander?"

"Yes, in fact it does. Keep track of those two women. Tell them we'll try to set things straight as soon as we sort everything out," Chan replied. "Can you chat with the other armless EE woman and get her story. I suspect she too is a volunteer with a contract."

He bowed and did so, shortly indicating Chan was correct.

The Wolf explained, "Well, we have the women here all figured out. It seems Bao and Huan have stolen a pair of their own volunteer women's bodies out of stasis pods. Interesting, eh. Now they are trying to sort out the men. That should be easier, I hope."

It was. Two men were technicians and two were caretakers for the seven men. "Now they are going upstairs to the place where the stasis pods are located to see what's there. Hang in there, gang," the Wolf explained.

Sometime later, the five could not tell how long, Lady Persephone returned to them. "I have some partially good news for you four. We found your bodies in the stasis pods. True, your arms had been amputated. I found them in a nearby dumpster last night. However, the good news is their eyes are still intact."

"That's something. At least we'll be able to see," Tilly admitted.

"Well, there's more and it's not good for these volunteers. There is only one other woman in the stasis pods; she is currently the other woman without arms. I'll be restoring her to her body soon. Bao and Huan stole two other volunteer women's arms, so I'm going to have to transfer those two out of their stolen bodies and put the volunteers back into their original bodies."

"Where will you put Bao and Huan?" Tilly asked. "How about these bodies? Serve them right," she lashed out. Lady Persephone laughed and agreed with her.

Lady Persephone continued, "Six of the male volunteers can be returned to their original bodies as well. However, one volunteer's body is missing. I'm going to have to figure out what to do with him. Petra, your situation is unique. This is still your original body, the one that was kidnaped. I can't temporarily restore your sight. I'm not entirely sure what to do for you in the immediate future. Anyway, I'll get started on the transference process right away, starting with you four. I hope the pain of the surgery will be bearable. Hopefully, they have healed some while in the stasis pods. At least you will have your sight back for now."

Three hours later, the four were back in their original bodies. Their shoulders throbbed, but were already healing well, thanks to the time spent in the stasis pods. While they were taken back down to the living quarters and fed lunch, compliments of the Chinese cook and the other three helpers, she transferred Bao and Huan into two of the vacated blind bodies. They didn't go quietly, but screamed and cursed until the transfer process began which knocked them out.

By suppertime, Lady Persephone had six male volunteers restored to their rightful bodies, along with the three female volunteers. The Chinese Feds captain promised them their wages would soon be placed into their bank accounts, once the Lin brother's funds were located. The remaining male, whose body had been taken by Master Yao Bing although no one knew this fact at this time, chose to be put out of his misery. He had long ago lost all will to live, even though he was originally a volunteer.

After supper, half of the Feds left, while the remaining men stood guard in case the Trikuza attempted to retake the foundation. The other half began dismantling the machines, storing them in an Air Liner. Once again, they would be taken to Lady Persephone's castle. Meanwhile, the large group of friends dined together, helping the five to eat.

Trying to make the best of her current situation, especially with her dearest friends, Beth said bravely, "Well, perhaps it is time that we four got our feet fixed up. Lisa manages really well and so has Petra for that matter. If we could use our feet like Lisa does, we probably can get by somehow."

Lady Persephone purposely kept quiet. Just how would the four and Petra react now? How badly did they want to keep their mutilated bodies? She had several solutions available, though she'd not mentioned them just yet.

"Yes, Lisa is amazing. If she can do it and get by so well, if we had our feet repaired, then I'm willing to try to learn," Jessica added, fighting back tears.

Tilly, though, spotted a facial flicker on Lady Persephone. "Say, My Lady, you've been mostly silent on this. You were thinking about such things happening to us. Do you have some suggestions? Perhaps you can start desensitizing us soon."

She grinned mischievously. "Ah, found out at last. Yes, I do have several solutions on board my EMAC. I've spent the past many weeks roaming around the outlying towns looking for casualties of the psychs and their antiquated implant machines, the old Model I. I have six EE women in stasis pods on my ship, one for each of you, along with three males as well. If I transferred you into these new bodies, you would be young Chinese EE women, looking very different than you do now."

"Great! We'd have arms again," Beth exclaimed, fighting from having to recite the litany once more.

"Yes, but you would look very different to your spouses," Lady Persephone pointed out. Four faces sank some.

"She's right. I suppose we'd just have to get used to looking vastly different to each other," Jessica admitted with a sigh. "What do they look like? Can we see them before we decide and all that?"

She laughed and said, "Of course. I only took the prettiest and best ones, but what concerns me most is your current bodies. Lisa does very well, so if you do go ahead and get your feet handled, perhaps you would also like to keep these."

"Say, what about having both, as Petra and Chan has?" Tilly asked. "I'm really partial to this one and Amanda's. I suppose if she and I looked completely different, then that wouldn't make a big difference in how we feel towards each other. We'd still be ourselves, just look vastly different to each other. Petra has been doing great with two. Can we try that as well?"

Lady Persephone smiled, "I was hoping you might suggest this. I'd prefer you four at least to try to handle two bodies each. I really don't have all that much faith in this whole darn transference thing. Just how long does the transference last? We know it does for years, but what if there are some as yet unknown factors that enter? This process has never been done before, and I don't trust the Lin brothers in the slightest. If something did go wrong, I'd feel a whole lot better if you at least still had your original bodies going."

"You think it might not be wholly permanent?" Beth asked, growing a little worried.

"Who can say? All this is new and highly experimental. All that we do know is that Mei was able to run Petra's body for thirteen years in the controlled living room environment. We've no idea if being out in the real world and as active as we are if the transference would last that long. I'm leery of it, personally. Take no unnecessary chances," she answered as honestly as she could.

"Okay, let's try running two bodies. I sure as hell don't want to wake up some morning and find I don't have any body anymore," Tilly said determinedly. The others agreed with her.

She carefully dropped her bombshell on them. "One other small possibility remains. If we get the implants desensitized again and if Beth and Tilly still have their current bodies, then we could try to use two of the males as your second bodies. Then you would both be males once more."

"What? Hey, I like that. I see what you are driving at!" Tilly exclaimed. "We would still have an EE woman's body to run, so if the implant kicked in, we could satisfy its behavior patterns, but still be able to be a man again."

"Hey, I like that too," Amanda broke in with a big smile on her face.

Jessica wholeheartedly agreed with Amanda. That settled it. They would make every effort to make this happen.

"I'll send word to the podiatrist and have him waiting for your arrival," the Wolf hastily offered, feeling somewhat left out of the conversation. He found this talk utterly strange, beyond his wildest imaginations.

"Excellent. Now then, what to do for Petra remains, that is, Mei-Petra," Lady Persephone approached the delicate topic, having laid the groundwork with Beth and Tilly.

"Say, would it be possible for me to also try a male body?" she asked, growing far more cheerful. "I suppose if it didn't work, I could take one of the new female bodies you have. I sure as hell don't want another armless one, unless there isn't any other choice that is. Beth and the others should have first choices. I go last."

"Yes, I would like to see if a male body for you would also work out, Petra. However, first we need your latest implant desensitized at the very least. I've no idea just how many times a person can safely be transferred into new bodies. I'm a little hesitant to do it any more than absolutely necessary, Petra. Do you suppose you could endure as you are for the time it takes us to get you desensitized? That way, we only have to make one transference."

"Sure, I'll do anything to get a male body, but make sure Beth and the others get handled first," Petra replied. "At least I can see with Chan. I think we can manage somehow."

"Excellent, Petra. I believe euthanasia is in order for the two blind bodies. What about the three armless women and the six armless men? What should be done with those empty bodies?"

"Hey, this is a moral dilemma isn't it?" Tilly responded. "If there is no being in the body, is it really a human? Are we committing murder, if there is no person in it?"

"I see, like putting down a horse with a broken leg?" Juan added.

"A horse? Those creatures still exist?" asked Amanda, who remembered a picture of a horse in one of her high school history books. Juan chuckled at her tease, since she'd obviously seen his old horse when he rescued them back in Montana.

"Precisely. Without a person in the body, is it acceptable to put them down, as Juan suggests?" Lady Persephone asked.

"Certainly so with the blind ones. They are completely helpless and useless. No one would ever want a body in that bad a shape," Tilly said passionately and with a shudder.

After some discussion, they agreed to put down the six male and the two blind female bodies. They were a bit reluctant to put down the remaining three females but decided to do so as well. None could conceive anyone actually wanting such bodies. Besides whomever had them originally were now long gone.

"All right then, tomorrow after the Feds get this place cleared out and we have searched the place thoroughly, we'll head first to my place to unload the stuff. From there, we'll go to Wolf's place and get your feet handled," Lady Persephone outlined her plans.

"Say, how come there were so few of those Trikuza around here?" Juan asked. He had been thinking about how easy this raid had actually been. Considering just how deadly these men were, he had been surprised so few were here to protect the place.

"My doing. I was here first, and when I checked on the second location the Greg sent us, I found your arms in a trash dumpster not far from here. I then headed for the first set of coordinates he'd sent, but I spotted Trikuza guards several blocks from here. After some scouting, I found this place was heavily guarded. Since the guards were loafing and since it was the middle of the night, I took out a few of them—ten in fact and actually entered the warehouse. Finding nothing, I left my calling card and a phone number. Whoever is leading this Trikuza mafia was wise enough to call. I suggested it was in his best interests to abandon guarding of this place, and apparently, he took my advice to heart. The five who were here were older men, sacrificial tokens. I wonder what the connection is between the Trikuza and the Lin brothers. I doubt we can get them to tell us, though. Had the Trikuza been here in force, the Feds might have been wiped out."

"Thank you, Lady Persephone," Lech replied, finally understanding why things had gone so smoothly.

"Yes, Lech, we need to start getting you fellows off Pytalon," Petra suggested, bringing a slight grin to his face.

"All right. There is one more detail to discuss," Lady Persephone took control once more. "What are we to do with the Lin brothers? They've proven resourceful and deadly. Personally, I'd like to stick one of my cards in their brain matter, but. . ." She paused.

"Well, they have provided useful information several times," Beth countered. "Still, what they did to us is unforgivable."

"True, plus they never mentioned this second foundation at all. Are there more secret foundations? If so and we kill them, those poor people trapped in there are going to be in big trouble," Petra spoke up.

"Want me to torture them and make them talk?" Lech asked, trying hard to follow the rapid conversation.

"I have a better way to make them talk. If I can safely say that there are no more of these hidden foundations, then I believe that the world has had more than enough of the Lin brothers and their nasty inventions," Lady Petra suggested.

"You can't kill us! We're geniuses. Our works have saved the world," screamed Bao, overhearing her suggesting her death.

"Gag them!" she ordered. Lech and his men were very happy to oblige.

The next day after breakfast and while the Feds were still busy dismantling and loading the building's contents into Air Liners, Lady Persephone injected a serum into Bao. After giving it some time to take effect, she began to question her, knowing she could not lie to her. Before long, she learned of the third foundation and its location, but was relieved to hear only backup equipment was stored there. Satisfied, she allowed the drug to wear off. Lech and two squads of Feds headed off to secure this additional site.

An hour later, he reported finding more machines in storage crates, but thankfully no humans were there. He and his men loaded the crates into another Air Liner for shipping and then returned close to lunchtime. After eating, the entire armada departed for home, though four Air Ships headed for Sussex first, along with Lady Persephone's EMAC.

The seven women were having major migraines, unable to carry out their implanted orders. Further, Bao and Huan had to remain gagged during the trip. They simply wouldn't stop bickering, complaining, and protesting loudly. Even so, everyone save Lady Persephone had reservations about outright killing the two. Later that afternoon while they were over the Pacific Ocean, the professor called and suggested they be brought to Phoenix and he would see to their secure but humane treatment.

A week later, Beth, Amanda, Jessica, and Tilly were resting up in the Wolf's hotel in southern Germany. The podiatrist had worked his magic on their feet and assured them that their feet would make a full recovery. The not so good part was they would need to remain off their feet for another five more weeks. Already boredom had set in on the four, moderated by the dull aches in their healing shoulders and their feet. Still, they had already accomplished the desensitizing of their recent implant.

Since the wording was essentially the same, the process had worked much more rapidly than before. Juan and the Wolf hovered over them as well as two of his female staff. "How are we ever going to survive another five weeks like this, sitting on a couch?" Beth moaned. "I'm going mad already and it's only been a week."

"Me too, I was on to something with the high school drop outs. I'm itching to find out more, but here I sit. What if there are more nasty groups out there causing problems I might have prevented, but am cooped up here doing nothing?" Jessica added her complaint to the mix.

"Well you're going to find some of the students we recruited into our organization, as well as some the professor recruited into yours," Bardulf replied. "I just hope that accounts for all them, excepting those who joined the Trikuza that is." She smiled.

"Hey, don't forget me," Tilly grumbled. "Not only can I not safely go out and do my observations, I can't even walk or scratch my nose. It itches again, Wolf. This is torture. Shoot, we can't even play a card game."

"I can't play anything. All I can do is eat. I don't want to get fat," Amanda protested as well.

"I can't even listen to my music," Beth complained.

"Beggars can't be choosy," the Wolf teased them, bringing a brief smile to their faces. "Oh yes, I've some news to share. Lisa and Greg are coming here for a visit with you, and she has a little surprise to share with you. They will be arriving tomorrow afternoon," Bardulf explained. He'd at least given them something to look forward to, relieving the monotony.

Back in Sussex, Lady Persephone had not been idle. While the Feds were unloading the equipment, she'd taken the four women to her stasis pod room where the "dead" bodies she'd been acquiring had been carried. "Okay, first choose who wants which female body and then who wants which male body. Petra will take the male you don't choose."

"This is so utterly weird," Jessica whispered. "Choosing what your body will be? Weird beyond weird."

"Tell me about it," Beth whispered back, uncertain why they were whispering. The bodies were in a comatose state and probably couldn't hear them anyway. "I know, Jessica, Amanda, you two choose the prettiest women. We will take what's left. If we are able to get male bodies, then we want you both to have the very best that you can."

"They are all very attractive, Beth, but I see your point. Okay then, I like that one there the best. Damn, I can't even point to her," Jessica grumbled and nodded her head towards one. Lady Persephone put a sticker with her name on that pod. Amanda studied the others for a while and made her choice. Beth and Tilly made their choices rather hastily, hoping to become males once more.

As the two looked over the three males, Beth suggested, "Tilly, you and Petra ought to have the two stronger looking bodies. I work with electronics and computers, so I'll take that one because it doesn't look as physically strong as the other two."

"Good point. I'll take this one and leave Petra to have what appears to be the stronger of the three," Tilly announced hers. "God, this is so utterly weird! I hope we really can become males again."

Amanda added, "You aren't the only ones hoping so, dearest." All four laughed. After then sending the others on to Germany to get their feet operated upon, Lady Persephone and Yan began desensitizing Petra's recent implant. They also discovered this time it went far faster and easier than before.

While Beth and her friends awaited the arrival of Lisa and Greg, Lady Persephone and Petra began their great experiment. Would Petra be able to handle a male body, now that her EE woman's implants were mostly quiet? They knew as long as her female bodies were pleasured regularly, Petra had no headaches and was able to operate normally. However, she also knew if she didn't indulge herself when the implant pressure began to build up, the implant would slowly build up in force until she did obey it's dictated behavior. This behavior would be impossible to replicate in a male body, but since she also had her Chan body, she and Lady Persephone were hoping that would allow her the outlet she needed to keep the implants at bay.

An hour later, the blinded Petra body was in a stasis pod. Lady Persephone then roused Petra, who now also had the rather muscular Chinese male body to operate as well as Chan's. "Oh my head. I forgot how much it hurts your head to do this. Oh! I'm speaking in a bass voice! It worked. I'm a man again. Hallelujah! Oh, I feel really strange," she said, feeling her body a little. Chan was leaning over the new male body, as was Yan. "Oh!" both Chan and the new male body exclaimed simultaneously. The sex organ certainly was working. "Well," the male Petra cleared her throat, slightly embarrassed. "I guess this is a good sign."

"Okay, up and at it. We need to see if this is going to work out. What should we call you in your male body?" Lady Persephone asked.

"Peter. I'll go back to calling myself Peter and Chan can either be Chan or Petra, which ever Yan prefers."

"I like Chan. I've always known you as Chan, but if you want Petra, that's okay too," Yan answered.

"Okay then, Chan and Peter Delius it'll be," Peter announced. "Got some clothes for me to wear? It's a little embarrassing like this," he hinted.

During the next few days, Lady Persephone put Peter and Chan through all manner of tests, but between them, they were unable find any faults. The transference was solid, and they agreed to terminate the blind body. That was risky, Lady Persephone thought. There were so many unknowns in what they were doing. Fortunately, neither Chan nor Peter felt anything happening to them as the blind Petra body slowly passed away. "Well, no turning back now," Peter commented when it was done.

"Look, if something does happen or come up, we can always transfer you to one of the remaining female bodies," Lady Persephone advised. However, nothing happened during the next few days, and the trio headed back to Chicago to get back to work. Peter promised to email her every day for a time, keeping her abreast of anything unusual he experienced or that Chan did. She fired off a full report to the four in Germany, hoping this news would brighten their days.

Lisa and Greg arrived at the hotel right on schedule. "Oh my! You're pregnant!" Jessica exclaimed the moment she saw Lisa and Greg walking into the huge lounge area.

Lisa giggled, "Yes, we're starting our very own family. The doc says it's a girl, but I wanted a boy, but maybe next time. I was a bit afraid she would have my birth defect, but I saw a sonogram and could see her tiny arms there. Isn't this just wonderful?" she bubbled. Greg just looked like a very proud father standing beside her with an arm around her.

Everyone poured out their congratulations and the two sat down to chat. Meanwhile, Bardulf's staff carried the two's bags up to their rooms. "You look so well, all of you. We rather expected to see you were in not so good a shape. It must have been utterly awful for you," Lisa chatted away. "But we're here now for a couple of weeks. After that, I'm going to Chicago on our way back and help them get more people trained to help get others off Pytalon. The Feds will be the first ones, Chan-Petra's orders. I can see why, what with those nasty mafia fellows, the Trikuza. I read about them once in history class, but the book said they were extinct. Well, the book is obviously wrong, isn't it?"

Lisa was definitely still a chatterbox, but the four welcomed her. Their utter boredom was broken, at least for a while. After they had their suppers, Lisa changed topics. "One of the things I'm to do while I'm here is to help get you ready to begin using your feet like I do. It's easy to do, once you get the hang of it. The main thing we need to work on first, while you don't dare use your feet, is flexibility. You need to be able to raise your legs up like this and touch your noses or your forehead." She demonstrated, adding, "It is getting harder for me now that I'm pregnant. Greg says that eventually I might need him to help me with many things. I suppose that will be so when I'm nearer my due date."

"Say, when is she expected? You didn't tell us your due date," Jessica asked, realizing this slight oversight. She should have asked Lisa that right away.

"I'm five months along, so it's due around Valentine's Day. Won't that be something? Be my darling valentine!" she giggled again. "Now come on; let's see how high you can lift each leg."

"Oh crap! This is pathetic, Lisa. You can stand there and touch your forehead, and I can't get mine much above my waist!" Beth complained.

"Stretching exercises and practice, Beth. That's why I'm here. Greg too. Now let's see how you do, Jessica," Lisa insisted. A bit later, Lisa admitted, "Well, I can see we have a whole lot of work do to here, but then we've the time to get you four all prepared, don't we? Another five weeks, they told us before we left." She chatted on while Beth groaned again—five more weeks—an eternity. No wonder they'd not had this done before now.

"Once you're allowed to use your feet and stand up and walk and all that, Greg and I will be back. Then, I can show you all the tricks I know about how to get things done," Lisa continued to chat away. She and Greg did keep the four interested.

More importantly, both took turns working on stretching their legs. By the time they left two weeks later, all four had the dozen exercises down pat and were beginning to be able almost to reach their noses. Lisa failed to point out they'd find themselves even more limber and the exercises far easier to do when the heavy foot casts were removed. She left that to be a pleasant surprise for her four friends. "Remember, let us know when the casts come off and we'll be back."

"Three more weeks of this," Beth complained after Lisa and Greg left them. "Funny how fast time flew when they were here. Lisa's quite the talker."

Jessica smiled. "She sure is and so full of life and vitality. Well, we best do our exercises, dear."

Bardulf added his encouragement, "Okay, if you continue to do your exercises diligently, I'll get you some voice-activated laptops."

Beth's eyes glowed. "Thank you, thank you, thank you, Wolf!" He grinned.

Several days later, Jessica was merrily back on her trail of high school dropouts while Beth was remotely checking up on the long running program that was searching the psych's database for implant "anomalies." Amanda and Tilly began to investigate all that was known about the Trikuza. Each had something to do, to occupy their minds, but Bardulf made sure they did their exercises each day before he turned their computers on for them.

***

During these weeks, Peter, Chan, and Yan headed back to Chicago. Now he faced a new situation. Would the Feds accept him now that he was male once more? He felt rather confident they would, since as Petra, she was the only female in the Feds. However, as Petra, she had been encouraging other high school girls to consider joining the Feds. If Peter took over, there would be no women again in the Feds, counter to what she'd been trail blazing. As they flew back across the Atlantic, she realized that was precisely what she had done and was doing, being a trailblazer for women in the Feds organization. "I owe it to women to continue to blaze this trail," Chan said to Yan. "Yet my Peter body is far better suited to the task. Damn, I never considered this before. What am I going to do? I really can pay attention to only one of these bodies at at time, Yan."

"I don't know, Chan, but now we can really have a family. We have Peter, and we both can have children and be mothers and raise a real family. Maybe we could even have a little house too. Maybe you and Peter could share being the commander. That way you would have time to have a baby too. With so much bad things going on, we need more babies that are free of the drugs and implants. Don't you think so?"

"Good point, dear," Chan replied. "A mother. Somehow, I really feel as if I should be doing that too, Yan. Sharing the duties of the Supreme Commander—I wonder if we could

460

somehow manage to do that. Say, I know. I still have to dress and appear as an EE woman and wear these six-inch stilettos, which makes me a distinct liability in the field. I can do the work in the office, while Peter does the work in the field. As long as I don't have to do them at the same time, it should work out, don't you think?"

"Yes, and you could then also have a baby with me. We could be mothers and have our family. Could we get a small house do you suppose?" Yan asked.

"Unfortunately, Yan, there aren't any houses close to the Feds building. We're in the heart of the city, skyscrapers all around. A house will have to wait a while, but we could easily make this work and start a real family. I really could be a mother and Peter, a father, couldn't we?" Chan replied.

"Oh yes. Peter can make it so for us." Yan beamed. She had grown up very significantly since she had found Chan in London. She'd seen much of the world and had worked out what was important to her and what was not. Being an EE woman was definitely not what she truly wanted.

Two days later when the trio entered the Feds building and explained what they now wanted to do, Lech broke into a smile, in spite of his drugged state. He replied in his monotone voice, "That would be more than perfect. Peter can have my back again, like old times. I won't have to nursemaid Chan-Petra in the field and can do my job better. It is more than acceptable; it is perfect. Make it so, boss."

They did so, and it began to work very well indeed. Peter sent a message to everyone outlining what they were now doing and that it was readily accepted. Lady Persephone, for one, breathed a huge sigh of relief, but continued to closely monitor how Chan-Petra and Peter were doing, considering the two EE women's implants that they shared. In her mind, so many things could go wrong. They were in uncharted territory with this new transference technology.

A week later, Lisa and Greg arrived, and the next day, Lech and five other Feds began their long sauna treatments, slowly coming off Pytalon. Again, Lady Persephone continued to monitor the situation with the Feds. With Lech and others now themselves once more, how would they handle Chan-Petra and Peter? Would they tolerate them? Would old male prejudices kick back in with the Feds? She imagined a number of awful scenarios and insisted on daily reports from her or him.

One thing Lady Persephone knew as fact: men could never be trusted with power. Egos and testosterone always led to abuse. She had the entire world as the ultimate example to prove her point, to say nothing of the Lin brothers or rather sisters now. Give men a taste of power and they invariable want more, never satiated. "Watch and see," she whispered to her walls. Her thoughts drifted to Juan Carlos. Well, perhaps not all men, she amended her conclusion slightly.

Naturally, those thoughts led her to the four women now in Germany. *It's women who are bringing the world back to rights, not men. Jessica has been the key all along, she and Amanda. Their bravery, their sense of rightness, their extreme courage, their unfailing support of what is right and just has brought us out of the perpetual, hopeless darkness this world has been in for two centuries, maybe more. Now, they're again called upon to put forth immense courage and determinism. God, I couldn't conceive how I could remotely handle what they are facing and dealing with now. Yet, they're doing so with grace and unfailing drive to continue work to say nothing of the constant support of their mates. I know I don't have either the courage or strength to bear what they are doing so without a complaint and no expectation of any tangible reward. All I can hope to do is to guard their backs and support them in any way that I can.*

Lady Persephone looked at her calendar on which she had marked key dates of the proposed recovery time for her four friends. December 12th their casts would come off, and they would then spend two more weeks getting physical therapy on their feet. She knew that would be the most critical time for the women, and she intended to spend those weeks with them. She knew the limits of her physical body well, thanks to her many years of martial arts workouts. All that she knew of healing, she fully intended to use on her friends. "They are determined to keep those damaged bodies and adapt, using Lisa as their model. Well, Lisa is a good role model, but she is a talker. However, will they be able to adapt? Lisa grew up this way. She's had years of practice and time to work things out. They don't and I fear for them, I really do," she explained to her walls. "I'll be ready with the replacement bodies, though I wish they were English and not Chinese, but then do they really care about nationality? Does anyone anymore?" She sighed; the entire world was such a strange place to live.

***

"Thank God the casts are coming off!" Beth gushed as the nurse and doctor began removing hers. It was the middle of December, and Lady Persephone along with Lisa and Greg were with them now. She suspected why Lady Persephone was here. There were too many what if's in play just now. Would their feet really be normal feet again? If so, could they really learn to be somewhat independent by using their feet as Lisa was? Lisa had grown up this way, while she and her friends hadn't. Beth had many doubts about this whole thing. Perhaps she should have just accepted one of the new Chinese female bodies and allowed hers to die. She glanced at Jessica, who was watching the proceedings eagerly. No, that wouldn't be fair to her mate, she decided. *I must do all that I can for her. Somehow, I must make this work for her sake too.*

"Well I have feet again," Beth declared, looking at them. "They look like feet and toes all right." Following the podiatrist's instructions, she wiggled them, and then with Bardulf and Greg supporting her, she gently rose and put her weight on them. It felt a little strange, a little stiff, but she stood. "Wow, my feet are flat on the floor. That's a very good sign. They're stiff. Is that right?"

"Oh my yes. That's what the therapy must handle," the doctor replied. "Now see if you can walk. Gentlemen, make sure she doesn't fall.

Slowly Beth took her first steps in over six weeks. "Stiff and sore, but they're working, I think. Fantastic, doctor!"

Jessica beamed, hope flooded over her face, as well as Amanda's and Tilly's. They were patiently waiting their turn to have their casts removed.

After Beth sat back down, Lady Persephone kneeled and began massaging her feet. "God does that ever feel good, My Lady! Heavenly. Oh, well not so good there."

"I know. I'm starting to get them flexed out more. Expect some twinges, Beth," she explained. "You've a long way to go to get your feet and toes, in particular, as flexible as Lisa's are. Takes time and patience." Mentally, she thought, and I hope you have plenty of both, for you will need them.

"Thanks. I objectively know that, but subjectively, it's another matter. At least our shoulders are fully healed. Greg has inserted more locator chips so we can't get lost again, though I don't expect we'll be needing them activated again," Beth chatted a bit, taking her mind off her feet a little.

Two days later, all four were walking normally and that alone drove their spirits and hopes up. Now Lady Persephone and Lisa began two parallel crash courses with the four women. She worked with them on increasing their motor skills and control of their feet and toes, while Lisa worked with them on life skills using their feet and toes. As Lisa suspected, the hours of exercises they had done paid off. All could easily touch their noses and foreheads with their toes. That alone gave Lisa hope that in time and with patience, practice, and guidance, her four friends could learn her ways of living and not be helpless women.

Two very awkward weeks passed quickly. Just trying to pick up a fork with their toes and feeding themselves proved intensely frustrating for the four who had always used their arms and hands. Then came learning to write with their toes and handling computers. The latter was, naturally, extremely vital for the four who spent much of their hours working with them. Lady Persephone carefully watched their frustrations as they rose and fell and rose again, repeatedly during the two weeks. Lisa did as well. At night, she and Lisa held lengthy conferences working out plans for the next day's therapy sessions.

On Christmas Day, while just trying to manage eating, their frustrations crescendoed. Beth exclaimed, "I'm never going to get this. What are we going to do? Lisa, it's going to take me years to get somewhat independent again! I can't even pick up my fork, which fell onto the floor."

"I know, Beth," Lisa sympathized with her. "Remember, I had several years of martial arts training too, which helps a lot. You mustn't expect to be completely independent in just two weeks. It takes a lot of time and practice and patience too. With most things, I'm slow compared to normal people."

"Aren't you jealous of normal people?" Tilly asked, just as frustrated as Beth.

"Yes," Lisa sighed and admitted, "there are times I get jealous of normal people, but not for the reasons you probably think. I'm often jealous of just how fast they can get things done, while I'm so slow. I'm not jealous of the fact they have arms and hands. I never had them in the first place."

"So what do we do now?" Beth asked again. "We have to get back to work. So many things are dependent upon our work. We can't spend the next year trying to pick up a fork off the floor."

Lady Persephone realized this was the time for her to step in. "I believe the time is right for you four to get your new bodies. Here is what I propose. After you get the new bodies and we're sure it's working, then I'll take you four with me to my castle in Sussex. I'll train you in some martial arts and, with Lisa's help and guidance, on living skills. Meanwhile, your four new normal bodies will go back to your safe house in East Peoria and continue your usual work. There is a six-hour time difference between us, so I'll work you four from say six in the morning until one in the afternoon. Over in the States, your other bodies will still be sleeping. Then when they wake up over there, over here you can lounge around and then sleep. This way, you'll only have to worry about one body at a time. What do you think about this solution?"

Beth sighed, greatly relieved. "Lady Persephone, I love it. This takes the pressure off us. We can get back to work right away while taking our time to learn how to do things. Thank you, thank you."

Once more, they were ignorant of the internal secrets of the Total Care Program. Had they fully investigated this organization, other solutions would have been possible. However, circumstances had yet to force them to explore Total Care fully.

"Then, let's get to it now." Lady Persephone and the others packed up after dinner. Bardulf received four loving, thank you kisses for what he'd done for the four, pleasing him immensely. At dawn the following morning, they were on their way to Sussex, arriving around ten. Conveniently, Lady Persephone had everything prepared in advance.

Beth went first. After lying down on the table, the electrodes were connected to her head and then to the male body she'd picked out. Some ten minutes later, the process finished, and Lady Persephone used smelling salts to rouse Ben. Yes, they had agreed to revert to their original names for their male bodies. "Oh my head. Oh! It worked. I have hands again," Ben said, sitting up and rubbing his head."

"Okay, Ben, now focus on your old body there. Right, here goes," Lady Persephone ordered. She roused the comatose female body. As it stirred, Ben's original connection to it activated.

"Oh, my head," she and her new male body said simultaneously. "Oh! Wow, I'm seeing double! No, from two places. Oh! Hey it worked," she exclaimed, staring at herself and himself. She broke into a hearty laugh. "I'm two now, way cool. Oops." Her male body responded to her female body, embarrassing the two of them. Juan handed Ben some clothes, which he hastily donned. Juan led the two off into the next room, allowing Beth and Ben to get used to the very strange situation. Meanwhile, Lady Persephone began setting up the machine for Jessica.

A half hour later, Jessica and Jess joined Beth and Ben. "Holy cow, Jess, you look fabulous," Ben admired the new Jess. She was tall and thin; her hair was thick, black, and extremely long, falling straight as an arrow down to her ankles. Currently, it was parted down the middle, with each half draped over her shoulders down her front and over her massive EE woman's breasts. It was almost twice as long as Jessica's lovely hair.

"Thanks, it's going to take some getting used to, Ben. Wow, you look handsome too, big fellow. I think this is going to work, but doing two things at once is tough. Hug," she said. He was very willing to oblige.

A half hour later, Tim and Tilly joined them, followed a bit later with Mandy and Amanda. Like Jess, Mandy had the typical very long black hair as well. Hers reached a few inches short of her ankles. "Oh, your hair is even longer than mine, Jess. This is something else isn't it? So hard to do two things at the same instant. Are you all managing it?"

"Er no, one thing at a time," Tim advised. "What are we supposed to do now?" he asked as Lady Persephone, Lisa, and Greg joined them. Juan was watching over the eight rather like a mother hen.

"Well, let's do some testing to make sure these transferences are holding strong," she suggested. They spent another day experimenting before she was satisfied all was well. Then Lisa and Greg took Ben, Tim, Mandy, and Jess with them back to the States, while Lady Persephone and Juan began working with Beth, Tilly, Jessica, and Amanda. Naturally, she insisted upon daily health reports from the four Stateside. She didn't stop fretting and worrying about the transference for a month. 2272 promised to be an interesting year, she thought.

Chapter 30—Following Leads

As the Chicago Feds were slowly coming off Pytalon at their new Detox Center, Chan-Petra and Peter began to pick up the pieces of the Chicago Feds. Lech retained his position as their top leader as Captain, while Peter and Chan-Petra continued to share the duties of Supreme Commander, worldwide. What demanded the interest of the three was the Trikuza. While Peter was concerned with the mafia's worldwide operations, Lech worried they had a branch office in Chicago. All three wanted answers, but the Trikuza had very effectively gone underground for the last two centuries. Digging them out was challenging to say the very least.

The only clues they had were the three dead gang members Juan and a security guard had killed during the kidnaping of the five EE women. Extensive autopsies were done. The only common thread so far was the fact all three men were of Chinese ancestry or descent, which was only logical since the Trikuza was historically a merger of the Chinese and Japanese mafia.

With so little to go on, Chan-Petra focused her attention on the only identifying mark, the right upper arm tattoos—a triangle with a dagger piercing it. Lech suggested all Asian men in Chicago be rounded up and their upper right arm checked for the telltale tattoo. Peter discounted that. "Look, once word gets out, those in the Trikuza will simply vanish, hiding until we go away. Besides, the gang members aren't likely to be on Pytalon or implanted. Your method will only work when you apprehend a possible suspect."

Lech sighed; that was his only idea.

Chan-Petra pondered the images of the tattoo for days, recalling seeing the same marking on the five who had been killed during the raid in Peking. All were the same black color, with a hint of shiny reflectiveness, rather a unique tattoo. On November 1, she got the idea to have one of the tattoos chemically analyzed. She reasoned, "Perhaps there is something unique in the pigments of the tattoo we can use."

On the 10th, the analysis came back from the CSI laboratory. She gazed at the printout. One detail caught her eye. It contained trace amounts of a rare isotope of Iridium, ^{191}Ir to be precise. She looked up Iridium, found it was a silvery-white crystalline, and realized this was what gave the black of the tattoo its shiny reflectiveness.

"So how does this help us?" Lech asked. Chan-Petra had just shown him and Peter the results, though obviously Peter didn't need to be shown, but Chan and Peter were being socially polite.

"That I don't know. I need Beth again. I wish she were up and running. Still, what else do we have to go on, except these tattoos? I suppose we could run a worldwide trace on Iridium production and see if we can find any connections to the Trikuza," she suggested.

Lacking any other real ideas, the Feds did just that. As December came, she ran into a dead end on that route. Frustrated, she dearly missed Beth's assistance, but knew Beth was still immobile, her feet in casts. Armless, Beth couldn't help her in the slightest. Now if she took one of the male bodies, then Beth would be back in business, she thought. She texted Lady Persephone about this, but accepted her reply that Beth wasn't mentally or physically ready for such a transference just yet. At last, she was forced to give it up until Beth returned.

She spent most of December reviewing the progress other Feds were having tracking down the implant "goofs" that Beth's long running program was still uncovering. Every major city had roughly fifty of them to check out. Chan-Petra constructed a chart showing the statistical results. On the average, a "goof" that needed Feds intervention and handling occurred once every thousand implants. Overall, she thought that was a good batting average. The psychs had done their jobs very well. Once the crucial ones were examined, then the Feds had to check up on the others that Beth's program spit out as possibly able to cause trouble. Here, the averages were a ten times higher, one in a hundred. However, worldwide, these were being routinely handled and seldom caused any real trouble, mostly "accidents at work." Of course, she now knew how bad such accidents could be.

During this time, she set up a large Recovery Center, placing the Southend Mission in charge of the new facility, designed to help and assist in any way needed those who were physically handicapped for whatever reason, greatly expanding what the Total Care Program provided for them. By mid-December, she had the Feds in all locations setting up similar facilities, along with spreading the word about these facilities on all the many billboards, replacing the usual "Sanity is" messages. As Christmas rolled around, Chan-Petra pretty much had these loose ends taken care of, one way or another.

Their personal life was going extremely well. As Peter, she fully satisfied both Yan and Chan, that is, herself. By the end of December, both women were pregnant, much to both women's great pleasure. Yan had her fondest wish; they were starting a family, a close one at that, though she still wanted a small cottage somewhere. For now, their penthouse suite would have to suffice. Both women were due sometime late September or early October.

When Ben, Tim, Jess, and Mandy arrived on January 7, 2272, Peter and Lech were at the main desk to welcome the four back into the Feds. After introductions, Peter gave them their new ID cards, which gave them full access to the Chicago Feds building and their ninth floor office. "We can't begin to tell you how much we've missed you four," Peter said as they headed up to his office, where Chan-Petra and Yan were waiting to greet them as well. "I for one am completely stumped on how we can find the Trikuza that may be here in Chicago. Chan-Petra has something to bounce off you, Ben, our only solid clue. Ah, here we are. Join us, Lech, please."

After introductions and hugs, Ben wanted to see just what Chan-Petra had uncovered, while Tim and Lech discussed possible avenues to track Trikuza activities in Chicago.

"I had their tattoos analyzed and found a rare isotope of Iridium in the black pigments—^{191}Ir to be precise. I was hoping you could work out a way we could somehow use this to help find Trikuza members, starting here in Chicago. Lord knows, I don't want a repeat of what happened last time. We all were extremely lucky. They could have just as easily killed us," she explained.

"So this Iridium gives it that shiny texture. Well, okay, I'll get on it. However, we have tons to do. Nothing like being gone for nearly two and a half months. Backlogs everywhere," Ben replied. He changed the topic, "Say, now that we four have become we eight, well as soon as our other bodies get trained some by Lady Persephone, we're going to have to move out of our safe house in East Peoria. No way could all of us fit down there. I was thinking perhaps it might be smart for us to move up here closer to the action."

"Now I like that!" Chan-Petra exclaimed. "Why not get a penthouse suit near ours? Yan and I are expecting sometime in September. We'd love to have you all close at hand."

Ben smiled and congratulated her and the grinning Yan, who looked very pleased indeed. Later that afternoon, Peter took them to look at a vacant large penthouse suite on the top floor of the building next to their own penthouse suite. This one was huge and luxurious, once the offices of a Pytalon executive, now deceased. All four liked the layout, especially since they could park their EMAC and EMAC bus on the roof just overhead. Ben and Tim took it, signing a five-year lease. To their surprise, the Feds paid for it. "Just to show you how much your work means to us," Peter explained.

They decided to keep their safe house in East Peoria anyway as a backup location if trouble came. Ben and Tim decided to get all new computer equipment and devices. Back at their Feds offices, while Ben and Tim began making orders for their rather large amount of new equipment, Mandy and Jess were ordering their new furniture and appliances. That done, they returned to East Peoria to pack up what they needed to take, making copious backup copies of everything and then putting the equipment back into the hidden storage room for safe keeping.

By January 10 and with helping muscle from the Feds, they had their new suite prepared. Each of the four had their own office area with their computer equipment and electronic devices, though Jess and Ben's areas were twice the size of Tim and Mandy's. Each couple also had their own large bedroom suites with attached baths, sharing a common kitchen, dining room, and living room areas. Taking a tip from Greg, Tim had all the doorknobs replaced with horizontal handle latches of the type Lisa easily handled. He wanted no barriers for their other four when they finally returned from Sussex. At last, the four finally got back to work in an optimum environment, setup just the way that was best for them.

Jess began reviewing their various recordings, monitoring various organizations worldwide. Tim and Mandy began work on formulas for predicting some actions of the Trikuza, while Ben put his full attention onto Chan-Petra's isotope problem. "Hum, half-life is seventy-four days, used in radiology. Not sure how this helps. Wait, as the ^{191}Ir decays it releases gamma rays. Don't we have satellites that can pick up gamma radiations?" Ben muttered.

Jess stood at the side of the low wall between their offices. "I think I saw a reference to that somewhere. Why gamma radiation? It sounds more interesting than these boring recordings. Not much at all has happened while we were gone."

"The strange isotope that's in the Trikuza tattoos emits gamma rays. I wonder if we could commandeer one of those satellites and if it is sensitive enough to detect such small amounts," Ben replied.

"Well, we're part of the Feds now, silly. We don't have to commandeer one, we can just requisition it, I think, if I understood Chan-Petra," Jess replied. "Want me to check?"

"Sure go ahead. I'm going to try to see if there is a way we can test it. They still have the three bodies on ice in the morgue—I've found out that much," he replied.

A half hour later, Peter joined them and helped Ben and Jess bring the defense satellite online and focused on the Chicago Feds morgue, located in the basement of this very building.

"Might not work, since there's so much material in the way," Ben grumbled. "I suppose we might get someone to carry one of the bodies out onto the street."

A bit later, Jess had the incoming false color images up on her monitor. "Wow, look at these hot spots!" Peter and Ben came around to look. Curious, Tim and Mandy joined them, looking over everyone's shoulder.

Peter was quite familiar with Chicago. "Say, I think those bright spots are the area hospitals. Can you overlay this image with a street map?"

"Sure, the center coordinates are in the corner there. Give me a second to find the map," Jess replied. Soon the false color image was superimposed on a Chicago map. She adjusted the scale and Peter proved his point.

"Yes, there, there, there, those are the major hospitals. Ah, these smaller ones are outlying health centers. Okay, zoom in on this spot here; that's us," Peter requested, becoming fascinated with this process.

"Ah ha. There, see those three tiny spots?" Ben said, pointing to them. "There are the three tattoos. Bingo. We have a way to spot Trikuza members!"

Peter patted Ben on his shoulders. "My god, you and Jess have done it again! Amazing. Now how can we make use of this to find the Trikuza in Chicago?" he asked, sending for Lech.

"Well, for starters, I would look wherever the largest concentration of those of Asian descent or ancestry lives," Ben suggested. "Sorry, I don't know Chicago." After showing Lech the image, he too was very impressed. He then gave them the location of the densest group. Ben and Jess reoriented the map, centering it on that location, and then zoomed in. The largest spot was a health care center.

Lech exclaimed, "I'll be damned! Right there. I see five tiny spots. I'll bet anything those are mafia members. What's that address? I'll take a squad there now!"

"Careful, remember they're the deadliest fighters in the world. Shoot first and ask questions later," Peter ordered. "And make sure a medic goes with you—hell and an ambulance. Jeesh, I don't want to lose you, Lech!"

Lech laughed, "Me either boss. We'll be careful. I suspect they'll try to run. If so, we'll shoot. Keep me posted."

"Right, they might be on the move. These are stationary pics," Peter pointed out. "How fast can new updated images be shown?"

"Once every five minutes," Ben replied sighing, "not too useful if they are on the run. Still we can track them. Maybe get to them at night when they are sleeping."

A half hour later, Lech and his squad of heavily armed Feds arrived at the designated location. The tiny dots hadn't moved appreciably thus far. Lech reported, "Boss, we are outside a tea garden. Going in now. Got five men outside ready to shoot any who flee. Video feed is now live."

Peter, Ben, Jess, Mandy, and Tim crowed around Ben's monitor this time. He'd tapped into Peter's live feed, and they saw the streaming video as Lech entered the tea garden. Quaint tables filled the large room, decorated with Asian characters and tapestries. Curiously, all five felt comfortable with them, but had no idea of their significance. Their bodies were Chinese and were born and raised around the Peking area. They were sensing body familiarity with the scene. People rose, some bolted. Lech had obviously made his announcement.

For a couple of minutes, chaos erupted on the screen. Then, things settled down, and they watched men raising their right shirt sleeves for the Feds men. They saw no tattoos. Lech's voice came through. "We shot three of them. Confirmed Trikuza. Wounded one; one got away, but I sent him a message. You can run but you can't hide from us any longer. Maybe word will get back to the leaders. Going outside now to show you the tattoos." Shortly, the images of three bloody men appeared, their right sleeves torn away. There were the tattoos. Ben smiled; his idea was working. At last, the Feds had a way to locate the otherwise invisible Trikuza mafia members!

A half hour after the initial deployment, Lech asked, "Okay boss, where are the two dots at now? We are ready to pull out and go after them." Ben and Jess had been monitoring the dots and gave him the two nearest crossing streets. As they watched the live feed, they saw a crowded street near lunchtime. For an hour, the Feds tried to track the fleeing two men, but with the five-minute delay in obtaining an updated position, Lech finally gave up, promising to try again at night when perhaps they would be stationary, sleeping.

Hours later, a bug-eyed, Jess gave up following the tiny dots, much too fatiguing. One by one, the others took turns keeping track of the two dots. Finally, the four had to give it up and head home to bed. Soon their other four bodies would be waking for another day of training and would demand all their attention. Hence, Peter took over for them, guiding Lech and his men towards the two dots around two in the morning. The wounded Trikuza didn't give up without a fight. When he was finally slain, he'd already wounded three of the Feds. The remaining member fled, presumable in an EMAC. Peter lost track of him.

The next few days, Peter and then Chan-Petra took over the project of scouring Chicago from the satellite images, looking for more tiny red dots, the mafia members. They hoped to locate other mafia members, but alas, they found no further trace of the lone man who had eluded Lech and his men. Satisfied and bleary-eyed, they gave up the search for now.

Chan-Petra fully documented the procedure, codifying it. She then sent the document to all the other Feds captains, along with instructions first to attempt to detect the number of mafia members in their cities and second to attempt capture or elimination of said Trikuza men, but only if there were a half dozen or less in their city. If there were more, they were to report the numbers to her. Obviously, with larger numbers, a combined Feds operation would be needed. Chan was certain that would be the case when the cities in China and Japan reported.

Next, Ben and Jess put their attention back onto the high school dropout problem. True, some were joining their own resistance movement in Phoenix and some were joining up with the Wolf. Still, that left two to four seniors from nearly every high school, depending upon the size of the class, who failed to show for their Assignment or Choosing Day. Of course, some were ill and showed up later on. Hence, her next action was to try to eliminate those from the final totals.

Several days later, the two stared at the final overall yearly numbers. Each Assignment Day, worldwide some five hundred teens went missing, a rather alarming number, since these were obviously now living completely outside the grid. In the last ten years, some five thousand were on the missing rolls. Where did they go? What were they up to?

Armed with these solid facts, Tim and Mandy set to work attempting first to categorize the possible scenarios the teens were following and second to come up with some percentage estimates for the categories. For example, "sabotage the system" was one such endeavor they could be following. "Joining a band of like-minded individuals" was another broad category, which encompassed many more specialized categories, including militias. Slowly the two began to work out their behavior prediction formulas for the many categories, based on wild guesses of the likelihood of each occurring. Both knew this was only a preliminary guess; they needed more facts.

They presented their initial work to Chan-Petra in late January, asking her for suggestions. The three mulled it over for a time before she got a bright idea. "Say, when I was giving all those assembly speeches for the seniors, I learned a number of people visit the high school during the spring, interviewing students for prospective jobs. Perhaps you could do the same. Interview students for us Feds, keep your eyes open, and do some spying.

Tim liked the idea immensely. Fieldwork. "God, I have been away from my love for far too long!"

"What, you don't love me?" Mandy teased him.

He flushed and said, "You know what I mean, my love. You could go too and get your feet wet with some real fieldwork. Usually, it's a whole lot of fun, but true, it can be dangerous at times. I wouldn't expect there to be any danger visiting a high school, though. What say you? Up for some fieldwork?"

"You bet. I'd love to see just what you do and how you gather the data that we need for the formulas. Count me in, dear," Mandy replied.

Chan-Petra made the arrangements for four of the larger high schools. Each one had their own week with the many job councilors so one company's representative could visit all the different schools. Four sounded like a good start, and Chan promised that if they needed more schools, she could easily arrange them.

The first week in February, Tim and Mandy, he dressed in a nice business suit and she dressed in a nice EE woman's gown with her usual six inch heels, entered the first high school. They were directed to the auditorium where a series of long tables and chairs were setup. Each representative had a sign over their location, and Tim put theirs up, while Mandy adjusted her long hair to her front and took a seat. Then, both surveyed the other representatives. Most seemed ordinary. There was one for Caterpillar EM machinery, one for Gen Dyn EM Motors, one for Ace Appliances, one for Allied Foods, and even one for MTE Constructions. This was the first year that a sign was present for the Feds.

Soon, the teens began filing in, ambling along, and looking over the signs. Theirs drew quite a bit of attention, rather unexpectedly Tim thought. While most were boys who stopped to make inquiries, a surprising number of girls did too. Many asked Mandy, "Do you have to be an EE woman to join up?" Their second most frequently asked question was, "Do you just make coffee and stuff, or do you actually do important work?"

Mandy laughed the first one off, "No, you don't. It is just I happen to have had that implant." However, she elaborated a good deal in answer to the second one. "I'm an analyst and do very key work, quite valuable. You need to be up on your math and computer skills, unless you want to work in the field and sometimes fight criminals like the men do."

Both were frequently asked, "Is it true none of us are going to have to get implanted or go on Pytalon when we graduate?" To this, both answered never again, unless you yourself choose that path. Of course, if you choose not to have either, then you are agreeing to help us restore our world and civilization." Both elaborated in more detail to the impressed teens.

During the lunch hour break, Tim and Mandy began visiting with many of the other representatives. Their objective: spot any suspicious representative. Exactly what that meant, neither could say with any certainty. It was, after all, fieldwork.

Visiting with the reps, quickly one aspect became apparent: most were glassy-eyed zombies, merely repeating the same descriptive sentences to each student who came by their location. Many had brochures outlining the benefits and job opportunities at their company. During the lunch break, these men and women said very little unless spoken to directly.

However, several men and women most definitely were not Pytalon zombies. Mandy whispered, "I thought Peter said everyone including the Feds was now on Pytalon. Looks like some were missed!"

"Most interesting. Let's see who they are," Tim suggested. "Of course, they might be intimidated by us since we're Feds." He moved through the milling group and approached one such man. "Hello, I'm Tim Hickory. This is our first time meeting with the seniors. Might I ask what is the MMS that you represent?"

"John Smith," the muscular man in his thirties replied somewhat gruffly. "Marshals Militia and Security. We provide corporate security for companies in the hot spots of the world, such as close to the Iran border. Never heard of the Feds recruiting. You must be getting desperate, eh?" he insinuated rather covertly.

"Not really, but we're willing to learn from others, such as yourself. I thought there was nothing left in that country, you know, after the war," Tim replied with a smile.

"Still troublemakers in that area. No regard for human life, other than their own warped lives. Feds have ignored all the world's hot spots, so it is up to the MMS to deal with the insane in those zones," he countered. "So what's the Feds done recently for Chicago, eh?"

"Oh nothing much. We've rid Chicago of the Trikuza mafia members. Just trying to make the city safe for everyone," Tim replied nonchalantly. John's eyes rose slightly, Tim now knew that he knew of their existence and just what they were. "Say, have you got a brochure on your MMS? I've come across several students who indicated that they might be interested in taking a more active role in securing our world from troublemakers. I could route them to your table."

John handed him a brochure and thanked him. He turned away, beginning a friendly chat with some of the EM company representatives, asking about stronger EM dozers for fieldwork. Carefully, Tim folded the brochure, making sure the man's fingerprints were preserved. A gut feeling told him this man was not to be trusted.

Meanwhile, Mandy milled around and edged her way up to a woman representative. She wore a plain blue cotton dress with flowers on it. Her brown hair was up in a tight bun. Her physical appearance was about as unattractive as she could possibly have made herself look, the total opposite of Mandy, whose sky blue satin gown, extremely long black hair, six-inch black patent heels, and enormous bosom caught the attention of many. "Hello, I'm Mandy Hickory, an analyst with the Feds."

The woman had an alto voice. "Betty Worth. Didn't know the Feds had any women in their organization, especially your kind, but then I imagine you have many other duties," she insinuated. Though she didn't say sex doll, her intention was quite clear from the look on her face and raised nose and eyebrows.

Mandy's ire rose. She wanted to tell her in no uncertain terms she wasn't the play toy of the office, not a sex doll. Instead, she controlled her flaring emotions and asked, "I really am an analyst. Good with math. Say, what is Bailey's Pond Antiquities? I've had a couple of girls ask me what it was and I couldn't answer, but I did tell them to come and ask you. I'm sorry I don't know. This is our first year here with the seniors. My husband and I are just learning the ropes, so to speak." There, I let her know I'm not an office sex toy, she thought.

"Thanks to your Feds and the world powers, all that the world once had is now lost to us forever," she began to explain. From her harsh tone, Mandy sensed that she was holding back a lot of anger against the "system" and the Feds, who were its enforcers. "We at Bailey's Pond Antiquities are doing our very best to find and preserve the antiquities for future generations who have never known what a movie is, what a CD is, what a rock band is. The list is practically endless. We only accept students who are willing to devote their lives to the location and preservation of the now long gone relics of what had been the greatest civilization on earth. They have to have a passion for the preservation of the ancient great things, which, thanks to your people, the psychs, and the drug companies, no longer exist or are even known by virtually everyone. Nor do they even care about such things." She spat out her ire and hatred.

"Things are changing, Betty. I, for one, love the ancient music from the fourteenth and fifteenth centuries. Give us time and you'll see positive changes, I truly believe," Mandy replied.

She then moved on looking for another who was not on Pytalon.

Neither got a chance to "visit" with several others who were "normal." It was back to counseling, as the students returned to the auditorium from their lunch break. However, Tim kept his eyes on the type of students visiting several other reps that he had under suspicion. Only strong, outspoken young men visited the God's Disciples representative. This he found most curious, since the name of the group didn't suggest the type of students who spent time chatting with the man. He rather wished he could overhear what they were saying. Strong, muscular lads also spent considerable time chatting with the man from Locki's Freedom Fighters. He made a note to check up on this group as well.

Meanwhile, Mandy kept tabs on several other reps. One married couple were representing Bensing's New Order. The woman there definitely was most submissive. Either that or she was the shyest woman Mandy had seen. Still more than once, she received a covert "dirty look" from the woman. Mandy didn't have to imagine what the woman thought about her. She also saw a fair number of girls visiting with the man from Markus Commune. Even more curious was the lone man from Jacobites Religious Retreat. He wore a robe over his suit and hardly any students spent more than a passing glance at his table. She didn't see anyone taking his brochures.

She also noted a fair number of attractive girls visited the EE Women's table. Many took the brochures the older woman had. Jess had thought the era of EE women was over, so she had a brief chat with the woman. "Oh no. There is still a demand for us beautiful, exotic escorts, as you well know. We must always look our very best," she replied. Jess continued to ponder this unexpected bit of news. She made a mental note to follow up on this point.

When the bell rang ending the day, Tim suggested, "Let's dally a little and see if they leave some of their brochures. If so, I want to pick up a few." Mandy agreed. She wanted the literature on the three that she found curious. An hour later, they had their brochures, and arm in arm, they walked slowly out of the school to their waiting EMAC.

After dinner, they shared their results with Ben, Jess, Chan, and Peter. They had seven groups that they wanted the four to look into for them. Also, Tim wanted the fingerprint he'd lifted analyzed. Peter took the brochure from him and rushed it down to the CSI lab for him. Meanwhile, Ben and Jess began doing what they did best: research.

The Markus Commune was just that, a cooperative commune community. From what they saw on the Internet sites, the type of people that were accepted into the closed community were pliable teens, ones who would accept communal living. According to Feds records, well more than half of their "registered" members were on Pytalon though. The commune grew its own food and was considered self-supporting, needing no outside anything. They didn't seem threatening.

The Jacobites Religious Retreat appeared to be a collection of highly religious men only. Their brochure stated successful applicants would be devoting their lives to prayer at a secret retreat. Ben couldn't determine where that retreat was located, however. Further, the representative wasn't in the Feds database, so he was in fact also off the grid entirely. Again, they presumed this group was not threatening.

The Bensing's New Order only accepted teens who were strongly anti-government minded, that is, they passionately hated the current system, and their IQs weren't high. Anyone whose IQ was over 110 wasn't accepted. This group, Ben decided, warranted further study.

Jess discovered Bailey's Pond Antiquities was just as advertised. This worldwide organization was tiny, barely one hundred members, all dedicated to the location and preservation of "old things," meaning ancient artifacts. In a way, Lady Persephone's collection was quite similar to the collections of this small group, whose headquarters was in Topeka, Kansas. Again, this group didn't appear to be threatening in any way and might prove useful later on if and when the society began to awaken from its drugged state.

Locki Freedom Fighters appeared to be a worldwide organization of individuals whose dedicated goal was freeing the world from insanity. At least that was what their web site stated. Jess decided these people deserved a closer look.

The fingerprint analysis came back after the four had to retire for the night to give their other four bodies in Sussex their full attention. Hence, Peter accepted the results and did more digging on the MMS or Marshals Militia and Security. John Smith was an alias. The man was really Edgar Hamilton, and he had a long overseas' rap sheet. That the MMS operated in the remote hot spots of earth was true. However, security was far from the group's goals. Peter found much more data on the MMS from the Turkish Feds database. Apparently, the MMS's idea of security was to annihilate any rebel opposition to the ongoing program of PDH implants and Pytalon drugging of the people in these remote areas of the planet. Edgar was wanted on a Turkish warrant for genocide of a remote village in eastern Iraq, close to the radioactive zone of Iran. Curiously, Mr. Smith failed to appear at the high school the next day.

Peter also researched God's Disciples and found they had nothing to do with religion. Rather they were based in LA and were reputed to be nothing more than extortionists, using threat of physical harm to get compliance with their wishes. The problem was just who they could extort these days. However, there were no outstanding warrants on their representative. Peter left the data for Tim to review the next morning. Curiously absent were Trikuza representatives, but then he didn't expect the mafia to be openly recruiting.

The next day, Chan-Petra fired off a lengthy document to all the other Feds offices in the world. In it she outlined their plan of action here in Chicago and the preliminary findings. She ordered the other offices to conduct similar high school meetings, where possible. After sending it, she wished all the results were back. Her interest was pricked to say the least.

As she sat brushing out her hair before bed, she began to realize just how much the entire world lacked true leadership and how much she had failed. There were no governments of any kind in any of the world's countries. In this "Sane World Society," in other words Total Care, there was no need for such things, and hadn't been for well over a century, once the majority of the world's population had been PDH implanted and/or on Pytalon, compliments of the Total Care Program. The governments merely ceased to exist. The psychs and the Pytalon companies effectively controlled the world after that, with the Feds enforcing their will, but lurking somewhere in the background was this Total Care organization.

She realized that in fact, none of the three actually ruled the world; they merely continued to obtain what they wished until they got too greedy. One by one, the psychs were put onto Pytalon becoming mindless zombies themselves, and then he, Peter Delius, had done the same to the remaining Pytalon company leaders and later even his own Feds. The world was leaderless, but at this precise moment, it didn't actually need it, because the Pytalon and implanted men and women merely continued their "programed lives" day after day—at least that was the apparency Peter saw.

Now with her friends and their unique system of checks and balances, they were starting to undo it. The lack of other leaders was acutely apparent to her. As Supreme Commander, she saw she knew absolutely nothing of what was going on beyond her own small patch of the world, pointed out acutely to her by a couple of these high school representatives. Hot spots? She knew nothing about them. The other Feds offices closest to them probably were handling them in their own zombie manner, but she had no data, no idea. Further, if she were to attempt to familiarize herself with the situations around the world, she'd be at it for years! This is what truly woke her up to the lack of country or local governments. It seemed to her they were beginning to awaken the world and that it would rapidly slip into utter chaos!

The next morning, she called the professor to discuss her revelations with him. "Petra, bloody well done! You're precisely correct in your observations. Yes, Tim and I knew this would soon become a huge problem, once we started taking people off the implant-drug route. It's up to us to fill in those missing leadership holes everywhere. I haven't been idle, but working on the problem that's soon to face us. Let me share my current ideas with you." She agreed eagerly.

"First, for the immediate future and likely for many, many years, we must continue to guide and lead the world back to sanity, until they're able enough to take over from us. Hence, as I see it, we have already put in the foundation, just not labeled it properly. You're correct; we must continue to have checks and balances upon us. Officially, we'll have three worldwide organizations to guide us. The Feds have always been worldwide, so your organization will enforce the rules and laws as you have always been doing. I would suggest you begin to organize the top structure so you're not overworked. Lady Persephone has agreed to head the World Court to handle the justice side. I'm working up a World Guidance Council, whose job will be to make the board decisions and 'laws' as needed."

"Yet, we're going to need to put three similar units in place within each country as well. I figure to use the AP-cops as the parallel group to you Feds or perhaps they would work better at the local level. Yes, we have a whole lot to work out, but it hinges on having men and women who aren't implanted and not on Pytalon to fill those posts and carry them out. We're going to see how this batch of graduating seniors work out and mesh with the 'Sane Society' around them and go from there. For now, see what you can do for your top most positions or you're going find yourself rather overwhelmed by the magnitude of what we're facing."

"I already am," Chan laughed. "Okay, I'll make this my top priority at the moment. Thanks."

She called up the Wolf. "Hi Bardulf. Chan-Petra here. Say, I want to bounce something off you. How would you like to become the head of the European Feds? Total control over all them. Please say yes. I need someone in that empty position that I can trust and have total faith in."

Bardulf roared with laughter. "Chan-Petra, two years ago if someone would've said I'd be asked to be the head of the European Feds, I would've thought them totally insane! Okay, I'll do it, if I can bring along my own trusted people to help staff it and if I have total control over the European Feds."

"Agreed. I remain as your boss, the Supreme Commander, but you'll be the European Commander. However, as you probably know, we're held in balance by the professor's guidance group and Lady Persephone's justice adjudications," Chan replied.

"Excellent. Then I accept willingly. How soon does this become effective? Will the local captains accept me?"

"I'll send out the official appointment documents today and tell them to expect your arrival soon. The old Commander had his offices in Brussels, but it has been closed down for some time now. It would make sense to have your offices in one of the larger cites, Berlin perhaps?" she replied.

"That would be better for us. Berlin it is. Have the Berlin Feds see about finding appropriate offices for us. We're making progress, aren't we?"

"Yes, but we need to establish some true organization within the top levels of the Feds. Right now, I'm trying to run all the worldwide offices myself, and it's way beyond what one person can do. Silly me, right?" Both chuckled. After chatting a bit more, she typed up the official documents and orders, sending them to the various captains of the Feds in Europe. Now she had to do the same for the other continental zones.

She decided she needed one in Africa, Australia, Asia, India, and South America at the very least. "What was the name of the translator I put in charge in Peking? He would be the only one I can trust there." She hunted through her emails and found him. Tao Liang. She called him up and promoted him, much to his great pleasure. A bit later, she sent the Asian captains the formal documents. "Two down, four to go. Now what? I don't know anyone in these areas. Wait, I need someone for all of North America too. Lech!"

A half hour later, a very pleased Lech began making his own arrangements for finding a replacement for his position as captain of the Chicago Feds and setting up his new offices. The previous US commander had made his office in LA. Lech decided to remain in Chicago, which he knew well. He didn't really want to move. "Don't worry, Lech. Whenever I need something done here locally, I will always go through you, old pal."

He smiled, "Amazing what all we've been through. Mind you, I still don't like what you did to me with that cursed Pytalon, but then you've paid handsomely for that move," he teased her.

She grinned, "Yes, I think I've finally grown up, Lech. Say, you should find yourself a wife."

He laughed, "I have been thinking along those lines, but you EE women are so darn sexy. She would have to be one, but not the usual dodo-head sex dolls. She needs to be like all of you."

"Desensitized to the EE implant. Yes, I know. I'll see what I can find. Blind date, eh?"

He laughed, "At least I'll know she's pretty. They have to be in order to be even considered to become an EE woman." Both smiled.

"I think I know someone who might just fill the bill for you. Bright, charming, very intelligent, and a superb organizer. She loves to help others less fortunate than herself. I'll see if she is still single, Lech. How about a blind date Friday night?" Chan-Petra suggested. Lech grinned and agreed.

After he left, she called up Phillip at the Southend Mission. "Hi, say Phillip, is Mary Lyons still single and around?"

"Sure, she helps out five days each week. Why?" he asked.

"I want to set her up with a blind date Friday night."

Phillip laughed, "Well, that sure will surprise her. Hang on a second. I'll get her. She's feeding one of the men."

After a pause, "Hello, this is Mary Lyons."

"Hi , I'm Petra, remember me? The Feds commander."

"Oh yes, we can't ever thank you enough for what all you've done for the mission and everyone here," she replied enthusiastically.

"Well, I've a blind date possibility for you. He's a nice man, and to be honest, he needs someone like you to help him with organization stuff. Friday night?"

"What? Me? Does he know I'm a helpless cripple?" she countered worriedly.

"Hey, you aren't a helpless cripple. You've only lost a hand. Look at what I was. You're gorgeous and about the same age as he is, but no, I haven't told him about your hand. I think you both should meet, and you see if you like him and let him see you're a fantastic woman."

"But what if he dumps me the moment he sees me?" she countered, still very much concerned. After her accident, no one wanted anything to do with her, for she was no longer "perfect."

"If he does, it's his big loss, not yours. Just be yourself and see how it goes. I've never played matchmaker before, but I'd rather have him accept me for who I am than what I look like. Still, he is highly attracted to us EE women. I think that'll be a big plus in getting acquainted. Once he discovers your true self, I think he'll come a courting big time. At least I know I would. How about it? You don't have anything to lose, not really. The worse that can happen is that you won't like him or he won't like you. Nothing ventured, nothing gained, as they say. How about it?" She agreed somewhat reluctantly.

Later she told Lech the blind date was arranged. "Say, I'd sure feel a whole lot better about this if you and Peter could join us. Less embarrassing for me. I'm rather old for a blind date, don't you think?" She agreed and made arrangements to dine at a fancy restaurant in the loop.

That settled, she went back to her problem of finding heads for the other four areas of the world. The immediate problem was there weren't any of the existing personnel who were off Pytalon in those areas. She couldn't appoint a zombie as Commander. She sent a text to Tim. South America, Africa, Australia, and India would have to wait a bit, she thought. The only other recourse was to bring up the personnel records of the men in those areas, study them, pick four and bring them here to be detoxified and sent back as her commanders. She was hesitant to do that, because she wanted people in charge whom she could trust to do a good job.

Tim and Mandy discovered very little else about the reps during their remaining days at the high school. However, he was allowed to look over student histories for Chan-Petra. Two students rather impressed him, and he asked them to meet with him on Thursday. Hana Rumanan walked up hesitantly to their table. "You wanted to see me?" she asked somewhat timidly. She was of Indian birth; her parents had been transferred to Chicago when she was a freshman in high school.

"Yes, Hana Rumanana, right?" Mandy replied, figuring the teen would feel more comfortable talking to her than to Tim. She nodded. "We've been looking over your school progress. You're exceptionally bright, good with computers, and the leader of your volleyball team."

"Thank you. Yes, I am, but that will all end soon, will it not?" she replied. Mandy detected a note of hostility in her voice. Rightly so, careers were made and begun in just a few short months.

"We've talked to some of your councilors, and they say you wish to return to India. Correct?" Mandy asked, knowing that was a certainty.

"Yes, I do, but with my parents here, I'm not able to move. I was hoping some company from India would be here to hire me, but none are," she replied, revealing the origin of her disappointment and hostility.

"That is not entirely true, Hana. There is a very high paying opening in the Feds in India. You have all the qualifications needed. Would you be interested in a job there? You would need to receive some training first, before being sent to India."

Her eyes lit up. "Oh yes, very much so. But what city must I go to?" she asked.

"In this case, it can be any city of your choosing, Hana."

"Yes, yes, this is my dream, to return to my homeland. Yes, what must I do? What is the job?" she asked rapid fire, coming alive.

"A high paying one, Commander of the India Feds," Mandy finally said.

Hana nearly fainted. All that she could say was, "But, but, but. . ." Mandy rose and led her off to the cafeteria to get some tea and chat.

Tim smiled, sure that Hana would work well for Chan-Petra. Now only if Ben Adir would work out. He waited for that senior to visit the table. A half hour later, Ben appeared and twenty minutes later, Ben was as excited and elated as Hana had been. Not only would he would be able to return to Cairo, but he would also be the Commander of the African Feds! Chan-Petra wanted "normal" people to fill these top posts and decided to give teens a chance. Time would tell if they would be able to handle these new positions of power.

Around five Friday night, Lech changed into his business suit as did Peter. Chan and Yan merely had to freshen up a bit before they were ready for the blind date with Mary Lyons and Lech. "What if she finds me a big bully?" Lech whispered nervously to Peter.

"Oh I doubt that, Lech. More like will you find her not only attractive but also an interesting person in her own right," Peter attempted to calm Lech's nerves. He still didn't tell his friend about Mary's accident and missing left hand. No, Lech would have to face that, as would Mary. After all, beyond seeing an EE woman, her missing hand would be the first thing anyone would see when meeting her. Both needed to be able to face that and move on, he thought.

A half hour later, they walked into an apartment building where Mary lived by herself. She was waiting just as nervously for them in her lobby. "Mary, you look good tonight," Chan-Petra said walking up to her. "I want you to meet Lech Smith. Lech, this is Mary Lyons. She lost her hand in an unfortunate accident, and of course, her Pytalon drugged sponsor dropped her. Now she helps out daily at the Southend Mission."

"It is my pleasure to meet you, Miss Lyons. That's a terrible thing to happen so someone as lovely as you are," he greeted her. She was about his age, he noted and a gorgeous blonde whose hair was full and fell just below her shoulders. She wore a red satin gown and matching patent heels, the usual six inch stilettos. Ignoring her missing hand, she was dynamite, he thought.

"I am sorry I'm not now perfect for you, Lech. I had to cut my hair shorter so that I could manage it myself."

"I think you look just, well ravishing, if you don't mind my saying so. Shall we?" he offered her his arm. Smiling and a little relieved, she took his. "So Chan-Petra tells me that you work at the Southend Mission? You know we Feds never knew anything about that nor about all the most unfortunate accidents or their needs."

She giggled a little. "No one does, not until Petra came to us. Now that has changed. So what do you do, Lech?" she asked.

"I've just been appointed Commander of the North American Feds, a huge task, most challenging, and I have little ideas where to start," he replied.

"You need to cope first and get things going and then organize well. If you do it right, why you'll be on easy street in no time," she replied.

He paused, grinned, and said, "Amazing. I was thinking somewhat along those lines, but hadn't quite put it into words just yet."

Thus began a most interesting evening for the both of them. As Chan-Petra hoped, their courtship began that night. He was enthralled with her, not only because she was a knockout blonde EE woman (his description), but she had a brilliant mind for organization. Soon, she became indispensable in his office. They were married a month later, and she was appointed his top advisor as well.

Chapter 31—A Shift in Power

During February, Peter received reports from some of the other captains around the US on their progress in the location and elimination of the Trikuza mafia members. As expected, most were found in the areas where large populations of Chinese were living. St. Louis reported the elimination of five. New York reported dealing with twenty-five, though they also lost five good men in the process. However, LA reported they had uncovered a den of at least fifty and requested help in handling so many extremely deadly mafia members.

Peter knew just how deadly they could be, recalling the four to one casualties the Feds suffered when they came to Petra's rescue in Peking last year. Thus, he didn't hesitate to request Lech coordinate a massive assault, using all the US Feds. Lech did so, scheduling the roundup for March 1, some three weeks away.

***

Cai Dong's reaction was the same as his four fellow Trikuza members. Run. The Feds had just marched into the tea garden in force, wearing full battle armor. None of the five had their heavy weapons on them, just daggers and throwing stars, concealed of course. He dashed for the back door as the gunshots echoed. Bo was right behind him, but Bo cried out. Turning around, Cai saw Bo was hit, and he helped him back to his feet. Both began a mad dash into the throngs in the street. Ordinarily, that was more than enough to elude the AP-cops and the Feds. Cai thought one Chinese man looked just the same as all the others to the Feds, and he and Bo relaxed.

After putting a few blocks between them and the raiding Feds, they entered Bo's place, and Cai tended Bo's wound. It wasn't serious, a through and through. After bandaging the wound, both men retrieved their blades. While they were discussing just how the Feds had known they were in the tea garden, they heard noises out in the street. A quick peak and both cursed. "How did they find this place?" Bo cursed angrily. "Has someone squealed on us? They're dead!"

"Come on. Let's get going. We can't take on twenty of them, unless we have to, Bo," Cai growled. He was the leader of their small pack. The two snuck out the back way, darting down an alley, putting a few blocks between them. Exhausted from loss of blood, Bo finally said, "They can't find us now. We should be safe here. I need to rest." The two men sat down behind a green dumpster and waited.

Again, they heard the approaching Feds. "How are they able to find us? This isn't right, Bo!" Cai exclaimed.

"You go. Find out. I'll hold them off, Cai. This must be reported." Cai bowed to Bo, who returned in kind, though it hurt to do so. Bo drew his sword and prepared for battle. Cai slipped silently down the alley, heading for the nearest public EMAC station.

An hour later, he made a phone call before boarding an Air Liner bound for LA. "Yes, I tell you somehow the Feds knew where we were at, not once but three times. I swear we lost them each time. No one besides us knew where we were. No, no one else was there, and yet the Feds found us. I tell you, something is up. Yes, I'm on my way to LA. You do that; check with other cities." He hung up and boarded.

***

Weeks later, Master Yao Bing paced his penthouse suite in downtown Peking. His body was sore from the intensive martial arts workouts he'd been enduring. Bo Bin Lin was right, while he knew his moves by heart, he had to train them into his new, youthful body. Still, such was a tiny price to pay for immortality. His lovely EE woman, Juan Wu, sat upright on their couch, looking stunning in her bright red silk dress with yellow and green dragons wrapping around her form. Her straight, long black hair was draped across her front, reaching the floor while sitting, and her ankles while standing in her knee-high, matching, red ballet boots. "Dearest honey, what is the matter? Come here and let me sooth you," she said coyly, batting her long eyelashes and curling her bright red lips.

"Something new has appeared in our highly ordered world, my delicious honeybee. Something very nasty. That I, Master Yao Bing, do not know of this is a grievous insult to my honor," he replied with a frown.

"Please, come sit with me, and Juan Wu will make it right. I snuggle and please you," she replied in perfect EE woman form. In fact, Juan Wu could do very little by herself now. While she too was "immortal," her new body had no arms. Though this pleased Master Yao immensely, Juan Wu was not. Under the heavy influence of her implant, she found she couldn't execute its prescribed behavior very well at all. She had

489

frequent headaches now, relieved only when Master Yao took her to bed with him.

"Dearest, now is not the time. I must hold a meeting. Yet to do so, I will lose much honor, much face among our people. Come. You must accompany me. We go to the tea garden," he said, coming to her side. Using his hand, he helped her rise precariously to her feet. Steadying her, the two moved slowly, but elegantly, to the door. They took the elevator down one floor where Chan's Garden occupied the entire eleventh floor. Chan's was the most elegant tea garden in Peking. Master Yao had already reserved the restaurant for this meeting with all his seconds in command, all ten men.

As he reached the entrance, a glassy-eyed doorman opened the doors for the two, whispering, "Sanity is doing a good job. I open the doors for you." Slowly the two walked into the tea garden. The ten seconds had already arrived and were taking tea, but their whispered talk ceased as Master Yao entered, leading his elegant EE companion. The ten hastily rose and bowed low, and he paused to bow back to them. He whispered, "Juan Wu, you go over to our table and take tea. I will join you in a while."

Part of her wanted to cry out, "But I can't do this myself! How will I drink my tea or pull out my chair." However, her implanted behavior pattern refused to allow her to say this. "Dearest, please don't be too long. I long to please you deeply." She planted a gentle kiss on his cheek before facing the long walk across the gardens alone and without any helping hands. She felt a rush of terror, but could do nothing about it.

Master Yao sat down and poured himself a cup. Everyone was silent until he took a sip. "Gentlemen. Do any of you have anything to report on this matter that concerns us most gravely?"

Kang cleared his throat, "Oh great Master Yao Bing. I have discovered the truth." Kang was from LA and had only recently arrived in Peking.

Master Yao looked at the young man of twenty-five, knowing well that here was the one who would disgrace him. "Speak freely, Kang." He bowed and Kang did likewise.

"We captured a Feds and made him talk using the truth drug we stole. It seems our tattoos are giving away our position. Something that is in them is traceable by Feds satellites. We can run, but there is nowhere we can hide from them. We learned the Feds are planning a full-scale attack against my LA

490

division on March 1, using perhaps all the Feds in the United States. We're preparing to take them on, Master Yao, that is, if you give us the word."

His information caused quite a stir among the many other seconds, and they asked him a number of questions about this. Master Yao was himself silent, allowing his seconds to vent their anger and ask what they would, clarifying Kang's report so that he did not have to. Already his disgrace was significant. Knowing this, the other seconds were minimizing it for him, taking some of the disgrace upon themselves.

Kang suggested, "We could cut off our tattoos. They could not track us then." That met with disapproval, for it meant eliminating their signature trademark that had endured since the merging of the two mafia members two hundred years ago.

When they finished, an attitude of resignation of defeat filled the minds of the seconds. All knew this new method the Feds had was working well. They'd run the Trikuza out of all the cities in the US except for LA, where many had fled from other cities during the many raids.

Kang said, "We will fight to the death, Master Yao Bing. We will eliminate the Feds," he added with steeled determination, but with a fatalistic mood.

"My great seconds, long ago in ancient times, there were the Triads and the Yakuza, and we were enemies, plucking the riches of the world, like pears from the trees. Then, the world changed and both faced extinction. Rather than succumbing, our ancestors joined forces together and survived. Still the world around them changed, and to survive, they went underground, as we are to this day. The Trikuza still exists, while the entire world has changed." Most nodded.

He took a deep breath and continued, "Yet, what have we become? I ask you all this because it is most important, perhaps the most important thing I have ever asked. What have we become? Our world is filled with implanted zombies, a world of no-change. Gone are all the objectives our ancestors had. There are no drugs except for Pytalon, which the world is consuming to their detriment. Such things as opium and marijuana disappeared two hundred years ago. There are no secrets to steal, for nothing new has been invented in two centuries. Money? What can it buy that we do not already have? Crime? There is none, save that that we sometimes do. Extortion? All we have to do is ask a zombie for money and they willingly give it to us. We don't have to threaten them, beat them—nothing at all. We have become as a cat in a world of no mice, as a fish in a world without a sea, as a butterfly in a world of no flowers, as a bird in the world with no worms. While we can rob a store, what is the point when we can just walk into the store and ask for something and the zombies give it to us?"

"True, we are the masters of the arts, unequaled in the world. True, we are masters of our physical bodies. Yes, even now Juan Wu and I are immortal. But to what end do we exist now? What is our purpose in life? This insane society has defeated us. We are the most powerful men in the world, but that world with its zombies has at last defeated us, leaving us with no purpose at all. A man without a purpose is a dead man."

Their master's words hit home to the ten men. While they lived a life of leisure and luxury, they really had no purpose. They had become mere tokens of the ancient past. He allowed them a few minutes to reflect upon his words.

Master Yao then played the final remaining card he had. "My superb seconds, I have asked you here today to ask something of you. It may be I will be able to find us all a new purpose in life, for our existence, a purpose worth fighting for and dying for, a noble purpose, one filled with much honor. If I can find us that purpose, will you follow me? Will you obey me and help me fulfill that new purpose for us all? One that will guarantee our safety and continued survival far, far into the future. Will you give me your allegiance?"

Kang spoke up first, "Master, we are sworn to follow you, always. I so swear. Give us this new purpose and we will follow." Hastily the other nine echoed his words, though several were rather annoyed Kang was obtaining most all the honor at this meeting. Certainly, he would rise above them all in their master's eyes.

Master Yao bowed deeply to his ten seconds. "I am most grateful for the honor you give to me, most unworthy. It is to Kang that we owe the honor of this day. I shall retire now and prepare this new, golden purpose. Stay here; enjoy the gardens until I return."

He rose and again bowed humbly to his men, whose bodies were all much older than his own at eighteen. He walked stately across the room to where the lovely Juan Wu was sipping her tea through a straw.

"Come my orchid flower. We must return to our room for a time before we dine." He gently helped her to her feet and adjusted her hair for her.

Juan Wu looked most pleased and again gave him a loving kiss. "Yes, my darling. Is it time for me to give you much pleasure?" she asked demurely.

"In good time, my dearest, in good time."

This she took to mean yes and held her head proudly as they made their slow way out of the tea gardens.

Once in their suite, he said, "First, I must make this phone call. Please, sit beside me that I may touch you as I talk. You are the orchid of my life, lovely Juan Wu. If this call is successful, Juan Wu, then I will marry you and make you a proper orchid."

Juan Wu beamed with happiness, believing this meant more times for her to give Master Yao pleasure.

"Yes, I wish to speak to the head of the Feds. Yes, your Supreme Commander. Oh, I see. Petra then," he explained calmly.

The switchboard operator buzzed Chan-Petra. "You have a long distance call on Line 1. A Master Yao Bing, he says. He asked for the head of the Feds, and the call has been routed here from our LA office."

How strange, she thought. Chan-Petra picked her phone. "Hello. Petra Delius here. How may I help you?"

"I am Master Yao Bing, leader of the Trikuza. I wish to discuss some things with you and with Persephone, the Assassin and the one who left the Ace of Diamond cards in ten of my men near the secret Lin Foundation some months back, shortly before your raid on the Foundation. When she is on the line with us, I will then speak. When you both are ready, call me back on this number," he explained and quietly waited for her reply.

Chan-Petra's eyes widened. "I'll put you on hold, Master Yao. I'll get her on conference call mode in a minute. Please hold."

She pressed hold and let out a yell. Hastily, many Feds jumped into action. They would trace this call for sure! Quickly, she dialed Lady Persephone.

"Yes, Master Yao Bing, head of the Trikuza wants to talk to you and me. He specifically asked for Persephone, the Assassin, who put the Ace of Diamond cards on his dead men. Conference call mode. One second."

"But what does he want? You're closing in on all his men in the States," she replied.

"He won't talk further until we both are on the line. The call is being traced. If nothing else, we'll have his location, probably in China somewhere. Okay, we're live now. Master Yao, I have Persephone on the line with us," Petra spoke clearly, hoping his English was up to par.

"I am here, Master Yao," Persephone said softly. "Wise is the man who accepts my message. Wiser still is he who does not break his promised word. The five volunteers died with much honor."

Master Yao nodded, stroking Juan's hair. "Ah, it is you then. I must thank you for your timely message that saved many lives. The honor is all mine. I will be most frank with you both. I know you Feds are now able to track the location of my followers and how this is possible. I am aware of your proposed March 1 assault on Trikuza members in LA."

Crap, he knows. So much for surprise. It'll be a blood bath. "Yes, I won't deny it," Petra said solemnly.

"I wish to propose a deal that may benefit both of our organizations and avoid many deaths. Over two centuries ago, we were the Triads. The Yakuza of Japan were our enemies. We both plucked the riches of the world, like pears from trees. Then, the world changed and both of us faced extinction. Rather than succumbing, our most wise ancestors joined forces together and survived. Still the world around them continued to change. To survive, they went underground, as we are to this day. The Trikuza still exists, while the entire world has changed. To honor our long standing agreements, we surfaced recently, as witnessed at the second Lin Foundation."

"Yet, what have we Trikuza actually become? I will tell you what I have just told all my seconds. This is perhaps the most important thing I have ever asked. What have we become? Our world is filled with implanted zombies; it is a world of no-change. Gone are all the objectives our ancestors had. There are no drugs to deal. Such things as opium and marijuana disappeared two hundred years ago. There are no secrets to steal, for nothing new has been invented in two centuries. Money? What can it buy that we do not already have? Crime? There is none, save that that we sometimes do. Extortion? All we have to do is ask a zombie for money, and they willingly give it to us. We do not have to threaten them, beat them—nothing at all. It has been many, many years since anyone came to us for our services. Zombies do not think and have no need for our services. We have been slowly dying these centuries."

Still stroking Juan Wu, he continued with a perceptible sigh, "We have become as a cat in a world of no mice, as a fish in a world without a sea, as a butterfly in a world of no flowers, as a bird in the world with no worms. While we can rob a store, what is the point when we can just walk into the store and ask for something and the zombies give it to us?"

"As you are both well aware, we are the masters of the arts, unequaled in the world. We are masters of our physical bodies. Now Juan Wu and I are immortal, but to what end do we now exist? What is our purpose in life? This insane society has defeated us. We are the most powerful men in the world, but that world with its zombies has at last defeated us, leaving us with no purpose at all. A man without a purpose is a dead man."

"So you see, Persephone, Petra, you are talking to a man who is nearly dead, though his body be not yet twenty. Yet, I must make this one last attempt to guide my followers, to lead them onto a new path with a new purpose for life, a purpose worth fighting and dying for, a noble purpose, one filled with much honor."

Lady Persephone commented, "I believe the Master Yao Bing is most wise and humble to say what he has observed, though I know it brings him great pain and much dishonor to admit these things to us outsiders. I am most honored he thinks highly enough of me to tell me these things." Politeness was imperative at this point, she knew. Honor was everything to this man.

"I know that you, of all people, understand, Persephone, the Assassin. I shall come to my proposal, then. I would like to bring the Trikuza into the Feds, to work with you in whatever will bring the best to our world. Rumors abound that you are spearheading, if that is the proper English word, changes, eliminating the implanting and drugging of our children when they come of age. Can you tell me more of these things that I may better align my proposal?"

"Yes, I can do that, Master Yao," Chan-Petra spoke up. Quickly, she outlined their proposed changes. "We are working towards getting the entire world off Pytalon and free from the terrible implants, though to be honest with you, I know I'll not see the final end of this in my lifetime. Still, perhaps my grandchildren will reap the benefits of what we do today."

"Excellent and most worth purpose, Petra. Now I know the path the Trikuza must take. Here is my proposal. The Trikuza will assist you in any way we can to further this goal. I will place the Trikuza at the disposal of the Feds. There are trouble spots in the world. We will help fight and do what is needed to further the goal of a free world once more. In return, I ask only one small thing."

"So you and your men would take orders from we Feds? Help us combat renegades who are trying to harm our world? You would follow our commands?" Petra inquired, hardly believing this unprecedented offer.

"That is what I said, honorable Petra. We will obey as long as the commands further the goal of a drug-free, implant-free world once more. My people would have a purpose worthy of their highest honor."

"That is most commendable, Master Yao. Indeed, we have need of strong, able fighters, but I must ask of you what is this one small thing that you ask of us," Lady Persephone inquired. She suspected a strong catch to this unheard of proposition.

"At such time as this body of mine is dying and/or that of my beloved Juan Wu, then you will provide us new young bodies, using the inventions of the Lin brothers, which you now have in your possession. In this way, I can continue to lead the Trikuza, guiding them on this path to a new world free of Pytalon and the psychs. Since no man can know the time of his demise, you should have new bodies for us prepared, much as Bo Bin had for us. If you give me your solemn word to do this small thing for me and for my Juan Wu, then I will guarantee you the full support and cooperation of the Trikuza. Perhaps we should meet face to face to discuss details. By now, you know my location. I will be here to welcome you, if that is your desire," he replied humbly, still stroking Juan Wu gently down her curvaceous body as she leaned on him. He added, "If not, then I will still be here and you may send in your Feds to slay us. I will not resist, but I cannot guarantee the others will be so like-minded."

"Can you give us a little time to discuss your proposal, Master Yao?" Petra asked.

"Of course. You have my number now. Let me know one way or the other. Soon, perhaps, for I do not know how much longer I can command the Trikuza without providing them the promised new purpose for our lives," he replied.

"Excellent, Master Yao. I will get back to you very soon then. Thank you for discussing this with us. I am most honored by your call," Chan-Petra attempted to emulate Lady Persephone's manner of speaking, though it was foreign to her. He hung up.

Chan-Petra immediately added the professor to the conference call. After hastily explaining what the head of the Trikuza had said, she asked, "Is this for real? Do we believe him? Should we accept his proposal? Help. I'm out of my league here."

"Bloody hell, what an unexpected development, Petra! The Trikuza on our side? I would never have believed this turn of events," he replied.

"I would," Lady Persephone commented. "It has become a matter of honor, which they hold sacred, above all other considerations. Look, exactly what crimes can be traced back to the Trikuza in say the last fifty years? None, as far as I know, save their rescue of the Lin brothers. In ancient times, they were the mafia, committing all manner of heinous crimes. However, in this world of ours, what remains for them to commit? It is as he said, there is nothing to steal, no drugs. There in no honor in killing or harming a zombie. They are fish out of water, and he has had the wisdom to see that. Yet, they are fierce, highly skilled fighters, which we could certainly use on our side."

"But giving him and this Juan Wu new bodies later on? Is this something that we wish to commit to, really?" the professor asked.

"It is something not to be taken lightly. Remember, it is all honor with them. If we agree to his request now, then woe be it to whomever breaks that agreement in say fifty years when he requests a new body!" Lady Persephone explained. "If we agree, then we must be fully prepared to honor it."

"Well, I'm inclined to accept his offer," the professor spoke up. "There are so very few of us who are truly able and so many billions who are zombies. However, I believe we should meet with him, face to face, as he suggested, and as soon as possible."

"I would rather find a peaceful solution this time. I'm dreading the casualty lists from the LA mission coming up, and there are only around fifty Trikuza there. We simply don't have enough men to clear them out of China," Chan-Petra stated factually. "Okay, are we agreed to do this?"

497

"Yes, I believe we are, but I would recommend only two go to visit him," Lady Persephone suggested. "If this is a trap, then I'm able to take care of myself. He knows of the transference process, so Peter can go with me. He will be more comfortable discussing things with a male than a female. Besides if it is a trap, Chan-Petra would still be alive and well here. He couldn't wipe out our top leaders." They agreed and Chan-Petra made the call, arranging the meeting for tomorrow noon. That was as fast as they could get there, pushing the Air Liners at top speed. Lady Persephone immediately packed a few things and pushed her EMAC at top speed towards Chicago. Meanwhile, Peter made the rest of their arrangements.

Around eleven the next morning, the Feds' Air Liner landed at the airfield in Peking. The two took an EMAC to the location indicated by their geo-navigation coordinates that they had from their tracing of Master Yao Bing's call, landing on his skyscraper's roof. There a middle-aged man was waiting for them. In broken English, he said, "Master Yao Bing awaits in tea garden. Follow me." They did so.

Shortly, they entered a luxurious tea garden, now empty save for a pair of eighteen year olds—a man and an EE woman, who was elegantly dressed in a red silk dress with yellow and green dragons wrapping around her very shapely form, contrasting sharply with her very long, black hair draped over her front side. She wore matching red patent, knee-high ballet boots, and both could not help noticing she was armless. The young man wore an expensive black silk suit. In turn, they saw a woman in black, a cat ready for a fight. Lady Persephone purposely wore her Righteous Vigilante outfit, less her head mask. Peter wore a good quality brown suit, and he followed Lady Persephone's lead, bowing to the young couple as they entered the spacious gardens. Fragrant flowers decorated the restaurant along with the odors of cooking food. The young man returned their bows and motioned for them to join him.

As the two walked across the room to their table, he gently helped Juan Wu to her feet. Again, they bowed respectfully to Peter and Persephone, who also bowed. "I am Persephone; this is Peter Delius, Petra's new body."

"Master Yao Bing and my most lovely and gracious Juan Wu. Please sit. Lunch will be served directly." He helped Juan Wu sit down without falling into her chair, and then sat himself. "I see you have also put the Lin brother's invention to good use."

"Yes, we have, Master Yao," Peter replied, thankful that he didn't have to provide a lengthy explanation, adding, "as you both must have also recently done."

He nodded perceptibly. "Ah yes we have. Juan Wu now has a most perfect body. Is she not prettier than an orchid?"

She smiled at the compliment, but Persephone could tell that she was silently reciting her implant litany and wondering if she should flirt with these two.

"The Lin brothers allowed me to pick our new bodies. I trust you will afford me the same courtesy when the time comes, that is, if you are here to accept. If not, please do not slay my lovely Juan Wu, for she is blameless in all things."

"We are not here to slay anyone, merely to discuss the details, Master Yao. It would be most foolish of us not to consider your magnanimous offer of support," Persephone replied, setting him at ease. He was unarmed, she noted, though he could well have a concealed weapon or two.

Peter took the initiative, "Indeed, your offer took us by surprise, though having had time to reflect upon it, I can see the wisdom in this decision. It benefits us both. I have searched our database, and to our knowledge, the Trikuza have not committed crimes within at least the last fifty years as far as the Feds know. That I find most significant. We have been battling several groups who have been trying to destroy our world. Only now are we starting to become aware of dangerous groups on the fringes of civilization who are threatening us all."

He continued, "Here is how we are moving towards the restoration of our world. We have three separate groups engineering the eventual recovery and salvation of our entire civilization. No one group has total authority. There are checks and balances on our powers." He elaborated on the current setup and the current programs being piloted.

"Now then, having outlined just where we stand and our methods and goals, do you still wish to become a part of the earth's recovery?" Peter asked. He felt it was necessary to have explained all this to the Trikuza leader. He didn't want him to break his agreement later on, citing he was unaware of what the overall plans and objectives were.

Master Yao bowed to Peter once more. "I too am most impressed. We believed the Feds was just another corrupt arm of this insane world, out to suppress everyone into implanted, drugged, unthinking zombies."

"Your view is not without merit, Master Yao," Peter hastily admitted. "Three years ago, that would have been a concise statement of the Feds operations. However, I have changed, and as the Supreme Commander, I have altered the objectives and methods of the Feds to what it is today."

Master Yao smiled, "Ah, that is good to hear. I was not mistaken. Few men can admit such a mistake and so change their lives. In answer to your question, yes, your goals are worthy ones. I find no fault in your methods or plans. Your checks and balances make an interesting concept. Does this limit your ability to make decisions that need to be made? In our organization, it is up to me to make those decisions, and I must live with what I have decided. Can you react sufficiently swiftly with all those checks and balances?"

"Thus far, there have been no problems with it at all, that is, as long as I have a good knowledge of what needs to be done and our overall objectives," Peter replied. "When something unusual comes up, I can quickly consult the other three groups as I have done so in this case with your proposal. All three groups are in agreement."

Master Yao nodded and said, "Then, I can see no reason for the Trikuza to oppose you. We should be helping you, since this is a goal most worthy of us. If you agree to my lone request, then I will put the entire Trikuza at your disposal."

"Ah the request," Lady Persephone spoke up. "As you can plainly see, we have had to make use of the Lin brother's Transference Machine. Our group is very small, and we cannot afford to lose even one member at this most critical stage. However, we do not kill others, unless in self-defense. I knew no other way to reach you about that second Lin Foundation. The Feds were on their way with a massive assault group, and yet I saw the Trikuza were protecting the foundation. Had I not acted in the manner that I did, the number of dead for both groups would have been too much to bear."

He replied, "You acted wisely. We did not know the full story, only what the Lin brothers chose to tell us. At that time, we also thought that the Feds were out to suppress everyone, forcing them to be implanted or be drugged. I thank you for alerting me in time to avoid such strife. Still, we had a very long-standing agreement with the Lin brothers. Honor was at stake. I could not simply ignore that agreement."

Lady Persephone replied diplomatically, "Of course not, Master Yao. To have done that would have brought great dishonor to you and to the Trikuza. That said, we do not and will not kill an innocent person just to obtain their physical body for our use. Rather, I have been most selective. Here in China, the psychs in many of the smaller towns are still using the ancient Model I version of the Lin brothers' PDH implant machines. Unfortunately, this initial production model sometimes kills the person being implanted. Perhaps that is the wrong choice of words, for we now know that the person, the spiritual being, cannot be killed. Rather the transference process convinces the person that all is lost and to flee, to leave the body forever. Thus, their physical body is left to die slowly. It is those bodies that we have used. If we are to honor your agreement, the bodies will have to come from these. Will this be acceptable to you?"

"Yes, they would have to be Chinese, naturally. However, Juan Wu must also have an EE woman's body. I do not want her to have to endure the physical trauma to a new body as it is made into an EE woman's body. It should also have no arms like hers now. If these can be met, then I am most satisfied," he replied.

This was a sore point for Lady Persephone, who had already spent nearly two months working with Beth, Tilly, Amanda, and Jessica, trying hard to help them adjust to just such a life. She wisely knew Master Yao must have his reasons for wanting Juan Wu to be as she now was. Hence, she took a slightly different approach. "May I ask if you would prefer her to have her implant desensitized so she can once more think and speak for herself and not be continually reciting her implanted script?"

"This can be done?" he asked, somewhat surprised. "She would still be an EE woman?"

"It does not alter her body in anyway, of course. Rather, desensitizing gives her back her own mind so she can think, feel, and express herself as we are now, Master Yao. Surely, you would wish Juan Wu to be her real self once more."

Master Yao didn't react as Peter thought he would. He hesitated and rubbed his chin in thought. Seeing this, Lady Persephone added, "Or are you afraid she will turn against you because you have put her into a body that is virtually helpless in life."

His face flushed slightly and he flinched perceptibly, though Peter didn't see it. She did and knew she had hit the mark dead on. "In my opinion, she deserves to have her own mind back, to be able to think her own thoughts, and to express them, and not be a slave to her implant, as she is now. All the billions of people on Earth deserve this, though it will likely take many, many years to get the needed help to all those who have been implanted."

"But will she still care for me as I so deeply care for her? She has been my constant companion for over fifty years now. I could not live without her at my side," he replied honestly.

"That I cannot say, Master Yao. If you have mistreated her, she might not wish to remain with you. Yet, if you have been most kind and considerate of her, she may well care most deeply for you as well. You will never know unless you allow her implant to be desensitized," Lady Persephone persisted on behalf of Juan Wu, who sat opposite her, smiling continually at Master Lao and not understanding any of what had been said.

Master Yao stroked her head lovingly once more. "You are right. I have been dishonest with her, but here in China, that is to be expected. Women have virtually no rights, dependent upon us men. It has always been this way. Still, I would like my Juan Wu to be able to think too. I consent, but perhaps you can have two different bodies for her so she can choose next time?"

"I can promise we will have an EE woman's body for her. I can't promise anything about its arms," Lady Persephone insisted.

He sighed and agreed. "What must we do to get her desensitized?"

"Well that is a bit problematical. Her implant words were undoubtedly spoken in Chinese. Right now, I don't have anyone who knows how to do this and who can speak your language. It is not hard to do, really," she replied. "Let me see if I can find someone who can come here and do it for her."

"Is this procedure something I could do for her?" he asked.

"The procedure is very simple, actually. It requires knowing the precise script the psychs read to her during the implant process. However, it demands a great deal of patience and understanding on your part. Whether or not she can desensitize it depends utterly on your skill, patience, and persuasive abilities," she replied. "If you are willing to accept the responsibility for her, I will get the script you need and instruct you on how to do it."

"I would be most grateful. I have promised to marry her if we make this agreement. I would prefer to marry her if she truly desires me as well," he replied.

That brought a smile to Persephone's face. "Okay then, let me see if I can get the script now." She typed a text message to Ben asking for it.

"You can get such things? So quickly?" he asked, impressed with her.

"Yes, we have access to many things as you will be seeing. Ah, he thinks he can get it to me within the hour. Shall we dine?" she asked.

She was also curious to see how Master Yao would handle Juan Wu. To her surprise, he fed her in a very natural manner, and she concluded he had been doing so for some time. She relaxed a bit, since he was obviously caring personally for her needs, and she gave him credit for this.

When they finished eating, Ben sent her the script, and she relayed it to his cell phone. Next, she went carefully over the procedure, making very sure he understood what his role was and how to persuade her when the going got tough, which it certainly would. She emphasized never to vary from the pattern, no matter how she responded, but merely to coax and persuade her to continue repeating the phrase or sentence.

"The first phrase to desensitize is the one that says she must constantly repeat all these sentences. You will be able to visibly see the results of the process and so will she, thus inviting her willingness to persevere on the rest of it."

"Thank you, Persephone. I will begin tonight. With our agreement settled, I must now explain this to my people and obtain their agreement. I will be in touch."

Both Peter and Lady Persephone gave him their personal cell phone numbers to facilitate any further discussions, and they left for home, the deal sealed, but only if he could convince his mafia gang members to go along with it.

While both would have liked to stay around and see just how well he was able to convince his members, Lady Persephone had to get back to her four charges, hoping somehow they'd managed on their own for the few days she was gone. Neither of the two had any idea the entire proposal actually hung on whether or not Master Yao Bing could desensitize Juan Wu! Yet, the seconds demanded to watch and see if the Feds actually did have a way to lessen the horrible effects of the PDH implants. They wanted proof the Feds really did have a workable plan.

All sat patiently observing their master coaxing and sometimes persuading Juan Wu to continue to repeat, "I must repeat these words to myself many times each day." They heard her complaining bitterly how badly her head ached and how hard their master had to work to get her to continue the process.

However, around ten that night, Juan Wu's splitting headache vanished, and she commented, "It is strange, my love, but I don't feel compelled to say all these things any longer. How strange, but I do need to pleasure you my dearest love."

The ten seconds grinned, nodding to each other. Later, they agreed to honor the agreement and left to relay this huge change to their own subordinates. In turn, he sent a text message to Peter and Persephone telling them his men agreed, when they saw the desensitizing process was working. He told them of the success he had on that first sentence.

Two weeks later, Juan Wu had all the implant words desensitized. Master Yao and his ten seconds were most impressed. It had worked just as the Feds had said it would. He breathed a huge sigh of relief because Juan Wu still cared deeply for him and readily accepted his marriage proposal. However, she also complained bitterly about being so helpless and dependent upon him.

"Do not worry my most beautiful orchid; I will always be here with you."

She accepted this, particularly because he did pay far more attention to her than she thought he had before her new body. He invited all his seconds to attend his wedding ceremony, as well as Persephone and Peter, to be held in the tea garden.

When she arrived, she wore her white gown, no longer feeling the need to hide her identity as Lady Persephone Briton. Her objective was to check up on the mental health of Juan Wu. She feared the young teen would be horrified by her awful physical condition. As she entered the tea garden, orchids were everywhere, their odor quite strong. Over two dozen varieties were present in a superb arrangement. She bowed respectively to the ten seconds, who wore their finest silken suits in their honor. Quietly, she took a seat behind the ten men. It was a small wedding. A traditional Chinese priest, she assumed, presided over the ceremony.

Before long, the two entered from a side door. Master Yao Bing, his supporting arm around Juan Wu's waist, escorted his lovely bride across the room, standing before the eleven and the priest. She did look very beautiful, Lady Persephone thought. She wore a white satin gown with matching white patent knee-high ballet boots. Her shiny black hose was clearly visible beneath her gown, though only a few inches could be seen. Her thick black hair was quite shiny and perfectly brushed, falling to just above her ankles. She did wear a touch of makeup, but it was minimalist, save for her striking bright red lips. Her eyes sparkled, and as far as Lady Persephone could tell, she was extremely happy. Well, that's a good sign, she thought.

The wedding was in their own language, and she didn't understand a word of it. Nevertheless, the intent was clear, especially when they kissed each other. For her benefit, the priest announced in English as well as their own tongue, "I present Master Yao Bing and Mrs. Juan Wu Bing." All ten men rose and bowed deeply, and she followed suit.

After that, he escorted her over to a table where food and drink would soon be served. His men congregated around him, congratulating him, though she didn't understand their words. Instead, she sat down beside Juan Wu. "You look absolutely stunning, Juan Wu, the most beautiful bride that I've seen."

"Thank you, honorable Persephone. It is all Master Yao's doing. I cannot do much like this. I do look my very best. We owe so much to you. I can think now. No longer does my mind constantly go over all those words, except occasionally. Now I am free to be myself and to show Master Yao just how deep my love for him is. Thank you."

"I am so glad I was able to come to your wedding and share your most precious day with you. I am also very pleased you are free to be yourself. I was very worried about you, that you would be very depressed because of your physical limitations," she tried to find a polite way to ask what she needed to know for her own peace of mind.

"Sometimes I am so very frustrated, but always Master Yao is so very much pleased with how I look now that I do not allow such thoughts to bother me. He is my world and I, his."

"That is as it should be in a marriage. I am so happy for you. I brought you a small wedding present. May I give it to you now?" she asked. She opened a small box and withdrew a large emerald on a golden chain, which she fastened around her neck. It rested just above her massive cleavage. Both Juan Wu and Master Yao were quite pleased with her gift, thanking her excessively, she thought. Later after a lavish meal, she took her leave, heading home as fast as her EMAC could go. Lady Persephone was satisfied with the situation and gave Juan Wu no further thought.

However, the seconds now wished to have their own EE women. In the past, none wanted anything to do with the implanted women—not because they were perhaps the flowers of the land, but rather because they couldn't think, continually whispering their litany, their whole focus upon their programmed behavior. These martial arts masters found such behavior to be "insane." Now that they saw how Juan Wu was acting, talking, and thinking, they too wanted such women at their sides, desensitized of course. They followed the proper procedure and made their requests at their local EE women's web sites, adding to the demand for such women, which Jess and the others had thought was now gone. Of course, once they had them, they had to desensitize their new EE women's implants.

By June, many Trikuza began operating with the various Feds units around the world. Most, of course, were with the Feds in China and Japan. Five were with the London branch and fifty were with the LA branch, for example. Slowly, the Feds were building up the strength needed to tackle the fringe areas of the world commonly known as the hot spots, which a year ago, Peter Delius didn't even know existed.

Chapter 32—Jessica Takes a Stand

During the spring, Ben, Jess, Tim, and Amanda were focusing their efforts on gathering intelligence on the suspected groups that were highly suspicious in senior recruitments for their organizations. The Locki Freedom Fighter and Marshals Militia and Security were at the top of their lists. Unfortunately, dig as they might, very little information was being uncovered. Of course, this led them to try even harder to figure out just what these groups were actually doing or threatening.

Mid-May, Jess became frustrated that she could find out almost nothing and her mind drifted back to the apparent increase in demand for EE women. At last, she gave up the searching and decided to do a little investigating of her own. Just what was happening with this new demand for EE women? She visited the Chicago EE Women's Office personally to find out.

Mary Bell greeted her in proper fashion and was pleased to discuss the new demand for their services. "Oh yes, this time last year, why, we all were being asked to find a husband. Rumors abounded this was the very end for us all, that there were no more proper sponsors for us women. I was particularly saddened. I've been here for thirty-five years now. We EE women are the very best that womanhood has to offer, you know."

"So what has changed?" Jess asked.

"We're now getting a lot of requests from high school seniors. It seems now that the implants and Pytalon are totally optional and that the graduates are being allowed the freedom to choose their own paths in life, many young couples wish to marry their sweethearts."

"Yes, but what has this to do with our situation?" Jess asked, a little annoyed at the slowness of the woman. Still, she was doing a good job in spite of her implant, which had not been specifically desensitized, but had lost its grip over these many years. Mary Bell was fifty-three, but still looked ravishing, probably because of the heavy makeup she wore, Jess thought.

"You see, the young beaus wish their wives to look stunningly beautiful, and their brides desire to look their very best for their new husbands. These are accounting for the increased demand, you see," Mary Bell finally answered her question. "Still, we do get other orders as well." She leaned closer to Jess and whispered, "I wouldn't be surprised to see a big increase in our numbers, Jess. I can't think of a more rewarding career for a lovely, young woman. Can you?"

Jess could, but thought better of saying anything. Instead, she politely thanked her and left, mulling over what she'd learned. "Would I consider becoming an EE woman just to please Ben or Beth?" She asked herself, and she found she didn't have a snap answer, only a feeling that she just might, rather surprising herself.

Back at her office, she began examining the many other EE women's sites in the major cities of the world, drawing up graphs of the yearly number of new EE women each center produced. Produced is perhaps a poor choice of words. The psychs and the doctors actually turned the women into EE women, but as soon as they were done, the women were automatically registered with their local branch. She chose twenty large cities to study. A couple of days later, she tiled the twenty graphs, nicely labeled, on her large flat screen monitor. Now she could see the relatively worldwide pattern.

For years, the line representing the new EE women was horizontal. Then three years ago, it began dropping, becoming very steep when the Feds finally believed they had gotten everyone who wasn't implanted or on Pytalon handled. This corresponded to the time when she'd gotten revenge on Peter Delius. Now the graphs were rising sharply once more. However, something caught her eye. London. Their graph showed no dip whatsoever. In fact, they had an alarmingly high increase during the last five years. Jess had found another anomaly. Now she simply couldn't just leave it be. What was going on in London, she wondered?

***

Adrianna Worthington was just finishing up her A levels, expecting to graduate at the end of the spring term on June 1, 2272. Her goal was to be a teacher, and she'd applied to teach first grade at Eldon's Primary. The lovely blue-eyed, curly haired blonde lived in Whiteley Village, South London. Actually, she should have called herself Lady Adrianna Worthington, but she was in a rebellious mood, had been since she was ten. Her father, Lord Worthington, was the CEO of Worthington Industries and had a newly built manor house on

508

part of what had once been the Burhill Golf Club some two centuries ago.

Both her father and mother were heavily dosed on Pytalon, though her mother was also an EE woman, as expected of the Lady of the manor. Adrianna rebelled because she saw neither parent actually doing anything remotely useful or constructive. They were mere zombies and barely paid the slightest attention to her. She vowed to do something with her life, which is why she mostly paid no attention to the many boys who tried to date her. No way was she going to become a Pytalon drugged housewife! No, she had already seen just what that meant with her best friend's mother.

Martha Bettingham was Adrianna's BF since they met in second grade. Martha lived in St. Georges Hill, just across the ancient B365 otherwise known as Seven Hills Road, now a popular hiking trail for the high school teens. Her Pytalon-drugged mother drove both teens half-mad with her constant implant and drugged chatter. Her mother saw to it that each day was exactly like the previous day, no variations. Like her friend, Martha ignored the many boys asking her out. There was no way that she would marry and wind up like her mother! She had auburn eyes and wavy brown hair. Both Adrianna and Martha were very attractive young teens; their bout of acne had cleared up their junior year. Their constant refusal to go out with boys earned them the label of snobs, particularly because Adrianna was supposed to be a Lady.

Nursing had appealed to Martha until she had a field trip and actually saw the implanted and drugged nurses. After that, she put her attention onto computer work. Both teens were excellent with computers, winning school awards for the best-designed web site.

Late spring when the announcement came that the Feds were hiring too, Martha decided she would apply there. "Look, of everyone we know, the Feds are the least likely to be zombies," she'd explained to Adrianna. "You should too."

Adrianna toyed with that idea, but had put in to teach first grade instead. She loved working with the younger children.

Adrianna and Martha were nearly inseparable. Each evening, they alternated studying at each other's house and often took strolls down the hiking trail B365. Sometimes they wondered what kind of vehicles used to travel its weed-strewn path of concrete and asphalt that was still partially visible underfoot. The night before their Assignment Day when they would learn if they were chosen for the job for which they'd applied, the two left the fancy manor house, walking the short distance to the Octagon Road, where the MTE began. Instead of taking it on over to St. Georges Hill, they stepped off onto the hiking trail, sometimes called Seven Hills Road. The late May evening was warm with just a trace of fog beginning.

"A hike will calm our nerves," Martha proclaimed. "I do hope we are chosen. At least the Feds did say we don't have to get implanted unless we want to, and I bloody don't want that!"

"Who would? We also aren't going to be put on Pytalon either, thank goodness. Maybe things will be changing, do you suppose?" Adrianna asked sounding a hopeful note. "I think I'd rather die than be like my mother."

"Same here, but mine's even worse than yours, a real zombie. Honestly, I don't even think she knows I'm her daughter anymore. How can anyone live as our parents do?" Martha asked.

Adrianna shrugged her shoulders and tossed back her shoulder length blonde curls. "Don'na know. Going to be a bit o' fog tonight." The two walked on down the path, enjoying the evening air and the smell of heavy moisture in the late spring air. Already the world had greened, and many birds were still announcing their presence to the world around them. Slowly the tensions seeped out of the teens, as it always did when they walked the hiking trail.

Unseen by the two teens, two men in black slipped out of the nearby trees and came up silently behind them. Suddenly both teens felt a rag over their nose and mouth. At once, they struggled to get free, but the chloroform on the rags quickly overcame them. Both slumped towards the ground, unconscious. The two men picked them up and disappeared back into the trees, stepping out further on beside an EMAC. Shortly after that, the vehicle took to the air.

Fifty-five year old Lord Vincent Wargrave, dressed in a fine black suit with matching cape, met the EMAC as it landed near the psych center in Central London. He stepped inside and examined the two teens, verifying his men hadn't made a mistake. He could afford none, not in his business. True, he was on Pytalon, but that only aggravated his "hobby." He nodded silently and led the two men carrying the teens into the building.

"I've brought my two women. Are you ready for them?" he said, "Sanity is always doing a good job."

"Aye, my Lord. Sanity is always doing a good job. I'll do a good job on them, as ordered. Return in the usual three days to pick them up," the psych man said in his monotone voice.

"Your instructions regarding these two are quite clear, my good man? Sanity is doing a good job. Nothing must go wrong," he replied, struggling a little against his own mental fogginess.

"I have your orders here, My Lord. Sanity is doing a good job. I'll do so with them as I always do," he replied. Lord Vincent bowed slightly, turned on his heels, and left. His two glassy-eyed men followed him.

***

"Lady Persephone, look at the graph I or rather Jess made of London's EE women created per year," Jessica asked. She'd struggled with her new laptop and using her toes finally got the chart up. "This is an anomaly. The other nineteen cities showed a marked drop when Peter finally got nearly the last normal people implanted or on Pytalon. That's when the EE Women's sites began notifying us to all get married. See, London actually shows a rise at that time, not a drop. Why?"

"Now that's a good question, Jessica," Lady Persephone tossed her hair back a little and took a closer look at the graph. "You should investigate this, Jessica. Try it. If you can't manage it, let me know, and I'll lend a hand. You have to try."

Jessica sighed, "Yes, I know. If I don't try, I'm going to end up a helpless woman for the rest of my life. It's just so darn hard, so frustrating."

"I know. It is for all of you. Still, Lisa manages well. Give yourself plenty of time and patience and you can too," Lady Persephone attempted to console her and give her the support needed. Inwardly, she again cursed the Lin brothers for having done such an awful thing to these four women.

A few days later, Jessica managed to do what she could have done in a half hour before. "I've come across something that is rather odd, Lady Persephone. Look at this," she pointed with her foot. She was sitting on the floor with the laptop in front of her.

"Bloody odd!"

"I know. Why would one man want so many EE women registered with him as their sponsor? Is he running a brothel or something?" Jessica asked, unable to imagine why one man would want to sponsor nearly twenty women. "Who is this Lord Vincent Wargrave anyway?"

Lady Persephone fought hard from taking over Jessica's computer and typing rapidly to find out what she could about this man. If Jessica was ever going to be somewhat independent and live a useful life, she had to be able to do it herself. "I don't know. Why don't you see what you can find out about him and let me know?"

Jessica sighed again. She wanted to know right now and wished Lady Persephone would have volunteered to take over for her, but she hadn't. Inwardly, Jessica knew why she hadn't, but sighed anyway. Painstakingly slowly, she began to enter her search criteria. Before long, she had his web page up. Wargrave's Ponies. *How strange, the man raises and sells ponies. Who wants a pony anyway? Where would you even keep such a thing? What would you do with it? Maybe ride it as Juan does with his horse?* She again called for Lady Persephone.

"Ponies? Who the bloody hell wants ponies? Well, he is Lord of Wargrave Manor and has his stables not too far from here. It is outside Wargrave, which is northwest of here. It is a quaint looking farm. I'll give him that. Why have two dozen EE women on a pony farm? Keep looking. This is only getting stranger," Lady Persephone suggested.

She did so. A bit later, she came across a purchase page with two links. One was labeled "Ponies" and the other labeled "Equine Ponies." The first link took her to a series of pages where small ponies were being sold with pictures and prices. She backed up and took the strange second link. Up popped a login box. She couldn't get to the second set without a proper login and password. Jessica was stymied and stared at this strange link. Equine ponies? She thought, how strange—of or having to do with the horse family ponies? Again, she called for Lady Persephone.

"Now that certainly is a strange wording. It doesn't make any sense. Why password protect this page? I think you're getting somewhere, but I've no idea where," she replied. "Keep at it, Jessica."

She knew she didn't have the computer system here that they had back home. Thus, she sent the link to Jess and asked herself to crack it and send it back to her.

"Now we're getting somewhere, Jess thought and cranked up her software that cracked such things. Actually, it belonged to Weasel, but she was now very adept in using it. A half hour later, she was into the site and sent the login data to Jessica so that she could show these unreal pages to Lady Persephone. What she saw appalled her.

"Oh my god! Lady Persephone! Come look at these! How awful!" Jessica called out loudly. She and the other three came dashing over to her laptop sitting on the floor. She'd found the EE women all right. They were wearing their usual satin gowns, but hemmed very short, just barely covering their bottoms. Over their gowns, they wore a strange looking harness. Horse bridles were strapped to their heads with metal bits in their mouths and several tall, feathered plumes rising over a foot above their heads. Their thigh-high boots looked like the familiar ballet style, except a round hoof was attached to the toes and heels and a metal horseshoe was attached to the bottoms. Several other pictures showed the women harnessed to small carts, pulling other women or men around a track. The header text read: Trained Ponies For Sale. The prices varied and were in universal credits.

"This is utterly criminal!" Jessica cried out. "He's a beast! Those poor women!"

Lady Persephone fumed. "Time for the Righteous Vigilante to strike again! Talk about perversion—this takes the bloody cake!"

Just then, Lady Persephone received a cell call from Chan-Petra. "Hi, say, I hate to bother you, but this one is in your area of England, I think. I just got a call from Captain Lark of the London Feds. He's accepted a graduating senior named Martha Bettingham into his office as an analyst. However, she has failed to appear and has apparently gone missing. He asked for my help on what to do next. Could you look into it? She lives not too far from you in St. Georges Hill, fairly close to a Lord Worthington of Whiteley Village. Another graduating senior, Adrianna, has also gone missing. Apparently, these two were best friends. They disappeared on the 31st."

"Okay, I'll look into this. Both places are not too far from here. Have you seen what Jessica has uncovered here? Pony women?" Lady Persephone asked.

"No, Jess has asked me to come take a look, but I got delayed by the call from London. I'll go now. That bad?" Chan-Petra asked. They chatted a bit before hanging up.

"Jessica, can you open a new browser tab and work your magic. Two teens have gone missing, Martha Bettingham and

Adrianna Worthington. See if there is anything on them, like AP-cop reports, pictures, and social networking chats, whatever. I've promised to look into their disappearance. When it rains, it pours," Lady Persephone stated flatly, controlling her rising anger.

Jessica struggled with her toes, growing frustrated with how slow she was in responding. Yet, Lady Persephone still didn't offer to take over, and she finally made a connection to their computer systems in Chicago. An hour later, she finally had the remote search going, with the result pages being sent to her laptop. What should have been five minutes at most had taken her over ten times longer to do, and she fought the temptation to break down and cry over it.

At first, simple pages came back, their social network pages, and she read their on line postings for a while before turning in for the night. Jess needed her attention now. She couldn't run two bodies at the same time, not yet anyway.

***

Adrianna finally wakened. She had no idea she'd been unconscious for three days. Her breasts hurt and her lips felt funny. Something metal was in her mouth, she felt very groggy and strange. Finally, her eyes fluttered and she opened her eyes. She was sitting on a bench; hay was all around her. She raised her hands to her face. Her arms collided with her massive breasts and she looked down. Her bosom was enormous. Her hands, knotted into fists, were hidden inside what appeared to be two black rubber balls strapped to her wrists and padlocked. She wore a white satin gown that barely covered her privates, but also some strange leather harness was fastened over her torso on top of the gown. She felt a harness over her head too, holding the metal thing in her mouth like a horse's bit. Her feet throbbed and she glanced down at them. The tight-fitting thigh boots had her toes pointing straight down. Now she recognized the style of boots, EE women's ballet boots and a wave of panic slowly began to sweep over her. The bottom of her boots seemed heavy as if weighed down by lead. She let out a scream of terror.

From some remote corner of her mind, she had the thought EE woman, but could not focus enough to bring it into full consciousness. She heard another woman screaming not far from her stall. Then she tried to speak, but could not. Nevertheless, the implant words came flooding through her mind as she played them back to herself, wholly out of her control.

She'd finally reached the end of the litany when a well-dressed man stepped into the room. She could see him over her stall door. "Ah, you are awake at long last, my gorgeous Equine EE woman, Miss Adrianna. Oh, yes, and Miss Martha you are awake too, I see. Welcome to Lord Vincent Wargrave's Pony Farm. You are both beautiful EE women now and fantastic pony women. These are your stalls where you will be staying now. If you are thirsty, push on the button on the water fountains."

He continued, "At meal times, you'll join the other ponies at the dinner table. During the day, you'll be trained to be super ponies, just as you are superb EE women. Oh yes, once a day, your hands will be freed so you may properly groom yourselves. Since you need pleasuring so frequently, your special panties will supply the stimulus that you need. All you have to do is walk around your stall to satisfy your needs. When you need to relieve yourselves, your dresses are quite short so just bend over the latrines there in your stalls and have at it. I'll give you an hour to get yourselves satisfied and watered before I begin your pony training. Until then my gorgeous EE pony women," he bowed slightly, turned, and left the "barn."

Satisfy? The word echoed in both women's minds. Suddenly, both knew they just had to have pleasuring. A massive migraine began forming. Instinctively both tried to stand up and follow his suggestion to walk around the stall. Their feet cramped and ached mercilessly, but both teens managed to take a few steps and their special panties worked as suggested. Ignoring the pain in their feet, both moved around until at last, they were satisfied, but then both began trying to recite their implanted litany once more, but the bits in their mouths prevented them from speaking the words. Instead, they went over them silently in their minds.

When she finished, for a brief instant, Adrianna's mind was a little clearer. She looked into the next stall only to see Martha. Now she could see what she must look like, and she tried to talk to Martha, but soon gave it up. The tight bit in her mouth made speaking intelligibly impossible. She began to cry. Unfortunately, a minute later, her crying ceased as involuntarily, she began reciting her litany once more, ending with "Sanity is being a good pony woman," to which she found herself agreeing with wholly. That she did shock her further. In the next stall, Martha was undergoing similar reactions.

A while later, the man returned and clipped reins onto her head harness and forced her to rise. She tried to tell him that her feet ached, but she couldn't understand herself.

"There, there, a good pony never speaks."

Ah yes, be a good pony woman. Don't speak. She became quiet. He led her to a two-wheeled cart and began fastening her torso harness to it. Before long, he led Martha to her side and hooked her up as well.

"There my fine young ponies, you look splendid. Now be good ponies and take me for a ride." He climbed onto the cart and snapped a whip. "Giddy up. Go, ponies," he commanded. He had to explain what he wanted them to do, and at last, both teens realized he wanted them to pull him in the cart. Adrianna tried to pull, but she couldn't get much traction standing on her toes in the very heavy boots. He snapped his whip again and she tried once more. With Martha trying as well, they began to move the cart, but her feet throbbed in pain. "Good ponies, good ponies," he said kindly, which allowed both women to begin to ignore the excruciating pain in the feet. Both now felt they were doing a good job.

Soon they were outside pulling the cart around a dirt oval track. The air felt fresh and clean. Somehow, Adrianna felt this was perfect, especially as the man kept on complementing her and Martha. They were being good ponies. They looked perfect, he said, which made both feel even better. Finally gasping for breath, he drove them back into the barn, which she could now see was a red brick building and not really a barn, but that observation was buried deep in her mind, far from the surface, obscured by both her implant and the large dosage of Pytalon she'd been given. As long as he kept on saying she was being a good pony, she felt calm. How strange trickled into the very back of her consciousness.

Sometime later, she was led into a dining room. She heard her heavy metal horseshoes clicking on the wooden floor. She was told to sit, and she and Martha sat down on the bench before the rather tall table.

"Now I'm going to temporarily remove your bits so you can eat your supper. No talking, now. Good ponies don't ever talk, and you both want to be good ponies, don't you?"

Adrianna and Martha found their heads nodding yes in reply. A metal bowl with a delicious supper lay before her. She looked at it confused. Her hands were still in the balls, and she saw no silverware around. She looked around and saw there were ten other EE women ponies eating here too. One took pity on her and tapped her gently with her balled hand, then showed her how to eat. Adrianna bent her head over the food dish and began eating with her mouth. In her mind, she found the thought, "Oh, I'm supposed to eat like a pony." Somehow, it made perfect sense to her, and besides, she felt starving.

Later, with the bit replaced, she was led back to her stall. Finally, her hands were freed, and she was given a brush for her hair. "Make yourselves pretty, my fine, good looking ponies," the man said.

Mechanically, she did as asked. When that was done, her fists were put back into the rubber balls and locked into place.

"Now it is time for all good ponies to lie down and sleep. Cover yourselves with the soft hay."

Again, involuntarily, she did as asked, satisfied she'd done a good job and was being a good pony. In the deep recesses of her mind, she was fighting. She didn't want to be a pony or an EE woman, but she could no longer remember what she had wanted to be.

***

After breakfast the next morning, Jessica skipped the start of their practice sessions to check for more results of her computer search for the two teens. While her worm had uncovered a number of results, one caught her attention immediately, and she cursed her slowness at getting that page up. Both names were listed on London's official EE Women's web site; they had just become such a few days ago. A fuming Jessica marched into the practice session room.

"Lady Persephone, they've been turned into EE women against their will. I bet anything they're in the hands of that monster of a lord what's his name!" She was quite angry and more than a little annoyed. "We have to do something fast! We have to rescue them and all the others. That lord fellow needs to be taught a lesson he won't ever forget!"

"Deep breath. Calm down. How do you know this?" she asked. Beth, Tilly, and Amanda stopped their practicing to listen in. Seldom had the three ever seen Jessica this angry.

"London's EE Women's web site. Their entries just got posted," Jessica replied. "Come see for yourselves." She turned and headed back to her laptop, annoyed that she had no way to have brought it with her to save time. Many things were annoying Jessica, and they all had to do with her disability.

Presently, the group, including Juan Carlos, looked over her shoulders at the entry. Beth suggested, "Login and see if their sponsor is listed." Jessica sighed, wishing Lady Persephone would just step in and do it. Five minutes later, she finally got in and scrolled down to these two newest entries. Sure enough, their sponsor was none other than Lord Vincent Wargrave! Lady Persephone swore a very nasty curse.

"Okay, first thing we need to know before we go charging in there is where are the two teens being held," Lady Persephone visibly calmed down. "We need a plan. Give me a second."

She closed her eyes for a moment and then spoke up, "Session is canceled for today. Jessica, you and I are going to pay a visit to this pony farm of his. We're in the market for a pair of young ponies to drive you around, be your chauffeur, since obviously you need it. I'll be myself, Lady Persephone Briton. Since he is a lord, he may well know of me or have seen me at some time or other. We'll specifically ask for brand new ponies, teens, so they'll have a long lifetime pulling you to where you need to go."

"But we aren't really going to make them do that are we?" Jessica asked, believing what Lady Persephone was saying. She was very believable. Then, she caught the grin on her face, and Jessica began to giggle, realizing she'd fallen for it too.

"I need you to dress very nicely and wear stocking and your heels, as hard as that is for you now. We must look like a proper English Lady and her EE woman companion. Can you do this?"

"Sure, come on you guys, you have to help me get dolled up. Wait, Juan, I'll need your help too. None of us can handle putting on nylons yet," Jessica replied, thinking fast.

An hour later, Jessica looked like a proper EE woman, wearing her red satin gown, black stockings, and her six-inch heels. Lady Persephone also put a bit of makeup on her for good measure. She wore her white gown and low pumps, looking every bit a proper English lady. Together, they headed out to her EMAC. Fifteen minutes later, they parked in the EMAC lot of Lord Vincent Wargrave's Pony Farm. Lady Persephone carefully helped Jessica manage the three steps to the ground. Together, they walked up to the main office.

Lady Persephone was also carefully noting what security measures Vincent had here. She spotted armed guards and a video camera system as they entered the office. A glassy-eyed woman was at a desk. "May I help you?" she asked, whispering to herself, "Sanity is asking customers politely."

"I have come to see Lord Vincent Wargrave about some ponies for my niece here. Please tell him Lady Persephone Briton is here," she said in the formal tone of an English lady of high nobility.

Shortly, the well-dressed Lord Vincent came into the office, slightly out of breath. "My Lady Briton. How good it is to see you, and this charming young woman is your niece, I presume. Lord Vincent Wargrave at your humble service," he bowed respectively to her.

"Yes, my wonderful niece, Jessica. We have a problem, and I've it on good authority that you are just the man to see."

"Please, do go on," he said most politely, but eying Jessica carefully.

"You see my niece has met with a rather tragic accident some years back. Getting around is now so very hard for her. If she had a pair of ponies, they could drive her where she needs to go. Of course, since she is so young, the ponies must be teens themselves so we can get a lot of use out of them. Perhaps you have recently acquired some young teens that could pull my niece around my estate? She does need to get out into the sun more often. With a fine pair, why, she could spend hours driving around my estate. Obviously, Lord Vincent, price is no object, especially if they meet our criteria. EE women, good looking, well behaved, that sort of thing. If they aren't yet fully trained, we can wait a while before we take possession of them. Oh, yes, could we also purchase a light two-wheeled carriage that Miss Jessica can easily get into and out of? You see, the one I have is a bit much for her to manage alone. If not, I suppose I can have one made especially for her."

"Why, as a matter of fact, you have come at the right time, My Lady. It just so happens I do have a pair of young teens in training even as we speak. Of course, they're not yet fully trained. Perhaps by next week they'll be quite ready. I give you my word as long as Miss Jessica tells them frequently they're very pretty and very good ponies, they will respond very well to her commands. Of course, if you chose to ride, My Lady, you can use the reins," he explained politely.

"Oh this is so excellent, Lord Vincent! I told her not to get her hopes up too high, that you might not have young enough ponies available and that she might have to wait some time for her ponies. Might we see them? If they are satisfactory to Miss Jessica, we will purchase them today in anticipation of their delivery when you believe they are quite ready for work."

"Certainly, My Lady. If you'll follow me," he opened the office door for the two. Once outside, he began walking towards his "barn." "This is my barn ahead. Not actually a barn, it's fully heated and all that, regular warehouse converted to appear as a barn for the mental sake of the ponies. I presume you have a stable?"

"Certainly, what manor house doesn't have a good stable?" she countered.

Entering the barn, they saw a number of stalls and the feathered plumes from the head harnesses of many of his ponies. "At this time, I have a dozen here, but only two will meet your criterion. Of course, if you would accept older ponies, you could have them today and not have to wait a week. You may choose the colors of their gowns if you like. Ah here we are. I've recently acquired these two good-looking young ponies. Stand up good ponies," he ordered.

Mechanically Adrianna and Martha rose on their aching toes, but didn't complain. Adrianna thought: *He called me a good pony. I am a good pony; that's right. Sanity is being a good pony.*

Jessica wanted to lash out at Lord Vincent on the spot. Had she arms, she might very well have! Lady Persephone, however, was as cool as possible.

"Oh my yes, these are very good ponies indeed! I believe they'll be a perfect match for my niece. Dear, with these two ponies in our stables, you'll be able to ride all over my estate. Fresh air and sunshine will do wonders for your complexion and health, I'm sure. Lord Vincent, we'll take these two when you deem them fully trained."

"Ah excellent, My Lady, excellent. Of course, you won't be asked to pay for them until they are ready to be delivered. I stand behind all my good ponies, but accidents do sometimes happen. I shall contact you when they're ready."

He chatted a bit longer and displayed several models of two-wheeled carts, which Jessica could manage to get herself into and out of on her own. Lady Persephone added one to her order. After shaking his hand, the two women left.

Chapter 33—Jessica's Discovery

"He never mentioned their price," Jessica pointed out, as their EMAC rose into the air and headed towards her castle.

"Between lords and ladies, price is never mentioned. We're presumed to be quite wealthy. Now then, let's go over what you observed while we were there, specifically about Lord Vincent," Lady Persephone couldn't help but turn this into a training exercise for Jessica.

"Well, he seemed terribly polite, but I didn't believe much of what he was saying; he's covert. He's a slick seller."

"That is just the surface. Dig deeper." Jessica tried but finally gave up. "We'll work on your powers of observation more in the coming days and weeks. His eyes. Did you notice his eyes? They were glassy-eyed. He's on Pytalon himself."

"But how can he talk so nicely and be a zombie?" Jessica asked.

"Easy. He was doing all this *before* he was put on Pytalon. Now he's like every other zombie, merely doing the same actions over and over. Besides whatever he normally does, he also runs this slave pony trade on the side. He just keeps on doing it. At this point, it's probably wholly out of his control. He couldn't stop it if he wanted to—the drug, you see."

"Does that mean he can't be punished for his crimes against all these women?" Jessica reacted badly to her explanation.

"Of course he certainly is going to suffer the consequences of his actions. Right now, we have to rescue all the women and somehow get them salvaged. They've been implanted, of course, but also they're on a heavy dose of Pytalon. Plus, we need to find others he has sold and rescue them, if possible. We've only just reconnoitered the land," Lady Persephone replied, landing the EMAC on her castle grounds.

Once inside, Jessica described what had happened to the others, while Lady Persephone and Juan talked in private.

"Yes, you and I can probably take out the guards and secure the place," Juan agreed. "We could let the four lend a hand getting the women into the EMAC for transport. Are we going to turn Vincent over to the Feds?"

"Definitely not! I have something else in mind for that creep. I'm not the Righteous Vigilant for nothing. No, we secure him and bring him back here as well. Then we will go over his place with a fine-tooth comb. We have to find the other women he has sold and get to them as well, Juan. We've our work cut out for us tonight."

"Okay, so when we get the women back here, how the devil do we handle them? Do they really think they're human ponies?" Juan asked.

"They are heavily drugged, and we don't yet know what their implant scripts were all about, but I think their behavior is mostly caused by Pytalon. They can't think at all—only obey. The phrase 'good ponies' seems to control them. We'll just have to see once we get them here. Glad I have a sauna in the castle, because we're bloody well going to need it, I'm afraid. Let's get as much ready for them ahead of time as we can. We still have some hours before suppertime."

Around seven that night, the EMAC landed just beyond Lord Vincent's estate. "I wish we could come with you, but we couldn't do anything but hinder you," Tilly said with a sigh, as the two dark clothed figures prepared to depart.

Persephone, the Assassin, whispered, "Your time will come once we have secured the place. You four will be in charge of getting the women into the EMAC and calm. Okay, let's take out this bastard!"

Juan smiled, "I'll get the perimeter guards as we've planned. See you later at the barn."

Nearly invisible, the two figures slipped off into the night. Only the distant London lights provided the illumination on the cloudy night. The ruddy colors from the low clouds created a somewhat picturesque pastoral scene with patches of dark trees here and there on the sprawling estate. One by one, Juan crept up on the drugged security guards, knocking each one out and tying him up before moving back into the shadows again.

Persephone, the Assassin, headed straight for the manor house, eliminating the lone guard at the main doors. She guessed there would be another guard monitoring the video cameras, but would he see her enter or not? As she quietly stole inside, she spotted a silent door alarm and assumed a guard would soon appear to check it out. She slipped into the shadows in the corner of the entranceway and waited patiently. A minute later, a guard came walking into the hall, gun drawn, glancing all around. She struck with blinding speed; his gun flew out of his hand before he fell unconscious to the floor. She caught his body as it fell and lowered it quietly.

Slipping silently from room to room, she found the rest of the first floor clear and headed up the stairs to the second floor, where she heard low voices.

"What?" Lord Vincent exclaimed. She'd opened the door, guessing from the sounds that he was some distance from the door and that she had time to get to him before he could react. She was precisely correct. He was talking to his wife. Both were on Pytalon and their reaction times were so slow that she reached him before he even registered what was happening. One precisely aimed blow and he collapsed unconscious. She turned to his wife, who looked rather blankly at this black clad woman who had mysteriously just appeared in her bedroom. Then, she too went unconscious. "Secured Vincent," she whispered into her headpiece.

Three guards down, one more to go at least. Hold a bit," Juan whispered back.

Meanwhile, she tied up the two and hastily checked the rest of the huge house. It was empty. By then Juan gave the all clear outside notice, and she headed to the barn while he brought the EMAC up as close to the barn as possible.

"That was fast! Barely five minutes!" Tilly exclaimed, as Juan climbed into the vehicle and fired up the EM motors.

"Yes, most efficient. Good thing the guards were all zombies. Okay, now the hard part starts. We'll need your help, gang," Juan explained, landing the vehicle some twenty-five feet from the entrance to the barn. Persephone had already entered and turned on the inside lights. Juan turned on an outside light on the side of the EMAC, illuminating the ground between the doors and the vehicle. "Okay, let's do this," he exclaimed, still feeling the rush of excitement.

One by one, Lady Persephone opened the women's stall doors, rousing them. They all just looked at her and did not respond. Juan and the others joined her. "They are just lying there. Do we have to carry them to the EMAC?" she asked.

"I have an idea," Jessica offered, going to Adrianna's open stall door. "Adrianna, good pony. Get up and follow me, good pony." The dazed teen rose and got her heavy boots firmly on the ground. "Fasten the lead rope to her and give me the other end, please," she asked Lady Persephone, who looked as if she were nuts, but did so. "Okay good pony, follow me." She held the rope between her shoulder and neck, giving a slight tug. Adrianna obeyed and began following her, her iron horse shoes clacking on the cement flooring.

Amanda followed her, leading Martha to the EMAC. One by one, Beth, Tilly, Juan, and Lady Persephone duplicated the way Jessica was handling Adrianna. A half hour later, the dozen women-ponies were seated in the EMAC, alongside of the four. Juan and Lady Persephone headed back inside and carried the unconscious Lord Vincent and his wife out and into the EMAC. A half hour later back at her castle, those two were securely locked in a windowless storage room, while the four had made three trips leading the women into the main foyer, where they stood in a daze.

Now the real work began. "It is time for you good ponies to get a nice hot bath before bed," Jessica explained to them.

One by one, Juan and Lady Persephone removed their bits, head harness, body harness, hand balls, and then their clothing and boots. However, once their heavy modified boots were removed, they all gasped. Adrianna's toes were crushed, broken in many places, as were Martha's. Their front half of their feet were swollen and very black and blue. Unfortunately, without the boots, they couldn't stand up, so she had them on their knees moving to the baths.

As the two removed the boots from the next pair who had been "ponies" for at least a year, based upon their age, which they guessed was nineteen or twenty, their toes were just as smashed, broken in many places, but they had healed.

"My god!" Beth exclaimed, "Their feet are worse than ours were!"

Upon further inspection, their ankles no longer bent fully. They were unable to stand on them. As they got to the older women, they found the same thing had happened to their feet. Their toes had been crushed, and their ankles bent only a little now. Calcification had definitely set in on their foot bones and joints.

Lady Persephone called out each woman's dress size and shoe size as she came to them. Jessica carefully wrote them down crudely by using her toes and a pen.

"Okay, tomorrow I'll make a fast trip to the EE women's store and get them some proper clothes and boots. Tonight, they can sleep in some of my nightgowns; they should be loose fitting enough," she explained. She and Juan headed to the bathroom to help the dozen women with their baths.

By ten, the last of the ponies had been put to bed in three of her guest rooms. More importantly, Jessica had shown each one where the bathroom was at in relation to their bedrooms. From their living conditions, she suspected they were ordered to use the latrine at one side of their stall. She surely didn't want to have to scrub one corner of the bedrooms!

That done, the six sat down for a spot of tea to talk about what to do next. "First, they'll need to come off Pytalon. We'll have to use the sauna. Tomorrow, I'll ask Sally Bates to come here and see these dozen through the detox program. I'll see her before I get them some clothes. I'm going to have to make a trip overseas for a few days too. Lousy timing. It will be up to you five to help care for them until I get back," Lady Persephone ordered.

The last thing Jessica did was fire off a message to Ben to try to see if he could find the psych's scripts for Adrianna and Martha. She would need them to help desensitize their EE implants. Sleep didn't come quickly for her. Part of her consciousness was in Chicago with her Jess body, part was also milling over the incredible mental states of the women and how she could possibly do anything for them.

All dozen insisted on eating their breakfasts by bending their heads down eating like a horse or dog, in spite of having their fingers free and silverware beside their plates. This confused and frustrated Jessica and the others. However, Lady Persephone was long gone, having risen at dawn. The women had just finished when she returned with a mountain of apparel and boots, which Juan and her two caretakers helped carry into the dining room. However, by the time that she had the clothing sorted out, Sally Bates arrived.

"Oh my, this is worse than you said," Sally exclaimed, as she was introduced to the dozen women. "Okay, sauna time for everyone. Juan, I'll send you out for vitamins and more salts, but after we get them started. I brought along salts enough for today. Maybe we should send for Lisa. I don't know if I can handle them."

"I'll talk with her today," Lady Persephone replied, "but don't hold your breath. She's a mother now. Amy is only fourteen weeks old, and I doubt Lisa could come here." Sally flushed, she already knew that, but it had slipped her mind as she faced this daunting task. "Okay then, I'm off. Back in a few days, I hope. Text me with your progress, everyone. Juan, lend me a hand, will you?"

Later when Juan returned with the vitamins and salts, the four and Sally already had the dozen women in the sauna.

"You have to tell them 'good pony.' Now I want you to do this, good pony," Sally explained. "I've got them watching the dozen. When one needs something, I handle it. Glad you're back. This is a bit much, isn't it?" Sally said.

"No kidding," he replied, pulling up another chair.

"So what did Lady Persephone want help with?" Jessica probed.

"Getting Lord Vincent and his wife into the EMAC. She's taking them with her and is arranging for someone to look after them. I'm supposed to search his place thoroughly and see if we can find records of who purchased other pony women of his. Guess it'll have to be later on, when their sauna time is done," he replied.

Later, Captain Henry Salisbury dropped by. "Been asked by Lady Persephone Briton to help you search Lord Vincent's place. Oh my god, are these the women?" the older man said when he got his first look at them. "Why do they keep saying good ponies to them?" he asked, baffled.

"Here, I'll show you," Juan replied taking him over to Jessica's laptop and showing him Lord Vincent's web pages. "It is worse than you can imagine. Their feet are completely ruined, as you can see for yourself. That man deserves to be drawn and quartered!"

"My god, I guess so. We had no idea something like this was going on here so close to London. Well, we best get searching for more women," he replied, all business having recovered from the shock. The two men headed over to Lord Vincent's manor house.

The women were in bed when Juan finally returned late that night. Captain Henry and Juan did find records on the man's computer, and the Feds leader took it with him. He also had someone take down Lord Vincent's web site, though Juan suggested he hold off on that. Why? Those who had purchased ponies from Lord Vincent might get paranoid and kill their women ponies before the Feds found them. Captain Henry disregarded Juan's notions.

Already, Jessica had intervened with Lord Vincent's bank account and had it frozen. Only the Feds could make any use of it now. Her thinking was to use some of the man's millions to reimburse the women, perhaps dividing it among them. She sent a message to that effect to Captain Henry and to

Lady Persephone, unsure whether the Feds had jurisdiction or whether the judiciary had it in this case. As it later turned out, Lady Persephone took control of the funds, dividing it among the women proportionate to the number of years they were held prisoner and forced to be a "pony."

Mid-morning on their second day in the sauna, Adrianna and Martha began screaming. "What's happened to me? How did I get here? I didn't want to be an EE woman. How did this happen?" Both said roughly the same thing and then began sobbing. The other women merely continued obeying their given orders, oblivious to the world.

"This is to be expected," Sally explained to a worried Jessica, who wanted to jump in the sauna and explain everything to the two teens. "You see, they were on Pytalon only a few days. While it was an overly large dosage, it's coming out of their systems very quickly, unlike the others who will probably take several weeks of this before they're rational again."

During the days that Adrianna and Martha were sweating it out in the sauna, Jessica was trying to work out how she could handle them once the drug was out of their systems. Obviously, the entire pony training thing had bundled a host of other "commands" on top of their EE woman's implant. Beginning that second day, quite often, she heard Adrianna and Martha reciting their implanted words, and she took note of them. She found no variations from the usual script, save the additional line to wear ballet boots. Yet, they still involuntarily complied with good pony commands. However, she had no idea what "script" Lord Vincent had used on them. "How am I going to desensitize the pony stuff?" she complained to the others.

"Oh, you will find a way, I'm sure," Beth replied, planting a soft kiss on her cheek.

Jessica was consumed with trying to figure out a way to help these women. Then, she began to realize something the professor had once said. The transference process proved the person was a spiritual being and had a mind. She knew this to be true, having been transferred from her current body into that of the armless and blind young Chinese body. She had all her memories. Then, she'd been transferred back into her current body. Again, she retained all her memories of being in that horrid body and what had happened during that time period. Now, she also was operating the Jess body and retained knowledge of what was going on with both bodies. What she saw, felt, and heard while operating the Jess body was right there with her when she woke up her Jessica body and vice versa.

This, she concluded, meant her mind and all her memories, good ones and terrible ones, were a part of her and not her body. In getting desensitized herself, she also realized some of her traumatic events couldn't be remembered until she was forced to desensitize the phrases and sentences that someone else knew must have been said to her while she was unconscious while being implanted or comatose. This, she found interesting.

"I couldn't consciously recall those trauma memories, not the details, only a vague notion that something must have happened, until I was forced to repeat the phrases. Then the pain, grogginess, and everything else began to reappear. I wonder if these women have also got unconscious memories of their trauma and that if I can get them to see them well enough, if that will somehow reduce their power over them?" She relaxed a little; she at least had an idea of how to proceed.

When the two were pronounced finished by Sally on the fifth day, both were still getting around by crawling on their hands and knees. Some of the awful black and blue bruising had begun to recede, but their feet were still to painful to stand the slightest walking. Jessica had Amanda join her with the two women, who were now sitting on the bed they were sharing.

"Amanda, you take Martha and follow my lead with her. I'm going to try to work on this whole implant mess." Amanda agreed.

"Adrianna, close your eyes. Can you recall when you were first abducted?" Jessica asked, figuring she probably couldn't.

"Yes, I have a picture in my mind. Martha and I were out for a walk the night before we were to learn if we were accepted for the jobs that we wanted."

"A picture?" Jessica asked. *Now this is interesting. A picture. So she may well have images of the trauma, which maybe I can help her see fully and desensitize her trauma. Have to try.*

"Hey, I do too," Martha added.

"Okay, then see if you can go through what happened. Tell me what you're seeing and what's happening to you, if you can," Jessica suggested.

Amanda hastily repeated this to Martha. Thus began a three-hour marathon! The more the two had the two teens go over their supposedly "unconscious" memories, the more detail became visible to the two teens.

"My god, I can really smell the chloroform on that rag he's holding over my face!" Adrianna exclaimed. On she went. Now she began to see her body lying on a table while a doctor was operating on her breasts and lips. She even "heard" the doctor whispering, "Sanity is doing a good operation."

A bit later, she described the horrible pain in her head and how groggy and dopy she felt. After a bit more work, she told Jessica what the psych man was saying to her. Jessica's eyes bulged! These were the very words she needed to desensitize! She wondered if her older method of merely repeating the words and phrases somehow brought this small portion of the entire trauma memory into view.

When they had to stop to use the bathroom and eat supper, both Adrianna and Martha were doing markedly better. Neither was repeating their implant litany. Neither were "playing pony" any longer, but they were also not cheerful. In fact, they were closer to grief over what had been done to them. After supper, Jessica and Amanda continued with the two, having them once more begin at the first moment they knew something was happening, going through it all, and telling them what they were seeing, hearing, and feeling. Jessica now added smelling to the mix.

Jessica was long past the time when she needed to cease doing much to allow her Jess body its daytime activities. However, she kept Jess in bed a while longer, persisting with Adrianna. Around nine that night, Adrianna began laughing. "I don't know what just happened, but all those pictures are gone. My head feels clear. I'm not groggy any longer. In fact, I'm really, really awake. I feel fantastic, except for my smashed toes and feet." Jessica smile and ended her work. Not long after that, Martha experienced a similar relief, much to Amanda's amazement.

"My god, Jessica! You and Amanda don't have any arms! How awful! I just noticed that. I'm so sorry for you. What happened to you?" Adrianna exclaimed, suddenly very much aware of her surroundings and of Jessica and Amanda.

"Very long story and it's late. Let's talk about that tomorrow, shall we? It takes me a long time to get ready for bed," Jessica replied, noticing the extroverted behavior of both Adrianna and Martha.

"Can we help you somehow? Please, you must let us help you," Adrianna begged.

"We are trying to learn to be independent, if we can, but when I need some help, I'll ask you, okay?" she replied diplomatically.

"Okay. Gosh, I'm so wide awake! I don't ever recall being quite so awake," Adrianna gushed.

"Me too, I'm so alert, wow," Martha added. "Whatever you did, it worked. Thank you, thank you, Amanda."

"Yes, thank you, thank you, Jessica!" Adrianna gushed. "Come on. Let's get you two to bed. I'll crawl along behind you and help you tonight, since it is so late for you," she volunteered.

A bit later as Jessica lay beside Beth, she told her mate what had happened. Beth listened until she finished and then said, "You know, love, I think you're inventing a real science of the mind somehow. I wonder if it'll work on the others."

"I'm sure going to try. Say, I wonder if it'll work on us too. I mean we've mostly gotten the words desensitized, but what about everything else that was part of the PDH implant thing and all the other stuff that's happened to us. When I have time, I'm going to try it on you, dear. You'll be my guinea pig."

Beth laughed and with some effort, turned onto her side and gave her a loving kiss. With the two teens fully recovered, the next day Jessica had Juan take the two teens and her to the hospital to have their feet examined. She doubted there was much that could be done for them, however. She was right. The doctor showed them the x-rays of their feet.

"I've never seen feet and toes this damaged before!" He went on and on about how badly destroyed they were, and Jessica wanted him to shut up, fearing he would upset the two teens.

"Yes, we can see they're mutilated and badly broken, doctor," Adrianna interrupted him, "but first can anything be done to fix them up and second how soon will the broken bones heal. We can't keep crawling forever."

"Oh. They are healing well. I would say you have another two weeks before they are fully healed. So you smashed them four or five weeks ago?"

Adrianna looked at Jessica and then Martha, before breaking into a hearty laugh. "No doctor, we broke them a week or so ago. I guess we heal fast."

Jessica now had something else to ponder. Their broken bones were healing at an alarmingly fast rate. Could that be a result of what she'd done with the two? She had more questions than she had answers for just now, but resolved to find out.

During the subsequent days, Jessica and Amanda closely watched the two teens, expecting them to have the usual EE woman symptoms from time to time similar to those that they had. However, neither showed any such tendencies. While they weren't pleased or happy about becoming a sex doll in appearance, they didn't display any of the EE woman implant behavior. Neither even remotely tried to flirt with anyone, including Juan. What have I stumbled upon here, Jessica wondered.

The next day, Adrianna and Martha were laughing while getting dressed. "Well, I guess we might as well wear these EE woman's gowns. Nothing else is going to remotely fit our monster boobs," Adrianna suggested.

Martha continued to laugh. "No way will any of my old tops fit. You can't buy any that will, except EE woman's apparel, but we could still wear our skirts and pants, I suppose. Let's put the boots on anyway, even though we aren't supposed to walk on them yet. They'll protect our knees some while we crawl around."

"Good idea. Let's!" Adrianna replied. "I wonder if they'll let me teach first grade looking as if I'm an EE woman."

"Gosh, Adrianna, I bet they won't! I wonder if the Feds will still want me," Martha asked. Adrianna shook her head. "I can't believe how heavy my knockers are!" Martha added. Both teens giggled.

"Maybe we should try to help Jessica and Amanda instead," Adrianna suggested, as the two crawled off to the dining room for breakfast.

***

Lisa's predictions held, as far as Jessica could tell. The longer one was on Pytalon, the longer it took to flush the residual drug from their bodies. A week later, another four finished up. They had been "ponies" for two years. Adrianna and Martha eagerly joined Jessica and Amanda and used Jessica's new method to run these four through their hideous nightmare times and implants. While it took a week of heavy slugging, the results were just as spectacular on these four as they had been for Adrianna and Martha.

Of course, they'd barely finished when four more finished their sauna time and needed this help as well. A month after the rescue, all the abducted women were salvaged. True, their feet were so badly malformed that they had no choice but to continue wearing normal EE women's ballet boots, but that mattered very little now.

Lady Persephone doled out compensation funds to all them, wiping out Lord Vincent Wargrave's bank account. Thus, this group of women now had independent means of support. Further, the London Feds were able to find another six "ponies" who were still alive and rescued them. Jessica and her group handled them as well. All the other sold "ponies" had perished.

Adrianna and Martha got their wishes. The London Feds hired Martha, and Adrianna was hired to teach first grade. Both young women decided to live together, and they rented a nice apartment in London about equidistant from their two workplaces. However, they were quite emphatic about continuing to help Jessica with others who needed help erasing their implants and addiction to Pytalon, volunteering to come when Jessica needed help.

When Lady Persephone was asked about what she'd done with Lord Vincent Wargrave, she replied, "He and his wife now have new EE women's bodies. They too must always wear ballet boots, and they are armless. I've relocated them to an EE center in Shanghai, China. I hope they learn to speak Chinese soon. At least they will be learning firsthand what they did to so many women. They are both eighteen once more." She didn't need to elaborate. Jessica knew from the hint that she'd transferred them to a pair of young Chinese women who had "died" from their Choosing time implants.

Yet from all this, Jessica and everyone else also learned about another aspect to their society, one that until now they hadn't paid any attention to: the Total Care Program. Shortly after they returned from the hospital where they learned the state of Adrianna and Martha's feet, a rather plain looking woman wearing a red business suit visited them at Lady Persephone's castle.

Carrying a small briefcase, she introduced herself, "Hello. I'm Abigail Trout from the Administration Office of London's Total Care. Sanity is serving our people." She had light blonde hair, shoulder length and curly, but she was obviously on Pytalon and implanted as well. Lady Persephone met her and brought her into the room where all the women were just finishing their breakfasts. "Oh good. Everyone is here."

She opened her briefcase, filled with forms, and laid them out. "I'm Abigail Trout from Total Care. As you know, the Total Care Program provides basic care for all people from their birth to their death, from the Cradle to the Grave, is our saying. Part of this total care package that everyone has is Health Care. Your recent visit to the hospital triggered my visit, you see." No one "saw," but she didn't catch this, continuing right along.

"Of course, there are no hospital charges for you to pay, compliments of Total Care. However, I was informed your feet are permanently damaged. Lady Persephone has also informed me that you four have suffered a terrible loss of both arms," she nodded towards Jessica, Amanda, Beth, and Tilly. "So today, I've come to settle your Total Care accounts in these matters. You see, Total Care aims to provide for the care of everyone, particularly when disability strikes, as it plainly has here."

"Total Care is here to assist you all, based upon which Case Category of the five you fall into. Fortunately, with everyone here and with one exception, everyone falls into Case C coverage. Lady Adrianna is obviously has Case B coverage."

"Excuse me, Miss Trout," Lady Persephone interrupted her. "We're unfamiliar with the various cases. Could you explain them more fully please?"

"Certainly, but after I finish with the formal presentation. Now where was I?" She was having a hard time keeping things straight. Pytalon's influence. Lady Persephone decided not to press the issue just yet. "Oh yes. So Lady Adrianna, as a Case B situation, you're entitled to have your feet amputated and will be given prosthetic feet, if you so desire."

Adrianna gasped. "Oh dear god! No! I surely don't want my feet cut off!"

"Excellent choice, Lady Adrianna," Abigail continued right along, displaying no emotion whatsoever. "So in your case, Total Care will be providing you with a one-room, efficiency apartment, and a stipend of five credits a day for food, guaranteeing you two meals a day for the rest of your life. All the rest of you will receive the same five credits a day for food for the rest of your lives. In addition, everyone will receive a clothing allowance of one new complete outfit per year, including shoes."

"It works this way, except for Lady Adrianna, of course. Each day, you present yourselves to your local Total Care Mission. There you'll receive your two meals in exchange for your five credits. If you have no place to stay, then your local EE women's shelter will provide a bed for you to use. Each June, you'll be given a voucher for one new outfit. You merely hand it to the cashier when you pick them up. You see, Total Care aims to provide this ultimate safety cushion for you. From the Cradle to the Grave."

"Now then, I need your signatures on these forms along with your addresses. Oh yes, and Lady Adrianna, I'll need your signature here showing that you are declining the option to have your mutilated feet amputated and replaced with prosthetic feet. I do compliment you on your choice, My Lady. It so saves us a good deal of money. Prosthetic feet are so expensive, but then I'm told they aren't that beneficial anyway." She began doling out the many forms to be signed, but looked quizzically at the four armless EE women, wondering how they could sign them. She looked to Lady Persephone for help.

Once the papers were signed, Abigail relaxed a good deal. Obviously, all this had required a great deal of effort on her part. Never had she had to handle so darn many at one time. Seeing her relaxing, Lady Persephone again inquired. "So what are the five case categories?"

Abigail sighed and recited, "Case B is for the wealthy Lords and Ladies, though some have other titles, such as corporate executives, presidents—you know, the top leaders. Case C is solely for EE women. Case D is for all the professional personnel and highly skilled workers. Case E is for all the unskilled workers, the common laborers."

"I've already explained the benefits of permanent disability for the Case B and C categories. For Case D, they also receive a yearly clothing allowance and the five credits a day food funds, but they're allowed a bed in one of the local Total Care Mission homes. Case E personnel are merely given the daily food allowances, nothing more."

"Of course, these are the permanent disability allowances. In case of severe injury situation, at any hospital, those who meet Case B requirements are given replacement organs, if those are available, such as a liver implant, prosthesis, and such things. Dental care provides for teeth implants, bridges, and even false teeth. Those who meet Case C requirements, EE women, aren't allowed to receive organ transplants, but are eligible for everything else. Now those who can only meet Case D or Case E requirements aren't allowed to receive prosthesis either, and bad teeth are merely extracted."

"As far as normal emergency care goes, everyone is entitled to first rate care of their illness. So if you get sick, you get healed. You have an accident and break a bone, it gets set. Total Health Care, you see. However, those who meet Case E requirements get the minimalist care needed to get them released, as befitting their lowest potential within our society."

"Finally, anyone is allowed to purchase better care. So Lady Adrianna, you could purchase new feet through the organ donor program, assuming a compatible organ donor could be found, though I must admit such are very rarely found, a compatible donor, so many medical things must be met, but then I'm not a doctor. Anyway, I did check on the listed price for that procedure, just in case you wished to purchase new feet. The rate is three million dollars per foot. However, being EE women, I presumed none of you could possibly afford the prohibitive cost of six million dollars to obtain new feet." Gasps from the group indicated she was correct in making that assumption. She added, "I also checked on the cost of arm replacement, just to be thorough. The going organ donor rate for a whole new arm is twenty million dollars, prohibitively expensive indeed, again assuming a medically compatible organ donor could be found."

"Now, if there are no more questions, I do need to get back to my office and handle all this paperwork. I've never had to do so many of you at one time before." She did seem somewhat confused by the mountain of paperwork, as she scooped the signed forms back into her briefcase.

Lady Persephone had also gasped. That even the technology to replace arms was available came as a shock to her. "Excuse me, Abigail. What about Case A? If there are cases B through E, isn't there a Case A?"

Abigail Trout looked perplexed and confused. "Well, I suppose there is a Case A, but that is classified. I've never even seen the requirements for Case A, let alone what their benefits might be. I'm sorry. I don't have that information. Here," she fumbled for a card and handed it to Lady Persephone. "This is the number for the head of our London Total Care Program. He might know, but I surely don't know." With that, she rose, definitely desirous of ending this meeting. She felt a headache coming on. All this talk about Case A was most annoying. Such didn't exist in her world or training. Wisely, Lady Persephone rose and escorted her to the door.

When she returned, Jessica commented, "Well, that explains a whole lot! No wonder we found so many men and women in dire straits at the mission in Chicago. Five credits a day for food? Get real. That won't even buy a proper breakfast!"

Tilly spoke up, "I wonder what this Case A business is all about? You know, we've been so tied up in the implant and Pytalon mess that we've not even looked into the entire Total Care Program. I think we should do just that. I smell a rat." Several chuckled.

In October of 2272, the four finally left London for home, joining their four other bodies in their new and very fancy penthouse suite in Chicago. Tilly and Tim now had an entirely new line of investigation to pursue—this Total Care Program.
The End.

A Favor to Other Readers

How about helping other readers? Many readers rely on reviews to make the decision whether to buy a book. You can help them make their decision by leaving your opinions and viewpoint in a short review of the positive things of this book. Writing the review and expressing your opinion only takes a few minutes, and other readers will appreciate your efforts.

Click this link: Reclamation Series Volume 1 For the Want of a Pill
scroll down to Customer Reviews; click on Write a Review, and enter your review. Thank you.

Author Information

Visit My Amazon.com Author Page
Vic Broquard Author Page

Follow My Blog
Vic Broquard's Blog

Follow Me on Social Media
Facebook
Google+
LinkedIn
YouTube

Other Books by Vic Broquard

Without Warning (fantasy)

The Trident Series: (fantasy)
> Volume 1 The Trident and the Book
> Volume 2 The Trident and the Scepter
> Volume 3 The Trident and the Resurrection

The Adventures of Elizabeth Stanton Series: (science fiction)
> Volume 1 The Evolution of the Path
> Volume 2 The Great Messiah
> Volume 3 Of Kings and Queens and Troubadours
> Volume 4 Chaos in the Aftermath
> Volume 5 Power Plays
> Volume 6 Age of Exploration
> Volume 7 Abducted
> Volume 8 The Emperor and Empress
> Volume 9 A Job Worth Doing
> Volume 10 Degradation
> Volume 11 The Second Crusade
> Volume 12 When Worlds Collide
> Volume 13 Dark Ages

The Lindsey Barron Series: (fantasy)
> Volume 1 The Rod of the Apocalypse
> Volume 2 The Board of Governors
> Volume 3 The Crown of Moses
> Volume 4 Dominus for President
> Volume 5 The National Health Care Program
> Volume 6 States Justice
> Volume 7 Cross and Double-cross

Zoran Chronicles Series: (fantasy)
> Volume 1 A Dragon in Our Town
> Volume 2 Dragons, Power, Courts, and War

Planet of the Orange-red Sun Series: (science fiction)
> Volume 1 When Kingdoms Fall
> Volume 2 Dark Ages
> Volume 3 Age of the Towers
> Volume 4 Difficillis Exitus

Volume 5 Age of the Lords
Volume 6 The Renegade Tower
Volume 7 Rebellions
Volume 8 The Aliens Return
Volume 9 Power Struggles
Volume 10 Guilds, Genetics, and Gods
Volume 11 Magi, Witches, Swords, and Superstitions
Volume 12 The Voyage of the Eagle's Seed
Volume 13 Eagle's Seed and Origins
Volume 14 Justifications
Volume 15 Responsibilities

The Return of the Wizards: Twelve Companions – The Making of Wizards (fantasy)

Slow Comes the Dark Series: (science fiction)
Volume 1 Creeping Darkness
Volume 2 Serendipity
Volume 3 Darkness Descends
Volume 4 Perversion Incarnate
Volume 5 Extermination Wars

Reclamation Series (science fiction)
Volume 1 For the Want of a Pill
Volume 2 Organ Donors
Volume 3 Total Care

Dragons, Magic, and Me (fantasy)
Volume 1 The Box